DREAMSCAPE

**Something's happening!
But is it love—or magic?**

Julian's seen her for months in his dreams—
now she's walked into his life.

Sybil's been slipped a love potion—
by a man who scoffs at magic.

David's a complete stranger—
but Annie remembers him. Intimately.

They're falling under a spell....

DREAMSCAPE

Relive the romance...

by Request

*Three complete novels by your
favorite authors!*

About the Authors

Jayne Ann Krentz—One of today's top contemporary romance writers, Jayne has an astounding twelve million copies of her books in print. First published in 1979, Jayne quickly established herself as a prolific and innovative writer, and her novels regularly appear on the *New York Times*, Waldenbooks and B. Dalton bestseller lists. Jayne lives in Seattle with her husband, Frank, and her "truly brilliant budgie," Ferd.

Anne Stuart—This bestselling author has been writing romances for more than twenty years. She's written Gothics, regencies, historical romances, suspense, romantic suspense and contemporary romances. Anne lives in Vermont with her gorgeous husband and two wonderful children, and when she's not saying outrageous things she's usually writing them.

Bobby Hutchinson—Popular author of over fifteen novels, Bobby's books have touched and entertained countless readers all over the world. Bobby began her writing career in 1984, and she and her husband make their home in Winfield, British Columbia.

DREAMSCAPE

JAYNE ANN KRENTZ
ANNE STUART
BOBBY HUTCHINSON

Harlequin Books

TORONTO • NEW YORK • LONDON
AMSTERDAM • PARIS • SYDNEY • HAMBURG
STOCKHOLM • ATHENS • TOKYO • MILAN
MADRID • WARSAW • BUDAPEST • AUCKLAND

HARLEQUIN BOOKS

by Request—Dreamscape

Copyright © 1993 by Harlequin Enterprises B.V.

ISBN 0-373-20095-1

The publisher acknowledges the copyright holders of the individual works as follows:

GHOST OF A CHANCE
Copyright © 1984 by Jayne Ann Krentz

BEWITCHING HOUR
Copyright © 1986 by Anne Kristine Stuart Ohlrogge

REMEMBER ME
Copyright © 1989 by Bobby Hutchinson

CONTENTS

He once vowed
he'd return and claim her.
He hadn't.

She once swore
she'd never see him again.
She'd lied.

GHOST OF A CHANCE

Jayne Ann Krentz

1

THERE WAS NO EASY WAY for a woman to start a conversation with the man who had once sworn he'd return to claim her. Not when the man had failed to keep his promise.

Ghosts of memories flitted through Anne Silver's mind as she raised her hand to knock on the cabin door. The ghosts were not only in her head tonight, she decided. They were howling in protest as they were blown about by the first bitter winds of approaching winter. The cold came early in these Colorado mountains. It was only the middle of October. Back home in Indiana folks were still enjoying a pleasantly crisp autumn. But here in the mountains the ghosts of the coming winter already heralded snow. With her luck, Anne thought, the storm would probably arrive tonight.

Perfect. Just perfect. She would have to contend with both the phantom of a love that had never had a chance to be born and the specter of snow. Life, Anne decided wryly, had never promised to be fair in its dealings. The only intelligent way to handle tonight's task was to treat the entire matter as strictly business.

But as soon as her small fist had struck the door she knew how utterly impossible that goal was. There was no way on earth she would ever be able to handle Julian Aries in a strictly business fashion. Not when her whole being burned with chaotic emotions just at the thought of seeing him again.

She had alternated between states of longing and fury for too many months. There was no longer any room in her for logic and superficial politeness. As soon as that thought entered her head she tried to banish it. *I'm a thirty-one-year-old woman. I can handle the coming scene as a mature adult. I will not let him know that I waited and waited....*

There was no sound of movement from behind the heavy wooden walls of the cabin but quite suddenly the door swung inward. Anne experienced a childish, irrational desire to flee as she faced the man who stood in the doorway. But thirty-one years and an ingrained determination came to her aid.

"Good evening, Julian. It's been a long time. May I come in? It's getting cold out here."

"Anne."

She couldn't tell if her name was a statement or a curse. It was spoken in the soft, velvet growl she remembered so well, but there was an edge to it that sent a chill down her spine. She kept her chin high and her gaze unflinching as Julian's tawny eyes swept over her.

She recalled the dark golden gaze as clearly as she remembered the voice, but there was something different about it, too, this evening. Even in the pale gleam of the porch light she sensed that the gold burned with an unnatural brightness. It was her imagination, Anne told herself. It had been six months since she'd last seen him and she was overreacting now. A gust of chill wind gave her an excuse to break the tense moment.

"Julian? It's freezing out here."

He stepped back into the firelit room. "Sorry. You took me by surprise. You must realize you're just about the last person I expected to find at my door this evening." He turned away, moving toward the overstuffed chair on one side of the fireplace.

Anne stared in startled fascination as she saw the limp that altered the flowing, catlike stride she remembered. "Julian, you've been hurt?"

"Sit down, Anne." The too-bright gaze willed her to the chair, and the soft voice contained the old element of command. "I'll pour you some brandy. I'm sure you could use it. And not just because of the cold."

Without a word she sat down across from him. The firelight flared briefly, illuminating one side of his rough-cast face. With a hunger she didn't want to acknowledge, she drank in the sight of him. The nose that looked as though it had once been broken, the heavily etched lines at the edges of his mouth, the cheekbones that gave him such a leonine look and the thick black brows that framed the tawny eyes. Everything about him was the same, yet everything was different. Anne felt another uneasy chill.

Then he leaned forward to pour the expensive brandy from a bottle beside his chair. For a moment his face was at a different angle in the firelight, and she saw the scar that ran along the edge of his jaw.

"Julian, you have been hurt," she whispered. "What happened?"

"Roughly what you predicted would happen," he retorted, handing her the balloon-shaped glass. The shadows concealed the scar again as he sank back into the depths of his chair and regarded her with his overbright eyes. "I can hardly take in the fact that you're here. The last time we saw each other you were yelling something about never wanting to see me again."

And you were swearing that you'd come back to find me because we had unfinished business, she countered silently. "Was I yelling at you?" she managed to ask almost calmly, determined to maintain her self-control at all costs. "I do remember I was trying very hard to get across a particular point."

He nodded, giving her a brief, unexpectedly savage smile. He looked his age tonight, Anne thought. She knew vaguely that sometime during the past year he had turned forty. With a touch of whimsy she wondered if he were an Aries by birth as well as by name. What had happened to him during these past six months? The man who sat across from her tonight was the same one who had left her, vowing to return, but there was a difference in him.

It was enough of a difference to make her both wary and oddly frightened. If only he wouldn't look at her so intently, as if she were prey. Those tawny eyes seemed more dangerous than the flames in the fireplace and that smile.... She'd never seen him smile in that brutal manner.

"You made your point six months ago, Anne. You wanted me out of your life."

"I was very upset at the time," Anne began carefully.

"You were hysterical," he corrected bluntly.

"You were hysterical," he corrected bluntly.

Some of the fury that had alternated with the unfulfilled longing inside her for the past several months flared briefly, "I was not hysterical. I was furiously angry. There's a distinct difference."

He poured more brandy for himself, his eyes never leaving her face. "All right, you were furiously angry. It was difficult at the time to tell the difference between anger and hysteria."

Anne's hands clenched into small fists in her lap as she struggled to retain control of herself. "I had a right to behave the way I did. What did you expect from me after what you'd done? I begged you not to take Michael with you on that last mission. Two weeks later you brought him home with a bullet in his chest.

He spent a week in that hospital. You didn't even hang around long enough to find out if he would survive. You were gone by midnight the same day you brought him back."

"Ah, yes. Your precious Michael. How is your brother, Anne?" Anne blinked and drew in a deep breath. "Back in a hospital," she returned flatly.

There was a faint pause while Julian considered that news. "Problems from that six-month-old wound?"

"No. Problems from being hit by a car in downtown Boston. This time he very nearly did die."

Something flickered in the tawny eyes, perhaps a flash of genuine compassion. "I'm sorry, Anne. I didn't realize. He seems to lead an adventurous sort of life, doesn't he?"

"Almost as adventurous as your own. Unfortunately, he doesn't have quite as much luck as you seem to have."

"He'll live?"

"Yes, he'll live."

Julian's gaze narrowed thoughtfully. "Why is it that instead of playing the loving sister by his bedside, you're wandering around these mountains at ten o'clock at night looking for me? Have you come to hurl accusations again? Going to find a way to prove that I was responsible for Michael being hit by a car the way you decided I was responsible for him being shot six months ago?"

Anne shook her head, trying to find the words. "It wasn't your fault."

The overly bright gaze hardened. The brief flicker of compassion was gone as if it had never existed. "How very magnanimous of you."

"Julian, please, I haven't come here to argue."

"Then why have you come? Actually, there are a number of questions that come to mind. Why don't we begin at the beginning? How did you find me?"

"Michael had your last letter in his files. The one you sent from Denver telling him you were going to take some time off and spend it at your cabin in the mountains. You invited him here to go trout fishing. There was a small map at the bottom of the letter."

"I was feeling a bit lonely at the time," Julian remarked dryly. "I've since recovered."

"From the loneliness? Or from your 'accident'?" Anne demanded gently. "Julian, what happened to you?"

"Nothing you need worry about. In any event, we're still working on my questions. So you found out where I was from that letter I wrote in a moment of sentimental weakness. That doesn't tell me what you're doing here. Or why you're not at your brother's bedside."

"Michael's fiancée is at his bedside," Anne told him stiffly.

"Lucky Michael. He never seems to lack for angels of mercy to soothe his fevered brow."

Anne ignored the cynical inflection in his voice, frowning as he swallowed another large sip of brandy. He appeared to have made severe inroads into the bottle this evening before she had arrived, and he wasn't slowing down now. "Lucy and Michael met about three months ago. They're planning on being married around Thanksgiving." Anne hesitated and then asked anxiously, "Julian, don't you think you've had enough brandy?"

He stared at her over the rim of the glass, and Anne instantly regretted the impulsive words. There was a strangeness in the laconic, derisive expression that shaped his hard face; some element she didn't recognize. Julian had changed. Or was it simply that she'd never had a chance to really get to know him six months ago? A restless wariness made her shift slightly in her chair. Seeking something to do with her hands she rearranged the red, brass-buttoned jacket she had worn over her jeans and sweater. The coat was lying across the arm of her chair because Julian had not offered to hang it up for her.

"Enough brandy," he repeated. "Is it possible to have too much, do you think?" He sounded as though he had uncovered an interesting philosophical question.

"Yes, it's possible," she shot back firmly. "Highly probable, in your case, I'd say. Julian, you're acting very strangely tonight. I think it's probably because you've had too much to drink."

"You're wrong. It's not because of the brandy that I seem a bit, umm, disoriented. It's because I opened my door a few minutes ago and found you standing there. A severe shock to the system, I assure you."

"You were always fairly adept at dealing with the unexpected."

"Perhaps I'm slowing down in my old age. I'm forty now. Did you know that?"

"I remembered. Six months ago you told me that forty was a good age at which to consider a career change."

"I may have miscalculated." He poured some more brandy.

It seemed to Anne that the glass in his hand trembled slightly and that Julian took great care setting down the bottle. Too much care for a man whom she recalled as having a lithe, assured grace. That masculine grace had seemed second nature in him six months ago. Was he drunk or had he changed in that respect, too? She had known tonight's meeting would be difficult, but she hadn't expected to find herself confronting a man who looked at her with a devil's hot eyes.

"Have I really upset you so much by showing up like this?" Anne asked quietly.

"How would you feel if someone you'd seen far too much of in dreams suddenly walked into your life?" His mouth twisted wryly.

Anne barely caught herself in time to keep from telling him that she knew exactly how it had felt. He had haunted her dreams for the past six months. The possibility that she had also been featured in his gave her a cautious flare of hope.

"Did you dream about me, Julian?"

"Dreams. Nightmares. Hard to tell the difference."

"Nightmares!" She felt crushed.

"How did you think I'd remember you? As a loving, generous woman? Not likely. What was it you said to me the night I asked you to go to bed with me? Something along the classic lines of 'not if you were the last man on earth,' I believe. No, you haven't figured in my dreams as a warm and tender memory, Anne. Every time I've seen you, awake or asleep, you've been telling me exactly what you thought of me. It wasn't very flattering."

The anger she had tried to bury blazed to the surface once more. "You've got a hell of a nerve being bitter, Julian Aries. I'm the one who has a right to be feeling resentful!"

"Resentful. What a bland word. Go ahead and feel resentful, Anne. It's nothing compared to how I feel." Julian leaned forward, cradling the brandy glass in his hands as he pinned her beneath a molten glare. "Want to know what I've felt during the past few months? I've felt like tracking you down and taking you away to someplace nice and secluded. Someplace like this cabin, for example. I've felt like stripping you naked and laying you down on that rug in front of the hearth. I've felt like crushing you beneath me until you had no choice but to wrap your arms around me. I've felt like taking you again and again until you couldn't do anything else except respond, until you could no longer hurl recriminations or accusations, until you could no longer even think, until you could only plead with me to stop and then plead with me to do it all over again. And do you know what I was going to do then?"

Anne was shaking; a fine, almost undetectable physical reaction that was similar to shock. There was no love or even real desire in his words. Each phrase was coated in icy lightning. She knew exactly how his fantasy would end. "When you had me broken and begging beneath you, you would laugh at me, remind me of how I had once told you I'd never let you make love to me and then you'd walk away. I have a fairly vivid imagination, Julian. You don't need to spell it out. I just hadn't realized how much you hate me." She leaned her head back against the chair, closing her eyes wearily. "Coming here tonight was a mistake. I can see that now."

He didn't move. "Why are you here, Anne?"

"It doesn't matter. I should never have appeared on your doorstep like this." It was going to be a long drive back to the nearest mountain town and a hotel. A very long drive. And she was so tired. She'd been on her feet for almost forty-eight hours. There had only been that brief nap in the airplane on the flight to Denver. The thought of having an excuse to see Julian again as well as the urgency of her errand had kept her going. But this strange man with the golden eyes was killing her delicate fantasy and all the hope that had nourished it. She had been a fool.

"Why are you here, damn it? Answer me."

Anne opened her eyes and instinctively tried to retreat farther back into the depths of the chair. He hated her, she realized wildly. This wasn't the same, totally controlled man who had left her six months ago. The firelight gleamed on the jet-black hair that was marked with shafts of slate gray, the flames were reflected in his eyes and the set line of his mouth promised no gentleness or mercy.

"I'll go," she promised, shaken. Awkwardly she tried to scramble from the chair. He stopped her with a hand on her arm. Even through the fabric of her sweater she could feel the heat in his grasp. She could also feel the strength in him. Whatever had happened to him during the past six months, it hadn't diminished the power in his hands.

"You're not going to anywhere," he rasped softly. "It was your decision to walk into the lion's den and now you'll have to live with it. In case you didn't hear it, the gate's already locked behind you."

Her eyes widened as she sat tensely chained in his grasp.

"What are you talking about?"

"If it isn't snowing out there by now, it soon will be. You'd need chains to get down off this mountain tonight . . . if I were inclined to let you go, which I'm not."

"Julian, I can see this was all a mistake. . . ."

"Not the first one you've made. But maybe the first one for which you'll actually have to pay. Why did you come, Anne?"

She caught her breath. "To ask for your help," Under the lash of the command in his voice, the words were out before she could halt them. To her surprise, they appeared to startle him.

"My help!" He released her and sat back. Above the rim of his glass he regarded her with puzzlement. "You came all this way to ask me for help?" He sounded incredulous.

Anne sat very still, afraid to provoke another show of physical strength. Against it she was helpless. Her only hope now lay in controlling the tense, highly charged situation she had created. "I don't know too many people with your particular qualifications, Julian. When Michael was nearly killed, Lucy and I knew we had to do something. I found his notes and his plans when I went through his desk. I decided to go ahead with his scheme but I'll need help."

He shook his head once, as if she were annoying him. "You're not making any sense."

"I'm sorry, I'm a little nervous."

"I always did have that degree of power over you, didn't I? Six months ago I made you nervous, too." He smiled bitterly.

"Maybe if I put my mind to it, I could really terrorize you."

"Stop it, Julian," Anne snapped. "Why are you acting like this? Because I refused your offer of a one-night stand six months ago? Come off it. Somewhere along the line you must have learned to handle a few minor rejections."

"You'll have to forgive me," he growled caustically. "Perhaps I'm not quite as forbearing as I once was. It's been a rough six months, lady. Let's skip the recriminations and get on to the business end of this meeting. You are here on business, I assume?"

Anne nodded cautiously. "I need your help, Julian."

"How badly?" He cocked a heavy, dark brow.

"I beg your pardon?"

"Forget it. We'll get to that part later. Why do you need my help?"

Anne touched the tip of her tongue to her lower lip in a small gesture of anxiety. Her fingers twisted in her lap. "Because of my brother."

Julian eyed her intently. "Michael's in trouble?"

"They nearly killed him, Julian."

"Who's 'they'?"

"The people who ran him over. The accident was labeled hit and run by the police. No description of the car. No witnesses. Michael can only remember vaguely that the car was dark blue."

"As a professional journalist I thought he had trained himself to make more accurate observations in the field," Julian said dryly.

"He nearly died. Under those circumstances it's tough to make accurate observations."

"He did a good job of it when I took him with me on that last mission. Even with a bullet in him he was busy making notes in a tape recorder until the moment he actually passed out."

Anne glanced away, concentrating on the fire. "He's a professional. That's something I didn't fully appreciate six months ago. I do now. He'll do whatever has to be done to get a story."

"What's this?" Julian mocked. "Are you actually telling me you realize it was his own decision to accompany me on that mission to the island? Does this mean I'm no longer the big bad wolf who lured him into danger and then got him shot?"

Anne's head swung around, her loosely coiled and knotted hair unraveling a little with the abrupt movement. "You approached him first. You needed him for cover, remember? You were going to play photographer and he was supposed to be the writing part of the team. His credentials were solid and you knew he wouldn't be questioned. As his photographer you could ride on those credentials."

"Aha! So I haven't been miraculously exonerated. I'm still the fast-talking agent who convinced him to risk his life for a story just so I could use him for a shield." Julian nodded judiciously, as if satisfied with his analysis.

Fast-talking agent, Anne echoed silently. Yes, Julian had been fast talking. Also fast moving and lethally swift at everything else he did. He had wanted her from the moment he'd met her and had made no secret of that fact. In the whirlwind week of planning and preparation that had preceded the mission, Julian had used every spare moment to break down her defenses. Anne knew she had been unable to conceal the desire he aroused in her, but she had managed to stop herself from surrendering completely.

"I told you I didn't come here to get involved in that old argument. It was over six months ago."

"Not for me, it wasn't. I had to go back to that island. With memories of you standing in the hospital corridor outside Mike's room telling me you never wanted to see me again and blaming me for the bullet in Mike's chest. Remember that little scene, Anne? It's very firmly etched in my mind. I've had a lot of time to think about it. So dramatic, with you slapping my face the way you did in front of the head nurse and her staff."

"You handled the whole thing with your customary self-control. You didn't even slap me back." She remembered that scene. Because in addition to blaming him for bringing her brother back wounded, she'd wanted to plead with him not to return and finish the mission. She would have gotten down on her knees and begged but she had known at the time that it was hopeless. Nothing she could have said or done would have altered his decision to complete the job. Julian had been assigned, by the vague government agency for which he worked, to gain intelligence information on a terrorist ring based on a remote island in the Caribbean. He was a professional. Anne had known that she was helpless to keep him from going back and risking his life. That sense of helpless frustration had fueled her fury that night in the hospital corridor.

"I thought later that perhaps I should have," Julian mused.

"Slapped me? That was never your way, Julian. You're the icy, controlled, macho type, remember? You let me throw a tearful, screaming tantrum in the hospital corridor and then you just walked away." *Promising you'd be back,* she concluded silently. *Only you never came back to me, Julian.*

"I hadn't realized I'd left such an indelible impression on you," he grated, helping himself to more brandy. "It's getting hot in here," he added in abrupt irritation. He opened the collar of the black, long-sleeved flannel shirt he wore with his jeans. "I should douse that fire."

"Maybe you've had a little too much of that brandy," Anne ventured as an explanation.

Julian sighed. "If it's the brandy that's making me feel so warm, I'll just have to suffer. I need the alcohol more than I need a change of temperature." He lowered his lashes, concealing the heat in his eyes. "Let's see if we can get this conversation back on whatever track it was trying to follow. You're here. Presumably because you need something, not because you were curious about whether or not I ever got back from that damned island. Tell me again about the car that hit your brother."

Anne wanted desperately to go on talking about each other, but the rational side of her nature warned against the danger. She had to take this slowly.

"Michael was working on a project at the time he was hit by the car. He was investigating a strange theft ring that operates in a very unique fashion. The people in the ring pose as . . . as psychic phenomena investigators."

"Which means?"

"Ghost hunters."

"A time-honored profession," Julian observed wryly. "Why was Mike bothering to uncover a few more false psychic types? Houdini exposed dozens, and all it did was increase the general interest in mediums and other fakes."

"I told you, it's a theft ring. These people pose as psychic investigators to gain access to beautiful old homes that are filled with valuable antiques and paintings and just plain cash. They prey on the gullibility of eccentric little old ladies who believe they actually have haunted houses, as well as on a certain, trendy type who decides it's chic to have a resident ghost in the family mansion. The ghost-hunting exercises make for unusual weekend parties for the owner and his friends, I gather. Once inside the house, the ring goes through its little rituals to exorcise the ghost. Séances, confrontations with the ghost, that sort of nonsense."

"Meanwhile they're casing the house? Making wax impressions of keys? Learning the ropes of whatever security system might be installed?"

"Exactly. Michael was fascinated. He's always had a secret interest in ghosts and psychic phenomena. He's done a few articles on the subject in the past. Just for fun, I suppose. At any rate, he made a lot of contacts during the year he researched the stuff. A few months ago he started hearing rumors about a particularly successful band of ghost hunters and his old curiosity was aroused."

"If everyone knows the ghost hunters are really stealing from the houses they're supposed to, uh, deghost, why don't the police take care of them?" Julian moved a little restlessly, unbuttoning another button on his black shirt. His gaze went to the fireplace. Outside, the wind began to howl more loudly.

Anne's uneasiness increased. Things were difficult enough as it was, trying to deal with a man who obviously felt nothing but hostility toward her. It seemed to her that she didn't need the added unpleasantness of a major snowstorm.

"No one does know the ghost hunters are carrying out the thefts," she explained. "It's a theory Michael has, based on the fact that some very valuable jewelry and other objects have since been reported missing at most of the houses that have employed the psychic investigators. The thefts aren't being discovered for months in some cases because, often, fakes have been substituted for the valuables. Paste jewelry, painting reproductions, that kind of thing. Michael hadn't discussed his theories with anyone because he wanted to break the story himself."

"And now he's back in a hospital for his trouble. You're sure there's a connection?"

"Between Michael's investigations and the fact that he was a victim of hit and run? Yes, I'm sure of it."

"Damn, it's hot in here." Uncoiling like a cat from the chair, Julian got to his feet and stalked to the front door. The impression of a cat was married slightly by the limp. A wounded cat, Anne thought. Few animals were more dangerous. She watched uncomprehendingly as he flung open the door.

Instantly the noisy gale swept into the room, bringing the first snowflakes and a blast of freezing cold.

"Julian, what's wrong?"

He slammed the door shut after inhaling deeply a few times. "I told you, it's hot in here." He threw himself back into the chair and stared at her broodingly. "Does Michael know you're here?"

"No."

"But his fiancée does?"

Anne nodded. "Lucy and I decided something had to be done. It's obvious the police aren't going to pursue the hit and run. They have no evidence or descriptions to go on. Michael had a plan. I'm going to implement it."

"You're going to implement it?" he scoffed tightly.

"With your help," she added determinedly.

"My help," he repeated, shaking his head wonderingly. Firelight glinted on the dark depths of his hair and illuminated the slate gray buried there. "What makes you think I'd help you?"

Anne's jaw tightened but she kept her voice steady. "I understand that you wouldn't go out of your way to do anything for me. I'm hoping you'll do it for Michael's sake."

He watched her impassively for a moment and then a new fierceness permeated his expression. "No."

Anne flinched. Using Michael's name had been her last hope. If he wouldn't do it for her brother's sake then she had nothing else with which to bargain. "Won't you even listen to the plan? It might . . . it might intrigue you." She glanced unconsciously around the cabin, wondering how long he'd been cooped up here alone. Perhaps something that took him out of these mountains might be good for him. Whatever had happened to Julian during the past six months had changed him, and not for the better. She found herself wishing he wouldn't look at her with that too-hot gaze. It seemed to Anne that she could feel all his anger and disgust as it radiated at her through those golden eyes. She had been an idiot to think this idea was going to work. A rather desperate idiot.

"There isn't much that intrigues me these days, Anne," he told her coolly.

"Not even the thought of getting out of this cabin?" she demanded. His own restlessness seemed to be affecting her. She didn't feel the overheated atmosphere of the room as he apparently did, but she was vividly aware of another kind of tension. The anxiety of crushed hopes, a determination to go forward with her brother's plan, even without Julian's help, and the realization that she was trapped in this place with a man who was dangerously different from the Julian she remembered all contributed to her disquiet. Anne picked up her brandy glass and took a steadying sip.

"I like this cabin," Julian said dryly. "It's the closest thing to a home that I've got. I'm sorry if it depresses you, but then, no one invited you here."

Anger flared in Anne. Well, she'd tried. That was all she could do. Setting the brandy glass down on the table with a sharp snap, she rose and collected the red jacket from the arm of the chair. "You're right. This place does depress me. You depress me. I think I'll make a stab at getting out of these mountains before the snow makes the driving impossible."

He was on his feet before she could turn around, his powerful hand closing over her shoulder. With the instincts of a rabbit being confronted by a wolf, Anne went very still, not daring to move.

"For you the trip out is already impossible. You should never have come here, Anne."

"I know that now." Her voice was a faint whisper. She realized she was trembling beneath his hand. What a fool she had been.

Slowly, inevitably he pulled her around to face him. The golden eyes were lit with a devastating, unnaturally brilliant fire, and the same heat was being conducted through his hand where it grasped her shoulder.

"Once I asked you to spend the night with me," he rasped softly. "The night before Mike and I had to leave for that island."

"I remember." And she did. All too clearly. Her mind had been at war with her body that night. She had known he was wrong for her—known there was no hope of building any kind of permanent relationship with a man who made his living the way Julian Aries did. Her mind had won the battle. It had drawn on her sense of anger toward the man who was taking her younger brother into a potentially deadly situation. She had used that fury to fight her own undisciplined desire.

"I let you walk away that night. I would be a fool to let you walk away again, wouldn't I? Not when you've been haunting me for six months."

The heat in him was reaching out to engulf her. A new kind of fear sizzled along her nerve endings. Something was wrong and she didn't understand it.

"Julian, are you all right?" she asked again, not knowing how to ask the real question.

"No, I'm not all right. You've played havoc with my mind, Anne Silver. You came and went in my head like a ghost, turning up whenever I needed you but always staying just out of reach. I wanted to catch you and chain you. I wanted to possess you—make it impossible for you to escape."

"You wanted to hurt me, punish me," she protested. "But, Julian, I don't deserve your anger. You didn't hate me when you left that night after bringing Michael back. You said we had unfinished business, but I didn't think you hated me. What's wrong? What happened? Why are you—"

"Be quiet, ghost lady. I'm going to exorcise you. I'm going to get you out of my head once and for all."

His strong hands locked behind her head, thumbs moving along the line of her jaw so that she was forced to lift her face for his kiss. Their gazes clashed and in that moment Anne knew her premonition had been correct. She was dealing with a Julian who was far different from the man who had walked away from her six months ago.

2

HER HAIR WAS the color of autumn leaves. Julian snarled his fingers in the thick stuff, tugging it free from the tortoiseshell clip that had anchored it. How he'd longed for the rich russet color of her hair in the middle of that endless green jungle.

He'd wished for the sweet, womanly scent of her when the thick smell of decomposing undergrowth had threatened to clog his nostrils. And at night he'd dreamed of having the soft fullness of her body next to his. The nights had been the worst. It was then that she had floated in his head, taunting him, always just out of reach.

Julian had never been quite certain why he had been so fascinated with Anne Silver. His business with Michael had accidentally brought him into contact with her. As soon as she had discovered why he was spending so much time with her brother, Anne had begun to fight him. She saw him as a threat and in the end she had been right. A week had been too short a time to override her fears.

But he had known she was intensely aware of him. Julian had tried to play on that undeniable attraction—tried to use it to break through the barriers she had erected against him. He had failed. Anne had resisted him steadfastly, backed by her fierce desire to protect her younger brother and by her own instinctive wariness of Julian himself.

Only in his head had he been able to touch her like this, thread his fingers through the enthralling russet hair. Her blue-green eyes had looked at him often enough in his dreams, at times filled with accusation, at other times warm with desire. It was when he saw those eyes filled with need for him that Julian knew for certain he was hallucinating. Those times were the most dangerous. In a way he had come to see that fantasy of desire as a warning that he was losing his grasp on reality. He had relied on it to let him know that he was near the edge. In real life, Anne would never look at him with such sensual invitation.

That knowledge had infuriated him but it had also saved his life on more than one occasion. It had forced him to think logically enough to save his own neck when he otherwise might have slipped too deeply into the quagmire of his fevered mind.

"If I hadn't been half out of my mind a lot of the time, you would have driven me crazy," he growled against her mouth. Such a soft expressive mouth. Her smile could be brilliant, full of laughter and feminine mischief. He'd tortured himself with thoughts of how many other men she had used that smile on during the past six months.

"Julian, wait—"

He crushed the protest back into her mouth and the action was a catalyst. It unlocked all the raging hunger, as well as the raging frustration and anger that had been simmering in him. Remembered pain, both physical and mental, crowded into his head, seeking to be assuaged at last.

She tasted as he had dreamed she would taste. Warm and damp and inviting. The trace of brandy in her mouth was a piquant spice, blending with the overwhelmingly sensual flavor. It was better than he had dreamed, Julian told himself fiercely. Far better.

He felt her tremble in his grasp, heard her soft moan, and a feeling of exultation swept over him. She was here in his arms and he could hardly believe it. This time it wasn't a hallucination or a fevered dream. This time she was real and she couldn't escape. He wouldn't allow it. Not when he'd waited so long for this night.

As he drank from her mouth, trying to satisfy a thirst that only grew stronger, Julian allowed himself the luxury of touch. The problem with hallucinations and dreams was that a man could never enjoy the exquisite sense of touch. His fingers moved along the delicate shape of her ear and then traced the line of her cheek.

She was no great beauty, he tried to tell himself for the thousandth time. The lines of her face were not classic. Rather they were a little rounded, slightly softened. Just as the lines of her body were round and soft. A man looked at her and knew she was all woman, capable of gentleness and fire. When she loved she would wrap a man in both, Julian thought. When she was angry she could be as fierce as any she-cat. The one thing Anne could never be was remote and distant. That knowledge gave him power.

"I've wanted you for so long," he ground out, as he reluctantly freed her mouth to explore the line of her throat. "So long . . . You should never have come here tonight, lady. You should have had enough sense to stay out of my lair."

"Julian, we must talk—"

The words were muffled against his shoulder and he ignored them, concentrating on the way she was responding. When he had dared allow himself the fantasy, it had been exactly like this. She would murmur the words of protest because he knew that intellectually she was afraid of him. But her body always trembled under his touch, just as it did tonight.

He could feel the desire in her now. It made her shiver slightly and press closer. Her palms were flat against his chest, fingers splayed as if she were uncertain whether to fight or cling. Julian gave her no option. He drew his hands down the length of her back, seeking the full curve of her enticing derriere.

His head was beginning to spin a little. Only natural, he decided grimly. Having a fantasy come to life was disorienting. Wanting her arms around him he freed her momentarily to grasp her wrists and pull them behind his neck.

"You're not going anywhere tonight," he told her thickly, "so you might as well give me what I need. Hold me, Anne. Hold me as if you'll never let go."

The blood sang savagely in his veins when she did as he demanded. Intoxicated now, Julian groaned and bent to lift her into his arms. He would take her into the bedroom, he thought. Away from the heat of the damn fireplace. Between the two of them they would generate more than enough warmth anyway.

"Julian, you aren't the only one who's had dreams."

The small confession gripped him for an instant. He came to a halt beside the quilted bed and gazed down at her face. She had closed her eyes against him and the moment. "If I've figured in your dreams, it could only have been as a devil. That's how you've always seen me, isn't it?"

"I've hardly seen you at all. A few times before you left for that island with Michael and then that night you brought him home."

"Tonight you'll find out if all your worst fears are true, won't you?" He dropped her down onto the bed, following heavily. "At least I look the part now, don't I?" he demanded as her hand came up to touch the scar on his jaw.

"Please tell me what happened," she begged.

Julian studied the depths of her sea-colored eyes. "The last thing I want from you tonight is pity. Save it for some other man who will be satisfied with that kind of response. I want the fire and the softness."

But he knew that deep down he didn't want to witness her reaction to the marks on the rest of his body. His hand swept out to find the lamp switch even as his mouth closed over Anne's again. It wasn't just that he didn't want the light. He also didn't need the extra heat from the lamp. It was already so hot, even here in the bedroom away from the fire.

Somehow the sudden darkness seemed to fracture the languid spell that had governed Anne since he had first kissed her in the living room. When his hand moved hungrily to the gentle curve of her breast she cried out softly. He felt the sudden resistance in her and groaned.

"Anne, no. Don't fight me. I've waited too long—needed you too badly. You came looking for me tonight and you'll have to take what you've found."

The tension in her radiated through his own body and fed his desire. So many nights of wanting and longing. He had thought he was hallucinating again this evening when he'd answered the knock on his door to find his ghost lady standing on the step. He'd half expected her to simply disappear. And then she had complained about the cold and asked to come inside. He didn't think ghosts felt the cold.

Julian was aware that his fingers were shaking a little as he determinedly tugged off the sweater Anne wore. The knowledge irritated him. He would not give in to the weakness of his own body. Not tonight when his whole being was intent on exorcising his very personal phantom.

"You don't feel like a phantom, though," he muttered as the sweater came free and he found the tips of her breasts. The fact that she was not wearing a bra pleased him. One less obstacle to overcome.

"I'm real, Julian. Please treat me as if I am," she whispered. "Don't punish me for your nightmares. I never meant to haunt you."

Her fingers laced into his hair, stroking down to his nape almost as though she were trying to soothe him. Julian told himself that he didn't want to be soothed and gentled. Deliberately he fought the impulse to halt the lovemaking and simply lay his head down on her breast and allow her to stroke him. Always in his dreams that had been a dangerous lure the ghost had used. Always she withdrew her gentle touch just as he accepted it.

But this time Anne was real, he reminded himself. Wonderingly he grazed his fingertips across one nipple. When he felt it grow taut and sensitized he growled his pleasure.

"I know this is real," he murmured, bending his head to taste the budding nipple. "And this . . ." He slid his palm down her stomach until he felt her quivering response. She knew he was going to probe further and her whole body was reacting with unbearable anticipation and tension. The sense of power in him skyrocketed. For once his ghost lady was under his control.

The spinning sensation in his head seemed to accelerate. A throbbing urgency was governing his body. The forces driving him tonight were too elemental to allow for a leisurely, carefully charted act of desire. Impatiently Julian fumbled in the darkness with the clasp of her jeans.

"Oh, Julian!"

He couldn't be sure if it was a cry of protest or resignation or desire. He only knew he liked the sound of his name on her lips. With a quick, stripping action he pulled the jeans down over her rounded hips, heedless of her fingers as she struggled to slow him.

"Please, Julian, I . . . oh, *please!*"

He had found the secret, warm place between her legs and she shuddered as he made the contact. Already he could feel her dampening at his touch. She wanted him. Whatever else she said tonight, she couldn't deny that she wanted him.

"Give me the words, ghost lady. Let me hear you say that you need me tonight as much as I need you," he ordered, tracing an erotic design on the most intimate spot on her body.

Convulsively her hands went around him, her nails adding small marks to the collection of scars on his back. "I told you. You aren't the only one who's had dreams, Julian. I've longed for you. You promised to come back and you never did. *You promised.*"

He heard the accusation and the pain in her voice and couldn't understand either one. But there was no way on earth he could fail to understand the sensuous twisting of her body as she moved pleadingly against him. His ghost lady was coming very much alive beneath his hands.

When he pulled away to fumble rapidly with his own clothing Anne murmured a protest. His shirt and jeans landed in a careless heap on the floor alongside the soft leather boots he had been wearing, and then Julian turned back to pin his phantom to the bed.

"There were times when I would have sold my soul to have you where you are now," he grated. "I won't let you escape, now that I've got my hands on you."

In the dark shadows he saw her lips part as if she were about to contradict him. Julian sealed them with his own, simultaneously pushing himself between her legs. The softness of her thighs around him was all he had ever dreamed it would be. For a moment he held back, not yet certain whether to believe.

"Closer, Anne," he commanded huskily. "Cling to me until I know you're real."

"I keep telling you, Julian, I'm very, very real." She sighed into his mouth and her arms tightened, pulling him to her.

He sensed the surrender in her and gloried in it. Head whirling with the satisfaction of knowing she was giving herself to him at last, Julian rasped her name and drove himself heavily into the snug, hot velvet of her.

"Anne, oh, my God, Anne . . . !"

No fantasy this, Julian thought dazedly. He could feel the instinctive resistance of her body as it gradually accommodated itself to the fullness of his manhood. There was an exciting, tantalizing tingle of pain as her nails flexed on his shoulders. And the silky feel of her legs was exquisite captivity. Nothing in his life had ever been so overwhelmingly real.

Frantically he forced himself to find the pace that would allow Anne to stay with him as he sought the promised satisfaction. He realized dimly that he had to make it good for her. In his fantasies he had always promised himself he would make it right for Anne, hoping that the sensual gratification would be an inducement to make her stay with him.

"Julian, darling Julian. Love me. Please, please love me . . ."

He was aware of the new tension in her, felt the gentle telltale shiver that coursed through her, pulling him along in its wake and suddenly it wasn't just his head that was spinning. It was the whole world.

"Anne!"

The cry was torn from him as his body exploded. Blazing satisfaction surged in him, and he held the woman in his arms tighter than he'd ever held on to anything or anyone in his life.

And then there was silence. Nothing but too much warmth and too much silence. He should have put out the fire, Julian thought vaguely as he closed his eyes. It was too damn hot.

Anne realized slowly that the forceful grasp that had held her was slackening. She came out of the too-silent sensual aftermath to find Julian sprawled across her body, his head on the pillow beside her. Uncertainly she opened her eyes to meet his, not knowing what to expect. After the shattering finale to the lovemaking there had been no words, no soothing caresses, no soft murmurs. Only silence.

Silence and heat, she corrected, frowning a little as she realized just how warm Julian was. Unnaturally warm. The tawny eyes that had seemed abnormally bright were concealed behind the only soft feature of his face—his lashes.

He was asleep.

So much for worrying about what a woman said in a situation such as this, she told herself ruefully. It looked as if she was going to be spared the humiliation of acknowledging her surrender to the man who had insisted on it.

Tentatively Anne lifted a hand to push back a swath of dark hair that had fallen forward across Julian's forehead. When her fingers brushed his skin she felt the warmth there.

"Julian?"

There was no response. He was deeply asleep. Carefully Anne began untangling her legs from his. In the shadows she could only make out the harsh angles of his face but she ran a palm lightly down his smoothly muscled back. There, just below his shoulders, was the ridge in the surface of his skin. She thought she had felt it during the moments of frantic passion. Another scar, she wondered.

Dear God. Julian had been hurt badly. A fierce anger welled up inside as she carefully explored the length of the scar. Anne was filled with a sudden hatred for whoever had inflicted the physical pain on her lover. She remembered the limp and her brow furrowed again. Perhaps no one had deliberately done this to him. He might have had an accident for all she knew. What was it he had said? Something about a rough six months.

As she pulled herself free of the weight of his body Anne became aware of the chill in the bedroom. The heat of the fire had not penetrated well in here, and apparently Julian had switched on no alternative source. Unless she counted the source of heat that was his own body. Lord, he was hot. Much too hot.

A curious lethargy in her limbs made it difficult to get to her feet. She felt as though Julian had just forced her to run a hundred miles with him. Every part of her remembered the feel of his passion and strength. It had all been more real than she would have expected. Having a dream merge with reality should have been a more ethereal experience, Anne told herself. Something warned her that Julian had left an impression on her that would never be confused with a dream. Already she was vividly aware of a soft soreness in her lower body. In making her reach the peak of satisfaction with him, Julian had not spared her.

Awkwardly Anne started to pull on her clothes and then realized what she wanted in that moment was a hot shower. She found the adjoining bathroom, turned on the shower and stood studying the few masculine items arranged around the sink while she waited for the water to warm.

Julian used only the essentials, she thought. There wasn't even any after-shave lotion, let alone any men's cologne. There was a small black comb but certainly no styling dryer for his hair. Unable to stifle an overriding interest in the man who lay sleeping in the other room, Anne opened the small mirrored medicine chest.

A toothbrush. A tube of toothpaste, which had been consistently squeezed from the middle rather than from the bottom, and a razor. One can of shaving cream. Feeling guilty at the blatant snooping, Anne was about to close the door of the cabinet when she noticed the bottle of tablets on the top shelf. Aspirin, she decided. If Julian really did have a slight fever she could give him some later. Hastily she shut the cabinet and stepped into the shower.

By the time she began responding to the invigorating effects of the hot water, Anne also began to take stock of her situation. In every fantasy she had ever spun concerning a reunion with Julian Aries, matters had always taken a different course from the one they had pursued tonight. She had dreamed of long, quiet talks while they finally got to know each other. She had imagined herself explaining that she now understood that Julian hadn't "lured" her brother to that island. Michael Silver had a reporter's instincts and a willingness to go wherever he had to go in order to get his story. The story Julian had offered him in exchange for providing journalistic cover had been too good to turn down.

Anne had planned to make her apologies and explanations and then wait to see if Julian still had any interest in pursuing the electric attraction that had flared between them from the first moment they had met. She had been prepared to accept the limitations his career would put on any relationship they built. Or at least she had told herself she was prepared to accept those limits.

In return she had wanted some answers. He had promised to come back for her and he had never kept that promise. She had to know if the attraction he had felt wasn't sufficient to make him tolerate her anger and the demands he undoubtedly expected her to make. For six months she had waited for him to make the first move.

In the end she had been forced to come to him. The result had been explosive but not at all illuminating or constructive. Deep down she had known that sooner or later physically, at least, she would surrender. It had been inevitable and she suspected that something in her had recognized that from the start.

The problem was that the sensual coupling could provide no real, long-term answers. It only served to solidify the chains that bound her to Julian. And she had no way of knowing if even that much had been accomplished from Julian's point of view.

He had claimed he wanted to exorcise her from his mind. Perhaps tonight was all he would ever need from her.

Tugging on the jeans and sweater and her warm socks, Anne finished dressing and padded back out into the dark bedroom. Julian still lay in a sprawl across the bed. The light from the bathroom shafted across the solid, lean lines of his body, revealing the angry scar across his shoulders and another forbidding line along the back of his thigh. Her heart turned over at the thought of the pain those wounds must have inflicted.

Even as she fought back the instinctive reaction, Julian moved slightly on the bed. There was a restless abruptness to the movement that alarmed her. He mumbled something and flung his hand out over the pillow.

"Julian, what's wrong?" She hurried forward and sat down on the edge of the bed, testing the warmth of him with her palm. "My God, you're burning up!"

In the few minutes she had been in the shower, the fever she had sensed in him had blossomed into a fire. Alarmed by the intensity of it, she struggled to get him under the bedclothes.

"Too hot," he muttered, pushing at her with his hands. "Much too hot. Put out the fire."

"Hush, Julian. It's all right. I'll take care of you."

Eyes closed he turned his head in the direction of her voice. "Ghost lady. Why are you here? It's dangerous . . ."

"I'm here to take care of you, Julian. Please let me." She managed to pull the sheet over him although his movements were becoming more disturbed. His strength was a problem. Even gripped with fever his hands retained a lot of their normal power. When he tried to rip aside the sheet she was helpless to keep it in place.

"Julian, try to lie still. I'm going to get something to cool you down."

He was far too warm. When a fever soared like this it ought to be broken in any way possible. Somewhere she remembered hearing that bit of first-aid advice. Anne stopped battling him for the sheet and went back into the bathroom. Opening the medicine cabinet, she reached for the bottle of tablets she had noted earlier. They weren't aspirin. Frowning, she read the unfamiliar chemical name on the label and noted that they were a prescription.

"Two tablets at onset of symptoms. One every four hours thereafter," she read, wondering if the fever was one of the symptoms for which the tablets had been prescribed. Carrying the bottle back into the bedroom, she tried to get a moment of rational attention from her patient.

"Julian, are these pills for your fever?"

"Damn pills. Won't take them anymore. Tired of being a weakling. Go away, ghost lady. Take the pills with you. I hate it when you see me like this."

His body was dry from the inner heat. She had to do something. Determinedly Anne ran a glass of water in the bathroom and came back to the bed. Firmly she cradled him with an arm around his broad shoulders and held the liquid to his lips.

"You're thirsty, Julian. You must be thirsty. Here, put this in your mouth and drink the water."

To her astonishment he obeyed, swallowing the tablet and most of the water. When she attempted to remove her arm, however, he protested angrily.

"Don't go. Not now. Too late now."

"I'll be right back, Julian," she soothed. "I'm going to get something to cool you down a little."

"You'll come back?"

"Yes."

"Can't trust you. You always fade away."

"Not this time, Julian. Not this time."

Desperate to relieve the frightening fever and knowing she would be physically incapable of dragging Julian from the bed and into a cold shower, Anne grabbed the sheet and carried it back into the bathroom. There she soaked it in cold water. Julian groaned when she covered him with the chilled, wet sheet and she wondered if she was doing the right thing. It had been so long since she'd had any first aid.

When the heat of his body had burned away the benefit of the wet sheet, she resoaked the material and applied it again. Julian didn't protest the damp cloth, but he continued to shift himself violently around on the bed and the muttered words became more and more difficult to comprehend.

"It hurts, ghost lady. It hurts. Can't tell anyone. Shouldn't even tell you."

"Where does it hurt, Julian?" Anne whispered, wondering if she ought to give him another tablet. If only she were absolutely positive they had been prescribed for this fever.

"My leg. It's bleeding. If I can't get it stopped . . ."

"Julian, the bleeding has stopped."

"No."

"Yes, darling. I've stopped it. You're going to be fine. Please believe me, darling. You're going to be fine."

Together with the damp sheets, she kept up the running murmur of encouragement and reassurance for the next hour and then, when she was contemplating whether to risk another of the strange tablets, she sensed that Julian was finally growing quieter. In another hour she was certain the fever had broken. He was suddenly soaking wet and it wasn't from the effects of the damp sheet.

The sweat that coated his body was the aftermath of the fever. Carefully Anne stroked it from him and then she realized that she was going to have to change the saturated bedclothes. Now Julian would need warmth.

It was a chore remaking the bed because Julian had fallen into a deep sleep. He lay heavily in the middle of the damp bed and it took all of Anne's strength to roll him gently to first one side and then the other while she redid everything.

The room was quite cold now. The fire in the living room had probably gone out completely. She had been too busy to rebuild it. Anne went searching for a thermostat and finally realized there were some baseboard heaters in every room. Julian hadn't turned any of them on earlier, apparently. It took a long time before they became effective.

Anne spent the rest of the night keeping watch over her sleeping patient. At one point she thought he was growing warmer again and managed to wake him sufficiently to get another of the tablets down his throat. Then he began to complain of the cold.

At three in the morning chills were shaking his body and he clutched at her when she came near. The tawny eyes opened briefly, pleading with her.

"So cold," he growled. "Keep me warm, ghost lady. I need your warmth. So cold."

"Oh, Julian," she whispered, allowing herself to be dragged down beside him. There she gathered him to her, holding him beneath the covers until the chills stopped racking his body. Again he slept. When she was certain he was resting quietly she disengaged herself and went back to her chair.

At times during the early morning hours she dozed, but every shift in Julian's position, every change in his breathing pattern brought her back to full wakefulness. At dawn she finally abandoned any attempt at sleep for herself and, after checking her patient once more, went out into the kitchen to see about some tea or coffee.

The blanket of snow outside the window startled her. She had been so busy tending to Julian that she had forgotten the approaching storm. Her unwilling host had been right about one thing; she didn't have any chains in the car she had rented at the Denver airport. Until the roads were cleared she was trapped with her patient.

"As if I could leave him in his condition, anyway," she muttered resignedly, as she set a kettle on the stove. "Oh, Julian, what have they done to you?"

She didn't even know who "they" were. Just as she didn't know what had happened to the man who had captivated her so from the start of their short, stormy relationship. But she knew she would take great pleasure in seeking revenge for her lover of one night.

One night. Wryly she shook her head, wondering if Julian would even remember the passion that had reverberated between them. The fever had raged so swiftly that it was possible he wouldn't have any clear memory of the hour or two before it had seized him completely. The thought of how brilliantly his eyes had burned when he had opened the front door of the cabin made Anne wonder how ill he had been even then.

She had been so wrapped up in her anxiety and anticipation that she hadn't read the signs of illness in him until after he had made love to her. The realization made her wince. On the other hand what could she have done to halt the inevitable flow of the lovemaking once Julian had begun it? Nothing she could have said or done would have stopped him. Not then.

Carrying the pot of tea and a cup back into the bedroom, Anne sat down in the chair by the window and pulled the faded cotton drapes. Julian didn't stir as she poured herself a cup of tea and sipped thoughtfully.

The thick layer of snow outside gave the mountains a deceptively serene appearance this morning. Stately fir and pine, heavily weighted with the white stuff made her think of postcard Christmases. She wondered where Julian had planned to spend the holidays this year. Never in the short while she had known him had he mentioned any family or close friends. But then she knew so little about him. There had been no time to get to know each other before he and Michael had left for that island. What she had learned of him and his background had made it painfully clear that there was no real hope for any kind of lasting relationship, even if the hostility between them could be appeased.

She wished there was a phone in the cabin. She could have called the pharmacy that had handled Julian's prescription, and made certain she was using the tablets for the right symptoms. Uncertain and no longer desperate now that the fever had been drastically reduced, she decided to hold off giving him any more medication until he was awake and coherent enough to tell her the pills were meant for this particular purpose.

He slept throughout the morning and Anne decided the rest was more beneficial than waking him for some food. As soon as he was more awake she would try to at least get some liquid down him.

Her own stomach began making demands around nine o'clock, however, and Anne traipsed back into the kitchen to find something to eat. She was slicing some bread for toast when a faint noise made her swing around in surprise.

"Julian! You shouldn't be out of bed."

He stood in the doorway, staring at her. The fever had left him looking exhausted and a little unsteady, but the intensity of his gaze made her realize he was fully aware of his surroundings once again.

"I told myself I'd dreamed the whole thing," he whispered harshly.

"Julian, please go back to bed." Anne dropped the knife she had been using and went toward him trying hard to ignore the fact that he was standing stark naked in front of her. "You mustn't get chilled again."

"Are you sure you're not a ghost?"

"Quite sure." Perhaps he didn't remember everything that had happened during the night. It might be easier now if he didn't recall the lovemaking, Anne thought as she gently took his arm to lead him back to bed. Easier on her.

He ignored her hand, continuing to gaze at her in fascination. "You shouldn't be here. You're not supposed to be anywhere around here. You should be neatly tucked away back in Indiana doing research for that old professor who employs you."

"This way, Julian. I'll get you some breakfast if you like. Some poached eggs on toast."

This time he yielded to her firm tug, allowing himself to be led back to the tousled bed. She straightened it quickly and then urged him back between the covers. Somewhat to her surprise he obeyed, although he never took his eyes off her.

"Julian, are those tablets in the bathroom medicine chest for this kind of thing? I've already given you two of them but it says on the label you should have more."

"Two?" He frowned as he sank back into the pillows. His hand moved briefly across his eyes. "Only two?"

"Do you think you should have another one?" She plumped the pillows around him, bending over as she did so.

"No!" Then he relaxed a little. "No, not unless the fever comes back. It's never gone away this quickly, not even when I've taken the full dosage. Maybe...maybe I'm finally getting over..." His voice trailed off as she continued to fuss solicitously with the blankets. "Anne?"

"Yes, Julian?"

His hand came up to rest on her sweater right over the full curve of her breast. She froze, her eyes going anxiously to his intent face.

"Last night. I didn't dream any of it, did I? I carried you in here and made love to you."

Quite suddenly Anne knew she had been right earlier when she had wondered if everything would be much safer for her if Julian didn't remember the hour of passion.

"You were very ill last night," she soothed lightly, stepping out of reach of his hand. "In fact you were hallucinating at times, I think."

"Probably," he agreed dryly. "I usually do. But I didn't dream up that scene between you and me, did I?"

"I'm afraid so," she said gently, smoothing the hair back off his brow. She managed a nurse's smile. "You were ill when I arrived and it wasn't long after that before you were in bed."

"With you."

"Well, I was here," she admitted easily, "but not in a particularly romantic capacity. I spent a lot of time dampening sheets and soothing your fevered brow."

"Anne, I never would have guessed you were such a little liar." He closed his eyes in weariness. "When I wake up next time you're going to tell me why."

He was asleep before she could think of a response. But as she stood looking down at the proud, tired lines of his face Anne told herself she would make an attempt to stick by her story. He had been delirious enough last night that he couldn't really be certain just what had been real and what had been a figment of his imagination.

She had been wrong using her brother's plight as an excuse to seek out Julian, Anne realized. It was true that she badly needed his help, but it had still been just an excuse to see the man who had haunted her memories for six months.

Julian Aries was like a wounded animal who would lash out at anyone who got too close. He needed time to heal his own wounds before a woman dared approach him to offer any kind of relationship. Even then she might find that he was incapable of real emotional commitment, let alone love.

Everything she had ever told herself about Julian was still true. He was a loner, a man who might pursue a woman in order to satisfy his desire for her, but who would never ask for or want feminine comfort or gentle concern.

If she'd ever needed proof of that, Anne thought, she had it now. Julian had retreated, sick and injured, to his lair after that last mission, preferring to lick his wounds alone.

She didn't try to fool herself. Anne knew very well that he wasn't going to be at all grateful for her nursing. When he came out of the aftermath of his fever he was going to be dangerous. He would be violently resentful of the fact that she had witnessed his weakness. Hurting as badly as he was he could easily turn on her and claw her, out of frustration and anger.

She'd had no right to track him to his lair, Anne told herself grimly, and had no one but herself to blame for the mauling that was bound to ensue. Trapped here now, partly because of the snow and partly because there was no way she could leave while he was so helpless from the effects of the mysterious fever, she knew her only hope was to protect herself as much as possible.

There was no chance of coming out of the ordeal unscathed, but if she was very careful she might keep from getting completely lacerated.

3

THE FIRST WARNING SNARLS came around lunchtime when Anne carried a tray of hot chicken-noodle soup and a small sandwich into the bedroom. Julian's brooding gaze was on her the second she appeared in the doorway of his room, and she knew he had been waiting impatiently.

"I hate chicken-noodle soup."

"Then why do you have six cans of it on your kitchen shelves?" With a determinedly bright smile, Anne adjusted the tray in front of him. He sat back against the pillows, glaring at the soup bowl.

"I didn't feel like doing a lot of grocery shopping on the way up here. I just scooped up whatever was handy at the store in town."

"Winding up with six cans of a soup you don't like will teach you to be a more careful shopper in the future, won't it?" Anne observed cheerfully as she sat down in the chair beside the window to supervise his lunch.

He slanted her an assessing glance. There was clear menace in the catlike eyes but there were also traces of pain, and it was all Anne could do to keep from going over to the bed and cuddling him. Prudently she resisted the impulse, knowing she could easily get herself slashed in the process. Weak as he was, Julian was nevertheless dangerous, and she would be a fool to forget it.

"Shopping," he stated, "has never been one of my favorite hobbies."

"What are your favorite hobbies, Julian?" Anne demanded chattily. "I've often wondered if you have any. We know so little about each other."

"You discovered one of them last night." Morosely he picked up the soupspoon and tried a taste. "When uninvited females show up on my doorstep I take them to bed."

Anne astonished herself by not even flinching. "I'm afraid I must have missed something, then. You were flying high on that fever long before we ever reached the bedroom. Don't you remember how you kept complaining of the heat?"

"I remember how hot you were," he countered bluntly. "Compared to you, the fireplace was an iceberg."

"Your imagination certainly goes into overdrive when you're under the influence of that fever," Anne noted smoothly. "What is it, anyway? Malaria?"

"Something similar." He tried another spoonful of soup.

"Have you had many bouts of it? Those tablets in your medicine chest..."

"I picked it up on that damned island. It comes and goes."

"But how often has it recurred?" she persisted.

"Three or four times."

"What do the doctors say? How long will it continue to recur?"

"They don't know. With any luck the bouts will get less severe and eventually stop entirely. But I haven't been a real lucky man lately," he added derisively. "Unless you want to count last night, of course. I haven't thanked you for that, have I? I realize I might not have been at my best under the circumstances, but then, you didn't give me much notice. Give me a couple more days to recover and we'll try it again. That is, if you're still stranded here because of the snow."

"You can bait me all you want, Julian, but we both know I'm the only one who really remembers clearly what happened."

"Want to bet? How's this: You showed up on my doorstep last night to ask me for help with implementing some wild scheme of Mike's. You said Mike had been hit by a car and is still in the hospital and that you're planning on trapping the people you think tried to kill him. A bunch of ghost hunters, you said." He gave her a defiant look, daring her to tell him his memory wasn't clear on that subject.

"It was shortly after I told you all that, that you collapsed," she assured him gently.

"Like hell. But leaving that business aside for the moment, tell me more about this crazy plan. Are you serious about going through with it?"

"Yes."

"What does it involve?" he growled.

"Mike has already set everything up. Even if they're onto him, I don't think they'll have any way of being aware of his scheme. He's arranged for a very wealthy acquaintance of his, an eccentric old lady, to hire the ghost hunters. She wants them to clear out the family ghost from the mansion in California that she's just inherited. At least that's the story. She's going to swear she won't move in until the ghost has been, uh, freed from its mortal chains. I'm going to pose as her niece—her younger sister's daughter—who's volunteered to deal with the ghost hunters since 'auntie' won't come near the place until they've done their job. The house is full of valuable antiques and some really fine jewelry and paintings. It should be a sufficient lure for the theft ring."

"What happens after they've gone through their routine and left the mansion?"

"That's the part where I'll hire a little help," Anne confessed. "I need someone who knows how to keep a house under surveillance and who can figure out how to catch the ghost hunters when they come back to steal the stuff they've decided they want."

He stared at her. "That part of the plan sounds a little vague," he noted dryly.

"It is. I think now that perhaps I'll hire a private detective," Anne explained assertively. "Private detectives ought to know about that sort of thing."

"You could wind up paying him for several months of surveillance. There's no telling when your psychic investigators will make their move. After all, if they've got keys or full information on the security system they can sneak back any time it's convenient for them. Presumably, long after anyone remembers that they were once in the house and thinks to connect them with the crime."

Anne drew a deep breath. "I'm supposed to let it drop casually during their first visit that 'auntie' is planning on installing a whole new electronic security system within a few weeks. Hopefully that will inspire the thieves to make their move quickly before all the locks are changed and the electronic detection stuff has been installed."

"I see."

Anne waited, expecting some sort of further comment. Even if he wasn't interested in getting involved in the scheme she thought he'd probably have some thoughts on the matter. But Julian said nothing, merely continuing to munch slowly on the sandwich. She realized he was tiring rapidly.

"Julian?"

"Umm?" He appeared preoccupied.

"What do you think about Mike's plan? I'm not asking you to help me but I don't have anyone else with whom I can discuss it and I could use the advice. I admit I'm a little out of my field."

"Yeah."

Resentment prickled Anne. "Well, come to think of it, I doubt you've had a whole heck of a lot of experience trapping fake psychic investigators, either!"

"True. But I've seen a lot of carefully set traps go haywire, lady, and this particular trap doesn't even sound carefully worked out. With you in charge it's probably going to prove a total disaster."

Angrily Anne got to her feet. "If you've finished mauling that sandwich, I'll take the tray." She scooped it up before he could protest and swept out of the bedroom. She was trembling with outrage and a carefully imposed self-restraint. The last thing she wanted was to allow Julian to provoke a full-scale argument and that was what he was clearly bent on doing. He'd tried first to bait her with reminders of last night's passion, and then he was obviously intent on making her scheme appear foolish and unworkable. She had better learn that any opening she gave him for communication was an avenue he would twist for his own purposes.

It was as she washed out the soup bowl that she admitted to herself that she had really wanted his advice. She was out of her depth trying to implement Michael's plan and she knew it. Julian might be too occupied with healing his own wounds to help her carry out the plan but she'd been hoping for at least a few practical suggestions. She was nervous about what she was getting herself into, she realized. No, she was more than nervous. She was downright scared. The people she was hoping to trap had already shown themselves capable of attempted murder.

In the bedroom Julian collapsed more deeply into the pillows, closing his eyes in a combination of weariness and disgust. The fever always left him weak as a kitten, and the condition infuriated him. It was bad enough dealing with it on his own, but having Anne witness it was the last straw. His fist clenched in helpless rage.

Why did she have to show up last night? Every time he had mentally planned his first encounter with her he had never intended it to happen that way. In all his fantasies on the subject he had never been on the brink of another bout of the fever. Nor had he still limped. And the scars had all been magically removed in his dreams.

He was right when he'd told Anne that he'd seen a lot of carefully set traps go haywire. The one he'd planned to set for her was a shining example. It was in ruins. The knowledge was maddening.

Everything was infuriating him this morning, his own physical weakness, the fact that Anne had been obliged to play nurse to him and the realization that she was determined to pursue her brother's idiotic scheme.

But the most infuriating thing of all was the way she calmly denied last night's passion.

He *knew* he hadn't dreamed up the lovemaking. No matter what she claimed this morning, he was sure of the way she had responded last night. Glowering savagely, Julian threw off the blankets and sat up on the edge of the bed. It took more energy than he had to spare, to make his way into the bathroom.

Leaning heavily on the sink he twisted so that he could see his shoulders in the medicine-chest mirror. Ignoring the slash of the scar he peered intently at the two tiny little scratches he had been only mildly aware of when they had been inflicted. They were small, only half a day old and would undoubtedly disappear completely by the end of the day. But they were evidence.

Julian turned away from the mirror on a wave of rough satisfaction and staggered a bit as he made his way toward the bed. He hadn't been hallucinating when she had left those marks with her nails. He had been making love to his ghost, and furthermore, she had been responding.

But she was acting as if nothing at all had occurred between them. The question of why she chose to pretend he had dreamed it all up in a delirium kept festering in him.

Perhaps she was angry at him because of the way he had forced her into bed and then forced a response. He knew she had always been a little afraid of him, and the way he had treated her last night probably hadn't mitigated that fear in any way. Her surrender had been complete and she might have decided to deny it both to herself and to him. His fever had provided her with the perfect chance at regaining her pride.

Nursing him was bound to reinforce her sense of regained control. Between denying her response in his arms and being able to treat him like a helpless child this morning, she would be firmly reestablishing her sense of self-control in front of a man who had always threatened it.

Julian rubbed his aching head with his hand, grimly pleased with his own analysis of the situation. If she was still a little afraid of him and intent on denying her reaction to his lovemaking, perhaps his wounds and his weakness hadn't ruined everything. Perhaps she was not consumed with pity for him.

It was the one thing of which he had been so afraid: her pity. It was the last thing he wanted and the reason he had hidden himself in these mountains. He had planned to go looking for her when and if he healed. He had dreamed of returning to her as the strong, self-contained man he had been the last time he had seen her, not as a scarred weakling who was at the mercy of a malady that came and went with no warning.

The headache grew stronger, and Julian debated about taking another tablet. He decided against it. So far he'd only needed two of the pills, apparently. It would be a victory of sorts if he could get through the entire siege on that amount. Not much of a victory, but these days he had learned to take what he could get in the way of small triumphs.

A faint, savage smile briefly shaped his mouth. Actually he had two successes to celebrate this morning. In addition to getting by on only a couple of the tablets, he had his certain knowledge of the passion he had aroused in Anne. Her own denial of that arousal didn't detract from his sense of victory in the least. It meant she was still wary of him.

Six months ago he hadn't wanted her to be afraid of him but today he knew her signs of caution were signs of hope for him. A woman who was cautious around a man was subtly acknowledging his power. And as long as she thought he had some power over her, Anne wouldn't start pitying him.

In spite of the headache Julian was aware for the first time in months of the faint stirrings of a masculine arrogance he had once taken for granted.

Fifteen minutes later Anne had finished the few dishes left over from lunch and was frowning at the layer of dust on the well-worn furniture in the living room. For some obscure reason it annoyed her.

"Anne!"

Her frown intensified as she answered the summons. "What is it, Julian? Why are you out of bed?"

"Stop glaring at me." He stood braced in the bathroom doorway. "Don't we have any aspirin in the house?"

Anne deliberately stepped toward the bed and began tidying it. "I don't know. Do we?" she asked dryly. "I'm new here, remember?"

He swore softly and started back toward the bed, clearly still shaky on his feet. "I guess I've used them all."

"Do you want another of those tablets in the medicine cabinet?" She kept her eyes averted from his unabashed nudity.

"No," he growled, crawling slowly back under the covers. The strain on his face told of his discomfort. "I just want some aspirin. I always get these damn headaches after the fever."

She eyed him dubiously, wondering if he shouldn't be taking his prescription tablets instead. "I was going to go out to my car and get my suitcase. I might have some aspirin with me. But, Julian, are you sure you shouldn't take some of your medicine?"

"Just get the aspirin," he ordered roughly, closing his eyes. "You must be feeling better. You're back to issuing commands with your usual flair," she told him tartly.

"We'll get along fine if you just obey them." But the weariness in his voice spoiled the arrogant effect. The dark lashes stayed shut.

Anne's expression gentled as she realized how hard he was fighting to handle the pain and his own sense of weakness. "I'll be back in a few minutes," she promised.

Outside she found herself floundering through a foot of powdery snow. The crisp air was fresh and invigorating and the leaden skies were beginning to clear. The rental car was parked beside Julian's four-wheel-drive vehicle, and as she opened her trunk to remove her suitcase she wondered about using the more rugged truck to get down out of the mountains. Perhaps Julian would lend it to her if, in a couple of days, the roads hadn't been cleared.

There was no rush, she decided. For one thing she couldn't possibly leave Julian until she was sure he'd recovered enough to look after himself. And she still had a little time before she had to play the role of helpful niece in her brother's scheme. As she slammed the trunk shut and started back to the cabin with the suitcase, Anne realized just how glad she was to have the excuse of staying with her ill-tempered patient.

He was watching for her as she lugged the red leather bag into his bedroom. The tawny eyes were open now but there was a solid line of heavy eyebrows framing them. The leonine face was drawn tight with pain.

"Are you sure a couple of aspirin are going to do the trick?" Anne unlocked the red case and began going through it. The bottle was in a small zippered pouch.

"They'd better. That's all I'm going to take."

"Well, maybe if we combine them with a few other measures, you'll get some relief," she said, rising to her feet with the bottle of aspirin.

"What measures?" He looked somewhat suspicious as he swallowed the white tablets.

Anne smiled in what she hoped was a bright, nurselike fashion. "Turn over on your stomach and I'll give you a head and shoulder massage. That should loosen some of the tension and the pain."

Grumbling, Julian submitted to the pampering massage. "I used to do this for Michael occasionally," Anne explained as she sat beside him and moved practiced fingers over the knotted muscles of his neck and shoulders.

"Who taught you how to do this?" Julian gritted into the pillow.

"A friend of mine who's in the physical-education department at the college where I work."

"A male friend, I assume. Some ex-football hero?"

Anne hid a flicker of surprise at the note of challenge in his voice. "I don't believe Allen ever played football. He's the team's physical therapist, though, and he knows a lot about this sort of thing."

"I'll bet. Do you let him practice on you?"

"What is this," she asked lightly, "an inquisition?"

"Just trying to keep up my end of the conversation," Julian retorted. She could feel the beginning signs of relaxation in his neck, however. "You and this Allen date a lot?"

"A few times," she answered honestly. "Not a lot."

There was silence for a few minutes and then Julian asked, "Who else do you date in that ivory tower?"

"You can't be seriously interested in a list of people I go out with, Julian."

"The question has arisen in my mind at least once a day for the past six months," he rasped.

That stopped her for an instant. "It has?"

"Just answer the question," he said with a sigh.

"Well, occasionally I date a professor of history I've known for some time and then there's Allen. Once in a while I go out with Eric in the English department—"

"That's enough," Julian interrupted gruffly. "I should have known better than to ask for a list. For a quiet little research assistant you get around, don't you?"

She didn't care for the way he said that. "I realize my life-style lacks some of the excitement of yours, Julian, but in my own conventional fashion I manage to inject a little fun into my life."

"It sounds like it." There was another short pause. "Why haven't you ever married, Anne? Mike said you'd been engaged once."

"This really is turning into a game of twenty questions, isn't it?"

"Why aren't you married?" he persisted.

She gave a small shrug that she couldn't see and told him the truth. "It's just never quite worked out. My engagement ended when my fiancé told me he needed to be free to 'find himself.' He was in the philosophy department," she added by way of explanation. "Philosophers worry a lot about finding themselves, I discovered."

"Better for everyone if they stay lost," Julian muttered. "The world already has enough conflicting philosophies. Did your ex-fiancé ever succeed?"

"In finding himself? I don't know. He did, however, find a charming young female student in one of his classes who wanted to help him in the search."

"I see. You don't sound particularly upset over it."

"I'm not. That all happened about three years ago and it was all for the best."

"And since then?"

"Since then nothing's ever gotten beyond the casual stage," she admitted. *Except with you*, she added silently. *And you've made it clear you're not cut out for anything permanent.*

"I don't see how any man could remain casual toward you," Julian said thoughtfully. "You must be the one who keeps your dates at arm's length. Are you regretting the fact that you didn't manage to do that with me last night?"

Anne faltered as he made the deliberate reference to the passion she was trying to deny. "Poor Julian. That must have been a very interesting hallucination you had last night. How does your head feel?" she added crisply.

"Incredibly better," he admitted, sounding vaguely surprised.

"I'll convey your appreciation to Allen next time I see him," she couldn't resist saying as she got up from the bed.

"You do that," Julian countered, turning cautiously onto his back, golden eyes gleaming up at her with faint menace. "Right after you tell him how you spent the night with me."

"Allen would be the first to understand that someone had to play nurse to you last night," Anne managed sweetly.

The menace in his eyes grew a little stronger. "Go fix me some hot tea before I risk renewing the headache with a little physical exertion," he suggested meaningfully.

Anne fled to the kitchen, not knowing whether to be glad he seemed on the road to recovery or annoyed because of his quarrelsome manner. Memories of when he had clung to her, not in passion, but to still the chills that racked his body made the decision for her. She would be glad that he was recovering.

That altruistic attitude lasted only as long as the next challenge Julian issued, however. She had awakened him for his dinner, pleased to see that his color appeared much better than it had at noon. He sat up in bed, surveying the meal of curried stew and a thick chunk of bread. He looked as though he had the beginnings of an appetite.

"Did you make this?" he asked curiously.

"Well, it didn't come out of a can," she retorted, sitting down in the chair to eat with him. "I scrounged around in your freezer and found a package labeled lamb. You also had a sack of potatoes and some onions and carrots." She lifted one shoulder as if the result were inevitable.

"Not bad," he remarked grudgingly. "If you keep putting meals like this together I might let you stay for a while."

"Gee, thanks." She dipped her chunk of bread into the stew and took a bite.

He looked at her intently for a moment. "When do you have to be back at work?"

"I've got a month's leave of absence."

"Because of Mike?"

"Yes."

"But he is going to be okay, isn't he?" Julian asked slowly.

"The doctors say he'll recover. But it's going to be a long process. Fortunately he has Lucy."

"His fiancée, you said."

"That's right." Anne dipped the bread into the stew again, enjoying her own cooking and the knowledge that in spite of his grouchiness Julian was enjoying it, too.

"Then you don't have to rush back to his bedside."

"No."

He nodded. "You can stay here for a while, then," he finally said.

"Only a couple more days at the most. I have to be in California this coming weekend in order to set up Mike's plan," Anne explained.

"Don't be ridiculous. You're not going to get involved in that mess."

She glanced up from her stew, startled more by the absolute certainty in his voice than by the words themselves. "Julian, I've already told you that I'm going through with it."

"The answer is no."

She blinked. "I don't recall asking permission. Advice, maybe, but not permission."

He slid her a chilling glance. "If you think I'm allowing you to go through with that nutty plan all on your own, you're out of your head."

Anne arched one eyebrow, mildly surprised now by his interference. She had assumed he would be glad to see her leave. "I hate to break this to you, Julian, but you don't really have a whole lot to say about it."

"Someone had better say something about it," he exploded softly. "Mike's apparently in no condition to do so. That leaves me."

"I told you, I came to ask you for help, not to get your permission to carry out the plan! It's obvious you're not in any condition to help me but I'm not going to cancel everything because of that. I'll find a way to make it all work."

Julian's bowl of stew was set down on the nightstand with a solid clunk. The next thing Anne knew, he was sitting on the edge of the bed, the blankets carelessly tossed to one side. One powerful hand reached out to take hold of her chin and the tawny eyes burned. Not with fever this time, but with male determination.

"I may not be at the peak of my physical ability and I may be a few months over forty, but if you think I can't handle you, lady, you're dead wrong. Last night should have taught you that much, at least."

She winced. "I think you're well enough to start remembering to put on a robe when you get out of bed in front of guests!"

"Why should I cover up what you've already seen?"

"Julian, stop acting as though you had some rights over me." She stood up abruptly and his hand fell away. "I intend to go through with Mike's scheme and I'm not going to let you stop me."

He got to his feet and, even though he had to flatten one hand against the wall to help him maintain his balance, he exuded more than enough intimidation to cause Anne to retreat uneasily.

"When are those ghost hunters supposed to show up at that mansion in California?" he asked too softly.

"At the beginning of next week."

"How long will they stay there?"

"Their usual routine lasts about three or four days," she answered carefully.

"Then you'll stay here where I can keep an eye on you until at least the end of next week. Until it's too late for you to do anything about that idiotic plan."

"I'm going through with it, Julian."

"No."

The cold denial infuriated her. "Where do you get off telling me I can't do as I damn well please? You have no authority over me, Julian Aries. Not one single right. I'm as free an agent as you are. You may recall that nothing I said or did could stop you from taking Michael to that island, and you made it very clear the night you brought him home that nothing could keep you from returning to finish your job. Well, I have a job to do now, too, and nothing you say or do is going to stop me."

He took a step toward her, releasing his hold on the wall. "There's no comparison between this crazy situation and the demands of my job six months ago!"

"Oh, yes there is," she countered, retreating to the doorway. "I'm as committed to carrying out this plan as you are to your precious supermacho career as a government agent. Michael was nearly killed by these people. I'm not going to let them get away with it!"

"Anne, you don't know what the hell you're doing," he raged.

"That's why I came here," she shot back. "To get a little help and advice. But since I'm not going to get either, I'll just have to muddle through on my own."

"I won't allow it!"

"You have nothing to say about it."

He stalked forward another step and Anne saw the effort it cost him. "Get back into bed, Julian. You need to rest," she said with sudden urgency, moving forward to take his arm. "Please, stop acting like this. You've been very ill and you have no business staging a major scene."

He didn't budge under her prodding. Instead his hand moved around her nape and he held her as though she were an annoying kitten. "I will stage any kind of scene I please," he bit out savagely. "And, weak as I am, you're still not big enough or strong enough to stop me. Understand?"

The wounded lion was roaring now and Anne knew he was right about one fact. Even weak and in pain he could still over-power her if he chose.

"I understand, Julian."

"Good." He released her and staggered back to the bed, throwing himself down on it with a groan. Eyes closed he drew a deep breath. "We will discuss this further in the morning," he announced in a tone that was icy with the force of his effort to control it. "I'm going to get some sleep."

"Yes, Julian," Anne agreed meekly, knowing his head was probably throbbing again. She ached to be able to comfort him. Hurrying into the bathroom she picked up the aspirin bottle and a glass of water and carried both back into the bedroom.

Julian accepted the tablets gruffly after first making certain they weren't from the prescription bottle. Then he turned over on his stomach, burying his face in the pillow.

Without a word Anne sat down on the bed and began to massage his neck and shoulders again. He allowed her to minister to him as if he were tolerating a minor nuisance. But beneath her touch, she felt him begin to relax.

Poor lion, Anne thought with a small smile. He didn't know how to ask for a little tender loving care, not even when he needed it very badly. She wondered at the years of isolation and self-contained living that could breed such a fierce aloneness.

Julian Aries needed a wife and a home. But, then, she'd known that much six months ago. His refusal to accept his own needs made her much the wary of him.

4

"YOU'RE GOING TO GO through with it, aren't you?"

Two days later, ensconced on the living-room sofa with an old striped wool blanket over his legs, Julian acknowledged the inevitable. He was not, Anne decided, a gracious loser. It had been a hard-fought battle, she reflected. Julian had used almost every trick in the book except one.

He had tried to intimidate her, argued that he had an obligation to her brother to keep her out of trouble, informed her that she was not very bright, tried to order her obedience and had finally resorted to calm, rational discussion in an attempt to dissuade her. The one argument he had not tried was that she couldn't go through with the plan because he needed her to look after him.

Of course, Anne thought, that was the one tactic he never would use. Julian could not admit that he needed anyone, especially her. The certain knowledge filled her with a sense of hopelessness regarding their relationship. He wasn't the only one who needed to accept reality this morning, she thought as she finished washing the breakfast dishes. She needed a dose of it herself.

"I'm going through with it, Julian. I told you that two days ago."

"Even though I have absolutely forbidden the whole scheme?" he gritted.

"I thought you'd given up on the intimidation approach," she observed. "We were trying logic and reason the last time I tuned in."

"I gave up on both when you made it clear they weren't going to have much effect." Julian drank his coffee broodingly, his eyes never leaving her as she went about the kitchen chores. "I don't know why you're so dead set on this crazy plan. When your brother is out of the hospital he can renew his investigation and set up another scheme to trap those ghost hunters."

"I'm going through with it because I've got a good chance of making the whole thing work. They're on to Michael now. He won't be able to get close to them again. But they can't possibly know about me. And I don't think, from what I've learned about them, that they can resist the lure of old Miss Creswell's mansion. It's a perfect setup."

"There is no such thing as a perfect setup and if you'd had a little experience trying to carry out 'flawless' schemes, you'd know what I'm talking about!"

"I'm sure a little experience would be extremely useful, but I don't have time to get it."

"So you tried to take a shortcut by coming here to get my help and experience?"

She focused on the scene outside the kitchen window. The roads had been cleared that morning but the blanket of snow still made a postcard setting. "That was the general idea."

"The best advice I can give you is to stay out of it."

"That's the one piece of advice I'm not willing to take." She dried the plates and stacked them neatly on the cupboard shelf. "Just as you and Michael wouldn't take my advice not to go to that horrid little island six months ago."

There was a tense pause from across the room. Then Julian stated coldly, "It was my job to go. And it was Michael's job to come with me."

"I know that now," Anne said simply. "I've accepted the fact that both of you felt you had to go. I haven't blamed either of you for a long time."

"Is that the truth, Anne?"

"Yes."

"Are you sure that on some level you're not still hating me for what happened to your brother?"

"Michael made his own decision. I understand that now," she said quietly. "He also told me that you saved his life that night he got shot. After the sniper wounded him you risked your own neck to go out into the open and drag him back to safety."

"He would have done the same for me. Michael and I were in that mess together. We had a job to do."

"So do I."

"The hell you do! This isn't an assignment you have to carry out. You're doing this strictly to avenge Mike."

"Same thing," she shrugged.

"Anne, this is ridiculous. Mike can take care of himself. He can handle everything when he's back on his feet."

"That could be a long time. They hurt him very badly, Julian," she said starkly.

"All right!" Julian roared. "If you're going to be totally unreasonable about this, there's nothing I can do...."

"No."

"Except go with you," he concluded bluntly.

Anne lifted her head, startled. "Go with me? But, Julian, that's out of the question. I realized that the first night I arrived. You've got too much recovering to do. All I'm asking from you now is a little advice. Or perhaps you know someone who could help me. You must have some contacts."

"We'll leave tomorrow."

"Impossible! You're not coming with me." She tossed the dish towel down on the counter and faced him with her hands planted firmly on her hips. "You've been very ill, Julian. You need rest. A lot of it."

"It's a stalemate, lady," he said wearily. "I can't stop you from going and you can't stop me from going with you. Both of us seem to have received an overdose of stubbornness somewhere along the line."

"Now you're the one who's being ridiculous, Julian. I am not going to allow you to come with me in your present condition."

He slanted her a glance that held mockery and menace. "What are you going to do? Tie me to the bed?"

"If necessary!" she shot back unwisely.

Julian was off the couch an instant later. The brown towelling robe he'd put on earlier at Anne's insistence flapped carelessly open as he swooped across the room. He reached her in three long strides, seizing her by the shoulders.

"The only way you can keep me in bed is by staying there with me," he gritted softly. "Anytime you want to repeat what happened between us that first night you arrived, just let me know."

"I've told you, nothing happened," Anne said very bravely, aware that she couldn't move under the grip of his hands.

"Don't give me that nonsense. We both know you wound up lying beneath me, all soft and sweet and on fire. I've been through enough hallucinations to know the difference between reality and dreams, Anne. Why do you keep denying what happened that night?"

Goaded, Anne lost her temper. "Because nothing did happen! I didn't come all this way just to go to bed with you. I wanted to talk to you, tell you about Michael. I wanted to apologize for the way I lashed out at you the night you brought him home. I wanted to see if we could put our relationship on a different footing. I wanted a lot of things, but I didn't want to go to bed with you."

"You're afraid of me, aren't you?" he asked.

The flicker of masculine satisfaction that she saw in his eyes made her want to strike him. "Maybe I am in some ways. It's only natural to be a bit cautious around a man who won't admit he's human, that he has needs like everyone else...."

"Oh, I'm willing enough to acknowledge my needs, sweetheart," he whispered, pulling her against his bare chest. The toweling robe had parted completely, leaving only the snugfitting jockey shorts as a shield between Anne and Julian's overwhelming masculinity.

"Julian, stop it. This isn't what I meant and you know it."

But he ignored her, crushing her against the cloud of curling hair that formed a shaggy triangle on his chest. His lips came down on hers in a hard, punishing kiss that effectively silenced any further argument. Anne felt the frustrated feminine fury welling up inside, even as she acknowledged the effect of the sensual punishment.

His mouth insisted on her cooperation, his tongue probing arrogantly into the dark, warm recesses behind her teeth. It wasn't until she gave up trying to fight him and instead leaned obediently against him that Julian lifted his head. The tawny eyes softened as he stared down into her defiant face.

"Now why don't you stop pretending that nothing happened between us the other night?"

"You indulge your fantasies, I'll indulge my own," she said bravely.

"Little coward." He was more amused than anything else by her bravado. Slowly, this time with compelling invitation, he lowered his mouth once more to hers. His hand moved lightly to her hips, shaping her with possessive, sensual care until she moaned softly. Then he deliberately cupped her buttocks and lifted her up into his hard thighs.

"Julian." Anne sighed and nestled closer out of sheer instinct. Fighting him was so very difficult. Her fingers clung to the warmth of his sleek back beneath the robe and she knew a shiver of need as he made her fully aware of his own mounting desire.

"I could take you so easily, make you want me...."

"Julian, please don't...."

"If you're afraid of me even though I'm in this condition, how are you going to deal with something really frightening such as that theft ring you're intent on trapping?" He nuzzled her nape, cradling her head against his shoulder.

"I'll manage," she gasped, intensely aware of the hardness of his body. The insistent pressure of his aroused male form was both a lure and a challenge that was as old as time. But she knew she had to resist. And he must have sensed it.

With resignation, Julian dropped his hands and stalked back to the couch. The limp was more pronounced now and she knew he was struggling to control it. "When you pack for me this afternoon, don't forget my razor or the can of shaving cream." He leaned his head back against the pillow and promptly went to sleep.

Anne stood staring at him for a long moment wondering how she was going to deal with all the ghosts, real and imagined, that seemed to have invaded her life. Chief among them was the ghost of a dream she had believed in for the past six months; a dream of building a lasting relationship with Julian Aries. She had been a fool to think this man would ever admit that he needed her on any level except a sexual one. The lion had been surviving on his own for too long. He was not going to risk the weakness of loving and needing.

Slowly Anne went into the bedroom to pack Julian's clothes for the trip west. She knew him well enough to know that he would be with her when she left tomorrow morning, regardless of what it cost him in terms of pain or exhaustion.

AT DAWN THE NEXT MORNING Anne stirred on the sofa she had been using as a bed since she had no longer felt it necessary to keep a watch over her patient. A sense of presence in the room made her open her eyes, and she stared in astonishment at Julian who was fully dressed and prowling around the kitchen, making coffee.

"Good grief," she complained, yawning hugely as she pushed back the blankets. "You're up early."

He threw her a quick glance before going back to the coffee preparations. "From what you've told me we have a long trip ahead of us and a lot to do after we arrive at the other end."

"Well, yes, but I didn't say we had to rise at the crack of dawn."

"When I'm not coming out of a bout of that damn fever, I usually get up at dawn," he said, shrugging. "Sometimes earlier."

"Part of the secret-agent ethic?" she grumbled, stumbling to her feet. Her long flannel nightgown floated around her ankles.

"Early to bed, early to rise, helps a guy catch villainous spies?"

"That's not too bad, considering just how early it is. Are you always that fast at this hour?"

"No. I was briefly inspired." Anne patted another yawn, suddenly aware of how disheveled she probably looked. Her hair was a tousled, russet mop and the flannel gown had been chosen for warmth, not seductiveness. Not that she wanted to seduce Julian, she reminded herself grimly. "Actually, you're looking fairly perky yourself, this morning. You must feel better."

He considered that. "I do, as a matter of fact. Better than I have in a long time." The information seemed to surprise him. He frowned and flipped on the coffeepot switch.

He did look good this morning, Anne thought as she hurried down the hall toward the bathroom. He was wearing a gray sweater, a pair of jeans and boots. His dark hair was clean from the shower and had been ruthlessly combed into place. Julian moved this morning with something approaching his former lithe grace, even though the limp was still hampering him. There was a sense of regained strength in the leanness of his body.

Anne was seriously asking herself whether or not she could take any credit for his sudden progress when she realized the probable truth. Julian was looking better and feeling better this morning not because of her careful nursing but because for the first time in months he was about to go back to work. He had a task ahead of him. A self-imposed task, to be sure, but a real one.

The realization was depressing. She should be glad that he might finally be showing some signs of enthusiasm, she told herself. After all, apparently he had been holed up here for the past several months, licking his wounds. His mental outlook must have been very dark indeed during that period. Perhaps a challenge was exactly what was needed right now to help complete his recovery.

But deep inside, Anne knew the notion wasn't nearly as heartwarming as it should have been. The reality of the matter was that she had been nourishing a secret hope that she would be the cause of his recovery. She had wanted him to need her. When was she going to stop building up her hopes, Anne wondered sadly.

Julian was accompanying her to the West Coast for a variety of reasons, but none of those reasons included love. He probably felt an obligation to protect Michael's sister, since he hadn't been able to talk her out of the scheme. And he might be finding some inner enthusiasm for the unexpected challenge. But he wasn't going with her because he had finally realized he was hopelessly in love with her.

Anne grimaced at her own crazy emotionalism and drowned her discontent under the pulse of the shower spray.

"There are a few ground rules we'd better get straight before we get on that jet," Julian announced a couple of hours later, as he locked up the cabin and held out his hand for the keys to the red Buick Anne had rented at the Denver airport.

"Such as?" Anne ignored his outstretched hand and opened the door on the driver's side.

"Such as the one about me being in charge of this crazy project." Deftly he snapped the keys from her fingers. "Get in on the passenger side, Anne. I'll do the driving."

"The car is rented in my name. I'm the only one authorized to drive it," she protested, annoyed with the way he was starting to take over completely.

"Those roads are going to be slippery. Icy in places. Something tells me you haven't had a whole lot of experience driving a mountain road after a snowstorm."

"The roads have been cleared!"

"They'll still be treacherous. Get in on the other side, Anne."

Grumbling about his tyrannical attitude, Anne did as she was told, making a production out of tightening her seat belt while he started the car. "You're certainly in fighting trim this morning. But then, you always were inclined to give orders."

"Yeah." He shifted into reverse and expertly backed the car out of the drive, which had been only roughly cleared by a helpful road crew. "I've always been inclined to give orders. Not take them. I'm made that way, honey. It's one of the reasons I usually work alone or with only a partner."

"Well, think of me as a partner," she retorted.

"Even when I have one, I'm the one in command. I mean it, Anne. You're way out of your depth in this business with the fake psychics and you know it. If this idiotic plan is going to have any chance at all it will be because you understand and follow my orders. Got it?"

"If I'd known you were inclined to be such a tyrant I would have thought twice about asking for your help."

"You know anybody else you could have asked?" he countered smoothly. "Your good buddy Allen, the physical therapist, perhaps? Or the guy from the English department? Something tells me you didn't go pounding on their doors before you tried mine, did you, Anne?"

"I'm sure if I had, they would have proved far more cooperative," she muttered.

"You don't need cooperation. You need effectiveness." His mouth hardened as he negotiated an icy curve. "I'm generally considered effective."

Anne felt a chill down her spine at the way he said it. "You talk as if you're an instrument or a tool that someone uses."

"That's pretty much what I was to the people I worked for, I guess," he said with an offhandedness that alarmed Anne.

"And that's the way you thought of yourself, too, wasn't it?" Before he could respond, she hurried on, frowning at his profile. "What's with the past tense? You're not officially employed any longer?"

"No."

"I didn't realize you'd quit your job," Anne said uncertainly.

"It was a mutual decision," he said coolly. "Both I and my employers realized that my effectiveness had been somewhat blunted at least as far as fieldwork goes. Forty-year-old agents who aren't as fast on their feet as they once were and who are prone to unpredictable bouts of incapacitating fever don't make good tools."

She heard the self-disgust in his voice and her own words were charged with sudden fierceness. "Well, it sounds to me like your career has taken a definite step forward. What an awful thing to think of yourself as a tool to be used by others."

"Happens all the time," he said, the words slicing through her like a knife. "Isn't that why you showed up on my doorstep a few days ago? Because you needed a convenient instrument to help you with your grand scheme?"

Anne went white under the shock of the sardonic accusation. The lion's claws were definitely not sheathed. In spite of the uneasy pact between herself and Julian, she was going to get mauled occasionally. The beast was still very dangerous. She wondered bleakly if he even realized just how much damage he could do to her. She was only beginning to realize how vulnerable she was.

"I didn't want to *use* you, Julian," she whispered.

"No?" He threw her a laconic smile. "Let's think of the arrangement as a bargain then, hmm? I'll do my best to help you implement Mike's plan and in return . . ."

She slanted him a wary glance. "In return?" she finally prompted.

"How about in return I get a few more of those rather interesting hallucinations like the one I had the night you arrived at my door?" he suggested.

A dark red stain replaced the paleness in Anne's cheeks. She studied the mountain landscape intently while her anger simmered. "I don't need to pay you off with fantasies. You've already proved you can dream up your own."

"Anne—"

She interrupted him with quiet savagery. "If and when I go to bed with you, Julian, and it's a mighty big 'if,' I promise you it won't be because I'm paying you off for your 'effectiveness.' And I think you know it."

"Do I?" he drawled gently.

"One thing's for certain," she got out, almost choking on her fury, "until you do know it, you had better believe you don't stand a chance of sharing my bed! I won't make love to a man who thinks I'm repaying him for services rendered."

"Then what shall I think the next time you give yourself to me?" he inquired blandly.

"I think," Anne told him imperiously, "that you had better concentrate on your driving. You were quite right about the road. It's very treacherous." *Almost as treacherous as you, my wounded love.*

He appeared satisfied at the small sign of retreat. Anne's irritation increased by several degrees. The only positive note in the whole situation as far as she could see was that Julian definitely looked healthier and stronger this morning. Apparently the aftereffects of the fever didn't last long.

"Tell me about the ghost," he said at one point after they had left the mountains and were on their way into Denver. "I thought all the real ghosts in the country were on the East Coast. Since when does California have ghosts?"

"California's history is every bit as interesting as that of the East Coast. The Spanish colonized it in the seventeen hundreds, and over the years a lot of legends have developed. We needed a house that had a genuine legend attached to it because the fake psychics will check that part out. Our ghost is Spanish, by the way. A charming young señorita who apparently had a mind of her own. It was a problem for women in her day. Got her into a lot of trouble, according to the tale."

"Figures the ghost would be female."

"I researched the story before I came to see you. Even though it's all nothing more than a legend, I wanted to get the details straight. I'm sure Thomas Craven and his friends will do the same thing."

"Craven?"

"He's the one in charge of these so-called psychic investigators. According to my brother's notes he works with a woman called Sara and a man called Dan Hargraves. Sara's the 'sensitive' of the group."

"She's the one who's actually supposed to be female."

"Right. She makes the contact and finds out what it will take to free the phantom from its mortal ties so that it can go wherever released ghosts are supposed to go. Beyond the veil or something. Thomas Craven and the man called Hargraves are the ones who then go through the rituals. Apparently the three of them can put on a pretty good show. Should go down well in California," Anne concluded sardonically.

"Have they worked out there before this?"

"According to Michael's notes, no, they haven't. As you said, most of the more interesting ghosts tend to be on the East Coast. Most of Craven's psychic investigations have taken place back there."

"How did your brother lure Craven out west?"

"Michael got an old acquaintance of his to arrange it. Someone he met when he was researching psychic phenomena agreed to help him set the trap. Miss Creswell's a strange old lady who had a sister who was a film star back in the thirties. The sister owned the mansion near Santa Barbara where we're going. She died a couple of years ago and left the place to Miss Creswell. Miss Creswell has agreed to let it be known that she plans on moving into the place in a few months and wants the mansion thoroughly deghosted. She's the one who actually hired Craven and his crew. And she's informed them that her niece will be their hostess. She herself won't come near the place until it's properly cleansed of ghosts. At least that's the story my brother got her to tell. Actually, she's very much into psychic phenomena herself. Can't stand phonies."

"And that's why she agreed to help your brother set the trap." Julian shook his head. "What a half-baked scheme. Who was originally supposed to play the role of niece?"

"Lucy Melton. My brother's fiancée."

"You jumped in and volunteered to take over so she could stay with Mike while he's recovering, I suppose."

"That's right. Why are you so negative about this?" Anne demanded in annoyance.

"Hasn't it occurred to you that if Craven and crowd have already made an attempt on your brother they're probably onto his plan to set him up?"

"They didn't cancel. Miss Creswell heard from them just before I left for Colorado. Craven gave her the date of his arrival," Anne informed him haughtily. She was getting distinctly tired of his obvious opinion of the project. "Besides, there's no way they could connect my brother with Elizabeth Creswell. Michael was very careful to keep himself out of the picture."

"So why did someone run him down in a car?" Julian asked politely.

"Probably because they decided Michael was getting too close to the truth. He told Craven he was doing a story on psychic investigators, and Craven allowed him to accompany his crew on a few investigations. Those all took place back East. Craven must have gotten suspicious about Michael's real interest, namely the thefts that seemed to follow in the wake of an 'investigation.' But there's no reason to think Craven knows the California arrangement has been set up by my brother."

"Maybe. Maybe not. Mike's good, I'll grant that. It's possible he kept his connection with Creswell secret and that Craven will be lured into the trap. But the whole thing sounds highly reckless and the only reason I'm having anything to do with it is because you've made it clear you're going through with it on your own if I don't. I meant what I said, Anne. You're going to follow my orders and you're going to do exactly as I say. Clear?"

"I appreciate your help in this matter and I will endeavor to cooperate with you in view of your vastly superior knowledge," Anne murmured sarcastically.

He shot her a mildly amused glance. "You're cute when you're trying to be arrogant."

"You're not."

"Cute?" He thought about that. "No, I don't suppose I am. I don't think anyone's ever called me 'cute' in my whole life."

"Then it's fortunate you never had to make your living as a male stripper, isn't it?" Anne retorted too sweetly. "Look, Julian, I'm willing to be reasonable about this and I do respect your, uh, unique abilities in certain areas. I'm prepared, for example, to admit you may know a lot more about handling unsavory characters such as Craven and his bunch...."

"Thanks. Always nice to have one's talents admired."

"Nevertheless," she continued, undaunted, "I want you to keep in mind that this is my plan and I have as much, or more, to say about how it's implemented as you do!"

"No."

"What do you mean, no?" she challenged.

"It's a simple enough word. Your problem is that you probably haven't heard it used too often. Do you always get your own way, Anne? Mike told me you've always been on the bossy side."

"Younger brothers always say that about their older sisters."

"Yeah, but in your case it was true, wasn't it? Had to be, from what Mike said. You had a lot of responsibility to handle after your folks split up. Your father disappeared from the picture entirely and your mother's new country-club husband didn't much care for a couple of teenagers around the house. Mike told me you moved out when you were barely eighteen and he went to live with you. He was only fifteen at the time, wasn't he?"

"You and my brother appear to have had some lengthy little chats." Anne kept her gaze on the roadside scene.

"You got Mike through some rough years," Julian went on musingly. "Made sure he went to college. Kept him out of trouble. You had a lot invested in him emotionally. No wonder you hated my guts when I asked him to go with me on that last mission."

"Could we get back to the original discussion?" Anne moved restlessly in her seat. "There's not much point talking about what's over and done. I've told you that I understand now that nothing could have kept Michael from going with you. He thrives on the excitement of going after the story. It's in his blood."

"Intellectually I think you do understand that. But how about emotionally? Are you sure you're not still blaming me for what happened to him on that island?"

"No, Julian," Anne said patiently. "I'm not still blaming you." She was secretly surprised that he was worrying about it. He knew he wasn't responsible for what had happened to Michael six months ago. So why should he care about her reaction?

"All right. Back to the previous topic," Julian said evenly. "There really isn't much more to say about it. I'll be the one in charge."

"Don't I even get to vote on the matter?" she taunted. He lifted one dark brow. "No."

"Concise and to the point. Okay, Julian, it would appear I don't have a lot of choice. You're in charge."

To her astonishment he threw her a quick grin, the first wholehearted expression of amusement she had witnessed in him since she had arrived at his cabin. "Being in charge of you should prove interesting." The brief laughter in his eyes disappeared almost immediately as he gave his attention to his driving again.

Anne was not at all surprised by his skill on the uncertain road surface. There was a fundamental competency and efficiency in the man that was an integral part of him. They were qualities that had allowed him to survive on his own in life and she wondered if, after forty years of depending on them rather than on other people, Julian could ever change. He would probably always be too proud to ask for love. She accepted that now. What worried her was the possibility that he would never even be able to accept his need of a woman on any other level than a sexual one.

There was little conversation for the rest of the trip. Julian was engrossed in his own thoughts and Anne maintained a respectful silence. She knew he was sorting through the information she had given him, looking for problem areas and trying to modify the plans where possible.

By the time they had turned in the rental car and bought the tickets for Los Angeles, Anne knew Julian was beginning to tire. She saw the lines of strain around his eyes and fretted. But there was nothing she could say or do. He wouldn't appreciate having the weakness pointed out and she knew it.

As he sank down into the seat beside her and buckled the seat belt he finally allowed himself to relax. Anne said nothing, but she watched him uneasily out of the corner of her eye as he leaned back against the headrest and closed his eyes. Perhaps she should get him some coffee from the cabin steward. Then again he might need the sleep. She was chewing anxiously on her lower lip, wondering how to comfort him without annoying him when Julian spoke. He didn't bother to open his eyes.

"Yes?"

"One other thing, Anne . . ."

"Yes?"

"How did you plan to explain me?"

"To Craven?"

"Right. He's expecting Miss Creswell's niece but he won't be expecting me. When your brother's fiancée, Lucy, was going to play the part, was she going to be alone in the house?"

"Yes, except for the housekeeper who comes in on a daily basis. Michael didn't think there would be any danger to Lucy. Craven's only interested in getting the layout of the place and earmarking the valuable stuff. Mike planned to stay in a motel in Santa Barbara. Lucy could have called him if she got nervous."

"So Craven's going to arrive and find the niece he expected but also a man he didn't expect to see. We need a story to cover my presence in the house."

Anne's mouth tilted upward as a shaft of mischief went through her. "Well, actually, I did have one rather clever idea."

"Umm?"

"How about if we dress you up in a suit and tell Craven you're the butler?"

Julian's eyes opened at that. He stared at her. "The butler! Are you serious?"

"You don't like it?"

"Do you really think I'd pass as a butler?" he growled.

"Aren't you clever agent types trained to be adaptable?"

"Ex-agent," he corrected curtly. "And, no, I wasn't trained to be that adaptable."

"Pity. It would have been rather amusing to see you running around in a suit fetching sherry for me."

"You'll have to get your kicks some other way, I'm afraid," he told her flatly.

"Well, we could pretend you're Miss Creswell's insane nephew who's been hidden away for years in the basement of the mansion."

"Your imagination is taking my breath away." He shut his eyes again. "Any other bright ideas?"

Anne's urge to tease him faded as she saw the weariness in him. He had seemed so much better this morning but it was obvious he was tired now after the long drive out of the mountains. He needed some rest. "There was one other, uh, possibility," she began tentatively. "Not as brilliant and original in concept as my first two ideas, but—"

"Let's hear it."

"It occurred to me that you could pose as my fiancé or lover or male friend, or whatever you want to call it," she said, stumbling over the words. "It would give you an excuse for being with me. Craven could think that the two of us were simply taking advantage of auntie's little task to enjoy a few days together at the mansion. You know, that we were making a short vacation out of it."

The dark lashes stirred on his cheek but he didn't open his eyes. "Your fiancé," Julian mused. "Yeah. I like it. We'll go with that."

He was asleep before Anne could start on her long list of why it wasn't such a good idea.

"THE MANSION WAS BUILT on the ruins of an old adobe hacienda," Anne explained late that night as she and Julian finished the long drive from the Los Angeles airport to the Creswell estate just outside Santa Barbara. "The original owners had received a land grant from Spain that extended from the coast to a point several miles inland. The hacienda was destroyed in an earthquake sometime during the eighteen hundreds, and the present mansion was built in the early nineteen hundreds. A lot of movie-star wealth and a certain amount of Hollywood tackiness went into the place according to Lucy, who talked to Miss Creswell. Lucy said she wants a full report on each of the bedrooms and the master bath, by the way. Apparently the designer was given free rein and a large budget."

"I can't wait." Julian negotiated the coastal highway, following the directions Anne read off to him. He looked much better again, she noted with relief. The nap on the plane had helped. All in all her patient was coming along quite nicely.

The realization that she was secretly taking credit for his improvement made Anne smile to herself in the darkness of the car. Julian had not offered one word of thanks for her nursing skills and attention but, knowing how much he had resented her arrival, she wasn't expecting any great show of appreciation.

"So our ghost is a holdover from the days when the old hacienda stood on this land?" Julian asked as they turned off the main road to wind up toward a high bluff overlooking the sea.

"Yes, according to my research poor little Carlota was the victim of an arranged marriage. Her parents sent her off to the wilds of California to marry a very wealthy landholder who was several years older than she was and who had already been married and widowed. She not only acquired a husband, she also acquired his three children and the responsibility of running the huge hacienda. She was only a teenager at the time."

"I can sense trouble brewing already," Julian groaned. "Young wife resents being tied down to an older husband and his three kids. Longs for the bright lights of wherever it was she came from."

"Mexico. Hers was a wealthy, landed family down there. Lots of old Spanish pride. And if we are to believe the legend, she longed for more than lights. She also apparently missed some of the admirers she left behind. Carlota was, from all accounts, a very lovely young woman and accustomed to a great deal of masculine attention."

"Let me guess. She found someone here in California who made up for the lack, right?"

"How did you know?"

"I could see it coming a mile away," Julian said wisely.

"I didn't know you were such an authority on the female psyche," Anne observed with interest.

"I'm not. But the only reason there's a ghost story left to tell is that Carlota somehow met with disaster, right?"

"Right."

"Given the ingredients of the story so far, I think it's fair to assume that the most likely sort of disaster for sweet little Carlota to have precipitated was of the male-female variety. In other words, she got bored running the hacienda and started fooling around."

"Hardly fooling around," Anne said with a sniff, feeling obliged for some reason to defend the other woman. "She got involved in a grand, utterly hopeless love affair with the dashing young son of the owner of the neighboring ranch."

"Bet I know what happens next. Carlota and lover are discovered in a more or less compromising position by Carlota's husband and . . . ?"

"And her husband killed her. Strangled her to death with his bare hands," Anne concluded sadly.

"I expect her husband was a little upset at the time," Julian pointed out, sounding totally unsympathetic toward the unknown Carlota. "What happened to her lover?"

"He escaped. His family shipped him back to Spain as fast as possible, apparently. Typical that only the woman in the triangle got punished."

"She must have known the risk she was taking. Husbands aren't noted for their tolerance in these matters. Not even to-day."

"You're an expert on that subject, too?" Anne demanded. "Let's just say I have a vivid imagination, okay? I have no trouble picturing how I'd react in a similar situation."

He sounded so utterly sure of his own reaction that Anne was rather startled. "You're forty years old and have never been married," she complained. "How do you know what you'd feel if you were a husband in that situation?"

Julian shrugged. "I just know how I'd react."

"You'd have strangled poor Carlota?" Anne was suddenly feeling inexplicably incensed.

"Well, I don't know that I would have gone that far," Julian admitted easily. "But I certainly would have beaten you to within an inch of your life."

"Beaten *me*!" Anne stared at him, aghast. "We're not talking about me. We're talking about some poor woman who lived over a century ago. We weren't discussing *me*!"

"Oh. Perhaps it's just my new role of fiancé that has given me an insight into the matter. I might have been overempathizing," he remarked dryly.

"It sounds like it," Anne snapped back tartly. "Now, to finish the story. The reason Carlota occasionally appears in the mansion, according to legend, is that she's looking for something."

"What?"

"No one knows. I expect Mr. Craven and his bunch will be only too happy to tell us, however."

"And, since the legend doesn't tell us exactly what she searches for, Craven can simply make up that part, right?"

"Right. It will be interesting to see what creative touches he'll add to the story. Look, there's the place, now." Anne leaned forward to peer at the large structure looming up out of the night.

"You were right about the Hollywood touch. Looks like something off the back lot of a movie studio," Julian decided as he parked the rented car in the wide, circular drive.

The lines of the mansion were vaguely classical but the designer had obviously been unable to resist throwing in some originality. The overall effect was of a storybook mansion, composed of elements drawn from several different architectural periods.

"I'll bet the original adobe structure was more attractive. I wonder how Carlota likes having this thing sitting on the ruins of her home." Anne opened her door as Julian switched off the ignition. "It doesn't look as though the housekeeper is here. I don't see any lights." She rummaged through her purse, searching for the key she had collected from Lucy.

Julian stood patiently with the luggage as Anne sounded the huge brass door knocker. When there was no answer, she used the key to let them into the wide hall. There she fumbled briefly before finding the light switch. She and Julian stood in silence, staring at the surroundings.

"I think," Julian finally commented as he surveyed the intricate oak parquet floor, the huge, multitiered crystal chandelier and the carved staircase at the end of the hall, "that I like my cabin better."

"Personally I'm reserving judgment until I see the bedrooms." Anne headed determinedly for the staircase. "Here, I'll take my own suitcase," she added quickly as Julian made to follow her.

He must not have appreciated the expression of concern in her eyes because he ignored her outthrust hand. "I'll manage," he growled. "I might not be up to carrying you up these stairs, but I can still handle a couple of suitcases!"

Anne held her tongue, unwilling to say more and risk another dose of his irritation. He must be quite tired by now, she told herself. Better not to provoke him. Actually, all things considered, it was always better not to provoke Julian. A dangerous pastime.

The housekeeper might not have been in evidence but it was obvious she had recently been on the scene. The half dozen bedrooms were all immaculate and fully prepared. It was clear immediately where the designer had drawn his inspiration.

"Good heavens! Each bedroom looks like a scene from a film," Anne gasped as she opened doors.

"Yeah. A love scene," Julian agreed laconically as he stopped to peer into what looked as if it could have been a stage set of Cleopatra's bedroom. The one across the hall was straight out of a thirties musical. Black-and-white stairs led up to a black-and-white canopied bed. "Which one do you want?"

"This one, I think," Anne declared with abrupt decision as she opened the last door on the right. "Definitely this one."

Julian came to stand behind her. "Well, I'll be damned. I never would have pictured you as the harem type."

"Ah, but this isn't a harem scene. This is the sheikh's tent from one of those Rudolph Valentino films," Anne announced as she walked cautiously into the flamboyant room. "Isn't it incredible?"

Hollywood's vision of exotic, Middle Eastern splendor reigned supreme in the gaudy room. The ceilings and walls were draped with an elaborately printed fabric. The bed was a huge round affair so covered with tasseled pillows that it was difficult to tell where it began and where it ended. Gossamer veils cascaded down over the bed from a wrought-iron hook in the ceiling. Underfoot an intricately designed rug completed the opulent effect.

"Are you sure this is the room you want?" Julian appeared doubtful. He began prowling around, opening the mirrored closet doors.

"Are you kidding? I'll probably never have another chance to sleep in something like this as long as I live. A once-in-a-lifetime opportunity." Anne enthused. She picked up her red leather bag and set it on a nightstand. "Which room are you going to use?" she asked as she began pulling out her toothbrush and a robe.

A moment later when he still hadn't answered she glanced up to see him watching her curiously.

"Well?" Anne prompted expectantly.

"We decided to pass me off as your fiancé, remember?"

"So?"

"So, I'll sleep in here. If you're really sure this is the room you want," Julian added in resignation. He eyed the draped bed morosely.

Anne took a deep breath, telling herself to take it carefully. There was something rather substantial about him as he stood in the middle of the fantasy room. In his gray sweater and dark jeans, he appeared as a solid, rather forbidding note against all the ornamental splendor of the bedroom.

"Julian, you're playing the *role* of my fiancé. You are not actually going to marry me, if you'll recall," she said dryly. "Our engagement is as much a piece of fiction as this room itself is."

He moved forward slowly, tawny eyes darkening. "What's wrong with a little fantasy, lady? Didn't you enjoy the dream we shared that night you arrived at the cabin?"

"Julian . . ." Anne stepped hastily back as he lifted a hand to stroke the side of her cheek. "Go find a room of your own. You're not staying here."

His expression darkened. "Craven will be suspicious if we're not sleeping together."

"No, Craven will not be suspicious. Why should he be? A lot of couples maintain a certain image of propriety during an engagement," she snapped.

"You and I," he stated with grave certainty, "would definitely be sleeping together. And I wouldn't care who knew it. I'd want everyone to know."

"Craven doesn't have to know you feel so strongly on the subject," Anne reminded him rather tartly. Matters were getting dangerous. Julian seemed to have convinced himself that playing the part of her fiancé automatically gave him a few rights. No wonder he had jumped at the idea when she had mentioned it on the plane. "If you don't climb down out of your macho tree, we will revert to plan B," she warned.

"What's plan B?"

"That's the one where you get to play the role of the insane nephew who's been kept in the basement for forty years. I always did have a preference for plan B!"

Julian's expression hardened and the hand on her cheek slid down to her shoulder where it faintly tightened. "Why do you fight me? You know you want me."

"Do I?" she challenged, stepping out from under his hand to return to her unpacking. A faint shiver of anticipation or fear moved through her as he once more closed the distance between them. She refused to glance up at him. The menace Julian was radiating was suddenly filling the room.

"Even if you won't admit that you want me, there's something else you can't deny," he said grimly.

"What's that?" Carefully she unfolded a white, long-sleeved shirt.

"Just the little matter of the fee for my services—"

He never got a chance to finish what he was going to say. Anne didn't even pause to consider her own response. She swung around in one swift movement, her right palm colliding against the side of his face in a violent slap that caught him totally by surprise.

"Don't you ever, *ever* imply that I would buy your help that way! You might be willing to sell your expertise that cheaply, but I'm not willing to pay that price. I would only sleep with you for one reason, Julian Aries, and it's got nothing to do with paying you off. If you bring up that possibility one more time I swear I will . . . I'll push you off that cliff out there!" The muted pulse of the surf far below the bedroom window backed up her enraged promise.

Julian narrowed his eyes. The mark of her hand was turning a dull red on his cheek and jaw but he made no effort to touch the injured area. Anne realized she was breathing much too quickly and that the adrenaline was pounding through her bloodstream. She was furious with him and at the same time utterly dismayed at what she had done. The last thing Julian needed was another wound. A woman's slap might not constitute much of an injury compared to what the sheikh had done, through but Anne felt terrible about it, all the same. She wanted to wrap her arms around him and tell him how sorry she was and knew she couldn't because he would not totally misread the gesture.

"Just occasionally," he suggested brutally, "you might try reminding yourself that you're the one who came looking for me. If you don't like what you found, it's hardly my fault. Good night, Anne. Let me know if the sheikh shows up."

Anne watched in frozen silence as he stalked through the room toward a door he had tried earlier. The limp was very pronounced tonight and she knew his leg must be hurting him. Too much sitting still in a car and on the plane. But his broad shoulders were arrogantly straight, and there was more than enough dangerous male temperament in Julian to keep Anne very still until he had slammed the door shut behind him.

On the other side of the door Julian flipped on a wall switch and grimly surveyed the bedroom that adjoined Anne's fantasy tent. At least this room had been done in a more sensible style. He didn't much care for the early Western film look but he was relieved that he wouldn't have to put up with a bunch of filmy drapes over the bed. Feminine nonsense.

He might have been willing to tolerate the netting, of course, if it had meant he could have shared a bed with Anne. He was willing to be reasonable in some area. If she liked the drapes he would have put up with them to please her.

He'd have put up with a lot if it meant coaxing her into bed with him. Idly he fingered the still-stinging side of his jaw. Anne probably didn't realize how close to the edge she'd walked when she gave in to that burst of fury. It would have been very easy for him to have taken the angry passion in her and translated it into another, more sensual kind. God, he wanted her. His body was still taut with the heavy hunger.

Disgustedly he tossed his suitcase down on the bed and sat down to take off his worn leather boots. His leg was hurting him. It had stiffened up during the long day. Rummaging around in his case he discovered that Anne had packed her bottle of aspirin in with his overnight things. He sat staring at the little bottle, absorbing the implications of her thoughtfulness. Then he unscrewed the lid. Gulping down two or three of the white tablets he went in search of a glass of water.

The bathroom he found opening off his room was obviously meant to be shared with the occupant of the sheikh's tent. Mirrors lined every wall and the ceiling. Three steps led up to the huge oval red enamel tub. The rest of the fixtures were also in red, and the faucets were in a heavily scrolled brass. Huge bath sheets designed in a vaguely Oriental motif hung from the towel racks and a thick white carpet cushioned his bare feet.

Anne was going to love it, Julian decided in gathering irritation. He found a glass, filled it with water and downed the aspirin. On the other side of the wall he could hear Anne moving about in the sheikh's bedroom. Wait until she found out he would be sharing the bathroom with her. Maybe he'd time it so that he "accidentally" walked in on her when she was in the bath. Serve her right. Besides, he'd enjoy seeing her covered in nothing but soap bubbles.

Julian's annoyance grew as he undressed and fell into the rough-hewn bed. After reaching out to turn off the bedside lamp, he folded his arms behind his head and considered his relationship with the woman in the room next door.

She had a lot of audacity to think that she could just walk into his life and turn it upside down. The way she was leading him around—as if he were a bull with a ring in his nose—made him want to shake her. Who did she think she was, he wondered violently.

She'd had no right to turn up at the cabin the way she did. No right to see him when he was in the grip of that blasted fever. He couldn't figure out why she hadn't fled in disgust as soon as the roads were cleared. Whatever attraction he'd held for her must have suffered considerably when she found herself having to deal with the effects of that fever.

She'd seen the scars on his body, witnessed the way he limped and she knew how exhausted the illness had left him. He was definitely not the man he'd been when he left her six months ago.

And he hadn't wanted to have her see him until he'd restored himself to some degree.

Julian remembered all the dark nights when he'd wondered if he would ever recover to the point where he felt confident enough to go in search of Anne Silver. Then she had disrupted everything by showing up in his life, long before he was ready for her.

He knew he'd been savagely short-tempered on occasion during the past few days. He'd been furious with her for seeing him in his weakened condition. But she'd tolerated the outbursts of temper. And she still refused to admit that she'd spent that first night in his arms.

Maybe she felt she had to have his help on this dumb project, Julian rationalized. Perhaps she'd put up with his illness and his temper because she couldn't think of anyone else who could assist her.

But Anne hadn't merely tolerated his illness. She'd offered comfort and compassion and a tenderness he'd never experienced before from any woman. Fleeting images of how she'd drained the unbearable heat from his body with wet sheets and then warmed him again when the chills had control came and went in his head. He couldn't remember details, had only hazy, dreamlike memories of those long hours when he'd been at the mercy of the raging fever, but he had been aware of the soothing voice and the comforting touch of her hand and Julian knew he'd never forget those images.

He could have chalked them up to feminine pity except for the fact that Anne didn't treat him as though she pitied him. She was still wary of him, still snapped back at him when she'd had enough of his uncertain temper and she still refused to admit to that night of passion. She was afraid to admit to her own surrender, Julian knew. Afraid to admit to his power over her.

No, she didn't pity him, he decided with some satisfaction. His hand moved to touch the side of his face where she had struck him so fiercely. A little hellcat, he thought with a wry twist of his mouth. Women who packed that much feminine outrage into a slap weren't feeling a lot of excess pity for their victim!

Julian turned on his side, automatically reaching down to massage his aching thigh. He didn't understand why she had tended him with such gentleness and why she hadn't found his weakness and his scars revolting, but he was sure now that she hadn't acted out of pity. He was instinctively certain, too, that she was nervous of his sensual power over her. Furthermore, she did need his help and protection while she carried out this scheme of Mike's.

He didn't understand her or what she felt for him, Julian realized as he drifted off to sleep, but he was beginning to think that maybe everything hadn't been ruined by her unexpected reappearance in his life.

Perhaps he had recovered more than he realized, because he was increasingly aware of the fact that he wasn't going to let Anne walk out of his life again now that he had her. He could handle his little hell-cat. The knowledge felt good. For the first time in a long while his sleep was untroubled by dreams of a ghost woman.

Anne was not so lucky.

She explored the bedroom after Julian walked out, delighting in the unabashed ornateness of the tent scene. When eventually she discovered the red, white and brass bathroom she made a mental note to remember every detail for Lucy. They had made a joke out of the anticipation over the bedrooms because Miss Creswell had told Lucy to expect a treat. When Lucy and Anne had decided to switch places so that Lucy could stay with Michael, her future sister-in-law had begged for a full report.

"You know we don't allow ourselves to get that tacky here in Boston," Lucy had said with a grin. "I was really looking forward to indulging myself out there in California. Now I may never have another opportunity to experience West Coast decadence."

But some of the pleasure had gone out of her exploration, Anne realized. That last confrontation with Julian had squelched her sense of humor. Damn the man! Why couldn't he stop using his claws on her whenever she got too close? Tonight he'd taken one too many swipes, and this time she'd really lost her temper. She'd half expected him to slap her back, but instead he'd simply stalked out of the room. She hadn't been able to read the expression in those tawny-brown eyes, but she'd sensed the tight control he'd been exerting over himself.

Anne tried to put the unpleasant scene out of her mind as she crawled beneath the gossamer veils. Positioning herself in the exact center of the round bed, she reached out to carefully arrange the frothy drapery.

"I should get a camera and take a picture of myself in this thing," she muttered as she switched off the lamp. "When I'm very, very old I can take it out and show it to all my friends at the health farm. Tell them this is how I spent my younger days."

It was a cinch that if she didn't make any more progress with Julian this fantasy bed was probably about as exciting as her night-life was going to get. The thought depressed her.

SHE NEVER REALLY KNEW what it was that awakened her. Anne was aware of a chill in the room when she stirred drowsily several hours later. There was no reason on earth she should be so cold, she thought. Not when the thick down quilts were piled on top of her the way they were.

Maybe there was a thermostat on the wall. This huge old place had everything else, it probably had central heating. Anne twisted in the tousled sheets, reluctant to leave the comfort of the bed, but knowing that she was going to be uncomfortably cold unless she arose and found the heat.

If her room was so chilled, Julian's probably was also. That thought goaded her into sitting up in bed. The last thing he needed was to be exposed to too much cold. Anne opened her eyes and reached for the transparent bed veil.

And then she saw the figure standing at the foot of the bed.

The scream seemed to be locked in her throat. Anne's fingers clenched in the fine fabric of the veil. Her heart began to pound with fear and she told herself she was dreaming. There was no other explanation.

Dreams like this went away, she thought frantically. All she had to do was open her eyes. But her eyes *were* open. She was awake. She could feel the tissue-thin drape in her hand, was aware of the cold in the room, felt the light weight of the quilt on her legs. Dear heaven, she was awake!

Frozen in horror she tried to focus all her energy on allowing the scream to escape. Julian was in the next room. He would hear her. There was no doubt at all in her mind that if she could just yell for Julian he would save her.

As if she sensed that Anne was about to summon aid the woman at the foot of the bed, and it was a female, Anne realized vaguely, even though she was dressed in a man's riding costume, shook her head. There was a pleading expression on the pale features. Anne realized that she could see the wall behind the apparition even as she looked at her. She was able to see right through the figure.

The shock of that realization finally freed her vocal cords.

"Julian!"

The ghostly figure held out a hand in demand or appeal. Anne could not be sure which. But already the phantom woman was fading. A split second later, just as Julian flung open the door between the two bedrooms, the wraith disappeared completely.

"Anne, what the hell . . . ?"

She struggled frantically to get through the bed veil. "Julian, oh, Julian, I've never seen anything like it. I must have been dreaming, but I *wasn't*. Julian, I . . . I . . ." She couldn't speak coherently and the stupid bed drape seemed to be deliberately impeding her escape.

"Take it easy, Anne," Julian soothed as he reached out and tore the veil aside. "What's going on? Why the scream?"

She threw herself into his arms, clutching at his solid form with every bit of strength she possessed. A part of her realized that he was naked except for a pair of jockey shorts, but she was in no shape to concern herself with what he was or was not wearing.

"Julian, there was a woman. I could see right through her. She was standing at the foot of the bed and she . . . she . . . "

"Easy, honey, take it easy." His hand stroked her hair while she buried her face against his bare shoulder. Sitting on the rounded edge of the bed, Julian gathered her close, holding her on his lap and murmuring calming words.

"It was incredible, Julian," Anne whispered. "I've never . . . never had a dream quite that real."

"That's all it was, Anne. Just a dream." Julian wrapped her a little closer, pulling her more firmly into the warmth of his body. "Just a dream. Don't you think I know what it's like to have ghost women invade your dreams? Believe me, I'm an expert."

"But, Julian, she was there. Holding out her hand to me as if she wanted my help. I think she was wearing riding clothes. Old-fashioned, Spanish-style riding gear. But it looked like a man's outfit. You've seen those pictures of the tight black pants and white shirts with the little jackets. . . . "

"I've seen plenty of them and that's probably why you dreamed that your visitor was wearing an outfit like that. One too many films of early California."

"But the figure in the dream was a woman. Wouldn't you think I'd have her in one of those beautiful, lacy gowns from the last century? Maybe a mantilla in her hair or something? I mean, why did I have her dressed like a man?"

Julian chuckled softly. "There could be some extremely complicated psychological reason for that," he pointed out gently.

"Uh-huh. Something along the lines of my subconscious trying to project her in men's clothing because even in my dreams I don't approve of the limitations placed on women back in Carlota's time? Maybe I tried to dress her in men's clothing because I wanted her to have the freedom of a man. Not a bad piece of analysis, Julian. Where in the world did you pick up dream analysis techniques?"

Julian's mouth crooked at the sharp note in her words. It was better than the panic that had been there a moment ago. "I've told you, honey. I've had a hell of a lot of experience in the subject. There were times in my dreams when you seemed so real I thought I could reach out and take hold of you."

She stirred against his chest. "Really? What did you plan to do to me after you had me?"

Julian looked down at her, studying her unexpectedly vulnerable expression in the shadows. "Well, there were times when I thought I might beat you."

"Thanks a lot!"

"Ah, but you deserved it," he assured her softly, not entirely humorous now as he remembered just how highly charged his emotions had been during those dreams. "You showed up just when I seemed to need you the most but you were always just out of reach. It was frustrating beyond belief. I thought you were going to drive me crazy and then, after a while, I realized you were an indicator of the status of my sanity. Whenever I saw you I knew I was hallucinating. When all I could see was jungle, I knew I was seeing reality."

She lifted her arms around his neck, her gaze wide and intently serious. "Julian, what happened after you went back to the island? Please tell me."

"Not tonight, Anne. You've had enough of a nightmare for one evening. Think you can go back to sleep now?"

"Are you ever going to tell me?"

"About what happened on that island? I doubt it," he said flatly. He felt her stiffen. "It's over, Anne. The best thing to do with nightmares is put them behind you and forget them."

"But you haven't forgotten. You remember every time your leg hurts or you come down with that fever. In fact, you probably remember the nightmare every time you look at me," she said with sudden, sad perception. "Oh, Julian, I never meant to do that to you. I don't want you to think of pain whenever you're around me. I should never have come looking for you."

"It's too late to have any second thoughts," he told her quietly. "You did come looking and regardless of what you intended, the result is what we both have to deal with."

"Meaning I've dragged the lion out of his lair and I have no one to blame but myself if I can't control matters?" she managed wryly.

"Is that how you think of me?" He was startled. "A lion?"

"I have a very vivid imagination," she explained apologetically. "Although, until tonight I had no idea just how vivid it could get!"

"The dream really shook you, didn't it?" Soothingly Julian began massaging Anne's nape. He liked that part of her, he realized. She was vulnerable there. Soft and vulnerable. And she seemed to respond when he stroked her like this.

"I've never had a nightmare quite that real, Julian." She leaned her head against his shoulder again, nestling into his warmth.

Julian found himself wondering at the unfamiliar sensations her trusting closeness was causing. Considering how badly he had wanted to make love to her earlier tonight it amazed him that he could be so content just to soothe her fears and cuddle her now.

She was really very vulnerable at this moment, he thought. He could easily lay her back against the pillows, talk to her a little longer until she was completely relaxed again and then gradually let his gentling touch grow increasingly sensual. He could have her in the palm of his hand with very little effort. It would be so simple now to make her admit to the passion that he had been able to draw from her the other evening. If he handled her right he could spend the rest of the night in bed with Anne making slow, overwhelming love to her. By morning she would be unable to deny his power to make her respond.

But even as he told himself how assured the passionate victory was, Julian realized he wasn't going to pursue it. Another desire in him was equally strong tonight—stronger, in fact. He wanted to offer comfort and reassurance and feel her respond to his gentling touch rather than to his passion.

It was an odd need, unlike the straightforward, uncompromising desire he had allowed himself to experience in the past around Anne. Six months ago the desire had been dominant. Whatever else he had felt for her was easily buried beneath the relatively safe, understandable, physical attraction. He had wanted her from the moment he saw her, and he had told himself that given time and opportunity he could make her want him.

But both time and opportunity had been denied him. He had returned from that godforsaken island knowing he was in no condition to pursue and seduce a woman like Anne Silver. She was a strong woman and his instincts told him she would respond only to a strong male. He needed time to recover at least some of the easy masculine power he had once wielded so casually.

Anne had shredded his plans and intentions when she had showed up in the middle of the night asking for help. The fact that he had been able to seduce her even though he had been on the verge of succumbing to the fever had restored a large chunk of his self-assurance, at least on the physical level.

By rights he should be pursuing that avenue of control. Instead he was taking a strange pleasure in being a source of comfort. Julian couldn't recall ever having offered a woman this kind of gentle reassurance. He couldn't recall a woman ever having asked for it. But, then, his relationships with the female of the species had always been a bit limited in scope.

Perhaps that was why Anne had gotten under his skin. Something in her had demanded more than simple passion from him and he had found himself wary of providing it. He wasn't even sure he had it within himself to give.

Tonight he began to wonder if he might have underestimated himself. Because tonight he was discovering that he did, indeed, have something other than desire to offer to Anne.

And judging by the way she was drifting off to sleep in his arms Julian could only assume that she needed what he was trying to give. It was a curiously satisfying realization.

6

ANNE CAME AWAKE the next morning with a gradual awareness of the fact that she was not alone in the theatrical bed. Julian's arm lay across her breasts and his heavy leg pinned her with unconscious ease. She allowed herself to savor the comforting warmth of him for a full minute before she opened her eyes and turned her head on the pillow.

It was a small shock to find herself confronting Julian's fully alert tawny gaze. Instantly Anne's focus moved to his shoulder in confusion.

"It's about time you woke up," Julian said equably. "We've got company."

"Company!"

"Umm. Probably the housekeeper. I heard the car drive up a few minutes ago. Someone came into the house and headed toward the kitchen. We probably ought to go downstairs and introduce ourselves."

"The ever-alert secret agent," Anne grumbled, trying to ease out from under Julian's weight. "I didn't hear a thing." Very carefully she avoided meeting his eyes. "What are you doing here in my bed?" she went on uncertainly. "The last thing I remember you were patting my hand and telling me not to fret about ghosts."

He blinked with catlike interest. "The last thing you remember?"

"Well, yes. I had that horrid nightmare and you came running...."

"After you screamed bloody murder," he pointed out virtuously.

Anne grimaced. "I suppose I did. She shook me up a bit appearing at the foot of the bed like that."

"You don't really think you saw Carlota, do you?"

"Don't look so concerned for my mental health," Anne muttered. "I know it was a nightmare. That's not the point. The point is, what are you doing here in my bed? You should have gone back to your own room after . . . after . . ." Her voice trailed off.

"After cuddling you until you went back to sleep?" Julian yawned magnificently. "Yeah, I probably should have. But it didn't seem right to just abandon you after all that passionate lovemaking. Besides, it was cold, and a little shared body heat seemed like a good idea at the time."

"What passionate lovemaking?" Anne blazed, sitting straight up in bed and glaring down at him.

Julian looked honestly astonished. "Don't you remember? I was busy soothing you and trying to coax you back to sleep and all of a sudden you were dragging me down into the sheets and making very interesting love to me. Maybe it had something to do with having seen Carlota's ghost. Perhaps she inspired you. After all, from what you've told me the lady was quite a little wanton—"

He got no further. Anne seized the pillow and shoved it briskly down over his face, cutting off the taunting grin and the teasing words. "That's enough out of you, Julian Aries. I know perfectly well that I went straight off to sleep last night. Don't try making me believe that anything else happened."

"Muumph," he growled.

Whatever Julian was trying to say through the thickness of the down-filled pillow was drowned out by the knock that sounded on Anne's bedroom door.

"Good morning, Miss Melton," a bright voice sang out as a middle-aged woman wearing huge round glasses and a pair of very tight jeans pushed open the door and stood poised on the threshold. "I saw your car in the drive. I'm Prue Gibson, by the way. I take care of this place for Crazy Creswell. Thought you might like a cup of coffee. . . . Oh, my goodness. I guess I should have brought two cups, hmm?"

Her inquiring blue eyes went to Julian who was removing the pillow from his face. For a moment the two stared at each other, and then Julian smiled with a graciousness that startled Anne. She'd never had occasion to see Julian making an effort to be polite and charming. She was stunned to discover that he could summon such casual aplomb under the embarrassing circumstances.

"Good morning, Prue. I'm Julian Aries. And, as you've already guessed, this lady with the startled look on her face is Anne Melton. Miss Creswell's niece and my fiancée. She's going to supervise the ghost hunters for her aunt and I came along for the free vacation. And a little honeymoon practice."

Glibly Julian used Anne's assumed name and the story she and Lucy had concocted. Miss Creswell had told the housekeeper and Craven to expect a "Miss Melton." She hadn't given Lucy's first name, so all Anne had to change was the last. She'd been practicing the switch silently for several days but Julian had had very little time to become familiar with the roles. It was a sign of his professionalism that he slipped into the cover story as easily as a sword into a sheath, Anne thought with an inner sigh. It was a little scary.

"Well — "Prue Gibson nodded amiably" —pleased to meet you both. I see you've settled in nicely," she added with a grin. "I'll just buzz back downstairs and set an extra place at breakfast. You two come down when you're ready." She closed the door behind her with a brisk slam.

Anne flopped back against the pillows, a disgusted expression shaping her mouth. "So much for preserving a little privacy and decorum!"

"Lucky we thought of the fiancé pose for me, hmm? It would have been a little difficult to explain that you were in bed with the insane nephew formerly housed in the basement."

"Go take your shower," Anne ordered, "before I decide to find out if there are any sharks down there in that cove beneath the window."

"You're thinking of using me as the shark bait?"

"You've got it."

He gave her a persuasive, slightly hurt look. "Are you really so upset about what happened last night?"

"Nothing happened last night!" Anne hurled the pillow at him. Julian sidestepped it lazily, letting the soft missile strike the bathroom door. He might not ever regain the full power and speed he'd once had, Anne decided wryly, but there was no doubt that, even after what he'd been through, Julian's reflexes were faster than those of a lot of men who had never been injured or stricken with unnamed jungle fevers.

"Far be it from me to contradict a lady," he murmured. He moved forward, leaning down to cup her face in two strong hands. "If you want to pretend that nothing occurred. . ." He finished the words against her mouth, kissing her with warm, male satisfaction.

Anne's body melted beneath the gentle heat, her mouth opening to receive him without any conscious thought on her part. She felt his fingers teasing lightly at her nape and knew the extent of her own vulnerability around this man. But there was something new in this enveloping caress, a softness that was unfamiliar in Julian. Anne realized she found it utterly enthralling.

"Nothing happened?" he taunted lightly, flicking his tongue intimately into her ear.

"Julian, I recall perfectly well what occurred last night," Anne shot back as repressively as she could manage. "And I do not want to hear another word on the subject."

"Hmm. A pity. Well—" he shrugged and released her, heading toward his door. "—I can play the gentleman on occasion." His hand was on the doorknob. "Oh, one more thing. I take it our new friend Prue Gibson thinks everything is straight and aboveboard?"

Anne nodded, confused by the way he'd halted the kiss so easily. "She believes the ghost hunters are just what they say they are and that I'm here merely to represent Miss Creswell in the matter. I gather she thinks Miss Creswell is a little nutty. What did she call her? Crazy Creswell?"

"Probably because she's into the psychic phenomena bit. All right, that's what I wanted to know. I shall do my best to maintain your brilliant cover story," Julian said chuckling, finally closing the door behind him.

Anne stared at the door and then drew a deep breath, composing herself before she got out of the rumpled bed. Julian's sense of humor this morning was unnerving. Just as she'd never really been exposed to his charm, she'd also never had much opportunity to find out whether or not he had a real sense of humor. Every time they had been together it seemed the circumstances were too overlaid with urgency and emotion to allow for any exploration of the softer sides of his personality.

But it wasn't just his teasing humor this morning that was difficult to assimilate. There was also his gentle soothing in the dark hours of the night after she'd had that nightmare. Anne paused on the edge of the bed and allowed herself to dwell on that for a moment longer.

Whatever he claimed this morning, she knew very well that there had been no lovemaking last night. Julian had held her and comforted her until she had gone to sleep. Then he had gone to sleep beside her. He had made no effort to take advantage of her emotional vulnerability last night.

All that left her with was a very big question. Why hadn't he taken advantage of the situation? She stood up and forced herself to consider the obvious answer. Perhaps he had simply been too exhausted!

That brought a rueful smile to her face as she went to the closet to find her robe. She would only be asking for trouble if she tried to read more into Julian's behavior than really existed. The man had been tired last night and he had every excuse in the world to be thoroughly worn out. He'd probably just gone to sleep without any further thought to the matter.

No, she must force herself not to read too much into Julian's actions. She would only be opening herself up to disillusion and hurt if she pretended that her wounded lion was beginning to gentle. For her own sake she had to remain extremely cautious.

Resolute in her decision, Anne flung open the door to the red-and-brass bathroom and stopped in her tracks. Julian was nonchalantly shaving in front of a steamed up mirror. And he wasn't even wearing the jockey shorts he'd had on earlier.

"Julian!"

He met her outraged eyes in the foggy mirror and grinned. "This wasn't exactly how I'd planned it, you know. I was intending to walk in on you. Preferably when you were sitting in a tub full of bubbles. Ah, well, the best-laid plans . . ."

He started to turn around and Anne hastily backed out of the room, slamming the door behind her. It was difficult enough dealing with Julian when he was wearing clothes. Confronting his unabashed nudity was quite another matter. There were definitely times when, for a woman, discretion was the better part of valor.

Prue Gibson was waiting for her two visitors downstairs. She surveyed them both with lively curiosity as they walked into the airy breakfast room, and immediately invited them to join her in the buffet breakfast she had prepared. Prue was clearly well into her second helping of fried potatoes and scrambled eggs. She was obviously not the deferential, retire-to-the-kitchen, classic type of housekeeper, Anne thought in amusement. Always expect the unexpected in California, she reminded herself.

"So you two are going to entertain those weirdos for Miss Creswell, hmm? Should be good for a laugh, if nothing else. I hope they're into séances and stuff. Always wanted to attend a real séance. When are the ghost hunters supposed to arrive?"

"This afternoon," Anne said calmly, helping herself to some eggs and a couple of pieces of whole-wheat toast. "What's your schedule, Prue? Are you here all day?"

"Miss Creswell phoned and asked me to stick around full-time during the days while everyone's here. My evenings are my own, though," she went on easily. "And if you don't mind my saying so, I've got better things to do than spend them here in this place."

"Afraid of ghosts?" Julian asked lightly as he poured himself a cup of coffee.

"What ghosts? That old tale of poor Carlota is pure garbage and everyone except the Creswell sisters know it." Prue Gibson laughed. "Nope, I said I've got better things to do with my evenings and I meant it. Just got married."

"Oh, congratulations," Anne said sincerely.

"We'll have to wait and see whether congratulations are in order. This is my third marriage. Harold's fourth. Nowadays it doesn't pay to jump to conclusions about how things will work out. Nice ring, though, don't you think?" She flashed the diamond solitaire with satisfaction.

"It's beautiful," Anne agreed politely.

"Harold's done okay in the stock market. In fact, he says he wants me to quit my job. I'm with one of those temporary help agencies," you know. Harold says we should go on a world cruise."

"Sounds like it would beat housekeeping," Julian observed, sipping his coffee slowly.

"I have a hunch it would," Prue said with a grin. "But when I took this assignment after the housekeeper retired, I promised the new owner I'd stay until she moved in and could line up someone permanently. This old place takes a lot of work on a daily basis. It can't stand empty very long or it really begins to look haunted."

"So you didn't work for my other aunt? The ex-movie actress who used to own this place?" Anne asked. She eyed Julian's cup of coffee with disapproval. So far he hadn't helped himself to any of the food.

"Nope. When she died, the housekeeper, who was getting on, retired. I understand the old actress was nice enough if you don't mind the eccentric type. She used to sleep in a different bedroom every night, I'm told. I see you two found one of the more interesting rooms last night. When are you planning on getting married?"

"We, uh, haven't set the date," Anne answered before Julian could open his mouth. She frowned across the table at her phony fiancé. "Aren't you going to have any breakfast?"

"I'm not hungry." He lifted one shoulder dismissingly.

"Well, you're going to eat," Anne declared firmly. She got to her feet and dished up a full plate of food. She had no intention of letting the man impede his own recovery by not eating properly.

"I said I wasn't hungry, Anne." There was an all-too-familiar thread of irritation in his soft growl.

Anne ignored the warning as she placed the plate in front of him. "You need the protein. Eat now and yell later."

Julian glanced down at the food and then looked over at an interested Prue. "Perhaps you can see why we haven't set the date for the wedding," he remarked meaningfully. "We have a few things to iron out between us first."

"You mean you aren't sure you can handle an assertive woman?" Prue shot back blandly.

"Is that what they call bossy, managing females these days? Assertive?"

"That's right," Anne assured him equably, watching in satisfaction as he began to fork up the eggs. "I'm assertive. Furthermore, I'm not the only female in this household who is. Prue, I'm sure, is on my side. Eat your toast."

"I appear to be outnumbered two to one." Julian picked up a slice of toast.

"Three to one." Anne smiled with an air of vast superiority. "Don't forget Carlota. From what I've read she was on the assertive side, too."

"That's right," Prue nodded pleasantly. "Legend has it, that little lady had a mind of her own and the guts to defy her husband. That took some doing back then."

It was Julian's turn to smile with cool arrogance. "Let's not forget what happened to her when she finally overasserted herself."

The comment effectively silenced the discussion on female assertiveness. Julian finished his eggs and toast with the air of a man who has just won a major victory.

It was after breakfast that Julian announced his intention to look over the house.

"Help yourself," Prue said airily. "I'm going to do some dusting and see that the rooms are ready for your ghost hunters." She started to step backward through the swing door into the kitchen with her hands full of dishes.

Anne recognized the routine and grinned. "How long did you work in a restaurant, Prue?"

The older woman looked surprised and then chuckled as she paused in the doorway. "Does it show?"

"Something about the way you back through that door reminds me of a part-time job I once had."

"No kidding. How long did you wait on tables?"

"Off and on for about four years. It was during the time I was in college."

"So what are you doing now? I mean, when you're not hosting a bunch of weirdos?"

Julian stepped in to answer before Anne could respond. "She's a research assistant at a fancy university back in the Midwest."

Anne was mildly surprised by the tone of his voice. She got the odd feeling that he didn't care for her job. "Don't look so impressed, Prue." She smiled. "I don't work in a lab or do any exotic testing. I have a background in librarianship and I know my way around a good research library. Mostly I work for a professor of history who's writing the ultimate book on the battles of the nineteenth century. Or thinks he is."

"Think anyone will ever read it if he gets it written?" Julian asked blandly.

"Oh, I'm sure he'll assign it to all his own classes. A small but guaranteed audience," Anne said with a chuckle. "The problem with history is not that people don't read it. It's that they don't seem to learn from it."

Prue laughed and disappeared into the kitchen. Julian continued to sit, staring thoughtfully at Anne.

"Do you really like that job?" he finally asked.

She wondered again at the faint hostility in his question. "It's a good job. Yes, I like it. It may lack some of the excitement and challenge your job has, but—"

"As my job *had*," he corrected quietly.

She frowned. "Julian, I know you're upset because you won't be going back to work at your old profession but don't expect me to sympathize. As far as I'm concerned you're well off out of it!"

"It paid well," he pointed out simply.

"So what?"

"So I could have offered—" He broke off abruptly, glowering down at his half-empty coffee cup. "Never mind. Unemployed males are occasionally moody."

"Is that right?" Anne grinned, tossing down her napkin. She leaned back in her chair, hooking her thumbs into her belt. "What next? Should we be making plans?"

Julian got to his feet. "Probably. That's why I thought I'd take a look around this place. I'm going to see what kind of security the house already has."

"Why?"

He gave her a mockingly patient look. "First, because if I know what kinds of locks and other security arrangements have already been made, I'll know what to expect if and when Craven and his bunch come back to carry out the burglary. And second, because I know a little bit about security in general. Supposedly this is the sort of expertise you came looking for when you came knocking on my door."

Anne lifted her chin. "You don't have to snap at me."

He closed his eyes in silent disgust. "I was not snapping at you. Not that you don't deserve it. Kindly do not treat me as though I were a small boy at the breakfast table again, Anne."

"You need your food," she retorted stubbornly.

Julian lifted one sardonic brow. "I'm well aware of my own needs. And I'm capable of going after whatever it takes to fulfill them." With that he turned and stalked out of the breakfast room.

Anne sighed and decided that what she needed was a long walk on the beach. Julian's uncertain temper was very wearing at times. Determinedly she went into the huge kitchen to find Prue and ask for some advice on descending the cliff to the rocky beach.

Twenty minutes later Julian stood at an upstairs window and watched broodingly as Anne picked her way down the little-used path to the cove below the old house. She was moving carefully, choosing her route cautiously, and he guessed that the footing was uncertain. When she got back he'd issue a few well-chosen words of warning on negotiating the cliff path. Not that she'd thank him, Julian decided grimly. The lady was stubborn, arrogant and definitely self-assertive. She was also soft and sweet and deliciously vulnerable in bed. The combination was captivating.

Telling himself he had work to do, Julian turned away from the window and went to examine the lock on her bedroom door. Anne might be here because she was determined to carry out her brother's plan. Julian, however, knew that he was here, not because of Michael Silver, but to protect Anne. If Craven really was a crook, the first order of importance would be to keep an eye on the assertive little female who had concocted the situation in which Julian found himself. And he'd do it whether or not she appreciated his efforts.

Not liking the fact that Anne's hall door could be opened with a key from the outside, he took a few minutes to jimmy the mechanism so that it could no longer be unlocked from the hall, only from the bedroom. The task was child's play for him. He certainly owed the government for having provided him with an unusual and probably highly unmarketable set of job skills, Julian thought sourly. Anne was probably only impressed by those in academic careers.

When Craven and his small team arrived in a car three hours later, one of the first things Anne noticed was that two of the trio were very much academic types. For some reason she was surprised. None of the three looked at all as she had imagined.

"Thomas Craven," the portly, genial man announced as Anne opened the door. "I believe I and my friends are expected?" He smiled a gentle, ingratiating smile and fussed a bit with the wire-rimmed glasses that were perched on his nose. Craven was in his fifties, Anne knew, but she hadn't realized he would look quite so much like the scholarly professor of history for whom she worked. Balding, with friendly gray eyes and a fastidiously maintained mustache, Craven could have blended in with the academic crowd of any campus.

"Please come in, Mr. Craven. I'm Anne Melton," Anne said pleasantly, having practiced using Lucy's last name. "Did my aunt warn you I'd be representing her?"

"Of course, of course. Poor Miss Creswell. I understand she's most upset about the presence in the house. No need to be so nervous about those who have gone beyond. I have yet to uncover an instance where a presence has actually caused any physical harm to the inhabitants of a house. But I certainly understand how unsettling it can be to have an astral entity about the place." He turned to gesture to the two people standing on the steps behind him. "This is Sara. Sara is a sensitive."

"A sensitive what?" Anne asked blankly. She was concentrating intently on the young woman in front of her. Sara was an ethereal beauty. Long blond hair, parted in the middle and falling to her waist, framed delicate, translucent features and a pair of dream-filled green eyes. Everything about the woman was as exquisite as fine crystal. She looked as if she'd shatter if someone shook her hand with too much force. Even as Anne asked her question, Sara was focusing on a silent Julian who stood waiting to one side.

"A sensitive is someone who has the ability to tune in to a presence, Miss Melton," Craven explained easily. "Sara has been gifted with a special kind of awareness. She's the one in our group who will actually be able to detect the presence, if there is one, and perhaps, if we're exceedingly lucky, communicate with it."

"How do you do, Sara," Anne managed politely. It didn't take any great sensitivity to see that Sara wasn't particularly interested in the formalities. "I didn't catch your last name."

"I have no last name," the young woman told her in a small, soft voice. "I'm just Sara."

"Oh."

"And I'm Dan Hargraves." The handsome man in his early thirties who stepped around Sara to offer his hand was refreshingly casual and open. "I'm Mr. Craven's assistant. I get to do all the research and keep all the notes. Glorified secretary, I'm afraid."

"I know the feeling," Anne said impulsively, responding to his easy manner before stopping to think. "I'm a research assistant myself. And there are times when I could have used a good secretarial course."

He grinned down at her as he shook her hand, his hazel eyes gleaming faintly. His hair was a light sandy brown, worn stylishly long. He was dressed more casually than the other two and there was a breezy charm about him that was quite attractive. Especially when it was contrasted with the dark, saturnine presence of Julian, who was still standing quietly, waiting for the introductions. Anne hastily made them.

"My fiancé, Julian Aries," she said quickly, nodding toward him. Privately she was rather relieved not to stumble over the word fiancé. "He's, uh, taking a couple of days of vacation."

"Really?" Thomas Craven eyed him interestedly. "And just what is your line of work, Julian?"

"My fiancée was being polite when she said I was taking a vacation," Julian replied dryly, slanting a glance at Anne. "Actually, I'm unemployed at the moment. Want some help with the luggage?" He started out the door, not waiting for an answer.

Dan Hargraves went to assist him.

"Are there just the two of you staying here, Miss Melton?" Craven asked politely as he stepped into the foyer.

"Just Julian and I and the housekeeper, Prue, who is only here during the days. You'll meet her shortly. She's out doing the grocery shopping. Please call me Anne, by the way." Leading the way toward the staircase, she went on chattily, "The bedrooms are a little odd but rather interesting."

"Fascinating," Thomas Craven observed as he and Sara followed Anne up the staircase. "Your aunt has inherited some excellent art, Anne."

"Oh, you mean the Ballards and the Renfrews?" Anne said easily, glancing at the watercolors that lined the staircase. "Yes, they are rather nice if you like that sort of thing. I've never been too fond of them, myself."

"Nevertheless, they're worth a fortune," Craven murmured, pausing to examine one in more detail.

"Ballard and Renfrew were friends of my other aunt. The one who originally bought this house. She was something of a patron to them when they were both young and struggling, I believe. They repaid her by giving her several pictures."

"Interesting." Craven smiled blandly.

Sara kept silent. She appeared to be lost in thought as she climbed the stairs behind Craven and Anne. Probably busy detecting presences, Anne decided uncharitably. Or else deciding whether or not to go to the bother of acquiring fakes to hang on the wall in place of the Ballard and Renfrew paintings, when the originals got themselves mysteriously stolen. Anne made a mental note to tell Julian that Craven had already shown an interest in the artwork.

Later that evening after dinner Craven helped himself liberally to the bottle of port in the living room and explained the procedure he and his companions would use to first detect the presence, as he called Carlota, and then remove her permanently. He was an excellent conversationalist, at ease with his audience, and in spite of what she knew about him Anne found herself listening intently to his stories. It was difficult to believe this was the man her brother had been trying to trap. For the first time Anne began to wonder if Michael might have been mistaken. But Lucy had said he was so sure it was Craven who had tried to get rid of him.

Uneasily Anne tried to sort through her impressions of the three ghost hunters as they all sat talking after dinner. When eventually Craven excused himself to go to bed she was no closer to any certainties than she had been earlier. In fact, she admitted to herself, she was beginning to feel very confused. Other than that Sara was definitely a bit strange, these people were all rather nice!

"I'm really looking forward to this assignment," Dan said pleasantly as he followed Anne into the kitchen after Craven had retired. Prue had long since gone home, and Anne was cleaning up the cups and saucers that had been used for after-dinner coffee.

"Anything special about this one?" Anne asked politely as the kitchen door swung shut behind them. She wondered what Sam and Julian would find to talk about alone in the living room.

"Mainly that it's taking place here in California," he said with a chuckle. "I've always wanted to visit California. Did you get to spend much time here when you were a kid?"

"Uh, no, my aunt didn't relish having kids around," Anne hastily temporized.

"Too bad. Can't imagine anything nicer than spending summers on this coast. When I was younger I always had a secret longing to follow the sun and become a full-time surfer." He set down the load of saucers he had been carrying and peered out the kitchen window. "Is the ocean really just down below us?"

"Yes."

"Mind if I step out on the terrace for a few minutes? I'd like to take a look at that cove you mentioned."

"You won't be able to see much at night," Anne warned. "There's not enough of a moon to . . ." Her words trailed off as Dan smiled and opened the kitchen door.

Curious, she followed him out onto the old brick terrace. The wind off the ocean was chilly, carrying the scent of the sea and promising a storm. What moon there was had already been obscured by clouds.

"Exciting, isn't it?" Dan murmured, as he leaned against the terrace railing and stared out at the night-darkened ocean. "A man could get addicted to the sea at night."

"It looks rather dangerous to me," Anne said with consideration, moving to stand beside him. Earlier that day the surf hadn't appeared to be too rough except where it broke over the rocks of the cove. But now, beginning to run before a storm, the waves looked and sounded considerably more violent. "But, then, I grew up in the Midwest. I've never felt entirely comfortable around oceans. I suppose I prefer lakes." She chuckled.

Dan laughed softly, and somehow he had moved a little closer. "Life is more fun when there's an element of danger in it. Maybe that's why I'm working as Craven's assistant."

"Is it dangerous?"

"Oh, not really, but one definitely encounters some strange tales and happenings in this line of work. To tell you the truth, Anne, I never believed in ghosts until I took this job with Thomas Craven. He and Sara have convinced me there are some really odd things in this world. Things that can't be easily explained by modern science."

"It must be fascinating," Anne observed cautiously.

"It is. Someday I'll write a book about it. Might as well use all the research for something useful."

Anne felt herself smiling in the shadows. "I've had the same thought from time to time. I spend so much effort doing research for someone else, and then I don't have the satisfaction of using it myself."

"Frustrating, isn't it?"

For a long moment they stood silently gazing out at the endless expanse of sea and then, with obvious reluctance, Dan drew a deep breath and straightened away from the railing.

"I suppose I'd better be getting upstairs to that wild Cleopatra-style bedroom. It's been a long day." But he didn't move for another minute or two, studying Anne's face in what little light emanated from the kitchen. "Yes," he said quietly, as if to himself, "I'm really looking forward to this particular assignment. And not just because of the ocean. Good night, Anne."

Anne watched in silence as Dan stepped back inside the house. A very nice man. Someone with whom she had something in common, too. The door closed behind him, and she was left alone on the night-shrouded terrace. It was very chilly and damp, and she told herself she should go back inside. She was about to do exactly that when Julian's voice came to her from the far end of the terrace.

"It's called 'divide and conquer' and although it's an old strategy it can be remarkably effective," he drawled in a low voice that sounded as though it had been roughened by the wind.

Startled, Anne swung around, searching for him in the shadows. He stepped silently out of the patch of blackness that had been created by a tall hedge. "Julian! I didn't hear you. Where's Sara?"

"Gone to bed. She said she was tired."

"She looks like someone who needs a lot of rest," Anne heard herself say caustically. "A bit on the delicate side, wouldn't you say?"

Julian shrugged. "Maybe she's encountered one too many ghosts. That's not what I wanted to talk about, Anne."

"What did you want to discuss? Your habit of spying on people from the shadows? How long have you been standing there, Julian?"

"Long enough. Don't give Hargraves any encouragement, Anne. He'll take advantage of it."

Anne bristled. "Really? And what about dear Sara? Will she take advantage of you?"

"If I let her, yes. Like I said, it's called 'divide and conquer.' Hargraves and sweet Sara are professionals, remember? Liars, thieves and possibly worse, if Mike was right."

"But they all seem so *nice*," Anne protested unhappily.

"Hargraves wants you to think he's the nicest guy to come along since Santa Claus. It's to his benefit to see that you're left with a really terrific impression of him. That way you wouldn't ever dream of connecting him with the robbery that's going to take place at some point in the future. All three of them are going to want us to think they're *nice*. I told you on the way out here that you're going to do this my way, Anne, remember? You're to follow my orders. And my first order is that you watch your step around Hargraves. Keep him at a distance. No more dreamy little midnight scenes on the terrace."

Anne felt her temper start to simmer. "You're being ridiculous."

"No, Anne. Ridiculous is what I'd be if I didn't make certain, right from the start, that you remember I'm the one giving the orders. Now go inside and go to bed. It's late and it's getting cold out here."

Anne blinked, a little shocked at the steel in his voice. Julian was not speaking out of annoyance or irritation. There wasn't even any of the familiar frustrated masculine temperament in his words. He was suddenly very hard and very professional and he meant to be obeyed.

As Anne walked back into the house, her head held defiantly high, she had a distinct feeling of apprehension, which had nothing at all to do with ghosts. It had everything to do with her sudden certainty that Julian Aries at work was going to be even more formidable than Julian Aries recovering from his wounds and his fever.

7

IT WAS THE WIND that woke Anne several hours later. At least, that's what she assumed caused her to stir within the confines of the tented bed. It was a howling, gusty wind that carried the driving rain in from the sea—a wind well suited to a haunting. Sleepily Anne wondered if Craven and company liked the added bit of atmosphere the storm provided.

She turned drowsily to punch up her pillow, and that's when she saw the figure standing at the foot of the round bed. Anne froze in cold shock, staring through the misty veil at the apparition.

"No," she whispered in stark denial. "No, please . . ."

"Did you think I'd let you sleep alone tonight?" The phantom moved in the thick shadows, coming toward her around the bed. "After witnessing that cute little scene with Hargraves out on the terrace?"

"Julian!"

"Tonight we're not going to play any games," he swore softly as he stood on the other side of the bed veil and methodically began to unclasp his belt and step out of his jeans. Anne could see the outline of his bare, hair-covered chest in the darkness.

"Julian, please. I don't know what you think you're doing, but I do know I don't want you here tonight." And it was the truth. She did not want this man until he came to her with love. Anne knew that now. But she wasn't at all certain she could deny him if he ignored her wishes. Her own love for him weakened her.

"I am here, Anne. This time I can promise you that in the morning you won't be able to pretend that nothing happened." He was out of the jeans now, pushing aside the gossamer netting of the bed veil.

Instinctively Anne edged back, her pulse beginning to throb as a mixture of intense emotions coursed through her.

"There's nowhere to run, lady. Not tonight. Not tomorrow. You haven't had a chance since you foolishly turned up on my doorstep." Julian came down on the bed reaching for her.

There was heat in him tonight, Anne thought dazedly as he touched her, but not the heat of fever. The tawny-brown eyes gleamed faintly in the unlighted room but not with the unnatural glow of illness. Tomorrow morning he would remember all too well the effect he had on her senses. Anne thought she knew what he could do to her, but he would use the information. If she succumbed to his aggressive passion tonight she would be handing him a weapon he could wield against her.

"Julian, you must know I'm not about to get involved with Dan." Anne lay still beneath the chaining grasp of his hand. Something told her that if she struggled he would respond by pinning her more firmly to the bed.

"I know that," he agreed. "And tomorrow morning you'll know it, too. You'll also know that there won't be any more professors of either English or history or any therapists from the physical-education department. In fact, after tonight there won't be anyone else for you except me."

Suddenly Anne became angry. "You're only doing this so that you can control me, aren't you?"

"The strange part is that for the past six months I wouldn't have guessed I could control you this way," he said huskily as he settled his heavy thigh over her lower body. "I told myself I needed someone stronger—that I would have to wait until I had fully recovered. I was too proud to face you until I knew for certain you wouldn't pity me or find me weak."

"Oh, Julian," she whispered, lifting her hand to touch the side of his hard face. "The one thing I have never felt for you is pity."

"I know that now. I think I knew it that first night. I seduced you that night at the cabin, didn't I? I carried you off to bed and made love to you until you were helpless in my arms. You surrendered that night and you knew it. It wasn't pity you were feeling. In fact you were a little afraid of just how completely you had surrendered, weren't you? That's why you denied everything the next morning." He lowered his head deliberately and grazed his lips along the line of her throat. When she trembled in reaction he muttered his sense of satisfaction. "Do you have any idea of how it made me feel to know that I had that kind of power over you? Even though I was on the verge of another attack of that fever?"

"Julian, I don't want it to be like this between us. I don't want you to make love to me because it gives you a feeling of . . . of power or control. It should mean something else—something more important."

He looked down into her pleading eyes and traced the line of her slightly parted lips with his thumb. "Honey, you don't know just how important it is to me to feel this sensation of power over you. You don't know how good it feels to know I can make you surrender completely. Believe me, after all these months of thinking I wasn't the same man you had been attracted to in the beginning, it was very, very satisfying to know I could still make you want me."

"You're so damned arrogant," she breathed helplessly. *And you know exactly how to disarm me,* she added silently. There was no way she could fight him tonight. Not after that small confession of his. It was incomprehensible to her that he could have believed she wouldn't be as attracted to him now as she had been six months ago. "And you're far too proud," she told him.

"But I can make you shimmer in my arms, can't I?"

"Only because . . ."

"Because?"

Anne sighed in surrender, her hands clinging to the solid planes of his shoulders. She couldn't tell him that she loved him. Not yet. Julian Aries wouldn't understand that emotion. He saw things in simpler, more fundamental terms. "Only because you're Julian."

He hesitated no longer. "Anne . . . !"

She felt his strong fingers on the buttons of her flannel gown and she cried out softly when he undid them all so that he could slip his hand inside.

"You're so soft," he murmured. "I dreamed of your softness—longed for it." His mouth moved hungrily from the base of her throat to the opening of the nightgown, seeking the budding tips of her breasts.

Anne felt herself being crushed back into the bedding. Dreamily she realized that the flannel gown had been removed completely and that Julian was exploring her body with bold wonder.

"Do you like my touch?" he demanded provocatively, trailing his fingers down her stomach to the dark mystery between her legs. "Do you, Anne?"

"You know the answer to that. Oh, Julian, *please*."

"I want to feel your hands on me, honey." His tongue moved tantalizingly over her nipple. He caught hold of her wrist and dragged her fingers along his side to his muscular hip. "Touch me, Anne. Let me know how much you want me."

She sensed the need in him and knew it was as great as her own. Perhaps he did think in terms of power and control. Perhaps recovering that purely masculine arrogance was a necessary part of his recuperation. In any event it was all he had to offer her now and Anne knew she would take what she could get.

Slowly she traced the hard male outlines of his body, thrilling to his obvious response. Maybe he did have power over her she thought wonderingly, but she also had a certain amount over him. And it was an intoxicating kind of knowledge.

Gently she pushed against his shoulders until he allowed her to roll him over onto his back. And then she found the base of his throat with her lips.

"Anne—" Whatever he would have said next was lost in a thick male groan of rising hunger as she strung tiny kisses down to the flat masculine nipples.

When she carefully let him feel the edge of her teeth he shuddered violently, his palms moving down her back to the curve of her buttocks. As she worked her way lower, so did he. Anne felt his hand slide down to the flowing heat between her legs.

Her fingers closed delicately on the shaft of Julian's manhood, drawing a fierce, swallowed sound of need from him. And then he was probing the moistness of her, using her own warmth to smooth and lubricate the sensitized flesh between her thighs. A feeling to give him back some of the passionate heat he was generating in her, Anne bent her head and brushed her lips intimately against him.

"My God, Anne, you'll drive me out of my mind." He uncoiled beneath her, pushing her back into the sheets again. "Out of my mind . . ." He trapped one budding nipple between his front teeth and tantalized his captive with incredible gentleness.

Julian's hand flattened on her stomach and then went lower. His mouth followed until Anne cried out and clenched her fingers in his hair.

The night and the storm flowed around them and through them, closing out all but the deep mysteries of passion. Julian made love with an uninhibited aggression that excited Anne beyond anything she had ever known. It turned her into a creature who both delighted and demanded. The scope of her own desire amazed her, and Julian's escalating response captured her senses.

When he finally moved to cover her body with his own, she pulled him to her with urgent little cries. He fed on the soft sounds, plunging his tongue forcefully between her lips a second before he filled her body with his uncompromising hardness.

"Julian, Julian," she gasped as he thrust completely into her. She was pinned beneath his weight, her legs forced widely apart so that she was totally vulnerable. Anne felt at once ravished and wanton—the one who is taken and the one who takes. She wrapped her body tightly to her, sinking her small, white teeth delicately into the muscle of his shoulder as the driving rhythm of his lovemaking grew in intensity.

When the moment of utter release descended on her, she clung to the man who had provided it, refusing to let go until he had joined her. She had the fierce satisfaction of hearing her name on his lips as he arched violently against her, and then the thick shadows enfolded them.

It was a long time before Julian stirred on her, uncoupling slowly, reluctantly, to roll to one side. Then he gathered her against him, his arm curved around her.

"Remember this the next time Hargraves turns on the charm," he rasped. "Remember that now you belong to me." Lazily he traced a circle around the tip of her breast. "You're the one who came looking for me, honey. And you're going to have to take what you found."

She raised herself on one elbow to gaze down at him. "You sound possessive," she whispered.

"I'm feeling possessive." His mouth curved with masculine content.

"Were you jealous of Dan?"

"Let's just say I'm taking steps to protect you from him."

"You were jealous," she accused softly.

Julian hesitated as if considering his words. "Hargraves is going to hold out all the bait I haven't got to offer."

"That's ridiculous!"

"Is it? He's going to show you how much you have in common, how similar your professional interests are, how charming and considerate he can be."

"He's involved with the people who tried to kill Michael. How could I possibly be attracted to him?"

"Tonight you were already questioning his involvement. All three of them were so *nice*, you said. Remember?"

"Well, they are. At least Craven and Dan are nice. I can't quite figure out that Sara. Isn't it a bit affected not to have a last name?"

"Goes with the image."

"I suppose. Julian, you don't have to worry that I'm going to forget the reason I'm here," Anne told him vehemently. "After all, I'm the one who set this up. It's my brother lying in that Boston hospital!"

"Honey, you're not used to dealing with real con artists. The nicer they are and the more charming they seem, the more you're going to question your own judgment."

"So you assaulted me tonight in an effort to remind me that you're in charge and I'm not to let myself get led astray by the opposition, right?" She flopped back on the pillow, pulling the comforter up to her chin and staring angrily up at the draped netting.

Julian turned on his side, regarding her with something between amusement and speculation. "Is that what you considered it? An assault?"

"You scared the daylights out of me by just appearing at the foot of the bed the way you did," she accused morosely. "At first I thought it was her. . . ."

"Her?"

"The ghost I thought I saw last night. The one in my dream. I couldn't see you very well through this stupid veil."

"I'm sorry I frightened you." He bent his head to brush his mouth against her ear.

"But you're not sorry you assaulted me?" she challenged.

"No. In fact, I'm seriously thinking of doing it again," he teased.

Anne turned her head in astonishment. "You are?"

"Umm. But first I want you to admit you do remember that first night at the cabin."

"Never," she declared loftily.

"Never is a long time. But not quite as long as the rest of tonight." He pushed his hand beneath the down-filled comforter and flattened his palm on her stomach. "There's no point denying it, honey. I know I carried you off to bed that night. I've gotten very good at telling the difference between reality and illusion lately."

Anne looked up at him from under her lashes. "Maybe I'm not quite so adept at it." And maybe that was the truth. How much of an illusion was she weaving for herself when she pictured a future of love with Julian Aries?

Then his hands were moving on her again, and she no longer cared about the difference between the real and the unreal. Only Julian's touch mattered.

WHEN ANNE AND JULIAN walked into the breakfast room the next morning it was to find that Thomas Craven had already preceded them. He was involved in a lively conversation with Prue Gibson, who was sparkling even more than usual under Craven's gentlemanly charm.

"Good morning, you two," Prue called out cheerfully, pouring coffee into two cups. "How did you sleep last night? That was quite a storm we had, wasn't it? I was just telling Thomas here that legend has it little Carlota was trying to make her escape on a night like last night."

"I've never quite understood why ghosts and storms go together," Thomas said genially as he sat back and sipped his coffee. "But there is a definite correlation. In many of the cases I've investigated the presences are felt most strongly during a severe storm. It will be interesting to see if Sara experienced any emanations last night."

"I expect ghosts and storms go together because people's imaginations seem to become more vivid under stormy conditions," Julian remarked coolly as he handed a cup of coffee to Anne and then helped himself.

"You sound like a skeptic, Julian." Thomas Craven smiled blandly. "Only to be expected. Most people are until they've actually experienced a presence or witnessed the results of one passing through. I myself used to scoff at the idea of ghosts, but in my line of work you quickly become convinced. I set out to disprove the legends and tales I had been collecting and found myself unable to ignore the evidence. But I still maintain a scientific approach to the matter, and in many of the cases I'm called in to investigate I wind up proving there is no presence. In other cases my friends and I have been able to provide tranquillity to homes that have been troubled."

Julian shrugged with evident disinterest. "Well, it's Miss Creswell's money. If Anne's aunt wants to pay you to de-ghost her house that's her business."

"Still," Dan Hargraves remarked from the doorway, "it must be a little galling for a man who is currently unemployed to see money being spent in such a frivolous fashion. Then again, I suppose you can afford to take the long-term view. After all, you're going to be marrying one of Miss Creswell's heirs, aren't you?"

The silence that followed the provocative insult was broken only by the sound of Anne choking on her coffee. She couldn't believe Dan had had the nerve to offer such a challenge to Julian Aries, even if he truly believed that Julian's motives were questionable. Dan had no way of knowing that the whole engagement was a farce, of course. He was reacting to the situation that had been presented, and Anne could only assume he was deliberately insulting Julian for a reason. She just couldn't imagine what the reason would be.

Neither, apparently, could anyone else in the room. Even Prue was momentarily silenced in astonishment. Craven looked pained. Anne was struggling to find words with which to smooth over the situation when Julian spoke.

He regarded Dan with laconic boredom, as if the younger man was a rather annoying rodent that had wandered into the house. "You can skip the not-so-subtle insults, Hargraves. Anne and I understand each other very well." His dark-gold eyes went to Anne's face, and only she saw the warning in those depths. "She knows, for example, just what holds our relationship together and it has nothing to do with money. Isn't that right, honey?"

Anne's temper flared. She knew he was deliberately setting a public seal on her. A seal that would accompany the very private one he had placed on her last night. The desire to tell him to go to hell was brought under control only with a great deal of difficulty. Instead she managed a smile while telegraphing her anger with her eyes.

"Oh, yes. Julian and I understand each other." But he didn't understand her. Not at all. And she was beginning to wonder if he ever would.

It was Sara, appearing in the doorway, who succeeded in dispelling the tension of the moment. Everyone at the breakfast table swung around as she made her entrance. And "entrance" was the right word. Pale, beautifully wan, a weightless smock of embroidered gauze drifting around her slender frame, Sara definitely looked a little ghostly herself this morning. The long blond hair had been brushed until it hung like a silken curtain around her shoulders, and it occurred to Anne that sweet Sara had taken a bit of time with her appearance. She wondered how much luck the blonde had with that fragile look.

"She's here, Thomas," Sara whispered. "I felt her presence last night. Oh, Thomas, she is in such agony. We must free her." Her voice broke on the last words and she rushed toward Craven. Thomas patted her with what seemed to Anne to be slightly more than a paternal touch.

"All right, Sara. All right, dear. Just calm yourself. Everything's going to be fine. Just fine."

Sara sniffed delicately, and a single, glistening tear appeared on her cheek. The woman really was overplaying her part, Anne decided, casting a wry glance at Julian. The glance became a glare as she realized Julian was staring at the other woman with fascinated concern.

"Did you actually see her, or were you only able to sense the presence?" Dan asked in a practical tone.

"Last night I could only feel her. She was there in my room. I think she came looking for me because she knows I can communicate on some level with her. She's desperate. She's been confined so long now, trapped in this old house because it was built on the ruins of her home. She is a very sad creature."

"What's the next step?" Julian asked interestedly.

"We must establish a more definite contact," Craven explained. "Sara can only do that by going into a full-scale trance of sorts."

"A séance!" Prue exclaimed, looking delighted. "How exciting."

"Well, it's really not that much fun," Dan told her in mild amusement. "It can be very traumatic on occasions, and it always leaves Sara wiped out for most of a day."

"Still, it's the only way we can determine exactly what the presence requires in order to be freed," Craven said with a sigh.

Anne remembered the tale she had researched. "According to the legend, Carlota returns to look for something. Will we actually have to find it for her in order to get her out of the house?"

"Not necessarily. Usually in cases such as this one the presence has somehow become trapped in a loop."

"A loop?" Julian asked. "You mean like a program loop in a computer?"

"Not a bad analogy," Craven nodded, pleased. "That's exactly what it's like. In a program loop the machine gets stuck going from A to B and back again and can't escape to continue with the program. One has to go into the program itself and correct the flaw that has trapped the machine. Presences who died in sudden violence occasionally seem to be caught in that sort of trap—unable to break free of their earthly ties, but no longer a real part of this realm. Their despair is often the first sensation Sara feels. Somehow we have to break the loop cycle."

"When do we get to hold the séance?" Prue demanded.

"I think this afternoon," Craven announced, glancing at Sara to see if that was all right with her. "It doesn't always work the first time, however. It may be necessary to hold two or three of them in order to achieve an adequate level of communication."

"I see," Anne said briskly. "Well, eat hearty, Sara. You look as if you'll need the energy. You look a little run-down," she added too sweetly.

Julian tossed Anne a half-amused, half-rebuking glance but Anne just smiled quite brilliantly.

THE SÉANCE THAT AFTERNOON was not at all what Anne had expected. There were no artificial trappings, no crystal ball, no velvet-draped surroundings. The fog, which was beginning to roll in from the sea, did manage to provide a certain air of gloom, but that was it as far as lighting effects went. Craven had decreed that Sara use the living room.

"We can build a fire in the fireplace," he explained. "Sara often gets quite cold when she's in a trance. The added warmth can be very comforting to her."

Julian did not offer an opinion on the subject. He just went about building the fire with casual efficiency. Anne was idly noting that his leg didn't seem to be bothering him so much today in spite of the foggy chill outside, when she realized that she wasn't the only one watching Julian lay the fire. Sara's pale, haunting gaze was also on him as he knelt to set a match to the kindling. In fact, Anne decided in disgust, Sara had been paying a lot of attention to Julian.

"Thank you, Julian," the blonde murmured in her gentle voice. "I shall soon be very grateful for the added warmth. I get so cold sometimes...."

"Maybe you should try wearing a sweater and slacks," Anne suggested, "instead of that little lightweight nightgown."

Sara gave her a reproachful glance. Julian, standing directly behind the blonde, sent Anne a warning glare. Anne ignored both.

"I have to feel free when I'm trying to communicate," Sara explained gently. "Wearing loose-fitting, light clothing helps me achieve that feeling."

"Well, now," Craven interrupted genially, "I think we're all set. Don't overexert yourself, Sara. Just go as far as you comfortably can. Let's see if we can even make contact."

"Do we all get to sit in a circle and hold hands?" Prue asked.

"I'm afraid that's an old charlatans' technique," Dan said chuckling. "Really not a necessary step at all. The fake psychics just wanted to make sure everyone's hands were occupied so that the people around the table wouldn't accidentally touch any of the rigged apparatus."

"Will we be able to see anything at all if Sara makes contact?" Anne inquired curiously.

"I'm afraid not. Only a true sensitive can see the presence and even sensitives often have to rely more on sensation rather than sight. Occasionally there will be a manifestation of noise but that's rare."

"How disappointing," Prue grumbled.

"If Sara does make contact, we'll be able to ask questions through her. That can be very interesting." Dan consoled the older woman lightly.

Craven decreed quiet as the group took their places in chairs near the fire. Sara sat on the floor in a lotus position facing the flames on the hearth.

Craven turned off the living-room lights, and Anne suddenly realized just how thick the late-afternoon fog had become. There was an eerie, gray, dimensionless feeling to the day, as if the strange old house were adrift in a sea of endless fog. Even the familiar noise of the surf seemed muted. Only the fire provided any note of warmth and light. Anne suddenly understood why Sara demanded it. A person could get so cold on a day like this. So very cold . . .

She shivered as silence fell on the room. Sara's eyes were closed and everyone else was watching the blonde. Anne thought seriously about getting up to change the thermostat setting, but for some reason it seemed like too much of an effort. And she didn't want to disrupt the mood of the quiet room. Not now.

It was almost unpleasantly cold in the room, Anne realized a few minutes later. Nothing had happened, but she had the strangest impression that someone had left a door open somewhere and that tendrils of fog had found their way into the living room.

Sara broke Anne's strange feeling of lethargy with a chant. The meaningless words disturbed something in the atmosphere. Anne moved restlessly, wishing the woman would shut up. She wanted to listen, pay closer attention to the flickering flames on the hearth. There was a message in those flames, a meaning. No, not in the flames—in front of the fire. The air in front of the fireplace seemed to shimmer faintly. Anne wished desperately that Sara would stop chanting. It was so annoying and it was disturbing whatever hovered in front of the fire. Then Sara spoke.

"We are here to help you, Carlota," Sara said in a singsong voice. "We only wish to help."

Instantly whatever had been there in front of the fireplace was gone. Almost at once Anne began to feel warmer. She shook her head in an attempt to clear it of the dazed, lethargic sensation and became aware of Julian's solid presence beside her. When she slanted him a glance out of the corner of her eye she saw him carefully watching Sara.

Craven sat with his eyes closed, his hands folded over his portly stomach. Dan was also watching Sara, but he looked quite relaxed. Prue appeared vividly curious and was focusing intently on Sara. None of them seemed to have felt the earlier chill in the room, and none of them looked even slightly dazed. Maybe she was one of those people who could easily be hypnotized, Anne told herself by way of explanation. But that didn't make any sense. The weird sensation had begun to occur before Sara had started in on her repetitive chant. On the other hand, Anne decided grimly, perhaps she'd merely let her own imagination run away with her.

"Help you, Carlota. Help you. We only want to help you. Tell us . . ."

Sara's low, singsong voice began to bore Anne. She was wishing she'd thought to fix some coffee before starting the séance, when suddenly the blonde's tone changed.

"Yes," Sara whispered. "Yes. I can feel you Carlota. Just as I felt you last night."

Craven opened his eyes and sat forward, staring intently at his assistant. Dan Hargraves also took on an air of focused attention. Prue looked hopeful, and Julian's expression didn't change at all.

This was utter nonsense, Anne thought disgustedly. There was nothing else here in the room with them. Not now at any rate. But Sara was beginning to carry on some sort of odd conversation.

"I know you need help. Can you tell me what to do?"

Silence. Presumably, Anne decided, the ghost of Carlota was answering.

"Yes, Carlota. I understand that you search. But for what?"

Silence again.

"Peace, Carlota? Justice? I don't understand. What do you wish of us?"

Everyone remained very still during the next stretch of silence, and then Sara gave a startled cry. The flames on the hearth flared abruptly higher turning a brilliant shade of green. The fluorescent green gave way to vivid blue and finally burned silver.

Sara collapsed, falling forward so that the curtain of blond hair was flung like a cape around her. Dan was instantly on his feet, lifting her and settling her into a nearby chair. Craven looked concerned but not unduly worried.

"She'll be all right," he told the others. "Just give her a couple of minutes. Have you any brandy, Prue?"

"Right over there on the cart. I'll get it." The housekeeper hurried across the room and returned with a large dose of brandy in a glass and held it to Sara's lips. A moment later the blonde opened her eyes and smiled wanly up at Prue.

"Thank you," she murmured, accepting a few sips of brandy.

"Did you really see her?" Prue asked expectantly.

"Yes. The presence is a very strong one. She . . . she wants to be released."

"Did she say how that could be achieved?" Dan asked quietly.

"She says the truth must be told. She said something about the legend being a lie. A lie that trapped her here. If the truth is told to us, the living, she will finally be able to go beyond and join her lover."

"The woman has a one-track mind," Julian observed. "Even as a ghost all she can think about is running off with her lover. No wonder her husband strangled her."

"Julian!" Angered by the lack of sympathy, Anne turned on him. "You know nothing about the situation. I'm sure Carlota was very much in love and feeling very trapped in an arranged marriage. All she wanted was to be free."

"And that's the one thing she still seems to want," Dan said mildly. "When do we get the whole story, Sara?"

"It was my fault things ended when they did," Sara said apologetically. "I couldn't take the full force of her presence in one sitting. She recognized that and said she would return when I had rested and could call for her again. She'll tell us the tale and then she will be free."

"What did she look like?" Prue demanded, obviously enthralled with the whole business.

"Very beautiful. Black hair, dark eyes. Very aristocratic looking," Prue smiled.

Anne didn't know what made her ask the next question. It was as if she couldn't help herself. "What was she wearing, Sara?"

Sara looked momentarily taken aback. She recovered herself quickly, however. "A lovely gown of black lace. A wide, full skirt. Her shoulders were bare, I think. And there was some sort of hair ornament. A comb trimmed in silver, I believe. I'm sorry, I wasn't paying that much attention to her clothing."

"I'm not surprised. Must be quite an experience talking to a ghost," Anne said quietly. And then she thought of the woman she had seen in her dream the first night at the house.

The phantom had been very lovely with dark hair and dark eyes. But she hadn't been wearing a lace gown. She had been dressed in a man's riding clothes. It was understandable that Sara's description of Carlota was the expected one. It could have been drawn from a portrait or a film.

Why had her own imagination turned up a Carlota wearing riding gear?

8

JULIAN SAT DOWN WEARILY on the edge of the Western-style bed, slowly unbuttoned the blue work shirt he was wearing and wondered how Anne would go about telling him she wasn't going to sleep with him tonight.

He was prepared for the small confrontation. He'd seen it coming all afternoon. The speculative glances she'd given him when she thought he didn't notice, the restless uneasiness in her when he'd sat down beside her after dinner and the hint of defiance in her bearing when he'd quietly announced it was getting late.

She hadn't argued when he'd deliberately risen to his feet and then waited for her to precede him up the stairs. Saying a polite good-night to Craven and his friends, she had obediently walked to the staircase and along the corridor to her room. There she'd smiled very coolly and closed the door gently in his face. Julian had been forced to use the hall entrance to his bedroom rather than the connecting door from Anne's room.

He could hear her now, moving about in the sheikh's tent. He wondered sardonically what she would do if he simply opened the connecting door, walked into her room and climbed into bed. At the very least he'd get a display of outrage and defiance.

Little did she know he wasn't going to make matters difficult tonight. He'd made his point last night. And he'd been reasonably satisfied with the results today. Whenever Hargraves had tried to maneuver too close to Anne she had warily, if politely, sidestepped. The distance she had put between herself and Hargraves was carefully maintained, at least whenever Julian was in sight. Julian had been careful to be in sight most of the time.

By dinnertime Hargraves had stopped making a serious effort to approach Anne. He seemed to realize she wasn't going to encourage the process and that suited Julian just fine.

Julian told himself he had accomplished what he'd set out to accomplish last night when he'd invaded Anne's room. If she hadn't fully accepted his claim, at least she wasn't going to defy him or his rule.

He cocked his ankle over one knee and started to pry off the worn leather boot. The small effort made him wince as his upper leg protested. Damn that leg. How many more months was it going to act up under the slightest provocation?

He'd thought the thing was improving. The familiar ache had been considerably lessened this morning. But then the damp fog had rolled in off the sea to shroud the house, and by evening his thigh was beginning to throb again.

He should probably dig out that aspirin Anne had packed. Somehow it seemed almost too much effort to get up, walk across the room and find it in the suitcase. Julian sat on the edge of the bed and thought that what he really wanted tonight was to have Anne massage his leg.

The realization darkened his expression into one of fierce denial. The last thing he would do was ask Anne for a massage. She'd already witnessed enough of his various and assorted physical weaknesses. It was intolerable to even think of telling her he needed her gentle touch. He would not risk undoing the bonds he had placed on her last night, and if she lost respect for him that was exactly what would happen. No, he couldn't ask for her help. Not tonight.

But, oh hell, it would be so good to be able to lie down and let her soothe the ache in his leg. So very good. Memories of the way she had massaged away the pain in his neck and head when he'd been recovering from the fever returned to taunt him. All he had to do was open the door and ask.

No. He wasn't that weak. Disgustedly Julian finished undressing, out of long habit leaving on only his shorts. He found the bathroom unoccupied and brushed his teeth. A brief notion of taking a hot shower to see if that would help the ache in his leg went through his head, but somehow it all seemed like too much work. He did manage to dig out the aspirin, although he was skeptical about how much good it would do.

Julian was throwing back the Indian-patterned blankets and climbing into bed when the tentative knock came on the connecting door. *Oh, yeah. The confrontation.* Little did she know that with the way his leg was hurting he was in no mood to play the demanding lover.

"Hello, Anne," he managed in a nonchalant drawl as he opened the door. "Come to seduce me?"

"Hardly," she retorted with a ferocious little frown, as she made a determined effort not to let her eyes drop below his chin. "I wanted to talk to you, Julian."

"I'm always willing to talk to a woman when she's standing in front of me wearing a nightgown," he murmured, opening the door farther and stepping aside. She looked rather sweet in that soft-flannel gown, he decided, in spite of the frown. Her hair had been set free from the sleek knot in which she'd worn it most of the day, and now the autumn-colored stuff was falling in undisciplined curls around her shoulders. God, she looked good. And her gentle hands would feel so wonderful.

"Julian," she began, her chin lifting with an imperiousness that amused him, "I would like to get something straight between us." She walked stiffly into the room and turned to face him again.

Some of Julian's affectionate amusement faded. It was bad enough that he didn't even feel he could risk asking her to massage his leg. He didn't particularly want to hear that she didn't want to sleep with him, as well. He understood that she needed to assert herself a little, after what had happened the previous night, but he didn't want to listen to the entire speech.

"It's all right, Anne, you don't have to worry about tonight." With an unconscious gesture of weariness he rubbed his jaw, realized what he was doing and stopped immediately. "I think we got the main points out of the way last night, don't you?"

"I'm in no mood for your macho attitude. I won't have you thinking you can control me with sex."

"It never occurred to me that I could," he told her dryly.

"No? You've been awfully cool and sure of yourself today."

"Is there some reason I shouldn't be sure of myself?"

A slight flush stained her cheeks. "It's just that I…I don't want you to think that because you invade my room and make love to me you therefore have a whole new set of rights over me. Julian, I don't want to argue. I just want you to understand that—" She broke off, glaring at him intently. "What's wrong?"

"What could be wrong? I'm getting ready to go to bed and you're standing here giving me a lecture on sexual ethics. It wouldn't be so awkward, I suppose, if you weren't wearing a nightgown but since you have invaded my room dressed like that, what am I supposed to think?"

"Lie down," she ordered briskly.

He gave her a speculative, narrow look. "Why?"

"I'm going to massage that leg for you." She was already moving over to the bed and arranging the blankets.

"The leg is fine, thank you. Now don't you think you'd better get back to your own room before I start misreading your intentions?" he asked.

"My only intention is to massage that leg for you. Lie down, Julian. Humor me, okay?" She gave him a bleak smile.

"Anne, I don't . . . Oh, hell. If it will pacify you, go ahead," he finally agreed, aware that he was growing at her and wishing he wasn't. "Where did you get all these maternal instincts?"

"Julian, I promise you, I don't feel at all maternal toward you." She sank down beside him as he stretched out on his stomach, his face turned away from her. Without further comment she went to work on his bare thigh, starting from the knee and working up toward the puckered scar.

So good, Julian thought, slowly beginning to relax. Her hands felt wonderful. She seemed to know exactly where to knead the muscles. This was what he had been craving all evening. "Just how much hands-on instruction in this kind of thing did you get from that football physical therapist?"

He sensed the smile in her voice. "Actually, the lessons stopped at the neck and shoulders. I'm improvising."

He submitted to the "improvising" with what he hoped seemed like disdainful reluctance, as if he were, indeed, just humoring her. But privately Julian admitted to himself that he had been longing for her touch. He tried to figure out a way to thank her without admitting just how much he'd needed the soothing massage. Perhaps he'd just say thanks very casually when she was done. Or perhaps he'd reach around, take her by the nape of the neck and pull her down onto the bed. He could make love to her to show her how grateful he was.

But would she understand that he was trying to convey gratitude and pleasure? She'd probably accuse him of trying to control her again.

"Julian?"

"Hmm?" His voice sounded too satisfied and lazy, even to his own ears.

"What made the fire flame in all those colors this afternoon?" He had to stop and think about what she meant. "Oh, yeah. The colors. You can make any fire do that with a certain powdered chemical that you sprinkle on the flames."

"But when and how?"

"Sara did it just as she cried out and collapsed."

"Oh."

There was a pause while Anne digested that. She seemed to be about to say something else but Julian felt her hesitate then change her mind. Vaguely he wondered what it was she had started to tell him. He wished she didn't feel she had to pick and choose her words.

But his leg was feeling almost magically better now, and the soothing quality of Anne's touch seemed to be the most important thing in the world at the moment. What was she thinking, he wondered. Then he recalled the way he had felt the night he had cuddled and gentled her after the nightmare.

Perhaps, just perhaps, she felt the way he had then; filled with a longing to offer comfort. If that was the case, if he knew for certain that she hadn't lost any respect for him because of his illness and his weakness, then perhaps he could risk letting her know that he wanted and needed her touch tonight, that he wasn't merely suffering through the attention.

Julian tried to think of all the ways he could test the waters before taking the plunge. He was seriously thinking of starting out with just a straightforward thank-you when all of a sudden the massage came to a halt.

"Good night, Julian. I'll see you in the morning." Anne pulled the wool blankets up around his shoulders and, after hesitating a few seconds while she apparently debated about whether or not to give in to the impulse to drop a kiss on his cheek, she quietly turned out the light and left the room.

Lying very still in the darkness, Julian gathered one hand into a fist and considered the many facets of frustration.

Anne slowly closed the connecting door and stood silently for a moment in the solitude of her own room. *Oh, Julian,* she thought unhappily, *can't you even tell me when you're hurting?*

No. He couldn't. Not yet, at any rate. Not willingly. And he certainly couldn't tell her that he was grateful for her care. The pride of a strong man was a difficult thing to handle, she thought wryly. And she very much doubted that she was the first woman in history to learn that salient fact!

Taking a firm grip on her too-vulnerable emotions, Anne finished readying herself for bed, turned out the bed veil. The day had been instructive in several ways, she admitted ruefully.

Ghost of a Chance

Number one, she had learned very quickly that she was not about to risk Julian's wrath when it came to dealing with Dan Hargraves. He was right, she thought. She'd asked for Julian's help, agreed to abide by his decisions since he was the expert in coping with nasty people, and it made sense that she should obey his orders now that the action had begun. But she was not in a mood to forgive him easily for the manner in which he'd chosen to enforce his commands. Nevertheless, she had found herself being very cautious around Dan today. Just as Julian wished.

Well, there was nothing she could do about that little matter. But it had taught her something about herself. On a very fundamental level she had submitted to Julian Aries. The realization was not particularly pleasant.

In an entirely unrelated matter she had found out that she was surprisingly susceptible to suggestion. It still astonished her that she had allowed herself to drift so easily into that strange, half-dazed state this afternoon. She would have to watch herself around the Craven crowd. All this talk of ghosts and legends was obviously getting to her.

Live and learn, Anne told herself, and promptly fell asleep.

IT WAS THE COLD that awakened her a long time later. The same mind-chilling, thick cold that she had felt during Sara's séance that afternoon. She was beginning to recognize it, Anne thought distractedly, as she stirred and groped for the comforter. It was a product of her overactive imagination and she must deal with it as such.

But this time there was something more accompanying the chill. There was a sense of urgency and anger and a distinct feeling that something was very wrong.

Anne opened her eyes and saw the black-haired, dark-eyed woman in riding clothes. This time she stood near the connecting door, and the sensation of stark urgency was a palpable force in the room.

Anne stared, not aware of the fear she had felt the first time the ghost had appeared in her dreams. Perhaps the natural fright was buried beneath the other emotion beating at her. The pale phantom said nothing, but there was no need for verbal communication. Anne got the message quite clearly that something was wrong and that the wrongness was endangering the man she loved.

Without even stopping to remind herself that the vision had to be a part of a dream, Anne pushed back the comforter and slid off the edge of the round bed. Her bare feet felt the cold almost immediately but it was a normal, natural cold, not the dank foggy chill that she felt on some other level.

"Carlota?" she whispered.

The woman in riding clothes shimmered and vanished but Anne knew she would not be able to rest until she had checked Julian's room. The sense of urgency had not disappeared with the specter.

Soundlessly Anne turned the knob on the connecting door and peered into Julian's room. The darkness she had left when she had turned out his lamp was pierced now with a shaft of light from his other door, the one that opened onto the hallway.

And silhouetted in that angle of brightness was Julian. He was standing in his jeans, his hand braced casually against the door as he greeted Sara.

"I am here because I must be here," Sara said with the deceptive simplicity of a Zen master. "I had no choice. The compulsion is strong. Too strong to resist. There is a natural kinship between you and me. I sensed it from the moment I entered this house. There is an essential oneness that must be completed. I have come here tonight to offer that completion."

"Is this all part of the de-ghosting rituals?" Julian asked with bland interest.

Sara shook her head very gently, just enough so that the heavy blond curtain rippled enticingly around her shoulders. "This is only between you and me. You are alone tonight, aren't you, Julian Aries? I saw you enter this room by yourself. The woman you say is your fiancée does not share your bed. I am also alone. I have been most of my life. Do you know what it is like to be a sensitive in a world of blind fools who will not accept what I can see? I exhaust myself in the effort to communicate with those on the other side, just as I did this afternoon, and most of the people watching see it all as just a parlor game. An amusing little trick."

"And it's not?"

"It's no game, Julian. Believe me, at times I wish it were. At times I wish I were just an ordinary woman with an ordinary occupation. But there are so few sensitives to make the necessary contacts. So many presences to be freed. I could never justify abandoning my calling. I would still hear the agony and the pleas of those I should be aiding."

"Sounds like you're trapped in the business, all right."

"We are all trapped in some aspect of life, are we not? Recognizing the trap is not something everyone can do. But I can, and I believe you are a man who also knows the traps of life."

Sara reached up to touch his face. "We have so few opportunities of escaping even for a short time. It would be a shame not to take advantage of each chance. Tonight you and I have such a chance, Julian Aries." She smiled wistfully. "Aries. The sign of the zodiac that promises much force and energy. Boldness and strength of will. A man born under that sign can be a dangerous opponent or—" she framed his face between her fingers "—or a demanding lover."

Anne watched the blonde rise on her toes, clearly about to kiss Julian, and decided the whole scene had gone far enough. She pushed open the connecting door and stepped into Julian's room.

"Then again, what's in a name?" she asked brightly, pleased with the way Sara jumped and dropped her hands from Julian's face. "Aries just happens to be Julian's last name, not the sign under which he was born. Sorry about the slight miscalculation, Sara. Because of such minor errors whole evenings can be ruined." She padded forward to stand beside Julian, aware that he was watching her with a gleam of amusement in his eyes. "Run along, dear, and don't fret about that business of essential oneness with Julian. I'm sure you'll both survive without it. Why don't you go have a chat with Carlota? She needs attention more than Julian does. As you can see, Julian really doesn't need to accept your generous offer. He's not alone, after all."

For an instant the wistful, haunted expression in Sara's eyes disappeared to be replaced by the flashing anger of a woman whose plans have been foiled. Anne took an unholy satisfaction in having been the cause of sweet Sara's ruined bedtime scheme. The other woman stared at her for a long moment, turned on her heel and walked briskly back down the corridor to her own room.

"I gave her the bedroom done in the style of a thirties' musical. You know, the one with the black-and-white bed. Lots of superficial glitz and glitter. A bit theatrical, but I thought it fit her nicely even though she does parade around like a refugee from the flower-child generation." Anne turned away as Julian reached out to firmly close his door but she knew she wasn't going to make it safely back to her own bedroom unscathed. Still, she made a valiant effort, her cold bare feet moving quickly across the hardwood floor.

"Not quite so fast, lady," Julian said behind her. A second later his hand closed solidly over her shoulder. She sighed as he spun her around to face him. "Mind telling me what that little scene was all about?"

"Scene? I didn't cause a scene. Sweet Sara what's-her-name was the one who caused the scene."

"Uh-huh. I know what sweet Sara was doing here. What interests me is what brought you to the rescue."

Anne met his gaze. "You wouldn't believe me if I told you. Frankly, I'm not sure I believe it myself."

Some of the wry humor left Julian's face. "What's that supposed to mean?"

"Well, what actually woke me was the same thing that roused me the other night. A dream about Carlota's ghost. Only it was so incredibly real, Julian. It's hard to describe. It was as if she was trying to tell me something and that it had to do with you. I felt the strongest compulsion to check up on you. I had to make sure you were all right."

"Did you now?" He stroked back a tendril of autumn-colored hair, his face softening in the shadowy light. "You know what I think happened?"

"What?"

"I think that you heard Sara's knock in your sleep and your subconscious translated that into a warning."

"You think I'd have heard her knocking on your door?"

"It's possible. It's just a few feet down the hall from yours, after all."

Anne frowned. "Perhaps." She remembered the shrouding cold that had accompanied the warning sensation. And then she recalled her own suspected weakness when it came to suggestion.

"In any event, you came racing to my rescue," he mused. "Were you jealous, Anne?"

"That little blond con artist has had her eye on you all day," Anne said with a sniff, trying and failing to move out from under Julian's hand.

"Probably because Hargraves was having so little luck with you," Julian murmured. "It was a two-pronged effort right from the start. When you made it clear you weren't going to be an easy target for Dan, Sara decided it was time to test the waters with me. Divide and conquer, remember?"

"You didn't look as though you were trying to fight her off."

"I'll bet."

Julian shook his head, his amusement growing. "No, seriously. I wanted to hear the pitch."

"You can hear a similar one on any street corner!"

"Well, I sure as hell wasn't hearing it from you."

Anne went pale under the almost casual cruelty. Standing unnaturally still under the restraint of his hand, she lowered her lashes. "No, you weren't, were you?"

Julian groaned and pulled her close, his fingers cupping the back of her head. "Damn, I didn't mean it like that, Anne. Sometimes I say things to you that I wish I hadn't. I don't know what it is about you, honey, I can handle myself so easily around most people. But with you I…never mind." He used his thumbs to lift her chin and his eyes moved searchingly over her face. "Were you really jealous, Anne?"

"In a way," she admitted starkly. "Were you jealous of Dan?"

He hesitated. "In a way." There was another pause and then Julian ventured very cautiously. "But it wasn't that I really believed you'd jump into bed with Hargraves."

Anne summoned a misty smile. "And I wasn't really afraid you'd take Sara up on her offer. I was just thoroughly annoyed that she was making it and that you were listening to it."

"I guess that's how I felt about Hargraves." His fingers moved lightly down to the soft line of her nape. "Except that I was more than annoyed. I was scared he'd con you into thinking he was an all-right guy. And I was furious that he had the nerve to make a pass. And I was mad at you for even listening to him."

"But you didn't actually think I'd let it go any further," Anne concluded softly.

"No."

"And I didn't really believe you'd invite sweet Sara into your bed."

They stared intently at each other for a long moment, then Anne said quietly, "It's called trust."

Julian's restless hands suddenly clenched around the curve of her shoulders. "Do you trust me, Anne?"

"I've always trusted you. Even when I thought I hated you. You've never lied to me." *Except when you told me you would come back for me. And I understand now why you didn't*, she added silently.

"I'll never give you cause to lose that trust," he whispered huskily. "I swear it."

Anne gathered her courage. "I want the same thing in return. Your trust."

"Yes."

It was the starkness of that single affirmation that told Anne just how rarely he gave the precious commodity. In a flash of perception she realized that Julian Aries had probably seldom trusted anyone or anything in his life. An aching sweetness flowed through her as she comprehended just how much he had given when he said he trusted her.

"Oh, Julian, I'll never betray you," she whispered brokenly, brushing her lips across his mouth. It was a vow and he accepted it as such, holding her fiercely to him so that she was crushed against the hardness of his chest. Her hair flowed over his arm and the hem of the flannel gown wrapped itself around his legs.

The silent bonding held them both in a strange thrall. Anne took hope and courage from it, telling herself that with both physical attraction and trust between them she had the beginnings of a solid foundation on which to build. Julian's love might be a long time coming and it might be an even longer time before he was capable of acknowledging his need of her on some level other than the physical, but she would be patient. Even if it took a lifetime. And in the meantime they would trust each other. A lot of people never got that far, she assured herself. She was lucky.

"Your nightmare," Julian murmured into her hair. "Did it frighten you tonight?"

"No," she replied absently. "It was strange but there wasn't that startled sense of panic I had last time."

"Oh." He went silent again. Then he went on more practically. "Just the same, I'll double-check your doors and windows before you go back to bed. You'll sleep better that way."

She sensed a question hidden in the statement but ignored it as another thought struck her. Anne raised her head away from his shoulder. "You never told me how the security measures looked in this house. You said you were going to make a survey of them."

He nodded. "Pretty dismal. Considering the amount of valuables housed here, I'm surprised Miss Creswell's sister didn't take more precautions. Those vases in the library look like they're worth a lot all by themselves. Not to mention the paintings and that fancy china."

"They're all worth a fortune. That's why Michael thought this would be such a tantalizing piece of bait for Craven and his friends. I have no idea why Miss Creswell's sister didn't install more efficient security measures. I guess she just never felt the need to bother. Probably never had any trouble."

"Times are changing. When this is all over someone should advise the new owner on what to do to protect her property," Julian said thoughtfully. "I wonder if she'd be interested in hiring me?"

Anne held her breath. It was the first time Julian had mentioned a future of any kind. "Are you a real expert on that sort of thing? Locks and bolts and stuff?"

His mouth curved wryly. "And electronic devices. Yeah, I guess you could say I'm an expert. One of the few skills I picked up during my, uh, former career. I just never thought of it as particularly marketable."

"Are you kidding? People pay a lot these days for security advice. Industry has a great need for it as well as private individuals such as Miss Creswell. She'd hire you in a minute to redo this place," Anne declared strongly.

"You think so?"

"Definitely."

"Hmm. Well, it's something to think about. My career options have seemed rather limited for the past six months," he growled. Then his eyes narrowed. "Are you sure that nightmare didn't bother you this time?"

"Worried I might yet have hysterics?"

"No, it's just that last time you were kind of upset."

Suddenly something clicked in Anne's brain and she stifled a small smile. "Yes, I was, wasn't I? Perhaps the only reason I didn't go bananas this time was because I was busy defending your virtue."

Julian didn't seem to see any humor in the situation. He appeared to be searching for words. "Now that you've saved me from a fate worse than death, I wonder if you'll have any trouble, uh, getting back to sleep. When you're lying all alone there in that silly bed you're liable to start remembering how real the nightmare was."

"It certainly did seem real."

"Maybe it would help you get to sleep faster if I rubbed your back for a while," Julian offered with seeming casualness.

It was no slick, double-edged offer, Anne realized. Julian really did want to rub her back. He was, in a very tentative, uncertain manner, trying to provide her with some of the comfort she had given him earlier this evening. And even if she didn't need it to help her over the effects of the nightmare, she hungered for it for other reasons.

It was another small step forward, Anne thought as she nodded her agreement to his suggestion and led him toward the connecting door. Julian might not know how to ask for tender loving care, but if he was learning to offer it he was definitely making progress.

"Thank you, Julian," she murmured as she stretched out on her stomach on the round bed. "You have no idea how real Carlota's vision seemed tonight. And the room felt so cold. It was very odd. Do you know that I thought I half felt her presence in the living room this afternoon when Sara went into her trance bit?"

Julian sat down beside her, his powerful hands moving over her shoulders with a strong, kneading action that was unexpectedly relaxing. "I think this whole scene is really getting to you," he declared seriously. "If we weren't so enmeshed in it and hadn't already exposed Miss Creswell's house to Craven, I'd seriously consider calling it off."

"It's too late for that. Besides, it should be all over soon. Sara will treat us to one or two more séances during which we'll hear the so-called truth about Carlota. Then she'll pronounce the poor woman 'freed' and away will go Craven and crowd. Phase one will be over. What happens next, Julian? Will you keep an eye on this place personally or hire someone else to do it?"

"Twenty-four-hour surveillance jobs are impossible to conduct alone. I'll bring in some outside help."

"Who?"

"I have some contacts," he said slowly. "Some people who could use the work."

"Other folks from your particular unemployment line?" Anne questioned dryly.

"I guess you could say that. My former line of work tends to have a few occupational hazards," Julian muttered. "A lot of people wind up taking early retirement," Julian muttered.

Anne hated the note of roughness that had entered his voice. His fingers seemed to be tensing on her shoulders. "Julian?"

"Yes?"

"Is Aries more than your last name? Is it also the sign under which you were born?"

His hands went still on the curve of her shoulders. "You mean you're not sure? Even after that little squelching speech to Sara?"

"I don't even know when your birthday is. All I know is that you had one during the past year. But I somehow think you might be an Aries."

"Why?"

She turned over lazily, her smile warm and welcoming in the darkness as her love thrummed through her veins. "Well, I suspect Sara was right about you making a dangerous opponent."

Gleaming desire began to replace the honest concern that had been reflected in his catlike eyes. "You think so?"

Anne nodded, feeling strangely shy as she found herself initiating the lovemaking. But if Julian could show her some TLC, she could show him a little tender love. He hadn't had much of it in his life and she had so much to give him.

"Yes, I think so. And I do know she was right about the other. You are a very demanding lover." Anne reached up to pull him down to her and heard the husky growl of unadulterated masculine pleasure that rumbled in his chest.

He came to her with barely restrained power, parting her legs with his hands to make a place for himself at her hearth. His weight bore her deeply into the sheets, cutting off the rest of the outside world completely. She knew the roughness of his chest hair against her flowering nipples, delighted in the impact of his hips as she raised her lower body to meet him.

Then, when she thought he was about to plunge into her she found herself being deliciously tormented by the feel of him at the threshold of her aching desire. Deliberately he teased and tantalized, thrusting into her only fractionally and then withdrawing almost at once. Again and again he repeated the wildly sensuous torture until Anne's fingers were clenched into the skin of his shoulders and her legs were a vise around his waist. Helplessly, demandingly, pleadingly she begged him to take her completely.

And when he did, Anne cried out his name in a litany of unraveling excitement.

Lost in the overwhelming assault on her senses, Anne didn't realize until much later that she still didn't know whether or not Julian was really an Aries.

The fierce, throbbing purr of the huge cat who had captured her was the only answer she sought to hear that night.

ANNE DID NOT SLEEP WELL that night and it surprised her. Considering the passionate demands Julian had made on her she should have been pleasantly exhausted.

His lovemaking had been different this time. She wasn't quite certain how to define the difference but it seemed to Anne that there was less of a sense of desperation in it. It was as if Julian had been trying very hard to accept the gift she was trying to give. He had seemed enthralled with her gentle boldness, fascinated with her willingness to initiate the lovemaking. And he had also seemed determined not to question his luck. Anne decided with a flash of perceptive humor. He had been tired earlier, and she knew the couple of hours' sleep he'd had before sweet Sara came knocking on his door probably hadn't been nearly enough to revitalize him. But Anne would never have known that, by the way he urged her on with husky words of excitement and need.

In all honesty, Anne thought, Julian wasn't the only one who had been rather astonished by her soft aggression. She herself had been more than a little surprised. She had intended to sleep alone that night. But the scene in Julian's room had changed all her intentions.

So why couldn't she sleep, she wondered, turning restlessly on her side. Julian was solidly out beside her, sprawled over a good portion of the round bed. His head was turned away from her, and the comforter had slipped down around his sleek shoulders. In the pale light of a watery moon she could see the scar that slashed across his back.

Anne wondered if he would ever tell her the full story of what had happened on that last mission. There was no point pushing for it. He had drawn some very fierce lines over which she dared not cross. Perhaps he would never be able to talk about it. What was it he had said? The best thing to do with a nightmare was to put it behind you.

A few days ago she was convinced she had been wrong to intrude on Julian's self-imposed privacy. Now she didn't know what to think. At times such as tonight, it seemed he was making progress. There had been talk of the future and talk of trust.

At other times Anne felt that she had no right to interfere with whatever form of healing Julian had chosen for himself. The risk wasn't just to him, she acknowledged bleakly, it was to her, as well. She was making herself far too vulnerable, leaving herself open to pain. Julian might be changing a little but his bitterness and pride still lay close to the surface. He was still capable of turning on the one who loved him and slashing her with a carelessly cruel swipe of his claws. She must not forget that.

But even that knowledge, as uneasy as it made her, did not account for the feeling of restlessness tonight. She lay staring over Julian's bare shoulders at the weak moon on the ocean. Some of the fog had cleared, she realized idly. But it would probably be back by morning.

Some of the fog had cleared. She found herself repeating the observation. Cleared enough so that, with care, a person could make her way down to the beach. It would be tricky, of course. The cliff face was treacherous even in daylight. But with caution and a flashlight it would be possible....

Good grief! Anne shut her eyes in momentary disbelief. It was utterly incomprehensible that she should even be considering such a thing. Was she out of her mind, she wondered. What idiot would think of going down to the beach in the middle of the night?

Carlota.

Anne drew a deep, steadying breath. Carlota had gone down to the beach on a night such as this. A night in late fall when the fog had been uncertain, offering both peril and concealment.

Uneasily Anne glanced around the darkened room, vastly relieved not to see any lingering shades of her dream ghost. She was getting fanciful. The night and the mystery of the house were getting to her. That was all there was to it. Julian had warned her obliquely that it could become difficult to tell the difference between reality and illusion.

Anne sighed and tried to make herself relax. But the vague restlessness didn't go away and she was still half awake when the pale glow of another fog-bound day finally arrived.

Julian opened his eyes to find Anne lying quietly awake beside him. He watched her in silence for a moment, aware that her attention was on the dismal weather scene outside the window. He was feeling better than he had in months, he realized with a sense of satisfaction. Well rested, no bad aches or pains and he was even feeling hungry. It had been ages since he'd had a genuine appetite for breakfast.

Breakfast wasn't the only thing for which he felt an appetite. With lazy anticipation he put out a hand to stroke the contour of Anne's throat. She looked so soft and tousled this morning. Memories of the way she had pulled him down to her last night flickered through his head.

But the moment his fingers touched her skin she stirred and turned too quickly. There was a tension in her he didn't understand. She had moved as if his touch had startled her.

"Anne?" He murmured her name, leaning closer to drop a possessive kiss on her mouth. "Everything okay? How did you sleep?" He smiled in anticipation of the appropriate answer.

"Fine."

Julian blinked, lazily aware that the small word was a lie and wondering why she would bother with such a tiny falsehood.

"Sure?"

"What time is it? It feels rather late." She twisted around to find the clock.

"It's not late. Prue won't even be arriving for another hour or so. Relax. We've got lots of time." Julian traced a teasing fingertip down to the opening of the flannel nightgown. Deliberately he pinned her gaze as he probed beneath the fabric. "Hungry?"

"No."

Julian hid his disappointment. Perhaps she hadn't understood the double entendre. "Not even for this?" He let his fingers glide warmly over her breast, delighting in the womanly fullness of her.

"Julian I . . . I'm not . . . that is, I don't . . ."

He could feel the way her nipple was beginning to harden under his touch. Surely she wasn't going to lie there and tell him she didn't want him! But something was wrong this morning. The tension in her was not that of physical desire but it was very real.

"Are you regretting last night?" he demanded gruffly, unaware of the way his palm suddenly weighed more heavily on her breast, as though he would trap her.

"Julian, I think... I think we may be rushing things." A vivid intensity swirled in her blue-green eyes.

"It's a little late to worry about that now, isn't it?" he tried coolly.

"I don't know whether it's too late or not. I only know I had no right to track you down in Colorado. You should have been allowed all the time you wanted to be by yourself. You should have the right to take your time...."

"Anne, we are discussing the possibilities of a little early morning loving, not my past or my future," he told her, aware of a vague irritation seeping into his voice. What was the matter with her? She had initiated matters last night. She had no right to change her mind this morning, he decided with a measure of masculine indignation. He was half tempted to demonstrate quite forcefully that he wasn't going to allow her to play the tease. He might not be quite the same man he had been when he'd left her six months ago but that didn't mean he was so weak she could now manipulate him.

"I'm sorry, Julian. It's just that I feel a little odd this morning. A bit nervous or something. I'll be glad when this is all over."

He didn't like the absolute certainty with which she made that declaration. It sounded very much as though she wanted to be rid of him. "Do you think," he growled in soft warning, "that I'm going to let you walk back out of my life after this business with Craven is finished?"

She seemed to gather herself. "I think we both need time, Julian."

Anger simmered now in place of the lazy morning passion that had been building in him. He knew it probably was reflected in his eyes because he saw the wariness that came into her own gaze. "I'm willing to give you time, lady, but I'm not going to let you blow hot and cold. You're not going to seduce me one night and then pull away in the morning. I never would have guessed you were the kind of female who uses sex to tease and confuse a man. But if you are, you'd better realize right away that I'm not the kind of male to let you play that game."

"Oh, Julian, I never meant to play games with you," she protested.

"Then why the coy act this morning?"

"I'm not being coy! I told you, I just feel a little restless. A little uneasy. I'm not at all sure we're developing this relationship in the proper way. In fact, I'm fairly certain I've handled matters all wrong."

"Like I said, it's too late to change your mind." But he was confounded by her very genuine agitation. She *was* nervous and tense, and he wasn't at all sure of how to deal with her. The last thing he wanted to do was drive her away, he thought. "Look, Anne. I'm not some kind of monster. Before you arrived at my door in Colorado I'd been six months without a woman…"

Instantly he realized he'd said something horribly wrong. He had been attempting to explain that wanting her first thing in the morning after having made love to her during the night was hardly abnormal. But she reacted as if he'd slapped her.

"Is that all you've been doing for the past couple of nights? Making up for six months of abstinence?" she hissed, scrambling off the edge of the bed.

"Anne, for crying out loud! You know that's not what I meant! What's the matter with you this morning? Last night…"

But she wasn't sticking around to hear his analysis of last night. The door to the red-and-brass bathroom slammed firmly behind her incensed figure. Julian threw himself back down on the pillows with a groan and cursed himself for being an idiot. When he was finished with that project he went to work on the female of the species, finding terms even less complimentary.

Julian had vacated her bedroom by the time Anne finished her morning shower. She opened the bathroom door cautiously, peering around at the bed before entering. There was a sense of both relief and disappointment in finding she had the sheikh's room to herself.

Hastily she dressed in a pair of olive-drab trousers and a matching designer version of a military style shirt. Together with the wide leather belt and the short cuffed boots, the effect was rakishly chic and it gave Anne a certain degree of inner fortitude. She needed it today she realized later as she headed downstairs alone. The strange restlessness was still invading her blood and she felt taut with a vague tension.

A walk on the beach after breakfast might be nice, she thought, as she entered the breakfast room and found Prue pouring herself a cup of coffee.

"Good morning, Anne. How did you sleep?"

"Fine." There was certainly no point going into uninteresting details of a restless night. "That coffee looks good."

"Umm." Prue sipped enthusiastically on her cup. "I had some before I left the house, but after driving through that fog, I needed another cup. It's like the inside of a can of gray paint out there."

"You shouldn't have taken the risk," Anne admonished with a frown. "I could certainly handle the cooking for this bunch for a couple of days."

"Well, if it's this bad again tomorrow morning, I might take you up on the offer. We get stretches of fog like this along the coast a few times during the year, and the car accident rate always skyrockets because of it."

"That settles it. Assuming it's safe enough to drive home this evening, don't you dare attempt coming to work tomorrow until it clears off."

"Thanks." Prue smiled. "My husband was a little upset. I told him you needed me because of all these ghost hunters to feed and tidy up after." Prue took another sip of her coffee. "A bit of a disappointment, isn't it?"

"What's that?" Anne was thinking again of a walk on the beach.

"This ghost hunting business. I mean that séance yesterday was rather bland. I expected a lot more excitement."

"I know," Anne said thoughtfully. "So did I." And she realized that was the truth. According to her brother's notes the Craven crowd usually put on a fairly exciting show. So far all the Creswell ghost had received was a somewhat half-hearted attempt at contact. She had expected that real phonies, such as Craven and his bunch were supposed to be, would resort to more theatrical effects. On the other hand, perhaps the calm approach convinced people they were genuine in their efforts. Then her mind returned to the beach.

Would it be possible to navigate the path down to the cove in this fog? Last night it would have been easier. At least then she would have had the pale moonlight. This morning she wouldn't be able to see more than a few feet in front of her.

Ridiculous. The very notion of going for a walk in this gray soup was idiotic. Anne shook off the idea as Sara walked into the room followed by Dan Hargraves. Both greeted Prue and Anne politely, Sara acting as if nothing at all had happened the previous night, and made casual comments on the weather.

"Does this kind of gloomy weather help in making contact with the ghosts?" Prue asked interestedly as she carted in a tray of toast and bacon.

"Surprisingly enough it does," Dan said easily, helping himself to the toast. "Atmospheric effects sometimes do seem to release more energy that a presence can, in turn, utilize for contact. That's probably why most of the old legends involve dark and stormy nights," he concluded with a grin.

"Perhaps it is that the sensitives are able to tune in more easily when the weather is unsettled," Sara offered vaguely. "Where is Thomas?"

"I saw him in the library with Julian," Dan said. "They looked pretty involved in a discussion. I didn't want to interrupt."

"A most interesting discussion," Craven said genially as he strode into the room followed by a quiet-faced Julian. "Mr. Aries was just telling me that Miss Creswell has plans to modernize the rather antiquated security measures in this old place. I certainly would, if it belonged to me. There are some extremely valuable items here."

If a silent message was passed among the three ghost hunters, Anne certainly couldn't detect it. Part of the scheme had been to put the pressure on them to make their move sooner than usual by implying that security was soon going to be tightened.

"When is she going to have the work done?" Sara asked idly.

"In a couple of weeks," Julian said as if rather uninterested. "Or so she said. Wasn't that the date she said the security expert would arrive and begin installing the electronics, Anne?"

"Yes, I think so," Anne managed politely. And wondered privately if this whole plan had even a prayer of working. Perhaps Michael had been wrong about Craven and crowd. Perhaps they were merely honest psychic investigators after all.

"When's the next séance going to take place?" Prue asked. Craven smiled and nodded at Sara. "It's up to her. How do the vibrations feel, Sara?"

"Weak but present. I think it's worth a try today."

"This morning?" Dan prodded.

"Yes, that will be fine," Sara agreed softly.

The second séance took place after breakfast and was set up in much the same manner as the first. Sara asked that a fire be built and Julian complied. Once again the small group sat in the living room of the fog-shrouded house and watched Sara chant herself into a trance.

But this time Anne felt no odd sense of disorientation. Rather the urge to take the walk on the beach seemed to be pushing out all other interests. Julian, more silent than usual, took his place beside her. He seemed aware of her restlessness and it appeared to annoy him. Several times Anne felt his brooding glance on her profile. Impatiently she ignored it and tried to concentrate on Sara's little show.

"Carlota, we have come to hear the truth. Tell us your story so that you can be free. We will believe," Sara intoned in her soft singsong.

Over and over again, eyes closed, seated in front of the fire in her lotus position, Sara called for the phantom lady. Anne felt her own impatience grow steadily. This was ridiculous. Carlota wasn't in this room. A walk on the beach would be far more revealing than listening to Sara's chanting act. She was seriously wondering if she could slip away from the group when Sara's body went suddenly taut.

"Yes," the other woman breathed almost soundlessly. "We are here. I can feel you, Carlota. Tell us . . ."

Silence descended on the group of people in front of the fire as Sara waited in a tense, listening pose. Dan was busy taping the session and Craven sat forward, his face steepled, his face a study in concentration. Prue was hunched in a posture of breathless anticipation. And Julian looked laconically bored.

Anne stared out the window, wondering how fogbound the path down to the beach would be right now. If she were to slip away she could be down in the cove before anyone knew she had left.

No, Julian would be well aware of her leaving the room. Annoyed at that fact, Anne continued to sit dutifully while Sara exchanged messages with Carlota's nonexistent ghost.

"We understand, Carlota. I will tell the others. They will believe."

Tension hummed in the atmosphere and Anne had to give Sara credit for creating it with her intense attitude and apparent belief in what she saw. Prue didn't look disappointed in today's séance, even if there were no visible manifestations.

And then, quite suddenly, it was all over. Sara sobbed heavily, taking great gasps of air, and then she collapsed attractively. Dan reached out to catch her. Once again brandy was brought, and Sara smiled apologetically as she sipped.

"A simple enough story," she explained as Prue asked for all the details. "Carlota says that she was not running away with her lover the night that her husband discovered and killed her. She says she and Diego, that's the lover's name, had agreed that their love could not be fulfilled without bringing dishonor on both households. She says she met with Diego one last time to say farewell and that her husband descended on them. He wouldn't listen to reason. She shouted for Diego to leave, saying she would explain it all to her husband. Diego fled but Carlota was unable to talk sense into the enraged man who thought he had discovered her in a thoroughly compromising position."

"So her husband strangled her instead of listening to the truth, hmm?" Prue nodded in satisfaction.

"The poor woman died violently and under a curtain of dishonor. In those days outward appearances meant everything. She died knowing that the world would think her a faithless wife. The last conscious thought she had was one of wishing for justice." Sara sighed in commiseration. "She wanted the world to know the truth—that, in spite of temptation, she had been faithful."

"That fierce, dying desire for justice combined with the violence of her passing must have been the factors that kept her bound to this house," Craven observed. "What now? Do you think she's been freed?"

"Thomas, I'm too exhausted to be able to sense her presence, even if she's still here. By tomorrow morning I will know. Every night I've been here I've been very much aware of her presence. If she's still trapped here, I'll sense her again during the night. If she's free, I'll know she's gone."

Craven nodded. "And if she is, then we can take our leave in the morning. Wouldn't want to charge Miss Creswell for any extra unnecessary time, would we?" He patted Sara gently. "Got all your notes, Dan?"

"I've got the session down on tape, but, as usual, I'll want to talk to Sara in detail before she has a chance to forget any pertinent information. How about it, Sara? Feel up to our usual analysis?"

"Yes, I think so," the blonde nodded, sitting up on the sofa where Dan had placed her after she collapsed. She set aside the brandy and smiled wearily. "It's fading fast, Dan. You'd better hurry up with your questions."

Dan glanced around at the others. "Mind if we do this part in private? It's difficult for Sara to reconstruct everything when she has an audience."

"Of course not," Anne said quickly, leading the way out of the living room. "Take your time."

The others followed her out but Anne didn't stop to discuss the events. She headed straight upstairs to her bedroom, closing the door firmly behind her. Then she went to the closet and dug out her red jacket. She had to get out of the house before this restlessness drove her nuts.

When she emerged from her room several minutes later she could hear the voices of Julian and Craven in the hall below the stairs. On an impulse, because she didn't want to bother with a lot of questions and explanations, Anne headed for the back stairs. They led down to the kitchen. Anne descended in silence and then let herself out into the thick, gray mist.

She had to take her time, but the going wasn't quite as treacherous as she had imagined. It was possible to see several feet ahead, and that was enough to be sure of her footing. The sound of the surf in the cove below the cliffs guided her in the right direction.

Cautiously, slipping a bit now and then on the damp rocky path, Anne made her way down the short cliff to the sea. She had taken a walk on the beach only once during her stay, and on that occasion had headed south from the cove. Today she would head north. She was quite certain of her direction.

Pebbles churned underfoot as she neared the bottom and Anne nearly lost her balance. She landed on her feet amid a shower of rocky debris a few minutes later.

The first thing she realized was that the tide was out. Getting around the jutting northern tip of the rock wall that formed the cove would be no problem this morning. Having always lived in the Midwest she knew little about the rhythm of the tides, but it occurred to her that there were probably times when the entire floor of the cove was under water. Little pools among the rocks testified to the repeated return of the sea.

The foggy mist swirled around her as she made her way toward the northern tip of the cove. For some reason the urge to explore that region was irresistible today. Doing so would pacify the restlessness that seemed to be flooding her bloodstream.

"Anne!"

She stopped suddenly as Julian's voice came at her through the fog.

"Anne, where are you?"

Irritation mingled with a reluctant realization that she would have to answer, so Anne halted.

"Julian!" she called back. "I'm just taking a walk. Don't worry about me!"

There was no response but she sensed that he was starting down the cliff face. Suddenly another thought occurred to her, one that made her forget her earlier decision to explore the northern end of the cove.

Julian had no business exposing himself to this dank, damp, chill fog. He should be keeping warm in the house. There was no telling, but the cold air might very well bring on another attack of his strange fever.

"Julian?" Frowning, she tried to determine his progress down the cliff by sound. He was moving much more quietly than she had. Another occupational skill he'd probably picked up in his former career, she thought wryly.

"Right here," he growled, startling her by looming out of the fog. He wore an expression of tight-lipped anger. "What on earth do you think you're doing?"

"What am I doing?" she retorted, surveying his worn leather jacket and jeans. "You're the one who should be asked that. I'm merely taking a walk. You have no business at all being outside on a day like this! Don't you have any common sense? Are you deliberately trying to bring on another bout of that fever?"

He came forward, his hands shoved into the pockets of the old jacket. "What kind of idiot takes a walk on a day like this?"

"I felt like it. There's no harm in it for me. You're the one who should know better than to be outside. Go back to the house, Julian, I don't want to have you getting sick again." She turned away, intending to start back toward the far end of the cove but found herself dragged to a jolting stop under Julian's rough fingers.

When he spun her around she realized that he was blazingly angry. Anne caught her breath as his tawny eyes glittered. His hand was clamped tightly around her shoulder. Instinctively she went very still, all thought of continuing her exploration forgotten as she confronted the lion enraged.

"I'm sorry if my being ill is a burden on you," he began savagely.

"Oh, Julian, I never meant—"

"Just keep in mind that I never asked you to deal with that blasted fever. You're the one who showed up on my doorstep in the middle of the night. You're the one who insisted on playing nurse. If you found the whole bit boring, you have no one but yourself to blame."

"Julian, you know perfectly well I never—"

"You wanted my help, you said. My protection. Well, you've got it. But one of the agreements we made is that I'm in charge, remember? You will do as I say. And right now I'm saying I don't want you going for lonely walks in the fog. This is treacherous country. You know nothing of tides and you know nothing of the terrain. Furthermore, since part of my job is to keep an eye on you, the last thing I'm going to do is let you wander off alone."

"I only wanted to take a walk, Julian. I've been feeling a little restless cooped up in that house."

"You've been acting very strange all day," he countered. "Ever since this morning when you flounced off to the bathroom in high dudgeon."

"Well, what did you expect after you implied you were trying to make up for lost time because you hadn't had a woman in six months?" she flared, angered to the point of recklessness.

"You'll have to forgive my animalistic desires along with my tendency to fall sick at inconvenient times. Just keep in mind that sometimes you get what you ask for in this life and you asked for me. You've got me. If I don't live up to your expectations, that's tough. You're stuck with me at the moment. Now get your sweet tail back up that cliff before I drag you up it."

Anne swallowed, knowing when she was definitely going to lose. No point in dragging it out. Julian was quite capable of doing exactly as he threatened. She gave him a bitter, resentful glare and then she stepped pointedly around him, heading for the path up the cliff.

She climbed in silence, aware of him directly beneath her. Several of the wet pebbles loosened by her passage undoubtedly struck him, but Julian said nothing. His anger beat at her as she moved upward, a tangible force that made her edgy and tense. Neither of them spoke until they were on top of the cliff, walking back toward the house. Then Julian said curtly, "About the matter of my, uh, animalistic desires—"

"What about them?"

He took a breath. "You misunderstood me this morning."

"Did I?"

"I never meant to imply that the only reason I wanted to make love to you was because I'd spent the past six months exploring the joys of abstinence!"

"Really?" she drawled flippantly.

"Anne, I wanted to make love to you this morning because . . . because I wanted you," he exploded tightly. "I've always wanted you. Since the moment I met you, in fact. And you know it."

Anne's hands clenched into fists in the pockets of her red jacket. "Do I?"

"Yes, damn it, you do! Because you've wanted me from the beginning, too."

Anne winced, unable to think of a fast counter to that. It was the truth. "Are you by any chance in your own inimitable style, trying to apologize for your rather gauche remark in bed this morning?"

"I'm not apologizing, I'm explaining," he snapped.

Anne suddenly grinned, unable to stifle the flash of humor. "Ah, yes, but for you, Julian, I think that constitutes an apology. Probably the only one I'll ever get. I shall savor it."

He eyed her warily. "Does that mean you're going to stop acting so oddly?"

"Have I really been acting that strangely?" she asked curiously.

"You've been, well, distant. As if you had something on your mind. Your temper is short and you haven't seemed particularly interested in the performance of our psychic investigators."

"I told you this morning that I feel tense. Restless. I can't explain it, Julian. I guess this whole thing is getting to me. I'll be glad when it's over."

"Is it this ghost scene that's bothering you or is it us?" he asked bluntly. "You said something this morning about wanting time."

Julian's eyes were straight ahead, focused on the huge dark bulk of the house as they approached it through the fog.

Anne sensed the tightness in him and knew he didn't know how to talk about their relationship.

"I think it would be a good idea," she murmured gently. "You have to admit that matters got out of hand this past week."

"Because we went to bed together? Is that what you call getting out of hand?"

"You, I take it, don't see it that way?" she asked dryly.

He shrugged. "No. As long as you and I are around each other, the sex is inevitable."

Anger flashed again in her. Today, in her unusually nervous mood, she seemed to be letting all his casual gibes get to her. "Well, if proximity is the only thing that affects your love life, we can certainly cure that. You can sleep in your own room to-night, Julian!"

SEX WASN'T THE only thing that was inevitable, Anne decided much later that night as she crawled alone into bed. If she stayed around Julian Aries she was going to find herself more and more firmly bound to him. But then, perhaps her love for him had been inevitable from the beginning.

Restlessly Anne fluffed her pillow and turned to stare out the window. The fog still clung. But for some reason she was quite sure that, with the aid of a flashlight, she could probably make it down the cliff.

Carlota had found her way down those cliffs one fog-shrouded night. But she hadn't been wearing a black lace gown when she tried it. She'd had on men's-style riding clothes that she had fashioned in secret.

Anne sat up suddenly in bed, startled at how absolutely certain she was of the facts that had just popped into her head. She *knew*, in a way she couldn't explain, that Carlota had gone down to the cove at night. There she had left something . . . something very important.

Annoyed with herself Anne tried to halt the direction of her thoughts. It wasn't as though she didn't have other matters on which to speculate! Julian, for instance.

Julian, who had said almost nothing to her since dinner. Actually, he'd said very little since he'd force-marched her back up the cliff. But he had appeared in the opening of the communicating door just before going to bed to remind her to lock her hall door.

"Are you worried about something?" she'd asked.

"Craven and his friends are leaving in the morning. I don't want them to get any last-minute ideas," was all he'd said dryly.

He had sealed himself in his own room before she could ask what sort of ideas. His irritation and impatience had been palpable. Anne knew she wasn't behaving with her normal degree of equanimity, but she was powerless to explain her own nervous tension. She lay in bed and wished Julian hadn't caught up with her before she'd had a chance to finish exploring the northern tip of the cove.

There was an answer down there, Anne told herself, staring wide-eyed into the darkness beyond the window. A finish.

The compulsion to go down to the cove became overwhelming. The air seemed to be shimmering between Anne's bed and the window. Tautly she waited for the figure in riding clothes to materialize, but nothing happened.

My God, Anne thought dazedly, *I must be out of my mind to be looking for ghosts.*

But the ghost had come looking for her, something whispered in her head. The answers and the ending lie in the cove. The northern end of the cove.

Anne shook her head, trying to clear it. The urge to go down the cliff only increased the unbearable intensity. Nothing could force her down to the cove, she knew with certainty. But there was a plea behind the compulsion — a plea that caught at her. She wanted to pacify that pleading — bring peace to whatever called. The other woman from a different time had appealed to her because she sensed that Anne understood the undeniable demands of love.

With sudden decision, Anne pushed back the covers and padded over to the closet to find her jeans and a white knit top. Hurriedly she tugged on her boots and found the jacket she had left lying across a chair. Then, very, very softly she unlocked her door and went out into the hall.

The house seemed to be filled with an inner gloom tonight that went beyond normal nighttime shadows. There was no noise and Anne found herself taking care on the staircase.

Just as Carlota had that fateful night.

Once more the unbidden knowledge flowed into Anne's head. Carlota had taken a lantern to the edge of the cliff. But this was the twentieth century, and Anne found a flashlight in a kitchen drawer.

She didn't turn on the light until she was outside, and then it barely cut a swath through the murky darkness. As it had that afternoon, the pounding of the sea served as a guide.

Anne was almost at the cliff's edge searching for the beginning of the pebbly path that led down to the cove when an uneasy prickling sensation made her whirl around.

"Who's there?" she demanded tautly, playing the flashlight across the murk. It came to rest on a curtain of pale hair. "Sara. What in the world . . . ?" And then she saw the ugly gun in Sara's fist. Anne went very still, aware of a surge of fear and adrenaline invading her system. "Sara, I have to tell you, you lose that sweet, flower-child appeal when you're holding a gun."

"Since the appeal didn't work on your lover, there's no point overdoing the act, is there?" Sara remarked, no longer sounding so wistful and gentle as she once had. Instead there was a hard, utterly cold note in her voice.

"Mind telling me why the gun?" Not knowing what else to do, Anne kept the light fixed on the younger woman.

"It's simple enough. Because your name isn't Anne Melton. Your name is Anne Silver."

Anne closed her eyes briefly. "How long have you known?"

"Since the beginning."

"Where's Craven? And Dan?" It was ludicrous, but Anne couldn't think of anything else to ask under the circumstances. It was obvious there was no point denying her identity. Stupid plan. Julian had been right.

"Craven and Dan are taking care of Mr. Aries," Sara assured her. "We all thought I'd be able to handle you by myself. And I think we were all correct, don't you?"

"I get the feeling you're enjoying this."

"I am," Sara acknowledged calmly. "It's rather satisfying to pull the rug out from under you. What did you hope to accomplish, Miss Silver? Did you think we would be so easily tricked? Your brother obviously did. Perhaps stupidity runs in the family."

"You tried to kill him, didn't you?"

"Next time we'll make sure we're successful." Sara smiled. "As successful as we're going to be tonight with you and Aries. What fools you were!"

"How did you know?" Anne knew she was going to have to start thinking clearly, but at this point all she could manage to do was keep the flashlight reasonably level and keep asking questions. What was happening to Julian?

"About you? Oh, it was simple enough. When Miss Creswell hired us and informed us she'd have her niece handle the arrangements we took the single extra step of finding out about the 'niece.' It seems there isn't one. Only a nephew who's stationed in Europe. We wouldn't normally have taken the trouble to check, but lately, what with one thing and another, we've had to be a bit more cautious. I'm sure you can understand."

"And tonight you're planning more accidents?" Anne breathed.

"An unfortunate fall over the cliff. Not here near the path, though. The cliff isn't high enough here to make it look effective. No, I think it will have to be out there at the far end of the cove. Might as well get ready. Move, Anne Silver."

Anne considered her options and found them exceedingly limited. "You don't dare shoot me. If I'm found with a bullet in me it's going to be a little difficult for the authorities to render an 'accidental death' verdict."

"Don't think we haven't planned this very well," Sara said chuckling. "I'll shoot if I must. It will be made to look like a lovers' quarrel in that case. Aries will be made to look as though he pulled the trigger and then committed suicide. Take your choice, the sea or a bullet."

"I might survive the sea," Anne pointed out calmly. Under a prodding motion from Sara's gun she began moving along the top of the cliffs. The water below was not particularly violent tonight. A rather light surf, in fact. And somewhere along here there was the deep pool where the waves surged in and out almost lazily. If one jumped while the waves were on their inward course there would be plenty of deep water to absorb the impact. Farther along, however, a person could easily get dashed against the rocks.

"You'll be unconscious when you go into the sea, I'm afraid," Sara explained kindly. "Both you and Julian. There's not much chance of surviving the ocean if you've been knocked out, is there?"

Anne said nothing, using the flashlight to pick a path along the rocks and occasionally allowing the beam to play over the water. A few more feet should bring her to the section of cliff that formed a backdrop for the deep water pool below. Sara followed from a safe distance but the other woman couldn't stay too far back. She couldn't risk losing Anne in the fog.

The mist roiled and twisted, sometimes parting to reveal a clear path and a stretch of water, at other times closing in so thickly that the beam from Anne's flashlight barely penetrated. Anne noticed that during the moments when the fog swirled most densely, Sara came closer to her quarry. As long as Anne

was holding the light, she realized, she was making a target of
herself for the blonde's gun.

"How did you know I'd left the house tonight, Sara?"

"We had planned to make our move tonight. I was about to
come and get you when you very obligingly opened the door to
your room and trotted down the stairs. I merely followed you
while Thomas and Dan went to finish the business with your
lover. You know, I was rather sorry my little play for Julian didn't
work the other night. He's quite interesting in some ways. In spite
of the limp and that scar on his face, there's something intriguing about him. Too bad he's unemployed and on your side. I
prefer my men rich and devoted to me." Sara laughed.

"Like Thomas Craven?" Anne hazarded, thinking of less-than-
paternal pats.

"Yes, Thomas is quite rich now and quite devoted. He doesn't
know I made that little side trip to see Julian last night. I'm afraid
he wouldn't approve."

"What about Dan?"

"Oh, Dan and I leave each other well enough alone. We're
merely business partners. We make a good team. Our partnership has been most lucrative."

"Sara . . ." Anne hesitated, her curiosity getting the better of
her. "Are you at all psychic or is the whole thing an act?"

"All an act. I'm afraid I don't believe in ghosts any more than
you do. Too bad you really didn't get the full benefit of one of
our performances. We just didn't feel it was worth the trouble to
bring on all the bells and whistles. After all, you weren't going
to live long enough to appreciate it. Normally we do the whole
bit. Even achieve a 'manifestation' of the presence. It's all done
with a lot of sophisticated gadgetry we normally carry around.
Most of our clients love it."

"I see. Then you saw or felt nothing during that first séance?"
Anne asked softly.

"I never see or feel anything strange during a séance, except
the gullibility of my audience," Sara murmured. "Slow down. I
wouldn't want to lose you now, would I? Blast this fog! I should
have brought my own flashlight!"

At that moment the chill wind off the sea parted the mist long
enough for Anne to determine that she was in the vicinity of the
deep water she sought. Almost immediately the fog closed back
in, whirling thickly around her. Anne knew she wasn't going to
get a better chance. She also realized in that instant that for a few

seconds the flashlight she held was the only point of visual reference Sara could possibly have until the momentary coil of fog lifted.

Anne hurled the flashlight from her, heedless of the direction, and threw herself down onto her stomach.

"Damn you!" Sara screamed in frustrated fury. A second later the gun in her hand roared. Before the sound had even faded into the night, the blonde, racing frantically forward, tripped and sprawled over Anne's prone body.

"Bitch!" Sara gritted the word even as she struck the ground.

Anne gasped for breath, having lost a fair amount of it when Sara's body impacted hers. Then she was scrambling madly for an arm or a leg or a hunk of that long blond hair.

The two women twisted in primitive combat on the rocky surface. Anne forgot everything she had ever learned about ladylike behavior. She kicked and shoved and lashed out blindly as the mist came and went around them. Sara fought fiercely, but fortunately with no more trained skill than Anne.

Grabbing a fistful of the pale hair that was whipping around in the struggle, Anne yanked violently as Sara went for her opponent's eyes. Sara rolled aside and Anne followed.

And then the bottom seemed to fall out of the world. Anne felt the horrifying sensation of air where hard rock should have been and realized that in their struggles, she and Sara had rolled off the edge of the cliff. There was no chance to grab for safety. It was all gone in the wink of an eye. She could only pray that the waves were coming in, not withdrawing.

Anne heard Sara's piercing scream as the two women fell and then there was a jolting slam as the chill seawater seemed to reach up to grab them both out of the air. Anne managed to catch half a breath before she went under. And then there was nothing but shocking cold and stunning silence as the huge roll of a wave gathered her into its maw.

JULIAN CAME AWAKE with a motionless, fully alert sensation he would have sworn he'd forgotten during the past few months. Lying perfectly still, his head turned into the pillow as he sprawled on his stomach, he tried to identify whatever it was that had awakened him.

Silence blanketed the house.

But it was not a normal silence. Instinctively he was certain of that, and Julian had long ago learned to trust his instincts. The old place was solid, built literally like a rock. It would not betray movement with squeaky boards or hollow-sounding landings. Noise could be heard if it was intentionally made. But someone was deliberately trying not to make any noise. He was as certain of that as he was of his bond with Anne. Both were gut-level realizations that did not need intellectual verification.

Someone was entering his bedroom from the hall. Someone who had a key to the old-fashioned door. He had jimmied Anne's door lock so that it could not be opened from the outside just as a precaution, but he had done nothing about his own. Partly out of curiosity, he supposed. You could get a lot of information about someone based on the simple observation of whether or not he'd go through a locked door.

Was it Hargraves or Craven, he wondered. And why tonight? Clearly the "foolproof" plan of Anne's had been far from *damn* foolproof. If he'd had time a few days ago he could have built in a few more precautions. But Anne hadn't given him time. She'd been set on carrying out the scheme on schedule. *When this is all over*, Julian thought, *I'm really going to lay down the law.*

At least he'd rigged the locks so that anyone trying to get to Anne had to go through his room.

It had to be Hargraves. Craven wouldn't be able to move that well. And there had been something about the light assured way Hargraves walked that told its own story. The real question, Julian decided, was how well he himself could still move.

No light had entered the bedroom when the door had been deftly opened, which meant that Hargraves had kept off the hall light. He would be working as much in the dark as Julian would be forced to work.

Another old, familiar sensation washed through Julian as he lay waiting. The tension of the hunt and the suspense of waiting to find out whether he was going to be hunter or prey released the cold awareness deep in his body. The energy hummed as the wait stretched out. Couldn't Hargraves feel it?

The soft rush, when it came, was not quite as professional as Julian had feared. Hargraves was good but he wasn't fantastic. Julian felt the launch of the attack the instant it started.

He twisted to one side, throwing himself off the edge of the bed even as something solid and very heavy landed where his head would have been on the pillow. Julian could see the shape of his attacker now, realized Hargraves was off balance as he put his whole body weight behind the blow. In that instant Julian knew he had him.

He came up off the carpet in a coordinated, spiraling motion that propelled him straight at Hargraves's midsection. The thudding impact as both men hit the floor managed to send a slight tremor even through the old, well-built house.

Julian didn't waste any time. His skills lay in his hands, and he used them efficiently. Hargraves recovered with surprising quickness, trying to throw off Julian's weight.

Both men rolled across the carpet, slamming into the wall. A small but heavy bronze of a rearing horse fell from the top of the bureau when Julian barely managed to avoid a chopping blow from Hargraves's fist. It struck the floor, missing Julian's head by inches.

The missed blow gave Julian the opening he needed. He aimed a short, crunching slice at Hargraves's chin and put all the strength he had behind it. Hargraves groaned once and went limp.

Julian gasped for breath, cursing the weakness of a body that hadn't been tested in many months. Lord, he was out of shape. He struggled to rise, aware of the pain from some of the blows Hargraves had landed. The other man's weight seemed exceptionally heavy as Julian rolled out from under the unconscious figure. Getting to his knees, Julian leaned down and put three fingers against the pulse in Hargraves's neck. The guy would live but he would be out for a while.

Glancing around the shadowed room, Julian remembered the lariat that had been hung as a decorative item on the wall. Stifling a grunt of pain as his bad leg protested the unexpected activity, he reached for the coiled rope and then turned back to tie his victim. He worked swiftly, thinking of his next move as he automatically checked the knots. He could take Anne out of the house by using her balcony-window exit. The keys to the car they had rented in Los Angeles were still in his pocket. Once free of the Creswell mansion he would make a few phone calls and get this mess straightened out.

And then he'd have a few words to say to Anne Silver.

But even as he made the dire threat in his head, Julian knew he was reacting to his own stupidity in allowing her to go through with the charade.

As if he'd had any choice.

The task of tying Hargraves completed, Julian got to his feet again, once more aware of the stab of protest in his thigh. Grimly he ignored it but as he reached for his jeans the bare toe of his already sore leg struck the bronze figure of the horse. Insult to injury, he thought savagely as he winced and swore very softly.

At this rate he was going to be forced to the conclusion that everyone and everything really was out to get him. He wouldn't be able to pretend he was merely suffering from a little paranoia. Bending down, Julian scooped up the heavy bronze and then shoved his feet into the boots.

He still had the bronze in his left hand when he quietly opened the communicating door to Anne's room.

"Anne?" he whispered, reaching out to flip on the light.

"Not here, I'm afraid," Thomas Craven announced cheerily as the light came on to reveal his stout figure standing on the far side of the room. "For some entirely incomprehensible reason, Miss Silver saw fit to take a midnight walk along the cliffs tonight. No harm done. It was the direction we had in mind for her anyway. Sara has gone after her. Wouldn't want the little lady to have any unplanned accidents, would we?"

"You prefer the planned kind?" Julian stood quietly, his fingers still hovering over the light switch as though the sight of Craven's weapon had rendered him immobile.

"Ever so much more efficient," Craven nodded pleasantly. "Except when things don't go quite right, as in Mike Silver's case."

"Yes, I'm afraid there was a slight mix-up in that instance. Either Mr. Silver's reflexes were better than Dan expected or poor Dan botched matters. He seems to be doing that lately," Craven went on musingly. He gestured significantly at the darkened interior of Julian's room. "I take it he didn't live up to expectations in there, either?"

"He's out of it for the duration."

Craven shook his head. "It's hard to get good help these days. Hargraves didn't even manage the simple task of seducing Miss Silver."

"That would not have been a simple task," Julian growled, aware of a new kind of anger ruffling his senses. Deliberately he tamped it down. Emotional reactions were guaranteed to bring disaster in situations such as this. He was experienced enough to know that. "I'm afraid that would have been an utterly impossible task."

"You must have made quite an impression on Miss Silver in a short period of time, then. Because according to our investigation she certainly is not engaged to you or anyone else."

"And that's why you thought Hargraves could try the seduction bit?"

"It was worth a try. Who are you, Julian Aries? Where do you fit into all this? Where did Miss Silver find you?"

"She tracked me down to my lair. At least I think that's how she sees it," Julian said softly. "As far as who I am, that's easy. I'm exactly who I said I was: the man who's going to marry her. Which is why Sara's seduction attempt wouldn't have worked on me any more than Hargraves's did on Anne."

For the first time since he'd met the man, Julian saw a flash of real emotion in Craven's expression. The emotion, interestingly enough, was fury.

"What seduction attempt? Sara was never assigned to seduce you, Aries!"

"Then what was she doing at my door the other night?" Julian inquired sardonically, recognizing that he'd finally hit a raw spot. About time. "Selling Girl Scout cookies? I haven't seen many Girl Scouts dressed in filmy little nightgowns—"

"You're lying! Sara is mine, she wouldn't dare—"

But Julian didn't wait to hear any more. This was as off balance as Craven was going to get. The other man's rage was the edge Julian needed. He hit the light switch with one hand, and as the room was plunged into temporary, blinding darkness he sent the heavy bronze horse hurtling toward the point where Craven had been standing.

The gun went off, whether by intention or out of a reflex action on Craven's part, Julian didn't know. In any event the shot went wide as a solid thud and a painful groan announced that the rearing horse had found its mark. Flicking the light switch back on, Julian leaped across the room, falling on Craven to finish the job. He had been right. The stout, middle-aged man could not move well at all. Craven was neatly unconscious in a few seconds.

Julian staggered back to his feet, telling himself that when this was all over he was going to con Anne into massaging his entire body. After all these months of inactivity he was really feeling the strain tonight.

Hurriedly he cast around for something with which to tie his newest victim and seized on the gossamer netting that hung down over the empty, rumpled bed. He yanked on it and the whole mass came into his hands. The silky stuff twisted very nicely into a tough strand of pliable rope. A couple of moments later, Craven was securely bound.

A fierce sense of urgency was pounding through Julian now. Anne was out there on the cliffs somewhere with Sara in her wake. Matters had deteriorated very rapidly.

Julian flung open the door of Anne's room, realizing that Craven would never have been able to enter so easily if Anne hadn't conveniently opened the door for him, herself. Another point to confront her with when this was all over, Julian decided as he headed down the staircase as quickly as he could. Each jolt of his injured leg as he broke into an awkward, off-balance run sent a message of pain throughout his nervous system. But the leg was performing after a fashion, and that's all he asked of it tonight.

He was about to head outside through the kitchen door when he remembered the flashlights housed in a nearby drawer. Not bothering to turn on the overhead light, he reached inside the drawer and grabbed the first one that he touched. It was bulky, sheathed in a rubbery plastic. It had to be one of the waterproof types, he thought briefly. The kind that would still work after a fisherman or a camper accidentally dropped it into a stream. Maybe it would even float.

Pulling open the door he glanced out into the darkness, trying to get his bearings. He scanned the swirling mists and saw a jagged ray of light sweeping through the air. It came to rest, sending a dull unwinking gleam back toward the house. Another flashlight, Julian thought.

The pinpoint of light served as a guide as he made his way over the rough terrain toward the cliffs. The utter motionlessness of the other flashlight worried him. It looked as though it might have been dropped. Julian didn't dare switch on his own light for fear of making a target out of himself. There was a good chance that sweet little Sara was armed, and he had no doubts at all about her being dangerous.

He came closer to the cliff's edge, following the unwavering beam of the dropped flashlight, and then he realized that he could hear sounds of a struggle over the roar of the surf. He was in the process of flicking on his light when a sudden scream rent the air.

"Oh, my God, Anne!" he cried out in agony as his beam caught the two women going over the edge of the cliff. "Anne!"

He plunged to the edge of the rocks, sweeping the churning waves below with the heavy-duty flashlight. Shock and fear clutched at his guts. He'd never experienced such a devastating emotion in his life, not even when he'd thought he hadn't been going to make it out of the jungle. Nothing had ever been like this.

"Anne!" he yelled in helpless rage, as the beam of his flashlight revealed nothing in the waves. "Anne, don't you dare do this to me!"

And then he saw pale hair floating on a wave. Sara. If Sara survived this and Anne didn't he would probably kill the blonde. He knew it deep inside.

But a second later a face surfaced next to the floating blond hair. It was Anne. And the only reason Sara's hair was floating on the waves was because Anne was struggling to keep the other woman's face above water.

"Anne, let her go. Just keep yourself afloat. Don't waste any energy on her," Julian yelled instructions as he kicked off his boots. "I'm coming to get you."

Clutching the waterproof flashlight in one hand, Julian launched himself into a dive calculated not to take him very deep. The shock of the cold, seething water was enough to knock the light from his powerful grip. But when he surfaced an instant later the floating flashlight was hammering against his shoulder, driven by the force of the wave.

"Julian! Over here!"

He twisted in the water, searching for Anne, his fingers closing once more over the flashlight. The heavy waves had a strong, surging action he realized but they were normal, not storm-driven. They could be handled if he kept his head.

The light fell on Anne's face, and Julian struck out in her direction.

ANNE FELT AS THOUGH she had swallowed a large chunk of ocean by the time she surfaced and found Sara floating limply nearby. Instinctively she had shoved at the other woman, trying to put distance between them. It was then that she realized the blonde was almost unconscious. She didn't know what made her grab Sara and attempt to keep her chin above water.

Coughing and sputtering as she adjusted herself to riding the swells of the waves, Anne looked up as the beam of a light flashed over her and she heard her name called out.

Relief and panic went through her simultaneously. But before she could decide which reaction to favor Julian was already launching himself into a shallow dive timed to coincide with the waves at their highest. He surfaced nearby.

"You pick some dumb times to go for strolls along the beach, woman," he gritted as he swam over to her.

"You choose some odd occasions to go swimming," she tried to retort but her heartfelt relief at having him with her took the sardonic quality out of her words. "Oh, Julian, I'm so glad to see you. I was so worried. How did you know—"

"Later." His powerful hand caught her arm providing welcome support. "What are you hanging on to her for?" he demanded indicating the groggy Sara who was starting to stir and cough.

"I don't know. It seemed wrong to just let her go."

Julian took Sara's weight. "I'll handle her if you're too soft-hearted to leave her behind. We're going to have a job getting back on shore. We can't climb up that wall of rock in front of us, and the cove farther along is going to be too treacherous with the tide in. We'll have to try another direction."

"Julian, over there, at the tip of the cove," Anne gasped. She set off in that direction, absolutely certain of her sudden knowledge.

"Anne, wait!"

But she knew he was following, dragging the barely conscious Sara. Anne headed toward the jutting rock. The waves broke heavily on either side of it, but getting to the tip itself was comparatively simple. The worn angle of rock functioned like the prow of a ship, dividing the surging water smoothly. Anne was careful to stay in the smooth section of thrusting water and found her footing fairly quickly.

"In here, Julian." She turned to see him struggling upright in the water behind her, dragging Sara rather carelessly.

He stood knee-deep in the foaming water and played the light over the dark opening in the rock face. "What in hell . . . ? It's a cave. How did you know it was here, Anne?"

"I'll explain later," she said, scrambling up into the dense darkness of the cave opening. "Here, hand me the flashlight and I'll help you get Sara up the side."

"The last thing we want to do is get trapped in that cave, Anne. The tide is still coming in. Water will be pouring into that opening in a few more minutes."

"No, it's safe. It opens out onto the beach on the other side of thio cove."

"Are you sure?"

"I'm positive. No need to explain just now why she was so positive, Anne told herself. Men could be stubborn at times and this was not a moment for excessive masculine stubbornness. She reached for the still-limp Sara.

"If you're positive you know there's another exit from this cave," Julian began with obvious reluctance.

"I am. And it will save us the long swim to a safe beach. Come on, Julian. That water is cold." And the last thing he needed was this kind of exposure, Anne thought anxiously. The threat of the fever seemed to be hovering over him in her mind. The water was cold and the damp night air was even colder. She had to get him to warmth and safety. Her own reserves were depleted drastically, and she didn't know where Julian was getting his energy.

Without further argument Julian lifted Sara into the cave and scrambled up the side after her. "Anne, this place could be a trap if you're wrong about the other opening."

"This way," she said, trying to drag Sara. The blonde groaned and twisted groggily.

"All right." Apparently having decided to risk trusting Anne's knowledge of the deep cave, Julian turned his attention back to the burden of Sara. "On your feet, Sara, or we'll leave you behind."

"No, I . . ." Sara sputtered, coughing up water. Her breathing, although ragged, was reasonably normal, however. She seemed dizzy, reaching out to the damp rock walls for support. And then she appeared to notice Julian. "Help me," she whispered in her soft, theatrical voice. "It's been a nightmare. You don't know what it's been like, having to work for that man. He's forced me to do the most awful things."

"I think you were right, Julian," Anne broke in, utterly disgusted with the woman's deliberate appeal to Julian. "Let's leave her behind."

"You can't do that. I heard you say the water would be coming in here," Sara protested distractedly, real fear twisting her beautiful face as the flashlight lit it briefly.

"Come on, then. I'm through carrying you," Julian announced. "Let's go, Anne." He pushed Sara into line behind Anne and then handed Anne the flashlight. "Here, you seem to be the guide. You'd better know what you're doing, honey, or I'm going to be a little short-tempered when this is all over."

"I'll bet."

Anne took the light and set off through the cave, her footsteps never hesitating on the uneven, rocky floor. She didn't like caves—hated the enclosed, claustrophobic sensation they gave her. Just as Carlota had hated it. But she knew the exit was up ahead and that it would open out onto high, dry beach.

Carlota had hurried through this tunnel, entering the cave at low tide. On the far side she would find her lover waiting. And in the soft, sandy mouth of the cave they would make passionate love until the tide began to return. Always the tide set the boundaries of their lovemaking. Carlota had to be back before the water entered the lower entrance of the cave.

Carlota hated the tides because they always seemed to conspire against her passions.

"It's okay, Julian, we're almost through. Just a few more feet." Following the winding twists and turns of the ancient, hollowed-out rock, Anne lost all sense of direction. No wonder Julian was questioning her. But it would be all right. She knew it. And then she tripped over a heavy object lying on the floor of the cave and went sprawling.

"Anne?"

"Honey, are you all right? Stay put, Sara." Julian came forward to retrieve the flashlight and help Anne to her feet.

"Yes, yes, I'm okay. Julian, let me have the light. Hurry," she whispered as a frantic feeling of excitement tore through her. The answer and the ending were here in this cave. "Julian, look!"

He peered down at the heavy, carved box over which she had tripped. It wasn't a large object and it was half buried in dirt and debris. This section of the cave was surprisingly dry, testifying to the fact that the water seldom, if ever climbed this high into it.

"It's just an old box someone left behind."

"Carlota left it behind," Anne said grimly, going down on her knees to pry at the carved chest.

"Carlota! Are you crazy?" Sara demanded, reaching out to cling to Julian in support. "We've got to get out of this horrible cave. We might be going toward a dead end. We'll be trapped!"

"Shut up," Julian said with a total lack of interest. He shook off her pleading hand and focused the light on Anne's scrabbling fingers. "Anne, we've got to get out of here. Leave that for now. We can come back some other time."

"I've almost got it," she said, yanking the small chest free with a desperate tug. As it came loose from a century of debris, Anne felt the sighing satisfaction and gratitude that suddenly filled the cave. She stood up, dazed by the flood of Carlota's emotion. "Julian," she whispered, "Julian, she's free. Carlota's free. She's going now, I can sense it."

Julian's face was lined with concern in the pale light that reached his features as he held the flashlight. "Come on, honey. Let's go. Everything's all right now, but we've got to get out of here."

"Oh, stop talking to me as though I'd gone crazy," she grumbled, clutching the chest and starting toward the far end of the cave. "I'll explain it all to you later."

Wisely, Julian held his tongue, reaching out to clasp Sara firmly and haul her along as Anne's pace quickened.

"There, feel the wind? We're almost on the beach."

Anne stepped out of the cave mouth a moment later. Overhead the stars shone with unexpected brilliance. The swirling fog had almost completely dissipated.

"I'm so cold," Sara complained.

They were all cold. Anne's fears for Julian's health returned in full measure. "Julian, Julian, we can't go back to the house. Craven and Dan will be there."

"Yeah. But they aren't going to cause us any trouble. I left them neatly tied up in our bedrooms. Now all we have to do is find our way back." He glanced around, sweeping the beach with the flashlight. "We've come farther than I thought."

"You're going to be chilled to the bone," Anne worried.

"So are you. Let's get moving," he growled.

"But the fever—"

He shot her a ferocious glance that shut her up immediately. Without a word, Anne followed him as he dragged Sara across the beach. In the distance she could see the bulk of the Creswell house, still in darkness.

Sara had gone mute right after hearing that Craven and Hargraves had been neutralized. She went sullenly along in Julian's grip.

They reached the silent house a short time later, and Julian dispatched Anne upstairs for dry clothes and some blankets. When she returned with her load she found that he'd started a fire.

"Julian," she said very carefully, "Craven is lying on the floor of my room groaning."

"He'll live."

In the face of that kind of professional callousness Anne wasn't sure what to say. She and Sara undressed while Julian turned his back and unabashedly stripped off his own clothing. Modesty was not the order of the day, but then, no one felt like peeping, either, Anne decided ruefully. When they were finished Julian picked up the narrow leather belt Anne had been about to fasten around her middle and reached for Sara's wrists.

Anne watched uneasily as Julian methodically and rather brutally strapped Sara's hands behind her back. Then he carelessly thrust her down on the couch and tossed a blanket around her. The other woman glared at him but didn't offer a protest. It was Anne who felt obliged to say something.

"Julian, she's hardly going to cause trouble now."

He slanted her a level glance, the golden eyes gleaming with an unnerving brittleness. Anne caught her breath at the ruthlessness she saw there. Then she remembered what Sara had said about an Aries man making a dangerous opponent.

"She tried to kill you. Don't expect me to treat her like a princess. Sweet Sara is lucky to be alive and I think she knows it. Go get us something hot to drink, Anne. I've got to make a couple of phone calls."

Aries men make dangerous opponents. Anne took one look at the shuttered, ruthless expression on Julian's face and recalled that she had once thought he might not be a very nice man when he was "working." "Talk about the understatement of the year," she muttered to herself as she scurried off to the kitchen. As she left the room Julian was already reaching for the phone.

Anne returned sometime later with a tray of cups and a jug of coffee. She felt better, but there still seemed to be a lingering chill in her body. The sea had been cold, and the shock of events had also taken its toll. Once more she worried about Julian's health, but one glance at his face as he finished his conversation on the phone was enough to convince her not to bring up the topic.

"Don't worry. All three of them will talk. I'll see to it. Just set things up with the local cops, Steve, I'll take care of the rest. I know, I know." He paused, listening impatiently. "Steve, haven't I always tied things up for you in a nice, neat package? Well, this time is no different." Another pause. "Okay, I'll be waiting. And thanks, Steve." He hung up the phone and turned his head to meet Anne's questioning gaze. "Good. Coffee. I need it."

Anne handed him the cup and was about to hand one to Sara when she realized the other woman couldn't very well accept it with her wrists tied.

"Forget her. She'll survive without a cup of coffee," Julian said.

Sara glared at him but there was an element of fear in her expression. Anne realized the other woman was very uneasy around Julian now. Ignoring Julian's advice, Anne held a cup of hot coffee to Sara's lips and let her take a few sips.

Julian just shook his head. "You're too soft, Anne." He leaned back in a chair, sipping his own coffee and scowling thoughtfully into the fire. "The cops will be here shortly."

"Did you call them?"

"Yeah. I also called a guy I used to work with. He's in charge of coordinating some federal law-enforcement activities in this part of California. He's going to keep an eye on the situation and make sure nothing slips through the cracks." Julian slanted a cool glance at Sara. "But somehow I don't think anything will. Sara and her friends upstairs are going to tell all to the cops, aren't you, Sara?"

"Bastard," Sara swore, hunching into her blanket with obvious discomfort.

"Yeah. I've been told that on previous occasions." He set down the coffee cup and got to his feet, running a hand through his still-damp hair. "I guess I'd better go upstairs and make certain Craven and Hargraves understand just how much of a bastard I can be when the situation calls for it."

"Julian?" Anne lifted her head anxiously.

"Stay here and keep an eye on our sensitive." Julian turned and walked toward the stairs with a grim determination that told its own story. Anne knew his leg was bothering him and she knew equally well that he'd never admit it.

"Who the hell is he?" Sara gritted furiously as Anne tried to hold the coffee to her lips again.

"The man I love." Anne pushed the rim of the cup rather forcefully against Sara's sullen mouth.

When the car pulled into the circular drive a moment later, Anne got to her feet, telling herself it had to be the law. A quick trip, considering how isolated the Creswell house was, she thought, reaching for the doorknob.

"Prue! Good heavens. What are you doing here at this hour of the night?"

Prue raised her right hand and displayed a small, wicked-looking gun. She sighed regretfully. "I was very much afraid that Craven and the other two might foul up even a simple plan like the one I'd made for tonight. And since you're the one answering the door, I can only assume I was right." She motioned Anne back into the hall. "Where's Julian?"

"Busy," Anne shot back defiantly, trying to adjust to the latest twist in events.

"I see. Then we'll just have to wait for him, won't we?"

"Prue," Sara called harshly from the living room as she heard the other woman's voice. "In here!"

"Shut up, you idiot," Prue Gibson snarled as she pushed Anne ahead of her into the living room. Then she glanced at the blonde's bound hands. "My dear, you make a splendid actress but you do have your limitations in other fields, don't you? Where are Thomas and Dan?"

"Upstairs. Aries is threatening them or something," Sara told her swiftly.

"Julian! It's Prue. She's got a gun," Anne yelled and then tried to dodge as Prue swung the barrel of the weapon toward the side of her head.

The gun caught Anne a glancing blow that sent her sprawling against the coffee table. She flung out her hand instinctively to catch herself and struck the dirt-encrusted chest that had come from the cave. It went flying onto the floor, the old rusted catch parting easily. The chest fell open, and a necklace came free.

"Pick it up, you little bitch," Prue ordered roughly, her eyes never leaving the heavy, ornate object that was now draped over the edge of the box. *"Pick it up!"*

Anne moved hesitantly to obey. There was no sound from upstairs and she wondered why Prue wasn't paying attention to the silence; the older woman knew Julian was up there. Why was she staring at the necklace as if fascinated, Anne wondered.

Prue wasn't the only one apparently captivated by the jewels, which no longer gleamed in their intricately carved setting. Sara, too, seemed hypnotized by the object.

"A fortune," Prue breathed. "It must be worth an absolute fortune. Where did it come from?"

"The cave. She tripped over it when we went through a cave on the beach." Sara bent forward, studying the necklace.

It was an interesting necklace, Anne had to admit, but she didn't see quite what there was about it to enthrall Prue and Sara. Still, she wasn't about to question their apparent fascination. Cautiously she moved toward the fallen chest, watching for an opening.

A shadow flickered at the corner of her eye and she caught her breath. Julian was in the doorway. As quiet as a ghost he'd made his way downstairs. Perhaps he'd used the back stairs, Anne thought vaguely. She knew she must not give him away.

Prue was scarcely even bothering to aim the gun now, so hypnotized was she by the tangled necklace.

"My God, those are emeralds," Prue whispered almost passionately.

"And the setting is gold. So much gold," Sara said, echoing the intensity of the other woman.

Anne wondered how on earth they could tell what sort of gems or metal lay under the century-old dust and grime. She moved to obey Prue's orders, trusting that Julian would know how and when to make his move.

"Hurry," Prue said roughly. "Pick it up and hand it to me."

Anne's fingers closed around Carlota's necklace, and in that instant she knew Carlota had given it to her. It belonged to Anne. Passing on the necklace to another woman in love was Carlota's ticket to freedom.

"You can't have it," Anne said quietly, straightening with the necklace in her hand. Over Prue's shoulder she could see Julian moving silently forward. "It belongs to me now."

"Take it from her," Sara snapped, her eyes vivid with a strange hunger. "Get it, Prue. Get it and then untie me."

"Hand over the necklace," Prue ordered, reaching out to make a grab for it. The gun wavered dangerously.

Anne pulled back, nearly stumbling against the fireplace. The heat from the flames licked at her as she caught hold of the mantel but she clung to the necklace.

Julian's voice cut through the tension. Almost casually he reached out and yanked the gun from Prue's hand. "That's enough, Prue. I was wondering when you'd turn up."

His calm, dark voice seemed to break the spell that held Sara and Prue. Clearly startled, and looking rather dazed Prue swung around. "Aries!"

"Julian, she talked about being the one who'd set up the whole plan tonight," Anne told him, dancing quickly away from the hearth. The necklace was still clutched tightly in her fist.

"I was pretty certain she had to be involved. No one seemed at all worried earlier about getting rid of the 'housekeeper.' Given the fact that she could have tied these three to our mysterious 'accident,' I thought that seemed a bit strange. There's no husband in Santa Barbara, is there, Prue? How long have you worked this little psychic bit?"

"For years," Prue snapped. "And it always went perfectly until that damn Michael Silver started poking around, asking questions."

"Umm. Did you always lay the groundwork for the various jobs by getting yourself hired on the domestic staff of whatever house was being set up?"

"I don't have to talk to you. I know my rights."

"Rights?" Julian looked politely curious. "Someone who organized an attempt to kill my woman doesn't get a whole lot of respect for her rights from me. I'm willing to let the law handle you if it can. If it can't—" he lifted one shoulder as if the rest were obvious — then I'll take care of matters in my own way."

Something about the way he said it must have gotten to Prue and Sara. They stared at him, reading the endless threat that swirled in the depths of Julian's tawny-brown eyes. They were still staring at him, strangely mute, when the sheriff's car pulled into the circular driveway.

IT WAS A LONG TIME LATER before Anne finally got the hot shower she had been craving since her swim in the ocean. The deep-down chill hadn't quite gone away although she hadn't been terribly aware of it during the scene with the law-enforcement officers. Julian had handled everything with a dispatch and cool professionalism that Anne found both a relief and an annoyance. She realized that while he could be a tower of strength in this role, he was also more unapproachable than ever.

Julian had used the shower in the bedroom next to Anne's, the one Sara had used. Anne knew he had not invited himself to share her hot shower because he hadn't wanted her to see just how much his leg was aching. Or perhaps he hadn't wanted her to know just how exhausted he was.

She was almost out on her feet herself, Anne realized. Her hand moved to stifle a huge yawn as she finished toweling dry and reached for her flannel nightgown—absolutely exhausted and still vaguely cold. She brushed her hair and then stood in the middle of the bathroom trying to decide which door to open, her own or Julian's.

A lonely bed or a wounded lion. It was a heck of a choice.

But there was another factor to consider tonight. Julian might or might not need her but she definitely needed him. The decision made, she flung open the door to Julian's Western-style room and found it empty.

It took Anne a couple of seconds to realize that meant he might have gone to her room to wait for her. Maybe he needed her tonight as much as she needed him.

For some reason that thought brought as much tense emotion as any of the earlier events of the evening. Cautiously Anne went back into the bathroom and opened the door to her room. Julian was stretched out on the bed, his arms folded behind his head. His eyes went to Anne's face as she stood silhouetted in the doorway.

"You look tired, honey. Come to bed," he rasped softly.

She hesitated and then padded toward the round bed. "I am tired," Anne admitted. "It was all so strange, Julian. I've never been through anything like that in my life."

"I should hope not," he said on a dry chuckle, reaching for her as she folded back the sheet. "You weren't cut out for this kind of thing, sweetheart. I want your word of honor that you won't get us involved in any more situations like this one."

"I ought to call Lucy and tell her it's all over."

"In the morning. It's late here, and it's three hours later back in Boston. She can wait until tomorrow." He stroked a hand along her shoulder and down her arm.

With a soft sigh, Anne yielded willingly to the soothing touch, and her own fingers met no withdrawal as she began to knead the upper part of his injured thigh.

For a long while they lay wrapped in silence, each soothing and relaxing the other. Anne nestled against Julian's bare chest as he worked his hand down her spine. He lay unprotesting as she continued the gentle massage of his leg with her free hand.

The mutual stroking and comforting grew from tentative to assured as the minutes passed, and finally Julian simply wrapped his arms around Anne and held her tightly against the length of his body. She rested her head in the crook of his shoulder and accepted the peace.

"Julian?" she ventured at last.

"Hmm?"

"I'll never be able to tell another soul and I'm sure you'll laugh at me when I tell you, but I've got to talk about it just once."

"About what, Anne?"

"Julian, I didn't know that cave even existed until I found myself swimming toward it. I had no way of knowing there was an opening on the far side. I went down to the sea tonight in the first place because I had to search for something. It was for Carlota's sake. Julian, I think I've seen her ghost a couple of times since we've been staying here. I . . . I went down to the beach because she wanted me to go down. She wanted me to find that necklace so that she would be free. And . . . and she was planning on running away with her lover that last night. The necklace was hers. Her mother had given it to her. It was all she took the night she decided to run off. It was to help finance the escape with her lover, I suppose. Both of them knew they'd be cut off from their families."

"Anne, honey . . ."

Anne twisted. "Please let me finish, Julian. I know it sounds crazy but I promise you that once I've told you I'll never bring it up again. I just have to get the whole thing out of my system. At any rate there isn't much more to tell. Carlota's husband followed her that last night and found her in the cave with her lover. In his fury he attacked her, and the man Carlota was in love with ran off like the coward he was. The chest containing the necklace was left behind, and no one realized it was missing. But somehow Carlota's spirit was bound to that necklace. She couldn't be free until the necklace was retrieved. She needed someone who understood and sympathized. Someone who would follow her to the cave and find the necklace."

There was silence from Julian. Anne shifted uncomfortably. "I'm sorry," she went on, embarrassed. "I know it sounds outrageous, and I know you probably think it's all a product of my imagination. I swear, I'll never talk about it again. I just had to tell someone once."

"Anne, honey, how can I laugh at your ghost story when I've got my own to tell?"

Anne held her breath, aware of a barrier crumbling—a barrier that had stood solid all these months since she had last seen Julian Aries. Afraid to move for fear of shattering the moment, she lay very still.

"I had plenty of visits from a ghost lady," Julian began slowly, his fingers threading through her russet hair. His chin rested on her head as he talked. "You were my ghost, Anne, and there were times when I thought that a ghost was all I'd ever have of you. That plus a few memories of you yelling at me for risking Mike's neck."

"Oh, Julian," she said sighing.

"I went back after bringing Mike to you. I had to go back. I had a job to finish, Anne. Too many people were counting on me. The twenty-four hours it took to fly Mike to you and return to the island were all I could spare. I shouldn't even have wasted that much time. But I couldn't just send him home alone. I knew you were going to hate me, but I had to face you." Julian moved restlessly and then went on. "At any rate I went back to finish the assignment and told myself, just as I had told you, that when it was over I'd return to straighten everything out between you and me. I had decided that would be my last job for the department. I wanted out. Other things in life had suddenly become much more important."

"Were you really going to come back for me?" Anne asked wistfully.

"Oh, yes. I knew that much. What was scaring the daylights out of me was the realization that I had very little to offer you. We seemed worlds apart in many ways. I didn't know how I was going to go about convincing you to give me a chance. Then everything about the assignment I was working on fell apart. There was a leak. To make a long story short, I was captured by members of the group I was supposed to be investigating."

"Captured!"

"Don't look so shocked. It was probably bound to happen sooner or later. I'd been playing with fire for a long time. I suppose it was inevitable that my luck would run out."

"What happened?" Her eyes wide with pain, Anne moved back a few inches to search his face. "Those bastards hurt you."

His mouth crooked wryly. "It's nice to know you're on my side. For a while there I thought the whole world was working against me. I got hurt when I managed to escape. They had plans for me, I was told. They wanted information and they wanted to make an example out of me. Either way I probably wasn't slated to survive captivity, so I made a try for the jungle one morning when the guard took me out of my cage."

"Oh, God, they kept you in a cage?"

"I'd used a broken piece of glass from a bottle that I'd found to cut the ropes on my hands and feet. When the guard came for me he wasn't expecting me to be quite so, uh, mobile. I took him by surprise. Then I ran for it. Straight into the jungle. But the guard got off a few shots and one caught me in the leg. I managed to get into the safety of the jungle and promptly blundered into a member of the group who was returning to the camp. In the process of coping with him, I got a little cut up." Julian absently massaged the scar on his jaw.

Anne sucked in her breath but she said nothing. A primitive anger was rising in her, however. Anger against an unseen foe who had done such things to the man she loved. Given half a chance she would willingly have tried to avenge him.

"By the time I got my leg to stop bleeding and had time to realize I was completely lost in that damn jungle, I was not in the best of moods or the best of shape," Julian went on. "The wounds got infected over the next couple of days and I started getting feverish. I'd wander for hours telling myself that I was following the direction of the setting sun and then I'd come to and realize I had just been moving blindly through the jungle. Half the time I couldn't even see the sun because the foliage was so thick. And throughout the whole mess you'd see fit to appear occasionally. And that's when I knew I was really in trouble."

"Did you hate me so much, then?" Anne asked sadly.

Julian shook his head. "I never hated you Anne. But during my lucid moments I realized you were thousands of miles away. I developed a pattern. Whenever I could see your ghost I'd know I was hallucinating. When I found myself alone I knew I was in my right mind, muddled though it was. I eventually stayed clearheaded long enough to find my way through the jungle to the ocean and from there I could follow the beach until I came to civilization. Three days after I got back to the States I came down with the first bout of fever."

"And you had your hands full trying to recover," Anne said gently, running soft fingers down the hard line of his cheek.

"The doctors didn't know what it was at first and finally diagnosed a nunfatiluke bug. They hope that the bouts will get less frequent and less severe over time, but they also don't know how many more there will be. Between that diagnosis and my wounds I knew I couldn't go back to work for a long time, I also knew I couldn't go after you."

"I understand, Julian. I think you were arrogantly proud, hopelessly macho and downright wrong in making that decision, but I understand."

"Honey, I wanted to come back to you as strong and healthy as I had been when I left. I was afraid the only reaction I'd get from you in my present condition was pity, and I also thought you'd still be furious with me for getting Mike shot."

"Julian, the reason I screamed so much abuse at you that night in the hospital was because I didn't want you to go back to that horrible island, and I also knew that nothing I could say or do would keep you from going."

He looked down at her. "Is that really why you were so upset that night?"

"Yes."

He groaned and pulled her close once more. "It's been a long six months, Anne."

"I know," she agreed simply.

"I have even less to offer you now than I did six months ago. Hell, I don't even have a job."

She smiled mistily. "Julian, you idiot, you don't know it yet but you have a lot more to offer now than you did then." *Now he could offer himself.*

He wanted to ask her what she meant but her soft fingertips were brushing the hair back off his forehead, and her leg was lying between his thighs. The flannel nightgown was a soft covering for an even softer body, and Julian's head was beginning to spin with desire. And he suddenly realized he wasn't feeling nearly as tired as he had earlier. Even his leg wasn't aching so much.

"Anne?"

"Yes, Julian?"

"Is your ghost lady gone?"

"Forever. I thought she had left while we were in that cave but she hadn't. Not completely. There was something of her spirit still clinging to that necklace when the box fell open. Something that managed to hypnotize Prue and Sara long enough for you to disarm Prue. At least, that's the feeling I had. But now Carlota is really gone."

"And my ghost lady has turned out to be quite real." Julian bent his head and kissed her with an odd gentleness.

Anne forgot Carlota and reached up to twine her arms around Julian's neck. He might not yet be ready to hear her verbal declaration of love, but she had no qualms about making it with her body. She needed him tonight—needed his warmth and strength, and he needed her.

Whether he knew it or not, he needed her.

The gentle understanding that had been borne between them metamorphosed into the desire that had always existed between them. The result was a limitless passion that swept through both lovers. Anne could feel the singing heat in her veins and knew it was echoed in the pulsing sensuality that caused Julian to shudder heavily when she touched him.

They moved freely together, touching, coaxing, demanding responses. Their bodies twined and flowed, hardness against softness, dampness against heat, strength against gentleness. Julian's hands caressed with wonder and need. When he traced erotic little designs on the inside of her thigh Anne caught her breath and arched against him with sweet abandon. She knew he gloried in her response. When she returned the caress, cupping the rigid shaft between his legs he responded in kind, thrusting himself more deeply into her gentle grasp.

The power and energy of their lovemaking both exulted and drained them. The fear and danger brought about by the events of the night faded as Anne was warmed by her lover's touch. Together they explored the farthest reaches of sensual comfort and sensual need.

Again and again Anne found herself at the brink of an incandescent excitement elicited by Julian's dancing, probing, thrilling caresses. Each time he felt her hovering at the edge he pushed her gently over until she thought she would go out of her mind.

Desperately she sought to take him with her, her tongue skipping lightly down his chest as her nails sank ever so carefully into the blunt tip of his manhood.

"I can't hold out any longer if you insist on playing with fire like that," he warned thickly as he moved at last to cover her.

"I want you with me this time," she gasped as he entered her, and he swallowed the sound of her words with hungry lips.

Then they were spinning through darkness and light, bound by passion in a manner that paralleled the way they had been bound together in danger. One kind of bond reinforced the other. In the end Anne could not imagine ever being free, or ever wishing to be free of this man again.

12

THE PHONE CALL to Lucy and Mike wound up being held in an astonishingly loud tone of voice. The irate noise level was mostly from Michael Silver's end and when he discovered that his sister and his fiancée had decided to go through with his original plan without telling him.

"How could we tell you, Michael?" Anne finally exclaimed in exasperation. "You had your hands full concentrating on getting well. We didn't want to bother you."

"Didn't want to bother me!" he exploded from his hospital bed. "I don't believe this. You went through with this thing without letting me know what was going on because you didn't want to *bother* me? Didn't you realize that the fact that someone had tried to run me down meant everything had drastically changed? Yet the two of you decide to just blithely go along as if nothing new had happened. As if everything could proceed normally. When I think of you out there alone in the Creswell house surrounded by that pack of wolves—"

"I wasn't alone, Michael," Anne snapped. Vaguely she was aware that she ought to be grateful her brother was feeling well enough to engage in the tirade. On the other hand she didn't envy poor Lucy having to take the brunt of his anger.

"You weren't alone?" he mocked. "Who the hell was with you? The ghost?"

"Well, I did have her help," Anne replied on a sudden note of humor. "But the one who saved the whole situation was Julian."

There was a beat of silence on the other end of the line. At last Michael said quite carefully, "Julian Aries? I thought he was holed up somewhere in the Colorado mountains."

"He was." Anne smiled, glancing across the breakfast table at the man in question, who was calmly eating breakfast. "I went and dragged him out and put him to work."

"You mean Aries was with you during this whole farce? Why didn't you say so?"

"You didn't give me much of a chance. Here, want to talk to him? I'm tired of having you yell at me." Anne handed the phone over to Julian who accepted it blandly.

"Hello, Mike. How are you doing? Good." There was a pause during which Julian's eyes met Anne's and his expression turned sardonic. "Well, I'm glad you're relieved to know I was here with her. Frankly, I had a few moments of extreme doubt, myself. But when I realized I couldn't stop her, there didn't seem to be any alternative to going along and keeping an eye on her." Another pause. "Yeah, it's all tied up. Prue Gibson was the real brains behind the plan. She'd set up a deal by getting a job on the household domestic staff whenever possible so that there would always be an inside person. Craven was the art expert and he took care of earmarking the valuables that were later to be stolen. Sara what's-her-name played the psychic and the guy named Hargraves was the muscle man. He was also the lock-and-key expert. He took care of determining how to get past whatever security measures were in place."

Julian helped himself to another slice of toast while Michael talked for a few minutes, then he agreed with something Anne's brother said. "I know. In this case it would have been child's play to get past these old locks." He took a deep breath. "I was thinking of asking Miss Creswell if she'd like an expert evaluation of her security system before I leave. She's got a lot of valuables to protect." He waited a little tensely while Michael said something on the other end of the line, and then he smiled with a trace of relieved satisfaction. "You do? Maybe I'll give her a call, then. Okay, okay, I will definitely give her a call. Thanks, Mike. What's that? Yeah. Something of a career crisis all right. Anne tells me it's all for the best, though."

He talked a few minutes longer and then dropped the phone into the cradle. Julian gave Anne a quiet, steady look. "Your brother thinks Miss Creswell would jump at the chance to have a real expert go through the house and update the security."

"Of course she will," Anne agreed blithely. "So will a lot of other people who have treasures to protect. Your background, disreputable as I happen to think it is, is just the sort to give people a lot of confidence in your security skills."

"It will be a while before the business builds itself into anything resembling a full-time career," he warned slowly, still watching her intently.

"About a year, I would imagine," Anne speculated cheerfully, munching toast.

Julian picked up his coffee cup, gripping it quite fiercely as he said in a suspiciously even tone of voice, "It will be at least that long before I'll be able to offer you much of anything. Anne, if I've made it in my new field a year from now, would you consider marrying me?"

Anne smiled very brilliantly, feeling her pulse pick up with happiness and excitement. "No."

Julian's face went very taut and the golden eyes pinned her. "No?" he repeated carefully. A strange mixture of emotions seemed to be passing through those tawny eyes. Anne read everything from pain to fear and anger.

"No," she said quite steadily. "I will not wait an entire year to marry you. I figure we can stop off in Las Vegas on our way back East to see my brother. No waiting period in Nevada. We'll be married by the time we reach Boston." She poured more coffee while Julian continued to sit staring at her.

"You'll marry me right away?"

"Julian," she admonished with mock severity, "you should have been proposing to me six months ago. I've waited long enough to wring an offer of marriage out of you. I'm not going to wait another year."

"Anne, are you sure?" he pressed roughly. "I have nothing to offer you now."

"You're wrong, you know," she said gently. "Now you can offer me yourself. Six months ago you were as hard and as self-contained as a chunk of granite." Anne paused to slant him a wicked little grin. "Sexy as hell, mind you, but still not quite human."

"You think I'm more human now?" he growled.

"Umm," she said nodding. "You're still arrogant and proud and capable of annoying me no end but you're very, very human. You're also everything a woman could want in a husband: strong, protective and passionate."

A strange smile curved his mouth. "That's funny. I was going to say something similar to you. You're everything a man could want in a wife: strong, protective and passionate. And you can cook."

"I don't do windows," she warned.

"Anne, I love you."

Anne choked on her coffee, certain she hadn't heard correctly. Sputtering and coughing, she managed to squeak, "What?"

He frowned. "You heard me."

"How long . . . how long have you known?"

His frown deepened thoughtfully. "And then he shrugged. "I don't know. Maybe I realized it on some level when I kept hallucinating about you in the jungle. I suppose I knew it for certain after those three days in the cabin. Until that point I knew I wanted you, but after that I began to realize that I—" He broke off quite abruptly on a sneeze.

Anne stared at him. "Julian?"

He sneezed again, using a paper napkin as a tissue. "Oh, hell."

Anne stood up and came around the table. "Are you feeling all right?"

"As a matter of fact, no." He sounded grimly furious.

"Actually, I've been feeling a bit off myself this morning. My throat's a little scratchy," she admitted. She put her hand on his forehead. "Hmm."

"Anne, if it's that fever again, I swear, I'll . . . " The sentence trailed off in frustration as Julian blew his nose.

"It's not the fever," Anne told him calmly.

He looked up at her over the cloud of napkin he was holding to his nose. "You don't think so?" There was a flare of desperate hope in his gaze.

She swallowed experimentally, feeling the slightly dry sensation in her throat. "Julian, I have a feeling you and I are about to experience a rather unique brand of togetherness. We're going to have to share an old-fashioned cold. Come on. Let's get a fire built. I'll make a large pot of hot tea with lemon, and we can sit in front of the fireplace and comfort each other."

"It's probably from that dip in the ocean last night," Julian offered, looking a great deal more cheerful than he had a moment ago.

"Possibly. Or perhaps one of those four turkey houseguests we've been entertaining was coming down with a cold and passed it along to us before we got rid of him or her. That Sara what's-her-name always looked a bit sickly to me."

An hour later, ensconced at opposite ends of the long sofa, their feet touching under a quilt, Julian toasted Anne with a mug of hot tea.

"Comfy?" he asked with a chuckle. He had a fire going and had placed a box of tissues at both ends of the couch.

"Perfectly," she murmured. "Julian, you never finished what you started to say earlier."

"About how I knew I loved you? I suppose I acknowledged that about the same time I realized I needed you." His face sobered. "I've never needed anyone before, Anne. It was a very strange sensation. And I've never really wanted anyone to need me. It made life simpler."

"And now?" she asked tremulously.

"And now I realize how much I want you to need me." He looked at her. "You love me, don't you?"

She didn't hesitate. "Yes."

He nodded in quiet satisfaction. "After I decided you weren't pitying me and after I realized that you could care for me one moment and come alive with passion the next, I knew that what you felt encompassed a lot more than physical attraction. Six months ago I thought the attraction was all we had on which to build—another reason why I didn't want you to see me while I was recovering."

"There was no need to worry," Anne told him dryly. "Even wounded and feverish you were quite capable of sweeping me off my feet!"

He grinned at that, masculine arrogance stamped plainly on his hard features. "Taking you to bed was the most therapeutic thing I'd done in six months, and you were going to deny it had even happened," he accused.

"I have my pride, too, you know," she reminded him gently.

"We both do. But it's not going to stand between us again, is it?" he asked very seriously.

"No, Julian," she whispered, her happiness brimming in her eyes. "I love you so much. I love you and need you and want you."

"Not any more than I love and need and want you." He set down his mug of tea, reached over to remove hers from her fingers and pulled her into the curve of his arm. "I'll take care of you, Anne."

"And I'll take care of you. It's all part of loving."

"No more ghosts?" he asked almost whimsically, ruffling her hair with his hand.

"No. How about you?"

"No more ghosts for me, either."

"I do have a question, however," she began deliberately.

"What's that?" He bent to drop a small kiss on the nape of her neck.

"You never did tell me exactly when your birthday is. Are you an Aries?"

He grinned — a slashing, piratical smile that caught at Anne's heart. "I'll tell you on our wedding night," he promised.

She thinks
he's a "reactionary old poop,
a narrow-minded old fossil."

He thinks
she's a "wispy spinster, with trailing garments,
vague eyes and the IQ of a toaster."

When they actually meet,
they're going to get the surprise of their lives!

BEWITCHING HOUR

Anne Stuart

For Lorelei Wheeler and Bev Young—
I couldn't have done it without you.

Chapter One

"Something's coming," Sybil Richardson stared down at the tarot cards covering her already littered desk, and her high forehead wrinkled in confusion. "I can't tell whether it's something nasty or not. But it's powerful."

"Did you try the I Ching?" Leona looked up from her position on the floor beside the rack of dowsing pendulums. The front rooms of the old house on Water Street in Danbury, Vermont, held the business offices of the Society of Water Witches, better known as SOWW. The back room held Sybil Richardson's occult bookstore, and Leona was in the midst of unpacking the latest stock of psychic and dowsing paraphernalia.

"You know you do best with Eastern forms of mysticism."

"The I Ching was even more confusing," Sybil said gloomily. "Why don't you do a tarot card reading? You have more talent than I have."

Leona rose to her full five feet, and her round face wrinkled in disapproval. "You know there's no such thing, Sybil. We all have psychic ability; some of us are just more in touch with it."

"I'm not within screaming distance today," Sybil said, pushing back in her chair and running a hand over her coil of dark blond braids that were, as usual, giving her a headache. "I just have this premonition."

"Then you should pay attention to it," Leona said firmly. She was a slightly comical figure, like a cross between Yoda and Mrs. Santa Claus, with a round plump body, a round plump face, small dark eyes that looked like raisins in a suet pudding and a halo of untidy white hair. She never told her age, but Sybil suspected that she was somewhere on the shady side of seventy, despite her limitless energy. "Premonitions have a purpose, and it's risking all sorts of danger to ignore them. You should go upstairs and meditate. I can watch the office."

"Can't do it," Sybil said with a sigh, shuffling the malevolent-looking cards back into an untidy pile. "The newsletter has to be typed; it's already three weeks late. And That Man's coming."

"What man?" Leona sank down onto a straight chair, her short little legs dangling like those of a child.

"Nicholas Wyndham Fitzsimmons." Her voice sounded as if she were naming a snake. "The one who writes all those snotty books, ridiculing everything he doesn't happen to believe in. Which ends up being almost everything that matters to us."

"Oh, dear," Leona said faintly. "If he doesn't believe in anything, why is he coming here? Not to write an exposé, I hope."

"Apparently the great man believes in dowsing. Real dowsing, as he puts it. The ability to find water using a divining rod or pendulum, and that's all there is to it. Just like the trustees."

"Oh, dear," Leona said again.

"Exactly. He thinks the be-all and end-all of dowsing consists of old men finding wells. And he's coming to do research on them."

"Well, we certainly have enough of them. As long as he leaves the rest of us alone."

"Hah," Sybil said. "I'm sure he's as obnoxious as his books. He'll be snooping around, looking down his aristocratic nose at us, and sooner or later I'll be driven to murder."

"Does he have an aristocratic nose?" Leona asked in her most prosaic voice.

"I wouldn't know. He doesn't have his picture on the cover of his books. But he teaches at Harvard; I imagine he's extremely aristocratic."

Leona rose. "Do you have any of his books in the shop? I don't remember seeing them."

"I keep them under the counter," Sybil began shuffling the cards again, frowning once more, "I have to have them in case some poor misguided fool wants to read his venom-dipped prose. But I don't have to advertise them." She turned over the Queen of Cups, moaned and flipped all the cards over.

Leona was looking at her oddly. "The Queen of Cups usually means romance for you. Just how old a man is this Nicholas Fitzsimmons?"

"Ancient," Sybil said. "All you have to do is read his books to know. He's a reactionary old poop, a narrow-minded fossil like most of the trustees. He'll feel right at home with them."

Leona breathed an audible sigh of relief. "Good," she said. "You know how I feel about romance."

Sybil grinned, and the smile lighted up her plain face and turned it into something close to beauty. "I know how you feel. You have your reactionary moments, too."

"If you wish to expand your horizons, to get in touch with the infinite inner and outer reaches, then you can't diffuse your energy with sex," Leona announced.

"I know, you've told me that a million times," Sybil said in a cheerful voice. "Personally I wouldn't mind a little healthy diffusion. It's just that everyone here is married, senile or just reaching puberty."

"And it's a good thing," Leona said sternly. "I'll take these pendulums back to the shop, and then you can sit still and I'll do a reading for you."

"Give me one first." Sybil held out her hand, and Leona dropped a metal, bullet-shaped object into her palm.

"I thought you didn't like dowsing."

"Only because I have such lousy results. Every time I try to dowse for what kind of baby someone's going to have it always comes up with the opposite. But nothing else is giving me any results today. Maybe for once the pendulum will work."

"It will work if you let it," Leona intoned. "You mustn't get distracted by simple bodily urges. Rise above them."

Sybil watched her sturdy little figure toddle away. "God, would I love to get distracted," she said mournfully. She shoved the cards into her desk drawer with a blatant disrespect for their antiquity, slammed it shut and lifted the small pendulum by its metal chain. She held it up, and it began twirling in concentric circles. "Clockwise for yes, counterclockwise for no," she informed it. It just kept spinning.

"Okay, pendulum," she said. "Is something going to happen?" It spun around in wildly clockwise circles. "All right. Is it something good?" The pendulum halted for a moment as if confused, then continued its aimless spin. "Will I like it?" Still clockwise. "So far so good," she muttered. "Does it involve a man?'' The pendulum got quite excited at this point, spinning in an arc that was almost parallel to the ground.

Sybil stared at the exuberant pendulum. "Okay, okay," she said. "Here's the hard part. Are my eyes brown?"

The pendulum dropped down, stopping, and then began a slow, counterclockwise motion. Sybil stared at it from her warm brown eyes and cursed. She dropped it into her desk drawer along with the much abused tarot cards. "So much for dowsing." And she turned to her long-neglected typewriter.

It was just an all-round bad day, she thought four hours later when she finally pushed her rolling chair away from the aging Selectric. She cast a cursory glance around the deserted office for the plastic cover, but as usual it was missing. She shivered as she looked out of the multipaned window to the snow-covered road. It was early December, dark at four-thirty, and it snowed or sleeted almost every day. November averaged less sunshine than any other month, but this December was giving gloomy November a run for its money. They'd had thirteen days without sunshine, ending with freezing rain last weekend, making travel impossible. The road still had a solid coating of ice beneath the fresh snow, and Sybil had every expectation of sliding home, even with the blessed amenity of four-wheel drive.

Still and all, the weather had its compensations. The roads were too bad for her to drive to the Burlington airport and fly down to see her family in Princeton. She could spend a few more weeks without the doubtful pleasure of her family's disappointment and well-hidden disapproval. Now if the fates could only come up with a blizzard on Christmas she'd be safe until one of her overwhelming family risked allergy and asthma to visit her. She might even make it till spring.

Not that she didn't love her family. Her father was bluff, kind and tactless. He was also the president of a bank. Her mother was clever, loving and concerned. She was a corporate vice-president. Her older sister, Hattie, was a gynecologist, with a solid-gold practice of rich, grateful patients and a national reputation; her middle sister, Emmie, was a lawyer in one of Philadelphia's most prestigious law firms; and her baby sister, Allison, was a career diplomat, on special assignment for the State Department. They were all very bright, very accomplished, very competent, astonishingly attractive and very kind. And then there was Sybil.

She couldn't be around them without feeling like a changeling. Their determined kindness only made it worse. Because Sybil had no great gift, no great talent, no frightening intellect that made strong men weep. She was just an ordinary sort of woman, with an ordinary amount of brain power that carried her through Bennington College with acceptable grades. She was passably attractive, with thick brownish blond hair, warm brown eyes and regular features that were pleasant enough. Her body was average height, average size, with an inch too much around the hips, but then, who didn't have that? Not her family, of course, but most mortals.

In any other family she would have been a more than acceptable member. But in the Richardsons, women conquered empires, ruled worlds; they didn't like to bake bread. In the Richardsons, women gathered advanced degrees as if they were collecting china figurines; they didn't have gardens and bumper zucchini crops. In the Richardsons, you strove until you dropped and the honors were piled at your feet. You didn't make a disastrous marriage to an unimaginative banker, leave him instead of having children and run away to Vermont, of all places. And you certainly didn't get involved in flaky organizations like the Society of Water Witches.

But thank God, all Richardsons had money. Their maternal grandmother had been the first female self-made millionaire in the New York stock market, and she'd left all her money to her granddaughters. When Sybil could finally take no more of her rigid married life in Scarsdale, she had packed her clothes, left Colin an apologetic note and taken off for the family home in Vermont. Her first act had been to acquire two springer spaniels, which quickly became six.

The dogs had kept the Richardsons at bay. Along with all their other qualities, all the Richardsons, except Sybil, suffered from intense allergies. They couldn't be in the same room with a dog without wheezing and coughing and resorting to inhalants. It had worked out beautifully.

And she didn't have to feel guilty. They hadn't used the house in Vermont for years anyway; it was only opened on an occasional Labor Day weekend, and even then half of the family couldn't make it. So it was Sybil's and she reveled in it, with her six dogs and her solitude and her fresh-baked bread that was directly responsible for that extra inch around her hips. Fortunately the zucchini crop helped to take it off.

No, if it weren't for the lack of eligible men, her life in Danbury, Vermont, would have been absolutely splendid. And she didn't really know if she wanted a man, she just wished she had the option of turning one down. But she had a job she enjoyed, friends and creative outlets that turned her family pale with horror. She was blissfully content, even on such a dark, gloomy, snowy day. If it weren't for this premonition.

Leona hadn't been able to come up with much in her tarot reading. The ancient fortune-telling cards were obscure, offering more vague warnings about diffusing her energies, warnings Sybil took with a grain of salt. It had been three years since her divorce, three years of celibacy, and her psychic powers didn't seem to be increasing. If Prince Charming happened to show up, it might be worth trying a new tack.

But it was Nicholas Wyndham Fitzsimmons who was going to show up. He had to be seventy if he was a day; the board of trustees didn't trust anyone under sixty-five. The last thing she needed was a gold-plated academic. Her ex-husband had been aristocratic enough. No, what she needed was some earthy, sweating hunk to warm her through the long winter nights. Or failing that, at least someone who didn't make her feel as inadequate as her family did.

But all her partially formed instincts and psychic powers told her it was going to be a completely uneventful winter, with no more passionate diffusing than went on in a convent. With her usual good humor she banished the incipient depression that crowded around her at the thought. There was a great deal to be said for peace, even at her miserably advanced age of thirty.

Her only problem right now was having to wait for the old man. The snow was coming down with more enthusiasm than she cared for, there was the monthly meeting of the psychic group to contend with, and by the time they were finished it would take her ages to get down the narrow road to her cottage. Damn the man, why couldn't he be there on time? If he didn't arrive by six, she'd leave him a note and he could find his own way around. Flicking off the desk light, she headed for the small bookshop at the back of the building.

NICHOLAS WYNDHAM Fitzsimmons's dark green Jaguar XJ6 slipped sideways on the snow-packed road. With deft precision he turned into the spin, gently tapping with responsive brakes, and felt the tires regain their traction and their forward momentum down the deceptively icy road. It was the fourth time he'd nearly lost it in the last half hour, creeping over the secondary roads from St. Johnsbury and I-91. Despite the loose clasp of his leather-gloved hands on the steering wheel, he was in the worst mood he'd ever been in. He'd been cursing steadily for the last ten miles, peering through the whirling, blowing snow for signs of his destination. It was with only a faint lessening of temper that his headlights illuminated a white painted sign that announced he was now entering Danbury, Vermont, established in 1793, home of the Society of Water Witches. Nick's lip curled as he slowly, carefully negotiated the left hand turn onto Water Street. It had been a stupid time of year to come up for research, but he hadn't had much choice in the matter. He was due in England by the end of January, and he had to have his information well in hand before he went. But damn, he wished he were back in his cozy little apartment in Cambridge.

Even through the blowing and drifting snow he didn't have any trouble finding the old white farmhouse that held the society's headquarters. A single light was burning in the front of the building, with more in the back, and one snow-covered station wagon was parked out front. At least the secretary had stayed to welcome him. What was her name—Sybil something? He knew just what to expect. Some wispy spinster in her fifties, with filmy trailing garments, vague eyes and the IQ of a toaster. He pulled the Jaguar to a stop and had the distinctly unpleasant experience of having it slide two feet more until it bumped gently against the snowy retaining wall. With a savage curse, he turned off the key and bounded out into the night air.

The door was unlocked. For a moment he just stood inside the hall, letting the heat and light surround him. There was no one in the darkened office, but he could hear music from the back of the building. Or at least, he thought it might be music. Shaking the snow off his head, he ducked under the low doorway and headed toward the noise.

SYBIL SAT BACK on her heels, surveying the display of dowsing rods with a critical air. She liked the small brass ones best—they could fit in one's purse and be ready for any likely occurrence. But they didn't fit the rack she'd built for the longer, L-shaped rods, and she didn't like them just huddled together on the counter. She picked up a pair, hefting them lightly in her hands. She had somewhat better luck with rods than with pendulums, but not much.

With a sudden, uncanny movement the twin rods shifted to the right, moving with precision and coming to a full stop. Sybil's brown eyes followed their path to discover they were pointing at a pair of snowy feet standing in the doorway. Slowly her eyes moved upward, way upward, past long, jeans-clad legs, past a fisherman knit sweater with melting snow glistening on it, way up to a face. She uttered a tiny sound of complete panic. She felt as if she were looking into the face of the devil himself.

He was standing motionless, watching her, and the eerie stillness of his long, lean body added to the sensation. She stared back, mesmerized, unable to move. He had a narrow, dangerously beautiful face, with a strong blade of a nose, a thin, sensual mouth and the most disturbing eyes she'd ever seen. They were a golden sort of topaz that seemed to glow with an unearthly light as they stared down at her. His hair was black, unfashionably long, and he had a widow's peak in front. His eyebrows were equally black and sharply defined, emphasizing those strange, otherworldly eyes. He stood there without saying a word, and those eyes seemed to hypnotize her.

Sybil stared up at him, unmoving, and gulped.

"I suppose you're Sybil." The vision shimmered, altered, moved and dissolved. The man standing in the doorway walked into the room, and she could see that he was only a man after all, albeit a good-looking one. Also an extremely bad-tempered one. "Don't they ever salt the roads around here? I've been sliding on sheer ice for the last thirty miles."

"Salt is bad for the environment," she said absently. "Yes, I'm Sybil Richardson. Who are you?" It was a stupid question. She didn't need psychic powers to guess, and to know that all her previous suppositions had been dead wrong.

"Nicholas Fitzsimmons. You were expecting someone else on a night like this?" he snapped. Even in temper it was a a charming voice, she had to admit that. Low-pitched, musical, as mesmerizing as his golden eyes had been. Except those eyes were so bad-tempered and blazing they no longer had any effect on her except irritation.

"Hope springs eternal," she said cheerfully, dropping the brass rods back onto the shelf and rising to her full height. On top of everything else her entire family was taller than she was, most of them topping five feet ten, and the lean giant in front of her brought out her usual feelings of inadequacy. A short, sweating hunk was what she wanted, she added to herself. "I'm sorry about the roads, but as I expect you'll realize, they're not my fault."

For a moment he seemed to collect himself. "No, you're right," he said grudgingly. "They're not your fault."

"Besides," she added with a trace of mischief, "they're not really that bad."

"When were you last out, Miss Richardson?" he demanded in a voice as icy as Route 15.

"An hour ago," Sybil lied blithely.

"Then why were there no tire tracks in the snow?"

She grinned. "I did what I always do in bad weather, Mr. Fitzsimmons. I levitated."

"Very funny," he said sourly.

Finally Sybil took pity on him. "You'll get used to them sooner or later," she said, flicking off the lights and moving toward him, forcing herself not to react to his intimidating height. "And you'll feel better after you've eaten."

He was still watching her warily. "Deke Appleton said you'd make arrangements for me?"

She smiled, only a twinge of guilt marring her composure. "And I have. First you're coming to a meeting of our psychic group. It's the best way for you to meet everyone, and we're having a potluck supper so you'll be well fed. You'll be spending the night at Deke's, and tomorrow we'll get you settled into the old Black Farm."

"What's wrong with the old Black Farm?"

She looked up at him. She was sure her voice had sounded completely normal when she'd mentioned it. "Why, nothing at all. It's got all the amenities, including electric heat if you get tired of dealing with the wood stoves. You'll be very comfortable."

He just looked at her, and those topaz eyes glowed slightly in the dimly lit room. "Maybe," he said. His voice sounded low, sexy and very skeptical.

Sybil, remembering the Black Farm's history, merely smiled.

Chapter Two

The temperature had dropped drastically since earlier in the day, and Sybil shivered as she pulled her down coat closer around her, ducking her head as she stepped outside. It had to be down in the teens, and the snow was falling at an unpleasantly enthusiastic rate. She looked at the sleek, beautiful lines of the Jaguar sedan and gave an audible sniff.

"No wonder you slid all the way," she said. "You need something a little more prosaic on these roads."

"Like that?" His tone of voice as he gestured to her aging Subaru was as contemptuous as hers had been.

"It'll get you where you want to go," she replied, sweeping the drifts of snow off the windshield. "Which is more than I can say of yours."

With an effort her unwelcome visitor controlled his temper, but she could see the irritation sweep across his handsome face. Good, she thought, ignoring her spasm of guilt. If he could be argumentative and bad-tempered, so could she.

"Would you care to place a small bet on it?" he said evenly.

"Nope. Deke lives on a back road and I don't want to spend hours digging you out of whatever snowdrift your elegant car chooses to slide into. You'll have to drive with me. We're late anyway, and the group likes to get started promptly during the winter months so everyone can get home early."

"Then you admit the roads are bad."

"Of course I do. We treat the weather and the roads with the respect they're due. We don't try to drive too fast in cars that are unequipped for the weather. I bet you don't even have snow tires."

"All-weather radials."

She shook her head. "Not good enough. Steve at the garage can fix you up with studded snows. That is, if you're still planning to stay for a while."

"I'm planning to stay," he said in a deceptively even voice.

"Sorry to disappoint you."

She gave him her dazzling smile, and for a second he looked startled, blinking those extraordinary eyes of his. "Oh, I'm not disappointed," she said. "I think you'll end up being quite entertaining. The cat among the pigeons, and all that."

"I aim to please," he said.

"I find that very unlikely," she said frankly. "I happen to have read your books, and your reactionary views aren't going to be very welcome. But winters are long and boring around here, and you'll provide fodder for some good arguments if nothing else."

"I'm glad I have my uses."

"Get in the car," she said, scraping the ice off the windshield. "Just dump the papers in the back seat."

He opened the door. "What about the Tab cans littering the floor?" he demanded.

"Kick 'em out of the way. Deke's farm is only three miles away—you won't even notice them."

"Don't you want to start warming up the car?"

"It wastes gas. We try to be energy-conscious around here."

He was shivering slightly as he slid into the front seat, and for a moment Sybil took pity on him. With an effort she hardened her heart. Nicholas Fitzsimmons mocked everything she held dear; she was damned if she was going to welcome him into her world just because he was the best-looking man she'd ever seen in her life.

Besides, it wouldn't matter. The moment he set those wonderful topaz eyes on Dulcy he'd be lost, and Sybil Richardson would be relegated to the status of a sexless maiden aunt. She'd seen it happen too many times, and it failed to disturb her. It wouldn't bother her this time, either. Dulcy would know just how to handle him; she wasn't sure that she could.

She climbed into the driver's seat, turned the frozen key that she'd left in the ignition and listened to the engine's customary whine of protest. Nicholas's tall, lean body was shivering beside her, his long arms were wrapped around his torso and his teeth were clenched. She turned the key again, and once more the engine chugged, sputtered and died.

"Third time's the trick," she said, turning it again. It caught, rumbled ominously and died.

"Why don't you dowse it and find out what's wrong?" Nicholas said cynically, the effect ruined by his chattering teeth.

"Good idea," Sybil said, whipping off her glove and running her fingers on the dashboard.

"What in God's name are you doing besides courting frostbite?"

"Dowsing. You can find all sorts of things besides water, you know. I run my fingers over any smooth surface and if it sticks the answer's yes."

"Or else your fingers have frozen to the dashboard," he snapped.

She ignored him. "Nope, the car's okay," she said, putting her glove back on. She turned the key once more and the engine zoomed into life. They sat there for a long moment, both of them listening intently. "What did I tell you?" she said proudly.

"Where's the heat?"

"It won't do any good to turn it on yet. It'll just blast cold air on your feet."

"Cold air is already blasting on my feet," Nicholas said.

"Turn the damned thing on."

"It's your funeral." She turned the blower on high, shoved the stubborn gear into reverse and backed out onto the icy road.

They drove in a silence only marred by the sound of Nicholas's chattering teeth. Sybil's guilt finally got the better of her.

"I have a blanket in the back," she offered.

"No, thanks. I like freezing to death," he said with mock politeness. "Did you say you were taking me to Deke's?"

"Only for the night. He and Margaret are leaving for Europe tomorrow. It's a shame, too. Besides being the president of the SOWWs . . ."

"Sows?"

"Society of Water Witches. SOWWs for short. Anyway, Deke's a water dowser, or water witch—right up your alley. You'll just have to find your own partisans."

"So what's this psychic group we're going to? Is it part of the SOWWs?"

"Yes and no. All the members of the group are members of the SOWWs, and they all believe in dowsing. But half of the society doesn't believe the stuff we're into. New Age stuff, like earth energies, sacred geometry, past-life regressions, trance mediums, nature religions."

"Nature religions like witchcraft?" he asked.

She steeled herself for his disapproval. "White witchcraft," she corrected. "And Native American religions. That sort of thing."

"You're a bunch of dangerous idiots," he said calmly enough.

The red haze of fury that formed in front of Sybil's eyes almost obscured the icy road. "And you're an opinionated turkey."

She felt rather than saw the meditative smile that lighted up his dark face. "As long as we have that clear in our minds."

"Quite clear."

"You do realize that I find you as infuriating as you find me?" he inquired as Sybil slid to a stop in the crowded driveway of the brightly lighted house.

"That's some consolation," she said sweetly, turning off the car. She turned to face him in the darkness, about to order him out into the cold, when she stopped, motionless, astonished. The heat had never come on during the short ride, and her breath was a billow of icy vapor that rose and met his, mingling with it in the confines of the old Subaru. She stared at the clouds of breath in front of her, watching them entwine and tangle like two lovers, and a frisson of premonition ran over her backbone.

She met his eyes. They looked almost as startled as hers did, and his breath, his mouth, moved suddenly closer.

"What are you doing?" she whispered, not moving, not backing away.

He stopped within millimeters of her, and she could feel the warmth of his breath in the cold car. "I'm not sure," he said in an equally soft voice. "I'm either making a pass at you or trying to intimidate you. Maybe both."

"Either way it's a lost cause," she said, her startled eyes looking into his.

"Oh, I'm not so sure...." He moved closer, but this time she did move, ducking out of his reach and out of the door before he could make contact.

"Bring those papers with you, will you?" Her voice sounded admirably calm. She kept her pace modest, decorous, as she headed for the front door, and he caught up with her before she made it.

"I don't suppose there'll be something hot and strong in there?" he asked, and the moment in the car might never have existed.

"Herb tea or hot cider."

"I was thinking more along the lines of coffee and whiskey."

"Drugs cloud the mind and affect your psychic concentration," she said.

"I have no psychic concentration. I just have a frozen body."

"I'm sure Deke will take pity on you."

"I don't know if there's any pity in the entire state of Vermont," he said morosely, following her into the light and warmth of the crowded old farmhouse. Sybil made no reply.

Sybil could never enter Deke and Margaret Appleton's place without a sense of disorientation. On the outside it was the perfect, rustic Vermont farmhouse, with narrow, white-painted clapboards and green shutters, a tin roof to repel the snow and cozy little dormer windows placed at haphazard angles. Inside it was pure Scarsdale, imported by the Appletons when they retired from their suburban New York home. From the baby-blue wall-to-wall carpeting that always got tracked with mud, salt and snow, to the beige chintz sofas that always picked up every trace of dog hair clinging to Sybil's clothing, to the spindly little Chippendale bamboo chairs that looked as if they wouldn't safely hold anyone over forty-five pounds and were now obscured beneath several two-hundred-pound-plus Vermonters, it was elegant, downstate and impractical.

Margaret Appleton had resisted the impulse to put up her Christmas tree the day after Thanksgiving, as far too many Vermonters had begun doing, but there were a few tasteful touches—a papier-mâché reindeer and sleigh on the mantel, some artfully arranged evergreens in a copper vase. Cat spruce, Sybil thought, wrinkling her nose at the litter-box smell. Trust a flatlander not to know the difference between balsam and its smelly cousin.

There was a good crowd tonight, despite the weather, she realized with a start of nervousness. The smells that filled the house were wonderfully down-home in contrast with the upscale luxury—the baked beans that were de rigueur for any potluck dinner, spicy chili and Leona's latest concoction, which always tasted of rosemary no matter what she cooked. The scent of the mulled cider mingled with the wood smoke and the faint, lingering trace of wet wool slowly drying in the warmth of the overheated house. She gave Nicholas a glance in time to see him wrinkle the nose that was just as aristocratic as she had imagined. Maybe she had more psychic ability than she thought. She certainly knew he'd have that disdainful nose. She just hadn't realized it would be surrounded by such a handsome face.

"Too many people," she muttered to a surprisingly patient Nicholas. "Let's find the kitchen." Without thinking she took his hand to pull him from the crowded, noisy room. It was a mistake—she wasn't used to touching men, and his hand was cool and strong beneath hers. But not for anything would she back off. She pulled him into the gleaming modern kitchen, shut the door behind them and leaned against the chrome and Formica countertop with a sigh of relief.

"They're a wonderful bunch of people," she said, pushing at the wisps of hair that were escaping her coronet of braids. "But in large doses they can be overwhelming."

"Why are we hiding in the kitchen?" he inquired. "Have you developed a sudden taste for my company?"

He was still looking a little blue around the edges, and Sybil no longer fought the guilt that she'd been flirting with. "I thought you might like a moment or two to warm up before you had to cope with the full force of the Danbury Seekers of Enlightenment."

"Oh, God," Nicholas moaned. "Who thought of that repulsive name?"

"I did. And I have someone I want you to meet. She'll be here sooner or later—she always ends up in the kitchen." She smiled, very pleased with herself. "I think you two will make a wonderful couple."

She'd startled him out of his bad temper. "Are you matchmaking?"

"Why not? It keeps me entertained."

"And my intended is some woman who always ends up in kitchens? I presume she weighs about three hundred pounds."

Sybil smiled. "You're a big man, Nicholas. You'll manage."

She'd pushed him too far. "Listen, I don't need matchmaking, I don't need the Danbury Seekers of Enlightenment and I don't need your wonderfully solicitous care. I need—"

The door opened at that moment, and Dulcy walked through, letting it swing shut behind her. "Hi, Sybil," she said with real warmth. "I wondered where you were hiding. I've been hearing about your contribution to our little gathering. Is this the Grinch Who Stole Christmas?" She gestured toward Nicholas's suddenly still figure.

Sybil nodded. "Nicholas Fitzsimmons, Dulcy Badenham. Make him welcome, Dulcy." And she slipped from the kitchen before anyone could stop her.

Nicholas watched her go with mixed emotions. No, they weren't mixed at all—they were pure regret. He turned back to the paragon who had entered the kitchen and allowed himself a long, leisurely look. One that Dulcy permitted with a faint smile of amusement.

She was quite a sight, he had to grant Sybil that. She must have been close to six feet tall, with a long, willowy body with just the right amount of graceful curves. Her hair was white-blond, and hung straight and thick to her tiny waist. Her eyes were a hazy, mystical blue, her skin was a flawless porcelain, her mouth a sensual rosebud. She was a perfect, untouched beauty, with even the amazing asset of clear intelligence and humor shining from those eyes that watched him watching her. And she moved him not one tiny bit.

Sybil had presented her friend with the air of one offering a great treat. The expression on her plain, dark face had been one of smug pleasure, certain that her matchmaking had succeeded. And all he wanted to do was chase after her and argue some more.

"Finished looking?" Dulcy had a deep, beautiful voice to match her appearance. With an effort Nicholas dragged his attention back from Sybil's dubious charms.

"Very nice," he said absently. "Where did Sybil disappear to?"

"Probably to get something to eat. Welcome to Danbury, Nicholas Fitzsimmons. Are you going to make fools of us in your next book?" She sounded no more than vaguely interested, and he smiled a distant smile.

"I doubt it. I don't think the Seekers of Truth are worthy of that much print space. There are any number of crackpot psychic groups all over the country—I doubt you have anything special to offer.''

"You might be surprised,'' she said tranquilly. "And we're the Seekers of Enlightenment. Better known as the Spook Group.''

"Who came up with that one?''

"Sybil, of course. She doesn't take herself nearly as seriously as you seem to.''

Score another point for Sybil, he thought. He looked at the glorious Dulcy, wondering why she left him so entirely unmoved. "Who are you, the resident familiar?''

"I'm a lawyer in St. Johnsbury. I have a fairly good-size practice in criminal law.'' She moved closer to him. "I'm also a white witch.''

"Sure you are.'' He was getting bored now, along with being cold and hungry. Dulcy might be a smart lady, but she had the same bizarre fantasies everyone else did. "What's on the agenda for tonight?''

"I think Leona is planning a presentation, with Sybil's help.''

"A presentation?''

The door opened, and Sybil reappeared, divested of her down coat, her knee-length felt-lined boots, her three scarves, her heavy sweater and her mittens. She looked like a thin brown elf, and her braids were sagging ominously around her small face.

"Past-life regression,'' she announced in answer to his overheard question. In her hands she held a plate heaped high with food, and she presented it like a sacrificial offering. "Leona's going to take me back to a previous incarnation. It's a fairly common technique. Leona will lead me back through time in a guided meditation and we'll see if we can pick up a past life.'' She shoved the plate into his hands. "Eat something.'' She looked back and forth with a hopeful expression between Dulcy's tall, elegant body and his own, and once more he was reminded of a sparrow in search of a juicy worm.

It wasn't forthcoming. "Matchmaking again?'' Dulcy inquired, not in the slightest bit embarrassed. "You've struck out. I'm not Nicholas's type.''

"Did she tell you she was a lawyer?'' Sybil hadn't given up yet.

"She did,'' he replied.

"Still no go, eh? I'll keep looking.''

"No, thank you. I can take care of my own sexual needs." She grinned. "To each his own."

"I didn't mean that," he began.

"Listen, you don't have to explain yourself," she said sweetly. "Eat your dinner. Leona's waiting for us."

"Us?"

"You might get to be a guinea pig, too."

"The hell I will—" She vanished again, and the door swung back and forth gently.

"Don't fight it," Dulcy counseled. "Sybil can be very determined."

He barely heard her. She had moved quickly, without Dulcy's grace, without the languid sensuality of most women of his acquaintance. As she darted away from him with a delicious grin on her dark face, he was conscious of a sudden uprush of desire more intense than he'd felt in years.

"So can I," he said softly, more to Sybil's vanished figure than to Dulcy's shell-like ears. "So can I."

Chapter Three

He didn't like Leona Coleman, not one iota. For all her dizzy charm, he had the odd feeling that it was an act. The other Seekers of Truth or Enlightenment, or whatever, at least seemed sincere enough. Leona struck him as patently manipulative. And he especially didn't like it that she was manipulating Sybil.

Particularly now that he was feeling decidedly mellow toward her. He'd eaten just enough of the highly spiced, unrecognizable food she'd handed him to still his hunger, and then he'd followed her back into the crowded confines of the Spook Group. He had met Deke and Margaret Appleton, a surprisingly mundane couple in their early seventies. He'd corresponded with Deke, one of the best water dowsers in the country, and he matched his expectations: a short, rosy-faced little man with dreamy blue eyes. His wife was a matriarch who topped him by almost a foot and had clearly turned her social tendencies to the material at hand. She was the perfect, overwhelming hostess in her self-consciously British tweeds and overloud voice, and Nicholas wished he had stayed in a motel for his first night instead of accepting Margaret Appleton's heavy-handed hospitality.

He had been standing there, bemused, listening to her holding forth on energy lines beneath the main altar at Chartres Cathedral when Sybil had reappeared out of the crowd. She put a hot earthenware mug into his hand and slipped away before he could break Margaret's stranglehold. He stood there, a polite prisoner, and took a sip.

Bless the woman. It was coffee—strong, hot, black, just the way he liked it. And there was enough whiskey in it to float a battleship. He took another long, appreciative sip and began to consider Sybil's undeniable merits.

But his temporarily sanguine mood had now faded. He was sitting on one of the chintz sofas, sandwiched between a dairy farmer from Walden and a librarian from Greensboro. The dairy farmer hadn't changed his boots since he'd done the evening chores, and the faint scent of manure mingled with and drowned out the smell of whiskey from his coffee. The librarian favored musky perfume and coy glances. If there'd been a spare inch in the now candlelit room, he would have moved to it. But every space was packed, a hush had fallen over the expectant group, and Sybil sat cross-legged on the floor, her hands resting comfortably on her knees, her thin shoulders relaxed, as Leona began her damned mumbo jumbo. Nicholas felt his tension increase.

It was a simple enough technique, he thought objectively, listening to Leona's voice drone on and on. She was hypnotizing Sybil, or aiding Sybil in hypnotizing herself, and the suggestive voice was creating a dreamy mood throughout the room. It would have been easy enough to succumb, after the long day and the generous shot of whiskey, but that was the last thing he had in mind. He was intent on watching Leona, catching her little tricks. Not that he planned to say or do anything about it. He merely wanted to observe.

He'd gone through just what Sybil was about to go through, had been guided by one of the best. Past-life regression involved self-hypnosis, being guided back through time until a likely period was picked, and listening to the fantasies come forth. His own had been quite colorful, involving the French Revolution and his sexual adventures with a Countess Félicité. He'd imagined himself to be some sort of revolutionary, and according to Swami Benana he'd come to a bad end, but it was entertaining while it lasted. He'd listened with real amusement to the tape the Swami, whose real name was Harry Johnson, had made.

But Harry, while he was absurdly gullible, had at least believed in what he was doing, and had done it in the spirit of fun. Leona was intoning in a singsong chant that was making his blood run cold. Sybil sat there, at her mercy, her eyes closed, waiting for God knows what.

"Where are you now, Sybil?" Leona asked gently. "Can you tell us what's happening to you?"

Sybil opened her eyes. They were dazed, with none of their earlier clever mischievousness. Nicholas quickly drained his coffee and tried to keep himself from putting a stop to this farce.

"It's long, long ago," she said, her voice dreamy. "I'm in a cold place. I'm wearing skins around my body."

"Tell me more," Leona urged.

"There are horses. I've been training horses," she murmured, and an appreciative gasp arose from the enthralled company.

Nicholas shook his head silently. She must have been reading Jean Auel. They were going to have to sit through half-baked retellings of the *Clan of the Cave Bear*. It might take all night.

But Leona wasn't interested in a secondhand Ayla. "Come ahead a bit, dear. Into the warmth and light. What are you wearing now?"

There was a long, eerie silence, and then suddenly Sybil giggled. It was an enchanting sound, sexy and delicious, and once more in the darkness Nicholas felt that astounding reaction.

"Not much at all. An emerald necklace," she said. "And diamonds around my ankle."

A sudden sense of horrified disbelief swept over him. He sat forward, intent, staring at the two women in the center of the darkened room.

"What day is it, my dear? What is your name?" Leona cooed.

Sybil grinned, an impish upturning of her suddenly sexy mouth. "It's July 13, 1789. And I am Félicité, Countess de Lavallière."

He must have groaned. There were sudden, hushing noises, glares in his direction. With an extreme effort he bit down on the protest he was about to make.

"I must have complete silence," Leona addressed the hushed crowd like a cross schoolteacher. She returned to her subject, her voice low and crooning once more. "And what are you doing, Countess? Why aren't you wearing anything?"

"Because I'm waiting for my lover, of course."

The librarian beside him sighed gustily, and the musk wafted around him.

"Who is your lover, Countess?"

"Oh, I'm not allowed to tell. It is very bad of me, very naughty, but I don't care."

Leona had clearly had enough of that low, sexy chuckle.

"Very well, let's move ahead."

"I don't want to," Sybil piped up. "I want to talk about Alex."

"We will move ahead—"

"He is so handsome," she said with a lusty sigh. "He has the most wonderful eyes, *au diable, et...*" Her musings had dropped into very idiomatic and graphic French. Her accent was perfect, and Nicholas understood every word she said. He wondered if he was blushing.

"We will move ahead," Leona said again, her tone brooking no disobedience. "It is winter now, and—"

Sybil's face had crumpled in despair. He watched in suspended amazement as her huge brown eyes filled with tears, her mouth trembled, her body seemed to cave in around her. "No," she screamed, and the sound was loud and shocking in the packed living room. "No, he can't be dead!" And she collapsed, weeping, on the baby-blue carpeting.

Nicholas had had enough. "Take her out of it," he ordered, his voice cutting across the excited murmur of voices.

"Really, it can't be interfered with," Leona protested stubbornly. "It's never worked this well."

Nicholas rose to his full height, knowing he made an impressive sight in the flickering candlelight, knowing and using it to his advantage in this group of gullible souls. "Take her out of it, damn you. Now!"

He was careful not to overplay. He kept his voice low, a silky menace, knowing that half of this scene was carefully staged theatrics and knowing his performance had to fit. But half of it was a woman weeping for her dead lover, lost in time, and he wanted her brought out of it with a desperation that amazed him.

"All right," Leona acquiesced with poor grace. "Though we're missing a wonderful chance...."

"Get her out of it," Deke piped up. "We don't want to see poor Sybil so miserable."

Nicholas knew he should sit down and keep silent. But Leona was shaking Sybil, her voice sharp, and still she lay there weeping, murmuring the name of her lover over and over again.

Without further hesitation he stepped over the people sitting on the floor in front of him and reached Sybil's side, brushing away Leona's rough hands and substituting his own gentle ones.

At the different touch she opened her eyes, which were swimming with tears. "Alex," she whispered in disbelief. "I thought you were dead." She spoke in French, and without thinking he responded in the same language.

"I'm right here, my love." And she sank into his arms.

He held her as Leona intoned her mumbo jumbo words, held her gently as she slowly returned from her self-induced fantasy. "You're back now, Sybil," Leona said, still sounding disgruntled. "You're here in Danbury, and Professor Fitzsimmons is holding you."

He felt her stiffen. Slowly he released her, preparing himself but still startled to see the expression on her face. It was a combination of surprise and irritation, as if he'd been too forward and she couldn't quite figure out why. The only thing at odds were the tears still swimming in her eyes.

"Copping a cheap feel, Nicholas?" she murmured under her breath. "I thought you took care of those things yourself."

"You ought to have your mouth washed out with soap," he muttered back, rising to his full height.

"Try it," she taunted, loud enough for Leona to hear.

"I must ask you to resume your seat, Nicholas," she said sternly. "We've lost valuable ground."

"You're not doing it again," he said flatly. "Not to Sybil."

"I most certainly am. She's been the most receptive subject we've had so far and—"

"No," he said. "Practice on someone else."

"I don't believe you have any say in the matter," Leona, too, could be silky-voiced. The two of them, along with everyone else in the room, turned to Sybil.

He could see her hesitate, and he knew damned well she'd like to spite him. But she wasn't a fool; she knew her limits.

"Not tonight, I think," she said gently. "That was pretty rough. Let's do it later."

"It may not work as well later."

She gave Leona a reassuring little pat. "If it's meant to work, it will. Haven't you always told me that?"

Score one for Sybil, Nicholas thought sourly. Leona had no argument left.

"Turn on the lights," the old woman announced. "I think we've all had enough. And I, for once, need sustenance. I feel quite depleted."

"What about you?" Nicholas hadn't moved from Sybil's side. The people around them had begun talking, filling the room with an irritating buzz, but for the moment he had the odd, pleasant feeling that they were alone there, surrounded by white noise.

"Drained would be a better word," she said, taking his hand and rising to her feet.

"It's amazing what tricks our minds can play on us," he said.

"Is that what you think it was? A trick?"

"Do you remember what you dreamed?"

"Dreamed," Sybil echoed. "Not much. Part of it was so horrible I don't even want to think about it." She shivered in the overheated room.

He hesitated for a moment, then on impulse quoted an old saying. "He who sits down to eat with the devil sups with a long fork." But he said it in French.

She looked up at him in complete confusion. "What?"

He began to repeat it, but she shook her head. "In English, please. My French is third-grade level and completely lousy."

He just stared at her. Her French had been superb, a precise, Parisian French. And he looked up, past her shoulder, to stare directly into Leona's triumphant little eyes.

THE DRIVE HOME from Deke Appleton's seemed longer than seven miles. The roads were icy, but the Subaru could handle them. The heater finally decided to work, and at least the snow had stopped. Sybil shivered slightly, wrapped her scarf around her aching head, and drove onward, her eyes watering from concentration.

So Dulcy and Nicholas hadn't hit it off. The thought should have depressed and disturbed her. There was no reason why she should find it such a source of secret delight. Doubtless he liked short, buxom brunettes instead of tall, willowy blondes. There was no way he could prefer plain ordinary women of indeterminate everything. She was still safe, if she wanted to be. Right now she didn't need her life complicated by someone like Nicholas Fitzsimmons. To be sure, he was a very handsome man; one couldn't help but respond to such good looks. When he wasn't wearing that bad-tempered pout he was even more irresistible. She'd brought him the whiskey-laced coffee as a peace offering, and the quick, grateful look he'd cast her way had almost taken her breath away. Not to mention the expression in those disturbing eyes of his when she'd awakened from Leona's induced nightmare to find him holding her with all the tenderness of a lover.

But then, there'd been that startled, disbelieving expression on his face when he'd babbled in French at her. She could understand a couple of words, but her grasp of the language had been rudimentary, to say the least. Languages were never her forte; she did better in English and art, less well in practical matters involving tenses and genders and declensions.

She hadn't even said good-night to him. She'd ducked out like the coward she was, before half of the Spook Group was ready to leave. She'd see him soon enough; Deke and Margaret were going to drop him back at his car tomorrow on their way to the airport. And she'd have to see him settled into the Black Farm. She'd hoped to foist that particular duty off on Leona, but the antagonism between the two of them made her own relationship with Nicholas seem like love at first sight. No, she'd have to do the dirty work. Maybe in the bright light of day he wouldn't have that odd effect on her.

Except that in December in northern Vermont there was unlikely to be any bright light during the day. Most likely more snow, maybe more sleet, certainly more gloom. Maybe she'd take the day off and go Christmas shopping—that would cheer her. Or maybe she'd just sleep in, play with the dogs and let Nicholas find the farm by himself.

No, she couldn't be that much of a coward. She'd get a good night's sleep, and tomorrow she'd be in much better shape to deal with a bad-tempered, dangerously handsome, surprisingly charming thorn in her side. After all, he probably hadn't spared an extra thought to her all evening. She'd get him settled, and they could forget about each other.

And maybe hell would freeze over.

THE BED WAS TOO SOFT, too narrow and too short. Nicholas was used to sleeping in a queen-size loft bed, and the narrow little cot to which Margaret Appleton had shown him resembled a torture chamber. He knew without asking that the Appletons were one of those couples who didn't own anything larger than a twin bed. With a grunt of frustration he punched the limp pillow and accomplished the impressive feat of turning over without falling off the narrow mattress.

Not that he would have slept well anywhere. For all the discomfort of his body, the discomfort in his mind far outweighed it. So far he couldn't find a way to reconcile himself with what he had seen and heard and, most particularly, what he felt.

But...

He didn't believe in past-life regressions. It was that simple. He didn't believe in reincarnation, either, or at least, he was still highly skeptical. Most past-life regressions were the result of a combination of self-hypnosis, fantasy and half-formed memories from bad historical romances the subjects had read in their youth. They had nothing to do with real life and hard facts.

But...

Sybil's French had been perfect. And the look of blank incomprehension on her face, when he'd spoken to her later, hadn't been feigned. Of course, there were explanations for that. People knew a lot more in their subconscious than their conscious let them realize. She'd quite probably assimilated a great deal of French from foreign movies and years of French class that her mind had resisted.

But...

She'd looked different when she was under hypnosis. That sensual grin, that sexy chuckle were nothing like the face she'd presented to the world at large yesterday. Perhaps yesterday was a bad day, perhaps she was usually like that gamine and the transformation had surprised only him.

But...

She'd known about Countess Félicité and the onset of the French Revolution. And she'd had a lover with his middle name, Alexandre, a lover who'd met a bad end. But Félicité was a common enough French name, and, of course, any fantasy countess would have a lover. They probably both got the name Alexandre from Dumas *père ou fils*. There was no way either Leona or Sybil could have known about his own fantasies, but coincidences do happen, and they must have happened last night.

But...

It still didn't explain his reaction. His eerie, half-submerged recognition when she chuckled. His body and his reluctant mind had been flirting with an unwanted attraction to her all night. When she'd wept in his arms, he'd given up the fight. For some reason he wanted her, more than he'd wanted anyone in a long time. The musky librarian left him cold, the glorious Dulcy had no effect on him whatsoever. For some inexplicable reason he wanted Sybil, and he couldn't get that wanting out of his mind.

He was going to have to watch Leona. He didn't trust her, and he didn't like her effect on Sybil. Then again, he didn't like Sybil's effect on him. Hell, right now he didn't like anything much.

Tomorrow it would begin to make sense. In the bright light of day, Sybil would lose whatever arcane attraction she held for him. He'd get settled into the Black Farm and begin his research, and avoid the Seekers of Enlightenment or Truth from now on. Superstition and mumbo jumbo had always been contagious, how could he have forgotten? He had to keep his mind clear and his options open.

And if one of his options included Sybil Richardson, he was open-minded enough to consider it. Though he knew damned well she was going to bring him nothing but trouble.

He punched the pillow once more, imagining Leona's round face beneath his fist. He'd never run from trouble before, and he wasn't about to start now. Sybil might prove a very delightful sort of trouble indeed. If he were one of her flaky friends, he'd run his hands along the side of the bed to dowse it. Instead of courting splinters, he turned over and finally went to sleep, only to be plagued with erotic dreams of a Countess Félicité who looked exactly like Sybil Richardson.

Chapter Four

Sybil Richardson had a headache, a nervous stomach, a scratchy throat and the worst case of nerves she'd had since she faced her assembled family last Fourth of July. She sat at her desk in the office of the SOWWs, thankful to be alone, and tried to talk herself out of her ill-feeling.

Sure she had a headache. When she had braided her hair this morning she'd been in too much of a hurry, not to mention in a bad mood, and doubtless had braided too tightly, then stuck hairpins into her scalp. Her stomach was nervous because all that she had managed to swallow all morning was black coffee. She had overdosed on that because for once Leona wasn't there to disapprove or to make her weak peppermint tea with too much honey in it, and Sybil had gotten carried away.

The scratchy throat wasn't unexpected on such a raw, blustery day, and the nerves were probably because she hadn't slept very well last night. And that must have been because of that disturbing nightmare, half terrifying, half erotic, all about the French Revolution.

She was lying to herself, she admitted with a sigh, taking another sip of the cooling coffee and slipping a few of the more lethal hairpins from her coiled braids. There was one reason for her current state of physical and spiritual unease, and one reason alone. And that reason was a man who had just been dropped off in the snowy driveway and who was now peering at his precious car like an anxious father.

She considered throwing on her coat and rushing out to forestall his invasion of her territory. The sooner she got him settled into the Black Farm the sooner she'd be rid of him. Or would she? Deke had already made it clear that Nicholas should have free rein over his office and the adjacent library on the second floor of the old building. With Sybil's luck he would be there every day, haunting her, driving her even crazier than Leona did.

Well, she could take it. She could deal with the reactionary old men who made up the board of trustees, she could deal with her family in small and even large doses, and she could certainly deal with one rather large, distinguished-looking gentleman afflicted with antiquated ideas and a bad temper. Sure she could.

She heard the silver bells on the front door ring, she heard the stamping of snow-covered feet in the hallway, but she made no move. Better to make him come to her, rather than to seek him out. She could sit there, cool, remote, a distant, amused smile playing around her mouth, while he blustered....

The footsteps moved away, back toward the bookstore, and Sybil swore, the amused smile vanishing. "I'm in here," she called out, disgruntled.

"I know." His voice drifted back, and if anyone was amused, he was. "I'm just checking your book supplies."

"Hell and damnation," Sybil muttered, shoving herself back from her desk and starting after him. The last thing she wanted was to have him poking around her shop, sneering at her choices, mocking her passions. "Wait a minute," she yelled. "I'll be right there."

She raced out of the office, not even bothering to put on her shoes, and the snow he'd tracked in sank into her wool socks. She cursed again, slipped on the next patch of melting snow, and barreled directly into a tall, immovable figure.

Hands reached up to catch her arms, strong, surprisingly gentle hands. Her eyes were level with his shoulders, her flesh still smarted from the impact of their bodies, and she waited for her usual feelings of irritated intimidation to wash over her. They didn't come.

She stepped back, yanking herself out of his grasp with only a trace of startled panic. "You tracked snow in," she said belligerently, staring at the unbuttoned top button of his blue wool shirt.

"You aren't wearing any shoes." His voice was warm, low and beguiling, with none of last night's bad temper apparent. She looked up, startled, directly into those topaz-colored eyes and for a moment felt very much as she'd felt last night, as if she had drifted into a hypnotic state. But dangers had lurked in that blissful lassitude, and danger lurked in those wonderful eyes of his. She stood there, wiggling her damp feet, reminding herself that he was Trouble.

"I don't wear shoes in the office," she said. "What did you want to see in the bookstore?"

"I wanted to see what percentage of your stock was purely dowsing and what was this new-age crap."

Any accord that might have begun between them vanished as swiftly as the snow had melted on the carpet. "As much as I want," she snapped. "Why?"

"Research, Sybil. I'm interested in how much other things have infiltrated the bastions of pure water divining."

Her reaction was quick. "Give me a break! No one wants to interfere with your prejudices and opinions. Leave us ours."

"I don't want to interfere, I just want to document them. My book isn't just on water dowsing, it's on the division between traditionalists and the new wave."

"And we know which side you're on."

"I have an open mind," he said loftily.

"Sure you do. While you check out the 'new-age crap' in my bookstore," she snapped, finally bringing her condescending smile into play.

He didn't appreciate it. "I never said I was tactful."

"You don't have to be tactful. You're a college professor, you get to cram your ideas down students' throats and no one will dare disagree with you. Well, I'm not your student, Professor Fitzsimmons. And I think you're full of—"

"Sybil!" Leona's soft voice cut her off in midsentence. She had just a moment to register Nicholas's look of irritation before that bland, superior expression swept over his handsome face as he turned to greet the newcomer.

"Hi, Leona," Sybil said sheepishly. "Nicholas and I were just having a discussion."

"I heard it," she said. "Do you realize the negative energy that is flowing through this place right now? Your aura is very tight and small, Sybil. Very tight and small."

"What about mine?" There was just the suggestion of a sarcastic drawl in Nicholas's voice.

"Bright red, Mr. Fitzsimmons. Red and small and tight and angry. This is not the kind of energy we need here in the office,'' she said. ''I think the two of you should keep away from each other.''

''I'm sure you do,'' he said softly.

Sybil cast him a brief, curious glance before rushing to placate her friend. ''Don't worry about it, Leona. I'm just in a bad mood today—I'd fight with Mother Theresa herself. And we'll get our negative energy out of here. I'm going to see Nicholas settled into the Black Farm while you watch the office. I should be back in less than an hour.''

''Perhaps I should go instead,'' Leona offered. ''You could stay here and clear the office.''

''Clear the office?'' Nicholas echoed. ''Isn't that a little extreme?''

Leona gave him a reproving look. ''Professor Fitzsimmons, you know enough about all forms of dowsing to know I meant psychic clearing, not a physical overhaul. Sybil can sit and meditate, sending waves of healing energy through this place to clear out the angry vibrations.''

''Does she do this on company time?''

Sybil couldn't help it. She giggled, earning Leona's further displeasure. ''Never mind, Leona. I'd probably do a lousy job of it. Why don't you take care of it while I'm gone, and I'll come back in a much more peaceful mood?''

''And how will you manage that, cooped up with the professor?''

''I'm sure I can come up with something,'' Nicholas purred, and the sexual innuendo was so clear that for a moment Sybil was startled into silence. ''And please, don't call me professor. It makes me sound ancient and stuffy. Call me Nick.''

Leona didn't blink her dark little eyes, and there was no answering smile to Nick's sudden use of charm. She turned to Sybil. ''And I can smell the coffee,'' she added accusingly.

''It smells wonderful, doesn't it?'' Nick said.

''It smells like death,'' Leona intoned.

''Oh, yuck, Leona,'' Sybil protested. ''That's going too far.''

''It kills the brain cells and destroys psychic receptivity,'' Leona stated.

''Yes, but it tastes so good,'' said Sybil.

''Get your coat on and take the professor over to the Black Farm. I'll pour out that nasty stuff and brew us a nice pot of peppermint tea. It'll be waiting for you when you get back.''

Sybil considered saying "yuck" once more, then dismissed the notion. Leona was clearly distressed, and Sybil hated to distress anyone. Unless it was the tall man beside her. "That would be lovely, Leona," she said gently. "I promise you it won't take me long."

THE HELL IT WOULDN'T, Nick there and then resolved. He had every intention of keeping Sybil Richardson at the Black Farm as long as he possibly could. Apart from the fact that he hated to give her over to Leona's tender mercies, he wanted to see if he could make her laugh again. That soft, unexpected giggle had the same effect on him that her transformation as the Countess Félicité had. And while he would like nothing better than to toss her down on the nearest bed Black Farm had to offer, he'd settle for just one more giggle, one more imperceptible lowering of that guarded distrust she kept wrapped around her.

Maybe he'd have to learn tact. It had never been a commodity he'd dealt in; he preferred brutal honesty cutting through all the social lies that wasted time and intellect. But clearly Sybil, for all her obvious intelligence, had a soft spot for some of the crackpot beliefs held dear by the fringe elements of the water witching community, such as it was. If he didn't want to spend all his time dodging her glares, he'd better learn to put a guard on his tongue. Given time, she'd see reason and learn that her auras and past lives and dashboard dowsing were nothing more than parlor games.

Given time. The phrase echoed oddly in his head. He was only planning to be in Danbury for less than six weeks—just through the Christmas season and into the first weeks of the new year—and then he was off for England. What made him think he'd have time to show Sybil Richardson the error of her ways? And what made him want to?

Hell, he must be getting soft in his old age. It had been more than a year since Adelle had moved out, and while he hadn't been lonely or celibate since then, maybe he was fool enough to want to fall in love again. But Sybil Richardson would be a hell of a lousy choice, worse than Adelle, and it hadn't worked with Adelle.

Of course, it had worked for a while. For three very nice, comfortable, fun years. But Adelle wanted to get married,

Adelle wanted babies, and Adelle had wanted them immediately. While he thought for a while that he could provide those things for her, when push came to shove they both realized he couldn't. Somehow, sometime, when they weren't looking, they'd fallen out of love and into friendship. And that friendship couldn't withstand the strain of marriage and an incipient family.

They'd broken their engagement, canceled the wedding, sent back the presents, and Adelle had moved out. Now she was married to an advertising executive in Dedham and her first baby was due in two months. She was supremely happy, he was happy for her, and not for a moment did he have doubts. Regrets, maybe, but not doubts.

So for the past year he'd been enjoying his freedom. He was only thirty-four, he had enough money and an enjoyable amount of limited fame, and he was considered attractive by attractive members of the opposite sex. Surely he could hold out until he found some nice, leggy British lady untainted by crackpot ideas.

Sybil returned from her office wrapped in a lavender down coat that was leaking feathers, a handwoven shawl around her narrow shoulders, her heavy braids sagging ominously around her small, narrow face and a wary expression in her brown eyes. Nicholas, knowing he was crazy, decided that maybe leggy British ladies weren't all they were cracked up to be. And maybe he'd learn tact after all.

She waited patiently enough as he brushed the snow off his car. This time her Subaru started without complaint, and she took off with a little more reckless abandon than he could have wished as he pulled out onto the snow-packed road to follow her. For a moment he wondered if she was driving too fast in hopes that he might go off the road trying to keep up with her, and then she could once more sneer at his beloved car. The moment the thought entered his brain he dismissed it. For one thing, she'd driven just as recklessly the night before. For another, he didn't think she was that petty.

No, what it all boiled down to, he thought as they sped in tandem over the narrow back roads, was that she was a lousy driver, and with his newfound determination to be tactful, he would say absolutely nothing about it.

"You know, you're a hell of a lousy driver," he said when he climbed out of his car. They had slid down a long, winding driveway, ending up in front of a good-sized red clapboard house. The barn beside it was in as good shape as the house, far better kept up than many of the farms he'd passed. Apparently the Black family hadn't been hit by the economic crunch most farmers were going through.

Sybil was staring up at the old house, an abstract expression on her face, and he waited for her spirited defense. "I know," she said absently. "That's why I have four-wheel drive, so I can get out of all the drifts I slide into." She reached into the pocket of her coat, pulling out a clanking set of keys, and a billow of feathers wafted into the air around her.

"Since I'm not a lousy driver, I expect my Jaguar will do just fine, then," he said, slightly distracted by the way the feathers were settling back onto her coat.

"Maybe."

"What have you got against my car? Most people consider it to be very nice."

"My ex-husband had one just like it," she said in a disgruntled tone of voice.

"Aha."

"Don't aha me," she snapped. "Colin's Jaguar was an essential part of his nature. Jaguars tend to be that important, and I'm assuming it's an essential part of you. And while they're very nice cars indeed, I don't like the kind of people who own them."

Ex-husband, he thought. *That's part of it.* "What if I told you that I'm not really a Jaguar person?" he said suddenly. "What if I told you that I bought it on an impulse, to cheer myself up?"

"Then it would depend on what kind of car you used to have," she said, giving him her full attention for the first time.

"A 1963 Plymouth Valiant."

Her mouth dropped open. It was a very nice mouth, with small, white teeth, and he wondered if he should take advantage of its vulnerability. Before he could move she snapped it shut again.

"I don't believe you."

"It had 367,000 miles on it when it died," he said solemnly. She grinned then, a wide, warm smile that brought the frozen Vermont temperature up at least ten degrees, and Nick felt the strands wrap tighter and tighter around him. "Then you deserve the Jaguar," she said. "What color was your Valiant?"

"Gold."

"Mine was pale blue," she said with a reminiscent sigh. "It didn't quite make it to three hundred thousand."

"I'm surprised it made it to one hundred, given your driving."

She stuck her tongue out at him, her brown eyes bright with mischief. "Come in and see where you'll be staying for the next six weeks."

He moved up behind her as she was fiddling with the keys. "I didn't think people locked anything around here."

"Oh, we lock houses when no one lives in them. There are plenty of lowlifes who rip off summer houses and sell the good stuff down in the big city."

"Big city?"

"Boston or New York. Though why they bother to lock this place..." She let it trail off as the door swung open into an old-fashioned hallway.

"Why shouldn't they lock this place?" he demanded, suspicious.

It was easy enough to tell when Sybil Richardson was lying. Her pale cheeks flushed pink, her brown eyes looked edgy and her voice grew light and breathless. "No reason," she lied. "Close the door and I'll show you around."

He did as he was told, biding his time. There was no way he was going to let her go back to Leona until he knew exactly why no one would break into the Black Farm. Looking around, he realized that it wasn't for lack of things worth stealing. The house was in perfect condition, renovated within the past twenty years with a lot more taste than Deke and Margaret Appleton had used. There was a large living room with shiny hardwood floors, Indian rugs in perfect condition, comfortable new sofas and beautiful old tables. A large wood stove stood in front of the fireplace, with piles of dry wood beside it.

"It'll be up to you if you want to heat with wood. This place has got electric heat—that's what's on now, but on a really icy day when the wind blows it isn't enough. Besides, it costs a fortune."

"I think I can afford it," he said dryly.

"I expect anyone with a Jaguar can," she said. "There's a full bath off to the left and a bedroom, and the kitchen's on the other side. There are four more bedrooms upstairs, but they're closed off right now. You can open them up if you want, but it'll make the place even harder to heat.''

"Okay," he said mildly enough.

"You can put your car in the barn if you want—there's no garage. Or you may just want to leave it out."

"Why would I want to leave it out in this climate?"

She shrugged, her cheeks flushed, her eyes looked edgy and her voice came out light and breathless. "No reason. I'll show you the kitchen."

He followed her with mock docility, waiting his chance. He saw the bedroom with its old-fashioned double bed and pile of pillows, the modern bathroom, the remodeled kitchen and woodshed. The whole place was warm, welcoming, completely charming. He couldn't figure out why it was empty, waiting to be rented, and why Sybil Richardson was lying her head off.

He stared at the bed, with its carved mahogany headboard and the snowy windows beside it. He could imagine long mornings curled up in that bed, with Sybil's small, compact body beside him.

"Where do you live?" he asked suddenly.

She blushed, and he wondered if she was coming up with another lie. "The last house on this road," she said with an odd trace of defiance.

"How far from me?"

"A mile and a half."

"And who's my closest neighbor?"

"Right now I am. We're not far from the lake, and in the summertime there are people in the cottages. They're all closed down now, and it's just you and me."

"Cozy."

"Don't count on it." She whirled away, heading back through the living room. "If you don't have any more questions I'm going back to work."

He caught up with her in the front hallway. She hadn't even bothered to take off her coat, and she'd left a trail of feathers behind during her sudden rush. Her braids were slipping down, and he wondered how she'd look with her hair full and loose around her defiant little face.

He felt her stiffen as he put his hand on her, felt the sudden surge of awareness shoot through her, the same awareness he was feeling. He considered letting her go, then dropped the idea. He kept his hands where they were, on her arms, holding her loosely enough, but holding her nonetheless.

"Just one more question, Sybil," he said. "What makes you so uncomfortable about Black Farm?"

"Maybe it's you," she said, squirming just enough to show her displeasure, but not enough to break the bond.

"That's not it. You manage to put up with me pretty well, all things considered. Do you want to tell me the truth this time, or are you going to lie again?"

"Why should I lie?"

"You tell me."

She wet her lips nervously, but her blush didn't deepen and her eyes were steady. She shrugged, but he didn't release her.

"Someone was murdered here."

"Somehow I'm not surprised," he said with a sigh. "In the barn?"

"You're quick," she said. "In the barn. Old John Black was kicked to death by one of his horses. Except that the barn was locked from the outside, and he'd withdrawn ten thousand dollars from the bank earlier that day and no one ever found it."

"Ten thousand dollars isn't very much to kill someone for, Sybil."

"It was in 1936."

"1936?" he echoed. "You mean I'm supposed to worry about a murder that took place fifty years ago? Or are you going to tell me his ghost haunts the place?"

"No one's ever seen a ghost," she said grumpily. "But there's a bad feeling about this place, a very bad feeling. No one stays here for long."

"Neither will I. Just six weeks, and then I'm gone. It's a lucky thing I'm not sensitive, Sybil. You might have me racing into your bedroom in the middle of the night, terrified of John Black's shade."

"Try it," she snapped, yanking herself out of his grip.

"Is that an offer?" He considered reaching for her again, considered and then dropped the idea. She'd probably bite him if he tried to kiss her.

"That's a veiled threat. I have six dogs, and they're trained to attack." She headed for the door. "I'm going back to work.

If you need anything, the telephone's in the kitchen. Call somebody else.''

"Yes, ma'am," he said meekly. "See you, neighbor."

Sybil snarled, slamming open the front door and exiting in a waft of feathers.

He stood there in the open doorway, watching her go. She did need the four-wheel drive—in her rage she drove off the narrow driveway twice, and the second time she nearly didn't make it back out of the drift. Then she was gone, tearing off down the road at speeds better suited to Indianapolis. He stared after her, a speculative expression in his topaz eyes, and turned back into his haunted house, shutting the door behind him.

Chapter Five

It had been too long a day, Sybil decided as she drove down the progressively narrow lake road to her house. First a sleepless night, followed by too much of Nick Fitzsimmons, followed by a lecture from Leona that was made even worse because it was so kindly meant. Add to that too much coffee followed by too much peppermint tea and her stomach was in an uproar, her nerves were screaming, and all she wanted to do was load the wood furnace, pour herself a large glass of Courvoisier and crawl into bed. She had a pile of books near at hand that threatened to topple over every time she climbed into her bed, and she had her choice of a range of subjects, from map dowsing to auras to pyramid power to crystal power to runes. Somehow she thought she might dive under the bed for the latest Jackie Collins.

She tried to keep her face averted when she passed the Black Farm, but curiosity overcame her. She could see the elegant tail of the Jaguar at the end of the road and detect a thick white plume of smoke curling upward in the darkening sky. He must have settled in well enough without the further help she knew she should have supplied. He'd find the small general store with no trouble, and Hardwick had a Grand Union if he demanded more variety. The state liquor store was only ten miles away, and clearly the man knew how to start a fire in a wood stove. She had absolutely no reason to feel guilty.

Her own driveway was only half a mile down the road, not the mile and a half she'd told Nick, but it never seemed farther away. She stomped on the gas pedal, slid sideways and careened into her well-plowed dooryard, just missing the Honda Accord parked there.

Her house was well lighted, and her own wood fires had already been tended. The front door opened and Dulcy's tall, willowy figure was silhouetted by the warm light behind her. The pack of killer dogs zoomed past her, barking wildly in the gathering dusk.

Sybil jumped out of the Subaru before twenty-four paws could do any more damage to the scratched-up paint job, then squatted down to welcome her vicious attack dogs.

The English springer spaniels swarmed over her, licking her, howling their pleasure at her return, panting and rolling in the snow and generally making a good-natured nuisance of themselves. The four puppies decided Sybil's shawl was a suitable toy, and it was pulled off and in the middle of a tug-of-war before she could retrieve it. She lunged for it, fell in the soft new snow and lay there for a peaceful moment.

"It's a good thing I'm still here," Dulcy drawled from directly above her, "or they'd find you frozen to death like something out of a nineteenth-century ballad."

Sybil rolled over and surveyed Dulcy's feet. "Not with my killer dogs. They'd keep me warm."

"Killer dogs? Your spaniels are so gentle and cowardly they'd probably lick a burglar to death. What's the problem—aren't the allergies enough to keep your family at bay?"

"Yup," Sybil said, climbing to her feet and rescuing her shredded shawl. "But I don't think Nicholas Fitzsimmons has asthma."

"If you're trying to keep Nick away, I'm afraid I blew it," Dulcy started into the house, her silver-white hair flowing behind her. "I told him I was on my way to feed your sweet little dogs and that he ought to come see them."

Sybil followed, shutting the cold and the romping dogs out, shutting her sudden surge of irritation in. "Thanks a lot. When did you see him? I thought he decided you weren't his type."

Dulcy smiled that secret, cat-got-the-canary smile and curled up on the sofa, picking up her cognac in one long-fingered hand. "He has."

"But you thought you'd change his mind?" Sybil kept her voice even as she pulled off her coat, dumped the ruined shawl into the overflowing wastebasket and kicked off her boots.

"No, Sybil. I was simply being a good neighbor. I dropped off some of my herb jam as a welcoming present for him. Even Leona sent over some of that nasty rosemary wine she makes. I'm sure you're planning to do the same."

"Guess again." She poured herself a glass of the cognac Dulcy had left out. Her friend had taken the one Waterford brandy snifter, so the Courvoisier had to settle for one of the Indiana Jones glasses Sybil had bought from Burger King. Neither the cognac nor Indy seemed to mind. "I've already done my part in welcoming him. From now on he can muddle through on his own."

"Then what's that casserole in the fridge?"

"Maybe I'm hungry." She took a defensive gulp of the cognac and then had to force back a choking gasp. Her eyes watered, but she remained calm.

"So why do you have two casseroles?"

"That was before I met the man. I thought he was going to be a crotchety old reactionary with a heart of gold. I figured I could charm him into being pleasant."

"And instead he's a crotchety young reactionary with a handsome face. Maybe your charm could be put to even better use."

"Forget it," Sybil said, throwing herself into one of the overstuffed chairs. "Leona says I'll diffuse my energy if I get involved."

"Leona is ..." Dulcy began sharply, then took a deep, calming breath. "Leona is full of opinions," she finished evenly. "There's no need for you to agree with all of them."

"I don't. But she makes sense."

"Sometimes. I never thought celibacy was all it was cracked up to be. Some of the great psychics of history have been fairly randy creatures." Dulcy took another decorous sip of her cognac. "And don't bite your lip like that. I know you're dying to ask me what the hell I know about celibacy."

"I wouldn't do that," Sybil protested, a small grin playing around the corners of her mouth.

"Only because you're too nice. But you thought it just the same. Why don't you use some of that niceness and some of that discretion on your new neighbor? He deserves it as much as Leona, maybe more."

The dogs were scratching wildly at the door. Sybil rose, let them in, then wrestled the puppies for the chair while Annie and Kermit, the two parents, took their dignified places on the sofa beside Dulcy. "Why don't you like Leona?" she asked.

Dulcy sighed, draining her cognac. "Who says I don't like her?"

"Everything about you. Your expressions, your polite behavior toward her. The only people you're polite to are people you don't like."

"Maybe you could learn to be as polite to Nick."

"Why don't you like her?" she persisted.

"Maybe I don't trust her."

"Why not? She's sweet, kind, and has the same interests we do. She even spends lots of time with the old ladies in the Davis Apartments, just as you do. I've never heard her say a single mean thing about anyone."

"Maybe that's why I don't trust her. Anyone without noticeable malice has to have a lot hidden away."

"Well, at least we don't need to worry about Nick having hidden malice. His is there for everyone to see."

"I don't think he's malicious, Sybil. Just a little...contentious, perhaps. I think with the proper handling he could be quite...lamblike."

Once more Sybil stifled the surge of irritation. "Well, go for it."

"Not me, kiddo. He didn't come to Danbury for me."

"He didn't come to Danbury for anyone. He came to do research on water witching."

"So he thinks," Dulcy said with her serene smile. "In the meantime, the poor man is going to open a can of corned beef hash for dinner. Do you think that's fair for a newcomer to town when you have chicken marengo in the fridge?"

"Life isn't fair," Sybil grumbled.

"It is the way you play it," Dulcy rose to her full, impressive height, pulling on her handwoven lavender cape, which only added to her ethereal effect. "Take him dinner, Sybil. I've loaded your stove, fed the dogs and walked them, so you've got nothing else you have to do. Be your sweet, fair self."

"For someone like Nicholas Fitzsimmons?" she argued, already talked into it.

"Especially for someone like Nicholas Fitzsimmons. Things don't happen without a reason, Sybil. He had a purpose in being here, and someone has a lesson to learn from it."

"And you think I'm that someone?" she said morosely, following Dulcy to the door, with the dogs trailing behind them.

"It seems like a possibility."

"I shouldn't listen to you."

"No, and you shouldn't listen to Leona, either. You should only listen to yourself, to your inner voices."

Sybil tried it one last time. "My inner voices tell me to go to bed and let Nick eat canned meat."

Dulcy smiled her secret, glorious smile, and Sybil wondered how Nick could have resisted it. "Do they really?"

Sybil gave up. "No, and you know they don't. My inner voices say to change my clothes, fix my hair and drive back to the Black Farm."

"Good girl. Listen to your voices." Dulcy started out into the chilly night air, now pitch-black. Her pale hair was a beacon of light in the darkness.

"You still haven't told me why you don't like Leona," Sybil called after her.

Dulcy didn't answer. She merely waved an airy hand behind her before climbing into her Honda.

Sybil went back inside, shutting the door behind her. The dogs had already resumed their spots around the wood stove, ready to settle down for a long winter's nap.

"I don't want to go out," she said plaintively. Annie lifted her black-and-white head and stared at her with gentle, disbelieving eyes. "No, I really don't. I want to stay by the fire and read trashy books and drink cognac and eat all the chicken marengo by myself."

Annie yawned, dropping her head down onto her paws, and one of her puppies rolled over, paws in the air. "I suppose I could call him. He's probably already eaten. After all, it's after—" she looked at the mantel clock "—quarter to six. Well, still, he probably doesn't want any more visitors. If Leona and Dulcy took goodies to him, then other people probably did, too. He won't need anything," Kermit shifted, his head flopping halfway off the sofa. "Okay, okay, I'll call him."

"The number you have called, 555-7740, is not a working number. Please call your operator for assistance." Sybil dropped the phone down in its cradle with annoyance. She didn't need to call the operator to know that she'd messed up. It had been up to her to have the Black Farm telephone reconnected—she should have called New England Telephone two weeks ago when she first heard Nick was coming. Now there was no question—she'd have to go back there, if for no other reason than to explain the phone situation.

NICK STARED at the phone in his hand in frustration. He should have had enough sense to try it earlier, when he could have driven out to Danbury and called the phone company. Even if he wanted to attempt it in the pitch-darkness, the business office would be closed and chances were the trip would be wasted.

Of course, instead of turning left at the top of his driveway he could always turn right. Somewhere down that road were Sybil Richardson and her killer dogs. He could show up, exert his long-lost charm and ask to use her telephone. If he played his cards right she might even invite him to dinner, and he wouldn't have to make do with the canned corned beef hash that had looked edible enough in the dim light of the almost empty cupboard.

He'd have to think of someone to call first—preferably someone who wouldn't be home, so he'd have to keep trying. It had been Sybil herself he'd been trying to reach when he discovered the phone didn't work, and that was for a lame enough excuse as it was. What it all boiled down to was that he was restless, bored and lonely. And he was restless, bored and lonely for Sybil Richardson.

Not that he didn't have visitors. There had been a steady stream of them, from Dulcy with her herb jam to Leona and two of her elderly cronies, bringing rosemary wine, of all the disgusting things, and hard little cookies made entirely of whole wheat. He'd forced himself to nibble on them, poured the rosemary wine down the sink, and wished he had thought to go to the store before the early winter sun set.

He would survive. He had gourmet Gummi Bears in his glove compartment, instant espresso in his travel kit. At first sign of daylight he'd hunt for a restaurant that would feed him. If worse came to worst, he could drive all the way back to St. Johnsbury and have an Egg McMuffin.

Unless he wanted to go searching for Sybil Richardson. The more he thought about it, the less he thought of the idea. He was hungry, he was lonely, but at this point things would be much better if she made the next move. He didn't want her to feel she was being stalked. Even if that was exactly what he was contemplating.

He threw himself down on the comfortable couch, glowering at the wood stove. Not even a nice fire to watch, he grumbled to himself. Nothing to drink, nothing even to read. It looked as if it was going to be a hell of an evening.

Now what would one of the Danbury Seekers of Enlightenment do in a situation like this? Certainly not sit there and sulk. He could always lean back and meditate, send thought waves across the frozen countryside to his neighbor. He slid down on the couch, stretching his long legs out, a cynical grin on his face as he closed his eyes.

"Come to me, Sybil Richardson," he intoned in a spooky voice that was a good match for Leona Coleman at her campiest. "Come to me and bring me food."

The dry wood in the stove crackled cheerfully in response, and Nick slid lower on the couch. "Come to me," he murmured. "Bring me food and drink and leave your killer dogs behind. Come to me, Sybil." His voice was low and eerie in the empty house, and for a moment he remembered John Black's fate fifty years ago, and a faint twinge of nervousness ran across his backbone. He opened his eyes, glanced at the shadows in the dimly lit living room and for a moment considered getting up and turning on every light in the place.

He dismissed the notion, figuring he was getting a little nuts with hunger. Maybe he should just go to bed. Maybe....

There was a loud rap on the front door. He could hear it all the way in the living room, and he sat up, startled. He hadn't heard a car, hadn't heard anyone approach in the stillness of the December night. Maybe it was John Black's ghost. Except that according to Sybil the place wasn't haunted, and she wouldn't have lied to him to spare his sensibilities. As far as she was concerned he didn't have any.

He headed for the hallway, pausing by the thick wooden door. Someone was rattling the lock, someone in a bad mood. He could guess who that someone might be, but it was too coincidental and downright creepy. He couldn't really have summoned her across the miles, could he? The knocking began again, loud and irritable.

"Who is it?"

"Who the hell do you think it is, you paranoid flatlander?" Sybil's irritated voice came from the other side. "Unlock the damned door."

A slow grin creased Nick's face. "How do I know it's really you and not a ghost?"

There was a long, furious pause. "If you don't open this door, I will leave, and I'll take my chicken marengo and my bottle of cognac with me."

Nick flung open the door before the last word was out of her mouth. She stood there, small and defiant, a basket full of wonderful-smelling goodies on her arm. "Red Riding Hood, I presume," he said thankfully, reaching out for her, reaching out for the basket. He tugged them both into the house, shutting the darkness out.

"Your phone doesn't work," she said flatly.

"I know. It's the damnedest thing—"

"No, it isn't," she interrupted. "I forgot to have them turn it on."

He stopped his rummaging in the basket long enough to look down at her. She looked like a resistant little kid, awaiting a deserving punishment. "On purpose?" he questioned softly.

"Of course not. I didn't realize you were so obnoxious. I thought you'd be a sweet little old man."

He laughed, too pleased with the smell of the chicken and wine to snap back. "And instead I'm a sour, big, not so old man."

"You got it." She stood there, making no effort to take off her shedding down coat. "Anything else?"

"You brought coffee," he said reverently. "And cream, and pie and..." A silence fell over the hallway. "Courvoisier," he said, and his voice was hushed with awe. "I could kiss you."

She was getting nervous, he could tell. She edged toward the place, and he was a tall man. She had a chance to get to the store," she thought you might not have had a chance to get to the store," she said on that breathless note. "Well, I'd better be going."

She opened the door, clearly hoping to dash out.

He put a quick stop to that, reaching over her head and slamming the door shut again. "You can't leave me. I'm not only starving, I'm lonely."

"I don't think I'd be the best company...." He set the basket down on the floor and became busy unfastening the buttons on the front of her coat. "Nick, don't..."

"Humor me." He moved closer, pushing the coat off her shoulders, his body almost touching hers. Simple intimidation tactics that were being amazingly effective. He could feel the heat from her small, surprisingly lush little body, could sense the battle going on behind those startled brown eyes.

It was a battle he lost. She reached up, yanked her coat back on and pushed him away. "Forget it. I have to feed my dogs."

He knew when to back off. He shrugged, moving away, but not before he saw a delicious flicker of disappointment in her face. "At least I was higher priority."

"I was on my way home. Otherwise the dogs would come first."

She was lying again. He remembered Dulcy's seemingly artless prattle that had told him a great many things he'd wanted to know.

"Well, thanks for the dinner," he said.

She grabbed the doorknob. "I'd do it for anyone."

"I'm not supposed to jump to any conclusions, then?"

"You got it."

"You want to tell me something, Sybil?" His voice stopped her as she stepped out into the chilly night air.

She hesitated, and he knew she wanted to run back to the Subaru. But she was made of sterner stuff than that. She turned. "Yes?"

"Why are you afraid of me?"

"I'm not afraid of anyone," she said with a weary sigh.

"Then why are you lying to me?"

"I'm not...."

"Dulcy fed your dogs. Your car drove past here to your house an hour and a half ago. I was outside and I saw it. Why won't you stay and have dinner with me? Are you afraid I'm going to attack you? I promise you, I can control my raging lusts."

"I'm sure you can." Her voice was as clipped and cool as the December night.

"Then why?"

She smiled sweetly. "Because I don't like you." And without another word she ran out, got into her car and raced down the driveway.

He watched her breakneck pace with smugness. "And that, Sybil Richardson, is another lie," he said. And he turned back to the house.

THE DOGS GREETED her return with their usual enthusiasm, but even their high spirits failed to help her gloom. She'd given him the last of the cognac, and she wasn't desperate enough to resort to her ever-growing cache of Leona's rosemary wine.

She let the dogs out one last time, loaded the stoves and pulled on her ancient and blissfully comfortable flannel nightgown. Climbing into bed, she pulled her battered copy of the I Ching from the pile beside her, sending the precariously balanced books tumbling onto the floor.

Of all the various bits of arcane tools she'd come across in her search for deeper meaning, her favorite was the I Ching, the ancient Chinese book of changes. By casting coins and reading the appropriate hexagram, she'd gotten herself through more difficult times than she cared to remember. She sat back, closed her eyes and tossed the three coins as she cleared her mind.

For now, her only problem was dealing with Nicholas Fitzsimmons, she thought, casting the coins for a second time. She didn't usually lose her temper like that, she wasn't usually so responsive to jibes and . . . was it flirtation? It had seemed uncomfortably close.

She tossed them the third time. Dulcy was right. There was a lesson to be learned here, and she was fighting it. Maybe the I Ching would show her the way.

She rolled the coins three more times, opened her worn yellow book and turned to the appropriate hexagram. She immediately slammed it shut, sinking down into her bed with a howl of despair that woke the puppies.

"Of all the hexagrams to have gotten," she moaned, "why did I have to come up with Marrying Maiden?" With a groan of surrender, she switched off the light beside her bed and buried her face in the pillow.

Chapter Six

It was a brilliant, sunny morning, the first in days, and Sybil decided she was going to enjoy it. Leona wasn't coming in at all, and with any luck Nick would be so busy settling in and doing the shopping that he would have forgotten about yesterday and she wouldn't see him, either.

Her mornings were traditionally allotted for office work: her afternoons were for the bookshop. She would finish the long overdue monthly mailing, then take her knitting into the back room, turn on her new tape and sit there in the sunshine drinking herb tea and feeling righteous. It was going to be a glorious, wonderful day.

Of course, she hadn't taken into account that she couldn't depend on Nick's absence. It took her twice as long as usual to finish up the mailing, since she kept getting up to see if his Jaguar was coming down the road. Every time the phone rang she jumped a mile: every time the wrong voice spoke on the other end she felt a wave of emotion drain through her—an emotion she called relief but that still felt a lot like disappointment.

She didn't finish till quarter past twelve, and by that time it was too late to go out for lunch. Business had been brisk in the pre-Christmas rush. She might have an unending stream of three or four customers in the afternoon, and she couldn't afford to lose a single one. She could afford to miss lunch, however, and if she had any hunger pangs, the tape would take care of it.

She shoved *How to Lose Weight without Trying* into the cassette player, climbed onto her stool by the old-fashioned manual cash register and pulled out her knitting. It was a rich, flame color and shapeless, with a wonderful texture that was mainly the result of dropped stitches. She hadn't improved much in the past two years, but she refused to give up. This latest would be a Christmas present for someone in her family, she still wasn't sure who. It all depended on what it ended up being. It had started out as a vest, turned into a cardigan and was now looking like a lumpy sort of afghan. It would probably end up as the same kind of ill-fitting pullover her other efforts had made. Sighing, she dug her needles in, keeping the tension of the yarn too tight, as the sound of waves washed over her and a mumbling voice whispered, "Food is for nourishment, not for pleasure. Food is for nourishment, not for pleasure."

Sybil remembered her missed dinner the night before, the yogurt that was two weeks past its due date for breakfast, and she sighed. "Food is for pleasure, not for nourishment," she muttered, dropping a stitch. "Food is for pleasure, not for—"

"I'm glad to hear that."

Sybil jabbed the knitting needle into her palm. Apart from that she managed quite well, looking up into Nick Fitzsimmons's golden eyes with only a faint quiver of alarm. "I didn't hear you come in."

"I have been told I have a light footstep," he intoned.

Sybil abandoned her knitting, temper forgotten in sudden interest as she recognized the quotation from *Dracula*. "You don't strike me as the vampire type." Which was a lie. With his black hair, commanding height and mesmerizing eyes, he could very well be a Transylvanian immigrant.

He moved into the room. He had already shed his jacket, if he'd even been wearing one, and his close-fitting navy sweater and faded jeans accentuated his height and leanness. "What type do I strike you as?" he murmured.

She cocked her head to one side, considering. One part Frank Langella, one part William F. Buckley, a dash of Dan Rather, a soupçon of Sting, a side order of Henry Kissinger and a tiny little streak of James Dean. It was a bizarre and potent combination, she recognized ruefully. "Miss Piggy," she said.

He laughed, placing a heavenly smelling paper bag on the counter beside her. There were delicious-looking grease spots leaking through the brown paper, and Sybil recognized the aroma of tomato-mushroom bisque from the restaurant in town. For a moment she felt faint. "How can you say such a thing when I have brought you a peace offering?"

He was toying with her, she knew he was, and there was a satanic gleam in those wonderful golden eyes of his. Only a devil would waft tomato-mushroom bisque under the nose of a starving woman.

"Peace offering?" She tried to make her voice sound cynical, but it came out in a plaintive bleat.

"Pleasure, not nourishment." He nodded toward the bag. "Soup, pastrami sandwiches and even, if I remember the floor of your car properly, Tab."

Sybil slid off her stool, contemplating temptation. According to the ancient legend, Persephone had been kidnapped by Hades and carried off to the Underworld. She would have gotten off free and clear if she just hadn't succumbed to hunger and eaten six pomegranate seeds. Surely there was a lesson to be learned in all that. This dangerous, disturbing man was standing in front of her, bearing gifts of pastrami and NutraSweet. Surely she could resist.

She wavered for an instant. "What do you want in return?"

His answering smile was blissful innocence itself. "Absolutely nothing. I'm returning your favor of last night and going you one better. I'm going to eat it with you."

She eyed him suspiciously. "Pastrami?"

"And Tab."

How could he know her know her greatest weakness, a weakness she'd been trying hard to conquer? "Well," she said finally, "if you are a vampire, the pastrami should keep you at bay."

"Don't believe everything you read. Vampires probably love garlic."

"Nothing's sacred," she said, leading the way into the old kitchen that was still part of the renovated farmhouse. "I take it you've found everything you need? Food store, restaurant, liquor store?"

"Actually, I made do with the Danbury C and E restaurant. I figured you could tell me where to go later."

"I'd be delighted," she murmured, setting out plates and silver.

"I didn't mean it that way," he said, unruffled. "What does C and E mean, anyway?"

"Come and Eat."

"Oh, no."

"The food's worth it," she pointed out, opening the bright pink can of Tab and breathing a blissful sigh as it hissed a welcome. "So what did you do this morning?"

"Nosy, aren't you?" He dug into his sandwich. "I went visiting."

Dulcy, she thought in sudden misery. No, Dulcy would be working. "I didn't realize you knew anybody in town," she said carefully.

"I met them yesterday. The Muller sisters came calling with your buddy Leona, and they asked me to stop in for morning coffee."

"And you did?"

"Why do you sound so skeptical? They're a couple of fascinating old ladies. They fed me coffee strong enough to keep me going for weeks, sticky buns and all the local gossip. I had a great time."

"I wouldn't think they'd be your style."

"We still haven't come up with what my style is. And I like little old ladies. They were very informative."

She drained the twelve ounces of Tab and started in on the soup. "At least my conscience is relatively clear—they couldn't have told you anything that embarrassing."

"Actually, we didn't talk about you."

She looked up sharply. "Sorry. I tend to become a little self-absorbed in the winter."

"Not because I didn't have every intention of pumping them about you, but we got off on the subject of their recent losses."

For some reason she felt better. "I know, isn't it awful? They lost every penny of their savings in that stupid investment program."

"So they said."

"At least they have enough to live on," Sybil continued. "They'll be comfortable, but that's about it. They won't have anything to leave their nieces and nephews."

"Miss Edla said they weren't the only ones."

Sybil had finished the soup and had gone on to the sandwich. "No, they're not. It seems as if half the old ladies in town have lost their nest eggs."

"Doesn't that strike you as odd?"

She stopped eating long enough to look up into his beautiful eyes. "No, why should it? Our farmers are all in trouble, too. The economy is lousy right now, and has been for a while."

"Not that lousy."

"Listen, people are making bad investments. I can understand how it happens. Half of them are farm widows. When their husbands die they sell off their farms and move into town and invest their capital. They've never had any major financial dealings before in their lives, and it's no wonder they run into trouble. Danbury is full of women with the same sad story."

"Have they lost it all in the same place?"

"Of course not. The Mullers invested in orange juice futures when there was a bad winter. Ally Johnson lost hers in a computer company. Merla Penney and Cleora Lyles invested in a wood stove company after everyone had already bought one. It's just been bad luck."

"If you say so."

Sybil pushed her plate away and stared mournfully at the empty Tab can. "Apparently you don't think so," she said. "What's your explanation?"

"I think they're being swindled."

"If they are being swindled, why didn't the crook take everything? All of them have enough to live on, they just don't have enough to leave their children and grandchildren. Have we got a crook with a conscience?"

"Not if we have one robbing helpless widows, we don't."

"Which I don't think we have," she said firmly. "I think you're imagining things. Cabin fever's already set in and you've only been here two days."

"Maybe it takes an unbiased mind to see what's going on right under your nose," he replied, an edge to his smooth voice.

"Well, if we're looking for an unbiased mind we're going to have to look farther than the great professor."

He opened his mouth to snap at her, then shut it again, and she could see he was making an effort at controlling his temper. She wondered why. "Keep that up," he said, "and I won't give you the other can of Tab I bought."

She nearly disgraced herself and begged. Instead, she drew herself up very tall. "That was kind of you," she said. "But I've already had one."

"You drank it in fifteen seconds flat."

"Nice of you to notice."

"I'm observant."

"I'm trying to quit."

He fished the second pink can out of the bag and set it on the table. "Don't let me tempt you."

She grabbed it before the words were out of his mouth. "You're rotten, you know that?" she said amiably enough. "I just hope you don't discover any of my other weaknesses."

He didn't say a word; he just grinned. It completely transformed his handsome, somewhat austere face. If he'd looked satanic before, now he looked like a fallen angel, and Sybil felt her heart doing a graceful flip.

"Okay, so if there's a crook, who do you think he is?" she asked, humoring him.

"She."

"I beg your pardon?"

"Who do I think she is."

Sybil stopped with the can of Tab halfway to her lips. "I don't suppose you mean me?"

"Wishful thinking. You're not evil."

"You think I'd want to be evil?" she demanded, outraged.

"I think you might flirt with the idea."

"So if it's not me, who is it? Dulcy? You're way off base with that one. Dulcy's spent half her time trying to help the old ladies. She's an advocate for the poor and elderly in St. Johnsbury and she does half her legal work for free."

"It could be a cover-up. You have to admit it would be a pretty effective one."

"I don't have to admit anything. You've been here two days and already you're concocting crimes and coming up with suspects. Don't you think you've got a lot of gall?"

Again that wicked smile. "Did you think I didn't? Besides, I didn't say I thought it was Dulcy. I just said I thought it would be a good cover-up. She's not the only one who's been a good friend to all the old ladies."

Sybil took a deep, furious breath, knowing exactly whom he was talking about. "Leona wouldn't hurt a fly," she said fiercely. "She's a little old lady herself; she wouldn't swindle one of her own kind."

"Who would she swindle, then?"

"No one. You make me so angry! You've been in town less than thirty-six hours and already you've been listening to nasty gossip and jumping to foul conclusions. Just because Leona's a newcomer—"

"How new?—"

"She's been here two years. As long as I have. I'm surprised you haven't decided I'm her accomplice."

"I haven't decided anything," he said in a maddeningly calm voice. "I just noticed some curious coincidences involving your good buddy. I'm not jumping to any conclusions."

"It sure sounded like it—," She was interrupted by the jarring ring of the office telephone. "I'll get it."

Nick was there ahead of her and his reach was longer. He picked up the kitchen phone. "Society of Water Witches," he said in an unctuous murmur.

"Give me that phone!" Sybil snarled, reaching for it.

She might have been a Pygmy batting at a giraffe. "I beg your pardon, whom did you wish to speak to?" he said, ignoring her futile attempts.

"Nick . . . !"

"Sara Lee?" he echoed.

With a howl of rage she ripped the phone out of his grasp. "Hello, Mother. Yes, it's me."

Nick just stood there, staring, and that fallen-angel grin of his spread across his face once more. Leaning against the doorjamb, he waited, all mischievous patience, as Sybil dealt with her surprisingly loquacious mother.

"Yes, I'll be down before Christmas. No, I can't leave the office for any longer than that. Listen, Mother, I'm very busy. Yes, one can be busy at the Society of Water Witches. No, that wasn't a nice man who answered the phone, it was a very nasty man. Yes, I'll call you back tonight. Goodbye, Mother."

"Nasty man?" Nick echoed as she replaced the receiver with far more gentleness than she'd wanted.

"Very nasty man." She braced herself, waiting.

"Sara Lee? As in pies and cakes and frozen goodies?" The laughter in his voice might at any other time be beguiling. But not when it was at her expense.

"Saralee. One word, named after my maternal grandmother, who never baked a day in her life. All she did was make money."

"Saralee," he murmured, his voice slipping over the syllables in an oddly erotic way. "It suits you. Far better than Sybil ever did."

"If you call me Saralee," she said calmly, "I will personally do everything I can to make your life hell. And I can do a lot."

"You've already been more distracting than I care to admit. Okay, Sybil." His voice mocked the name. "Show me where I can work and I'll keep out of your hair."

She had to admit that Sybil didn't sound half as nice as Saralee did in his rich, sexy voice. Had to admit it to herself, not to him. Maybe she would wangle more vacation time, fly down to Princeton and the bosom of her family and stay there until Nick was ready to leave.

No, she must be out of her mind. Even Nick wasn't as bad as the assembled Richardsons with their tactful concern. Besides, she couldn't close the bookstore during the Christmas season—it was the only time she made any money. And she wouldn't let Nick Fitzsimmons drive her out of her comfortable home in Danbury.

She'd have to warn Leona, of course. She'd had a hard enough time, coming into a tiny, tight-knit community like Danbury without having Nick give her trouble. It was all absurd, of course, but it wouldn't do any good to tell Nick that. He would believe what he wanted to believe.

"Deke's office is at the top of the stairs," she said, her expression giving nothing away. "The library's in the room next door. But careful with the books—some are very old and rare."

"On water witching?"

"On everything. We even had a couple of ancient books of curses and spells someone's ancestor brought over from England. They're practically indecipherable but fascinating enough."

"Don't tell me you believe in spells and witchcraft?"

"No, I don't believe in spells and witchcraft," Sybil snapped. "They're a curiosity, that's all. Go away, Nick. Let me get back to work."

"I take it the truce is over?" He stood there, still blocking the doorway. She wished he were six inches shorter and six times uglier. "My bribe didn't work for any longer than that?"

She reached over, drained the second Tab, and gave him a flashing, gorgeous smile. "Ten minutes of sweetness per Tab," she said.

He looked startled, then straightened up and headed toward her out of the doorway. She ducked underneath his arm, brushing past him as she went. "Thanks for lunch," she called back, heading for the bookshop and her private phone line.

"Give Leona my love," he called after her.

Sybil, trying to remember where she'd be able to reach her friend that day, shivered.

DEKE APPLETON'S OFFICE was small and cramped, with the sloping ceilings proving a decided menace to a man who topped six feet three. The library was a little better, the table provided more work space than Deke's desk, and it had a view out over the small, picturesque little village. All he needed to make it perfect was Sybil Richardson in plain sight.

She was right about the books. There were real treasures there, including books from the nineteenth century on water witching that he'd heard about but had never been lucky enough to see. The books on regular witchcraft were in a locked, glass-door cabinet, cheek by jowl with Aleister Crowley and his ilk. For a moment he was tempted to go back and get the key, then thought better of it. Sybil—no, Saralee—needed some time away from him. He had to be very careful not to push her too far or too fast.

For that matter, it wouldn't do him any harm to ration his exposure. For some reason, the more he saw her, the more attracted he was to her. And there was no earthly reason for it. He was used to women with a great deal more physical beauty, and certainly more charm of manner. He was used to statuesque blondes who flirted, not sullen little sparrows who every now and then looked up at him out of those melting brown eyes.

So, okay, here he was, finally able to start work on the dowsing book and, instead, he was standing there having erotic fantasies and suffering from the expected physical reaction such fantasies usually provoked. If nothing else, he could at least make a catalog of the books he was planning on using. And if worse came to worst, that glass-door cabinet would be a simple matter to open, even without the key. He could distract himself by reading some ancient witch's prescription for syphilis.

Or he could think about how he was going to trap Leona Coleman without her little champion getting in the way. Because he had no doubt at all that Leona was everything he suspected, and worse. And while her pernicious influence on Sybil was at this point only psychological, he didn't trust it to remain that way. According to the Muller sisters, Sybil had

"Money," though she didn't care to use it. If it were up to Leona, she might no longer have that option.

Gingerly he lowered himself into a chair, stretching his long legs out in front of him and contemplating the quiet, musty room. His plans were simple. He had to research his book, trap Leona and break through Sybil's defenses until she was ready to be involved, both physically and emotionally. He still wasn't quite sure why he didn't want to settle for a brief affair, but the longer he was around her, the more he wanted, and he wasn't getting anywhere rationalizing about it.

He had to accomplish all this within six weeks. He was going to have a busy time of it, and the only way to accomplish everything was to get started. First things first, he told himself, and headed straight for the book of spells.

Chapter Seven

Sybil couldn't get through to Leona. She'd gone off to Hanover with Mary Philbert and they weren't due back until dinner. By the time darkness had closed down around the old building, she no longer wanted to. After all, she thought, adding row upon tangled row to her knitting, what would be accomplished by passing on Nick's infamous suspicions? They were patently absurd, no one else would even dare imagine such a thing, and to tell Leona would only hurt her feelings. It would be much better if she kept an eye on Nick, to keep his nosiness under control, rather than worry her elderly friend with pointless gossip.

She just had to hope he wasn't crass enough to start spreading those sorts of malicious tales around. For all his faults, and they were countless, he didn't strike her as the vindictive sort. He probably didn't for one moment believe that about Leona; he probably made it all up just to torment her.

But on the off-chance that he did believe it, on the vague possibility that he would start harassing Leona on some misguided suspicion, she would have to be doubly observant, and very careful. She would have to keep an eye on Nick Fitzsimmons, to make sure he wasn't causing any trouble for her friend. She couldn't just ignore him, as she told herself she longed to; she'd have to keep close tabs on him. The thought was infuriating and depressing, but highly stimulating.

She had her busiest day in the entire year, with a grand total of eight paying customers and almost a hundred dollars' worth of business. She almost forgot the presence in the office upstairs—forgot, until she heard the measured tread, the shifting of a chair, an absentminded cough.

The Mullers came at the end of the day. Miss Edla, the plumper and more talkative of the two, peered at her out of nearsighted, fading blue eyes that were quite mischievous, while Miss Minna devoted her attention to choosing between a lapis lazuli pendulum and a tiger's eye one for her totally uninterested niece.

"We like your young man," Miss Edla said, leaning over the counter confidentially.

Sybil dropped another stitch. "My young man?" she managed to say in an admirably bewildered tone. "I don't know who you're talking about, Miss Edla."

The frail old lady giggled. "Of course you do, Sybil. I haven't lived for eighty-three years without learning something. We had your young man to tea this morning."

"Oh, you mean Professor Fitzsimmons?" she said in a voice that would have fooled half the population of northern Vermont. "He's not my young man, Miss Edla. We don't even get along very well."

Miss Edla wasn't fooled. "He was asking all sorts of questions about you. We didn't tell him much, just enough to whet his interest. And when he left we dowsed it. There's no question about it, Sybil. He's your young man."

Sybil didn't use rude language in front of little old ladies, so she gritted her teeth into a semblance of a smile. "Not if I can help it," she said.

Miss Minna looked up from her perusal of the pendulums. "I don't know if you can, dearie," she murmured. "We've got a very good track record in predicting these things. We haven't been wrong yet."

No, they hadn't, Sybil remembered gloomily. "There's a first time for everything," she said.

"Of course. But this isn't it. Here . . ." Miss Minna removed the knitting from Sybil's slack fingers, pausing long enough to cluck in dismay over the tangled mess, and replaced it with a jade pendulum. "Try it yourself."

"Miss Minna, you know I can't dowse—"

"Everyone can dowse," Miss Edla said sternly. "Go ahead, try it."

With a long-suffering sigh, Sybil held the pendulum over her left knee. "Clockwise for yes, counterclockwise for no," she ordered in a bored voice. As usual the pendulum responded. "Are my eyes brown?" Yes. "Am I thirty years old?" Yes. "Do I love my family?" A less enthusiastic yes. "Are the Muller sisters with me?" Yes.

"Try something a little harder, dear," Miss Minna ordered, her blue eyes bright in the afternoon.

"Will there be peace in our time?" she asked, and the pendulum swung back in a depressing no.

"Not that hard, Sybil. You know what to ask."

She did indeed, and she didn't want to. Her results had been far better than usual—for once she was trusting the answers the pendulum was giving her. She didn't want an answer that could turn her world upside down.

But the Muller sisters were watching her, their matching blue eyes curious and trusting. And not for anything, not even Nicholas Fitzsimmons, would she let herself be a coward.

She hedged her bets just a trifle. "Will Nick and I ever get along?"

The pendulum wasn't sure about that one. It swung clockwise for a bit, then looped around to counterclockwise, then swung aimlessly.

"You see," she said to the sisters. "I told you we can't get along."

"That's not the question, Sybil." Miss Edla used to be a schoolteacher, and she hadn't lost the iron touch. "Stop avoiding the issue."

Sybil sighed, staring at the tiny piece of jade that was ordaining her future. "You tell me what the question is, Miss Edla."

"Will you and Nick fall in love?"

"No!" she said violently.

"I didn't ask you, Sybil. That's for the pendulum to answer."

"I'm not asking that question."

"Then phrase it your own way."

Sybil stared at the pendulum, then took a deep breath. So intent was she on the question she was formulating that she didn't hear the footsteps, the admittedly light footsteps, on the hall stairs.

"You asked for it," Sybil muttered, "you got it. Will Nick and I be lovers?"

The pendulum stopped its aimless twirling and began a slow, clockwise motion. It grew in intensity, moving faster and faster, so that it was spinning around in her hand, parallel to the ground in the enthusiasm of its positive response. "Damn," she muttered. And looking up, she stared directly into Nick's golden eyes. Those eyes were bright with malicious amusement.

"Parlor games?" he questioned, walking into the tiny bookshop, which was suddenly crowded to overflowing with his large presence.

Sybil stared up at him. She could always hope that he hadn't heard her question, but fate wasn't usually that kind. Besides, he wouldn't have that grin on his face if he thought she'd been asking about the weather or water veins under the building.

She closed the pendulum in her fist and shoved it into the pocket of her jeans. "Parlor games," she agreed.

"I'm heading home now. I'm taking a couple of books with me. Do you have any problem with that?" He was carrying a couple of the oldest leatherbound volumes, and Sybil knew she should put up a token protest.

"Not in the slightest. I think you'll be more comfortable working from home."

"Oh, I have no intention of doing that. There's no suitable place in the Black Farm to spread out. The library upstairs suits me just fine. As long as I'm not distracting you." It was said so innocently. Sybil wanted to stamp on his foot.

"You're not distracting me," she said through gritted teeth.

"I'm glad to hear it," he said, his eyes still bright with mischief. "Where's the best place for me to get herbs around here? And I don't mean the supermarket kind, I mean homegrown."

"Dulcy." She came up with the answer quickly, knowing if she hesitated she wouldn't want to send him there at all. One more inconsistency in her bewildering behavior.

"Oh, my yes. Dulcy has the finest collection of herbs in New England. She grows them, dries them and even manages a small mail-order business," Miss Edla volunteered. Sybil was doubly glad she hadn't hesitated. Nick already thought he knew too much about her and her reactions to him.

"Why don't you sell them in your shop? You have everything else under the sun."

Sybil smiled. "There are a few areas of disagreement between Dulcy and myself. One of those areas is her herbs and the uses she puts them to."

"Dulcy's a white witch," Miss Minna offered. "She grows her herbs for spells."

"And healing," Sybil added fairly. "But it's an area I tend to keep away from. I think it's dangerous to mess around in things I can't understand."

"That's what I've been trying to tell you," Nick said mildly.

"Only when it comes to witchcraft. It's an area where there's been active work toward causing harm. Even white witchcraft makes me uneasy, so I keep away from it."

"Very wise. I'll give Dulcy a call this evening."

"Do that," Sybil said evenly, ignoring the irrational stab of jealousy that had come over her once again. "Why do you want herbs?"

Nick only smiled, and his clutch on the ancient leather books tightened. "Parlor games, Sybil. Parlor games."

The Muller sisters left with him, thank heavens. The last thing she wanted to do was answer any more questions, deny any more suppositions, defend her skepticism or her honor. She watched them leave. A light snow was falling, illuminated by the street lamp that was one of seven in the entire town of Danbury. Standing motionless in the front window of the old house, she watched them go, and she reached into her pocket for the pendulum.

She pulled it out, watching it swing aimlessly. She wouldn't be proved a coward in front of the Mullers, and she was damned if she'd be a coward with only herself watching.

"Will Nick and I fall in love?"

Yes, said the pendulum, swinging clockwise, and Sybil bit her lip. Might as well go the whole way.

"Will we live happily ever after?"

Again that aimless swinging, that irritating refusal to answer. She was about to pocket the piece of jade once more, when an irresistible question came into her mind.

"Is Leona harmless?"

Once more the pendulum began to spin, but it turned in a negative, counterclockwise circle. Sybil stared at it, opened her mouth to ask another more specific, damning question; then she shut it again and shoved the jade back into her pocket. After all, if the pendulum was clearly wrong about her and Nick, it couldn't be trusted about Leona, either. She would have to rely on her own instincts, either, and her instincts told her. . . .

Damn, she didn't care. She didn't even trust her instincts anymore. Her instincts told her to trust the pendulum. It was only her brain that knew better. And maybe it was time to listen to her brain. It could hardly get her into the kind of trouble her instincts and the pendulum seemed intent on leading her.

Parlor games, she thought, locking the bookshop and heading for her coat and boots. It was her own fault for not treating the pendulum with proper respect. No wonder it lied to her. Hadn't it?

NICK TOOK A DEEP, meditative sip of his cognac and surveyed the various oddments laid out on the kitchen table in front of him. The ancient book of spells and curses lay propped up behind them, open to a page entitled "Love Philtres for Reluctant Partners." The herbs lay in front of him, encased prosaically enough in Ziploc bags, and the wooden salad bowl, still slightly redolent of rubbed garlic, waited nearby.

Dulcy had proved more than helpful. Not only did she have everything he requested, from something as mundane as lemon thyme to something as arcane as wormwood, she had been willing to drop them off on her way to a meeting that night. It had been too late when he realized he had forgotten to ask for the orrisroot, and when he called her back she had already left. He'd kept the book carefully hidden when she arrived. He had politely offered her a drink and politely offered her recompense for the herbs, both of which she refused.

"Part of my housewarming present," she said, tossing that silvery mane over her shoulder. "Just make sure you follow the instructions."

"What instructions?" he'd asked, looking properly innocent.

She had only smiled, that wise, knowing smile. He didn't like deliberately mysterious women, and he didn't like ethereal smiles. And he certainly didn't like self-styled white witches. But he had been polite enough, waiting with barely concealed impatience for her to leave, and then had taken his basket of goodies into the kitchen to dump them onto the scrubbed pine table.

Everything was there. He stared down at the neatly marked packages, a cynical smile on his face—one that faded when he picked up a package marked orrisroot.

Coincidence, he firmly told himself, taking another warming sip of the cognac. To prove he didn't put any stock in Dulcy's claims, he mixed the potion with a deliberately casual hand, stirring the fragrant herbs and muttering the various incantations required. The vodka was the final ingredient. It would have to suffice—heaven only knew where he'd get honey mead in this century. He poured generously, the liquor releasing even more of the rich aroma. It was supposed to sit for an hour. Then, somehow or other, he was supposed to administer it to his intended victim.

That might prove easier said than done. For one thing, after today she was highly unlikely to show up at his house again. For another, even if she did, the concoction didn't smell all that appetizing.

He drained his cognac, moving back into the living room and the wood stove that was a poor substitute for the glow of a fire. Sooner or later he'd find a way. The idea had fascinated him since he'd run across the recipe for the potion, tucked between those of dangerously costive disposition. It was a combination remedies for the French disease and a potion efficacious for of boredom, lust and too much Courvoisier that made him determined to finish what he had started. He was never a man to admit defeat, particularly in something as minor as an ancient love spell.

Maybe he would discover a real aphrodisiac. Think of the chaos he could unleash upon the world—the idea boggled the mind. Think of the money he could make for such a discovery. But no, he didn't particularly need or want a lot of money. He could patent it, and then only sell it through Sybil's pathetic little store. Then she'd become rich and famous, and in her gratitude she'd turn to him....

But if the love potion happened to work, she would have already turned to him. It was an unquestionably appealing thought. Now if there were only some way he could get her over here, if worse came to worst he could hold her down and pour the nasty stuff down her throat.

No, subtlety was the ticket. The phone company had outdone itself and fixed the phone late that afternoon. He could call her up, invite her over on some irresistible trumped-up excuse, and then ply her with that concoction. Or maybe he could just ply her with the cognac—it had proved quite effective over the centuries in seducing reluctant maidens, and he had no gentlemanly qualms about taking advantage of her. He wanted her any way he could get her. Maybe the simplest plans were the best. Though he would still like to see how she reacted to the orrisroot punch.

First things first. What in all creation would get her to enter the lion's den at quarter past eight on a Friday evening? Leaning back on the couch, he took another sip of his cognac and put his inventive brain to work.

SYBIL STOOD OUTSIDE the doorway, huddled in her down coat, telling herself she was crazy. Nine o'clock at night was no time to be visiting Nicholas Fitzsimmons. As far as she was concerned, there was no time to be visiting him at all. She had the weekend ahead of her, two days of uninterrupted peace. So why had she driven back out on this snowy night, looking for trouble?

She could admit her first reason. She wanted to see if Dulcy's blue Honda was still parked in front of the Black Farm. She only intended to look, then to turn around and go back and congratulate herself on her matchmaking abilities.

But Dulcy wasn't there, and that same incomprehensible relief swept over her. All she'd meant to do was turn around in the end of his driveway and head back home, but somehow she found herself driving down toward the farm.

Well, she had excuses enough. She was still worried about Leona. Having the damned pendulum confirm Nick's suspicions was distressing, and sitting home worrying about it didn't help matters. She needed to prove that smart-aleck pendulum wrong, and she could do that either by proving that she wasn't going to fall in love with Nick Fitzsimmons or by convincing Nick his suspicions were unfounded.

Either way, she couldn't just let the situation with Leona fester in the back of her mind like an untended wound. She was someone who faced up to things, unless they were connected with her family. And facing up to Nick, nerve-racking as it threatened to be, was better than sitting home worrying about it. Right?

Right, her cynical brain replied. *Stop looking for excuses and knock on the damned door.* And raising her gloved hand, she did just that.

It took him a moment to get there. She'd practiced all the things she planned on saying, rehearsed all the pithy little comments she planned to make. When he opened the door, tall and dark with the light behind him, his topaz eyes gleaming down at her, all conscious thought left her brain. She stood there, silent, staring, unable to shake the sudden, uneasy suspicion that she confronted a creature of the night.

The creature of the night broke the silence. That fallen-angel grin lit his face, and he reached out and pulled her into the warmth and light. "Welcome to Carfax Abbey."

"You still don't make it as Dracula," she said, hiding the sudden shiver that swept over her backbone. She moved out of reach of those long, graceful hands of his. "Is this a bad time?"

"A bad time for what?"

"A bad time for a visit. I wanted to talk to you, and since your phone doesn't work . . ."

"Actually, it does. They fixed it late this afternoon. And you couldn't have picked a better time for a visit—I just made some of an herb drink I found in an antique recipe book. You can be my first victim."

She gave him a long, suspicious glance before shrugging out of her down coat. "I don't need anything. I won't be staying long."

"You'll be staying long enough to have a drink. Don't be graceless, Saralee. You can certainly manage the amenities for an hour or so." Once more he put his hands on her, warm, strong hands, and he pushed her gently in the direction of the living room. "Go in and have a seat and I'll bring you your drink."

"Is that what you've been having?" she demanded.

He smiled, a curiously mischievous smile, and she wondered, if she looked closely, whether she might discover fangs. "Cognac," he replied. "A little too much, but it won't do me any harm."

"Then I'll have cognac too."

"Sorry, I drank it all." He was lying; she knew it, but there was no way she could prove it. He gave her another gentle push toward the living room, the warmth and light spilling over into the darkened hallway. "Come into my parlor," he murmured, and she could hear the laughter beneath his deep voice.

"Said the spider to the fly," she snapped back. "Stop showing. I'll go along quietly."

"And you'll drink my herb drink? It's the least you can do when I keep you supplied with Tab."

She stopped inside the doorway, turning to stare up at him, all her suspicions aroused. He just smiled at her, with such sweet innocence that she knew she was in deep trouble. She could always run while he was getting his herb drink.

But no, she wasn't a coward, and she wasn't going to let Nick intimidate her. She'd sit there, drink his damned drink and calmly, rationally, convince him that Leona had nothing to do with the recent raft of bankruptcies among the old ladies of Danbury. Then she'd leave, immune from any sort of attraction, and when she got home she'd give the pendulum to the dogs to eat.

She smiled up at him with equal innocence. "I'll drink your herb drink," she said. "If it's good, we can make up a batch and sell it in the bookstore."

"You know, I thought of that," he murmured, a devilish light in his eyes. "It would be . . . interesting."

She turned away from him, moving into the warmth of the living room. "I'm sure it would."

Chapter Eight

It was amazing, the subtle changes someone's presence wrought in a room. Already the living room of the Black Farm was altered, different, a chair pushed closer to the wood stove, books scattered on the coffee table, a sweater tossed over the back of the sofa. It looked and felt less like an empty house with an unhappy history and more like a home, and it was undeniably welcoming.

She perched gingerly on the edge of the chair nearest to the wood stove. For all the deceptive comfort of the place, she was already regretting her rash visit. Nick was up to no good, that much was clear, and his mysterious herb drink had something to do with it.

Maybe it was just some of Leona's rosemary wine, and he wanted to see whether it had some nefarious hallucinatory powers. Or maybe he had concocted a hallucinatory potion himself. She rose quickly when he entered the room, that seraphic smile on his satanic face, and the brown liquid in the tulip-shaped wineglass looked unpromising indeed.

"Here you go. I promise you, the stuff is completely innocent. It's just a simple mixture of common herbs and a bit of vodka to bind it together."

She eyed it warily. "It's a love potion, isn't it?"

His grin broadened. "My, my, you do have a high opinion of yourself, Saralee. Why should I want to ply you with a love potion?"

She didn't even blush. "Because you've got an odd sense of humor. You took the book of spells and potions home with you, Nick. I've read it from cover to cover, and the only potions of any interest are for love potions. Unless you're trying to cure me of syphilis or help me conceive, I think you are probably fooling around with the aphrodisiac."

"Guilty."

"Let's try it and see." He moved closer, his tall body dwarfing hers.

"It doesn't work."

"I don't have to try it. I made some up a long time ago and tried it then. Nothing happened. Besides, it tastes very nasty. Like liquid cigarettes."

"Humor me."

She shook her head. "I can't imagine why you bothered doing it. You're the great skeptic—compared with you I'm Rebecca of Sunnybrook Farm, and even I don't believe in love potions."

Nick set the glass down on the mantel, reaching around her, and for a moment she felt trapped. And for a moment it felt good. When he moved away she released her pent-up breath, silently, so that he wouldn't hear it. "I was curious. Bored, too. And you accused me of having a closed mind earlier today. I wanted to prove you wrong."

"Messing around with antique spells isn't going to prove me wrong, it's just going to prove a waste of time."

He smiled, a slow, devilish smile. "So if it's harmless, ineffective and a waste of time, you won't mind trying it."

She opened her mouth to protest, then shut it again. "Okay," she said finally. "I'll drink some. Then I want to talk about what I came over here for."

"What's that?"

"Leona and your outrageous suspicions."

"I don't want to talk about Leona," he said flatly. "She bores me."

"Then I can leave right now." She started toward the hall, but he reached out and caught her, his strong hands a deceptively gentle restraint.

"Okay, we'll talk about Leona, and you can tell me how pure and innocent and kindly she is."

"She is!"

"I'm sure," he said. "But we'll talk about it after we try my experiment."

Sybil sighed. "Okay. Hand me the potion."

"Not yet. We have to do this in a scientific manner."

He was standing very close to her. He hadn't yet released her arms, and his topaz eyes had a gleam that made her very nervous. She swallowed once, wishing she could move back, away from him, unwilling to let him know how he affected her—particularly since she wasn't sure herself.

"Okay, we'll do it in a scientific manner."

"We need a basis for comparison."

"How do you plan to do that?"

He smiled. "Simple. I'll kiss you before you drink the potion and we'll see how you respond. Then I'll kiss you after the potion."

"What if the potion works? I may fling you to the floor, rip off your clothes and have my wicked way with you."

"I'm prepared for that eventuality."

"Nick . . .",

"Stop arguing. This is for the sake of pure science." His hands slid up her arms, pulling her closer, so that she was within inches of him. For a moment she panicked, struggling, and his hands were very strong. "What's the matter, Saralee?" he whispered, his breath warm and sweet on her upturned face. "Afraid I'll be irresistible?"

She stopped her useless struggles. "Not likely. Do your worst, then."

"I have every intention of doing my best." His mouth descended, touching hers, briefly, gently, a mere flirtation of a kiss that left her astonishingly aroused and longing for more. She kept her eyes open, and they looked up into his golden ones with more than faint mistrust.

She tried to pull away again, but he still held her firmly. "That was just to get you used to the idea," he murmured, a thread of laughter in his voice. And pulling her into the warmth of his body, he kissed her again.

She tried to keep her mouth closed against his, but it was a losing battle. Slowly, seductively his tongue reached out, breaching her defenses, slipping into her mouth, invading her, possessing her, as his hands molded her suddenly pliant body against his. He tasted of brandy, she thought as her eyelids fluttered closed. He tasted of love. And she moved her hands up to rest against his shoulders, and her fingers clutched at him.

She would have liked to think that she had been the one to pull away, but she doubted it. After all, it had been more than three years since she'd been kissed like that. Hell, maybe she'd never been kissed like that. When she opened her eyes she was standing alone, and despite the roaring fire in the wood stove she was cold.

"Ready for the potion?" he inquired innocently.

She looked at him. He appeared totally unmoved by that kiss, he just stood there, waiting patiently. But when she looked closer she noticed the rapid rise and fall of his chest. It would have been too crass to let her eyes drop lower, but while she had been concentrating on what he was doing to her mouth, the rest of her body still felt the imprint of his. And it hadn't been the imprint of an unaroused male.

Two could play at that game, she thought. If it took every ounce of her ability, she could appear undisturbed, too. She smiled coolly. "Ready." She stepped toward him, taking the wineglass from his hands and holding it to her lips.

It looked like weak tea with cigarettes crumpled in it. It would probably taste worse. "Here's mud in your eye," she said deliberately, toasting him with the glass. She took a cautious sip.

"You've got to have more than that," he protested when she grimaced in distaste.

"How much more?"

"Half the glass at least."

"Nick . . ."

"For the sake of science."

She looked up at him suspiciously. When it came right down to it, if she didn't drink the nasty stuff he'd have no reason to kiss her again. And she very much wanted another kiss—just one, and then she'd stop. Surely one more couldn't hurt her.

She took a deep gulp, drinking most of it, then handed him the glass. "For the sake of science," she said.

"You want to sit down for this one?" he inquired, setting the glass on the mantel.

"You think you're going to sweep me off my feet?" she responded. "It hasn't begun to affect me yet, Nick. I'm still wonderfully impervious to your charm."

"Sure you are, Sybil. So why don't you sit down so we can do a proper job of this?"

She managed, just managed, to emit a long-suffering sigh before sinking down on the sofa. She spoke no more than the truth—she wasn't overcome with any sudden upsurge of uncontrollable lust. She'd been suffering from that from the second time he kissed her.

He sat down beside her, very close, a light of humor and something else in those hypnotic eyes. His hands were warm and strong as they reached out and touched her neck, cradling her head, his long fingers stroking her jaw. He must have felt the trembling in her pulses, there was no way he could have missed it.

"What I don't understand," she murmured, putting off the inevitable, "is why you bothered trying this on me. Why not on Dulcy, or someone more amenable?"

"If I tried it with someone more amenable, it wouldn't be much of a test, would it?" His thumbs were tracing the line of her lips, a gentle, erotic caress that Sybil felt in the very center of her being.

"No, I suppose it wouldn't," she agreed, trying to sound prosaic. Her voice came out breathless, her lips moving against his thumbs were a tentative kiss. "But I would have thought you'd at least try it with someone you really wanted."

His eyes were dancing with humor and something more. Something even Sybil had to recognize, whether she wanted to or not. "Oh, Sybil," he said, his voice soft, "what makes you think I don't want you? I don't know if I've ever wanted anyone so much in my life." And before she had a chance to do more than open her mouth in astonishment he pushed her down on the sofa, his mouth claiming hers as his hands held her still for his shattering kiss.

A white hot spasm of longing swept over her, one so intense that she practically cried out. Her hands reached out to pull him closer, her tongue touched his, shyly at first, then with renewed hunger, until all that existed were their mouths, twining, joining, thrusting and retreating, heat and love and desire all tumbled together. Somewhere in the back of her brain Sybil reached for sanity, trying to tell herself that it was simple hormones, it had nothing to do with magic potions, nothing to do with a man she was sure she disliked. He simply knew how to kiss, and she was normal enough to respond. She told herself that as she clung to him, fighting the reaction that was threatening to turn her into a helpless victim of a passion that was nothing but trouble.

Just when the last bit of her control was about to shatter, just as she was about to do what she'd joked about and begin to rip off his clothes, he pulled his mouth away, mere inches, far enough for her to catch her breath, far enough for her to reach for the fast disappearing traces of common sense.

"What do you think?" he whispered, his voice husky. "Did it work?"

She was stretched out on the sofa, and he was lying half beside her, half on top of her. The weight of him was hot and strong, arousing and protecting, and she wanted to pull him all the way over her, into her. She could feel his heart racing against hers, feel the hardness of him pressed against her hips, could see the dazed look of desire he was trying so hard to keep from his eyes. And she knew she must look even more vulnerable.

She took a deep breath. "Nope," she said.

He moved so quickly she was taken by surprise. One moment she was cradled in his arms, in the next she was lying alone on the couch, chilled by the sudden withdrawal of his heat and strength. He was over by the mantel, and his eyes were hooded.

He shrugged. "It was worth a try. Guess we won't market it quite yet."

"Want some coffee? It'll only take me a moment."

She sat up, pulling her clothes together with hands that trembled. She supposed he could see that she was shaken; he probably knew perfectly well that she was lying. It didn't matter. He'd chosen to let her be, and his insistence that he really wanted her had been just one more manipulative trick.

She rose, giving him a regal smile that was only slightly lopsided. "No, thank you. I think I've had quite enough stimulation as it is."

He paused. "You found it stimulating?"

She met his gaze fearlessly. "You do know how to kiss," she said. "I certainly grant you that much. You just aren't much of a potion maker."

He nodded. "Would you like some cognac, then?"

"I thought you said you drank it all."

"I lied."

So did I, she thought with just a trace of mournfulness. "No, thank you."

He grinned then. "Another shot of love potion?"

"Don't push it, Nick," she warned. "I think I'd better just go home."

"I thought we were going to talk about Leona?"

"I don't feel like it now."

"Why not? I thought you were impervious to my charms."

"I'm impervious," she said. "I'm just tired. I'm sure by Monday you'll realize your suspicions were all ridiculous."

"Monday? Is the office closed on the weekend?"

"It is. I'm sure you'll find something to entertain you. Maybe you could try coming up with a cure for constipation out of that book."

"For those of a dangerously costive disposition? I might have a hard time finding a guinea pig."

"If you do with that book what I'd like to suggest you do with it," Sybil said sweetly, "then you can practice on yourself."

It took him just a moment. Then he laughed, a rich, delighted sound that was almost as beguiling as his kisses. "Saralee Richardson," he said when his amusement had died away, "I think maybe that potion backfired on its maker."

"I'm sure you'll be able to come up with an antidote." She moved toward the hallway, and this time he made no effort to stop her. She could feel his eyes following her, their gaze distracted, and for a brief moment she reveled in the tiny sense of accomplishment. If Nick Fitzsimmons had thrown her for a loop, she had at least disturbed his seemingly invincible amour propre.

He'd left her coat hanging over the banister, and she pulled it on without any help from him and headed toward the door without a backward glance. He said something beneath his breath, and for a moment she was tempted to ask him to repeat it. It had sounded like "I'm not sure I want one."

"I'll see you Monday," she called over her shoulder and stepped out into the chilly night air.

"If not before," he replied, still in the living room.

She shut the door behind her and walked to her Subaru. It had a light dusting of snow mantling its battered exterior, making it look almost as elegant as Nick's Jaguar. If one didn't have a good eye for beautiful lines, she thought, climbing in and offering up a silent prayer that her station wagon would start on the first try.

It started on the second try, and Sybil let out her pent-up breath as she let out the clutch, zooming up the driveway at breakneck speed. The sooner she got home, back to the safety of her house and the companionship of her dogs, the happier she'd be. For a few minutes back there she'd felt the solid foundation of her universe shift and slide, like geological plates during an earthquake. Everything she held dear, everything she believed in, had shimmered and dissolved for a brief moment when she was in Nick's arms. And she had to wonder whether the damned potion had worked after all.

"DULCY?"

"It's seven in the morning, Sybil," the tired, cranky voice came back over the telephone wire. "Saturday is my only morning to sleep late."

"I know that, Dulcy. And I wouldn't have called you this early if it weren't desperately important."

Her first response was a long-suffering sigh. "What is it now?"

"How do you know it's not something life-threatening?" Sybil countered, much aggrieved.

"Trust me, I'd know. Don't play games with me, Sybil, it's too early. What's the problem?"

"I need some herbs."

There was a long pause on the other end, and then, to Sybil's amazement, Dulcy laughed. "Do you indeed? Shall I waste my time asking why, or do I just guess?"

Sybil bit her lip. "I don't suppose you'll believe that I want to do some cooking."

"No. I think you must have fallen prey to Nick's little experiment. Don't tell me it actually worked?"

Sybil ignored the unmistakable glee in her friend's voice. "Of course it didn't work!"

"Then you don't want an antidote?"

"You're not making this any easier for me, Dulcy."

"I don't intend to. If you don't want an herbal antidote, what are you calling me for? Do you want to try a love potion for him?"

"God, no!" she said quickly, before she could even consider the enticing idea. "I don't need an antidote, the damned potion didn't work, but I decided it wouldn't do any harm to try one. You and I both know that it's the power of suggestion that makes spells and curses work, not actual magic. And I've simply fallen prey to the power of suggestion."

"Did you sleep with him?"

"Don't be absurd. He doesn't even know I had any reaction to the filthy stuff."

Dulcy laughed. "I wouldn't be too sure of that. Nick struck me as a very observant man."

"Then it was wishful thinking on his part," Sybil snapped. "My main problem is the nightmares."

"Nightmares?"

"Well, perhaps not really nightmares," she admitted, running a hand through her heavy mane of hair, which she hadn't yet confined in braids. "Just disturbing dreams."

"You can tell me about them when I get there and we'll analyze them," Dulcy announced.

"Forget it. You're too young."

"That raunchy, eh?"

"No... yes," Sybil admitted finally. "That raunchy. I probably won't be able to see the man without blushing. I'm sure it was just tension and lack of sleep. But I figured I'd hit all bases."

She could practically hear the smile in Dulcy's voice. "I know just what you need. Make a big pot of coffee and I'll be there in half an hour."

"Bless you," Sybil said with real relief. "I knew I could count on you."

Dulcy's delicious chuckle, the one Sybil had learned to distrust, came over the line. "You surely can, my friend. I have just the thing."

Slowly Sybil replaced the receiver, telling herself her sudden qualms were no more than part and parcel of a sleepless night. She would have been better off if it had been sleepless—her dreams had been so erotic and so real that she was still quivering from an advanced state of sexual tension that nothing seemed to diminish, not a cold shower, not Saturday morning cartoons on the TV, not meditating on the sins of Nicholas Fitzsimmons.

But Dulcy was coming; Dulcy with her common sense and her bag of herbs would take care of things, put her back on the straight and narrow. Wouldn't she?

But somehow, Sybil couldn't rid herself of the suspicion that she'd gone from the frying pan to the fire. With that gloomy thought breakfast came to mind, and she headed into the kitchen, the dogs trailing behind her. Maybe food would drown her sorrows. Or at least blunt her unmanageable cravings. Sighing, she opened the refrigerator.

"Damn you, Nick," she muttered to the link sausages. "You and your love potions." Slamming the door shut, she sat down at the butcher-block table to await her deus ex machina in the unlikely form of a white witch cum lawyer named Dulcy Badenham.

Chapter Nine

Dulcy wasn't long in coming. The coffee had just finished running through the drip machine, Sybil had thrown on a loose pair of jeans and a tiger-striped sweatshirt, and the dogs had had their morning romp. The wood stove was cranking out enough heat for two houses, and the dreams of the night before seemed a distant aberration. Until she remembered them, and felt herself growing hot all over again.

Dulcy was dressed in lavender, wispy clothes and wonderful handwoven woolens that played up her otherworldly air, an air that was instantly dispelled as she strode into the house and dumped her huge multicolored tote bag on Sybil's table.

"Pour me some coffee," she ordered, stripping off her cape and diving into the bag. "And I'll get things started. You can also tell me all the details about last night."

Sybil was already pouring. "There are no details. Did you know what Nick had in mind when he asked you for the herbs?"

Dulcy smiled, pulling out a pile of Ziploc bags. "Any fool could guess. Didn't you know what he was plying you with?"

"Thanks a lot. I don't happen to be a fool, either; I knew exactly what he was giving me."

"Why didn't you refuse?" She took the wooden salad bowl Sybil handed her and began sprinkling herbs into it.

"Because I knew it wouldn't work."

"So why am I here at quarter to eight on a Saturday morning, mixing up herbs?"

Sybil sank down in the chair, staring morosely at the rapidly growing pile of herbs. "Because I'm gullible. You know it and

I know it. My common sense will tell me it's all ridiculous, but my subconscious won't listen."

"The subconscious is a powerful thing," said Dulcy, taking a sip of her coffee and pouring a generous slosh into the salad bowl.

"You don't have to tell me that. That's what killed people during the Middle Ages; it's what kills people in the Caribbean who've been cursed. All they have to do is believe they're going to die and sure enough, they do."

"You're not going to die, Sybil," she said in a prosaic tone of voice. "Got any vodka?"

"Not at this hour in the morning."

"For your antidote."

Sybil lifted her gaze from the disgusting concoction. "Are you sure you know what you're doing?"

"Why did you ask me to come if you don't trust me?"

"Oh, I trust you," Sybil assured her. "I'm just tired and cranky."

"And if you don't believe Nick's potion really worked, it won't matter what I give you as an antidote, as long as your subconscious is convinced it will do the trick. Right?"

"Er…yes," she said doubtfully. "But you might as well give me the right one while you're at it. It wouldn't hurt to touch all bases."

"All I need is vodka and it'll be ready to drink."

"Yuck."

Dulcy's antidote didn't taste any better than Nick's vile brew, she thought as she dutifully downed a glassful, picking out the herbs from between her teeth. Mind you, it didn't taste any worse. As a matter of fact, it tasted exactly the same. She looked up at her friend. Dulcy was sitting back in one of the kitchen chairs, her long, slender fingers wrapped around a mug of coffee, a smug expression on her otherworldly face. "You're certain this is the right antidote?"

"Of course I'm certain. The proper antidote to the love potion in the Hungarian curse book is simply to administer a different love potion. I just whipped you up the one from the old English book of charms and curses. I realize it tastes much nastier than that nice lemony potion Nick gave you, but nasty medicine works better."

Sybil sat listening to this artful chatter with a growing sense of horror. "He didn't give me any nice lemony brew, Dulcy,"

Her friend set the coffee cup down very carefully, her pale blue eyes meeting Sybil's with just the right amount of concern. "What do you mean?"

"He fed me something that tasted exactly like your antidote."

Dulcy sat back in her chair, chagrin washing over her face. And if Sybil could see a light of amusement in the back of those fine eyes, it wasn't strong enough for her to call Dulcy on it. "Oops," she said.

"What do you mean, oops?"

"I gave you the wrong antidote."

"I knew it," Sybil howled. "Things couldn't be this easy! Couldn't you tell from the ingredients Nick asked for last night that it was this potion?"

Dulcy shrugged. "I didn't pay any attention. I felt sure he would have taken the Hungarian book home with him. It's so much more interesting than the English one."

"It was the English one, Dulcy." Sybil resorted to another cup of coffee, her third, both to wash the taste of the love brew out of her mouth and to give herself courage to face this latest trauma. "Do you have what you need for the Hungarian potion?"

"Why should I need stuff for that?"

"For the antidote," Sybil said patiently. "If the English potion wipes out the Hungarian, surely . . . surely. . . ."

Dulcy was shaking her head. "Sorry."

"Well, you must know something?"

"I hate to tell you this, kid, but there's nothing I can do. One dose of love philtre I can combat: two, and you're a sitting duck."

"Great," Sybil grumbled.

"Look at it this way—you don't really believe the stuff works. Just exert a little mind over matter. A glassful of nasty-tasting herbs isn't going to make you fall at Nick's feet. Not if you don't want to."

"I don't want to!"

"Of course you don't," Dulcy soothed her. "And you could meditate, mentally surround yourself with a healing blue light. No, on second thought, that might not be a good idea."

"Why not? It sounds like an excellent idea."

"Because if you surround yourself with a healing blue light you might get more than you bargained for. Who's to say that lusting after Nick Fitzsimmons isn't the healthiest thing you could do right now?''

"I do," she snapped, immediately resolving not to meditate.

"Cheer up, Sybil. You and I both know it doesn't really work. And look on the bright side of things. At least you're better off than Mary Philbert.''

All thought of love potions vanished from Sybil's mind as she felt a sudden dread. "What happened to Mary Philbert?''

"The same thing that's happened to too many people. She lost all her savings.''

"How?'' Her voice came out raw and raspy.

"Some bad investment or something. I don't know all the details, but it sounds as if she's another victim.''

"Victim?'' Sybil echoed.

"Of the bad economy. Or were you thinking she was a victim of something else?'' Dulcy was nothing if not shrewd. "Or someone else?''

"Of course not.''

"It's been awfully coincidental.''

"Dulcy, it's happening all over the country.''

"It's happening too much here. I'm planning to go visit her later this morning, to see if there's any way I can help. Maybe it wasn't just bad luck, maybe I might be able to trace some sort of fraud.''

Sybil set her mug down, banishing the last of her self-absorption. "I'll come with you. I didn't have anything planned anyway, and Mary's always been one of my favorite people.''

"She's an old sweetie. At least the other ladies are rallying round. A lot of them have been through the same thing, so they'll be as helpful as anyone can be at a time like this. It's a shame Leona isn't around.''

"She isn't?''

"She and Mary were in New Hampshire yesterday, and apparently something came up. She drove Mary back and then went on to Burlington. Something to do with her investments. Let's just hope she's not the next victim.''

"Yes, let's hope so,'' Sybil mumbled, not entirely sure she meant it. While losing one's life savings was a devastating blow, if Leona were similarly hit it would at least clear her of any suspicion.

Not that anyone was suspicious, just that slimy Nick. Even Dulcy, who had strong reservations about Leona, didn't seem to suspect anything.

Probably Nick didn't, either, she thought, as she watched Dulcy drive away. He probably just came up with that theory to worry her. He had a definite talent for it, a definite talent for upsetting and exciting and arousing. . . .

"Hell and damnation!" she said out loud, slamming her hand down on the windowsill. "I am going to stop thinking about him."

The dogs looked up at her out of soulful spaniel eyes, and Annie's openmouthed pant looked just a tiny bit like derisive laughter. "Yeah, I know," she muttered, pouring out the last of the coffee. "Fat chance."

"IT CERTAINLY SOUNDS suspicious, Nick, but I don't know how you think I can help." Ray's thick Boston accent came over the other end of the line. "After all, I'm just a vice cop in Boston—I wouldn't have any jurisdiction up in Vermont."

"I'm not asking for jurisdiction, Ray. I'm asking for information. You've got access to the most advanced information system in the world. All you've got to do is punch a few buttons and find out anything."

"You academic types." He sighed. "How many times do I have to tell you, it just ain't that simple."

"Are you telling me you can't help?"

"I'm telling you it isn't as easy as you think. I'll do my best for you, buddy, but I can't promise anything. And these things take time."

"I hate to hear that. You're shattering all my illusions about the wonders of the computer age."

"Ain't it a crime," Ray said with sarcastic sympathy. "Just like telling you there isn't really a Santa Claus. Tell me this old bird's name one more time."

"Leona Coleman. She's around seventy, no taller than five feet, heavyset, dark eyes, white hair. She's lived in Danbury for two years, and I haven't yet been able to find out where she lived before that. I think she gets close to the old ladies and gets them to invest in fraudulent schemes, either by simple friendliness or through her phony psychic stuff. I wouldn't put séances and all that hogwash past her, though if she goes that far it's pretty much of a secret around here. She's trusted and well liked, God knows why, and she's able to cover her tracks. No one's lost her money in the same way, and no one's made any connection between the sudden financial reverses and the sweet little friend.''

''But you have?''

Nick leaned back in his chair, propping his feet on the kitchen table that was serving as his desk. ''I have. I think it's a question of people being too close to the situation to notice. It takes an outsider to realize something's wrong.''

''Have you mentioned your suspicions to anyone?''

Nick grimaced, glancing over at the dregs of his foul-smelling potion. ''Just one. She had a minor fit, accused me of harassing the poor old dear. She's not going to listen to reason until I come up with some proof apart from my dastardly suspicions.''

''And you want her to listen to reason? I take it this isn't one of the little old ladies.''

''You take it right. And I don't want her to listen to reason, just to a few indecent suggestions.''

''Lucky Nick. You always manage to fall on your feet,'' Ray said with a wistful sigh. ''Heard anything from Adelle recently?''

''Just that she's happy and big as a house.''

''No regrets?''

Nick thought about it for a moment, probing at the thought as one might prod a sore tooth to make sure it still hurt. Nothing, not even a twinge. ''No regrets, Ray.''

''I'll do what I can for you. Chances are she's using a phony name, and we don't tend to cross-reference people by height. It'll probably take me a while but I'll get back in touch.''

''I appreciate it. There's a bottle of Jameson's in it for you.''

''Don't go bribing a policeman, my boy, or I'll have to report you to my superior. And he'll make me share the bottle.''

''Now that would be a crime. Take care, Ray. Give my love to Connie.''

Good old Ray, Nick thought, sweeping away the remnants of last night's psychic punch, draining his second cup of coffee and setting the dishes in the iron sink. It was handy to have a friend in the Boston Vice Squad, even if Ray, with his paunch, his balding pate, and his thick Irish face looked a far cry from the glamour of Crockett and Tubbs. He'd gone to school with

Ray's elegant wife, Constance, and the mismatch of the century, Ray's broad South Boston sturdiness and Constance's Brookline breeding, had proved the marriage of the century. They had three great kids, and he was godfather to all of them. It was only when he was at their overcrowded ranch house in Newton that he thought about Adelle and the baby with any nostalgia.

Hell, he would have married her. Would have fathered her baby. And it would have lasted maybe till the kid was out of diapers, maybe not that long. Whatever they'd had, and it had been strong and intense, had died, leaving him alone, restless, a little empty, and leaving her with a yuppie husband, a home in the suburbs and a baby on the way.

One final, fading twinge, he thought, rinsing the dishes and setting them in the rack to dry. Even in their earliest stages they hadn't talked much. Adelle had, of necessity, devoted all her time and energy to her career. Advertising was a demanding calling, leaving little time for home and hearth. When they did find the occasional time together, out of bed, they would find they had nothing to say to each other. It had been depressing, but they'd been busy enough so that those moments hadn't come very often. And when they had, the relationship faded and died.

He looked out the kitchen window at the forest behind the house. Just another cloudy day in paradise, he thought with a grimace. Flurries again, sifting through the gray sky and settling on everything in sight. Sure, it was beautiful, the crisp clean air, the tall, dark pines, the blue-gray haze of the mountains in the distance. But it would be a hell of a lot prettier with the sun shining.

So here it was, ten-thirty on a Saturday morning, and he was bored, lonely and restless. Not to mention frustrated as hell. That little romp on the couch with Saralee Richardson had taken its toll on his sangfroid. Even in his sleep he hadn't been able to get her out of his mind. "Obsession" was an ugly word, but it came close to describing his feelings about his unwilling neighbor.

He wandered back into the living room, crammed another piece of wood into the stove, then roamed over to the front window. It wasn't as if he didn't have plenty to do; along with the book of English spells, he'd brought home two of the oldest manuals on dowsing. He could sit down and start taking notes; in no time at all he'd get caught up in the subject.

It was getting started that was the problem. All right, if he didn't want to spend the day at the kitchen table poring over dusty old tomes, he could do some of the fieldwork. Three of the finest water dowsers lived within twenty miles of Danbury, and he'd already laid the groundwork with letters. They were expecting him anytime he cared to show up.

He knew where they lived—all three had given him careful instructions. Or at least he thought he knew. Maybe, just to be sure, he should check with Sybil. After all, he didn't want to end up hopelessly lost on the spider's web of back roads around here.

He could call her. She might even be willing to come along, if he swore it was purely business. Even better, he could take that long-delayed right turn at the top of his driveway and find her place for himself, come face-to-face with her killer dogs and see if he couldn't wheedle a little hospitality from her. It was clear she wasn't usually as hostile as she was with him. Something about him rubbed her the wrong way. But he knew as well as he knew his own name that beneath that hostility was a sensual awareness she was doing her damnedest to ignore. And he had every intention of making that downright impossible.

He was humming under his breath as he gathered notebook and pens together, all his lethargy and melancholy vanished. He'd even promise not to mention Leona. After all, he'd done all he could with that for now. He'd wait until Ray came up with something before broaching the subject once more.

Until then, he'd do his absolute best to be charming. It would take a lot of effort, but in Sybil's case it just might possibly be worth it. Because no matter how much he tried to dismiss the notion, he had the funny suspicion that they might have a hell of a lot to talk about, in bed and out. And he had no intention of giving up on her until he found out.

SYBIL SAT IN HER KITCHEN watching the snow fall. There hadn't been much she could say or do for Mary Philbert, nothing more than add to the litany of woe the other ladies of the Davis Apartments were reciting.

As for Mary, she was a tough old bird. She'd spent the first eighty years of her life on a farm, the last two in town in an apartment smaller than her old kitchen. She still had enough to stay in that apartment, she had enough to eat, and the government was supposed to take care of the medical bills for people her age. God willing, she wouldn't have any, she said, but could just go quickly when her time came.

The Greek chorus of mourning old ladies each took her turn, telling of her own financial downfall. For the first time Sybil listened intently for details. But they had nothing, absolutely nothing in common. Once again she told herself Nick had to be half crazy or a victim of city paranoia. Maybe he just watched too many cop shows on TV.

If that were the case, he wouldn't be having much fun at the Black Farm. It was down in a hollow, getting maybe two channels if he was lucky. Even Sybil, with an outside antenna, a rotor and a signal booster, had to make do with four, and one of them was in French. Watching reruns of *Dynasty* in another language lost its novelty before long, and she hadn't yet succumbed to the temptation of buying a VCR. After all, she'd left Scarsdale and moved to Vermont to simplify her life, get back to basics, not to clutter it up with technology. Even if she grew wistful at the thought of all the movies she never got to see.

But she was bored, lonely and restless. It would be nice to curl up in front of some nice old movie instead of *Wide World of Sports*. This time of year all they ever had was boxing anyway, and even the educational station showed European soccer matches all afternoon. It was enough to depress even the cheeriest of spirits.

What she needed was some distraction. What she needed was for Nick to come and take her away from all this, to needle her and argue with her and maybe kiss her just once more. Just to see if the potion was still having its insidious effect. What she needed was Nick.

She didn't hear a sound. Some instinct alerted her and she looked up, out the kitchen window to her dooryard. Just in time to see a dark green Jaguar pull silently into place. There were too many coincidences for her peace of mind, she thought, staring out at the elegant vehicle, the elegant driver climbing out of the driver's seat and heading for her front door. With a shiver of apprehension that wasn't all unpleasant, Sybil headed for the hallway, the dogs romping around her feet, barking cheerfully in anticipation of a treat.

Chapter Ten

He heard the dogs barking long before the door opened. They sounded like a pack of braying hounds, like something out of Arthur Conan Doyle, hounds of hell ready to rip his throat out. For a brief moment he considered the final indignity of racing back to seek shelter in his car, then resolutely stood his ground. For all that Sybil called them killer dogs, Dulcy had assured him they were harmless. While he didn't think he could trust what either of them said, at least Dulcy was more likely to be straightforward in the matter.

The door opened, and for a moment his eyes rested on Sybil's small, slim figure. Then that vision was obscured by a blur of black-and-white and liver-and-white fur, as a dozen furious dogs leaped at him.

"Kill," Sybil ordered cheerfully.

He wasn't knocked flat on his back, but it was a near thing. Dogs were leaping and prancing over his feet, licking his hands, sitting back and howling a melodious welcome. It took him a moment to sort out two grown dogs and four puppies, none of them with an ounce of dignity.

"Hey, guys," he said in a low, crooning voice, squatting down to their level. Their joy increased as they wiggled and danced around him, uttering little yelps of glee. "Calm down," he murmured, and slowly they obeyed, now and then butting a silken head beneath his hand for a caress.

He rose to his full height, meeting Sybil's dazed eyes. "Killer dogs, eh?"

She didn't even blush, just held the door open for him. He was nearly knocked over once again by the wave of dogs rampaging through around him, but he held his ground. "You're good with them," she said grudgingly.

"Dogs know who's trustworthy and who's not."

She snorted. "Tell me another one. These critters love everybody under the sun. They'd welcome Jack the Ripper with open arms."

"Yes, but could he calm them so quickly?"

"Oh, I admit you have a certain hypnotic effect on dumb creatures," she said.

"Including you?"

"Don't push your luck, Fitzsimmons," she warned. "What are you here for?"

They were still standing in her slate-floored hallway, snow melting around their feet. Charm, he reminded himself. "I was bored and lonely and I decided I ought to visit my dearest friend in Vermont."

"So why didn't you?"

"I'm here, aren't I?"

That threw her. "Nick, with friends like me, you don't need enemies."

"Come on, Sybil," he coaxed. "Invite me in, give me some coffee and listen to a proposition I have to offer."

"You're propositioning me?"

"Not that way. Though we can, of course, discuss that, too."

"Never mind," she said. "Go into the living room and I'll bring you some coffee. How do you like it?"

"Why don't you dowse it and see?"

"Why don't you . . ." It took a great deal of effort for her to bite back her no-doubt colorful suggestion, but she did so, reminding him that if she could do it so could he.

"Cream and sugar," he said quickly, repenting.

She looked at him for one long, suspicious moment. "Cream and sugar," she repeated. "I'll be right with you."

He liked her living room. It was small, cluttered and bright, with lots of windows, an old sofa with a beautiful quilt tossed over it pulled in front of the wood stove, colorful and artistically hideous paintings on the white walls and books everywhere. Tucked in corners of the couch, piled under tables, balanced on windowsills, there looked like enough books to stock a small library. He sat down on the comfortable couch, jumped up and pulled a small tome from underneath him, then sank back down with it in his hand. Past-Life Regression, it said in tiny gold letters. Leaning back, he opened it, searching for some logical explanation of his and Sybil's twin fantasies.

The book was snatched out of his hand. "Do you mind?" she said in her most frigid voice. The coffee she placed in his hand was almost as cold, and she moved to the chair opposite him, perching on it as if she were ready to jump up and escape at any moment. "What did you have in mind?"

He paused for a moment, looking at her sitting there, small and defiant. Her dark blond hair hung in one thick braid down her back, and wisps were escaping, curling around her narrow face. Her brown eyes were staring at him stonily, but that pale mouth of hers looked curiously vulnerable. And infinitely kissable.

But that wasn't what he was supposed to be thinking of, he reminded himself, or he'd be trying to get her on this comfortable sofa with him. Taking a drink of the cool coffee, he controlled a shudder of distaste. "I thought I'd do some fieldwork," he said. "And I wondered if you wanted to go with me."

He'd managed to surprise her. Whatever she'd been expecting, it wasn't something as innocent. "What kind of fieldwork?"

"You have three of the best water dowsers in the country within twenty miles of Danbury. I'd planned to visit them, find out how they operate, and today seemed as good a day as any."

"Perley Johnson, Lester MacIntire and Julius Collier?"

It was his turn to be surprised. "How did you know?"

"Don't be naive. It's not latent psychic power; I happen to be the secretary of the Water Witches. I know every dowser around here."

"Of course." He'd only been rattled for a moment. A moment, however, that she'd noticed and been highly amused by. "That makes even more sense, then. I've written to the three of them, and they told me they'd be glad to see me, but I might be more welcome if I brought you along."

"I'd be more than happy to go with you," she said, "but there are problems. Three of them, to be exact. Perley Johnson's already gone to Florida for the winter and won't be back till after mud season, Lester MacIntire's hunting mad and he's gone to Maine to try to push the season a bit, and Julius Collier's over in Burlington at Mary Fletcher recovering from surgery. None of them is around."

"What's wrong with Julius?"

"Hemorrhoids," she said succinctly.

"Clearly he didn't try the potion for those of a dangerously costive disposition."

She tried to keep from grinning, then lost the battle. "Guess not," she said finally.

"Any other dowsers of their abilities around?" he ventured.

"Not really. Not right now. I'm afraid you're out of luck."

He did his best to look pathetic. "Does that mean you're going to send me back to that cold, lonely house?"

"It's not cold if you know how to work the wood stove," she said. "Or you can turn up the electric heat. And maybe John Black's ghost can keep you company."

"*La Belle Dame sans Merci*," he said. He remembered her fluent French followed by her schoolgirl incompetence. "I suppose you don't know what that means, either."

"Sure I do." She smiled that wicked, beatific smile that was three times more powerful than any ancient love philtre. "The beautiful lady who never says thank you."

"No, it's—"

"Spare me, Nick. You don't have to know French to know it's the beautiful woman without mercy. However, you're wrong. I'm neither beautiful nor without mercy. If you can't stand your own company anymore, and I can't say I blame you for that, you can come shopping with me."

"Shopping," he echoed faintly.

"Shopping. Food shopping. Christmas shopping. I'll even go all the way and treat you to lunch at McDonald's."

He eyed her warily. "I should have known you'd like junk food," he said with a sigh.

"You should have known," she agreed. "Are we on?"

He was going to have a hard time making another pass at her if they were driving around from store to store. Then again, he'd have plenty of time to try it later, and in the meantime he could pump her for information about her good buddy Leona. He hadn't given Ray much to go on, and the more stuff he came up with the better chance he stood of getting results. "We're on," he said. "My car."

"My car. And I drive." She dared him to object.

He shuddered delicately, setting down the half-drunk cup of coffee on the pile of books in front of him.

"We who are about to die salute you," she translated blithely. "My Latin's better than my French. Don't worry, Nick. I always consider my passengers when I drive."

"That's what I'm afraid of," he said faintly.

IF THERE WAS A PRIZE given for stupid ideas, Sybil thought, this one had to take the cake. Here she had the entire weekend stretching out in front of her, a weekend free of Nick Fitzsimmons's disturbing presence, and she'd been fool enough to invite him along. It wasn't as if she even wanted company. There was nothing worse than trying to Christmas shop with someone tagging along. They always wanted to linger around auto parts, browse through videotapes or price washing machines.

When Sybil shopped for Christmas she was organized, fast and efficient. No peeking at the nightgown she'd always wanted, which was now miraculously on sale, no looking at novels or pricing new cars. And she certainly had no time for anyone else's more haphazard style of buying presents.

But Nick had been a pleasant surprise. He'd gone where she'd gone, been ready to leave when she left, and had even come up with one or two excellent suggestions concerning her brothers-in-law. He'd been patient as she'd fiddled through her coupons at the grocery store, enthusiastic when they stopped at the state liquor store, and tolerant at McDonald's, despite the presence of two birthday parties and a busload of Girl Scouts jamming the seats. She noticed he hadn't hesitated when he placed his order, hadn't wasted time looking overhead at the menu, all of which bespoke a certain familiarity with the fast-food restaurants he disdained. But with their newfound, temporary accord she refrained from teasing him about it. She realized as they were heading back on Route 2 that she'd actually enjoyed herself, despite her doubts. For a moment she was sorry she couldn't think of an excuse to extend the day.

Her only delay was a dangerous one. She ought to drive him back to her house, get rid of him and finish her last errand. But it was two and a half miles out to her house, another five if she were to go back and forth again, and the early dusk of mid-December had settled down around the icy road. The fitful snow seemed to be coming down in earnest. Bold as Sybil was, she really didn't feel like traipsing around any more than necessary.

"Does it snow every day in Vermont?" Nick asked lazily. He'd even been tolerant of her driving, moaning only once when she nearly hit a pickup truck. All in all, he'd been a charming companion, and her suspicions were fully aroused.

"Only in months with an 'r' in them," she said. She hesitated, then made her decision. She wasn't going to spend the evening driving all over creation. She'd simply have to trust Nick, even if it seemed tantamount to trusting a snake. "I have one more stop to make."

"Fine. I'm in no hurry."

"I have to feed someone's cat."

She could feel his golden eyes watching her in the gathering darkness of the car interior. For once she kept her attention on the road, trying to ignore the heat of his gaze. "Whose cat?"

They'd managed to avoid the subject all day, but she should have known her luck wouldn't hold. "Leona's," she said.

"Leona's out of town?"

"She had to go over to Burlington for a few days. She asked Mary Philbert to ask me to feed her cat. I usually do when she goes away."

"Does she go away often?"

She wasn't fooled by his casual tone of voice. "Just when she needs to deposit the money she stole from her friends," she replied coolly.

"Whose money does she have this time?"

"Why don't you lay off her? She's a harmless old lady, as innocent as the rest of them. Why have you picked her to harass?"

Nick shrugged. "Maybe because I don't like her influence over you."

"She doesn't have any influence over me!" she cried in exasperation. "We're friends."

"Okay, I'll buy that. I still think her behavior is suspicious."

The Subaru skidded to an angry stop outside the converted farmhouse that now served the tiny town of Danbury as apartments for the elderly. The Davis Apartments were a model of warmth and efficiency and easy access for the less than nimble, and their waiting list was a mile long. It had only been through an extreme stroke of fortune that Leona had managed to get a spot when she first arrived in town. Helen Sinclair had had a bad fall, sending her to the hospital for a month, and when they finally released her it had been to the nursing home. And she sublet her apartment to her new friend, Leona, who had been visiting at the time of the accident.

No one had ever figured out how that skateboard had ended up at the top of the back stairs outside Helen's apartment. There wasn't a single inhabitant under the age of sixty-five, and they weren't in the habit of riding skateboards. But no one could come up with an explanation other than the carelessness of a visiting grandchild, and no one had come forward and confessed. And Leona had moved into Helen's apartment and stayed.

"Stay in the car," she ordered, not giving him any choice.

"It'll only take me a minute."

He was out before she was. "The hell I will," he said pleasantly. "It's cold and dark out here. You can watch and make sure I don't steal anything from Saint Leona."

She stood there for a moment, wondering whether she ought simply to get back in the car and drive away rather than risk having Nick invade Leona's privacy. Snow was falling more rapidly now, clinging to her eyelashes, dusting Nick's shoulders.

"You touch anything and you're dog meat," she growled, turning on her heel and stalking toward Leona's front door.

"For your killer hounds? I think I'm safe. What's that in your hand?"

She was fiddling with the front lock. "What do you think it is? It's a key. Leona gave me one for times like these."

"I thought no one locked her house around here. I thought it was so safe and bucolic that people didn't worry about burglars and their ilk."

"Leona does. It's not her fault; she comes from Buffalo, where there's been a lot of crime." The moment the words were out of her mouth she could have bitten her tongue. The last thing she wanted to do was give Nick anything he could use against Leona. If he wanted to delve into her past he could do it without her help.

But he didn't seem to notice her slip. "Then it's understandable," he said smoothly, following her into the compact little apartment.

As always, it was spotlessly neat. Sybil used to tease Leona that she lived more like a monk than a little old lady. Every other inhabitant of the Davis Apartments had knickknacks, oddments, owl collections and spoon collections and Avon bottle collections and even Danish porcelain collections. Leona had a narrow bed with white sheets and a plain white bedspread, a desk, two hard chairs and a black-and-white TV. She didn't even have any books.

"Cozy little place, isn't it?" Nick murmured behind her.

"Leona lives an uncluttered life. You only have to look at her apartment to see what little use she has for the things money can buy."

"Uh-hum," he said, peering around the place. "Doesn't she have any family?"

"Why do you ask?"

"No pictures. Not even a snapshot. Was she ever married?"

There was no reason not to answer him—the questions were innocuous enough and the answers were common knowledge. "She was married. Her husband died ten years ago, and they were both only children with no kids of their own. The only kin Leona has is Gladys."

"Gladys?" he echoed.

"The cat," Sybil said. "And she doesn't look pleased to see you." That was an understatement. Gladys had never been the most even-tempered of cats, but the low, scratching sound in her throat was ominously close to a growl. She had just stepped out of the kitchen, her fat, marmalade-colored form delicate as always, when she caught sight of Nick and began that threatening rumble of sound.

"I usually get along with cats," he said.

"Maybe Gladys is more perceptive than most."

"Is she?"

"Actually, she's nastier than most. She's the sort that if you pet her she turns around and bites you," Sybil admitted with a sigh. "I don't know why Leona puts up with her."

"Maybe they're kindred spirits."

"Nick..."

"Sorry. Why don't you go feed that ravaging beast before she decides I'd be a tasty morsel?"

"I don't trust you."

"So what else is new? I'm not going into the kitchen with that damned cat, not even for you, Saralee. Go and feed the little monster and we'll get out of here."

"You won't touch anything?"

"What is there to touch?" he countered, skirting the issue.

Besides being a royal pain, Gladys was a picky eater. She turned up her nose at the open can of kitty tuna in the almost empty refrigerator, ignored with a look of disdain the can of salmon surprise Sybil offered, and finally, grudgingly accepted the can of Bumble Bee albacore that Leona kept for feline emergencies. Gladys cast her one evil look, as if to say, "Don't you dare pat me," and then settled down to pick at her feast.

Sybil didn't make a sound as she walked out into the main room. Nick was standing there in front of Leona's now open desk, staring at the contents.

"Don't you have any conscience?" she demanded.

"Not a trace," he replied instantly. "Come here and see this."

"I don't want to. You may have no qualms about invading someone's privacy, but I do." Her feet were edging toward the desk anyway.

"I'm forcing myself," Nick said.

Curiosity finally got the better of her. "What did you find?"

"That's what's so interesting. There's nothing here."

"Well, that's good."

"No, that's bad. Any normal person would leave canceled checks, letters, bills lying around, if for nothing else than for taxes. This desk is completely empty."

"Maybe she knew you were coming," Sybil snapped.

He shrugged. "Maybe she doesn't trust you."

"That's a lousy thing to say!"

"Then why are you peering into her desk yourself?"

Sybil jumped back. "You tempted me."

"The devil made me do it? I don't know if that would hold up in court."

"Damn it, Nick . . . ," she began, beside herself in fury, guilt and that continuing, niggling doubt.

"Who's James Longerman?"

"What?"

"The only thing I found was a scrap of paper that must have missed her eagle eye. It was stuck in the back of the drawer and it says James Longerman, 32650. Any ideas?"

"Not the slightest. Close the damned drawer and let's get out of here. I'm feeling rotten enough as it is."

"Anything in the kitchen?"

"Nick!"

"Well, we've already gone this far," he said reasonably. "May as well be hanged for sheep as well as lambs. Besides, wouldn't you like to know your suspicions are unfounded?"

"My suspicions?" Her voice was high-pitched with rage. "You're the one with suspicions, not me."

"Wouldn't you like to prove me wrong?"

"I don't think an affidavit from the pope himself would convince you," she shot back. "And there's nothing in the kitchen."

"Nothing?"

"Just food," she said. "And not much of that. Leona leads an austere life."

"Leona leads a mysterious life."

"We're leaving," she announced.

Gladys chose that moment to reappear in the main room of the apartment. When she caught sight of Nick, her fat back began to arch, her elegant tail to thicken and that low, evil growling began once more.

He was eyeing the cat. "We may as well. There's nothing more to discover here."

"That's because there's nothing to discover!"

"Maybe," he said, his voice showing strong doubt. And he followed her out into the night air with only a single backward glance.

Chapter Eleven

Sybil stared down at her tangled knitting. She'd been working on it since October, and while it was steadily getting bigger, it wasn't getting any better. Of course, there'd been that three-week period when she couldn't remember how to decrease, and it was only Leona's providential return from a trip to Buffalo that had saved the sweater from growing to gargantuan size. As it was, it would fit Emmie's husband, the six-foot-one beanpole. It would fit someone who was six feet three and had broad shoulders even better. And the color matched his eyes.

She was not going to give Nick a Christmas present, she reminded herself sternly. If there were only some way she could juggle her schedule, she'd be happy if she never saw him at all. But duty and finances insisted she stay at the Society of Water Witches all morning and work in her tiny bookshop all afternoon. And all that time Nick worked overhead, his measured footsteps vibrating through the old house, vibrating through her sensitive body.

He'd been in Danbury for ten days, and things weren't getting any easier. To be sure, he'd been remarkably, frustratingly polite during office hours. So polite, in fact, that she'd been tempted to slash the brand-new studded snow tires on his beloved Jaguar just to see his reaction. She'd controlled the temptation, just as she controlled the almost hourly urge to head up the narrow staircase and ask him some trumped-up question. If he could be immune to her, she could return the favor.

It would be nice if her dreams would stop. Every morning she dutifully wrote them down, then did her best to analyze them over morning coffee. Most of them were erotic and embarrassingly detailed. Fortunately, dreams seldom meant what they at first appeared to mean. Just because she had explicitly sexual dreams about Nicholas Fitzsimmons and woke with her heart pounding and her body covered with sweat didn't mean she actually wanted him. No, it had to mean something else, but she was damned if she could figure it out. And despite Dulcy's prying, there was no way she was going to share the intimate details with her nosy friend, even if it meant discovering that fantasies of making love with Nick in the library of the SOWW building meant she didn't trust her father.

No, that was Freudian, not psychic, she reminded herself. But Nick was becoming tantamount to an obsession. Thank God she was flying down to Princeton that very afternoon.

It was the first time she'd looked forward to visiting her family in years. Usually their glorious perfection did nothing but intimidate her, but not this time. This time she was going to revel in her mediocrity, blend into the woodwork and not even think of Nick Fitzsimmons, much less dream about him. She'd be so busy fending off her family's well meaning suggestions that she wouldn't even remember his existence.

According to the ladies at the Davis Apartments, Leona would be back sometime tomorrow. She wasn't usually gone for such long periods at a time, and Gladys had gotten progressively nastier as Sybil tried to tempt her with shrimp salad from the Come and Eat, frozen haddock fillets and even herring in sour cream. What she usually got for her trouble was a disdainful sniff and occasionally a hostile swipe from Gladys's cookie-size paw.

But Mary Philbert would take care of her tonight, and tomorrow Leona would return. Dulcy had already taken the dogs back to her house. For the time being Sybil's only duty and concern was for her family, and that was more than enough to keep her busy. If she could just weather the five days down there, then she'd be free to concentrate her energies on resisting Nick's seemingly irresistible attraction. And if she couldn't resist . . .

Sybil set the knitting down, cursing. Somewhere along the way she'd dropped another stitch, and if she didn't notice when she did it there was never any way she could get it back. It would serve Nick right if she gave the sweater to him. Not even her worst enemy deserved such a mess.

Not that Nick was her worst enemy. He was simply a distraction, an irritation and a royal pain. It was bad enough when he was hanging around, flirting with her. It was worse having him ignore her.

Maybe it would help if she had Christmas more in hand. For some reason she was reluctant to throw herself into the spirit this year. She'd made herself decorate the offices and the bookshop, she'd even earmarked the perfect Colorado blue spruce growing in the field behind her house. It would make a lovely Christmas tree, and thank heavens she didn't have to deal with some damned man.

They were the orneriest creatures when it came to Christmas trees, she knew to her sorrow. Send them out to buy one, and they came back with the scraggliest, scrawniest, most pitiful reject ever to make it to a Christmas tree lot. But send the dear man out to chop one himself, or even worse, go with him, and you were in for an all-day marathon, a twenty-mile hike and a case of the sullens when he finally had to compromise his high standards and settle for less than perfect symmetry.

Her father had been like that, her brothers-in-law, her ex-husband. She had no doubt whatsoever that Nick would fit the pattern. She was lucky indeed that she didn't have to deal with anyone's standards but her own.

Well, it was time to get into the proper holiday spirit. When she got back she'd drag the decorations out of the attic, she'd start wrapping the presents she'd accumulated, she'd bake sugar cookies and ginger cookies and *kringler* and *julekage* and stollen and eat anything she wanted. And she wouldn't even think about Nick Fitzsimmons.

Of course, it didn't help that every time she looked at her tangled knitting she thought of his mesmerizing topaz eyes. And it didn't help that all the cozy sentiment of Christmas made her long for someone to curl up with on a snowy winter's evening. Maybe that was why she was avoiding it.

There was no pleasing her, she thought in disgust. It would be the best possible thing for her to get out of town. It would be worth putting up with her family, worth everything just to be in another state away from Nick Fitzsimmons. With all his nose-to-the-grindstone hard work he'd probably be finished with his research way ahead of time, maybe even have moved back to Cambridge by the time she returned.

No, that was impossible. She was only going to be gone a week. Nick would still be here, still burying that aristocratic nose in those ancient books upstairs, still having tea with the ladies at the Davis Apartments, still roaming the countryside, without her, talking to farmers and such about water witching. No, he'd still be here when she returned. Thank God.

NICK STRETCHED his long legs out under the library table, turned to stare out into the winter afternoon and shivered. The upstairs rooms at the Society of Water Witches weren't the warmest places on earth, and if he didn't think Sybil above such petty actions he'd suspect she had turned the heat down on purpose. He could see the wind whipping the snow past the frosted window, however, and knew his suspicions were unfounded. When the wind blew, there was no way this drafty old building could stay warm.

He sat back, listening to the wind howl around the eaves, to the creaking of freezing wood settling, to the sound of Sybil singing to herself one floor below him. She didn't realize how every sound, every sigh, every breath carried up to him. She didn't realize he could sit there and hear every word of her conversations with her various customers, conversations that would, more often than not, involve the interesting newcomer to Danbury.

To his surprise Sybil was always charitable. Much as she tried to detest him on a one-to-one basis, she was unfailingly generous when answering the Muller sisters' curious questions. She even put up with their sly matchmaking attempts with admirable calm, a calm that never failed to amuse him.

She didn't like the distance he'd been putting between them. A brief grin lit his face as he put his fingers together and contemplated that distance. It was almost harder on him than it was on her. Of course, he had the advantage of knowing he was in control, that he was playing the game most suited to driving her crazy and into his arms. That still didn't mean he wasn't frustrated as hell, knowing she was one floor below, knowing if he pushed it he could have her.

But he also knew he wouldn't have her for long. Not if he got to her on anything less than optimum conditions. No, she needed to accept that she wanted him. And the only way for her to realize that was for him to be devious, manipulative and downright sneaky.

It was almost time now. He'd been distant, as charming as he knew how to be and out of reach for more than a week. When they were in the same room he'd move just close enough to invade her space, to make her physically aware of him, and then he'd retreat before she could complain. But he could see from the confused, frustrated expression in those wonderful brown eyes of hers that it was working.

The weekend was coming up and it was time to make his move. He'd have to be subtle. He didn't want to blow all his hard work and deprivation. Maybe he could deliberately slide off the road just past her driveway. What it lacked in inventiveness it made up for in believability.

Or he could get the Muller sisters to invite them both to tea. They needed no encouragement to matchmake and they'd taken a fancy to him. There was nothing they'd like better than to cook something up between him and Sybil.

Or maybe, just maybe, he could stop by with some of his notes, ask her for clarification on Perley Johnson's history, for instance, or Lester MacIntire's success ratio. Then he could casually ask her out to dinner, woo her with diffident charm and have his wicked way with her when she asked him in for a nightcap.

He liked that last option the best, probably because it involved a more immediate outcome. He could even set it up ahead of time, mention that he might stop by so she wouldn't get too suspicious when he showed up at her doorstep. Maybe he wouldn't even wait till Saturday.

He heard with disbelief the unmistakable sounds of Sybil locking up. He checked the thin Rolex on his wrist, just to make sure it really was only three o'clock. Sybil never closed up before five, no matter how bad the weather, and while it was a gray, windy day, for once no snow was falling. Maybe she was sick. He hadn't heard any sniffing or sneezing or rushing to the bathroom at frequent intervals, but you never could tell. Maybe she needed a ride home and someone to tuck a quilt around her and feed her savage dogs and ply her with chicken soup.

He slammed shut the book, choked on the cloud of dust that wafted into his face and forced himself to head downstairs at a leisurely pace. He'd pretend he hadn't heard her locking up, pretend he was just coming down for coffee.

"There you are," Sybil was standing in the hallway, and he noticed what he hadn't noticed before. She wasn't wearing her usual corduroys and denims and shapeless sweaters. She was wearing a dress, probably silk, of a pale rose color that did wonders for her coloring and wonders for the body he knew existed beneath the bulky clothes. She had breasts—not too big, not too small—round, luscious hips and a small enough waist to set off both those attributes. She'd even fixed her hair into a loose sort of bun and it framed her small, solemn face. He controlled himself with a strong effort.

He looked down at her feet, shod in neat little leather pumps, at the suitcase beside her, at the cloth coat over her arm and then back up to her face. "You're going somewhere?"

She sighed, and for once something else was overshadowing her reaction toward him. "I'm visiting my parents in New Jersey. I can't make it at Christmastime so we're celebrating early."

"Why can't you make it at Christmastime?" Stupid question, he chided himself. Until he saw the flush that warmed her pale brown skin.

"Because I don't want to. Besides, Dulcy usually goes up to Canada to visit an aunt and I can't count on her to watch the dogs. So my family gets me now or not at all."

"You don't like your family?"

"Of course I do!" she snapped.

"Well, then, why don't you sound happier about going?"

She took a deep breath. "Because my family, much as I love them, are overbearing, interfering and more than I can handle. Just like you."

He grinned. "Does that mean you love me?"

"That means I wish there were someplace I could go where I didn't have to deal with any of you," she said wearily. "I'll be back next Wednesday. There's a key on my desk, so you can come and go as you please. Leona's going to fill in for me—try not to harass her, okay?"

"Leona's back?"

"She will be tomorrow. I hope you've gotten over your absurd suspicions."

Nick smiled his most angelic smile. "What do you think?"

"I think Leona's a match for you," she said. She was pulling on her coat, covering that lovely little body of hers. "Try to behave yourself, Nick," she added.

He couldn't resist, even if it meant blowing all his hard work. He slid one long arm around her waist, under her coat, and pulled her against him. He caught her chin with his other hand, turning her startled face up to his. "I just want to see if the potion's still working," he murmured, and set his mouth on hers.

Her response was gratifyingly instantaneous. Her hands clutched his shoulders, her head tilted back and her mouth opened beneath his with only the slightest pressure. Suddenly he felt slightly desperate. He pushed his tongue past her teeth, into the warm dark hollow of her mouth, and her own tongue met his, sliding against him, flirting with him, and her breasts seemed to swell and press against his chest, as her fingers clutched more tightly, and he heard a tiny little moan deep in the back of her throat. A moan of wanting, a moan of surrender. He wondered for one brief moment whether he could carry her up those stairs to the uncomfortable couch in the library. Maybe the table would be a better surface.

Then she began to withdraw and he knew better than to hold her against her will. Even as his mind howled a protest, his mouth left her and his arms released her, and they were standing inches apart, breathless, staring into each other's eyes.

Her mouth was slightly swollen, he noticed. And her nipples were hard beneath the silk dress, hard despite the warmth of the hallway. Her eyes were dazed and hostile.

"It didn't work then," she said, "and it doesn't work now."

For a moment he couldn't remember what she was talking about, and then he realized. A slow, seductive grin lit his face. "What doesn't work? The love potion or the kiss?"

"Neither."

"Liar."

She took a deep, calming breath. He noticed her thick, silky hair was falling out of that bun she wore. And for the hundredth time he wondered how that hair would look spread out on a pillow beneath him.

"Goodbye, Nick," she said evenly, picking up her suitcase and moving past him toward the door.

He watched her go, forcing himself to remain motionless, even as her silk dress brushed against his thigh and the faint whisper of her flowery scent danced in his nostrils. "Hurry back," he said.

"It'll be a cold day in hell." She slammed the door behind her, the last of her calm deserting her.

He leaned against the panes of glass that surrounded the door, staring out into the gathering shadows of the December afternoon. He watched the Subaru peel out into the road, watched her drive away. A gust of wind blasted between the cracks in the old wooden door.

Nick shivered. "Honey," he said out loud, "it already is."

Chapter Twelve

Sybil had had worse visits in her family's house on Hodge Road. Growing up there had been sheer torment, always over-shadowed by her three sisters and her parents, always feeling like a changeling. If it weren't for the fact that she looked exactly like her father's mother, she might have thought venerable old Princeton Medical Center had made a mistake and switched babies. Maybe the real Saralee Richardson was Brooke Shields or Jane Pauley or the president of NOW. A real Richardson wouldn't be happily buried in the north woods, running a tiny little occult bookstore and working as a part-time secretary for a bunch of kooks.

No one said anything, of course. Their questions, their expressions of kindly interest were so well done that anyone outside the family would have been fooled into thinking they really cared, that they really respected the way she had chosen to live her life. But she knew them too well. She intercepted the meaningful glances that passed between her parents and her sisters, heard the vague explanations of her life-style to family friends, and she wasn't fooled for a moment.

It would have been so much easier, she thought, sitting alone in the bedroom that had been left just as she had always kept it, if she didn't love them and they didn't love her. But she did and they did. She was loved just as much as her more glorious sisters. She just wasn't one of them.

She stared around her room, at the looming posts of her canopy bed. Her parents had bought it for her one Christmas when she was twelve. She'd longed for it, begged for it, and when Christmas morning rolled around she'd received a photograph of it with the promise of delivery in one week. While a photograph wasn't as exciting as the real thing, she'd been overjoyed. Until she watched her sisters opening their big presents.

Hattie was eighteen, already fascinated by medicine. Her parents gave her a skeleton with all the bones named and numbered, and Hattie was entranced. Emmie got a set of law books, and was ecstatic. And baby Allison, two years younger than Sybil, got the oak file cabinet and electric typewriter she'd been begging for.

Sybil had hated that bed from then on. She'd never said a word, she'd slept in it for six years until she left for college, she slept in it every time she came back. She stayed amid the pink chintzes her mother had chosen, chintzes that made her look like a brown elf, and she looked at the dolls lining the shelves, dolls her sisters had discarded by the time they reached third grade, and she never said a word. If she couldn't be glorious, at least she could be pleasant.

She was just as glad she wouldn't have to be there when they opened their presents. Despite their cries of appreciation, she always had the suspicion that they were being just a little too happy about the Vermont maple syrup, the handwoven blankets, the wooden sap buckets and the homemade blackberry jam.

As usual, her parents tried to give her a new car, and as usual she refused. Another excuse for not visiting more often was the age of her Subaru, and while its replacement with an all-wheel-drive Audi was tempting, she resisted. If she really wanted one, she could afford to buy one herself—her trust fund just sat and increased. But she valued her excuses more than a new car, and she resisted the latest offering with only a small twinge.

She had flown down on Wednesday, it was now Saturday evening, and she only had four more days to go, she thought, counting them off on her fingers. She'd make it—nothing horrendous had happened so far. The only bad thing about the visit was Nick. Her dreams had only gotten worse. It was no wonder, considering that kiss he'd planted on her just before she left. She'd driven the two hours to the airport, alternately fuming and dreaming. Maybe she was overreacting. Maybe, despite Nick's many irritating qualities and beliefs, there was nothing wrong in getting involved with the most appealing man she'd met in a long time.

After all, sex hadn't even interested her for years. Part of it was Colin's fault—his lovemaking was polite, energetic and boring. And part of it was the lack of men around Danbury—the closest she got to a possibility was Ducy's younger brother and, at age fourteen, he was just a tiny bit too young for her. No matter what his other drawbacks, Nick Fitzsimmons was a devastatingly attractive, dangerously sexy man. And she should be pleased that she was healthy and broad-minded enough to notice.

Except that she was doing more than notice, she was being sorely tempted. Ever since she'd had that double dose of love philtre, it had simply gotten worse and worse. Even his distance during the past ten days hadn't helped. Even being four hundred miles away in the bosom of her distinctly uncomfortable family didn't help. Nothing helped; the attraction grew whether he was there to feed it or not. She had the uneasy suspicion that the next time he kissed her she was going to kiss him back.

Except that she was already had. And the next time she was going to do more than kiss him back. Maybe giving in to temptation would get him off her mind.

Maybe she really was as big an idiot as she always suspected, even to consider such an outlandish idea. She rose from the oversize chair, built more for tall men and women than for someone of her delicate stature, and flicked on the light. The closer she got to Nick Fitzsimmons the worse it got. He certainly wasn't the type she wanted to spend the rest of her life with, even if he happened to be insane enough to want it. He was too much like the rest of her family—too tall, too handsome, too talented, too bright. What he lacked in Richardson charm he made up for in wit. And she was going to find a short, stocky hunk, wasn't she?

She could hear the noise from downstairs; hear the clink of ice and glasses, the sound of laughter and bright conversation. Her mother had told her it was a small pre-Christmas cocktail party, only about fifty guests. Every one of those fifty would make her feel inadequate, despite the turquoise silk dress that Hattie, with her excellent eye for clothing, had chosen for her. At least Allison was planning an announcement. She'd been very secretive about it, but they all knew she'd been seeing someone in Washington. Someone important, it was whispered. And one more Richardson would make a wonderful marriage.

Of course, Sybil thought as she wandered down the hallway, her own marriage had been a Richardson one. Colin had started his own law firm at thirty-two, been named to governor's commissions, been quoted in *Newsweek* and had letters published in *The New York Times*. Her wedding day, with the four hundred and seventy-five invited guests, was one of the only times she had felt like a real Richardson. She had also felt absolutely miserable.

Well, she'd done her duty, stayed in the marriage far longer than it or Colin had deserved and now was free. It was up to Allison to do it right this time.

"Chin up, Sybil," she ordered herself softly as she descended the stairs. "It can't be as bad as you're expecting."

"Saralee!" Allison stood poised at the bottom of the stairs, and a tall, handsome, strangely familiar man stood directly behind her, one strong hand clasping her shoulder in a possessive gesture. "Come meet your future brother-in-law."

Sybil reached the bottom of the stairs, plastered a suitable smile on her face and looked up. Directly into Geoffrey Van der Sling's beautiful blue eyes. Eyes that didn't, for even one moment, recognize her.

"I THINK YOU'RE CRAZY to fly back into a storm," Emmie said, casting her sister a worried glance as they sped along the New Jersey Turnpike toward Newark Airport. "You don't even know if you'll be able to get on a plane, much less know if any are flying out."

"The weather is fine," Sybil said, huddled in the passenger seat of Emmie's Mercedes. "Just a little cloudy and overcast. We should have no trouble taking off."

"But there's a blizzard in Vermont!"

"No, there's not. Just some heavy snowfall. And the plane I'll probably get on has to stop at Logan on the way up. By the time we get to Burlington, the snow will have stopped and the roads will be clear. If not, I can always spend the night in a motel and drive to Danbury tomorrow."

"Why don't we turn around and go back to Princeton and you can fly out tomorrow? Better yet, stay till Wednesday when you planned to leave anyway. Why do you have to go back so early? It's only Sunday; surely your dogs will be fine."

"I told you, Annie just gave birth to seven puppies," she lied blithely. "I can't leave them with Dulcy."

"I don't believe you," Emmie said.

Sybil looked over at her sister, at the pregnant belly pushing against the leather-covered steering wheel, the concerned blue eyes. Emmie had always been the one she could talk to, the one who understood what it felt like to be a changeling.

Sybil opened her mouth to lie again, then shut it. "You're right."

"You want to tell me what the problem is? It was something that happened last night, I know that much."

Sybil stared down at her gloved fingers. "It was Geoff," she said.

"Geoff?" Emmie echoed. "Allison's Geoff? The senator?"

"The youngest senator in the history of New Jersey, the bright star of the Republicans, the charming, handsome, brilliant Geoffrey Van der Sling. Yup."

Sudden comprehension washed over Emmie's face. "I remember. You went to school with him, didn't you?"

"Yup," she said again, her voice morose.

"And you hate him?" Emmie ventured. "I can't see why. I mean he's a tiny bit pompous and certainly more conservative than you are, but then, everyone's more conservative than you are. What do you have against him?"

"Nothing."

The word hung in the heated interior of the Mercedes. "Oh," said Emmie, finally comprehending. "Now I remember."

"Yup," Sybil said a third time. "I had the biggest, most passionate, most desperate crush on Geoffrey Van der Sling that any adolescent has ever suffered through. I used to write his name all over my journal, I used to plan our wedding, I used to pick names for our children."

"Sybil," Emmie said patiently, and once more Sybil blessed the fact that of all her family, it was only Emmie who no longer called her Saralee, "you can't still want him."

"Of course not. As you said, he's pompous, conservative and to someone like me, boring."

"Then what's the problem?"

Sybil took a deep, shaky breath. "He didn't remember me."

"Should he have?"

"Of course not," she said bitterly. "No one ever looked twice at me, then or now. Not with my sisters around. I worked with him on the school newspaper, I acted with him in the school play, I even joined the Young Republicans and managed his campaign for student council."

"You joined the Young Republicans?" Emmie echoed, fascinated. "True love indeed."

"I spent hours hanging on his every word, running his errands, doing his bidding. And he didn't even remember me," said Sybil.

"Okay, I'll grant you, that stinks. But I don't see why you're running away because Geoff Van der Sling has a lousy memory. Unless you still want him, deep down inside."

"I don't want him," she said firmly. "I wouldn't take him on a silver platter. And I think that's part of my problem. I don't care about him, I don't want him, and I still feel absolutely lousy. It's irrational, but all I want to do is get back to Vermont and hide."

"Okay. And I don't think it's that irrational," Emmie added. "It's just one more thing to give you that absurd illusion of inadequacy."

Sybil managed to conjure up a grin. "I love the way you put things."

"That's why you let me drive you to the airport," she said, calmly making a turn in the midst of dense traffic that would have had Sybil tearing her hair. "I'm going to tell you something I promised Henry I wouldn't."

"What would your husband want you to keep from me? I'm hardly any danger."

"We've had ammo on this baby, since I'm thirty-five. We're finally getting a girl after two boys. And we've agreed. This one is Sybil."

She stared at her in amazement, swallowing the sudden rush of tears that threatened to choke her. "But what about the others? Or shouldn't you name her after Mother?"

"Not Rebecca," Emmie said firmly. "Not Hattie, not Allison and not even Saralee. She's Sybil, and she's your godchild in another month. So cheer up. That's better than marrying a senator any day."

"You're right," she said, her voice husky with emotion that Emmie understood without her having to say anything. "And with Allison's luck she might end up in the White House."

"Poor thing," Emmie agreed, commiserating. "Let's count our blessings and see if they have any restaurants in the terminal. As usual, I'm starving, and your plane isn't due to leave for another hour."

"Sounds good," Sybil said. Reaching over, she patted Emmie's huge belly. "You better keep my niece well fed."

"Don't worry," Emmie said with a groan. "At forty pounds and counting, I'm keeping her roly-poly."

THE PLANE was due to leave at three o'clock Sunday afternoon. Emmie finally headed back down to Princeton at five, they let the passengers board the plane at six, ordered them off at seven, put them on another at nine, and took off at eleven-fifteen.

Logan Airport was a madhouse. Planes were still flying in and out, skidding on the snow-slick runways, darting through the fog and swirling sleet, landing safely with all the passengers gripping their armrests and gritting their teeth. Sybil filed off with the others, thankful to be out of the claustrophobic plane for at least a few minutes till her connection to Burlington was ready to board. The airport was jammed with people, waiting for delayed and canceled flights, college students starting their Christmas vacations, skiers trying to get back to jobs. The loudspeaker was playing Christmas carols, with the same high-pitched, nerve-racking arrangements usually reserved for department stores, the kind that made people nervous enough to spend too much money just to get out of the place.

But no one was going anywhere from Logan. They were keeping the runways open, the snow was heading north and planes would be flying. Even if it meant a delay.

Sybil had always had strong doubts about using Ransome Airways, simply because of their name. Ransome reminded her of kidnapping, kidnapping reminded her of hijacking, hijacking reminded her of terrorists, and she never flew without feeling paranoid and uneasy. And their planes were much too small.

At least they weren't crowded, either. They were merely a connector for one of the larger airlines, and tonight most passengers didn't feel like making that connection. As she walked down the increasingly deserted corridors toward Gate 67A, she wondered if they'd make the flight for one passenger, or make her wait till they had more to fill up their tiny little plane.

The waiting area was dimly lit, a single clerk was standing behind the counter, waiting to check her in, and one lone figure was sitting over by the windows, staring out into the snowy night sky. They'd make the flight for two passengers, she thought in relief, proffering her ticket.

"Flight's two hours late," the clerk announced in a bored voice.

"Will we be getting out tonight?"

He stamped her ticket and handed her the boarding pass that read Number Two. "Who knows? Snow's supposed to be letting up, but things are bad up in Burlington. Even if you can take off here, they may not let you land."

"But . . ."

"Take it or leave it, lady. You want your boarding pass or you wanna arrange for a flight tomorrow?"

She surveyed the almost empty passenger area, the dim lights, the swirling snow beyond the plate glass. In her rush to get out of Princeton she'd left with only twenty dollars in cash, and she didn't believe in credit cards. Even if she wanted a motel, even if they weren't booked solid around the airport, there was no way she could pay for it.

Besides, she desperately wanted to get home. It would be worth sleeping in the airport, driving through a blizzard, just to get back.

"I'll take it," she said evenly. "Two hours, did you say?"

"At this point" was his discouraging reply.

"Thanks." She walked into the waiting area, casting about for a suitable seat. The dark figure of the man had the prime spot, looking out over the landing strip, but she didn't feel like making friends on such a dismal night. Even though she wondered where in the world he'd found that delicious-smelling coffee.

Sighing, she sank down in the row behind him, rummaging in her purse for the glitzy novel she'd been reading. The man in front of her moved, but she kept her head down, not wanting to catch his glance, not wanting to encourage a no doubt lonely businessman looking for some distraction.

It didn't do any good. She could feel his presence, see his shadow move around the seats, pause at the end of her row and then steadily advance toward her. She ducked her head lower, determined to ignore him. Really, she had no need to be nervous. The clerk was still standing there, still patiently bored, and even if the man pounced there were plenty of security guards roaming the place. Even if no one was in sight, there were plenty of stranded passengers within screaming distance.

Besides, she wouldn't have to resort to outside help. All she had to do was look up, fix the importunate giant with her most quelling Richardson glare, and he'd subside like a scurrying rat.

He sank down in the seat beside her. Out of the corner of her eye she saw the long legs encased in expensive wool trousers, the handmade leather boots. At least it wasn't a wino accosting her. Slowly she lifted her head, turning to glare at the intruder.

"Want some coffee?" asked Nicholas Fitzsimmons.

Chapter Thirteen

His first impression was that she looked like holy hell. There were shadows under her eyes, her face was pale and her mouth, as it dropped open in stunned amazement, was tremulous. She'd been crying sometime in the last twenty-four hours, crying a lot, or he'd miss his guess. And he wanted to put his arms around her and hold her, just hold her, until she lost that waif-like look and became the termagant he was used to.

Of course, he did no such thing. "Coffee?" he prompted again, holding out the plastic cup. "It's not bad for airport brew."

She ignored it. "How did you know I was here?" It was an accusation, pure and simple.

Nick grinned. "There's that ego again. I had absolutely no idea you'd be here. How could I? You told me you were going to Princeton, not Boston. And you weren't supposed to be back till Wednesday. Why would I expect to find you stranded at Logan Airport at—" he checked his Rolex "—one-thirty in the morning?"

The spark of anger left her eyes, leaving her pale and deflated once more. "You're right," she said.

"Well?"

"Well, what?"

"Do you want some coffee? And are you going to tell me what you're doing here?"

"No."

"No coffee?" Nick echoed, puzzled.

She took the cup from his hand, took a deep swallow and managed a half smile. "No, I'm not going to tell you."

Half a smile was better than none. "Don't you want to know what I'm doing here?"

"I imagine you came home for a visit," she said diffidently, clearly not caring.

Well, if that's what she thought, it was fine with him. He'd flown back to Boston this weekend for the sole purpose of pushing Ray into finding something more about Leona Coleman. So far, everything he'd tried had turned up blank, but he had high hopes for James Longerman, 32650.

Ray couldn't make any promises. Boston had a slasher loose, and every minute of computer time and every law enforcement professional were being called into play. As soon as he had a spare moment he'd get on it, and with that Nick had to be satisfied.

He looked at Sybil, thought for about a moment, then pounced. "I expect you went back to Vermont early, found out I'd gone to Boston and you came tearing after me."

"Why in God's name would I do that?"

At least he'd managed to get her interest. She was finishing his coffee, but that was a small price to pay. If she cheered up he might even tell her where the soft-drink machine was. "I can think of several reasons. One, you might be worried that you'd driven me away, so you chased after me to apologize and beg me to come back."

Sybil managed a genteel snort. "Not likely."

"Or you could have chased after me to make sure I stayed away."

"A better possibility, but not worth my time and effort." She set the empty cup down on the chair beside her.

"Or you could have missed me so much that you couldn't stand it, and came after me to announce your undying love and to drag me into bed. I still don't believe that love potion didn't work."

It was exactly the right thing to have said. Her backbone stiffened, her gaze sharpened and every trace of the woebegone elf vanished. "Fat chance."

He shrugged his shoulders. "I admit it doesn't seem likely. You want to tell me why you're here?"

"I don't suppose I have any choice if you're going to keep bombarding me with stupid suppositions," she snapped. "It's very simple—my family is a little ... overwhelming, and I decided to come home sooner than I had planned. The only flight

I could make had me change at Logan, so that's what I'm do-ing."

"Your family must be extremely overwhelming for you to take such a roundabout flight during a winter storm."

"They are."

"I don't suppose you've had a chance to look at this from another angle," he murmured, enjoying himself.

"What do you mean?"

"Well, don't you think it's odd that we both ended up in the same place at the same time? Don't you think it's fate, or kis-met, or somehow meant to be? I know how gullible you are—don't you think this is a sign?"

"If it's a sign, Nick, it says stop," she warned.

"Maybe I think it says yield," he said gently.

She closed her eyes and let out a long, weary sigh, one that still had the faint catch of distant tears on it. "Get off my case, Nick. It's been a long weekend, a long day, and it's not over yet."

"Why don't you end it, then? There are any number of mo-tels around—you could spend the night and take the first plane out in the morning. The weather will be better and you'll be more rested."

"Can't," she said succinctly. "I don't believe in credit cards and I don't have enough money."

"We could always share—"

"Shut up, Nick," she said. "I've had a lousy, miserable last few days and I've had just about enough."

"What was lousy and miserable about it?"

She glared at him. "You never stop, do you?"

"Not often. What was lousy about it?"

"Nothing, nothing at all. My younger sister is marrying someone I had a schoolgirl crush on, but that's just part and parcel of the whole thing."

That little twinge in his stomach felt uncomfortably like jealousy. Except, of course, that he wasn't the jealous type, never had been, never would be. "And you've still got that crush?"

"Of course not. Geoffrey is perfect, and perfectly boring. I think he's just right for Allison—she'll know how to handle him."

"But you feel rotten anyway?"

"Yes." Her nervous hands were wrinkling the trashy novel she was holding. "It's irrational and stupid, but it just makes me feel more like an outcast."

He reached out one large, strong hand to cover hers, to stop her fidgeting. To his surprise she didn't jerk away. "Cheer up, Saralee," he murmured. "You've got me."

"Some consolation," she grumbled. But her hand rested beneath his.

He stared at her for a long moment. Her profile was slightly averted, and his eyes ran down the line of her face, the short, slightly upturned nose, the warm brown eyes, the soft mouth and high cheekbone and the untidy mass of dark blond hair. He still wanted to put his arms around her, wanted to pull her into his lap and comfort her. It was an odd feeling—he didn't usually feel protective toward women. And someone as prickly as Sybil Richardson didn't need a self-appointed protector.

"All right," he said, "tell me which dowsing device you think works best: pendulums, L-rods, Y-rods or bobbers? Which sell the best, and why?"

He couldn't have picked a better subject. Her swift, suspicious glance told him she knew he was deliberately distracting her, knew and appreciated it. "What sells best doesn't necessarily work the best. It's a judgment call, anyway. They all have their merits. Which do you prefer?"

"I don't dowse."

She stared at him in openmouthed amazement. "You're kidding."

"No. I can write, I can analyze, but I can't dowse."

"Everyone can dowse."

"Not me," he said flatly. "But I'm hell on wheels at mixing up potions."

"The Arkansas bobber," Sybil said firmly, "is an obscure but extremely effective device...."

He sat there, a faint smile on his face, as she proceeded to instruct him about every obscure dowsing device known to man. He noticed she hadn't offered to teach him how to dowse, nor did she offer any of her own amazing success stories that most dowsers trotted out by the dozen. A sudden, delicious suspicion swept over him.

"... while Y-rods have been documented as far back as the tenth century—"

"Can you dowse?" he interrupted her.

She frowned. "I told you, everyone can dowse."

"But can you?"

"Yes," she said flatly.

"How good are you?"

"If you want more research for your book, forget it."

"I have enough interviews. I want to know how good a dowser you are."

She glared at him, and for a moment he was afraid he'd blown all his hard work. Then a slow, rueful smile started in her eyes, moved to her lips and bubbled up into a laugh that was nothing short of enchanting. "Lousy," she said. "Absolutely lousy."

By this time two or three other late night travelers had straggled into the waiting area, which was just as well. His gut-level reaction to Sybil was powerful enough to make him lose whatever sense of propriety he had, and now was neither the place nor time for unbridled passion, he thought, staring out into the night. The swirling snow had lightened to no more than an occasional flurry, and outside their row of windows he could see one of Ransome's small planes being readied.

He opened his mouth to say something, but the bored clerk forestalled him. "We'll be boarding in the next five minutes. Please have your boarding passes ready."

"Do you think it'll be snowing in Vermont?" Sybil asked, eyeing the snowy runway with a worried expression she couldn't quite hide.

"It's always snowing in Vermont," Nick said gloomily. "But I don't think they'd fly out unless they were reasonably sure they could land." He put his hand under her elbow, helping her to her feet. "Come on, Sybil. You can drink your way to Burlington and sleep the rest of the way home."

"How am I going to do that? I have to drive."

"No, you don't. The roads will be bad enough as it is; we both don't need to risk life and limb. I'll drive, you can sleep and we'll pick up your car tomorrow when the storm clears."

"How about I'll drive and you sleep? I'm the one with four-wheel drive, remember?"

"I also remember that you're the one who drives like a bat out of hell. If it makes you feel any better, we can drive home in your car, but I'll do the driving."

She glared up at him, yanking her arm out of his grip, "Just when I think I might like you," she said behind clenched teeth, "you blow it."

"Stop looking for trouble and accept your fate, Sybil," he murmured. "We've been thrown together for a reason; if you'd stop fighting it, maybe we could find out what it is."

"You were put on this earth to plague me," she muttered.

Adele had been an amazon. He'd always gone for long, leggy women, not little sparrows like the defiant creature standing there under his nose. Before he even realized what he was doing, he leaned down and kissed her, swiftly, briefly on her pale mouth. "I was put on this earth to tempt you," he said. "And sooner or later you'll give up fighting it."

"Sooner or later you'll give up trying."

He grinned. "Don't count on it. I can be very stubborn."

"So can I."

"Yes, but this time we both want the same thing. It's just taking you a little longer to realize it." She opened her mouth to protest again, but he stopped her. "Give the man your boarding pass, Saralee. We want to get home before dawn."

THERE WAS NO REASON why she should feel comfortable with him, Sybil thought as she leaned her head back against the seat in the Subaru. She shouldn't have sat with him in the plane, trading barbs and witticisms that grew steadily more sexual and more heated in nature; she shouldn't even have allowed him in her car, much less let him drive; she shouldn't have spoken to him at the airport. In retrospect, she had had other possibilities. Her cash would have bought her a taxi ride to her old college roommate's home in Milton, and Margie would have put her on a plane the next day when the weather cleared. But she'd been too miserable and too self-absorbed to think of it, and once Nick had appeared, too busy battling him and herself to think of such practicalities.

So here she was, halfway between Burlington and Danbury in the midst of a full-blown winter storm, trapped in the cave-like cocoon of an overheated station wagon with a man she found far too attractive for her own peace of mind.

She didn't need complications like Nick right now. She needed her own bed, the comfort of the dogs and maybe a glass or two of Courvoisier and one of her favorite books. All together they'd make her forget her miseries. But she'd finished the cognac, the dogs were at Dulcy's, her house would be cold with only the inadequate kerosene space heater going, and all her favorite books were lusty romances. Right now lust and romance seemed a very dangerous pastime.

"Aren't you asleep?" His voice was deep and sexy as he kept his concentration on the snowy highway ahead of him.

"Yes," she said, watching him. She had to admit, if she'd tried to describe the perfect man for her, at least in a physical sense, that Nicholas Fitzsimmons would fill the bill. He had an absolutely beautiful body. Too tall, of course, and his legs were too long, but damn, they were nice. His shoulders were just broad enough, not too overwhelming and not too scrawny. His hands were especially erotic, with their narrow, beautiful palms and long, artistic fingers.

Not to mention his face. She couldn't look into those topaz-colored eyes of his without thinking of the devil—not the frightening devil of fundamentalist religions and fire and brimstone, but the mocking seducer who tempted and twisted and stole people's souls. And people went to him willingly, just as Sybil wanted to go.

She liked his thick black hair, the widow's peak, the black eyebrows that only added to his satanic image. But most of all she liked his mouth, that thin, sexy line that could do the most devastating things to hers.

Or maybe he reminded her more of Dracula—not the vicious, blood-sucking monster but the erotic, elegant lover who sipped blood and drained souls. She could picture herself, stretched out on a bed, Nick leaning over her, his teeth on her vulnerable neck, as she reached for him....

Why was she letting herself have these erotic fantasies? She needed to remember what a pain Nick was, how infuriatingly pedantic and small-minded and incredibly devious he was. How could she have admitted she was a terrible dowser? He'd never let her forget it.

With a nervous hand she reached up and unfastened her coat. The car was hot, much too hot, though she could see he only had the heat halfway up. There was something otherworldly about the night, the utter quiet of the snow falling around them, the emptiness of the highway. Even the usually obstreperous engine was being more refined than usual.

"Go to sleep, Saralee," he said. "It's slow going—we won't be home for another hour."

"Why?"

"I used to hate that name," she said quietly.

"It's the name I grew up with," she said. "The name I associate with being a misfit, a changeling, a small brown wren in a family of peacocks. Every time I hear that name I feel small and inadequate."

"I can't really see you as a Sybil."

She sighed. "No, neither can I. It was just wishful thinking on my part. I was hoping I'd grow into it, be the sort of person who conversed with gods, but it hasn't happened. Not yet, at least. I haven't given up hope."

"Have you ever been called by any other name?"

She laughed. "Lots. Skinny, Short Stuff, Tubs . . ."

"Tubs?"

"I was fat when I was twelve. Also Cupcake, because of Saralee, Sis, and then of course my husband called me dear."

Nick wrinkled his nose. "Sounds pretty tepid."

"Colin was tepid."

"Who called you Cupcake?"

Sybil laughed. "A camp counselor. My family couldn't have a fat child sitting around, so they sent me off to fat girls' camp that summer. Very degrading at first, but I had one of the best times of my life. You see, no one else in my family had ever been fat, so none of them had been there. I was judged on my own merits, not as Hattie Richardson's little sister."

"Somehow I can't see me calling you Cupcake."

"Don't even try it," she warned. "Actually, I hate to admit it, but I don't really mind when you call me Saralee. Somehow it sounds different when you say it. Not so disapproving."

"Saralee it is," he said. "Unless you prefer me to call you dear?"

"Try it and I'll break your nose," she said sleepily.

"Or darling," he continued. "Or sweetheart, or honey, or hot stuff, or angel, or sweetmeat, or . . ."

"Cut it out, Nick," she murmured. "Two can play at that game."

"Go to sleep, Saralee. You can think of endearments when I get you safely home."

Saralee, she thought. She liked it too. She especially liked it in Nick's rich, sexy voice. She also liked the way he said darling, and sweetheart and honey and even sweetmeat. Did he really think she was hot stuff? He certainly seemed difficult to discourage, and she had offered him Dulcy on a silver platter. Maybe she was being a fool for fighting.

Fool or not, she didn't have any fight left in her. She had just enough energy to sink down lower in the seat and prop her head against the iced-over window. A few moments later she was fast asleep.

When she woke up an hour and a half later she was curiously disoriented, as if she were floating through clouds and space. It took her just a moment to realize that was exactly what they were doing, except that the fluffy white cloud was a snow squall with zero visibility and the floating feeling was all four wheels of the Subaru out of control.

Nick was cursing under his breath, slowly and savagely, as he deftly turned into one skid, then into another, somehow, by sheer force of personality or superhuman driving skills or demonic power keeping the car on the road when he couldn't even see the road. They were sliding down a steep incline, and for all Sybil knew they were heading off a cliff.

She jammed her feet into the floor, instinctively searching for the brakes that didn't exist on the passenger's side, as she clutched the seat with numb hands and began some cursing herself.

"Damn you, Nick, don't you dare kill me," she threatened.

"I'm not going to," he said calmly enough as they slid to the left. "At least, not unless I do it with my bare hands at some later time. We're almost home."

"Can't you stop the damned car?"

"I'm trying to." Beneath the calm there was a note she didn't care to encourage. Gritting her teeth, she hunched down in her seat, fingers clenching the cracked vinyl beneath her.

The car slid to the right, straightened out for a brief, glorious moment as the tires caught a last bit of traction, and then lost it again. This time there was no getting it back. Endless moments later they were tilted sideways in a ditch, the nose of her car crushed against what had to be the hardest maple tree in the state of Vermont.

They sat there for a brief, stunned moment. Nick reached over and turned off the lights that made no dent in the swirling white-out, then the ignition. "Are you all right?"

"Just peachy."

"We were only going about seven miles an hour when we hit the tree," he said in a damnably even voice. "With luck it didn't do much damage."

"Do you have the faintest idea where we are?" she demanded, unable to get too worked up over a car that had failed her in a crisis.

"Halfway down my driveway."

"Thank God," she breathed. "At least we aren't going to freeze to death."

He looked over at her. He'd left the overhead light on, and the dim bulb provided faint illumination in the darkness. "You're wearing a skirt, stockings and high-heeled shoes. The driveway hasn't been plowed, and even if we manage to head in the right direction we'll be slogging through at least a foot of new, wet snow. There are no lights, I don't really know how far we are, and—"

"We'll freeze in the car," she said.

"Right." He tried to open the door, but it was wedged shut against the snowbank. He shoved again, cursing, and then turned to her. "Lead on, Macduff."

Chapter Fourteen

Pulling the handle, Sybil shoved at the passenger door with all her strength. It didn't move. She grunted, shoving at it again, and panic began to creep up her spine.

"It might help if you unlocked the door," Nick said mildly.

"It's not locked. I never lock it."

"I locked it while you were asleep. I didn't want to risk having you tumble out onto the highway."

"Damn you, Nick...."

"Just unlock the door, Sybil. We'll argue about it later."

It was a waste of time to fight him. She pulled her thin gloves on, unlocked the door and shoved.

A moment later she was lying face-first in cold, wet snow. She lifted her head, blinking away the slush that clung to her, but she couldn't see a thing. It was a curious kind of chiaroscuro, the blackness of the predawn sky, the invisible whirl of white snow.

Nick's strong hands pulled her to her feet, and she clung to him, ignoring any remnants of pride, as he made a futile attempt at brushing the snow off her. He was right, the snow was at least a foot deep, and she might as well be barefoot for the protection her high heels and stockings afforded her.

Well, she was the tough Vermonter, he was the flatlander. Or at least she had two years' seniority on him. It was up to her to get them out of this mess. "Come on," she muttered, pulling away from him and heading out into the storm.

She didn't get far. His hands caught her, jerking her back. "You're heading in the wrong direction," he said, his voice muffled by the driving wind. "The house is back this way."

"Of course," she said, shivering, wrapping her thin cloth coat around her and wishing that she had her ratty down one with her. Not to mention boots and pants and long underwear.

"Let's go." She took two steps back the way she came, her high heel collapsed beneath her, and she tumbled full-length into the snow again.

For a moment she just lay there and cried, hot tears pouring down her icy face. This time Nick didn't help her up; this time he picked her up, tossed her over his shoulder like a sack of potatoes and started off into the blinding snow.

She started struggling, but a swift, hard smack on her well-padded bottom shut her up. "The sooner we get out of here and into the house, the happier I'll be," he shouted through the howling wind. "And we'll get there a lot faster if I carry you."

She subsided, doing her best to lie there passively, not liking it one tiny bit. There was nothing about the situation she liked, not the cold, not the snow, not the wind and not the company. Or at least, not in her present position.

He slipped once, sending both of them sprawling, but before she could scramble to her feet and try to make it on her own he was up again, carrying her with seemingly no effort at all and heading directly into the storm.

She dropped her head down, thankful that he had a better sense of direction than she did. She had absolutely no idea where they were going, it seemed to be taking five times as long as it should have, and for all she knew they were bypassing the Black Farm and heading directly into the woods. Maybe John Black's ghost decided to make an appearance and lead them to their doom, and they'd die locked in each other's arms.

It wasn't that unpleasant an idea. If they made it safely to the house, to the warmth and comfort of the old farm, then maybe she ought to find a suitable way to celebrate their close escape, maybe she ought to give in to those ridiculous potions and—

The breath was knocked from her as Nick walked directly into a solid unyielding object that turned out to be the old farmhouse. Once more they ended in the snow, and this time Nick didn't reach for her again. He was too busy cursing.

Sybil ignored him, pulling herself up on shaky, frozen legs and groping for the door. Of course it was locked, and Sybil's own curses matched Nick's.

"Calm down," he muttered, taking forever to find the lock in the pitch blackness. "We're almost inside."

"Almost isn't good enough," she managed through chattering teeth. "Haven't I told you you don't need to lock your doors around here?"

"Old habits are hard to break." The lock gave, the handle turned and the door opened. The two of them tumbled in, into the dark, warm cavern of safety, and collapsed on the hall floor. Nick kicked the door shut behind them and lay there, half on top of her, his breathing deep and labored.

As for Sybil, she was sheer ice from the hips down and from the waist up, her hair was frozen, her hands were frozen, her teeth were chattering so hard she could barely speak. No doubt Nick would count that a blessing.

"Didn't you turn down the heat when you left?" she grumbled in his ear, trying to shift out from under him. In his present snowy state he was only making her colder.

"No, thank God," he said, his voice infinitely weary.

"Thank God," she echoed. "You . . . w-w-want to get off me? You're like a blanket of snow."

"Always willing to oblige a lady," he muttered, rolling off her and standing. He pulled her up beside him, and her legs buckled. She fell against him, against his cold, snow-covered body, and she quickly pushed away. Standing on her own shaky two feet was preferable to embracing a polar bear.

He flicked on the light. The glare was so strong she shut her eyes against it, swaying slightly in the warmth. "I want you to go in the bedroom and take off all your clothes," he said.

"Forget it."

"And then get into the hottest shower you can stand, and stay there until you've thawed out. I'm not talking about sex, Saralee, I'm talking about survival. When you're warm enough, you can find some clean clothes in my drawers. In the meantime I'll get a fire going and find us something to drink."

"No love potions," she mumbled. "Two doses are more than enough."

"Two doses? Who gave you the second?"

"Never mind." She opened her eyes just a crack against the glaring light. "Point me in the right direction."

He gave her a gentle shove and she stumbled away from him, through the darkened living room into the bedroom. She fumbled with the light, staggered into the bathroom and began peeling off her ice-stiffened clothes. She didn't even bother to close the door. If Nick was so hard up that he had to resort to being a Peeping Tom, then that was his problem. All she wanted to do was melt the three layers of ice that had solidified around her body.

At first the water hurt her frozen flesh. Gradually the numbness faded, blood began to flow and her limbs began to move freely again. She stood there and let the blissfully hot streams of water rush over her, stood there behind the smoked glass door, ignoring the sounds from the bedroom beyond, ignoring Nick's shadow as he scooped up her wet clothes and took them away, ignoring everything but the warmth pouring over her frozen body.

It wasn't until the water began to lose its heat that she aroused herself from her stupor and turned off the tap. With warmth, sanity had returned, and so had at least a trace of her sense of self-preservation. It had to be close to five o'clock in the morning, in another couple of hours it would be light and she'd have no trouble making it home. That is, if her car wasn't totaled by its close encounter with a maple tree.

So she just had to make it through two hours of Nick's admittedly tempting company. Hell, she could do that. All she needed was something hot to drink, maybe something to eat, and she could face anything.

The bathroom was deserted, bereft of human presence and her wet clothes. He'd left a couple of towels for her, thick maroon ones he must have brought with him from Cambridge. No Vermont farmhouse ever boasted such wonderful towels.

She peeked out into the bedroom, but it, too, was empty, the door chastely closed. He'd left a silk dressing gown for her, a shimmering, sensual piece of apparel that was the last thing she intended to appear in. Particularly since the tie would be much too easy to unfasten. The dressing gown was lying across the bed, and the covers were turned down. Never in her life had Sybil seen a more inviting bed. It was an old-fashioned one, high off the ground, with maroon sheets that matched the towels and a patchwork quilt that had been there before John Black's time. She wanted to climb up into that bed, pull the covers over her wet head and fall sound asleep. And she'd like it even better if she could fall asleep wrapped around a long, lean body.

Forget it, she told herself. Instead, she headed for his closet, dismissing the wool and linen suits, settling instead for a huge blue plaid flannel nightshirt that came practically to her bare ankles. Rummaging in his drawers, she completed her outfit with a pair of thick woolly knee socks and a towel wrapped around her sopping mane. She surveyed her reflection in the mirror, grinning. If he'd had any thought of a last-minute seduction, this should put him off.

He was standing by the wood stove, leaning against the mantel, and he had a glass of cognac in his hand. He'd changed his clothes while she'd been showering, and he was dressed in black sweatpants and a sweatshirt, with no socks on his long, narrow feet. He looked warm, sexy and dangerous.

He caught sight of her standing in the doorway, and that thin mouth of his twisted in just the hint of a smile. "You didn't like the bathrobe?"

"Not warm enough," she lied, moving forward. "Got some of that for me?"

His smile broadened. The room was warm, hot even, and the dim lighting added to the sense of coziness and heat. "Some of what?"

"The cognac?"

"We have to share." He held out the snifter, watching with unconcealed amusement as she did her best not to touch him.

She took a deep, warming sip, feeling it burn its slow, languorous way down into her stomach, and immediately she knew it was a big mistake. The room, the warmth, the narrow escape and, yes, the company all combined to put her in a far too receptive mood. She'd have to keep all her wits about her if she didn't want to end up back in that comfortable-looking bed. And of course, part of the problem was that was exactly where she did want to be.

She sat down on the sofa, cross-legged, the thick wool socks showing to advantage. She took the towel from her head and began to rub it briskly through her long, wet hair. "How does the snow look?"

"Impenetrable. Why?"

"It'll be light in a couple of hours. I thought I could make it the rest of the way...."

"I smashed your car against a maple tree."

"But not badly, didn't you say?" She knew her eyes were anxious. She couldn't walk home, not in this kind of storm. And she couldn't stay here with him.

"Bad enough. And it's stuck sideways in a ditch. Even with four-wheel drive we'll need help getting it out."

"I'll need help getting it out," she corrected, shaking the long wet strands around her face.

"We'll need help getting it out." He took the brandy back from her, ignoring her start when his warm flesh touched hers. She was still cold, deep within the core of her, and there was only one way to get warm. "Stop fighting, Saralee. It's a waste of energy."

"I'm a born fighter."

"That you are," he said, his voice deep with approval. "But you don't have to fight me." He moved forward, squatting down beside the sofa, and his hand reached out and brushed the loose neckline of the oversize nightshirt. "Was this supposed to keep me away? I hate to tell you, darling, but this nightshirt is one of the sexiest things I've ever seen on anybody in my entire life."

She jumped a mile at the touch of his burning skin on her cool, trembling flesh. "You must be crazy," she said.

"Maybe. Who gave you the second love potion?"

She didn't even hesitate. "Dulcy. I called her for an antidote."

"Why did you need an antidote? I thought it didn't work."

"Of course it didn't work. But I ... I had nightmares. I figured the power of suggestion might be working, so I thought I'd do something to combat it. So I called Dulcy, and she mixed up a second potion to combat the first one. It was supposed to be a different one, and the two should have canceled each other out."

"Did they?"

Sybil grimaced. He was so close she could smell the cognac on his breath, and for a moment she wondered what it would taste like on his tongue.

"Dulcy made a mistake."

"Did she?"

"She thought you'd made a different potion. A Hungarian one, with completely different ingredients. Instead, she just gave me a second dose of the one you mixed up, and then she said there was nothing she could do."

"She lied."

She would have liked to insist that Dulcy never lied, but her own innate honesty stopped her. "You mean there was something she could do?"

"I mean she knew exactly what I had whipped up. She was the one who gave me the ingredients for it, how could she have not known which one I mixed?"

"You're right," Sybil said, unaccountably depressed. "I can't even trust my best friend."

He still hadn't moved. He was much too close, and as long as he stayed there she couldn't think quite clearly enough. "Maybe she thought it would be good for you," he suggested softly.

"And maybe she just wanted to cause some trouble. Dulcy likes to stir things up."

"Are you stirred up?"

She looked at him then, her wary brown eyes staring into his slightly hooded, hypnotic ones. She was crazy to get involved with him, he was nothing but trouble, he was everything she'd run away from. She was crazy to resist him, he was the sexiest thing she'd ever seen in her entire life and for some strange reason he seemed to want her.

"Are you?" he prodded, his voice low and mesmerizing, and the fingers that had been lightly toying with the flannel night-shirt slipped inside the loose neckline, to brush gently against her cool flesh. He was hot, so hot, and she'd been cold for such a long time.

"Yes," she said, her voice a mere whisper of sound, of reluctant surrender. "Yes."

He sighed then, a small sound that might have been relief, and his eyes drifted shut for a moment. The hand that was stroking her skin slid around behind her neck, pulling her gently to him as he leaned toward her. And his mouth touched hers, briefly, softly, and his lips tasted of cognac.

It was the last possible moment. He moved just inches away, his eyes fluttered open and stared down into hers. "One last chance, Saralee," he whispered, but he lied. It wasn't a chance at all, not with his long fingers still cupping her neck, not with his mouth so close to hers, not with the drugging sensuality of his golden eyes burning into hers. She didn't have a snowball's chance in hell.

She crossed the inches that separated them, rising onto her knees and sliding her arms around his neck. Never in her entire life had she wanted someone as much as she wanted this very dangerous man hunkered down in front of her. It could be the three years of enforced celibacy, the close brush with death or her own exhausted emotions. It could even be the double dose of non-Hungarian love philtre. It no longer mattered. She was through fighting it. For now.

Slowly, hesitantly she pressed her mouth against his. Her lips were trembling, her hands were shaking and he was holding himself very still, giving her no assistance, almost savoring her suddenly clumsy efforts. His mouth was soft, damp, responsive against hers, and she could feel his accelerated heartbeat as she pressed her breasts against his chest. It was more than enough encouragement. Very shyly she touched the tip of her tongue to his lips. They parted instantly, his own tongue caught hers before she could retreat. And the taste of cognac swirled around them, cognac and passion.

He surged upward, carrying her with him, and for a moment she dangled there in his arms, inches off the ground, as they kissed. He was hard against her, very hard, the soft fleece of his sweatpants leaving nothing to the imagination, and she gave a small moan of panic and anticipation. Slowly he lowered her to the floor, his hands sliding down to cup her rounded hips and hold her against him, forcing her to feel his need. It was a need that matched her own.

She slid her hands under the velour sweatshirt, trembling as she felt the hot, lean flesh of his stomach with its light covering of hair. He was hard all over, his stomach, his arms, his shoulders, everywhere. And she trembled, softness against his hardness, and pushed her hands higher under the shirt, to cup his flat male nipples.

He pulled his mouth away from hers with a groan, burying his mouth in the vulnerable curve of her neck. And the hands that had been cupping her hips were busy pulling the oversize nightshirt up and over her head, breaking them apart long enough to toss it across the room, leaving her in nothing but a pair of knee socks.

She tried to move back against him, half in shyness, half in desire, but his hands on her shoulders held her away, and his eyes as they drifted down her nude, aroused body were as powerful an aphrodisiac as any ancient love potion.

Then he pulled her back, and his hands on her flesh were unbearably arousing. She reached for his sweatshirt again, but he forestalled her, pulling it over his head and tossing it after the nightshirt. And catching her hand, he pulled it down between them, to that pulsing maleness that was turning her dizzy with want and a primitive panic. She wasn't used to this, she wasn't used to him, she wasn't sure....

He took her hand and slid it inside the waistband of the sweatpants. As her fingers curled, willingly and wonderingly, around his flesh, his hand found her, hot and damp and ready for him.

It had been so long, she thought. And it felt so good. No, "good" was too tepid a word. It was splendid, it was glorious, it was unbearably sweet. She was trembling all over, covered with a fine film of sweat, and her legs threatened to buckle beneath her. He was hot and hard and heavy in her hand, he was damp and ready for her, but still he made no move, content to stroke her, driving her past all conscious thought, and she knew if she had to wait a moment longer she wouldn't be able to stand it.

"Please," she whispered, her face crushed against the hot, smooth skin of his shoulder. Her free hand clutched at him, the nails digging into his flesh. "Please, I can't stand it."

"What do you want, Saralee?" he whispered in her ear, his voice soft and low. He couldn't be human, she thought. She had physical proof that he was ready to explode, and he could still taunt her, ignoring his own needs.

"I want you," she said. Stupid words, how could he fail to know that? "I want you inside me. Now."

He took his hand away from her, and she cried out in pain at the loss. He pulled away, out of reach, only for a moment, to strip off the black sweatpants. His eyes were glittering in the darkness, and the last little bit of fear shot through her. Was she a fool to want him?

Wisdom no longer had anything to do with it. Or sanity, or self-preservation, or even ego. Sybil no longer existed, neither did Nick. There was just woman, and man, and something dark and light, elemental and very complex, there, waiting.

His hands were hard and strong as they lifted her, up, up, into his arms and carried her into the bedroom. Then she was falling, they were falling, toward the bed, and he was over her, around her, in her, filling her with a deep thrust that left her breathless, and she was pulling him closer, wrapping herself around him, locking him in her arms, her legs, her body, imprisoning him as she was imprisoned by his invading maleness. Each thrust was a demand, a painfully sweet demand that she answered with the arch of her body, seeking that which retreated, only to advance again.

She was trembling, he was trembling, she was crying. Then the tempo shifted, jerked, swung crazily and exploded. *Too soon, Sybil thought dizzily. Not yet. Don't let it stop.*

And it didn't. For countless, endless moments it held, beyond reality, time and space. It held, so achingly pleasurable that it flirted with pain, then melted back into pleasure, until they collapsed together in a damp tangle of limbs and hair and heat and love.

She couldn't move, couldn't think, couldn't even open her eyes. Every ounce of strength she had left was spent on making her heart beat, her lungs fill with air.

Nick recovered faster, but then, he must have felt this incredible obliteration before. It was unlike anything Sybil had ever experienced in her life. She lay there, barely breathing, unable and unwilling to face him.

A finger touched her eyelid, and she flinched. Despite her best resolve she looked up to see Nick smiling down at her, those eyes of his bright with laughter, his fingertip wet with her tears.

She knew her expression was dazed, solemn, but there was nothing she could do about it. She watched him, waiting, waiting for heaven knew what.

"You're mine now," he said, his thin, sexy mouth curved in a smile that was oddly tender. "I just won your soul." And leaning down, he bit her lower lip, just hard enough to hurt.

"Got that, Saralee?"

She was too weary to fight. Her heart was working, her lungs were working, but her brain was still on automatic pilot. "Got it," she murmured in a rusty voice. And closing her eyes again, she shut him and all the troublesome world out, falling into a sated sleep.

Chapter Fifteen

He looked down at her, lying so sweetly, so peacefully, curled up in his arms. Her long, damp hair was wrapped around both of them, her warm brown eyes were closed in sleep, and one small, defenseless hand was pressed against her shadowed face. The other was resting against his shoulder in an unconscious expression of trust.

Who would have thought it? he brooded, stretching out in the small bed that had become pleasantly smaller with the addition of a much-longed-for companion. Who would have thought he'd fall in love with someone like Sybil-Saralee Richardson?

Adelle had been much more his style—leggy, sophisticated, ambitious, not a trace of fantasy in her elegant, cynical body. The woman lying next to him was, at best, passably pretty. Until she smiled, and his heart turned over. Or frowned, and he wanted to kiss her. Or looked abstracted, and he wanted to tickle her. In fact, no matter what she did, she captivated him. Illogical as it was, he was lost.

And the woman lying next to him believed in the most ridiculous things. What had that character in *Through the Looking-Glass* said? "Sometimes, I've believed as many as six impossible things before breakfast." He had little doubt that Saralee Richardson bettered that record.

She'd left elegant suburbia and a yuppie marriage for the rustic simplicity of wood stoves and blizzards, she wore cottons and corduroys and seemed oddly shy about sex. And the depth of his feeling for her left him shocked past denial.

She murmured something, shifting closer to him, and the hand tightened on his shoulder for a moment. He could see the mark of his teeth on her soft lower lip. That sudden act of possessive savagery startled him in retrospect. He'd always prided himself on his open-mindedness when it came to relationships; he believed that he'd never hold a woman if she wanted to leave.

Well, those noble days were over. If Sybil put up much more of a fight, he'd kidnap her and carry her off to Cambridge....

No, he wouldn't, much as the fantasy appealed to him in his current weary, semiaroused state. He'd be patient, charming, tolerant; he'd win her over by hook or by crook or by surreptitious doses of every love philtre known to man. And if that didn't work, then he'd kidnap her....

It was still snowing, and the rising sun had a hard time making inroads on the storm. He ran a tender, inquisitive hand down her back beneath the heavy quilts. Her skin was warm and responsive, even in sleep, and she murmured something low and definitely erotic. He ducked his head down to capture her lips again, but something about the shadows under her eyes, the faint trace of distant tears, stopped him. She'd only been asleep for less than an hour; he could give her a little time. With a storm like that still raging outside, there was no way she could run away. They'd have time.

SHE HAD NIGHTMARES. In the calm light of day she knew she wasn't being completely honest, to call them that. But they were the same sort of dreams she'd been plagued with ever since Nicholas Fitzsimmons had arrived in Danbury. Erotic, explicit dreams, full of sexual detail that seemed, to Sybil's uninformed mind, to be frankly impossible, combined with the typical imagery, which was even more disturbing. She could interpret the dreams in a hundred different ways, but one thing she couldn't avoid—she was physically obsessed with the man.

Not that it should be a surprise, she thought sleepily, curling up against him, nuzzling her face against the smooth, warm skin of his shoulder. Why else would she be in bed with him?

Her energy had certainly gotten diffused last night. If what Leona maintained was true, she wouldn't be able to dowse right now to save her life. Although dowsing was the last thing she had in mind at that point.

His hand was traveling up her back, slowly, gently, the touch of his lightly callused fingertips exquisitely arousing. She should open her eyes, tell him to take his hands off her and climb out of this bed.

But if she didn't open her eyes, she wouldn't have to face anything, would she? She could just lie back and enjoy it, pretend it was just one more of those deliciously, frighteningly erotic dreams she'd been suffering—"suffering" was hardly the word for it. She could just lie there....

"Open your eyes, Saralee."

How did he know she wasn't a heavy sleeper? She kept her breathing deep and steady, gave a realistic little wiggle and kept her eyes shut.

His hand slid around her hip, over her flat stomach, as his mouth gently brushed her lips. Her own mouth felt bruised, delightfully so, and it was all she could do not to open her mouth for him and kiss him back. But she kept her eyes shut.

"Open your eyes, Saralee." His voice was muffled as he trailed kisses down her neck, pushing her damp tangle of hair out of the way as he went. She wanted to help him, wanted to move closer, she wanted his hands and his mouth on her breasts. She kept her eyes shut.

He pushed the heavy quilts out of the way, and the cool air danced across her flushed skin. One hand stayed beneath the covers, stroking her trembling, fluttering stomach, the other slid under her shoulders, pulling her closer.

"Open your eyes, Saralee," he whispered, as his damp, open mouth captured her breast, his rough tongue swirling around the tightly aroused nipple. Her body arched in immediate reaction, her fingers clenched the sheet beneath her and she could feel the heat and dampness burning between her legs. She kept her eyes shut.

He was holding her as if she were a feast for his delight. His mouth was a bold devourer on her breasts, his hand was trailing across her stomach, sliding lower and lower, slipping between the legs that opened obligingly for him. His long, clever fingers knew just what they were looking for, and her body arched again in helpless response. A small, hungry moan sounded from the back of her throat.

"Open your eyes, Saralee," he whispered, moving his mouth from her aching breasts back to her bruised lips. She opened her mouth for him, for his plunging, invading tongue, and she opened her legs for him, for his clever, clever hand. But she kept her eyes shut.

A thousand tiny wings beat at her brain, a swirling mist of impenetrable snow surrounded her. She wanted him, she needed him, ached for him, so much that she was afraid she would weep with longing. And he knew it; he was too experienced a man not to recognize the signs. He had no qualms about taking advantage of a sleeping woman, and she had no qualms about faking sleep. She lay there, drowsy, passive, as his hands pulled her to the center of the soft bed, arranging her body for his invasion.

She could sense his shadowy presence above her in the dim light behind her eyelids. And then she felt him, hot and hard and ready against her.

He pressed against her, entering her very, very slowly, the pleasure of his measured advance sending shivers through her body. She arched up, wanting all of him, wanting it now, but he wasn't to be rushed. His control was absolute, his breathing labored but steady, as he filled her with unhurried, deliberate care. Then he was there, filling her completely. Her body was covered with a fine film of sweat as she tightened around him, savoring the feel of him, the size and strength and wonder—

And suddenly he was gone, pulling from her.

She arched up, reaching for him, but his hard hands held her down on the bed. "Open your eyes, Saralee," he said, and she knew it was for the last time.

Her eyes flew open, looking up into his intent, glowing ones in mute appeal. He still didn't move, and she could feel him there, waiting, teasing, pressing against her with his heat and power.

"That's better," he said, and the raw note in his voice was the only sign of strain. She saw the knotted muscles in his long arms as he held himself away from her, the sheen of sweat on his brow beneath the widow's peak, the gleam of his topaz-colored eyes. "I want you to know what you're doing. I want a participant, not a victim."

She lay there in the center of the bed. The old mattress dipped in the middle, cradling her, and he loomed over her, so that she felt trapped, imprisoned by the bed and Nick's hot, aroused body.

"I know what I'm doing," she said, and her voice wasn't much more than a whisper.

He looked down at her for a long, troubled moment. "Lord, I hope so," he said. Then he brought them together again, this time in a low, hard thrust that pushed her deeper into the hollow of the bed.

They took their time. The bed was soft and warm, their bodies relaxed and comfortable after their first, fevered coupling. This was the time to learn each other, to find what pleased them, where to stroke, where to kiss, where to nip lightly with sharp teeth. When to be fast, when to be blissfully, agonizingly slow, when to be soft and gentle, when to be just the tiniest bit rough.

The windows were covered with snow, and no one could look in. The telephone was off the hook; everyone thought she was still out of town. No one would look for her, no one would question her. She had nothing to do but learn Nick's body and learn a few surprising things about her own.

At first she'd tried to hurry him, being accustomed to her ex-husband's efficient attitude toward lovemaking. But Nick wouldn't be hurried; he wanted to savor, and savor he did. There wasn't an inch on her body he hadn't kissed, he moved her from position to position with gentle, demanding hands, and each new position carried her to new heights. Each time, when she thought she couldn't possibly feel any more, he'd showed her that she could.

Finally it was up to her. It was time to shatter his control as he had shattered hers, time and time again. She pushed him back on the bed, rolled him over and sat astride him, her long dark blond hair rippling down her narrow back, her brown eyes blazing in delight as this time she set the pace. When his hands reached out to cup her hips she moved them away, pressing them down on the mattress as she rocked, back and forth, teasing him as he had teased her, until he was panting and sweating, his golden eyes glazed, until he lost the last trace of his control and arched up into her downthrust, spilling himself into her with a raw, guttural cry that echoed in Sybil's heart as her body exploded around him one last time.

She sank down on him, her body drained and numb. She could hear his heart racing against her cheek, she could taste the salty tang of his sweat, she could feel the faint tremors that rippled over his body, tremors that matched her own. She realized she was smiling, a stupid, goofy smile against that warm, pounding chest, and for a brief moment she wondered what in the world had gotten into her. An old line came back to her—the devil made me do it. A little shiver ran down her backbone.

It was followed by the lazy stroke of Nick's hand, and that odd trace of nervousness temporarily vanished. "I hate to think what would have happened," he said huskily, "if that love potion actually worked."

It took all her energy, but she lifted her weary head to look down at him. She liked what she saw. He looked sleepy, dazed and completely satisfied. He even looked, just a little bit, like a man in love.

"If that potion had worked," she murmured, "you'd probably be dead."

He managed a tired grin. "I'm not quite sure that I'm not. I think," he said, "I've unleashed a monster."

"I think," she said, "maybe you have."

WHEN SYBIL AWOKE the next time the digital clock next to Nick's bed said twelve-thirty and the storm was over. Bright, glaring sunlight was pouring in the uncurtained window, reflecting off the thick white blanket of snow that covered everything. She closed her eyes against that glare, lying back in the bed, alone and sticky and sore.

The house was empty, she knew that without question. For a moment she had the wishful thought that Nick had seduced her and had run, back to Cambridge. At that moment she would have been very happy never to see him again.

But she knew that was too much to hope for. She straggled out of the bed, pulling the top sheet with her, and wandered into the living room. The wood stove was kicking out heat, and somewhere she could smell coffee. Nick might be part and parcel of that coffee, in which case she could do without it, but she didn't think so. The house had an indefinably empty feel that was unmistakable.

The coffee was sitting in its automatic drip pot, keeping warm just for her. The note was lying beside it.

"Couldn't wake you this time. Steve at the garage towed your Subaru in and is giving me a ride to Burlington to pick up the Jaguar. Be back around five. Be here."

Short, succinct, she thought with a curl of her lip, crumpling the note in one fist. There was writing on the back, and out of curiosity she flattened out the paper. "P.S. There's some extra love philtre in the refrigerator."

She ripped the note into tiny pieces and left them on the floor. She poured herself a cup of his coffee, because without it she would die, and stomped back into the living room.

She had no reason to be mad at him. He hadn't taken unfair advantage of her, it hadn't been rape, it hadn't even been seduction. It had been mutual, and that was what she couldn't accept. She would have been all right if it had just been last night. It would have been all right if she'd fooled him into thinking she was asleep this morning. But no, he had made sure she was wide awake and completely aware of everything he was doing to her more than willing body. And everything she was doing to his.

And the big question was, was there any future in it? In them? Was she a convenient roll in the hay, a challenge, a bed warmer for the cold Vermont nights? Or was it something more than that? And did she want something more than that?

She stretched out on the sofa that had been the beginning of her downfall last night. She pulled the maroon sheet around her body and slipped the strong black coffee. To be perfectly fair, she had to admit that there had been advantages to last night. While Colin's lovemaking had never been unpleasant, and What's-his-name in college had been exciting in an illicit sort of way, nothing had ever been as overwhelming as the last few hours had been. For years she had wondered if she were capable of feeling those kinds of reactions. Now she knew she was, and if Nick could bring them out in her, so could someone else. Couldn't they?

Couldn't she be grateful, enjoy the sex and wave a cheerful goodbye when he left? After all, she had a life she enjoyed up here, away from the pressures of modern life. She didn't want to go back, did she? And he certainly wasn't going to stay. So couldn't she just lie back and enjoy herself?

"No." She jumped before she realized she'd spoken the word out loud. But she said it again, for good measure. "No."

It simply wasn't in her nature, or in the nature of most women, for that matter. She couldn't give a man her body without giving him her heart. It was that simple.

It was also, she realized with a sense of shock, too late. Somewhere along the line, while she was fighting with him, and hiding from him, baiting him and avoiding him, somewhere along the line she'd given in. She'd fallen in love with the man. Before she'd given her body, she'd given her heart and mind and soul, and that was exactly why she'd been fighting so hard. What was the use of giving your heart and mind and soul to someone who didn't want them? It was downright degrading.

She'd already failed at one marriage. She wasn't cut out for connubial bliss, for suburbia and two-point-three children and happy ever after. Colin had been sweet, tolerant and undemanding, and she had suffocated to the point that she would have killed to escape.

How much worse would it be with a narrow-minded, overbearing tyrant like Nick? Someone who mocked everything she believed in, who rode roughshod over her objections and second thoughts. How much worse could it be with someone she loved to the point of obsession?

What had he whispered last night? "You're mine now," he'd said. "I just won your soul." And he'd bitten her.

A stray hand reached up and touched her lip. It stung slightly, and she pulled her hand back, trembling. She'd almost forgotten that odd, possessive interchange. Now that he had her, would he still want her? And for how long?

"Be here," he'd ordered. Well, that was definitely out. If she had to walk through a howling blizzard, she was getting home, away from him for long enough to think this mess through. If she stayed here she'd end up back in that high, soft bed, and heaven knows if she would have the determination to climb out again before he headed back to Cambridge.

"Damn," she muttered, draining the coffee. The sheet slipped off her as she stood, and for a moment she surveyed her body, from the tips of her toes, still clad in knee socks, up the nude length of her. Her winter-pale body had bruises, bites and other signs of her occupation during last night and this morning. At no point had Nick hurt her, but he'd certainly left his mark on her.

She sighed, pulling the sheet back around her. First things first, and the first thing she had to do was get the hell out of there. She headed directly toward the phone, dialing Dulcy's number. No answer.

She only hesitated a moment before hanging it up and dialing again. If this one failed her she'd walk.

Three long, fateful rings, and then a cozy little voice murmured, "Hello?"

"Leona," Sybil said, almost weak with relief. "Thank God you're there. I need your help."

Chapter Sixteen

"Didn't I warn you?" Leona questioned in her most plaintive voice, her tiny dark eyes glued to the snow-packed road ahead of them. She drove very slowly and carefully, so slowly and carefully, in fact, that it took her half an hour to traverse a stretch of road that took Sybil five minutes and a normal driver ten.

But beggars can't be choosers, Sybil thought, huddling down farther in the car seat, shivering in her cloth coat, silk dress and bare legs. She'd been lucky to find that much of her clothing; she'd even considered borrowing something of Nick's, but common sense had warned her against it. For one thing, he was more than a foot taller than she was. For another, it would give him the perfect excuse to come over and get whatever she borrowed.

"Yes, you warned me," Sybil said quietly.

"The man," said Leona, "is trouble."

Sybil sighed. She'd taken the shortest shower on record before Leona arrived, trying to wash the scent and sight of him off her body. She couldn't wash away the feel of his hands on her thighs, his mouth on her breasts, his hips . . .

"And you're not the only one who's suffered at his hands," Leona continued.

The flush that had heated Sybil's cheeks paled as an emotional fist slammed into her stomach. "He's been seeing someone else?"

"I hadn't even realized, dear girl, that he was seeing you. No, Professor Fitzsimmons has other interests. Unfortunately, I seem to be one of them."

Guilt swamped all of Sybil's other tangled emotions. "What do you mean?" she asked innocently. Damn, she should have warned her.

"Your friend seems to think I have something nefarious in my past. He's been making inquiries...."

"How do you know?"

Leona kept her face turned firmly toward the road as they crept along at a snail's pace. "Friends," she said mysteriously. "Friends told me people have been asking questions."

"But there's nothing to find out...."

"I'm afraid there is," Leona corrected her with a sigh. "I haven't lived a blameless life, Sybil. No one can live to my age and make that boast. I've made mistakes, but I've paid for them. They were long in the past, I thought gone forever, but your professor seems determined to rake them up."

"Not my professor," Sybil said firmly. "Er, what sort of mistakes, Leona?"

"Nothing dreadful. I have many gifts, and I haven't always used them wisely. I've been used by other people, evil men out for gain, and not realized it soon enough. When they were caught, I appeared guilty, and in a way I suppose I was. I should have realized what they were doing."

"What were they doing?"

"Cheating people out of their money," she said simply, and for a moment Sybil's heart shrank. "Exactly what your professor thinks I'm doing now."

"Not my professor," Sybil corrected absently. "What happened?"

She sighed. "It was all so long ago. My husband, and I'm afraid he was a major part of it, was convicted and sentenced to an obscenely long sentence. He died of a heart attack before he had served even two years of it. It was so long ago I don't even like to think about it," said Leona, dabbing a plump hand toward her dry eyes.

"Oh, Leona, I'm so sorry," Sybil said, her heart breaking.

Leona shook her head. "Don't be. I don't often think about it, only when something unpleasant comes up and reminds me of it. It was a sad time in my life, but I've put it behind me. Sybil, I wouldn't think of cheating my friends. You know me, I don't have such ruthlessness in me."

She knew very well that Leona had a great deal of ruthlessness when it came to small matters, but she dutifully shook her head. "Of course you don't," she soothed. "Nick must be crazy.""

"But will he convince the others? He's a very persuasive man.""

"Not that persuasive," said Sybil.

Leona spared an instant's attention from the road to cast a surprisingly knowing look at Sybil's attire. "Isn't he?" She blushed. "We won't let him railroad you."

"I'm afraid it might be too late. If he's started rumors...."

"I don't think he has. And we can fight back."

"I can't imagine how, my dear," Leona murmured with uncharacteristic fatalism. "I'll just have to move away from the first place that's felt like home—"

"You will not," she said firmly. "We'll think of something."

"Of course, we could always distract him," Leona suggested.

"Not the way you're thinking."

"Of course not!" Leona was affronted. "I wouldn't think of trading your purity for my peace of mind."

Sybil was feeling decidedly impure that morning, and not averse to a good enough excuse to continue that particular impure pastime, but she accepted Leona's protests. "Then how do we distract him?"

"Let me put my thinking cap on," she said with her usual coyness. "A wild-goose chase might be just the thing. Keep him so busy with phony clues that he won't have any time to spare for harassing me."

"Or me," said Sybil, only slightly mournfully.

"Especially not you, my dear," Leona said firmly. "We don't want you falling prey to his entrapments any more than me. Between the two of us, my dear, we'll put up a maze that no one could get through." She pulled to a stop in front of Sybil's snowed-in house. Thirty-five minutes that day, Sybil thought. An all-time record.

"Wonderful," Sybil said morosely. "You can count on me."

Leona gave her her kindest smile. "I knew I could, dear. I'll head back to the office, shall I? It wouldn't do to have the place unmanned."

"You do that," she said, setting her high-heeled, stocking-less feet in the deep snow and repressing a shiver. "I'll be in tomorrow."

Leona nodded. "We'll plan something then."

There were no dogs to leap about, greeting her with their usual doggy enthusiasm when she opened her unlocked door. The kerosene space heater wasn't adequate for the house—the most it could do was keep the heat above freezing so the pipes wouldn't burst. She had snow halfway up her thighs, her silk dress was soaked, her feet were blocks of ice and all she wanted to do was throw herself on her couch and weep.

But Richardsons, even changelings, were made of sterner stuff than that. She kicked off her shoes, headed straight to the bedroom and changed into warm long johns, baggy jeans and a thick wool sweater. She pulled on leg warmers and her warmest pair of socks, and headed for the living room and the wood stove.

It was an hour before the chill was off the house, an hour Sybil spent huddling in front of the hot cast-iron stove, shivering. She was too cold to call Dulcy again, too cold to read, to cold to do anything but stand there, hopping from one foot to the other, trying to get warm.

Her stocking foot landed on something hard and metal, and she let out a curse that would have done Nick at his most angry proud. It was a small brass pendulum she'd lost months ago. She picked it up, holding it in one freezing hand, watching it with unconcealed fascination as it twirled aimlessly.

Did unbridled lovemaking interfere with one's psychic concentration, as Leona contended? There was nothing to do but conduct a little experiment.

She ran the pendulum through a series of standard questions, and for once it was surprisingly responsive. Eyes brown, water running under the living room, snow falling, all of these things the pendulum agreed with.

"Am I going to live happily ever after?" She asked the question softly, half embarrassed.

The pendulum dangled, refusing to answer. "Will I ever find someone to love?"

It gave her an enthusiastic yes. Encouraged, Sybil pushed onward. "Will he love me?"

Another enthusiastic yes. "Will I meet him this year?"

The pendulum dropped, hanging there, and for one crazy moment Sybil had the odd impression that the pendulum was disgusted with her obtuseness. All right, the time for being coy was over.

"Is it Nick?"

The pendulum once more began its clockwise spin.

She stood there, watching it, biting her abraded lip as it spun, around and around and around, higher and higher. She must have thrown it. It couldn't have spun out of her hand, winging itself across the room. It was simply because she was tired and overwrought that she couldn't remember hurling the damned thing.

It was only because she was miserable that, search as she tried, she couldn't find a trace of it in the corner where she saw it land.

DULCY ARRIVED with the dogs sometime in midafternoon. Sybil hadn't called her again, but with her usual sixth sense Dulcy somehow got the message, not only about Sybil's return, but about her morose state of mind. She brought the dogs, she brought take-out Chinese food from St. Johnsbury, and she brought the largest size bottle of Courvoisier the state liquor stores offered.

Together they ate the food, giving the extra egg rolls to the dogs. Together they made a respectable inroad on the bottle of cognac. Dulcy left promptly at five o'clock, refusing to stay longer or to protect her from Nick's probable return.

Not that Sybil told her what she wanted to avoid. She'd been remarkably discreet, but Dulcy had gathered up her cape and her trailing scarves, had taken one look at Sybil's face and laughed.

"Lost your innocence, have you?"

Sybil's back stiffened. She was sitting on the living room couch, surrounded by dogs, and she had no intention of moving. "I don't know what you're talking about."

"Sure you do. I can read between the lines. You smashed up your Subaru at five in the morning and waited until afternoon for a ride home. You must have been doing something all that time."

"I was sleeping on the couch."

"Sybil," Dulcy protested, shocked. "Don't lie to me. For one thing, it's a complete waste of time. For another, it hurts my feelings. I'd rather you told me to mind my own business."

"Mind your own business."

"Don't throw him away, Sybil." She blithely ignored the order. "He's worth the effort."

Sybil gave up fighting. "I offered him to you first."

Dulcy shrugged. "He didn't want me. He'd already seen you."

"I'm hardly the type to overshadow you, Dulcy."

"You aren't the type, my friend. You were *the one*. Nick wasn't looking for a roll in the hay, a pretty face, a gorgeous body."

"Thanks a lot."

"Not that he didn't get all three," Dulcy said hastily.

"Who says he got them?"

"Your face does."

"Well, he's not going to get them again. Not if I can help it," Sybil said, leaning against the couch.

"Why not?"

"There are a million reasons."

"Name one."

Sybil leaned forward, intent, and one of the puppies slid onto the floor with a startled yip. "I'll give you two excellent ones. For one thing, he's out to get Leona. He's had her investigated, he's harassing her, trying to railroad her—"

"You're breaking my heart," said Dulcy, never a great fan of Leona's. "Don't you think Leona can take care of herself? You're not her mother, for goodness' sake."

"I don't like to see helpless old women victimized," Sybil said stiffly.

"Neither do I. But Leona's never struck me as the victim type. She's the sort who'll always come out on top. If I were you I'd spend my energy worrying about the Muller sisters and Mary Philbert. They're the real victims."

"Damn it, Leona didn't steal their money!"

"Is that what Nick thinks?" Dulcy murmured, fascinated.

"I hadn't thought of that."

"It's not true."

Dulcy merely smiled. "Give me your second excellent reason for avoiding Nick."

"He's everything I came here to get away from. I've spent my entire life running from people like him, from perfect lives and brilliant people and complicated, stressful life-styles." The moment the words were out of her mouth she wished she could call them back.

Dulcy smiled, seeing the unhappy recognition in Sybil's warm brown eyes. "Do I even have to say it, Sybil? Isn't it time you stopped running away? Isn't it time you face what frightens you? Maybe then you'll realize that there's nothing to make you feel inadequate."

"Go away, Dulcy."

Unfortunately, Dulcy left. Sybil looked around her, depressed. It was getting nerve-racking close to Christmas; maybe she should start to get in the spirit. She'd been so busy fighting her attraction to Nick that she hadn't even made a wreath. Maybe this year she ought to buy one. Her wreath-making talents were decidedly iffy, with the results looking more like an oval than a nice circle. She always stuffed too many dried herbs and flowers in them, to cover the inadequacies, but she usually got those herbs and flowers from Dulcy, and right now she'd die before she asked her for anything.

Think Christmas, she told herself, dragging out the large box of decorations from the attic. Think peace on earth, goodwill to men...to all, she corrected herself absently. To all but Nick Fitzsimmons.

She put a tape of medieval carols on the stereo, poured herself another cognac and set to work, with crocheted snowflakes in the windows, antique wooden toys on any surface not cluttered with books, candles of varying sizes and colors all around.

Each time the phone rang she jumped a mile. Steve at the garage called to say the Subaru was bloody but unbowed, her parents called to make sure she'd made it through the storm safely, Leona called to tell her she'd drive her to work tomorrow morning and they could discuss a plan she had. Even Edla Muller called, to tell her she was glad she was back.

But there was no word from Nick.

Well, of course she didn't want there to be. The problem with men, she thought as she strung delicate golden beads from the rafters, was that the moment you fell in love they disappeared. As long as the sensible female fought it, the man responded to

PLAS
AND

★ Excit
★ Plus

THE
LUC
SWE

1. Play Lu
2. Send b
   Super
   $3.50
3. There'
   anythi
   shipm
   numb
4. The fa
   mail fr
   conve
   new n
   our dis
5. We h
   to ren
   conti
   up on
   glad y

the challenge. As soon as she was fool enough to give in and lose her heart, he lost interest.

Well, she could lose interest, too, she promised herself grimly, ignoring the unfairness of her generalizations and rationalizations. She wasn't so far gone that she couldn't fight it once more. If he kept away, she wouldn't be as obsessed tomorrow, she'd be less so on Wednesday, and by Christmas she'd have forgotten all about it. Christmas, 1999, perhaps.

The dogs were lying all over the living room in various attitudes of doggy complacency. They did no more than raise their sleepy heads when Nick walked, silently and unannounced, into the living room.

Sybil was balanced somewhat precariously on a chair, trying to hook a strand of German crystal beads around the hanging lamp. He was heading toward her with a purposeful expression in those wonderful eyes of his, and for a moment she stood there, motionless.

During the day she'd managed to blot out just how good-looking he really was. His face was captivating, almost haunting in its beauty, from the thick black hair that came forward in a widow's peak, the satanic eyebrows, the narrow, almost austere mouth and mesmerizing eyes. If she looked into those eyes, those hungry, hypnotizing eyes for a moment longer, her resolve would vanish. Then who would protect poor Leona from him? And who would protect poor Sybil?

She jumped down before he could reach her, scampering behind the chair. He stopped his forward stride, his eyes met hers and his mouth curved in a cynical, resigned smile. "I don't suppose you're skittering away from me like a scared rabbit because I was a few hours late."

"Are you?" Her voice was husky and breathless.

"It's eight. I thought I'd be back by five or six at the latest, but the Jaguar had been plowed in at the airport and it took a while to get it out."

"I wasn't expecting you."

His sigh was loud, long-suffering and bordering on irritated. "Is it because I took off this morning? Believe me, I tried to wake you up. You were sleeping like the dead. I left you a note."

"So you did. As I recall, it said, 'Be here.'"

"Is that the problem? I can be dictatorial, I know. You'll have to cure me of it." He smiled at her, and her heart began to melt.

Think about Leona, she warned herself sternly. *Think about the Richardsons.* "That wasn't the problem. I just ignored it."

"Then what is it?" He advanced upon her, and then his hands were on her, his long fingers caressing her arms through the heavy sweater, and she could feel her knees tremble.

"Nick, this isn't going to work."

"Sure it is," he murmured, enfolding her in his arms, ignoring the token struggle.

"You're not the kind of man I want."

"Sure I am," he said, and she could feel him against her, the heat and hardness of him, and miserably she had to agree.

"And if I'm not, I'll change."

"Nick . . ."

His mouth caught hers, midprotest, in a slow, lazy kiss that was as thorough as it was arousing. Desperately she clung to the last shreds of her resistance, but it was fading fast, disappearing like wisps of wood smoke on a windy morning. One of his hands had slipped beneath her loose sweater and was already cupping her breast, and she could feel the tight curl of desire deep in the center of her, twisting outward.

He lifted his head for a moment, looking down at her, and his eyes were glittering with desire. "So what else is the problem?"

It was time enough for the last bit of common sense to intrude. If he hadn't stopped, if he'd just kept kissing her, she would have ignored her worries and concentrated on the moment at hand.

"Leona," she said.

He held himself very still, his arms still holding her, but she could sense the withdrawal, the slowly building anger.

"What about Leona?" he said with deceptive mildness, but the fiery depths of his golden eyes had turned flat and opaque.

"I can't have you railroading her."

"Are you telling me you'll sleep with me if I leave Leona alone?" The question was gently worded, but there was no way she could ignore the tight lash of anger beneath his even voice.

"No," she said bravely, ignoring the fluttering nervousness that had replaced, or almost replaced, the wanting. "I'm telling you to leave Leona alone, and that I won't sleep with you anyway."

He was very angry, very, very angry indeed. He pulled away, slowly, and with the withdrawal of his heat she felt cold, deep in the very heart of her. "I don't think," he said, "that I'll even bother to ask why. You'll just come up with more crap about how I'm not the kind of man you want, and it'll be a waste of time. Anyone who could dismiss what we shared this morning, ignore that rare kind of magic, is a fool. When it comes right down to it, Saralee Richardson, you're not the kind of woman I want."

He whirled and stalked, absolutely stalked, toward the hallway, fury radiating through his tall, gorgeous body, leaving Sybil staring after him, miserable, doubt-ridden, half ready to run after him.

She'd taken one step in his direction when he turned, and he was so angry he didn't notice the misery and doubt on her face. "And as for your friend Leona," he said, "I'm going to mop the floor with her." Without another glance in her direction he slammed out of the house.

Chapter Seventeen

He shouldn't have lost his temper like that. He knew it, regretted it, but right now he was so mad he wanted to pound on the leather-covered steering wheel and scream obscenities into the chilly winter night. How could she be so childish, obtuse, criminally stupid? Didn't she realize how rare last night was? You don't just throw something like that away because you're too damned scared to face life.

And that was it. Sheer, simple cowardice on her part. Sex that good didn't come from physical sources alone. There had to be love, love on both sides, to bring the act of making love from a satisfying physical experience to something approaching heaven. When he'd left her this morning he'd been dazed, shaken and more than a little frightened himself. His feelings for her—physical, emotional, even spiritual—were like nothing he'd ever felt.

Right now his intellectual feelings for her were so intensely furious that they threatened to wipe out all those blissful emotions. He should have turned her over his knee and spanked her. Except even that thought was erotic. Damn her, damn her, damn her!

Well, she could have it her way. He'd leave her strictly alone, back in her safe, celibate world for a while, and see how she liked it. Within two weeks, by New Year's Eve, she'd be climbing the walls. And he'd be waiting for her, and this time it would be on his terms.

In the meantime he was going to do exactly what he said. He wasn't going to rest until he found out exactly what was going on with Leona Coleman. He had little doubt he had her to thank, at least partially, for Sybil's sudden withdrawal. Sybil wasn't going to trust him completely until she found out what a scheming, devious criminal Leona really was.

Of course, there was always the remote possibility that he was wrong about her. So far Ray hadn't been able to come up with a thing, but what with the Boston Slasher the police hadn't had much free time to play around with computers. All his instincts told him that Leona was a crook of the first order, and his instincts seldom lied.

Those same instincts told him that sooner or later Sybil would come to her senses, come to him, where she belonged. He just hoped this wasn't the one time wishful thinking took the place of those infallible instincts.

He was driving too fast down the snow-packed road, but he didn't care. Not that he was in any hurry to get back to the Black Farm. It would be cold, dark and lonely there, and the rumpled bed, so much smaller than the queen-size one he had in his apartment in Cambridge, would seem very large indeed. And would continue that way, for all the nights afterward that he had to sleep alone.

He'd give Ray another call tonight, see if he could prod him into finding something. Sybil Richardson was a very stubborn lady; it would take time or solid evidence that she was wrong to move her. And right now, time was the last thing he wanted to waste.

While he was at it, he might as well make a call to his real estate agent. There was no way six springer spaniels would fit into his current apartment.

"DON'T WORRY," Sybil said wryly as Leona popped her snowy white head around the front door of the Society of Water Witches two days later, "he's not coming in today, either. I think he's gone back to Boston for a few days."

"I knew that," Leona said, straightening to her full five feet and moving forward with dignity. "I dowsed it before I came. I just wanted to make certain."

"Don't you trust your dowsing?" The moment the words were out of her mouth Sybil could have bitten her tongue. It was all Nick's fault, this sudden doubt that was plaguing her. He was shaking the foundations of everything she held dear, from dowsing to Leona to what she wanted in life. Why couldn't he just go away and leave her alone?

Except, of course, that was just what he'd done for the past three days. And she didn't like it one bit.

"Of course I trust my dowsing. But your professor—"

"Not my professor—"

"... is a changeable man. Unpredictable at best. That's why we have to do something about him." Leona plopped herself down on the straight chair beside the desk, her short plump legs dangling.

"I suppose so," Sybil said warily. "Do you have anything in mind?"

"It's got to be something to send him back to Massachusetts and away from us. Or at least something to keep him too busy to be chasing after me."

"Amen," said Sybil, thinking of her own particular chase.

"And I've come up with the perfect idea. We'll send him to see Everett Kellogg."

Sybil just stared at her with a mixture of doubt and admiration. "No one can get near Everett this time of year. I always wonder whether he'll make it through the winter up there, but every spring he shows up, hale and hearty. He must be past ninety."

"I expect he is. He's also one of the best dowsers around, and certainly the oldest. There are things he knows that no one else would, things that happened back at the turn of the century that would be invaluable to someone like your professor."

"Not my professor. And of course he'd be invaluable. That's exactly why I haven't mentioned him to Nick. There's no way, short of a helicopter, to get through to Everett before the spring thaw. And Nick's the sort of man who wouldn't believe me if I told him it couldn't be done."

"Exactly," said Leona, swinging her legs back and forth. "All you have to do is tell him about Everett and warn him that he can't make it. Your... Professor Fitzsimmons will do the rest."

"He could be killed, Leona," Sybil said quietly.

"Nonsense. He'll try to drive up through Gillam's Notch, wreck his fancy car and have to walk back down. He's supposed to be in England in less than a month; he won't have time to replace his car and finish his research. Even if he does, he'll be far more interested in getting to Everett than prying into my background."

"He's going to England?" Sybil echoed faintly.

"Didn't you know? He's here for research, and then he's going to Oxford for a year on a teaching and studying fellowship."

"Oh," Sybil said in a flat voice, trying to ignore the sense of betrayal that was rapidly building. Why in the world should she care if Nick was leaving the country? She wanted him out of her life, didn't she?

"The plan isn't foolproof," Leona admitted. "But it's better than nothing. With luck he'll get pneumonia. That should put him out of commission!"

"Leona!" Sybil hadn't liked the sound of malicious satisfaction in her friend's voice one bit. "Why can't we just send him a fake telegram or something, tell him he has to go to England sooner?"

"Because he'd check. Professor Fitzsimmons isn't the sort just to pack up on a moment's notice. He'd probably fight a summons like that just to be contentious. It's going to have to be Everett."

Sybil looked across at Leona's round, cherubic face, the dark, shining little eyes, the pursed little mouth, the plump little legs swinging back and forth. "No, Leona," she said gently. "It's too dangerous. We want him to leave us alone, but we don't want to risk his life. You haven't thought it through."

"Of course I thought it through. Do you think I would endanger someone's life, no matter how much he deserved it?" She was clearly affronted. "I dowsed it. I read the tarot, I cast the runes and, just to make certain, I even used the Ouija board, antiquated as it is. It will be perfectly safe."

Sybil just looked at her. Everything was on the line; the moment was upon her faster than she'd ever dreaded. She was being called upon to risk Nick's life, and the only guarantee he'd be safe was Leona's powers—things Sybil believed in, worked for, things intrinsic to her very being. But could she risk Nick's life for them?

She would risk her own life, no question about it. If she was afraid of a dangerous situation and a dowser told her it was safe, she'd go into that situation full of trust. But she had no right to risk Nick's life. And when it came right down to it, was she trusting her beliefs, or trusting in Leona? No one was infallible, particularly in matters like these.

"No," she said firmly. "I can't let you do it."

For a brief moment Leona's face went perfectly blank. Then she shrugged her plump shoulders and smiled. "Well, it was a thought. We'll just have to come up with a better notion."

The tension that had been singing through Sybil's body vanished, and she smiled with real relief. "Don't worry, Leona. We'll figure out some way to get him off your case.'"

Leona smiled sweetly.

EVERY NIGHT when she drove past the Black Farm she searched for signs of habitation. It wasn't until four days before Christmas that she saw the lights down at the end of that long driveway, the thin plume of smoke swirling up into the blackening sky.

For half an hour she considered trumped-up excuses to visit him. For another half hour she berated herself for her weakness. For the third half hour she made plans. Whether she liked it or not, he had a devastating effect on her. The hoped-for lessening in her libido hadn't yet taken effect, and the last thing she wanted was to immure herself in that old building with only Nick around, with his mesmerizing eyes, thin, sexy mouth and absolutely luscious body....

Christmas shopping. Three days to Christmas, and she had a million things left to do. Her tree was standing in the corner farthest away from the drying effects of the wood stove, and the handmade ornaments and tiny white lights were beautiful and curiously depressing. Maybe if she bought some colored lights instead. And she had to get stockings for the dogs, presents for Dulcy and Leona and the Mullers, and some wool for her next project. The flame-colored sweater was finished, and it was her worst job ever. It was too big at the top, too narrow at the bottom, the arms would fit an orangutan and the color turned her sallow. If worse came to worst, she'd give it to Nick; it might give her a malicious thrill to see him forced to wear it.

But not tomorrow. She wanted a day to compose herself, a day just to do what she wanted without having to worry about Nick. He'd been gone for almost six days; no doubt he expected her to fall at his feet. Well, she wasn't about to warm his bed for a couple of weeks before he took off for England. He could damn well be just as celibate as she'd been. Or could go after Dulcy.

The next day wasn't everything Sybil had hoped for. Leona was more than willing to fill in at the office, and as Sybil drove by the Black Farm she saw a tall, familiar figure climbing into the dark green Jaguar. Her reaction was like a fist to the stomach. She stomped on the accelerator as hard as she could, fishtailing up the snow-covered road toward town.

Eschewing the limited pleasures of St. Johnsbury, she headed for Burlington, for yuppie stores with gourmet chocolate and Liz Claiborne and Celtic music and imported cheeses. She didn't get there often, and had every intention of spending a fortune.

She bought half a pound of Godiva chocolates and ate them all on the way home. She bought raspberry liqueur for the Muller sisters and a crystal for Leona. She bought dog stockings for the springers, silk stockings for Dulcy and nothing for herself. By the time she reached Danbury in midafternoon, the sun was already sinking lower in the gray December sky, her stomach was protesting the surfeit of chocolate, and she was very close to tears.

The green Jaguar was parked outside the Davis Apartments. For a moment panic swept through her, and then she remembered that Leona would be at the office. They'd hardly be in the midst of a dangerous confrontation. And he couldn't be in there searching her apartment—Gladys would have ripped his throat out.

She drove past, very slowly. He was parked in front of the Mullers' door. Sybil looked back at the liqueur. She had been planning to stop in on her way out to her house; she shouldn't let Nick's presence stop her. But was she ready to see him? She'd spent an almost wasted day in Burlington, simply to avoid him. Why spoil a perfect record of misery?

She reached the deserted center of town, pulled a skidding U-turn, and headed back to the Mullers, just in time to see the Jaguar pull away, heading out toward the old road to Barton.

Edla and Minna were just finishing up their tiny little glasses of sherry, and nothing would do but they had to share another with Sybil. She could see the third empty glass, the crumbs on the plate of Christmas cookies, but with great effort she waited, eating Miss Minna's freshly baked spritz cookies and sipping the sweet cream sherry.

It didn't take long to get to the subject, and Sybil didn't even have to bring it up. "I am worried about the professor, dear," Miss Edla said.

"Are you?" Sybil picked up a cookie shaped like a Christmas tree and licked the green sprinkles off it.

"Do you think what he's doing is particularly safe?"

She raised her head sharply, her brown eyes meeting Miss Edla's faded blue ones. "What do you mean?"

"Well, if Everett Kellogg wanted visitors, I don't think he'd live up in the Notch. And I think Leona must be wrong—the road must be impassable by now. I don't think the professor should be heading out. . . . Where are you going?"

"After him." Sybil had crammed the cookie into her mouth and jumped for her coat. "Was he going there this afternoon?"

"Somehow he got the idea that it was the best time to go. I think Leona must be very confused—she told him that the road went all the way through in the winter. Of course, we don't drive, but as I remember the road ends rather abruptly."

"Did you warn him?"

"Well, no, dear. After all, Leona gave him complete instructions, and she does drive. I couldn't very well contradict her, now could I?"

She crammed the hat down on her head. "He's heading for the Notch? He wasn't going anywhere else first?"

"He seemed to think we were due for another big storm, and if he didn't go now, then he wouldn't see Everett at all," Miss Minna said. "Funny, the weatherman didn't say anything about a storm."

"Damn," Sybil said. "Bye, ladies."

She ran from the apartment, slamming the door behind her, and leaped into her car like a stock car racer. The Subaru purred into life, bless its engine, and she tore into the road, narrowly missing a milk truck while skidding sideways toward several parked cars, and finally straightening herself and her four wheels. She took off down the road like a bat out of hell, cursing under her breath.

Leona simply didn't realize how dangerous it was. The temperature was hovering around ten degrees, and there wasn't a cloud in the sky. By the time the sun set and the half-moon had risen, the temperature would plummet, well below zero. And Nick would be out there, stuck in a snowdrift, with his damned city shoes on and his damned city clothes, and if he didn't get frostbite or worse he'd be a lucky man.

She should have known Leona wouldn't be discouraged so easily. She was a very stubborn woman, unfortunately convinced of her own infallibility. If her pendulum told her it was safe, she'd walk on water. And probably manage it, too, Sybil thought with a ghost of a smile. But Leona's self-assurance wasn't enough to keep Nick safe.

It was quarter to four, and the shadows were deepening around her on the deserted road. The old road to Barton was paved for the first three miles, and the coating of ice was treacherous indeed. Since the road went nowhere, only to a couple of farms, and then ended halfway up Gillam's Notch, it wasn't a high priority with the road crew. By the time she reached the gravel part, it hadn't even been plowed since the last storm.

The Jaguar tracks were ahead of her, narrow and elegant even with studded snow tires. But the green car was out of sight, heading for a road that ended in a snowbank or a cliff. He could take his pick.

And if it was dark, and he didn't know about the cliff, he might swerve to avoid that wall of snow left by the plow. There might be enough snow buildup along the side of the road to keep him from plunging over into the gulch, and there might not. Sybil shoved her booted foot down farther on the accelerator, ignoring the needle as it pushed past sixty.

The Subaru didn't like the speed. You weren't supposed to use the optional four-wheel drive at speeds above fifty, but there was no way she was going to careen down this road at any speed less than her maximum, and no way she'd do it in two-wheel drive. If the poor car self-destructed, well, cars can be replaced. Nick Fitzsimmons couldn't.

She left the dim lights of the last farmhouse behind her and started climbing. It was getting very dark now, that twilight time when headlights made no dent in the thickening shadows, and Sybil kept cursing and praying under her breath. She tried to send a mental cloud of healing blue light around Nick, but her anxiety and panic kept interfering with it. All she could do was curse and pray and drive on.

Higher and higher she climbed. In the darkness she couldn't remember where the road usually ended, and out of necessity she slowed her desperate pace. As long as he didn't go over the cliff, she'd get there in time. But despite all the heavy snow of late November and December, snowbanks along the narrow road were less than a foot high. A determined driver with the power of a Jaguar could go right through them.

In the end she almost crashed into him. Rounding a corner, she saw the taillights of the car, jammed into the wall of snow ahead of them, and she slammed on her brakes, skidding sideways, heading directly toward the driver's seat of the Jaguar, directly toward Nick's waiting figure.

It took endless moments as she lifted her panicked foot off the brakes and began to pump them, gently, as she'd always been told to do and had never quite mastered. It would be a hell of a note, she thought, with her mind floating miles away, if she smashed into him and killed him while she was trying to save his life.

The Subaru slowed, slowed, slowed, sliding like a graceful figure skater, crossing the last few feet and coming to a gentle, delicate stop against the door of the Jaguar with no more sound than the gentle whisper of metal on metal.

Nick turned and glared at her as she sat there, dazed. With shaking hands she turned the key, only to find that the car hadn't stalled out after all. The starter shrieked in protest, and she shifted it into reverse, backing away, slowly, carefully, taking green paint with her.

It was a colorful gash down the side of the Jaguar, a rip in its elegant hide, but barely a dent to mar it. Nick climbed out, very tall, very angry in the moonlit darkness of the mountain, and stalked over toward her.

She sat there, unmoving, not even opening the window. He yanked open the door and pulled her out. "What the hell are you doing here?" he demanded.

"Wrecking your car?" she offered, her voice a nervous thread.

"It's not wrecked." He didn't even bother to give it a cursory glance. "Steve can tow it out tomorrow. I want to know how you knew I'd be up here."

"The Muller sisters said you were going to find Everett, and I didn't think it was safe . . ." she faltered.

"Leona said it would be."

"Leona hasn't been up here in a while. Besides, I told her it would be passable until after Christmas, but then, I thought about it and realized it wouldn't be, and when I heard you were coming up here I figured you might not make it..." She was stammering and stumbling as the lies bubbled forth, and it was all a waste of breath.

"I don't believe you," he said flatly. "I think you found out Leona was trying to set me up and you came after me. I don't know if you did it to save me or to keep Leona from making an even worse mistake."

"Leona didn't realize—"

"Why did you come, Sybil?" The anger was gone. His eyes were dark and glittering in the moonlight, his face silvered and dangerous.

"I didn't want you to freeze to death," she said, shivering a little herself.

He just looked at her. "Then come here and warm me up."

Her feet crossed the short space that separated them, and she went into his arms. She was right, he was wearing city clothes and city shoes, and he was cold, so cold. She opened her down coat to press her own warmth against him, wrapping her arms around him and pulling him closer. It seemed only natural for her mouth to reach up for his, only natural to kiss him, breathe her warm, sweet breath into his mouth, rub her tongue against his, her hips against his, her legs against his.

She found she was shivering, not with cold, but with another basic need that threatened to overpower her. And she wished it were a hot summer's night instead of hovering around zero.

Nick lifted his head, and his breath was frosty in the night air. "I think I'm warm," he said. "As a matter of fact, I think I'm burning up. Let's get out of here."

Sybil took a deep breath, looking around her. "We're going to have to back all the way down the mountain."

"That's all right," he said with the ghost of a smile. "As long as you let me drive."

"I'll let you drive," she said. *I'll let you do anything,* she thought. And moving away, she climbed into the passenger seat and waited.

Chapter Eighteen

It was a long, slow drive back down the mountain. Sybil stayed silent, sitting there beside him as he maneuvered the treacherous twists and turns of the narrow roadway. The heater was on full blast, making a small dent in the rapidly chilling air, and she shivered slightly, pulling her unzipped coat closer around her. She hated to think of what might have happened, of Nick trying to walk the five or so miles down the mountain to the nearest farmhouse.

Once he'd made it to the bottom of the hill he turned the Subaru deftly, heading onto the straightaway with his eyes trained outward. She spared a cautious glance at his profile. It looked cold and severe, grim and unyielding, and she shivered again.

"I know what you're thinking," she said.

He didn't spare her a glance. "Do you? I thought you said your psychic abilities were extremely limited."

"A maple tree has enough psychic ability to guess what you're thinking," she snapped, flustered. "It was a mistake, Nick."

"Humph," he said.

"I'm sure Leona had no idea the road was impassable. She doesn't drive up this way; she wouldn't know that it was already closed."

"Really?" His tone was unpromising.

"I know that's hard to believe when someone is as paranoid as you are, but it was entirely coincidental. Leona isn't the monster you seem to think she is; I'm sure she just wanted to help you out."

"Help me out of this mortal coil, don't you mean?"

"Don't be absurd. You wouldn't have died, anyway. You'd have made it to a farmhouse before you froze to death."

"Unless I went off the cliff."

Sybil shivered again. "She doesn't know the terrain. It's just lucky the Mullers told me where you were heading. Leona will be beside herself when she finds out what happened."

"Beside herself that I didn't go over the cliff."

"You're going to believe what you want to believe," she said wearily. "How can I convince you that she meant no harm?"

Nick turned to look at her, his face illuminated by the bright winter moonlight reflecting off the snow. "I should take everything she told me at face value?" he countered softly.

There was a trap, she knew it, but she was too overwrought to guess what it was. "Absolutely," she said.

"Then if what she told me was true, why did you leave me the message about Everett Kellogg?" he said in a silky voice. "According to Leona, you told her to tell me about him. It was your suggestion that I take the Notch road, and not bother to wait until morning. What happened, Sybil? Did you change your mind, decide maybe it wasn't time for me to meet my doom?"

She was shocked into a profound, utter silence. "You don't believe that," she said finally, her voice rusty.

"Give me an alternative. I'll be interested to see how you do it without implicating your good buddy. Either Leona lied to me and did her best to get me killed or at least incapacitated, or you're feeling a great deal more hostile than I imagined."

"Neither."

He glanced at her, and his thin mouth twisted in a smile that was only half cynical. "Okay. Let's hear your explanation."

She took a deep breath. "It's very simple," she said. "Leona must have misunderstood."

"Sure she did."

"I . . . we talked about Everett this week," she said, thanking heaven that much was true. "And we wondered whether it was too late for you to get up to see him. We were going to check with the people who live out this way, to see if the road was still open, before we told you. You're so headstrong you'd have come up here anyway, even if I told you it was impassable."

"I would have done it in broad daylight, driving slowly, with the proper clothes on in case I got stuck. So you and Leona were going to check and see whether it was safe, were you?"

"Yes," she said, grateful he was swallowing it. Enough of it was true—Leona had to have misunderstood the dangers of the situation. Leona was so certain her dowsing was infallible; she really would be horrified when she found out the danger Nick had been in. Wouldn't she?

"You're lying."

She swiveled around in the seat, staring at him as shock and hurt sliced deep within her. "How could you believe that I'd want to hurt you? I want you to go away and leave me alone, but I want you to go in one piece, of your own accord. How could you think . . . ?"

"I don't think you sent me up there, Sybil," he said as he turned the Subaru down her driveway. "I think you're covering up for Leona, and even worse, I think you're still trying to convince yourself that she wasn't trying to kill me."

"Nick . . ."

"But right now I don't really care. I'm taking your car, whether you like it or not. I'm going home and take a hot bath, and then I'll call the garage and maybe, just maybe, the police."

"How can I convince you—"

"You can't." He slammed the car to a stop, turned off the ignition and glared at her.

She considered pleading with him, considered and then abandoned the idea. He'd do what he had to do; nothing she said would change his mind. She'd already come up with the best excuses, and none of them worked. Worst of all, she couldn't rid herself of the suspicion that he might be right.

"When will I get my car back? I have to work tomorrow."

"Call Leona," he snapped.

She unhooked her seat belt and slid out of the seat, shivering in the icy night air. She could hear the dogs howling and scrabbling at the front door in their desperation to get out and greet them properly. "Better get out of here fast," she said in a subdued voice, "or the dogs will follow you halfway home."

There was no sound from the aging engine as she headed toward her front door. She could feel Nick's eyes on her, but she didn't look back. The back seat of the car was filled with the Christmas presents she'd bought that day in Burlington, and they could damned well stay there. The sooner he was out of there the better.

The dogs swarmed over her, yipping a joyous greeting, wiggling and twirling in midair in their enthusiasm. They made so much noise she didn't even realize that Nick had come up behind her.

"You're half frozen," he said gruffly over the barking of the dogs. "And so am I." He pushed her, gently enough, through the open door, and the dogs swarmed after them.

At least the house was still relatively warm. The temperature had only just begun to plummet, the banked fire in the wood stove had kept the heat at a bearable level, and it took her no more than a few nudges with the poker and a couple of pieces of dry wood to get a satisfying blaze going. Closing the cast-iron door, she turned to look up at Nick.

He was standing there, towering over her crouching body, tall and dark and menacing. He was dressed in black—black cords, black sweater, a long black topcoat better suited to city streets over everything. He'd unbuttoned the coat and was in the midst of shrugging it off when he caught her quizzical eye.

"I thought you wanted a hot bath," she said.

"I could always take one here."

"No, you can't," she said.

A faint smile creased the stern contours of his dark face. "Are you throwing me out?"

She rose to her full height, her muscles and bones protesting the cold and her own weariness. "I'll give you coffee and cognac to warm you," she said grudgingly. "And then you can leave."

"I can think of better ways to get warm."

"I'm sure you can," she said. "But I'm not in the mood for a little slap and tickle right now." She began unwinding her tattered scarf from around her neck. She'd left the Christmas tree lights on, and their glow was an unwanted romantic touch in the cluttered, cozy living room. With chilled fingers she began to unzip her down coat, ignoring the cloud of feathers that floated around her.

He moved so quickly she had no time to duck, if she had even wanted to. His hands brushed her numb ones away, unfastening the coat and pushing it off her shoulders. It landed in a feathery pile at their feet, but they both ignored it.

"What are you in the mood for, Saralee?" he murmured, his voice low and seductive.

She didn't sound terribly convincing, and he made no move to release her. "What if I said I don't believe you?"

"If I had any sense at all I'd mean it." She pushed against him, a token protest. To her dismay he released her, moving across the room to stand looking at the Christmas tree.

"Do you have any sense?" The question was idly spoken; he seemed more interested in the way the silver tinsel fluttered against the green spruce than in her answer.

"Sometimes I doubt it. And sometimes I wonder if I wouldn't have been far better off if you hadn't started messing with potions, if Dulcy hadn't decided to interfere, if I just weren't so damned gullible," she said, her voice raw with the effort her honesty cost her.

He turned his face from the tree, and she could see the tiny white lights reflected in his golden eyes. "You think magic is to blame for this? You think spells and potions and Dulcy's disputed powers are responsible for the attraction between us?" His voice mocked her. "You are too gullible."

"It certainly wasn't common sense that made me fall in love with you," she shot back, stung, too angry to catch the words before they flew.

He was very still now, watching and waiting in the dimly lighted room. The fire in the wood stove crackled cheerfully; the Christmas lights danced around their motionless figures.

"In love with me?" he echoed, startled. As if considering something new, she thought bitterly. "As in get married, have babies and live happily ever after fall in love?" he asked.

Sybil was busy cursing her unruly tongue. "I never said anything about that."

"I did."

She stared at him, astonished. She shook her head, as if to clear away the mist of confusion, and sank down in the corner of the sofa, curling in on herself in an instinctive posture of defensiveness. "Don't play games, Nick," she said. She'd wanted her voice to be cool, sharp. It came out absurdly wistful.

"I'm not playing games." Still he moved no closer. "I'm asking you to define your terms. You just said you're in love with me. What does that mean?"

"It means I'm lonely and depressed and ready to fall for the first good-looking man who comes my way," she said somewhat desperately.

His eyes were alight with cynical amusement. "So at least I qualify as a good-looking man."

"But you're the wrong man for me. We both know it. All my life I've been programmed for someone like you; I even married someone like you when I was too stupid to know what I was doing. But it didn't work, and it wouldn't work this time. I need someone gentle, supportive, undemanding, someone who shares my beliefs and interests, who loves the outdoors and winter and the simple life. I don't need an upscale, cynical professor and a yuppie life-style."

"I don't remember offering."

"You didn't. I'm just making sure you don't."

He nodded, the grin vanished. "So what you're looking for is a cross between Alan Alda and Frosty the Snowman, maybe with a touch of Saint Francis on the side. And you think that will make you happy?"

"It's what I need."

"Bull." He crossed the room in two long strides, and he was looming over her, staring down at her, all frustration and sexual menace. "I'm what you want, you stupid little fool, but you think you don't need me. I'm what you need, but you tell yourself you don't want me. You sit there and lie to yourself, telling yourself some mythical creature will solve all your problems when I'm right here, waiting for you."

His voice was clipped, furious, as he continued. "Sooner or later you're going to have to grow up. Sooner or later you're going to stop playing these mystical parlor games and accept the fact that what we think is true, what we want to be true, isn't always the answer. You'd walk all over your dream lover, you'd get bored with him in a matter of days. If you ever found him at all. And as long as you keep looking for him, you're safe from the demands of real life, you're safe from me."

She didn't move, didn't say a word, just sat there, staring up at him, as the words lashed over her. "Well, lady," he said, slowly straightening up, "I'll give you what you think you want. And I'll give you what you think you need. I'll leave you alone."

She managed to pull herself out of her dazed stupor. "Good," she said, her voice a whisper.

His mouth twisted into a dour smile. "I'll be waiting, Saralee. But I won't wait forever." And without another word he slammed out of the house, leaving his topcoat behind.

She sat there, listening to the sound of her driveway, listened until it faded into the distance. The room was warm; it was time to damp down the stove. It was now just two days before Christmas, her tree was beautiful, and she had just gotten rid of a nuisance.

His coat was lying at her feet. Reaching down, she pulled it around her, wrapping the warmth and scent of it around her. And leaning her face against the sofa, she shut her eyes and wept.

"WHAT ARE YOU DOING for Christmas Eve?" Dulcy carried a tray of empty punch cups into the kitchen at the Society of Water Witches. She and Sybil were cleaning up after their traditional Christmas Eve open house, and for four hours Sybil had managed to forget the ache in her heart.

Of course, Nick's failure to appear helped matters, she told herself as she tossed the plastic cups into the trash and shoved the forty-seventh sugar cookie into her mouth. She hadn't seen him since he'd stormed from her house two days ago. Steve had brought the Subaru back for her, and all her devious attempts at pumping him got her exactly nowhere.

For that matter, Leona had been pretty scarce. The next day Sybil had tracked her down and read her the riot act about Nick's near miss. Her reaction had been everything Sybil could have hoped for. Shock, dismay, disappointment, all showed quite clearly on Leona's cherubic face. If Sybil wondered whether those emotions reached her tiny, dark eyes, she knew it was only Nick's contagious suspicions that made her doubt her old friend.

Leona hadn't showed up today for fear of running into Nick. And Nick probably hadn't showed up today for fear of running into either of them. For all she knew he might have gone back to Cambridge for the holidays. He probably had family somewhere; he couldn't have just appeared out of nowhere. Somewhere there must be parents, siblings, close friends, all of whom wanted him a great deal more than she did.

"Well?" Dulcy said patiently.

"Well, what?"

"What are you doing tonight? I know you've managed to put off your family again. Do you want to come over to my place, or do you have other plans?"

"You don't celebrate Christmas, Dulcy."

She shrugged her elegant shoulders. "Saturnalia's close enough."

"Somehow I just don't think so," Sybil said. "Pagan festivals and earth religions are all well and good, but when it comes to Christmas I get very traditional and sentimental."

"When it comes right down to it you are a WASP, aren't you, darling? A good little white Anglo-Saxon Protestant, with all those Christian hang-ups?" she mocked lightly.

Sybil refused to rise to the bait. "It doesn't do any good to run away from what you are." No sooner were the damning words out of her mouth than she bit her lip.

Dulcy smiled. "Exactly what I've been trying to tell you, Sybil. Think about it."

"I'm not going to think about anything but a good night's sleep," she said firmly.

"Then you're not going to see Nick?"

"I don't even know if he's in town."

"He's in town, all right. He's going to be all alone at the Black Farm this evening. He has to go back to Massachusetts tomorrow, but for now he's— Why are you looking at me like that?"

Very carefully Sybil set the last tray of cookies down on the counter, very carefully she took a gingerbread girl and bit its head off. "Since you seem to know so much about his plans," she said gently, "why don't you go and keep him company?"

Dulcy threw back her head and laughed, a delightful, full-throated trill of mirth that left Sybil stonily unmoved. "Your jealousy is reassuring, darling. I was afraid you were too far gone. I know all about Nick's plans because I asked him. And I asked him when he called me on some trumped-up excuse to find out what you were doing. I've told you before, Sybil. He doesn't want me, he wants you. You're not usually so obtuse."

Sybil crammed the rest of the cookie into her mouth. In the past two days she hadn't gone a waking hour without eating, she'd probably gained fifty pounds, and all the sugar was making her hyper and sick to her stomach. She reached for another cookie, this time a gingerbread boy, and contemplated where to bite first. "It won't work, Dulcy,"

But Dulcy was tired of arguing. "If you say so," she said, whisking the remaining cookies out of Sybil's reach and dumping them back into a decorative tin. "If you change your mind, give me a call. I'll be home casting spells for the New Year."

"Not on me," she begged.

Dulcy only smiled.

Chapter Nineteen

There were distinct advantages to living alone, Sybil told herself later that evening. You could do exactly what you wanted, when you wanted and how you wanted. The trick was, taking advantage of all that freedom.

The Danbury Church of Christ had an early service on Christmas Eve, and Sybil had dutifully attended. When she got home at half past eight she turned out all the lights and lighted every candle in the house; she roasted herself a Cornish game hen stuffed with wild rice; she poured herself a glass of the best Chardonnay to be found in the state of Vermont; and she dressed herself in her favorite Christmas dress, made of red velvet, with a deep, square neckline, leg o' mutton sleeves and a full swirling skirt that reached the floor. She even put on lacy underwear and rhinestone-clocked stockings, and turned the radio to a station with the mushiest, most sentimental Christmas music she could find. With the dogs around her, she settled down to enjoy her Christmas Eve.

Normally her taste in music was somewhat more sophisticated, but for now she abandoned the Montreal-based New Wave station and settled for Mel Torme roasting chestnuts on an open fire, with Nat King Cole nipping at his nose. She sat there in her living room, the spaniels around her, picking at her game hen, sipping her exquisite wine and letting the sentimental images of Christmas pile up around her like a midwinter snowstorm.

It wasn't the first Christmas Eve she'd spent in solitary splendor. She usually enjoyed herself tremendously, far more than if she were dragged from cocktail party to open house in the determinedly festive environs of Princeton. Their family celebration had usually consisted of a massive, formal dinner on Christmas Day, followed by the anticlimactic opening of a few, very expensive presents, followed by more parties. There were times when her family seemed addicted to their hordes of friends; certainly a celebration like Christmas seemed more an excuse for socializing than for family get-togethers.

No, she was much happier up here in her snug little cottage, with a light dusting of snow falling outside, a real blue spruce she'd cut herself and dragged home shining cheerfully in the corner, her dogs around her and nowhere to rush off to.

Sybil wrinkled her nose as the radio played a particularly syrupy Andy Williams song, full of candy canes and holly and easy imagery. She preferred Mel Torme's elegant simplicity, or "White Christmas," no matter how many times she heard it.

She gave up on the game hen. It was delicious, but after two days of nonstop eating she'd suddenly lost her appetite. Even the Chardonnay was dull. She took her dishes out to the kitchen, dumped them in the sink and wandered back into the living room.

The presents beneath the tree were wrapped in brightly colored paper. Maybe she was more like her parents than she expected—she was feeling depressed, restless, lonely. She could change her clothes and take Dulcy her present, even visit the Mullers. But no, the Mullers would be at the party held for residents of the Davis Apartments. And Leona would be there, and right now Leona was the last person Sybil wanted to see.

Dulcy would be home, alone. But when it came right down to it, Dulcy wasn't whom she wanted, either. Sybil sank down on the ancient Persian carpet in front of the wood stove, leaning her back against the foot of the sofa, hugging her red velvet knees. For the first time in years, she didn't want to be alone on Christmas Eve.

"Don't be a fool," she said out loud, and Kermit raised his head and woofed softly. "You're well rid of him." With a sigh, she rested her head on her knees.

Andy Williams faded in a rush of strings. Then it was Judy Garland, younger than Sybil had ever been, singing "Have Yourself a Merry Little Christmas."

It was the last straw. She sat there, her head on her knees, and wept, tears of loneliness, misery and despair, as the snow drifted down outside her windows and the tree twinkled brightly in the cluttered living room. The dogs moved closer in mute sympathy, but nothing helped. She sat there and cried, tears pouring down her face and running into her long mane of freshly washed hair, cried until she started coughing and choking, cried until she began pounding the floor in fury.

The song on the radio had long since switched to something more saccharine when Sybil finally raised her tear-streaked face. "You complete, utter fool," she said softly. "What the hell are you doing, sitting alone on Christmas Eve, crying, when the man you love is less than five minutes away?"

It took her fifteen minutes to get ready. It was already past ten, and she didn't bother to change her clothes, didn't bother to braid her long hair, didn't bother to do anything more than scoop up Nick's present, pull her leaking down coat around her and call Dulcy. And even that was eerily abrupt.

"Dulcy?" she said, slightly breathless. "Are you going to Canada tomorrow?"

A low, friendly laugh answered her. "I'll come and get the dogs."

"But—"

"That's what you wanted, wasn't it?"

"Yes."

"So run off to your nemesis. Give him a kiss for me," Dulcy said cheerfully.

A sudden, peculiar suspicion flitted through Sybil's mind. "You didn't really want him, did you?"

"Truthfully?"

"Truthfully."

Dulcy's laugh was only slightly strained. "Let's just say I would have been willing to try. But he came here for you, not for me, and I learned long ago not to fight what was meant to be. You can have him with my blessing, Sybil. Just don't throw him away without a good reason."

"Dulcy . . ."

"I'll get the dogs. Merry Christmas, Sybil."

"Merry Christmas, Dulcy."

Her knee-high rubber barn boots were a little strange with the long red dress, and her long hair was covered with snow as she trudged out to the Subaru, the package under her arm. She decided against giving him any warning. Last time she'd seen him he had slammed out of her house. He might need a bit of persuading. Then again, she thought, remembering the burning light in his amber eyes, he might not.

She drove with far more than her usual care down the road to the Black Farm. Tonight of all nights she didn't want to risk sliding off the road; tonight of all nights she wanted to take her time, to make sure she knew what she was doing. The closer she got to the farm, the stronger her self-assurance grew. When it came to being half a mile apart and alone and miserable, or together and happy, there really wasn't much of a contest.

He'd learned his lesson well—the front door was unlocked. The Jaguar was parked by the barn, and Sybil winced as she spied the long, jagged scar along the door. The Subaru had definitely come off the best in this encounter, probably because it had less to lose.

She didn't knock; she just stepped into the hall and shut the door silently behind her. The living room was deserted. She could hear the sound of dishes in the kitchen and the faint sound of someone humming. Clearly he wasn't as bereft as she was, to be humming cheerfully to himself. For a moment she considered leaving, then steeled herself, slipping off the rubber boots and dumping her coat on the floor.

She moved across the chilly floors silently, the package crinkling in her hands. He'd found himself a Christmas tree, slightly lopsided, with multicolored lights and shimmering glass balls. He'd opened up the wood stove to expose the fire, the lights were low, and he was playing the same radio station she was. Had he heard "Have Yourself a Merry Little Christmas" and thought of her? Or had he preferred Andy Williams?

She set the package under the tree. Then, on impulse, she sat beside it, cross-legged, her long hair hanging around her shoulders; sat there and waited.

The scent of freshly brewed coffee mixed with the rich scent of pine above her. It was another five minutes before he appeared in the living room, a steaming mug in his hands, his gaze abstracted. He walked over to the sofa and sank down on it, never once glancing in her direction.

He was wearing the black sweat suit he'd worn the night they were caught in the storm. He looked weary, dangerous and very, very sexy. Sybil just sat there, waiting for him to notice her, waiting for some reaction.

What she got was the fifty-third rendition of "Little Drummer Boy." The fire in front of Nick crackled and popped, illuminating his shadowed face, his distant eyes. Sybil got tired of waiting.

"Ahem," she said.

"Jesus Christ!" Nick swore, almost spilling his coffee. He caught it in time, leaping up from the couch, and he opened his mouth to curse again. Then he saw her.

"It is His birthday," Sybil said demurely, keeping the mischievous grin off her face with a Herculean effort.

Nick stood very still, his anger vanishing as swiftly as it came.

"And what are you? A birthday present?"

Sybil shrugged, her thick honey-colored hair bunching around her narrow shoulders. "Birthday present, Christmas present. Whatever you prefer."

"How about a wedding present?"

She could feel the color drain from her face. Once more she tried to drum up excuses. He wasn't what she wanted, he wasn't what she needed, it would only end in disaster, she should run like hell.

"Yes," she said simply. "Yes." And she held up her arms to him.

"YOU'RE MAKING a big mistake," she said. Her voice came out slightly muffled, since her face was pressed against his bare shoulder and her mouth was busy trailing lazy, satisfying kisses on his warm, sweat-damp skin.

"Am I?" he murmured sleepily, pulling her closer into his arms. A trail of clothing led from the bed into the living room, with the red dress a swirl of color under the Christmas tree. The fire had burned down low, and the multicolored lights from the tree were the only illumination in the bedroom. Sybil could feel his tawny eyes on her, watching her with sleepy satisfaction.

"I'm not the right sort of wife for you," she said, feeling it only fair to warn him. "I'm not cut out to be a faculty wife, I don't want to live in a condo, I don't want you to wear a tweed coat with leather patches and smoke a pipe."

"I hate pipes. And I'm not tweedy. And we'll buy a house in the country, with plenty of room for the dogs."

"But I'm not the kind of woman you want," she wailed, miserable at the halcyon picture she could so easily imagine. It snowed in Massachusetts, just not so damned much, and they

SHE DIDN'T GET OUT OF BED till late morning, and by that time Nick had already left. There was no way he could get out of it; his old friends Ray and Connie were counting on him. He'd drive down, have Christmas dinner with them, invite them to the wedding and be back before midnight. The Jaguar was capable of highly illegal speeds and the interstates down to Boston were kept clear.

She didn't put up any arguments. Indeed, she wasn't in the mood to argue about anything, from wedding dates to guest lists to the uses of dowsing. And he never brought up the subject of Leona.

If she'd had any doubts, the Christmas presents wiped them out. She had finished the flame-colored sweater, despairing of its shape and size. As always the hips were too narrow, the sleeves too long, the shoulders too big to fit anyone, but she'd

could have a barn and a pond for the dogs to swim in and babies....

"No," he said. "You're not the *kind* of woman I want. But since you happen to be *the* woman I want, I guess I'll have to make do."

"I failed once," she muttered against his skin. "I couldn't be what Colin wanted me to be."

"You already are what I want you to be," he said, his hand trailing down her backbone, stroking, strengthening, soothing.

"But what if you change your mind...?"

"What if you change your mind? There aren't any guarantees in this life, Sybil."

"No," she said, doubt and misery thick in her voice.

"The only guarantee," he said, "is love."

She moved her head then, to look up at him. He looked so beautiful he took her breath away. "Do you love me?"

He smiled, a slow, infinitely tender smile that banished the last of her doubts. "Completely," he said, rolling her onto her back and leaning over her.

She looked up at him. "I can fight love potions," she said, "and I can fight Dulcy's interference. I can even fight my own heart. But there's no way I can resist you, too." Sliding her arms around his neck, she pulled him down to meet her hungry lips.

wrapped it to give to Nick anyway, partly because he'd teased her about it, partly because the color of the wool complemented the fire in his disturbing topaz eyes. He laughed when he opened it, laughed when he pulled it on. It fit perfectly.

"I give up," she said, falling back against the pillows. "Everything I knit comes out looking like that. I must have known you were coming."

"Via your Ouija board?" he mocked gently.

"Tarot," she said lazily. "Where's my present?"

"What makes you think I got you anything? Last I knew we weren't speaking; as far as I knew I wasn't going to see you again."

"You knew," she said amiably enough. "What have you got for me? I can just imagine."

She caught it when he tossed it, a small black velvet bag with something heavy inside. A stone of some sort. She opened it, and a deep blue pendulum tumbled out onto the bed.

"I don't believe it," she whispered. "It's Cleopatra's pendulum."

"A copy, I'm told," he drawled.

"The real one is in a museum in Alexandria. I heard they had made a few copies, but I never hoped to own one," she said, picking it up with reverential fingers. "It's beautiful. It must be lapis lazuli. How did you guess that I desperately wanted one? I wouldn't have thought you even knew they existed."

"I dowsed it."

She grinned up at him. "Sure you did. Did Dulcy tell you?" Carefully she squashed down the tiny spurt of jealousy, cradling the wonderful weight of the pendulum in her hand.

"The Mullers," he said.

"Do I have time to thank you properly?" she murmured in a dulcet voice.

"Do I end up like Marc Antony and Julius Caesar?" he responded, moving closer.

She slid her arms around his waist, up under the soft wool sweater that fit him so well. "Not so long as you behave yourself," she said. "Anyway, I wasn't talking about sex. I thought I could dowse whether or not you'd have a good trip."

"I'd rather have sex."

She grinned. "We could always do both. You'll have to take off the sweater, though—you'll give me a rash."

"I wish I could say the same for the pendulum," he said morosely, stripping the sweater over his head and climbing back on the bed.

SYBIL WAS SINGING her own mangled version of "Have Yourself a Merry Little Christmas" as she brewed herself a cup of strong black coffee. Judy Garland in her prime, she wasn't, and she didn't know all the words, but at least she could carry a tune. And that particular tune had become even more special to her since last night.

The doorbell rang and Sybil jumped, cursing slightly as the boiling coffee slopped over her hand. "Come in," she called out, wiping up the spilled mess. It was only one o'clock, too early for Nick to return. She ran her damp hands down the sides of Nick's nightshirt and headed for the door.

Leona was standing there, small, huddled, her dark eyes shining. "I thought that was your voice I heard," she said.

Sybil immediately steeled herself for the disapproval she knew would be her lot, but for some reason it wasn't forthcoming. "Is the professor here?" she murmured, wandering past her into the living room.

Sybil had picked up the trail of clothing, but if she hoped to fool Leona it was a wasted effort. Not that she had anything to hide, she reminded herself forcefully.

She moved ahead of her diminutive friend, diverting her from the bedroom. "He's gone down to Boston for the day. He'll be back sometime after midnight."

Leona allowed herself to be led toward the couch, her face calm and oddly abstracted. "Just for the day, eh? We'll have to move fast."

"I beg your pardon?"

Leona looked up at her, her cherubic face wreathed in smiles. "I can see you two have cleared up your differences. I'm so glad."

"You are?"

"Of course. I had my doubts about your professor when I first met him. And he certainly has been more than mistaken about me. But I'm sure we'll have everything cleared up in the next few days, and we'll all be great friends. Did he...did he say what he was going to Boston for? To see his family, perhaps?"

"Old friends," Sybil supplied, sitting down in the chair and crossing her legs under her. "I'm glad you're so understanding. Nick's just got this weird fixation about you. I'm sure it'll be a simple enough matter to prove him wrong, if we just all sit down and talk it out."

"I'm sure," Leona murmured. "So here you are on Christmas Day, alone, with nothing to do."

"Oh, I have all sorts of things to keep me busy. I was going to bring the dogs over, and then maybe fix something fancy for dinner."

"None of that will take very long," she said. "Indulge an old lady, Sybil. Give me a couple of hours of your time today as a Christmas present."

"Didn't you like the Herkimer diamond I got you?" Sybil teased. "You can't imagine how much trouble it was, finding that particular crystal."

"Of course I did. And that's what I want you for. If we do another past-life regression, with you holding the crystal, there's no limit to the possibilities. We both know that any meditations, any dreams we have while holding on to a Herkimer diamond are increased tenfold." Leona's eyes were shining with unfeigned excitement. "We never did finish that night—your professor misunderstood. Give me one last chance, Sybil. Who knows when we'll have another one?"

Sybil sat very still. For some reason she didn't want to, she didn't want to give over her trust to Leona; she didn't want to search back for past lives, especially for that poor Frenchwoman with her murdered lover. She wanted to stay here, alone, with maybe her dogs for company, and wait for Nick to return.

But what she wanted and what she was going to do were two different things. She'd be leaving Leona soon enough, it would be their last chance, and she owed it to the old lady. Besides, what harm would it do? She'd never been afraid of anything she might find out before; now wasn't the time to start.

"Okay," she said. "Let's do it."

"Not here."

"What do you mean, not here?" Sybil looked over her shoulder at the comfortable, welcoming room.

"The vibrations are crowded and uncertain. A skeptic has been living here, and a man was brutally murdered here long ago. The auras still linger."

Give me a break, Sybil thought, and then was shocked at her irreverence. "Okay. Where do we go?"

Leona smiled—a smug, pleased little smile—and her raisin eyes were like little lumps of coal. "I know just the place."

Chapter Twenty

"Congratulations!" Ray slapped him on the back, grinning like a fool. Nick knew he was grinning back, equally foolishly, and then Connie flung herself into his arms.

"It's about time!" she said. "Who's the poor girl? Another amazon? Let me guess—a lawyer? Someone who works for PBS? A museum curator?"

"A psychic," Nick said, and watched with real delight as absolute incomprehension swept across their faces.

"A what?" Connie gasped.

"A psychic. Except that she doesn't have much talent. A dowser, but she can't dowse. She runs an occult bookstore but it's always in the red. She knits passably well—" he gestured to the sweater hugging his torso "—and she's the secretary of the SOWWs. Society of Water Witches to you guys."

"But you don't believe in most of those things," Connie said helplessly.

"No. But I believe in Sybil."

"Have you two got anything in common at all, Nick?"

"Sure. She believes in everything until it's proved false, I doubt everything until it's proved true. We'll balance each other out."

"But—"

"Don't worry, Connie. All you have to do is meet her and you'll understand."

"I don't believe it," Ray said softly.

"Don't believe what?"

"The man is finally in love."

"I was in love with Adelle. Not in the same way, but..."

"No, you weren't," Connie said firmly. "Take it from an expert, I know love when I see it, and you and Adelle weren't in it. And Ray's right. You've got a wicked case of it right now, praise God. I couldn't ask for a better Christmas present. I just hope she deserves you."

"I hope I deserve her."

"Humility and everything," Ray said in disgust. "Come on in and have some eggnog. The kids have torn the living room apart, but we should be able to find a small corner of peace and quiet. Then I can tell you about your friends the Longermans."

"The Longermans?" Nick trailed after Ray's portly figure, stepping over the dismantled plastic monsters, the wadded-up wrapping paper, the crushed candy canes.

"Leona and James Longerman. James is in Attica right now, doing ten to fifteen for fraud. Apparently he was making a nice little living, bilking little old ladies out of their life savings. Leona got off with a slap of the wrist, but it was clear she was the brains behind the operation. James is up for parole tomorrow, and it looks as if he's going to get out in time to celebrate New Year's Eve with the little woman. Unless you've got something to keep him in there."

"Damn her," Nick swore. "I knew it, I just knew there was something going on. She's up to her old tricks, ripping off the widows in Danbury. God knows what she's done with the money...."

"I wouldn't be surprised if it was stashed up in Canada. You're not far from the border up there—it would be an easy thing to do. She's probably been building up a nest egg, waiting for James to be released."

"I don't suppose you brought any proof home with you? Sybil's not what I call trusting."

"I thought you said she was gullible."

"Unfortunately, not where I'm concerned," he said. "She's very loyal." He heard the telephone ring in the background, but its beep blended in with all the noise from the electronic toys around them.

"I have computer printouts. Will that be enough to shake her loyalty?"

"It should help." He took the cup of eggnog Ray handed him and sighed. "I just hope I don't have too hard a time convincing her."

"Nick?" Connie appeared in the doorway. "Telephone's for you. A woman."

"Sybil," he said, stepping over recumbent children.

"Nope," said Connie. "Someone named Dulcy. How many women do you have up there anyway?"

Nick ignored the sudden premonition that gripped him. "Just one, Connie. Just one."

"ARE YOU SURE you want to drive up here?" Sybil asked, huddling deeper into the passenger seat. She was wearing her red dress, another pair of Nick's knee socks, a heavy cotton sweater and her down coat. For some reason Leona hadn't wanted to stop at her house, even though they drove right past her driveway before they turned off onto the lake road.

The road wasn't in the best condition. No one lived out there this time of year, and while the road crews made an occasional pass at it with the grader, drifts could pile up for days on end with no one noticing.

"I'm sure," said Leona. "Just lean back and relax and we'll be there in no time. We need a quiet, peaceful place, with no one to bother us, so we can concentrate."

"But we'll be back before it's dark? You did promise, Leona. I have to call my parents and wish them a Merry Christmas, and I really should get my dogs."

"Of course. It's just after two now—it gives us till four-thirty. More than enough time."

"But where are we going?"

Leona smiled sweetly. She was driving faster than usual, her sturdy American car slipping slightly on the snowy roads. "The perfect spot. I've borrowed the Barringtons' house."

"But that's closed up for the winter! And impossible to get to—it's down a long driveway that must have three feet of snow on it."

"It's been plowed. The Barrington grandchildren were up for the skiing—they left this morning. We'll have no trouble, and no one will even know we've been there."

"You mean you didn't ask?"

"I dowsed it," Leona said with dignity. "It's perfectly all right."

"Leona," Sybil said, "when are you going to realize that dowsing isn't the answer to everything? We can't just walk into someone's house without asking permission because a pendulum told you it was okay. A pendulum tends to tell you what you want it to."

"You would never have said such a thing a month ago. The professor has had a very negative effect on you, Sybil. I'm disappointed."

"I'm just trying to be reasonable. Listen, I don't think this is such a good idea. Let's go back to my house. I'll make us some herb tea and we can do it there."

"We're almost there, Sybil."

"I don't feel right about breaking into someone's house," she said, trying to stifle the overwhelming sense of uneasiness that was washing over her. "I want to go home."

Leona pulled up in front of the old frame cottage. The pine trees grew tall and dark around it, shielding it from the lake road, closing them in. "I don't think so," she said very gently. And reaching into her dowdy cloth coat, she pulled out a very small, very shiny, very nasty-looking gun.

"DAMN HER," Nick muttered under his breath, shoving his foot down harder on the accelerator. Damn her for not listening to him. If she'd just paid attention to his suspicions she wouldn't be in this mess.

Of course, what proof did he have that she was in a mess? Just Dulcy Badenham's nebulous doubts, nothing concrete at all. Except those nebulous doubts were enough to send him racing out of Ray and Connie's Newton home and heading back to Vermont at the speed of light, or the Jaguar's equivalent of it.

Sybil and Leona were seen driving down the deserted lake road a little after two. And no one had seen them since. Now, perhaps Dulcy was simply being paranoid, but she thought Nick might want to know.

Nick did indeed want to know. If Dulcy was paranoid, Nick was panicked. The drive from Newton usually took close to five hours—he made it in two and a half. It was lucky the interstates were empty this late Christmas afternoon. He couldn't afford the time it would take to get a ticket, particularly since he was driving close to twice the speed limit.

He roared into Danbury at half-past six, heading straight for Leona's apartment. The door, like all the doors in Danbury, was unlocked, and his worst fears were confirmed when he opened it.

Gladys, the devil cat, was gone. So was every stick of furniture, every piece of paper, every trace of human habitation. Only the shades remained, drawn against the eyes of nosy neighbors. Leona had decamped.

And taken Sybil with her? He slammed out of the apartment, racing down the carefully shoveled walk to the idling car. He tore off down the road to the Black Farm, his hands sweating, his heart pounding, muttering under his breath a savage litany of prayers and curses. *Please God, let her be there.* He'd strangle her if she wasn't. *Please, let her be all right.* He'd kill her if she was hurt. Damn it, and damn her for being a trusting fool. If she was in one piece, he'd beat her for scaring him to death. If she was in one piece, he'd never let her go again.

The darkness of the old Black Farm warned him, but he stormed inside anyway, calling her name, his voice echoing with a ribbon of desperation threaded through it. There was nothing, no word, no sign that she'd even been there. Except for his plaid nightshirt, lying across the neatly made bed, waiting for her return.

Dulcy answered the phone on the first ring. "Where is she?" he barked into the receiver.

"I don't know. Are you back already? You must have come back by broomstick."

"Cut the crap, Dulcy. This isn't the time for jokes. Leona's cleared out her apartment in town; whatever she's planning she's not coming back. Think, for God's sake! Where would they go?"

"Nick, I haven't the faintest—"

"Can't you dowse it? Read the tarot, look into a crystal ball, do something! You're the witch around here, you're the one with a direct line to the infinite."

There was an ominous, insulted silence on the other end. "I don't know where she is, Nick, and I can't find out. I've tried everything feasible."

"What about the dogs? You have them there, don't you? Wouldn't they be able to trace her?"

"Those dogs would chase after the nearest rabbit. They love everything and everybody; they'd just get in the way," Dulcy said patiently. "Let's be logical about this. They were seen heading down the lake road in Leona's car."

"Where does the lake road lead?"

"Around the lake. As far as I know, most of the houses are closed for the winter. A few of the summer people come up for the holidays, but I don't remember if anyone did this year."

"Big help," Nick snapped.

"We've got two possibilities," Dulcy continued, ignoring his temper. "It could be either the Montebellos or the Barringtons. Try the Montebellos first. They're the second house past the schoolhouse. The Barringtons are farther in, maybe three miles from the Montebellos. You should be able to tell from the tire tracks."

"Why are you worried?" he said suddenly. "I thought Leona was a good buddy of yours."

"Leona is the sort of person who gives witches a bad name," Dulcy informed him. "Do you want me to meet you at the Barringtons'?"

"Stay put. I'll call you if I need help."

The moon was almost full, lending an eerie brightness to the snow-covered landscape. At least he didn't have to contend with another storm that night. All he had to deal with was a swindler-cum-witch run amok, who'd kidnapped the woman he loved. *Piece of cake,* he snarled to himself, skidding out of the driveway. *Goddamned piece of cake.*

"How LONG are you going to keep me here?" Sybil inquired in her most even tones. She was sitting by the fireplace, huddled there for warmth, her feet tucked up under her, the down coat wrapped around her. The sun had set long ago, but Leona had refused to turn on any lights, for fear it would signal their presence to any nosy passersby. Not that anyone passed by this deserted area even in the best of times. And surely everyone had something better to do on Christmas night.

"As long as I need to," Leona replied. "I really expected better of you, Sybil. Your professor was so enamored I would have thought he wouldn't have time to interfere with me. I must have miscalculated."

"You really did rip off the old ladies at the apartments?"

"Of course. You needn't be so disapproving, Sybil." Leona was sitting opposite her, the gun in one tiny little hand, a mug of instant coffee in the other. It was the first time Sybil had ever seen her drink coffee, but then, she'd never seen her hold a gun, either. It was a day for surprises. "I always left them enough to live on. None of them will want for anything. They just won't have enough to leave their children."

"Don't you think that's fairly rotten?"

"Not at all. The children never visit; they set their widowed mothers up in nursing homes and rest homes and retirement apartments and wait for them to die so they can cash in. Why should they get the money when they can't even come to see the old ladies?"

"Very touching, Leona," she said cynically. "But Mary Philbert's children come every weekend; they take her everywhere, even on their summer vacations. As a matter of fact, she used to wish they'd leave her alone. And you ripped her off, just like the others."

Leona shrugged her plump little shoulders. "What can I say? When it comes right down to it, I'm a rotten human being."

"You won't get an argument from me on that one," Sybil mumbled. "Are you going to kill me?"

"Heavens, no! I don't hold with physical violence. I'm simply going to keep you here until it's safe to let you go. When Nick starts looking for you he'll find a note at your house, telling him to sit tight and keep his mouth shut or they'll find your body in the spring."

"I thought you said you don't hold with physical violence," Sybil said, leaning back in the wicker chair. The mantel, like the mantels in half the summer cottages, was cluttered with golf tees, cross-country skiing wax, melted candles, sprung mousetraps and golf trophies. Old Mr. Barrington had won more than his share—there were cups and platters and even statues, all black and tarnished and forlorn-looking. Sybil eyed them wistfully.

"It's an empty threat," Leona said, and she wished she could believe her. "You see, my husband comes up for parole in a couple of days. We need everything peaceful and quiet until that goes through. Then I'll meet him in Canada and we'll live quite happily on the money I've been making."

"I thought your husband was dead."

"You also thought I was a nice person and your professor a danger. Let's face it, Sybil, you're not a great judge of character."

There was the quiet sound of teeth grinding, and then Sybil smiled. If there were only some way she could edge closer to the mantel and its nice heavy trophies. "So you're going to keep me here to keep Nick quiet until your husband gets out of jail. Then what will you do?"

"Tie you up, leave you and call Nick from the border. It's only an hour away, Sybil. You'll survive."

"What if you don't call him?"

"Then they really would find your body in the spring," she said in a comfortable tone of voice. "Be sensible for once in your life. Swindlers have a much lower law enforcement priority than murderers. I'll make sure your professor rescues you, whether you deserve it or not."

"I wish I could believe you."

"It doesn't matter whether you do or not," Leona murmured. "I have the gun."

"So you do." Sybil stretched her legs out in front of her, letting the coat slide down her lap. "I don't suppose you feel like letting me take a nap. I didn't get much sleep last night."

"I imagine you didn't," she said with a nasty smirk. "You can sleep right there in that chair. It's only eight o'clock—"

"We've been here six hours!"

"We're going to be here a lot longer than that before I'm through.... What was that?" She swiveled around at the muffled thud outside the door, the gun pointing away for a brief moment.

Sybil didn't dare hesitate. She leaped up, throwing her coat over Leona's tiny figure. She grabbed a large pewter platter from the Men's Handicap of 1978 and smashed it over Leona's head. She kept struggling, so the Men's Scotch Foursome cup followed suit, crumpling nicely. The gun went off, a bullet went whizzing through the coat to embed itself in the pine-paneled walls and a cloud of feathers filled the air. The Juniors' Handicap of 1941 was the last casualty, its cup parting company with the granite base, and Leona lay still beneath the coat and the feathers.

She heard someone at the door but ignored the sound as she moved toward Leona's motionless body. She knelt down, gingerly lifting the corner of the coat, steeling herself for a gory sight. Leona lay there peacefully enough, an imminent black eye purpling her skin, her plump hand clasped loosely around the little gun. Her breathing was even and steady. With a sigh of relief Sybil stood up, taking the gun with her, and headed for the door.

It wasn't an evil accomplice; it was Nick, looking terrified, furious and wonderfully worried about her. She was in his arms before he even charged through the door, hurling herself at him with enough force to knock him backward onto the snowy porch.

"Are you all right?" he demanded, his hands running over her body, searching for injuries.

"Fine. I knocked the old witch out."

"Good for you." He kissed her, hard, fast and deep on her trembling mouth. "Now if you'd just listened to me in the first place...."

"If you're going to say I told you so," Sybil warned, resting her head against his chest, "then the marriage is off. We'll just live in sin the rest of our lives."

"I won't say I told you so."

"Thanks."

"Not when you already know it."

"Nick ..."

"Is there a telephone in this place? We need to call the police, we need to call Dulcy...."

"How did you find me? Did Dulcy know that Leona had taken me?"

"Dulcy guessed. She called me in Newton and had me hightail it back here. I think I broke the speed record."

"I imagine you did. Thank God for Dulcy."

"What about me?"

She grinned up at him. "Oh, I've been thanking God for you for weeks now, whether I knew it or not."

"I'll make the appropriate response to that after we call the police," he said in a deep, sexy voice. "Where's the telephone?"

She led him past Leona's recumbent figure into the kitchen. "Is she okay?" Nick queried as Sybil began a tortuous leafing through the telephone directory.

"She's fine. I clubbed her as hard as I could, but only the good die young. You want to see if the Barringtons have anything alcoholic in their cupboards while I try to find the state police?"

"Can't you dial 911?"

"Not up in the boonies, you city slicker. Look over there." She flipped through the thin pages, deliberately ignoring the noise in the living room, raising her voice so Nick wouldn't hear. "Anything will do, even cooking sherry. I've never needed a drink so much in my entire—"

"What was that?" He whirled around, turning from the row of bottles.

"I don't know. Maybe—"

"Damn it, she's escaping!" Nick dove through the swinging kitchen door, with Sybil at his heels.

"Let her go, Nick," she called after him.

He stopped on the porch, staring into the moonlit landscape, listening as the sound of a car faded into the distance. Not the rough, sturdy sound of Leona's Pontiac. It was the elegant purr of a Jaguar disappearing into the night.

He turned to glare at the unrepentant Sybil. "She stole my car."

"I'm sorry about that."

"But you wanted her to escape, didn't you?"

She considered denying it, then dismissed the idea. "Yes."

"Why?"

"I don't know. Maybe as a Christmas present. So she's a slightly wicked old lady. I still didn't want to see her in jail."

"Even though she kidnapped you?"

"Even though she made a complete fool of me," she said, moving closer and wrapping her arms around his tall, stubborn body. "So I'm stupid and sentimental. Let someone else catch her—they will soon enough. I just don't want to be the one responsible."

He sighed. "I'll grant her one thing—at least she shot your damned leaking coat."

Sybil looked over his shoulder at the feathery mess. "You'll have to buy me a new one."

"You're ridiculous, you know that?" he said gruffly, bringing his arms up around her.

"I know," she said wearily. "Are you sure you want to marry me? Maybe you'll regret it."

"The only thing I regret," he said, his hands running down the length of the red velvet dress and cupping her hips against him, "is the years I spent without you."

"I won't be a yuppie wife," she warned.

"You'd be foolish to try. You're going to terrorize the stately environs of Harvard, you'll probably start a Cambridge branch of the Seekers of Enlightenment, I'll be stepping over pendulums and L-rods and springer spaniels and piles of books wherever we live, and my children will all be witches."

"Probably," she said, loving the sound of it.

"And I wouldn't have it any other way."

"Neither," she said, "would I." She reached up, feathering her lips across his. "Merry Christmas, Nick."

He pulled her closer, that demonic glint in his eyes promising wonderful things. "Merry Christmas, Sybil. Let's go home."

"Home," she murmured. "That sounds heavenly." She pulled away, scooped up her shredded coat and headed for the door. "The one thing that puzzles me in all this . . ."

"One thing?" He flicked off the light and shut the door behind them, stepping out into the chilly night air.

"How did you know where to find me?"

"Dulcy told me."

"But how did she know?"

"Someone saw you driving this way."

"Nick, we didn't pass anyone."

"Well, she just used common sense."

"Nonsense. She must have dowsed it."

"Don't be ridiculous, Sybil, she couldn't have—"

"She could have. After all, she's a white witch."

"I don't care if she's a purple witch. Besides, there are no such things as witches."

"Have yourself a merry little Christmas," Sybil sang. "Somehow I don't think our troubles will be out of sight."

He grinned at her from across the expanse of Leona's old blue Pontiac. "Honey, they're probably just beginning. Are you scared?"

She looked at him, her eyes clear and brown. "A little. What about you?"

"A little. Don't worry, if I get rowdy you can always have Dulcy find a spell for me."

"Or you can dose me with Hungarian love philtre."

"Or maybe," he said, "we can take care of it ourselves. Get in the car, Sybil, before I remember what happened to my Jaguar."

"I never liked it anyway," she murmured, climbing in.

"Do we need to stop at Dulcy's on the way back?"

"Nope," Sybil said with a sigh. "She'll know everything's all right. After all, she's a witch."

"She is not."

"Is too."

"Not."

"Is . . ."

He wants to be part
of her future.
She knows he's part
of her past.

REMEMBER ME

Bobby Hutchinson

Strangers drawn from the ends of the earth, jewelled and
        plumed were we,
I was Lord of the Inca race, and she was Queen of the Sea.
Under the stars beyond our stars where the new forged
        meteors glow
Hotly we stormed Valhalla, a million years ago . . .
They will come back, come back again, as long as the red
        Earth rolls.
He never wasted a leaf or a tree. Do you think He would
        squander souls?
—Rudyard Kipling, *The Naulahka*, ''The Sack of the Gods''

CHAPTER ONE

"Will he really make the cage and the birds disappear, Annie?"

Seven-year-old Maggie balanced her narrow behind on the very edge of her seat, round blue gaze fixed on the spectacle unfolding before her on the stage, squeaky voice full of wonder.

"It looks that way, Mag." Annie Pendleton's whispered response went unheard by her small companion, because now the magician was gesturing at children in the front row, inviting them to join him onstage.

Annie swallowed against the sudden constriction in her throat. What was going wrong with her? Her heart was hammering and she could feel perspiration dampening her palms.

"Come on up here and hold this cage down for me, won't you?" His baritone voice was gentle, full of humor, filling the auditorium. It was amplified by the small microphone Annie could see clipped to the open collar of his casual blue denim shirt, and it seemed to reverberate in her head.

What was it about this man?

Unlike the other amateur Vancouver magicians who'd appeared this afternoon, this one—The Sorcerer, he called himself—wasn't wearing the magician's traditional uniform of top hat and tails. He had on jeans and comfortable loafers, and his shirtsleeves were rolled up his forearms. He was probably a few years older than Annie's thirty-four years. He was attractive, but not startlingly handsome.

So what was he doing, affecting Annie the way rock stars affected teenyboppers?

Children were thronging from their seats now, eager to be part of the fascinating activity onstage, and The Sorcerer was arranging them around the twittering canaries' cage, which sat on an ordinary wooden table.

"Go on up there, Maggie," Annie's son, Jason, urged, but Maggie shook her head vehemently, making her long blond braids fly.

"You go, Jason. You go. I'm scared."

Jason groaned, torn between wanting to be close enough to study the spectacle about to unfold, but convinced he was far too old and jaded at thirteen to join "kids."

"It's just magic. There's nothing to be scared of, for Pete's sake, Maggie. Go up and see what's goin' on for me, please?"

But Maggie's round blue eyes were threatening to pop from her skull, and she shook her head as the other children ringed the bird cage, their hands overlapping on its surface. The Sorcerer held his hands in the air, staging the illusion to come.

"I bet the table has a false bottom, Mom, so the cage just drops inside."

Thirteen-year-old Jason didn't bother continuing his scoffing explanation to his mother. Jason had read every book on professional magic he could get his hands on, and he wasn't about to be fooled by any of this amateur stuff. He'd done his annoying best all afternoon to explain each trick to Annie and Maggie as it was being enacted . . . and had successfully spoiled the illusions for everyone within hearing distance.

"There isn't room, Jason. You can see underneath from here." Annie made a concerted attempt to sound normal.

This was the final act of the amateur magic show and Annie had been relieved that the afternoon's clumsy performances were finally coming to an end.

It was hot and stuffy, and her neck had started to ache by the time The Sorcerer was scheduled to appear. Maggie and Jason were becoming restless on either side of her.

Then this man had strolled casually onstage, and from that moment on Annie and the rest of the Saturday afternoon audience had paid close attention.

It was obvious right away that despite his casual garb, The Sorcerer was a consummate magician. During the first part of his act, he'd smoothly made scarves appear and disappear, pulled a small white squawking pigeon from the depths of an empty box and retrieved with a butterfly net a small army of white mice from the seemingly empty air in front of him.

Clever sleight of hand, but with it he had presence, a sense of timing and rapport with his audience the other performers had lacked.

And this trick with the bird cage was unusual, if he was actually going to make it disappear with all those kids holding on to it. In the third row from the front, Annie tried to look away from the stage, focus her gaze anywhere except on the magician.

The fact was that this Sorcerer was having a peculiar effect on her. A distinct chill shuddered its incongruous way down Annie's neck and back, a chill that had little to do with the clever tricks being enacted on the nearby stage, and everything to do with the uncanny feeling of familiarity she'd experienced from the first moment the tall, dramatic man had ambled out from behind the dusty stage curtains and taken command.

"It's done with fishing line, I bet it is," Jason concluded once again.

A middle-aged woman in front of them turned and glared, and then shot Annie a look that suggested she do something about Jason and his comments.

But Annie was impervious. Her attention was still riveted to the man onstage as he held both arms high in the air, and with a sudden loud exclamation, brought them down.

The bird cage disappeared, and a collective roar of amazement issued from the group of children who'd been resting small hands all over its surface.

"Humph." Jason made a noise like a balloon deflating, and his red-brown hair stood on end as he sat forward on his chair, brows beetled together in a concentrated effort to figure out what was really going on.

Annie narrowed her eyes and studied the commanding figure on the stage, unconsciously frowning herself. Her heart was pounding in an unnatural rhythm, and she felt confused, a confusion that had nothing to do with the trick, and everything to do with the man performing it. She was shivering, and yet the air in the auditorium was warmer and stuffier than ever, with its evocative reminders of yesterday's sweaty bodies and years of smelly gym shoes.

You've never seen that man before, you know that, she silently reprimanded herself, wiping cold, sweaty palms in slow motion down the sides of her red cotton skirt.

Then how, from the very first instant, had she instinctively known exactly how he'd turn his body... like now. She anticipated that slight arrogant tilt to his leonine head an instant before it occurred... and there, she knew the exact way his strong, clean features mirrored amazement and delight at his own sleight of hand, subtly making him one with his audience, projecting the impression that he was having as much fun as they were.

In his deep, shadowed eyes Annie also knew for certain that warm blue lights flickered like candle flames, that kindness and bottomless compassion were reflected in the dark irises.

Rubbish, she admonished herself. She couldn't even see his eyes from where she sat.

Ah, but she knew their expression as well as she knew the soft and voluptuous rounded lines of her own body.

She recognized his long-boned, rangy shape with its deceiving muscular strength. She remembered the way his wide, narrow mouth tilted in a wicked grin, the way it was tilting now.

How could she know these things about someone she was certain she'd never seen before? A mild form of panic made her heart pound and her breath come in shallow gulps.

This whole thing was ridiculous.

"How did he do that, anyway?" This time, the puzzled query came from Jason, poised on the edge of his seat. Maggie had been clapping her hands with delight, along with the rest of the audience.

Annie felt familiar, unaccountable pride and admiration mix with the other confused emotions racing through her consciousness.

He had such presence. He'd always been able to hold children in the palm of his hand, command their attention from the first instant he appeared among them. It was one of the innumerable things about him that delighted her, his love for children.

It was what made him such a fine doctor.

The thought had almost evaporated before she examined it, dissected the discrepancy there, and shuddered again.

Always when, Annie? And how do you know what kind of doctor he is?

Before, an impatient ribbon of rebellious thought insisted. *When before? You've never laid eyes on him until today.*

She swallowed hard, aware that her face was burning hot now, her fingers trembling.

Suddenly he made a dramatic gesture, and out of nowhere, the bird cage appeared and settled in his right hand, its silver paint sending shards of light glancing outward from the strobes overhead.

Jason expelled his pent-up breath in a long whoosh of admiration and wonder.

"Jeeze, that's ace. I never heard of any trick like that before, making it disappear and then come back out of thin air. Did'ya see that, Mag? Mom, you're going to interview this guy for your research, aren't ya? He's ace. Hey, Mom, when ya talk to him, find out for me how he did that trick, will'ya please? Jeeze, that's excellent." Jason slid back onto his chair, shaken completely out of his role as debunker of magic.

The Sorcerer set his cage back on the small table, smiled his crooked smile, bowed to his clapping audience and disappeared behind the dingy curtain.

The brown velvet closed behind him, and something totally unexplainable happened to Annie. As if the light at the core of her being had been switched off, utter desolation swept over her, an ancient, searing loneliness in her soul so intense and hurtful she had no armor against it.

Hating herself and feeling an utter fool, but unable to stop the onrush of puzzling emotion, harsh sobs rose in her throat and Annie began to weep, frightening Maggio and absolutely horrifying her son.

AN HOUR LATER, sipping iced tea in the familiar jumbled order of Cleo Fowler's kitchen, Annie felt embarrassed and apprehensive as Jason related the entire afternoon's drama in minute detail to his mother's best friend.

"And so help me, Cleo, I never heard of any prestidigitator..."

Cleo rolled her eyes heavenward, and suggested, "Can't you just say magician, Jason? Just say magician, for Lord's sake. I'm a simple, uncomplicated woman and it's easier for me to follow you if you use one-syllable words."

"Any—any—sorcerer—," Jason supplied triumphantly. "That's what he called himself, see. Sorcerer. I mean, he actually made a bird cage disappear, with a dozen kids holding on to it. Honest to, honest to goodness, he did. It's a super trick, Cleo. And it made Mom bawl like anything, didn't it, Mom? Man, I never thought you'd start to bawl about something like that. I mean, it was outrageous and all that, but still...cryin' over it..." Jason's recently unpredictable voice suddenly shot into a higher octave and he screwed his freckled face into a masculine grimace of horror and distaste at the memory of his mother's embarrassing fit of tears.

In a no-nonsense tone of voice he well recognized, Annie said, "Isn't it time for your paper route? Go home and fold your papers, Jason. I heard the van deliver them a few minutes ago."

Rolling his eyes in an exact parody of a habit his mother had, Jason ambled toward the screen door leading out to the wide porch.

"Can't you just say when you guys don't want me around, Ma? I mean, don't...prevaricate, okay? I mean, I'm old enough to handle the unvarnished truth. I'm not an adolescent anymore. I'm a teenager, Ma."

"Jason." There was a definite steeliness in Annie's voice this time, and her son speeded up his exit.

"He's driving me nuts," Annie said, staring at the door he'd slammed after him. "I've let him go too far, and now he's driving me crazy."

Cleo agreed. "Single mothers like us shouldn't have to cope with precocious teenage kids," she sympathized. "There ought to be a good home we could send 'em to until they turn twenty. And just think, I've still got the girls to live through all that with, and I'm barely over thirty."

Actually she was thirty-two.

"Anyhow, school starts in another week, so that should help," Annie said.

Cleo nodded, making her mop of soft, prematurely white hair look more than ever like dandelion fluff as it floated and resettled on her well-shaped skull. She turned her astute green gaze on Annie, noting the unmistakable silver tracks of dried tears on her friend's flawless skin, and the hint of pallor under the apricot tan.

"So what's up, pal?" she demanded. "Why fits of weeping over some dumb magic show, huh?" A look of concern passed over her angular features, and she added, "Hey, it's not your back again, is it?"

Cleo banged an exasperated hand down on the table between them. "Damn, I knew you shouldn't have been lugging Paula around like that yesterday morning. That kid may be only three but she weighs a ton."

Annie shook her head. "It's not my back, Cleo. My back's been fine for quite a while, apart from the odd twinge, and anyhow, it's not carrying kids around that affects it."

Cleo's eyebrows rose.

"So what did happen this afternoon?" she demanded with quiet persistence. "What happened to that famous Pendleton control, huh?" Her eyes widened. "Hey, you didn't have another call from Michael, did you? Honestly, you'd think when your son's father has been invisible for all these years, he wouldn't have the nerve to start bothering you again about wanting back into the kid's life."

"He hasn't called for two weeks now, Cleo. No, it wasn't Michael, either, that set me off, although heaven knows I wish he'd take a one-way flight back to India and stay there. It was just, it was . . . ," Annie stammered, and felt herself flush. How could she explain that wrenching gut reaction to a total stranger that even now made her stomach twist with anxiety? For no known reason? A man she'd never even met?

"It wasn't anything, anything . . . physical today," she lied, taking a long, slow sip from her tall glass, and then meeting Cleo's curious, steady expression with a helpless shrug.

"Or maybe it was entirely physical," she confessed with a long, drawn out sigh. "The simple truth is, I really don't know what came over me. I don't have the foggiest clue why I started crying, and I feel embarrassed as hell about it. It had something to do with that magician, some absolutely stupid feeling I had that I'd known him somewhere before. Not just casually known him, either." Annie slumped back into the wooden chair.

"Well, do you? Know him, I mean?"

Annie shook her head. "I know for certain I've never even met him, Cleo. I mean, the rational part of my brain knows that. It's this other feeling that . . ." Her words trailed off and her forehead drew into a frown. "Anyhow, why should that make me start bawling?" Annie paused, her soft brown eyes reflecting puzzled exasperation. "I've never felt remotely like that before, and I don't want to ever again. It's . . . disconcerting. Weird. Besides which, I'm going to have to meet him now, in the flesh, because I phoned yesterday when I got the tickets and made an appointment to interview him next week." With one slender finger she traced the ring her glass had made on the Arborite tabletop, and added, "I found out he's a pediatric surgeon at Vancouver Regional Hospital, named Dr. David Roswell, when he's not being The Sorcerer. The way I feel right now, I'd phone and cancel the interview, but you know what a hard time I've had to locate a decent magician to talk with for this next book I've got planned. And this guy was exceptional. He was really good."

"Jason certainly thought so," Cleo remarked, still studying her friend. "And Jason's about the most knowledgeable kid I've ever met when it comes to magic shows."

Annie nodded, a tiny grin masking the worried expression in her deep brown eyes. "Yeah. It was because of Jason's fascination with magic that I originally decided to do this book. He does know a lot about it. I figured once or twice today that the three of us were going to get tossed out, he was so vocal about how all the tricks were done."

"I told you to let the kids sit by themselves," Cleo teased. She paused, and then asked with disarming casualness, "How old do you think this Dr. David Roswell would be? Was he good-looking, tall, sexy? What? Give me a verbal sketch here."

Annie gave her a narrow-eyed, warning look. "The next thing you're going to ask is, did I notice a wedding ring?"

Cleo, not at all abashed, demanded, "Well, how old was he? Just take a guess. And yeah, did you happen to notice if he wore a ring? I know you're not interested in romance in the least, Annie, but think of me. I have to consider the potential of every single male we come across. I'm a tough case for any matchmaker, let's face it, and I haven't any intention of growing old without a sexy man to keep me company, even if you intend to."

"Cleo, you're impossible." Annie grinned all of a sudden, an infectious grin that lifted her winged eyebrows over her deep-set, wide eyes, making them sparkle with mischief and gamin devilry. Annie's grin was contagious, and as always, it drew an answering fond smile from Cleo.

"Let's see now, this candidate was about thirty-eight, forty maybe, and yes, you could say he was good-looking." Annie's lighthearted tone belied the sudden acceleration of her heart as, without effort, her brain formed a clear picture of David Roswell.

"He's tall, slim but strong, long arms and legs, good broad shoulders, crisp dark brown curly hair, a lopsided smile and sort of...aristocratic features. Thick eyebrows, really nice blue eyes."

"Aristocratic? You're as bad as that son of yours with words. What the devil is aristocratic supposed to mean?" Cleo interrupted, but Annie ignored her.

"And no, Cleo, I didn't look for a ring. But when I interview him on Tuesday," she forced herself to add, "I'll be sure to sound him out about his feelings concerning gorgeous divorcées with collections of kids." Annie was grateful that Cleo seemed unaware of the effort behind her lighthearted nonsense.

"Only two kids of my own," Cleo corrected. "The others are here part-time, on loan, seven-to-five, weekdays. Make that clear whenever you're advertising me, lady. And let's skip the 'gorgeous,' shall we? Say I'm witty, say I'm faithful, say I'm amazingly good in bed...if I remember how after all this time...but gorgeous I'm not."

Annie smiled at Cleo's matter-of-fact assessment, but it was a strained smile, and Cleo noticed this time and stopped her bantering.

"Don't worry about this thing today, Annie," she said softly, reaching across to touch Annie's hand. "Sounds to me like you just had a severe attack of what they call déjà vu or something. Everybody has experiences like that now and then. Maybe this guy just reminded you of someone you knew when you were a tiny girl, someone you don't consciously remember knowing, some doctor your mom took you to or something. That happens sometimes. I remember hearing...." Cleo launched an involved story about a friend of one of her aunts recognizing someone unlikely at a funeral, and Annie finished her lemonade, nodding vaguely now and then but not really listening.

The image of a tall, lean man with intense blue eyes...she absolutely knew his eyes were that certain royal shade of deep blue, and she refused to wonder again how she knew...kept getting in the way of Cleo's husky, animated tones.

When the story ended, Annie got to her feet.

"I have to go, Cleo. Thanks for the drink. Pop over later if you feel like a coffee. I'll be home all evening just as usual. I've got to work."

"Maybe after Maggie and Paula are asleep."

"Jason will come over and baby-sit for them if you like," Annie promised. "He'll be watching TV anyhow. They're doing reruns of *Star Trek*, and he can watch here as easily as next door. Besides, you always have better snacks than we do. Quote."

Cleo reached out to put a staying hand on Annie's arm. "You sure you're okay, friend? You're kinda pale. If you feel like company, you know you and Jason are always welcome to stay for supper. I've got a tuna casserole...."

Annie smiled at her generous neighbor, and shook her head.

"I'm fine, Cleo, honest. And thanks, but I really do have to get some work done. The synopsis on this magic book is due in two weeks, and all I have so far are a dozen scraps of paper with notes on them."

And an upcoming interview with a man she dreaded meeting.

She made her way down the rickety back steps, across the wide expanse Cleo optimistically called a lawn with its sandbox and swing set and wading pool, to the small gate in the high wooden fence that connected her property to Cleo's.

The lots in this older section of Vancouver were large, and Annie's back garden was a private, shaded welter of flowers, shrubbery and huge weeping willows.

Jason earned spending money by taking desultory care of it for her, mowing the lawn and giving the flower beds random attention, but his thirteen-year-old ambitions didn't extend to intensive neatness or dedicated gardening. Thus the yard had a careless, casual appearance she loved, as if no one interfered unduly with nature's whims.

She walked slowly up her own backstairs, in better repair than Cleo's because she'd hired a workman last fall to replace the rotted boards with new ones, and unlocked her back door.

A long, deep, indrawn breath revealed the myriad scents of living; the pleasant muted yesterday smells of cooking; the echo of the flowery cologne she habitually wore, the more pervasive sad perfume of the lilacs she'd placed on the narrow hall table.

She glanced down at a pair of filthy, ragged sneakers and a tattered jean jacket tossed just inside the door and she grinned.

Add to all those aromas the definite tang of a half-grown boy who hated soap and water, and you had the unique essence of the Pendletons' habitat.

Home. Annie never entered without experiencing a rush of warmth and wonder that she'd managed to actually buy this house for herself and Jason. Her fifth children's book, a tale of medieval demons and dragons, had unexpectedly sold its fanciful way out of bookstores and gone into a second and then a third printing, selling not to the children she'd intended it for, but to college students suddenly intrigued by all things medieval.

It didn't make her rich by any stretch of the imagination; her mortgage was a constant concern, and a writer's income was anything but predictable. But since then, three other books had also sold reasonably well, and now there was even a slender balance most of the time in her bank account—at least, on months when she didn't have to pay the orthodontist.

Life was stable, pleasant and she was a self-supporting, proud single mother. Annie planned to keep it that way.

She wandered through her well-equipped kitchen, on down the narrow hallway to the winding staircase. Halfway up, a window overlooked Cleo's backyard, and she smiled down at the foreshortened figures of Paula and Maggie, busy enacting some housekeeping game of their own in the wooden play-house Annie and Jason had devised for them.

Having Cleo Fowler and her kids living next door had been the best bonus possible in living here.

The huge, skylighted study she'd created by having work-men knock out the wall between two bedrooms was to the left at the top of the stairs. Directly ahead was an old-fashioned segregated bathroom, with the toilet in one small room and the bathtub and sink in another. To the right was her bedroom. It still felt strange to have the entire top floor to herself.

Jason had taken over the large finished room in the base-ment last fall, the day he'd turned thirteen.

"I'm not a kid anymore, Mom, scared of the dark. We both need more privacy," he'd declared, and Annie remembered now the confusion of emotions his words had caused her. Baby son had become small boy, and boy was fast becoming man. It was a progression she wasn't ready for. Yet.

Annie turned into the study, her mouth twisting in acknowl-edgement of the controlled chaos inside the door. The room was exactly the way it always looked when she was busy on a book. Cleo had described it as a bird's nest mixed with an egg beater.

The flecked gray wool rug was littered with scraps of paper and reference books and notepads. Scribbled notes were also tacked in haphazard fashion to the huge cork bulletin board along one wall, along with pictures torn from magazines, addresses, reminders to herself, and the most recent colorful, crayoned drawings Paula and Maggie had made for her.

Annie studied them for a moment and a wistful smile came and went. Paula's artwork was a mélange of three-year-old scribbles and lines, but Maggie's drawings were always of families, mother, father, and two children, stick arms joined, happy smiles bisecting round balloon faces.

Cleo joked about finding a man, but Maggie's drawings were silent and heartrending reminders that the little girl longed for a father figure in her life.

Dear old Mags, Annie thought as she moved to her worktable. *If only dreams came true just from wishing.*

The computer shared space with used teacups and assorted crumbs, and over the back of her comfortable chair hung the old grey T-shirt she pulled on against the chill of early mornings or late nights. The opposite wall held matted snapshots of Jason and Paula and Maggie, framed cover art from her published books and a coveted review *Maclean's* magazine had given her most popular book.

This room was the core of her home, the place where Annie worked and dreamed and spent most of her time. It was her surrogate womb, she had once told Cleo.

Now she sank into the padded desk chair in front of the computer, staring blankly at the dark screen. She'd worked there for several hours this morning, losing track of time as always, and then had to race to get ready to take the kids to the magic show as she'd promised.

She glanced up at the wall, at the huge face of the clock Cleo had given her last Christmas. Five hours ago. Only five short hours had passed since she'd last sat here. Such a minuscule span of time. Yet something had changed deep inside of her during those few hours; something had tugged at curious buried strings and made them resonate. It was disturbing.

There'd been a break in the even cadence of her comfortable life, a crack like the terrifying chasm an earthquake might create, and it both scared and angered her. She didn't want surprises. She didn't want upset.

Making an impatient noise deep in her throat, she chose a diskette from the plastic container beside the machine and inserted it in her computer, forcing her attention on the familiar messages that appeared, giving the automatic commands that would access her work.

The world outside this room could disintegrate and reform without her being aware, as long as she had her work—or so she'd thought until today.

For the rest of the August afternoon, as the late summer day dwindled and the sky overhead took on the hues of evening, she tried to center every ounce of attention and energy on the preparation of her book outline.

But just beyond her conscious thought, somewhere above and behind her in the deepening gloom, disturbing questions without answers lingered like specters, hovering and waiting to pounce the instant she relaxed her guard.

Questions like who was David Roswell, and how could she possibly remember how it felt to be loved by a man she'd never met before?

CHAPTER TWO

DAVID ROSWELL, still thinking about an intriguing conversation he'd just had with a colleague over lunch, strode down the hall to his office a few minutes after 1:00 p.m. Tuesday afternoon.

He thrust his outer office door open in typical energetic fashion and burst into the small room like an unleashed energy force, making the woman sitting on a hard wooden chair beside Phyllis's desk jump, and then leap to her feet. Phyllis was obviously still out on her lunch break.

"Sorry." He smiled in apology. "Didn't mean to startle you. I'm Dr. Roswell. How can I help you?"

Annie had spent the past two days convincing herself that whatever reactions she'd had to this man were pure imagination.

It took an eighth of a second, standing three feet from him, to realize how wrong she'd been. Her entire body signaled awareness. He seemed to exude an electric force that radiated outward and connected with her own aura.

Trying to control the sudden trembling in her legs and arms, the dryness in her throat, she drew in a deep breath and prayed her voice would have some semblance of normalcy.

"Hello, Dr. Roswell." Not too bad, only a trifle shaky. "My name is Annie Pendleton. I arranged with your secretary to interview you this afternoon."

Damn. Some kind of reporter. If Phyllis had mentioned this, David certainly didn't remember. And in typical fashion, he'd neglected to even look at the daily reminder on his desk. Now Phyllis would have to get hold of Calvin and let him know David couldn't break off early as he'd planned to have a quiet dinner with his old friend. There was also that consultation, and now and those overcautious parents he wanted to reassure, and now this interview would take a good hour or so of an already overloaded afternoon.

Besides, he'd have to be careful what he said until he found out who she worked for. There were several publications that were blistering in their objections to organ transplants, especially those involving children.

"I phoned last Friday, and your secretary said to come in today at one...."

This Annie Pendleton had a nice voice anyway, he decided. Soft, mellow, with a shy, endearing quality to it. She seemed a trifle nervous for some reason.

"Of course, Ms Pendleton. C'mon in here, have a seat...."

She was suddenly convinced he was covering up the fact that he'd totally forgotten about the interview, and a flash of unreasonable anger flared in her.

She'd spent the past two days and nights thinking of nothing else but him, and he hadn't given her a single thought.

Annie, you dope, why should he? she chastised herself in an effort to be rational. *The man's never even met you. His secretary arranged the whole thing. You know that.*

"Can you give me some clues as to what this will be about?" he was asking with a charming grin. "Is it to do with that TV interview I did about organ transplants for children?"

Organ transplants? Damnation. He really didn't know who she was or why she was here, despite the careful briefing she'd given that woman on the phone when she set up the interview. So his snippy secretary hadn't told him anything about it.

Had Phyllis told him what this was all about, David pondered?

Probably, but if she had he'd simply not been listening. At any rate, this woman looked and smelled delightful—some light floral scent he must have smelled before, because it was familiar.

He rubbed a distracted hand through his hair, feeling the way it curled down over his shirt collar at the back. He needed a haircut, but that was nothing unusual. There was never enough time for things like haircuts. And he knew without any doubt that he smelled of antiseptic soap, with an undertone of disinfectant.

He grinned suddenly. She wasn't interviewing him for bachelor of the year. Why the sudden concern about his admittedly roughshod grooming?

"This isn't to do with medicine at all, Dr. Roswell. It's about magic. You see, I write books for children. I'm planning one about magic, and I wanted to interview a magician."

He expelled his breath in a relieved sigh. Magic, huh? This was going to be enjoyable after all. "Why not just call me David, and I'll call you Annie. Let's make this informal, all right?"

She nodded, trying not to look straight into his eyes because when she did, she found herself stammering.

"All right, ah, David." Swallowing hard, she fell back on the carefully prepared introduction she'd gone over and over the night before when she ought to have been sleeping.

"My books are usually aimed at the nine-to-twelve age group, and have to be absolutely accurate. Kids that age are fascinated by magic, and I wanted to talk to you about your magic act last Saturday, at Thompson High School auditorium?"

David sat back in his chair and relaxed.

"So you were at that benefit show on Saturday, Annie? Weren't those kids a great audience?" It gave him a subtle sense of pleasure, using her name. Besides, it suited her perfectly. Annie. Simple and unpretentious. Intimate and easy. He repeated it to himself. Annie. Not the formal Anna, or the cool Anne. Just Annie.

"The organizers tell me it was quite successful financially, that show," he remarked. She had soft hair, he mused. Hair the color of . . . he tipped his head to one side a little, considering the exact shade.

"I was there, yes. I—enjoyed your performance. You're an excellent magician, doct . . . ah, David." She was uncomfortable using his first name. It made it much harder to maintain the emotional distance she felt she needed between herself and him.

Oak, he concluded with a sense of satisfaction. She had hair the shade of oak, that same lush richness undershot with gold and a bit of red that the best wood displayed. It must be quite long, because she had it wound in a plump knot at the back of her head, with soft wisps curling before and behind small ears.

"I'm very much an amateur," he assured her. "Magic is a combination of skill and showmanship, and I'm wise enough to know my limitations." He winked in a conspiratorial way. "I concentrate hard on showmanship."

"But you also do illusions that aren't ordinarily performed by an amateur," she persisted. "That bird-cage disappearance, for instance. My son was really impressed by that one. He has dozens of books on magic and neither of us could locate anything like that trick in his books."

So she had a son. He felt let down, and realized he'd been assuming she was single.

"The bird-cage illusion actually originated with a French magician called Bautier de Kolta, who died in 1903," David explained, watching Annie take out a yellow spiral notebook and begin jotting in it as he spoke. "Two well-known American magicians, Carl Hertz and Harry Blackstone, also presented the bird cage in their shows early in the 1900s. And currently, Harry Blackstone, Jr. does a version of the vanishing bird cage in his act. I saw him perform it several years ago, when a medical conference I was attending in New York coincided with a worldwide gathering of The Magic Circle."

Blackstone's interpretation wasn't the one David used, however.

She was scribbling with furious intent, and he took the opportunity to study her. He liked the tiny frown of concentration between her winged eyebrows, the length of the gold tipped lashes as she bent over her notebook.

She looked up and caught him at it, and her eyes and his locked for an instant. She looked away, determined to get through the questions she'd prepared. Staring into David Roswell's eyes wasn't going to help any.

"How did you learn the bird-cage trick, David? Wait. First tell me how you began doing magic. What made you start learning? Aren't sorcery and medicine mutually exclusive?" she queried with a small smile, watching him tip his head a little to the side, knowing just the way his deep blue eyes would change with gentle humor as he answered her question.

He deliberately skipped the first question and went on to the others, hoping she wouldn't notice.

The bird-cage illusion should have been beyond his skills. But he'd read about it, found a limited description of technique in an old, tattered book and been able to master the whole thing with amazing ease, making the illusion entirely his own. Even he didn't fully understand how a complex illusion other magicians were puzzled by should come like child's play to him.

He never revealed the secrets of the bird cage, and he wasn't about to now, no matter how beguiling he found Annie Pendleton.

He told her only that he had a weird kind of superstition about the trick, as if it were an heirloom to be passed from father to son and guarded with care. Not that he had a son.

"Actually magic and medicine have a great deal in common, Annie, particularly so-called mystical magic," he began, leading her off the track of the bird cage.

"Mystical magic relies on a combination of hope and fear, which are the same emotions that send modern-day patients to visit a doctor. Mystical magic was the handmaiden of sorcery, witchcraft, alchemy, all of which have contributed in some way to modern medicine."

He was accustomed to lecturing, she noted. His deep voice was devoid of awkward pauses, even and flowing, full of confidence and that ability she'd recognized last Saturday, the knack of commanding the attention of an audience.

He sat forward, interested in what they were discussing, his long-fingered, scrubbed-looking surgeon's hands resting on a closed file folder. The nails were cut short and square. He wore a ring with a green stone on the small finger of his left hand, but he had none on his ring finger.

"The amateur magician of today is a long way from practicing mystical magic, however. The kind of magic I do is known as entertainment magic, providing amusement through interesting deception."

"How did you get interested in magic?" she asked again.

Maybe he was married and just didn't wear a ring.

"Oh, that started about the same time I developed an interest in medicine."

She had plain silver drop earrings suspended from pierced earlobes. With that coloring, he mused, she ought to wear only gold.

"My interest in magic started with a book my uncle Edward gave me for Christmas when I was ten. It came with a box of tricks, and I bored everyone nearly to death with my bungled attempts at making things disappear." He laughed at the reminiscence, and the sound made her smile. His laugh was deep and hearty, and it was just the way she'd known it would sound.

"When I wasn't smoking out the house with some concoction that had gone wrong, I was driving Uncle Edward crazy bungling a card trick,'' he added. ''But you must have gone through the same trials if your son is interested in magic. How old is he?'' he asked.

She was aware once again of his voice, a rich, deep voice, with a resonance of ironic humor that evoked a memory she couldn't quite hold on to.

''Jason's thirteen. Actually I had two kids with me on Saturday. They both considered your act the high spot of the day,'' she managed to say.

''Your own kids?'' he queried with what he hoped sounded polite, detached interest. He was surprised for a moment at her having a teenage son. He'd have guessed her too young.

''Only one of them is mine. I'm a single parent, and so is my neighbor, so we usually combine the gang for outings.'' Annie felt the heat of embarrassment slide up her neck and over her face. Fool, she chastised herself. He's not interested in your marital status. Whatever had made her volunteer that bit of trivia, anyway?

But David considered it anything but trivial to know she wasn't married, and Annie knew it by something in his eyes. In tandem, her glance and his went down to her left hand, to its naked third finger. She met his gaze and felt hot color burning her face, and just as quickly draining away beneath his steady scrutiny.

''I'm glad they liked my act,'' he said, bridging the awkward moment. ''Kids are difficult to impress these days because magicians have become so good. There's television's Doug Henning, there's David Copperfield, Harry Blackstone, Jr. Each of them brings a vastly different viewpoint to their performances, too. What particular slant on magic will your book have?''

''It's not a how-to book,'' Annie explained. ''It's fiction, the story of a physically handicapped boy who learns to do a trick that hasn't been done for centuries, one that has baffled magicians over the years. There's an element of the supernatural, of mystery.''

Now that was a coincidence for you. David thought of the bird-cage illusion, of how close her idea was to what had actually happened to him, almost as if she'd picked the idea for the book right out of his mind. It was uncanny.

He decided to dismiss that reaction as ridiculous. He concentrated instead on how alive her eyes became when she described her writing, shining behind that curtain of thick lashes.

"The biggest problem I'm having is finding an illusion that's conceivable, but not easy to execute. Like your bird cage."

"I can see that would be a problem, all right." He knew she was hunting, and he regretted having to refuse her. But the bird cage was his and his alone.

They exchanged a smile that admitted each knew what the other was thinking, and David went on studying her.

Lush was the word for her hair and lashes, all right. Lush was the best word for the rest of Annie as well, he concluded. She had sun-stained skin that refused to pale to nothingness in the cruel fluorescent light overhead, and the modest mint-colored shirtwaist she wore did nothing to hide full breasts and generous hips beneath its prim buttoned-up front.

"Have you written many other books for youngsters?" he asked, not paying as much attention to what she said as to what his roving eyes were observing.

Trim waist. Wonderful legs, crossed at the knee and sheathed in skin-toned hose, so narrow at the ankle he was sure his thumb and forefinger would fit like a bracelet.

"...and with the fifth one, I just got lucky. It was published almost the very week that the board game Dungeons and Dragons became so popular, and the same group that was fascinated by the game began to buy my book. This one will be my ninth."

She stopped speaking abruptly, and he met her forthright, deep brown eyes with a trace of guilt, conscious of having been looking anywhere but at her eyes. An unexpected wave of sexual need swelled in him, so intense and throbbing and full that he was grateful for the concealing desk between them.

"Have we met somewhere before?" he asked with a sudden frown, and Annie watched the vertical line appear between his thick, dark brows, waited for and then saw that one eyebrow tilted in a question mark as the other lowered, just as she'd known it would.

She shivered, feeling goose bumps cover her arms and legs and lift the soft hairs on the back of her neck.

"No, I'm quite certain we've never met," she said with firm emphasis, avoiding his puzzled glance and beginning an inventory of objects littering his cluttered desk, because a ridiculous feeling made her certain she was telling a lie.

Files, with papers bulging out, two Styrofoam coffee cups with black sludge in the bottom of each, and, half hidden under loose papers and an open medical book, a smooth, polished alabaster egg resting at a crooked angle in a silver cradle, all reminders of those diverse interests of his, sorcery and science.

No framed photos of wife and children.

"Funny, I just have this weird feeling I know you from somewhere...." David realized after he'd said it how trite such a line must sound, and for a moment he, too, was flustered.

"I've a lot of books about magic, if you care to...," he blurted, and then was even more flustered. He'd been about to invite her to his apartment, to browse through the library of esoteric and ancient volumes he'd collected over the years, a library he was proud of having.

He realized in time that it might sound like an invitation to view his etchings. "Tell you what," he amended. "I'll look through them and see what I can find that might work for your book. Most illusions are variations of ancient deceptions, going back to Egyptian times, and there are very few that haven't been documented. But I'll see what I can find, if you like."

"I'd really appreciate that," Annie said sincerely. "I've been using my local public library branch, and the best area seems to be the children's section. The adult stacks have a book or two on Houdini, one on Mother Shipton's prophecies, and that's about it. My son has more reference books than they do."

"Give me a number where I can reach you, and I'll see what I can do," he promised, and she did, writing her home number on the pad he handed her.

For the next ten minutes, Annie asked technical questions about the paraphernalia magicians used and where they obtained it.

At that point, a tall, austere-looking woman in her late sixties poked her steel-gray head in the door, looked with disapproval at Annie and snapped at David, "I'm holding your calls, but you're running late again, Doctor," before she disappeared.

Annie leaped to her feet, but David waved a staying hand. "Relax," he commanded. "That's just Phyllis. Her mission in life is to run mine for me. I've told her before she's far too obsessed with time," he commented with the half smile Annie had been waiting for without being conscious of it.

"Really, I must go. I have stayed too long," she assured him, and he got to his feet, moving from behind the desk to stand beside her. He came far too near. She moved several steps away.

"Thank you very much. You've been super, giving me all this information," she gabbled, thrown off balance by his physical proximity and the devastating effect it had on her. Every pore was aware of him; her hands ached to reach out and touch him.

She moved another step toward the door, and the sudden awareness that she was leaving, that she probably wouldn't see him again, swept over her with shattering effect.

He followed behind as she fumbled for the door handle, and then he reached out a hand to shake hers in a gesture of farewell.

It was such an ordinary, everyday movement; yet she had to lift her own hand by force of will, make herself put it in his, deal with the tumult of having him so near she could smell the faint odor of his body, the warm, clean man odor, peculiarly his, that lingered in her memory in some mysterious fashion.

"I enjoyed this past hour, Annie." He smiled, a different smile this time, a whimsical smile, just a bit uncertain, as he held her hand.

Touching him was agony. It reaffirmed all the messages her emotions had been telegraphing, that this man somehow affected her as no other had done in her entire life, and she was compelled to look up, deep into his eyes.

He held her warm hand an endless moment too long, aware that her hands were rather wide and strong, that the skin on the back of her fingers felt soft and smooth.

"I'll call you soon, with that information I promised," he was saying as she all but wrenched her hand free and struggled to open the door.

She hurried through the outer office, oblivious of the curious glances Phyllis was giving her, intent only on escape before she disgraced herself the way she had at the magic show the other day by bursting into tears like an idiot.

It wasn't until she was in the hallway that Annie realized David was still close behind her.

"Annie, Annie wait…," he started to say, and she turned around, just as a woman's teasing call sounded from farther down the hall.

"David, you dope, where were you last night? I thought you promised me you were coming to Jenna's party," the slender dark-haired nurse scolded, sweeping past Annie as if she were invisible, and putting a familiar, restraining hand on David's white-coated arm. "I know eligible bachelors are at a premium in Vancouver, but playing this hard to get is ridiculous," she went on, smiling up at him with beguiling beauty.

Annie's heart felt as if it were about to stop beating. She felt a powerful rush of primitive fury, and for an instant she contemplated grabbing the nurse and flinging her away from David.

In another instant, Annie's brain cataloged what was happening to her, and she was appalled at herself. She was jealous, she was having a fit of violent jealousy over a man she hardly knew.

Saints in heaven, what was happening to her? She'd never been truly jealous over any male in her entire life.

Feeling anger and shame combine in a white hot rush, she whirled around and hurried a few more steps down the long, green painted corridor. When the first stab of pain shot through her neck and back, she ignored it.

But a moment later, a cry of agony she couldn't suppress was torn out of her to echo down the hallway. The pain was so sudden and extreme that even her vision blurred beneath its onslaught, and she staggered as if she'd been drinking, lurching to the side and catching herself by placing a hand on the wall.

It was her back—the old, dreaded, familiar pain that spread through her neck and shoulders and head. She'd thought it was gone, this persistent torment that had recurred at just such unexpected moments as this, all through her life. She gasped as the spasms shot down her arm, up into the back of her head, deep into her spine.

Over Betty's head, David was frowning, conscious that something was happening to Annie, but unable to pinpoint exactly what it could be.

Then he heard the cry, saw Annie stagger and, wrenching his arm away from under Betty's proprietary grip, he moved with the speed of an athlete down the corridor.

He was barely in time to catch her before she fell, and she was only dimly aware of his arms encircling her as the torment grew and engulfed her.

CHAPTER THREE

THE WORDS PENETRATED Annie's foggy brain in a persistent stream.

"Can you describe the pain? Is it constant or intermittent? Is it like the thrust of a knife, or dull? You say you've had these attacks since early childhood, Annie. Is there ever any warning, perhaps a difference in color of your surroundings, a buzzing in your head, a sense of unreality? Who's your family doctor? What medications has he prescribed for this in the past?"

David's rapid, professional questions were endless, and Annie, stretched out on a narrow, wheeled bed in the corridor near his office door, wished between spasms that her stupid problem had occurred anywhere in the western hemisphere but here, that she'd had this attack in front of anyone but him.

Nice going, Annie.

She answered his questions, aware every horrible second of being prone and helpless, of feeling stupid and vulnerable when she'd wanted above all to appear professional and capable to him.

There was a coffee stain on the front of his white coat that she hadn't noticed before, and she tried to center her attention on it, attempt the relaxation techniques that one of the endless list of specialists she'd visited had suggested as a last resort when these attacks occurred.

Annie heard Phyllis's irritated voice announce from somewhere overhead and behind her bed, "I have Dr. Simpson on the line now, Dr. Roswell."

David moved away, and Annie felt profound gratitude that her old family doctor had been in his office this afternoon. At least he'd confirm what she'd been gasping out for the past twenty minutes—that the pain was not life threatening, it had no known medical origin, and it usually went away by itself after an indeterminate number of hours.

Relax your toes, relax your feet. Relax your ankles, your calves, your knees . . .

Aghh. A moan escaped despite her best intentions.

When the pain was at its worst like this, it felt as if her neck were breaking, as if her spine were cracking in two.

"Dr. Simpson agrees that a strong muscle relaxant will give you some relief," David was saying, and the nurse who'd been hanging on his arm and flirting a short while before was now sponging Annie's arm with antiseptic, efficient and oozing professional concern.

Annie wanted to object—she'd had these shots before, and they'd turned her into a vegetable for hours.

"I don't want . . ."

But she had to close her eyes and bite her tongue against the pain as it swelled, reaching a nauseating crescendo. She panted and felt perspiration break out on her forehead. The minor prick of the needle in her upper arm barely registered.

"I want to go home," she managed to say next. "There's no need to keep me here, I want to go home. Now." She opened her eyes, and stared straight up at David.

He was bending over her, one arm resting beside her shoulder on the narrow cot, and she felt a ridiculous happiness for an instant, just having him this close to her.

He was frowning, and his blue gaze looked concerned and puzzled as he met Annie's eyes.

A tiny muscle around her mouth jerked as she strove to stay in control.

Then Annie could feel the drug beginning its numbing journey through her veins, and she felt a desperate, urgent need to escape this place before her eyelids grew heavy and sleep overcame her as it always did as a result of this shot.

She didn't want to fall asleep here in the corridor, helpless in front of Phyllis, in front of the dark-haired nurse. She didn't want to be vulnerable in their presence. She wanted to go home.

"Did you drive over, Annie? Where's your car? Is there someone I can phone to come and get you, a . . . friend, perhaps?"

David was unaware of holding his breath in tense anticipation for the time it took her to answer. She was lovely. There had to be a male friend, a lover. There wasn't time to wonder why he cared, why it should be an urgent matter to him.

"Nobody except my neighbor, Cleo, and she's taken all the kids camping till tomorrow," Annie said with a dejected tone to her voice. She could feel herself beginning to slur the words, too. "Please, just call me a cab. I'll arrange about my car . . ."

"Nonsense." The plan had formed the instant she answered, and he acted on it. "Phyllis, arrange a special permit for her car. What make is it, Annie? It's in that lot at the side of the building? See that security understands it will be there until tomorrow at least. And Phyllis, have the attendant in the underground park bring my car to the side entrance. Nurse, find me a wheelchair."

Everything was growing vague and distant in a pleasant, giddy way, and the torture in her neck had dulled now to a blissful, almost bearable ache.

She heard David issuing instructions, canceling appointments, and she paid little attention. Everything was receding, getting farther and farther away, less real to her.

Soon she was going to be asleep, and the reluctance she'd felt moments before no longer mattered at all.

Annie gave a wide yawn as the nurse helped her slide off the stretcher bed. Then she was strapped into a wheelchair and pushed down the corridor.

A polished silver-gray car, roomy and sleek, was parked close to the curb, engine running. With the nurse's help, Annie struggled in, drawing the rich leather upholstery smell deep into her nostrils.

She watched the young driver slide out and David come hurrying over, tugging on a tweed sport jacket and handing the boy a large tip and a word of thanks as he slid in behind the wheel.

A muted protest sounded deep inside, but it didn't reach her lips. It was just too much trouble.

Sinking back into the luxurious gray seat, expelling a huge sigh, Annie closed her eyes, willing to let whatever fate was in control carry on as if everything was normal.

"Hey, sleepyhead, you have to give me your address," his voice was saying.

Even with her eyes closed, she could envision the way the beginning of a smile was tilting the corners of his wide mouth, the way an eyebrow arched with gentle humor. He was watching her. She could sense his gaze, but she didn't mind. She loved having him look at her.

After a moment's thought, while a tiny frown creased the smooth skin in the middle of her forehead, she slowly, with great effort, repeated the numbers and the street.

"Gotcha," David reached across her, grasped the seat belt and drew it over her prone form, snapping it in place and allowing his hand to graze the satin skin of her arm before he jerked away and in one easy gesture guided the car free of the curb.

For Annie, there was no memory of time between that moment and the next, when she came out of sleep and became aware of David's hands unlocking the belt around her, his strong arms half lifting her out of the car in front of her house.

"We're here, Annie. Do you want me to carry you?"

"No, I don't. I can walk by myself," she protested with groggy dignity.

He took in the defiant tilt of her rounded chin and the hazy confusion in her sleepy eyes. She stumbled a bit when her shoes touched the sidewalk. With an amused half laugh he looped an arm around her waist, and even through the effects of the drug she shivered at that contact.

"I'm sure you can, but just let me help a bit. Neck all right?" he inquired, distressing her because his lips were close to her ear.

The burning sensation in her back was still intense, but the pain was far-off, and she told him so as she struggled to control her knees and make her feet go where her brain ordered. They progressed inch by inch up the cement path to her front door, and then Annie fumbled for endless moments in her straw handbag for her key. She finally located it with numb fingers and handed it to David.

"Can you unlock it please?"

"Sure can." It was more difficult than he'd anticipated, however. When he released his hold on her for the slightest bit, she began to crumble in slow motion toward the ground. Finally, with a sigh of relief, he managed to release the lock, and he half carried her in, looking around for somewhere to put her. There was a huge, soft sofa in the living room to the right of the door.

She gave him a sleepy, friendly grin as he laid her down and tucked a pillow beneath her head, and with a supreme effort, she drew her legs up one by one so they rested on the sofa.

Her shoes were still on, and David hesitated, then struggled with the straps on her high-heeled sandals, muttering an oath under his breath as they defied his best attempts. Finally he settled for inching the straps over her heels without undoing them. He dropped the shoes on the floor.

"I thought magicians were good at undoing things," she mumbled, and David laughed at the unintentional innuendo of her words.

"I guess I haven't practiced much on women's shoes," he confessed, and she nodded as if that made perfect sense.

"Are you going away now?" she said next, and the intense anxiety in her voice and eyes surprised him. "I know you must, but I wish there was more time. . . ." Her voice trailed off into a mumble.

He had been planning to return to the hospital right away. By now, Phyllis would have canceled his most urgent appointments, but there was always paperwork to catch up on, and of course the dinner date later with Calvin. He hadn't told Phyllis to cancel that.

For some inexplicable reason, he decided to stay a while. He deserved to play hooky once in a while, and today was that once, he assured his conscience.

He walked back into the entrance hall, down the short passage that led to the high-ceilinged kitchen, searching for a phone. There was one on the spacious counter.

"Phyllis? Listen, cancel all my appointments for the rest of the day." He listened, and added, "Yeah, cancel dinner with Calvin, too, please. I know he won't be too happy, but do it anyway and don't bitch at me, okay? Oh, and Phyllis, call the Quinlans, Carrie's folks, and ask them to meet me in the coffee shop tomorrow morning at ten and I'll give them all the details about her surgery."

He hung the phone up and looked around. Nice, homey kitchen, really well equipped. He'd bet Annie liked to cook. The place had an efficient yet warm feeling to it, and there were well-used utensils hanging over the stove.

Why had he suddenly decided to stay here? Well, he rationalized, Annie shouldn't be left alone. The powerful relaxant he'd administered would affect her for at least another few hours, and it was possible that she might try to get up, fall and hurt herself.

And that was a crock, he admitted with a twisted, honest grin. He wouldn't be here if she were a man, or anyone at all except Annie, because there was no real danger.

He walked back into the living room and studied the lines of her face against the pale rose pillow. Her eyes were closed. A pang of intense emotion clenched at his insides.

She was desirable, stretched out limp like that. Her skirt had ridden up above her knees, and her long legs were curled to one side, her arm folded beneath her. Soft tendrils of hair, a rich red-brown streaked with golden highlights, had come loose from the knot on her neck and lay in disarray across her ear and shoulder. Her skin was flushed a bit, and he had the most intense desire to lean over her, stroke his hand across her cheek and smooth the hair away from her face, just to test its silk texture on his fingers.

What the hell's getting into you, Roswell? You're a doctor, and technically, she's your patient. That's why you're here, remember? You're responsible for her well-being, which doesn't include sensuous stroking when she's half asleep, for Pete's sake.

Sound asleep, he corrected, looking at her again. Annie's breasts rose and fell beneath the pale green dress, and she sighed.

There was a knitted afghan in shades of rose and blue across the sofa back, and he hurried to shake it out and cover her with it, neck to toes. When that was done, he moved away, undecided again as to what he should do next.

Annie's home was welcoming and cheerful, quiet, with pleasing mixtures of bright colors scattered here and there. Purple and rose and blue throw pillows hugged the couch where Annie lay, and a wall of shelves held books and small objects. Blue venetian blinds at the windows contrasted against muted cream walls and a darker blue rug.

David wandered over to the stereo, curious about the tapes arranged on the rack over the machine. The mixture of musical tastes represented was a vivid reminder that Annie had a teenage son: Michael Jackson and Ravel's "Bolero." Men Without Hats and Glen Campbell. Willie Nelson and Prince, Neil Diamond and Lori Anderson.

A few muttered words from behind him brought his attention back to the woman on the sofa.

"...hear the birds. Is that a mockingbird in the apple tree?"

David strolled over to her. It was obvious she was dreaming. But when he drew close, he realized her eyes were open, and seemed to look straight up at him, the pupils dark and dilated.

"Are you awake, Annie?" he queried in a soft voice. "Do you mind if I play some music?"

Annie could hear him, from a far distance, asking her about music, but it was difficult to separate the dream from reality because his voice blended with the other voice she could hear. Present and beyond were fading into each other.

Something strange was happening to her, strange indeed. Her eyes were open, and she understood for brief seconds that she was in her own living room, but it was as though a movie screen stood between her and the reality of her home, as if she could watch the movie and act in it at the same time.

Then the images grew too strong to resist, and her living room faded, and she was young, in love, in some far distant place.

SHE WAS SO GLAD to have him with her this afternoon. Overwhelming tenderness for the man walking close at her side, holding her hand, filled her heart with joy. She loved him, and it made her happy.

It was a summer afternoon. Bird song filled the air along with the smell of earth and growing things. Now and then a pungent farm odor from the small holdings that lay along the fertile loops of the river made her wrinkle her nose, but even that had an earthy appeal.

Wildflowers bloomed, and the air was heavy with summer's warmth.

"Hear . . . music?"

Her lover's question wasn't clear, but she turned her face up to his and smiled into his deep blue eyes.

"It's just the birds, and the wind in the trees," she murmured. "Remember, darling, this is where we sat and had our lunch that other afternoon."

She gave him a shy glance, full of meaning. They'd lain there naked under the sheltering trees, as close as it was possible to be, and moved in each other's arms, moved in each other's bodies, until the world shattered and erupted in hot ecstasy, and she'd cried out and held him there inside her with her legs, and then wept afterward, and he'd stroked her tears away with his tongue.

She loved him with an intensity that frightened her, and as she looked up into his beloved face, she felt a foreshadowing trace of pain and fear that formed a constricting band around her heart that made her struggle to escape the dream. But it was woven in firm tendrils around her, and she couldn't escape its fabric just yet.

"Love, don't go, will you?" she begged him.

THE PASSIONATE WHISPER, the disconnected sentences she spoke were no doubt part of her dreaming, and David stood over her, observing the naked longing on her face, unable to look away from the tenderness and passionate feeling mirrored there.

Who was she seeing with eyes so heavy with love? Who inspired that devotion on her features, that soft moistness around her full, parted lips?

He felt strong emotion well in him, a feeling that might have been jealousy, and he dismissed it with impatient reason. Surely her dreams were private, and he should respect them as such.

"You won't go yet, beloved? You'll stay with me until night comes?" Her whispering voice was husky, heavy with a sensuousness that captivated him.

David couldn't stop himself. He bent over her, and placed his lips on hers, a light caress, almost innocent, allowing only his lips to touch her, but needing in some obscure way to make his presence known to her, to woo her away from that dream lover who held her captive.

He felt the heat of her, the petal softness of her lips against his own. He could detect a faint acid vestige of the drug he'd given her on her breath, along with a sweetness only Annie's.

She felt his mouth, locked in her dream, and she knew only that the lips on hers were those of her lover, her soul companion, and there was nothing else in the world she wanted or needed or desired. Only him, only his love. Forever.

"Sleep well, Annie. I'll stay until you wake up," David whispered, straightening, tugging the afghan closer around her shoulder, stroking a knuckle lightly down her flushed cheek.

It had taken a definite effort of will to take his mouth from hers. He shoved his hands into the pockets of his trousers, walked over to the window and stared without seeing out at the overgrown greenness of the backyard. Kissing her that way had left him unsettled, a trifle guilty, but excited as well.

He wanted to know her, know the real, waking Annie. He wanted to strip away the social mask he'd seen her wear that afternoon when she was interviewing him, locate instead this passionate, fiery woman she became in her dreams. He wanted to kiss her when she was awake, when she knew it was him instead of some damned fantasy.

He gave a deep sigh and a small, rueful smile crept across his mouth as he searched the recordings for one he'd noticed of Zamfir playing the pan flute.

The eerie, haunting music filled the room, and David chose a book at random from the shelves and settled himself in a comfortable armchair near the window, where he could glance over at Annie.

A thought occurred to him, and he smiled again. Magicians about to create an illusion often referred to putting their audience under the "fluence." The woman sleeping there had David Roswell under her "fluence," and he wanted to be part of the illusion of love she'd created in her dreams.

He would be part of it. He settled back and waited without much patience for her to awaken.

CHAPTER FOUR

ANNIE NOTICED SHADOWS creeping into the corners of the room.

She'd opened her eyes a moment before, but the delicious lassitude that filled her body and her mind made it impossible to move quite yet. And really, there was no need, was there? A sense of utter relaxation, of thick and heavy peace permeated her being.

"Annie? Are you awake?"

The deep, questioning male voice seemed a natural part of her waking at first, but as she grew more aware, surprise filled her.

"David? You stayed here this long? How late is it, anyway?" She cleared her husky throat and squinted at the evening shadows, raising her head with caution, anticipating pain. But there was only a dull ache as she wriggled to a sitting position, moving the afghan away from her body and tugging down the skirt of her crumpled green dress. Then she stretched her legs out to flex their cramped muscles.

He was over by the window, in her favorite armchair, and she was grateful that he allowed her these waking moments in relative privacy.

"It's . . ." He glanced at his wristwatch and his voice registered his own surprise when he said, "Hey, it's nearly seven. You slept four full hours. Is the pain gone?"

Annie again moved her head first one way and then the other. A relieved half smile touched her lips and she nodded. "Completely gone," she said on a long, relieved sigh.

He got up and came over to her, and she noticed that his suit jacket was now off, his tie hanging loose at his open shirt collar, the cuffs on his off-white shirt rolled to his forearms. The dark, curling hairs on the back of his wrists made a sharp contrast with the pale cotton fabric.

A wave of shyness rolled over her. There was an intimate feeling about being here with this man after he'd watched her sleep. He must have covered her with the afghan. He'd taken her shoes off; she did remember that much.

She'd been dreaming, a weird, crazy dream, undoubtedly caused by the drugs. But her brain was beginning to function again, and she gave him a puzzled look. "I'm grateful, but there wasn't any need for you to stay with me, David. I would have been fine on my own."

He nodded agreement, and his wide mouth tilted upward at the corners. A quizzical expression came into his eyes.

"You probably would have been fine, yes. The simple truth is I wanted to stay." His glance slid away from her to take in the details of the room.

"I enjoyed being here. You have a comfortable home, Annie. I took the liberty of using your tape deck and browsing through your books. It's not often I have a chance to just laze away an afternoon." His smile was conspirational and warm.

Annie frowned up at him, trying to make sense of it all and failing. He must have had appointments today with others besides her, things that demanded his attention, and yet here he was, looking relaxed and perfectly at home in her living room.

She reached up to brush away a tendril of hair and realized that she must look a complete mess. The careful chignon she'd fashioned was undone, any makeup she might have had on must be gone, and her dress was a wrinkled wreck.

"Besides, I'm starving," she blurted out, and he laughed as if he'd guessed the rest of her thought pattern.

"That's proof positive that you're feeling better," he teased. "Now that you mention it, so am I hungry." He hesitated an instant, and then said, "Shall we go out and find a restaurant?"

Annie stood, testing her body and finding it back to normal.

David seemed much taller when she wasn't wearing heels. "How do you feel about leftover lasagna?" she said with impulsive zeal. "I've got some in the fridge. I could heat it up in the microwave and make a salad."

"Are you certain you feel like doing that?"

She nodded and he smiled with pleasure. "Sounds great to me. As long as you let me help. I'm not bad at making salads, if you steer me toward the ingredients and a sharp knife."

"Give me a minute, and I'll be right back." Annie headed for the stairs, calling over her shoulder, "I think there's a cold beer in the fridge if you'd like."

Did he drink beer, she wondered? *He liked wine.*

Halfway up, she paused for a moment, staring out the landing window at Cleo's darkened house and wondering what in hell she was doing, inviting a man she barely knew to stay for dinner. She hadn't had a man at the dinner table for—how long?

Well, no big deal, she rationalized. Leftovers, Annie, just leftovers. No candles, no wine, no spiderwebs. What made her think he liked wine?

Look, idiot, you owe him. He drove you home, took care of you, took off your shoes and covered you up.

A wispy memory of lips brushing hers with urgent softness came and was gone again before she could pin it down. She shook her head and three pins fell out on the carpeted stairs, reminding her of what she was supposed to be doing.

She hurried up to the bathroom and let out a groan when she caught sight of herself in the full-length mirror.

Fifteen minutes later, dressed in worn jeans and a bright red patterned rayon shirt tied in a knot at her waist, feet bare, Annie entered the kitchen. She'd washed her face and left it clean of all but pale lipstick and a touch of mascara. She'd brushed her hair and braided it, letting it hang in one long, thick plait down her back.

David was standing at the counter, a drawer open in front of him and an unopened bottle of beer in his hand.

"Can't find the opener to save my soul," he said, turning toward her. He looked her over with unabashed interest. "You look different," he added, studying her naked face, letting his gaze rove over the snug jeans and casual blouse. "You look about fifteen years old."

"Sir, this is the real me," Annie said with an attempt at flip humor, hoping he didn't notice the flush of color she felt at his words. "That other outfit was just a clever disguise." She located an opener, handing it to him without meeting his eyes, then turned away and started taking things out of the fridge.

"I'm a peasant at heart."

"You enjoy cooking," he said. It was a statement rather than a question.

Annie smiled at him over her shoulder. "I sure do. If I didn't, heaven knows what it would cost me for take-out food for my kid. Teenage boys have appetites that have to be witnessed to be believed."

"So I've heard. I still can't believe you have a teenager."

"You don't have any kids?" The question was out before she could censor it.

He shook his head. "My wife didn't want any," he explained, and then added with deliberate casualness, "My ex-wife, that is. We've been divorced for four years now."

Overwhelming relief engulfed Annie, and she bent down and started pulling lettuce and green onions out of the vegetable tray so he couldn't see her face.

"How about you? How long have you been alone, Annie?"

She stood, avoiding his eyes, and plunked the salad makings on the counter.

"Always," she said in an even tone. "I decided not to marry Jason's father at all. So you see, I'm not a divorced single parent. I'm a single parent, period."

"And do you sock everybody who asks you why you decided to stay single?"

She looked up at him in surprise, unaware of how belligerent she'd sounded. Humor deepened the blue of his eyes as well as the tiny wrinkles surrounding them, and she had to smile back at him as he took the leaves of lettuce and started rinsing them under the tap.

"You know, hardly anyone's ever asked me why? Most people want to know if I get any support money."

"So why did you decide to stay single?"

He was persistent. Annie took a knife out of a wooden holder and started peeling an avocado. Her forehead creased in a frown.

"It's hard to explain. I was in love with . . . with this guy named Michael McCrae . . ."

Why was it always difficult for her to even say his name?

"Or thought I was. He was an engineer, five years older than me. I wasn't a kid at the time, either, I was twenty-one years old. He wanted the baby, wanted me." A shiver ran down her spine, remembering. "And the worst part was I didn't decide not to marry him until the day before the wedding."

"Deserted at the altar. So he was a touch annoyed with you." Once again, it was more statement than question. She glanced up and found David watching her.

"Yeah, you could say that he was a bit put out, all right," she said with ironic lack of emphasis.

"What happened?"

Michael had been more than angry. He'd been furious, livid. His absolute rage had terrified her. When he had finally understood that Annie meant what she said, that she had no intention of ever marrying him, he'd launched a vicious court battle for custody of his still unborn baby that had lasted until Jason was born and well over a year old.

"He fought me for custody. The thing was, I felt that it wasn't so much because he wanted the baby. It was simply that he wanted to hurt me any way he could."

His actions had underlined for her the rightness of calling off the wedding. Michael had illustrated the very things Annie had begun to sense about him; that underneath his quiet surface, there was a deep possessive strain, a jealousy and potential for violence in Michael's nature that frightened and repulsed her.

"He fought me for five months before Jason was born, and a full year afterward. Thirteen years ago, that was quite unusual, a biological father fighting for custody of an unborn child. I often think he might have had a much better chance now than he did then." Annie kept her tone as impassive as she could, hiding the deep and bitter hurt that still lingered over those long-ago memories. "Anyway, he lost. Thank God."

It was significant that she didn't say instead that she'd won. There hadn't been triumph for her that day after the court decision, only profound relief. And physical terror such as she'd never experienced before or after. The scene in front of the courthouse that afternoon twelve years before was still fresh in her mind, the horrifying moment when she'd come, by accident, face-to-face with Michael.

"Bitch, you cheating bitch, I'll kill you for this."

The murderous rage in his eyes was seared forever into her soul. He'd lunged toward her, and grabbed her by the shoulders. She'd felt his hands digging deeper and deeper into her flesh, sensed the muscles in his arms contracting, and with awful certainty she'd known that he was going to shake her like a rag doll, until her neck snapped.

Adrenaline surged even now at the memory, and the knife in her hand slipped, just missing her fingers.

David swore and took it from her.

"Let me do that. I'm quite good with knives. We surgeons have to practice on salads before they turn us loose on people." He smoothly sliced a tomato into thin pieces and when he spoke again the light, teasing note was absent from his voice. "I'm sorry, Annie. I didn't mean to upset you. I had no right to pry."

She shrugged with an attempt at nonchalance that failed. "I didn't have to answer you."

The astonishing thing was that she had answered. It had taken Cleo well over a determined year to uncover the things Annie had just told David.

"True." He nodded, and began chopping the lettuce while she found a wooden bowl and rubbed its inner surface with a cut garlic clove.

"Maybe that stuff you injected me with was actually truth serum," she teased. It took real effort to move away from those memories of the past.

He shook his head. "Nope, we sorcerers never have to resort to anything like that. We just cast a spell—nothing to it—and from that moment on, we see and know all."

Annie smiled at his banter, even as she acknowledged the ironic truth in what he said. She actually felt as if David had cast some sort of spell over her and could see into her heart. She'd been aware of it from the very first moment she saw him up on that stage, and now the feeling intensified.

When she took plates and cutlery to set the table in the dining room, David motioned to the small wooden table under the kitchen window, where Annie and Jason normally ate, and said in a plaintive tone, "Can't we have dinner right here? I have this thing about kitchens. We always ate in the kitchen when I was a kid and I loved it."

So she wiped off the battered wooden surface and used the everyday straw mats. Dusk became darkness outside, and Annie twisted the venetian blinds shut, encompassing the two of them in the warm and cozy room.

Deliberately she turned their conversation to books, and then to music, and as she served their meal, David related amusing stories about magic tricks he'd attempted and failed at with spectacular and funny effect. He told of wild things that had happened during performances. He described for Annie the ingenious ways magicians had of covering mistakes and making them appear part of their act.

He made her laugh and he laughed with her. Their laughter filled the room, the easy spontaneous delight of two people who find the same ridiculous things amusing.

And as time drifted by, Annie found herself filing away the things he revealed about himself, almost as though they were souvenirs she could take out and fondle again when this strange evening was over. Would she ever see him again, or was this all they'd ever share?

"Let's move into the living room where it's more comfortable for coffee and dessert," she suggested, not daring to think beyond the moment.

Together they cleared away the dishes and stacked them in the dishwasher. He helped her carry the coffee tray she prepared into the living room, and they sat on the sofa, the tray between them on the low coffee table.

"When I came to your office today," Annie ventured as she handed him a bowl of ice cream smothered with her own preserved brandied cherries, "you said something about a TV interview, which had to do with heart and liver transplants for children. Is that an area of medicine you're particularly interested in?"

She watched as he swallowed a mouthful of the dessert, tracing the strong muscles in his throat with her eyes.

"Yeah, Annie, it sure is." He stirred cream into his coffee. He sat forward on his chair, setting his bowl down. His voice took on a new intensity.

"Not performing the operations. I don't have the training or the skill for that. But teams of skilled professionals are available as soon as the facilities are in place here. At the moment, B.C. has no provincial budget for such procedures, and the kids needing them have to go out-of-province. But there's also the problem of donors, you see. There has to be a major educational campaign, and that, too, takes money."

"Do some of your patients need these operations, David?"

His face was bleak for a moment. "They sure do. Four kids right at the moment. They'll all have to go out of the country if they're going to have the operations they need to live."

Both he and Annie forgot their dessert as David explained the stress and almost overwhelming strain such trips placed on both the children needing them and on their parents.

"I'll give you an example. There's a patient of mine, this little kid named Charlie Vance. He's nearly three. His folks live in a small town in interior B.C. called Enderby, and his dad's a truck driver. They don't have much money. Charlie was born with a liver disorder, and his only hope is a transplant. You've probably seen Charlie's picture in the daily papers, because his folks have no choice but to exploit his cuteness and his plight in order to raise the formidable amount of money required to take him to a U.S. medical center for treatment. They have another baby, a little girl, and it looks as if she's inherited the same problem Charlie has."

Annie made a despairing sound in her throat at the unfairness of such a destiny.

David nodded. "Can you imagine the agony these young parents go through, having to exploit one desperately sick child just to raise money for a procedure that ought to be available here.... will be available if the mills of government ever decide lives are on an equal level with roads? And the only thing the Vances have to look forward to is going through the whole damned procedure all over again with their daughter, because I can't promise those parents that when baby Angela's condition demands a transplant as well, we'll be able to perform it here at home."

David's voice was bitter but resigned. "Chances are they'll just have to undergo the same media exposure, the same demeaning hands-out-for-donations performance that they're going through right now for Charlie."

Annie felt shaken. She'd read the articles in the papers, looked at the appealing photos of children like Charlie. She'd even donated money to such causes, without ever once personalizing the experience, or questioning why a child should be in such a begging situation. Her ignorance made her feel ashamed.

The depth of David's caring was evident in every word, and his passion was revealed through his voice, the way he leaned forward, the graphic motions his hands made as he spoke.

"We need the facility desperately, and we need it now," he concluded. "The feeling among most of the hospital board is that there's no real urgency because there aren't hundreds of kids standing in line to use it. There are relatively few in relation to the other problems we treat. But every day of delay for those few like Charlie means that their chances for life grow slimmer, their families' chances of survival as a unit grow fewer.''

Annie was silent, thinking over what he'd said, and also what he hadn't had to say. It was obvious David Roswell loved his job more than anything else in his life. There was none of the detachment she'd always expected in him, none of the distancing she'd always heard was essential for a doctor dealing with high-risk patients. He cared and he showed it. He was open and honest and vehement in his convictions.

Her soul responded, *Hasn't he always been this way?*

''Did you always want to be a doctor, David?''

He was gulping coffee that had to be stone-cold by now, and he waved away her offer to reheat it.

''You mean did someone give me a little doctor's bag the way my uncle did that magic kit?'' He shook his head and laughed. ''I think being a doctor is born in some people, like having six toes or a white streak in your hair for no reason. As far back as I can remember, I knew I'd be a doctor. There was never any question in my mind.''

''Did you come from a large family?'' The need to know about him was insatiable, and he seemed willing to answer her questions.

''Nope, I was an only child. I grew up in Toronto, and my parents were professional people. Dad was a research analyst for a chemical company, and my mother taught high-school English. So in many ways I was fortunate because there was enough money for education, and they were supportive of me in every way.''

''They must have been very proud of you.'' Annie thought for a moment of how bitter and disappointed her mother had been with her until she achieved some success at writing. That disapproval and the pain it had caused her had made Annie vow that whatever Jason did with his life would be fine with her. That awful, crushing sense of parental disapproval wouldn't ever be part of her son's life if she could help it.

David had finished his dessert, and now he carefully put the bowl and spoon down before he looked over at Annie.

''My parents died several years ago in the Mexican earth-quake,'' he explained. ''They used to go to the same isolated resort every year, to an old hotel run by a family they'd come to love over the years. The roof collapsed, and mostly everyone was killed. Their bodies were finally uncovered about a week later."

"David, I'm sorry." The words sounded inadequate. Annie could imagine that having both parents die suddenly must have been awful for him.

David was as open about his feelings as he'd been about everything else she asked. "It was a shock at the time. I miss them, but it's exactly what they'd have wanted, given a choice. They both had a horror of being old and helpless, and they were very much in love even after all those years of marriage. This way, neither had to suffer losing the other."

This time his smile was enigmatic, with more than a trace of sadness, and his eyes seemed to caress Annie's face as he added, "They misled me, you see, those parents of mine. Because of them, I grew up believing that marriage was a wonderful institution. When mine failed, I wasted a lot of time trying to figure out where I'd gone wrong before it finally dawned on me that my parents' relationship was the exception rather than the rule, and that more often than not, marriage simply doesn't work. Nobody's fault."

Marriage wasn't something Annie felt she could discuss with any expertise at all, but his conclusions about most marriages were basically the same as hers.

"I was an only child, too," she confided. "My father died when I was eleven, and my mother never remarried. From what I remember, their relationship was nothing like the one your parents had, but it was workable. I had a good, solid childhood."

"And you were never tempted to even try marriage after that first time?"

Annie shook her head. "Nope."

"That's unusual. You're a beautiful, sensual woman, Annie. You obviously love children. Don't you ever get lonely?" His voice had deepened, and Annie's heart began to pound, at the intimate tone as well as his actual words.

"Of course I do," she said, and her voice was ragged despite her efforts at control. "But I'm aware that not everyone's cut out for marriage. You said as much yourself. I'm not—I know that. Besides, how many marriages do you know of that are happy, besides the one your parents had?"

He looked distressed, and reached a hand out and laid it on her bare forearm, showing her how tense her body had become. She was also aware of his long, smooth fingers touching her skin, making every nerve ending come alive with a sensation almost painful, and causing the delicate hair on her forearm to stand on end.

"Annie, I'm not criticizing you. I'd never do that. I'm simply trying to understand. I want to know you better, that's all."

Wasn't that exactly what she wanted as well—to get to know this man who managed to stir such confused responses in her?

She made a conscious effort to relax. "Sorry. I guess I'm paranoid about this marriage thing. There's a lot of pressure when you've got a mother with traditional values constantly lecturing about how hard it is to raise a teenage boy without a strong man around. She's spending a year in Florida with a friend, and believe me, it feels like a parole not to have her watching my every move with Jason."

This time his voice was cool and cautious. "And there isn't a man around?" He didn't quite meet her eyes this time.

A tiny, delighted smile flickered across her lips. She sensed by his attempt at nonchalance that the question was important to him, and a glad rush of joy surged through her, knowing that it mattered.

"No," she said. "There isn't a man around."

Time pulsed, and pulsed again.

"I'm glad, Annie."

David drew his breath in and let it out again in what could only be a relieved sigh. Silence fell between them, a charged silence during which Annie repeated his three simple, complicated words in her head...I'm glad, Annie...and reflected on the strangeness of having him, sitting beside her...and on the conviction that being with him this way was right.

"This afternoon I found several of the books you've written over there in the bookcase," he remarked after a while. "I didn't have time enough to read them thoroughly, but what comes through is how well you remember what it's like to be a child. You manage to incorporate fantasy and reality in a believable way. It's no wonder your books sell, Annie."

She flushed with honest pleasure and thanked him just as the phone in the kitchen began to ring.

"Excuse me, David." She answered it, still smiling.

"Annie, I hope I'm not disturbing you," the familiar male voice said, and she stiffened and turned away from the living room.

"But you are disturbing me," she said in a low, passionate tone. "I've told you a million times that I don't want you to call here, Michael."

And why did he have to call now, at this moment? It was almost as if she'd somehow initiated this call just by mentioning his name earlier. Frustration filled her, and the impotent anger and unease that talking with Michael McCrae roused in her churned her stomach into a knot.

His tone was quiet and patient. "I apologize, but you do see that going through you is the only rational way for me to arrange to meet my son, Annie. Whatever you feel about me, Jason is my son, and I want to get to know him. With your full approval."

Annie knew that this new, quiet, reasonable persona Michael had adopted since he'd reappeared in her life was all a clever act designed to lull her into acquiescence.

"This isn't a convenient time," she insisted with stubborn emphasis.

"Then you set a time and place, and I'll meet you and we can talk this thing through." A deep sigh sounded over the wire.

"Please, Annie. I don't want to have to go through another court battle with you. Think what it would do to Jason. He's not a baby this time."

"I'll . . ." She turned and shot a glance into the quiet living room, knowing that David had to be overhearing her end of this conversation, hating the uncomfortable situation Michael was forcing on her, hating the need to deal with him at all.

"I'll think it over and let you know. That's the best I can do."

"You have our number, Annie. Call anytime at all."

She hung up and when the connection was broken, realized that the palms of her hands were sweating. She rubbed them down the legs of her jeans and drew in a deep breath, expelling it bit by bit before she made her way back into the other room.

David was just sliding a tape into the deck on the stereo, and soft music filled the room.

"Everything all right?" he queried, and she knew his penetrating glance was assessing her strained features and the new, stiff movements of her body.

"Sure, everything . . ." She paused. Within her was the unreasonable, overwhelming conviction that she shouldn't ever lie to this particular man, but her private nature made it impossible to confide in him any more than she'd already done tonight.

Besides, it was embarrassing. How could she blurt out any more of the convoluted tale of her association with Michael McCrae, explaining that for twelve blessed years, he'd all but disappeared from her life?

After the trial, he'd gone to India on assignment for the engineering firm he worked for, eventually taking an Indian woman as his wife. He'd stayed on and on. As the years passed, Annie had slowly come to believe she'd never see him again, and it gave her an immense feeling of relief.

Then, for some inexplicable reason, Michael had returned to Vancouver three months ago. And, like a bad dream, the whole problem of access to her son had started all over again, started with phone calls like this one, with Michael wanting to share part of Jason's life.

After all these years. He had no right, no right at all.

"Annie?" David came over to her and put a hand under her elbow. "You're pale again. Not feeling dizzy, are you? Your neck's fine?"

She forced a wide smile, hoping it didn't look as phony as it felt. She looked into David's clear blue eyes and wished with all her heart that her life was just beginning right here and now, that there wasn't any Michael to contend with, that she was free to just . . . belong . . . to this man.

But life wasn't that simple, was it? There were no brand-new beginnings, unburdened by baggage from the past.

"I'm fine, David," she insisted. "Everything's fine."

"Good," he said. And then his other arm came around her and he drew her into his embrace. She felt her body come into contact with his, separated only by clothing, and a part of her mind registered how well their spaces still fitted each other. She absorbed the welcome warmth he exuded, and she knew this was the only place in the entire world she longed to be at this particular moment.

At any moment.

He slid one hand up her back, along her neck and under the heavy braid, fingers tender, playing along her scalp.

"Annie," he said, as if saying her name pleased him. He studied each detail of her face, unhurriedly, questioningly, and then he bent his head and his lips covered hers.

CHAPTER FIVE

AT FIRST HE ONLY BRUSHED her mouth with the tenderest of kisses, soft, elusive, tantalizing, as questioning as the look he'd given her a moment before. But with the full meeting of their lips, the caress changed. His arms tightened around her and a low groan rose in his throat.

Annie's lips parted in eager welcome, and suddenly they were locked together in a scalding, drugging embrace, his lips and hers moving with hungry need, intent on discovering every way possible of tasting, teasing, shaping to suit and delight the other.

Annie's body filled with heat, softening and melting against him, and it was glorious to feel the ripe hardness of his erection against her belly.

Mindless, she moved her hips in cadence with the rhythm pounding through her blood, the rhythm of his tongue thrusting and withdrawing, plunging deep into her mouth with sweet, hot abandon.

As unexpectedly as it began, the kiss ended. Annie wasn't sure which of them drew away first. She knew only that she was standing on legs that trembled, a few feet away from him. His hands were on her shoulders, his grip almost painful, and he looked at her with eyes still clouded with desire.

"Lord," he whispered, his voice hoarse. "I want you, Annie. I want to take you right here on the floor, right now. I don't understand how this could happen so fast, but it has."

His words sent a shudder coursing through her, because it was so exactly what she wanted as well. But the tumult of emotions he roused in her were too new, too complex. She felt as if an integral part of her might shatter, irreparably, if the depth of feeling he roused was taken to its sensual limit tonight.

She didn't have to try to put the feeling into words, because he pulled her into his arms for one last, quick hug, and then, obviously reluctant, dropped his arms and with deliberation stepped away from her.

"Because of that damned injection, you're still technically my patient tonight," he said with rough irony. "And I don't seduce my patients." A rueful grin came and went. "But I'm severing our professional relationship as of this moment, Annie. After tonight, I give you fair warning, we're simply man and woman." Again his crooked smile played across his lips, but Annie knew he meant every word. "You'll have to find yourself another doctor, Ms Pendleton."

He turned and retrieved his tweed jacket, still tossed over the sofa arm where he'd left it earlier, and shrugged the garment on with careless grace.

"I'm leaving now, because I can't promise I'll be this honorable for even another five minutes."

At the door, he leaned toward her and brushed a light kiss on the tip of her nose.

"Thank you for supper, Ms Pendleton. Will you be home tomorrow?"

She nodded.

"I'll call." He gave her a formal little bow.

He was gone then, moving with the litheness that was somehow familiar to her.

Annie stood in the open doorway until the engine of his car purred to life. The night was star-studded, the neighborhood quiet until, a few blocks away, a fire truck began wailing, its undulating cry slowly receding as the taillights of David's car disappeared down the street.

She closed the door as if doing so took all the energy she possessed.

It was a full week before David kept his long overdue dinner appointment with Calvin Graves.

If David were to describe his old friend, he'd begin by saying the man had incredible energy. Calvin was fifty-six, but it would have been difficult, David always thought, to pin any age on his small-boned, tidy frame.

Tonight, as always, he was impeccably groomed and tailored in a charcoal-gray pin-striped suit and a silky white-on-white shirt. He'd looked askance at David's comfortable, albeit crumpled navy pants and well-worn tweed sports jacket. Calvin shook his head.

"I'm going to have to drag you forcibly to my tailor, David. Clothes may not make the man, but you must at least have heard the expression 'dress for success.'"

David had given him a deadpan look. "And you must have heard about rough cut stone. Give it up, Calvin. I'll never make the pages of *Gentlemen's Quarterly*."

They were meeting tonight only because Calvin had appeared at the office that afternoon and insisted. He'd all but dragged David off to this small but elegant French restaurant hidden away on one of Vancouver's downtown side streets. Calvin prided himself on always knowing the best new place to eat before it became popular—and thus no longer attractive to him.

Calvin had finished his typical ritual with the waiter, finding out what fish was caught that day, what exact spices the soup contained, and precisely which vintage of wine was best to complement the meal.

It usually drove David crazy to sit through the performance. In his opinion, it was a pretentious act, and it irritated him when he was out with Calvin.

But tonight, David hadn't noticed. His thoughts were all for Annie, just as they'd been every spare moment of the past seven days. Soft music was coming from the overhead stereo speaker, a French Canadian chanteuse whose husky tones reminded him of Annie's voice. There was a trace of the same shyness he'd noticed that first day in his office.

"...wondered what your opinion was on the hospital board's decision to cut back spending on the administrative level?"

David looked at his friend with a blank expression.

"Sorry, Calvin," he apologized as the waiter arrived with the soup. "I was thinking of something else."

"Apparently." Calvin's face creased in an ironic smile. "You've been woolgathering this way all afternoon. What's up, David? Tough case? Want to talk about it?"

Calvin was a renowned cardiologist who'd been in semiretirement for several years. He now accepted only those cases that intrigued him, or those that brought him the most recognition because the patients were well connected in the community. Calvin was a rare blend of medical doctor and sharp businessman.

"No, no," David assured him. "Nothing to do with work."

"Then it must be a woman," Calvin joked, and David had to smile at the outright amazement on Calvin's face when he answered, "Yes, as a matter of fact, it is a woman. Her name's Annie, Annie Pendleton. I met her a week ago."

The relationship between the two men was complex. Calvin Graves had taken an interest in David when the younger man was still an intern, and in important ways, he'd influenced David's career over the years, always in a positive manner, although in a way that negated any sense of David's being indebted to him, although David was well aware of the favors Calvin had bestowed on him.

There was an unpaid debt between him and Calvin Graves. It wasn't a conscious, nagging awareness that kept David awake at night. It was simply an acknowledgement that no one helped another's career or investment portfolio to the degree Calvin had helped David's without there being repayment somewhere along the line.

Their relationship had changed as time passed from that of student and mentor to the status of friendly equals, and then by a curious twist of fate, changed again to that of relatives through marriage. It was through Calvin that David had met his ex-wife, Sheila.

"It's sad. The combination of doctor and lawyer was ideal from a career standpoint," was all he'd said to David. "It's unfortunate you couldn't go on with it, just as a business arrangement."

Sheila was Calvin's niece, and the older man had been pleased when the two young people married—although he'd tactfully hidden most of the disappointment he felt six years later when they divorced.

David had told himself later that the remark couldn't have been as cold and heartless as it sounded, even taking into consideration the fact that Calvin and his niece had no strong emotional bonds. Perhaps it was just a comment on the fact that Calvin had never married. In fact, Sheila had referred to Calvin more than once as a cold fish.

So it wasn't exactly old family ties that kept David from discussing with Calvin the other women who'd wandered in and out of his personal life since his divorce.

Well, he amended, maybe it was partly out of respect for Sheila. Their divorce had been as amiable and good-natured as that legal procedure could possibly be. Sheila was a litigation lawyer, and her firm had handled the details for both of them.

Neither Sheila nor David harbored any ill will toward the other. Their marriage had simply run down, like a clock nobody cared enough to wind, with Sheila pursuing her legal career and David focusing his life around medicine. Heaven knew either career could eat a person's time and energy, leaving nothing to give a marriage.

But it hadn't seemed honorable at first for David to mention the women he casually dated to Sheila's own uncle.

However, years had gone by since the divorce, and Calvin of course knew that David hadn't taken any vows of abstinence. But neither had David deliberately introduced or discussed any of his women friends. Until now.

"Pendleton, Pendleton," Calvin repeated, as if he were tasting the name. "Don't think I know anyone with that name. What does she do, David? Is she in medicine?" Calvin took a long, judgmental sip of the white wine the waiter had poured moments before, and pursed his lips in grudging approval.

"She's a writer. She writes children's books. She has a thirteen-year-old son, and she's warm and funny and bright...," David struggled to find the words that would best describe Annie, and felt that none of them were adequate. "You'll have to meet her."

Calvin nodded, his penetrating pale gaze on David's face. "Who was this Pendleton man she was married to?" he inquired, taking an experimental bite of the mushroom-and-spinach salad.

"She's never been married."

The bare statement of fact, Calvin's slightly raised left eyebrow and disapproving expression gave David just an inkling of the type of reaction Annie must have encountered over and over, and it disturbed and angered him.

"For crying out loud, Calvin, plenty of people these days choose to be single parents," he exploded, unaware of the amazement his outburst created.

David was normally the most even-tempered of men, and Calvin noted his reaction with interest, and hidden concern.

"There's absolutely no social stigma attached to it anymore."

"Of course there isn't," Calvin soothed. "You mustn't be so defensive, David. I'm not exactly a prude. In fact, I'm looking forward to meeting your, uh, Ms Pendleton."

There was charged silence between them for a while.

"Isn't this an unusual hot dressing on the salad?" Calvin chewed with the slow appreciation of a gourmand.

David had already wolfed down half his bowlful without tasting it at all.

Calvin's calm voice went on commenting on the food, his manner relaxed and at ease so that gradually, David relaxed, as well. For the rest of the sumptuous meal, nothing more was mentioned about Annie.

Over coffee, they discussed local politics and the disturbing cutbacks the government was making in health care. Inevitably, the subject touched on David's pet project, the heart and liver organ transplant unit at Vancouver Regional Hospital.

"There are long-term plans to set up the unit sometime in the next five years, but nobody I know of is really pushing the plan, either in Victoria or here on the hospital board. Which means it could easily get shelved and we wouldn't get financing for who knows how long," David complained.

It wasn't the first time the subject had been discussed between them. Calvin listened, as always, and not for the first time, expressed his views.

"There's only one effective method of making changes, David, or of getting the specific things you want, like this heart and liver transplant unit. You can't rely on others to do it. If you care enough to make changes, you know the route, through the governing body of the hospital, which in turn has the ear of the Ministry of Health."

Calvin sat on numerous committees, and had a quiet finger on the pulse of hospital administration. Although he kept a deliberately low profile, David suspected he also had a great deal of influence in many political areas.

Calvin enjoyed pulling strings, manipulating power from the back room. David often thought of Calvin when he watched documentaries on the invisible men behind the scenes in politics.

"I've mentioned before," Calvin said with offhanded detachment, "that it wouldn't be at all difficult to get you an appointment as Advisor to the Board, and from there it would be simply a matter of time and opportunity before you became a junior board member.''

David's answer was long-standing and automatic.

''Thanks, Calvin, but no thanks. Hell, I'd have to invest in a whole new wardrobe just to attend meetings.''

Calvin smiled at David's attempt to take the sting out of his refusal. As always, the political machinations of the hospital were the last things David wanted to be involved with. He was busy enough with his practice, never mind taking on a whole new sphere of problems.

''Well, your wardrobe would be a drawback,'' Calvin teased. ''But you really should give the idea serious consideration this time, that is, if you're sincere about wanting to implement that transplant unit. I'm afraid that what you said about it getting shelved is all too probable. Will you give me your word that you'll at least think it over?''

Surprised, David glanced up from pouring rich cream into one last cup of coffee. Calvin sounded much more emphatic about the subject than he ever had before, and David found himself wondering with a trace of suspicion if perhaps the entire evening had been a way of leading up to this particular discussion.

It wouldn't be the first time Calvin had quietly pushed his young friend in the direction he thought best for him to go. And that tactful pushing had always been very much to David's benefit.

A little boy with huge brown eyes, a boy named Charlie Vance, filled David's mental vision for a second. He saw Charlie's trusting wide smile, symbolic of a personality persistently cheerful despite incredible physical restrictions and pain that would have destroyed a lesser spirit long ago.

The child was only one of several. There were others out there like Charlie. The unit David envisioned would at the very least simplify their lives, allowing them to undergo treatment here at home. How he wanted that damned facility.

Calvin was still waiting for an answer. David looked across at his old friend and said, his tone devoid of humor, ''All right, Calvin. I promise you I'll give it some serious thought.''

Calvin was wise enough to drop the subject then. He ordered them each a snifter of excellent brandy, and launched into a good-natured argument about free trade.

But before long, David couldn't resist a surreptitious glance at his watch. Would it be too late by the time he got home to give Annie a call? She'd mentioned that she often worked long past midnight.

He found himself bolting his brandy and wishing impatiently that Calvin would get a move on.

"ANNIE? HI, IT'S DAVID. I hope I didn't wake you."

"Not a chance. I'm finishing this synopsis at last."

Her heartbeat accelerated right on cue, and she knew the pleasure she felt at hearing his voice was reflected in her voice.

"I've been up here in my study ever since Jason went to bed." She glanced up at the wall clock. It was past one, and just as usual, she felt mild amazement that four hours could pass without her knowing.

"Heavens, I didn't realize how late it really was. But I think I finally managed to get this outline right, anyway," she remarked with a contented sigh, leaning back in her chair and trying to get the painful kink out of her shoulders.

"I was out with Calvin Graves for dinner. I just got home," David told her. "He's the friend I mentioned to you the other day."

"I remember." She got up, pulling the telephone cord with her as she moved the short distance to the window. She pulled up the vertical blind so the dark night sky and the rooftops of the neighborhood were visible. "Did you have a good dinner? Where'd you go?"

It still amazed her that she was able to chat with him in this casual way. They'd learned a great deal about each other in just one short week, Annie reflected. The initial intensity had never lessened between them, but they were more comfortable in their conversations.

And to her relief, most of those conversations had taken place on the telephone. David's job was a consuming one in terms of both time and energy, and for now, Annie considered that a blessing. She remembered all too well the overwhelming passion his kisses had evoked, and the promise he'd made her, that from that first memorable evening on, there would be no holding back as far as he was concerned.

Which seemed to put the ball in her court, and she wasn't at all certain about that. Annie had built a fortress around her heart in the past years, a barrier sturdy enough to withstand persuasive attack from outside. There had been several determined, attractive men who had set out to court her despite her reticence. Because of that reticence, maybe?

And that fortress had also managed to withstand the more insidious demands of her normal, healthy woman's body as well as the crippling loneliness that came like a virus every so often to torment her.

Her reaction to David had been so unexpected, so intense, that she was thrown off balance. But during the past days, she'd had time to reflect, time to regroup and make a firm, cautious decision to go slowly.

He'd called her often, beginning the very morning after that first real meeting. He'd taken her out for lunch one afternoon, and dropped in two nights ago for a few hours. Jason had been home that evening, and at first he'd been awed and excited at the prospect of meeting "The Sorcerer."

But after the first hour, the evening had disintegrated. It was no fault of David's. It was Jason. He'd come very close several times to being out-and-out rude that evening, leaving Annie furious with him as well as puzzled by the encounter. Jason was normally as polite and well mannered as a thirteen-year-old could manage.

"Why did you act that way, Jason?" Annie had inquired with open anger after David left. "You were smart mouthed and rude, and David was my guest. There's no excuse for rudeness. I won't tolerate that kind of behavior."

Jason's eyes were dark and resentful. "I just figured he'd be different than that," was the only mumbled explanation the boy would give. Annie had ordered him to bed, but she still didn't understand what was going on in Jason's head.

Annie listened now as David described the restaurant and the meal, smiling at his witty, sometimes wicked descriptions of the patrons and the serving staff. As usual during these telephone conversations, the content didn't matter to her half as much as the cadence and pitch of his baritone voice.

She sank back into her chair, closed her eyes, and let that voice become her universe. But her eyes snapped open and a pang of anxiety went through her when he said after a few minutes, "Tomorrow's Saturday. I'm not on call this weekend, so I'd like to take you and Jason out for the day if you haven't made other plans."

The uncomfortable first meeting between Jason and David was vivid in Annie's mind. An entire day spent trying to control Jason's unpredictable behavior would be difficult for her at best. She'd be on edge, forced into a role of diplomat and peacekeeper between the two males.

Drat her ornery kid. Why had he chosen David, of all people, to resent?

"I'm sorry, David," she heard herself saying. "I've already asked Cleo if she wants to come with me and take all the kids down to the park for the day," Annie improvised, praying her friend hadn't made different plans.

"Mind if I join you, then?"

Annie swallowed hard. What could she say to that?

"No, not at all, except it might not be much fun for you. You do realize we have three kids between us? Cleo's girls are still pretty small...."

"Hey, Annie, slow down. I like kids, remember? And healthy ones are exactly what I need at the moment to take my mind off work."

She'd done it this time. There was no way out.

"All I can suggest, then, is that you wear something washable. You're bound to get spilled on," she warned, and he laughed, a low, pleasing rumble of sound.

"I'll meet you down at Stanley Park then, say at the entrance to the zoo, at what? Eleven in the morning too early?"

"Great," Annie said with phony heartiness, and the moment he hung up, she dialed Cleo's number in a frenzy, hoping this was one of those nights her friend was propped up in bed, engrossed in some book or other. Thank heavens Cleo was a voracious reader and a nighthawk as well.

"Cleo, I'm in a mess. Please tell me you and the kids can come to the park tomorrow morning," Annie blurted the instant the phone was lifted on the other end.

"Do you often get these uncontrollable urges for our company at 2:00 a.m.?" Cleo sounded wide-awake.

"David wants to spend tomorrow with me and Jason, and..."

"He wants to spend the day with you, and you're inviting us along? Annie, my friend, have you taken leave of your senses?"

"I can't handle this alone. I told you how Jason acted the night David was here. I can't bear the thought of a whole day with that rotten kid of mine being either silent or snotty by turns."

Cleo was silent for a long moment.

"I have to say I think you're making a big mistake here, Annie," she finally said. "If you're going to go on seeing this guy, the best thing you could do would be to force the two of them to work it out, without any buffering from you. Or me, for that matter. That's what the psychologist from Parents Without Partners advised at that lecture I went to, the one about single parents forming new relationships."

"Yeah, well, I'm not that brave. In fact, I'm plain old chicken about this. So will you come?"

"The other thing you haven't considered," Cleo went on, "is that you're taking an awful risk, letting that gorgeous hunk of masculinity get a good look at me in a pair of shorts. My legs are my best feature, remember, and I did happen to catch a glimpse of Dr. Roswell through my front window that evening he came over. He is a hunk, capital *H*."

"I noticed," Annie said with dry humor. "Maggie told me you sat at the window the better part of an hour with your binoculars trained on my house. I'll have to change even your magnificent legs in this," Annie sighed. "Now come off it, Cleo. Say you'll come before you drive me frantic."

"Of course I will. I'll even bring a large kerchief to tie around your kid's mouth if the going gets rough."

"Cleo, you are a true friend," Annie sighed. "Seriously bent, but a friend all the same."

"Yup," Cleo agreed, adding in a different tone, "You know what's wrong with old Jason, don't you, Annie?" Her voice was gentle.

"No, quite frankly, I don't know. This one's got me flummoxed."

"Well, when was the last time a man sent your blood pressure soaring? When was the last time you cared enough to see someone more than twice, or introduce him to your kid?"

"I see what you mean. You figure Jason senses this damned reaction I have to David, and he's plain old jealous?"

"Something like that, but more complex. Kids are super-quick to pick up on emotions in their parents." Cleo was quiet again, and then she said abruptly, "Have you thought any more about letting Jason meet Michael and his wife?"

Annie had confided in Cleo long ago about Michael, and she'd told her friend about the ill-timed phone call from him the first night David was over.

"I suppose you figure I ought to give in on this," Annie said with more than a trace of irritation in her tone. "I suppose you're gonna tell me that Jason might feel a lot more secure around men if he actually got to know his own father."

She found herself wishing for an instant that she'd never told Cleo anything. How could an outsider understand?

But then she was ashamed of herself. Cleo was truly her friend. She'd proven that many times. And maybe, Annie forced herself to consider, just maybe Cleo could see something here that Annie was missing.

"Yeah, I guess I do feel that," Cleo was saying now. "Every kid wants to know who his parents are, both parents. Jason's no different. You told me Michael sounded calmer, more mature than he was when you knew him. He's been married quite a while to this Lili, you said. Maybe it would be good for Jason to get to know them. And with Michael pressuring you about it, well, it just seems maybe it's meant to be, but then, what do I know? You're the only one who really can decide."

Cleo's voice became wistful. "Heaven knows I'm the last one who should be handing out advice. I have no idea what I'd do if that bum who fathered my girls turned up again and wanted to see them. I can't say whether I'd let him or not."

Johnny Fowler, according to Cleo, had been lovable, handsome and fun, but he'd proven as well to be dishonest and totally irresponsible.

The day after Cleo had told him she was pregnant with their second child, Johnny had said he was driving to the store for a pack of cigarettes and hadn't been heard from since. He had taken the car, cleared out their meager bank account and helped himself to a diamond ring Cleo had inherited from her grandmother.

Cleo had managed, somehow, to survive, and it never failed to amaze Annie that she harbored very little bitterness about the hand Fate had dealt her. She often referred to herself as an incurable optimist, and Annie had to agree with that assessment.

They made the arrangements for the day ahead and ended the conversation. Annie took a long, hot bath and went to bed, but hours passed and she still lay awake, tangled images of Michael and David and Jason chasing one another through her thoughts.

"MOM? HEY, MOM, WAKE UP."

Jason's voice and the smell of fragrant coffee finally penetrated the foggy dream Annie was having. She opened her eyes with difficulty to find her son standing by her bed balancing a tray and grinning at her.

She dragged herself to a sitting position, gave a huge yawn and straightened the oversize T-shirt she wore as a nightgown.

"Morning, kid." She squinted toward the open window.

"Gosh, it's broad daylight out there. What time is it?"

Jason settled the tray on her knees, rescuing the mug of coffee before it slopped over.

"Nine-thirty. You work really late again last night, Mom? You sure were out of it. I called you before but you didn't move a muscle, so I figured the only solution was breakfast in bed just this once."

His eyes, exactly the same shade of soft brown as Annie's, twinkled at her. The truth was, he brought her breakfast in bed almost every weekend morning.

Annie smiled at her redheaded son, and took stock of the tray. It held a fried egg, over easy, just the way she liked, two slices of buttered toast and a carefully peeled and sliced orange as well as the coffee.

Ever since he was barely able to reach the countertops, Jason had been cooking and bringing her these breakfasts in bed. His first efforts had been pretty bad, but Annie had praised them and pretended to enjoy them, touched at the effort he'd made to please her. It had paid off, because now her trays were wonderful to wake up to.

His efforts made her feel pampered, and her delight made Jason feel proud. It had become a wonderful tradition.

"So how does it feel to be in junior high school, kid?"

School had started the week before, and Jason had made the transition from elementary to junior high.

"It's okay, I guess. It's funny to go from being the biggest guys in the school to being the runts again, though."

Annie smiled in sympathy, and they chatted about his teachers and his hopes about making the junior rugby squad. She sipped her coffee, and as they talked she wondered how best to introduce the plans for the day. She chewed her toast and forked up the egg, while her son sipped his own mug of chocolate, sitting on the wicker chair by her bed.

"We're going down to Stanley Park this morning, with Cleo and the girls," Annie finally announced with casual aplomb.

"Hey, neat. There's a new baby whale in the whale pool. Can we watch the show? I've got my own money."

"I suspect so," Annie said, adding, "David is meeting us at the entrance to the zoo at eleven, so I'd better finish this and get my act together."

"That doctor? Dr. Roswell? He's goin' with us?"

Annie was certain Jason knew exactly who David was, but she nodded anyway.

"Yup, that doctor. Alias The Sorcerer, remember?" she added with forced heartiness. "He's meeting us there, and we'll all spend the day together."

Jason set his empty mug on the tray, avoiding Annie's eyes. "Maybe I'd rather not come along after all, if that's okay, Mom. Larry and I figured maybe we'd work on his model today."

Annie felt exasperated. "Jason, I want you to come with us and that's that. I know you've taken some kind of weird dislike to David, but I can't see any reason for it. He particularly mentioned wanting to get to know you better."

"Yeah, well that's his problem. Do I have to come?" Jason's voice was martyred.

"Yes, I'm afraid this time you have to come."

His mouth curved in mutinous, silent rebellion, and Annie sighed with irritation. "Jason, I simply don't understand what's going on here. Clue me in, okay?"

Mute, he stared off into the middle distance, and she knew there wasn't any way to get him to talk when he was in this mood. Annie sighed again and finished her food in silence, the atmosphere between them strained as they got ready for the day.

STANLEY PARK was one of Vancouver's landmarks. A verdant thousand-acre peninsula jutting into Burrard Inlet, it contained beaches, picnic areas, playgrounds, swimming pools, as well as the zoo and the public aquarium, and it was already well populated this warm September morning by Vancouver residents who found it a great place to get away from it all.

It seemed a miracle when Annie found a parking place almost right away in the lot closest to the zoo entrance, and the little girls in their crisp cotton shorts sets tumbled out, with Jason following much more slowly, trailing far behind Annie and Cleo.

In an untidy group, they made their way through the crowd, and with uncanny precision, Annie picked out a tall male figure lounging against a low stone wall that bordered a pond where elegant swans floated to and fro.

He was waiting, just as he'd promised he would.

The trees, the sound of birds, the water . . . a flash of something that had to be a dream filled her senses, and for a brief instant, she knew that this man had waited for her in a setting very much like this, time after time.

And to Annie, the crowd was gone. The chattering of Maggie and Paula no longer penetrated the private world she inhabited.

She knew only that the greatest love she'd ever known was embodied in that tall waiting figure, and she had to go to him, just as she had gone so many other times.

With a smile full of joy, a radiance that brought stares and answering wistful smiles from those around her, she hurried toward him.

CHAPTER SIX

"I FEEL LIKE A PERVERT around the two of you," Cleo complained hours later, sipping the coffee Annie had bought from the nearby vending stand.

It was three in the afternoon. They'd toured the zoo and the aquarium, taken the girls for rides on the miniature train and eaten hot dogs and fries washed down with soda.

Annie and Cleo were sprawled on a grassy knoll, watching David and Jason. The two males were tossing a Frisbee in the field nearby, while Maggie and Paula provided an enthusiastic backup retrieval system.

"I feel like a pervert," Cleo declared, "because every time you and that hunk of man look at each other, it's like an X-rated intimate encounter." She sat up and crossed her legs Indian fashion so she could prop her coffee on one bare knee.

"The vibes between you two are hot, Annie. As in sexual. But then I suppose you might have suspected that without my telling you?"

"Has anybody ever mentioned that you're not exactly a subtle conversationalist?" Annie asked with sweet sarcasm, her eyes always on David, now sending the Frisbee flying across a wide expanse so Jason had to run hard if he were to catch it.

"You have a definite tendency to go straight for the jugular, friend." Annie's tone was light and teasing, but her cheeks grew hot beneath their tan, because Cleo had pinpointed what Annie knew to be true.

Try as she might to keep everything casual, there was an impossible-to-ignore undercurrent of strong emotion between herself and David. It was disconcerting to find out that others were aware of it.

Cleo was undisturbed by Annie's comments. "It's best to bring things like this out in the open," she said with complacent ease. "Just in case you've hibernated for so long you don't recognize good old sexual vibes anymore, I figured I ought to mention it. And you have, you know, Annie. Hibernated. For all I know, you'll mistake good, honest desire for premature hot flashes or something, and this whole thing will be ruined. As your friend and advisor, I can't let that happen, now can I?"

She crumpled the plastic cup and tossed it at a nearby garbage container. "Actually this is giving me back my faith in pure, unadulterated romance," she went on, flopping back on the grass and folding her arms under her head. She narrowed her eyes at the blue and cloudless sky and smiled.

"It's like that song, remember the one about some enchanted evening, meeting a stranger and knowing you'll see him again and again?"

Though Cleo pretended to tease, there was an undercurrent of wistful envy there as well.

"That day after the magic show, you told me something weird happened, Annie, that you felt as if you'd known him before, remember?"

Annie nodded. How could she forget?

"And seeing the two of you together today, even I get the damnedest feeling that you belong together." She squinted up at the blue of the heavens, her shock of white hair dramatic against the green grass, her voice thoughtful.

"Ever think that for all the scheming we do, Annie, we really haven't any control over destiny, that the whole thing is planned out on some master computer somewhere long before we're even born?"

"Mommy, Paula's going to have an accident."

From a distance, Maggie's piercing voice carried clearly to several families picnicking nearby, causing a faint ripple of laughter, which Maggie ignored.

"She has to go right now, Mom, and she won't let me take her, either," Maggie was panting as she tugged her roly-poly younger sister up the incline. The two of them stood over their mother's prone body, waiting with impatience for Cleo to take action.

Cleo rolled her eyes and sprang to her feet. "Straight from the mysteries of the universe to the reality of the bathroom. From the sublime to the ridiculous, that exactly describes being a mother. C'mon, kid, and be sure you hold it till we get there." She swung the curly-haired Paula up on her hip and hurried off in the direction of the public washrooms.

Mission accomplished, Maggie plopped her skinny bottom down beside Annie and heaved a huge, loud sigh. Annie couldn't help laughing, because Maggie so often gave her the impression that Cleo's household would collapse if Maggie didn't manage it.

"Mag, you're a case." Annie looped an affectionate arm across the girl's shoulders and planted a kiss on her blond head.

"Tired, peanut?"

Maggie shook her head vehemently. "We're havin' the best day, aren't we, Annie?"

Annie smiled down into Maggie's round blue eyes. "We sure are. I'm glad you're having fun, honey."

"I like him lots, that David guy," Maggie declared, with a decisive nod of her head. "He said we could call him David. But he's The Sorcerer, too, y'know, Annie. He knows magic and everything. Wasn't it neat at lunch when he made my hot dog disappear and then it came out of Paula's shoe?"

Annie nodded. "Yup, that was a neat trick all right." David had charmed the girls silly with his sleight of hand, and even Jason had looked as if he were enjoying himself every now and then, until he remembered he wasn't supposed to and deliberately assumed his glum look again.

Maggie sighed again. "I think he ought to marry you, Annie."

Annie swallowed hard. "What makes you say that? Marrying is serious stuff, Mags. And anyhow, why me? There are lots of other ladies around."

"'Cause he likes you better, silly," Maggie said with matter-of-fact innocence. "He likes us all, but he likes you best."

"Did, umm, did David tell you that?"

The child shook her head again. "Nope."

"Then how do you know?" Annie put her nose down against Maggie's.

Maggie drew back and gave her a look she reserved for imbeciles. "I just know, Annie. 'Cause he looks at you all the time, same as they do on TV when the man likes the lady and then he kisses her."

"I see," Annie managed to say. She stared down at the innocent face for a long, thoughtful moment.

First the mother, now the daughter, somehow both aware of whatever this thing was between her and a man she'd known only a short while.

What was it that made the two of them seem emotionally transparent to Cleo, to Maggie?

To Jason? She had no doubt Cleo had pinpointed the problem when she suggested Jason was plain old jealous of whatever he sensed between herself and David, if it was as evident as this to everyone.

Irritation sparked in her, and an old deep-rooted fear. She didn't want this complication in her life just now. She didn't need it.

Against her will, her eyes were drawn once again to the tall, lithe figure off in the field, laughing and leaping high in the air to make a difficult catch Jason had just pitched, and try as she might, Annie couldn't stop the telltale warmth that spilled through her just at the sight of him.

He'd finally come back to her....

The fleeting wisp of memory was gone before she could pin it down. But something deep in her responded, something in her knew that it was so, even while her rational conscious mind rejected it.

It was simply ridiculous, she chided herself.

Annie scrambled up, clasping the grubby paw Maggie held out to her and pulling the child to her feet.

"Let's go have a swing, what d'ya say, kid?"

"Yeah, I'll beat you to the swings, Annie." Maggie dashed off to the playground nearby, and Annie followed at a slow trot.

"I'm beating you, Annie." Maggie's shrill voice floated back as she ran hard for the swings.

Two rambunctious boys, three or four years older than Maggie, were racing with wild abandon from one set of swings to the next, grabbing the ropes and giving the wooden seats a mighty push so that the six swings were all in frantic motion within minutes.

Annie, her mind still on David, saw them pull the nearest swings back and heave them as hard as they could, and at the same moment, she saw Maggie dashing along, her head turned back toward Annie.

"Maggie, look out...,"

"I beat you, I beat...," the child chanted, at the same instant Annie screamed the warning. The swings came flying forward, with Maggie directly in their path.

Annie leaped ahead in a desperate attempt to reach Maggie in time, but one of the wooden seats connected fully with the girl's forehead an instant before Annie could snatch her away.

The dull, sickening thunk of the blow mingled with Maggie's sharp, startled cry of pain as Annie grabbed for the girl and missed, barely deflecting the second swing as it also came hurtling toward them.

Maggie went flying up and then down again, tossed forcefully to the ground. Her skinny little figure, clad in bright red shorts and a gaily patterned T-shirt, lay sprawled motionless, like a discarded scarecrow on the hard-packed earth below the swings.

"Maggie! Oh, sweetheart—"

Annie flung herself down beside the child, noting the bright blood surging and then seeming to erupt in a torrent from a long, ugly gash just above Maggie's left eye.

The girl was unconscious, eyes half closed and rolled back far in her head. Was she even breathing?

Annie opened her mouth and hollered as loud as she could, the only name she could think of.

"David, David, come quick...."

She peered in the direction of the open field, to see if he'd heard her, but other people were hurrying over, crowding around in a tight packed knot, and someone yelled, "Hey, this kid's hurt bad. She's bleeding. Someone better call an ambulance...."

"Stay back," Annie ordered, her voice loud and fierce. "Get back, do you hear me?" She sounded so forceful that the people crowding in actually moved away again, muttering but giving her and Maggie room.

A bolt of white-hot pain shot through Annie's neck and shoulders, and she gritted her teeth against its intensity.

"David," she screamed again. "David, David...."

Not now, please not now....

One moment she was alone, and the next David was kneeling on Maggie's other side, fingers on the child's pulse. Maggie's eyelids were fluttering, and a faint whimpering sound came from her throat.

"What happened here?" he said with calm control.

"The seat on the, the sw-swing, David. It hit her head."

Annie gulped and David's eyes moved from their intense study of Maggie, meeting Annie's stricken gaze for an instant before his attention returned to the swift and thorough examination he was conducting on the child.

The pain in Annie's neck eased a little, and a cold sweat broke out on her body.

"It's okay, love, don't look like that," David said, too low for the onlookers to hear. "She'll be fine. There's always more blood than an injury like this warrants," he assured her. "Did she lose consciousness immediately?"

Annie nodded, trying to release the tightly held air trapped in her chest, trying to relax the knotted muscles in her neck. It felt as if a vise were squeezing tighter and tighter, constricting her breathing, pain escalating . . .

David's here, he's a doctor, she told herself. Everything will be all right because David's here. Like a mantra, she repeated the words in her mind.

Jason came hurrying over just then, carrying the black medical bag David must have sent him to get. He quickly handed it over and then came to kneel beside his mother, taking her hand in a gesture that was comforting to her.

Annie squeezed the grubby, warm paw hard, then said, "Honey, please go find Cleo. She went to the washrooms with Paula. But try not to scare her, won't you, Jason? Just tell her . . . tell her . . ."

Annie's voice trembled and faded.

"Should I just say Maggie got a little bang on the head, and you and the doctor are here with her?" he queried, and at Annie's nod, he tore off.

By now, Maggie was awake and wailing at the top of her lungs, and it seemed the best sound Annie had ever heard. David's medical bag was open, and he was sponging off the deep gash in her forehead with a square of cotton and liquid from a small vial, chatting to her all the while.

"Want to sit on Annie's knee while we put a bandage on your head?" he asked at last, and after a second, Maggie stopped sobbing and gulped out a shaky "Yes, please."

He lifted the child with care and set her in Annie's lap while he secured a temporary dressing to the cut.

Annie's arms trembled uncontrollably as she held the fragile little body against her. How easily, how quickly, a child could be damaged. . . . Her love for Maggie and her fear mingled in a wrenching tumult of feeling.

With a final check of her pulse rate, David stuffed his equipment back into his bag and was snapping it shut by the time Cleo came hurtling through the crowd.

Her face was drained of color, but she did her best not to show alarm in front of Maggie. She knelt beside Annie, and the women transferred the girl from one lap to the other.

Cleo cuddled Maggie with one arm and grabbed for Annie's hand with the other. She squeezed it tight, needing support as she turned toward David, her green eyes begging him for reassurance.

"Is she, do you think there's any danger to her eye...."

"None at all. She's going to be fine, Cleo," he interrupted, his calm voice and easy reassuring smile causing an immediate response in the fingers gripping Annie's hand.

Cleo relaxed a trifle, her shoulders losing their tense stiffness as David went on, "She's going to need a couple of stitches, however, to close that gash, and we should take some X rays to make sure there's no other problem. We'll take her over to the clinic right now in my car, Cleo. Maybe you could take the other kids home in yours and wait for us there, Annie? We won't be long."

Annie nodded, and the quick smile he gave her warmed her heart.

"Maggie was unconscious for a very short time," he told Cleo, "so you'll have to keep an eye on her tonight, just in case of concussion, but you can probably do that at home. There's no need to admit her unless the X rays indicate otherwise." He got to his feet and reached out to help the two women up, one after the other. His hand was strong and comforting around Annie's cold and perspiring fingers.

IT WAS AFTER NINE that evening before Annie and David were alone together at last.

She'd brought Jason and Paula home and gotten them involved in helping her make pizzas out of a wild assortment of leftovers and odds and ends of cheese and cold meat she dug out of the fridge. Jason was touching in his attentiveness to the little girl, answering the same questions about Maggie's accident over and over, reassuring Paula that her mother and sister would soon be home, making her giggle at his antics with the pizza dough.

Watching them, Annie was reminded that just that morning, Jason had acted like a naughty child when she'd told him the plans for the day. She'd wanted to throttle him.

Now, a few short hours later, he was being mature and supportive in a way that foreshadowed the strong man she hoped he would someday become. It was confusing, trying to keep current with a boy growing up.

If his swiftly changing moods were difficult for her to understand, she mused as she watched him, they must be doubly difficult for Jason.

She flexed her shoulders and kneaded the warm yeasty smelling dough she'd mixed up, aware of the intense burning in her shoulder that had been there ever since the accident that afternoon. But at least the pain in her neck hadn't gotten out of control this time. It was there, a smoldering ache that stabbed her now and then, making her catch her breath.

David brought Cleo and Maggie home, and they all ate the hot pizza picnic fashion in Cleo's kitchen, so that Maggie could rest in her own bed. By now, Maggie was feeling a bit pleased at being the center of attention, but she was also prone to quick fits of tears.

Cleo gave her a hot bath and let her sit at the table with everyone for a short time, but soon Maggie's eyes drooped and her head nodded.

"Can I carry her up to bed for you?" David asked, and Annie felt a pang of tenderness go through her as the strong man lifted the fragile child in her pink flannel nightgown and trotted her upstairs. Maggie's arms were twined around his neck.

The accident had somehow bridged any awkwardness the women and children might have felt about having David included in such a homely scene this early in their friendship with him.

The fact was, he'd charmed the little girls, and charmed Cleo as well. Paula, shy but determined, demanded to sit on his lap after dinner, and when Maggie woke up for the second time, feeling sick, she accepted his presence beside her bed.

Cleo raised her eyebrows at Annie as David loped up the stairs to tend the child. "Think he's got a twin brother?" she whispered as she passed Annie's chair. "I wish."

It was a pleasant, intimate gathering. Only Jason had been quiet, eating fast and then hurrying away to deliver his papers.

As soon as Cleo's kitchen was tidy, Annie suggested she and David go back to her house. Cleo needed time alone with her children, and Annie found herself longing for a few private moments with David.

"Coffee?" she suggested as they came in the back door and she turned on lights.

"Sounds great," he agreed.

"With brandy?" she suggested, tossing her blue sweater on a chair and filling the drip coffee maker.

"Sounds even better," he said with a grin.

David ambled around the kitchen as she gathered up mugs, cream and sugar, a tray. He spent long moments looking at the dramatic prints she'd framed and hung on one wall, modern, cheerful studies of kitchen utensils and herbs and sunflowers.

"I like this one," he said after a moment, and she glanced up from filling the sugar bowl. "It's different from the others. Is it an old family picture?"

It was different. In fact, the picture he was studying would have looked quite out of place among the modern prints she'd grouped on the other long wall, so she'd decided to hang it by itself in a narrow space near the door to the hall. Usually no one noticed it there but her.

It was a small, simple watercolor of a thatched roof farmhouse in the country. Annie liked to think the scene was right after a rain, with fresh-washed fields stretching off in the distance and an orchard of apple trees beginning to bloom pink in the background, rambling down a slope with a wide river just visible in the distance. The colors were muted, misty green and gold and blue seeming to run together in the favorite fashion of some of the French Impressionist painters.

"I found that in a junk shop down on Water Street years ago, and for some reason it appealed to me." Annie was waiting for the last of the coffee to drip through, and she slid the pot out an instant too soon. Coffee dribbled over the counter and she swore under her breath, adding without thinking, "I guess when you live in a city, there's always a part of you that longs to return to the country."

"Did you grow up in the country, Annie?" He was still studying the picture, hands tucked into the back pockets of his jeans.

"Heavens, no. I've always been a city girl. I hardly know one end of a cow from the other," she said with a laugh, picking up the tray and leading the way into the living room.

"When you said that the scene makes you long to return to the country, I just wondered," he said, one eyebrow lifted quizzically as they sat down side by side on the sofa.

She had said that. A stab of irrational irritation with herself niggled at Annie and she forced it away. Her mind was playing tricks on her, had been ever since the day of the magic show.

There was the recurring dream she'd been having about walking through farmland beside a river, for instance. Perhaps it had originated with the picture on her kitchen wall, but it seemed strange she'd never dreamed it before now. And she was irritable these days, which wasn't like her.

Well, she rationalized, today her vague irritation was no doubt a result of this mild but persistent pain in her neck, combined with the trauma of Maggie's accident.

"Has Maggie had a similar accident before, a bad blow on her head?" David queried.

"Not that I know of, and I'm sure Cleo would have mentioned it. Why do you ask?"

David shrugged. "When I was taking her up to bed tonight, Maggie asked if I remembered that other time she banged her head. She seemed to be convinced I'd treated her then as well. It was probably just a child's imagination, and a result of the shot she had for the stitches, combining to make her a bit muddled."

Annie nodded agreement and poured them each cups of steaming, strong coffee, adding generous dollops of brandy. They sipped, and almost at the same time they both relaxed, sinking back into the cushions and expelling mutual sighs of relief.

They caught each other's eyes then, and both of them started to laugh without a single word being exchanged. The incongruity of the day's happenings suddenly struck them both funny.

"Some nice relaxing day you had, huh, away from the hospital and all that chaos," Annie teased. Then she sobered. "It meant a great deal to have you there, David, caring for Maggie. I was so darned scared. I thought for a moment her eye was going to be damaged." Annie shuddered. "I'm afraid I'm not very rational when one of our kids gets hurt."

"You're very close to Cleo and her children, aren't you?" he inquired in a tender tone, and Annie nodded.

"Very, especially Maggie. I love both the girls, but Mags could easily be my own child. I felt it the moment I met her, which was the day Jason and I moved in here. And Cleo is like a sister to me. Even though she had so little to spend on groceries, Cleo came over that first day with a big tuna-noodle casserole for us, and I asked her and the kids to share it with us."

The details of that meal suddenly made Annie giggle. "Cleo'd been so excited about our moving in that she forgot to put any tuna in the casserole."

David laughed with her, and Annie went on, "That was three years ago. Paula was just newborn, Cleo's husband had walked out on her only months before and they sure didn't have much to go on. Cleo's a strong, brave woman, though. I watched her pull herself together and start a day-care center to support herself and the kids." Annie paused and thought for a moment.

"I do feel this particular bond with Maggie, though," she admitted. "Probably because I was like her when I was a girl, a weird combination of bold and timid, outgoing and introverted."

"You still are that way," he said, and Annie caught her breath as his fingers touched first her hair, and then slid down her cheek, stroking her skin, outlining her ear, making her shiver.

"You're as bold as hell at times, like when it comes to protecting the kids. I heard you order that crowd today to stay back out of the way." His index finger was resting just beside her lips, and now he used it to outline them, tracing their full shape slowly once, and again. His eyes followed the movements of his fingers, and his voice came from deep in his chest, a low thoughtful rumble.

"But when it comes to this, to lovemaking, I think you're timid. I can feel you holding back, trembling. I can feel you wanting me, and still resisting it." His words were wistful. "Can't you let yourself trust me? Trust whatever this is that's happening between us, let it grow? It's neither trivial nor ordinary, Annie, not to me." His finger journeyed back across her lips. She shuddered, and his hand cupped her chin, then released it when she resisted the gentle pressure he exerted.

Nervous, she reached out toward the low coffee table for her cup, wincing as pain shot through her shoulders and down her back, forcing herself to ignore it, to hide it from the man beside her.

"It's just that I need to go slowly, David," she said as she sipped the now lukewarm coffee. "I'm...I guess I'm out of practice," she joked with feeble humor. "I'm not used to this yet."

The truth was, she was terrified of being in his arms. The passion he roused made her lose any control that might have existed, and that loss of control frightened her.

"We've got plenty of time, Annie. There's no hurry." He studied her for a moment, and then he frowned.

"Your back is giving you problems again, isn't it?"

She opened her mouth to deny it, and said instead, "How'd you know?"

"You move differently when it's hurting. Your eyes change. They get darker and sort of glossy, and I can see the strain in your face, the way your jaw tightens."

She attempted a shrug and aborted the movement with a gasp when a spasm of white-hot pain shot once again through her neck.

"Damn it. Yes, yes, it is bothering me, but it's something I've had all my life in varying degrees, so I try not to think about it. It started this afternoon again when Maggie got hurt."

"Would you agree to a thorough evaluation if I set up an appointment for you with some friends of mine?" David didn't wait for the denial that would follow the quick negative shake she gave her head at the suggestion. She'd been through the same thing before, and she had no desire to submit to still another round of medical testing.

Before she could say no, he went on, "We're learning new treatments all the time. Diagnosis is better than ever before. I know you've already gone through careful testing. Your doctor told me he'd sent you through the whole business several years ago. But if there's even a remote possibility something could be done for you, it's worth another try, don't you think? Nobody should have to live with pain." The compassion in his eyes reminded her of his role as physician.

"I'd like you to think about it at least. Will you, Annie?"

She was spared an answer. The back door opened and slammed, and Jason yelled excitedly, "Hi, Mom. Hey, Mom, guess what? Mrs. Thompson wants me to take care of her budgie while she goes . . .''

Jason appeared in the doorway to the living room, his denim jacket half on and half off, his bright hair standing on end. The torrent of words stopped in an instant when he saw David, arm still looped around Annie's shoulders.

The animation faded fast from Jason's mobile features. His expression became stiff and remote. "Sorry, Mom. I didn't know you still had company," he mumbled.

"David's not company," Annie said, more sharply than she had intended. She tried to moderate it. "Why don't you get a glass of Coke and come talk with . . ."

Annie's invitation stopped in midsentence. Jason had already turned away. He was opening the door to the basement, and before she could call to him, he hollered belligerently, "You oughta warn me when you're having your boyfriend over, Mom. I'd make myself scarce so you could be alone to make out."

He slammed the door shut with enough violence to shake the house. Annie heard his footsteps pounding down the stairs.

A moment later his bedroom door also slammed, and then there was silence.

Annie felt her face burn with embarrassment. She couldn't meet David's eyes. Jason's words had made her self-conscious and horribly angry and ashamed of her son all at the same time.

"I'm sorry. He's not usually this way," she stammered, and then blurted out, "Damn that kid. I'm afraid he's jealous of you, David."

"Of course he is," David agreed. "It's natural he would be. You've been alone with him for a long time." He paused, and then added, "You know, Jason talked about his father quite a bit today. Does he see him often?"

Annie's entire body stiffened with shock and she gaped at David.

"Jason talked about . . . But that's impossible. Jason has never even met his father. What on earth could he say about him?"

David was frowning at her, confused.

"What do you mean, never met him? Jason's never met this Michael McCrae?"

Annie shook her head. "Michael went to India shortly after the court case when Jason was a baby. He stayed there until three months ago. Since his return, I'm certain he's never been in touch with Jason. What on earth did Jason tell you about Michael?"

"Let's see. He told me his father was a famous engineer, that he'd built three important dams in India but that now he was back in Vancouver for good. I naturally assumed he and Jason spent a lot of time together."

Annie slowly shook her head. Why did the unwelcome feeling that she was being shoved against her will these days, in directions she didn't want to go?

"What Jason told you is technically correct. Michael is living here now, with his wife. But I haven't allowed—I haven't agreed to their meeting or to Michael spending time with Jason."

David, watching her face said, "I see. Still, the boy must think about it a lot, Annie, because he talked about his father several times today. He also said McCrae had been a wrestler at university, and that he, Jason, is also in a wrestling club at the community center. He even knew how many matches his father had won years ago."

David gave her a lopsided grin. "In fact, I had the distinct feeling that Jason was letting me know that he's a pretty tough guy, like his dad, and not to be messed with. That he was warning me off you, maybe."

Annie was astounded. "I didn't know he was even interested in all that stuff about Michael. He must have gotten hold of some old yearbook from the university. And my mother goes on a lot about Michael. She never forgave me for canceling the wedding. I just can't believe this," she stammered. "Certainly he's asked me about Michael, more in the past months than ever before, but he hasn't talked to me that much about him...." Her voice trailed off as she admitted to herself that Jason's questions about Michael had always annoyed her, so she'd been short-tempered about answering.

Kids were smart. She guessed he'd just stopped asking her and found ways to learn about his father himself. It made her feel as if her own son was becoming a stranger, hearing all this from David.

"Sometimes I think I don't know the first thing about raising kids," she remarked in exasperation. "Maybe I ought to take a course or something."

David was sympathetic. "I've never even had kids, Annie, so there's a hell of a lot I don't understand about them, either. And my ex-wife used to accuse me of not knowing the first thing about women, even after living with her for six years. So I'm anything but well qualified at kids and women. But if you decide to give me a chance, I'll try my best with both of you. With Jason, and with you."

You don't have to try at all with me, David, her heart answered. *I'm yours, whether I can accept it or not, whether you realize it or not. I've been yours from the beginning.*

Before the beginning.

Her mind snapped back in gear.

"I'll have to have a long and honest talk with that boy," she said, more to herself than to David. It wasn't going to be easy, either. Jason was her son, but it seemed that whether she wanted it or not, he was also his father's son.

"Speaking of talking to people, there's a cocktail party this Thursday that I've been railroaded into attending," David was saying. "It's a business obligation of sorts, and it will probably be as exciting as watching paint dry, but it would give me a chance to show you off, as well as introduce you to Calvin. Would you come with me, Annie? We could get through it fast and then go somewhere quiet for dinner."

"You make it sound worse than a visit to the dentist," she said with a weak grin. "With the promise of ice cream later if I behave."

"You got it," he confirmed with his charming, lopsided smile. "Will you come?"

She looked at the lines of his face, and recognized the complications of the question. He was moving them away from her familiar ground, from the privacy of her insular world to the scrutiny of the much larger arena his work entailed. Perhaps it was a test of sorts, for both of them. It took courage to venture there with him.

"Yes, I'll come," she said after a moment. The simple word seemed to echo in her head after she'd said it. Yes, and yes, and yes again.

She was amazed to find she wanted to go with him. Her reward was the pleasure his blue eyes reflected in the soft light from the lamp in the corner, and the kiss he planted full on her lips.

She allowed it to go on much longer than she had intended, but at last with reluctance, she pulled away.

"Jason . . ." she murmured in apology. "He's liable to come upstairs for something, and I'd rather not . . ."

"Yeah," David said, and he moved back on the sofa, putting distance between them. "Yeah, I understand, Annie."

There was a faint trace of constraint and disappointment in his voice, however.

She felt guilty. To bridge the moment, and because it was something she wanted to know, she said, "Tell me more about Calvin Graves, David. If I'm going to meet him on Thursday, I ought to have some sort of road map to go by. What's he like, what kind of man is he?"

Annie listened as David sketched his friend in words. "Calvin's image conscious, always perfectly groomed." David smiled and added, "He's forever threatening to send me to his tailor. I'm afraid clothes never mattered all that much to me."

David's casual disregard for style was one of the things Annie found endearing about him. She'd always had reservations about men who relied on clothing to convey an impression of themselves. She didn't say so now, though. It would sound like a criticism of Calvin.

"Did I tell you that Calvin was my former wife's uncle? It was through knowing him that I first met Sheila."

Annie was surprised and also in some obscure way, disturbed by the disclosure. She hadn't realized that the men's relationship was as complex as that. "Was he upset when you divorced, then?"

The man had every reason to hate her on sight, considering. "Not on a personal level, no. He and Sheila had never been close. From a professional standpoint, however, I think he felt Sheila and I suited each other. I think I told you that she was a lawyer, and Calvin figured that was a great combination."

Annie was beginning to suspect that she and Calvin Graves might have very different outlooks on life, and the thought of meeting him began to make her nervous.

"I'll pick you up at seven on Thursday," David confirmed as he was leaving a short time later.

"I guess I should wear something pretty fancy?" Already she was mentally sifting through her closet, choosing and discarding from her rather meager supply of dresses suitable for a cocktail party. Maybe she'd have to buy something, and she hated shopping.

Already she was having second thoughts about getting herself into this.

David was holding her in his arms in the darkened hallway, and now he kissed her hard before he answered. There was a smile in his voice.

"I'm about the last person you ought to consult about what to wear." His lips grazed across her ear, and he whispered, "Don't you know by now that all I want to do is take off whatever it is you're wearing, Annie?"

It was all she could manage not to start undoing buttons on the spot.

CHAPTER SEVEN

"Ooops...excuse me. I didn't spill any of that on you, did I, dear? How awfully clumsy of me."

"No harm done," Annie lied as she swiped at the darkening stain the red wine had left on the sleeve of her brand-new off-white dress. She held on tightly to the stiff smile she'd worn ever since she and David had arrived half an hour before at the opulent mansion on Marine Drive.

She tried to pretend polite nonchalance as the sleek and lovely woman gushed over David while keeping a precarious grip on the wineglass she'd just spilled on Annie.

"Merv Kanmill introduced us at the Christmas party. You do remember, don't you, David? I'm Gillian Fraser."

"Hello, Gillian. This is Annie Pendleton."

Gillian's adroitly made-up eyes slid across Annie and then returned to rape David's features.

"Nice to meet you," she murmured, taking hold of his arm with her free hand and adding without a pause, "Come with me, David. There's someone over here you simply must meet."

David tried to tug Annie along with them, but she held back, and she caught the helpless glance he shot her as he was propelled away. Gillian's talonlike fingers secured around his forearm.

Annie wriggled her fingers at him and winked, trying to pretend she didn't mind one whit being left alone in the middle of this roomful of strangers. The truth was, she did mind, something awful.

Five minutes after walking into this huge chandeliered room, she'd begun wishing that she'd never agreed to attend the cocktail party with him, and that feeling had escalated with every succeeding minute.

The large group was comprised of people who either seemed to be intimate friends, or at least knew of one another by family name or political connection. It was a slick, plastic "in" group, and Annie felt decidedly out.

She was familiar with many of the faces present. She'd seen them before in the society and gossip sections of the daily papers. She'd just never wanted to meet any of them in person. Their world and hers were poles apart.

"Hello there. You must be Annie Pendleton."

The well-modulated male voice came from just behind her, and Annie turned toward it. Relief flooded through her for a giddy moment. At least whoever this was, he knew her name and he'd be someone to talk with for a few minutes.

"How do you do? I'm Calvin Graves," the well-dressed small man explained, giving her the faintest of faint smiles and extending a polite hand. "I saw you arrive with David, but he seems to have disappeared, so we'll simply have to introduce ourselves."

"He's just over there," Annie gestured to the group surrounding David, and then added, a beat too late, "How do you do? David's mentioned you several times." She remembered all her faint misgivings about this man, and found herself hoping that none of them were well-founded.

He seemed formal, a bit old-fashioned, perhaps? Should she call him Doctor? Mr. Graves? Calvin?

He didn't enlighten her. In fact, he barely touched her hand with his own before he withdrew it. He was not the hearty handshake type. Annie was also becoming aware that his pale, cool eyes were taking in every detail of her face and hair and clothing, and registering not one sign of approval or warmth.

It didn't make her feel at all comfortable.

"David tells me you're a writer, Annie. I may call you Annie, may I? Children's books, isn't that it?"

Was there something patronizing in his tone, or was this damned party simply making her paranoid?

"Annie's fine. Yes, I write fiction for kids. I'm working on one about magic at the moment. That's how I met David. I needed to talk to a magician and attended one of his performances at a school one afternoon. I found out later that he was a doctor masquerading as The Sorcerer. You're a doctor, too, aren't you?"

Damn, now he was making her babble.

One precise nod. "Semiretired, yes." He took a careful sip of the martini he held and swallowed with deliberation.

Uncomfortable silence formed a pool in the midst of the party clamor around them.

"You and David have known each other a long time," she finally commented, more to bridge the awkwardness than anything else.

"Yes. We've been close friends for years, even though we're in the unusual situation of being at opposite ends of our careers. Mine is winding down, and his is accelerating. Which is exactly as it ought to be."

He paused a long time again, seeming to consider his next statement with care before he said it. Each word was precise, though devoid of emotional emphasis as he went on, "David is a gifted young doctor with unlimited potential, but of course I don't have to tell you that. I'm sure you're aware of his capabilities. He's mentioned his aspirations to you, of course?"

Annie nodded, feeling a little confused. "The organ transplant unit at the hospital—yes, he did tell me about it. I hope the funding becomes available. It sounds like something the city needs."

"These things are never easy to achieve, you understand. They never happen by accident. They require hard work and a great deal of cooperation, as well as a dedicated man to hurry them along. And the right connections, of course. David has the potential, the charisma, to make quite a difference, and of course when he succeeds . . . Well, my dear, it's quite possible he might have a future in politics. Who knows?"

"I'm sure I don't," Annie said, mystified by the conversation. It was as if he was talking to her on several different levels, with undertones of meaning she wasn't sure she understood. Could he be hinting that she wasn't quite good enough for David?

"I understand you have a son." The rapid shift in subject confused her still further.

"Yes, I do. Jason is thirteen."

"Hmmmm."

The noncommittal sound made Annie's hackles rise for some unexplainable reason. What was that supposed to mean, exactly?

"A difficult age, thirteen," he said with pursed lips.

What the hell was she supposed to make of any of this, when it came down to it? Annoyance and apprehension mixed into the knot that had been in her stomach ever since she'd arrived.

She didn't like this man.

Calvin Graves was the kind of person who made her feel she must have food stuck in her teeth and smudged eye makeup. He also made her feel as if she wasn't quite bright enough.

It was disappointing, but David's friend just wasn't the sort of person she could ever feel comfortable with. He had all the warmth and animation of a two-day-old salad, and she had the definite impression that he was weighing her on some private scale and finding her wanting. Well, she didn't have to stand here and let it go on any longer.

"If you'll excuse me, I think I'll wander over there and get some food," Annie said with a final, polite, strained smile.

She moved away fast. She was loading a tiny plate with lobster mousse and chilled shrimp and caviar, swearing under her breath, when a warm hand slid around her waist.

"Get rid of that stuff quick. I'm gonna feed you, but not here. We're getting out of here right now," David breathed into her ear.

"Thank heaven," she sighed. With casual aplomb, she abandoned the overflowing plate on one of the side tables and with her hand tight in David's soon found herself reclaiming the exotic shawl she'd borrowed from Cleo and being whisked out the door. Three people intercepted them on the way, and David somehow managed to slide past while still being polite and friendly.

Annie caught a glimpse of Calvin Graves talking with a group of dark-suited men near a stairwell. He glanced their way and made an imperious, beckoning gesture at David.

"David, a moment please—"

David waved with utter nonchalance and kept right on toward the door. Annie felt wicked triumph as the door closed behind them.

Take that, Calvin Graves. One mark for the girl from the wrong side of the tracks.

Freedom at last. The night air was salty and damp, and when the thick door had closed behind them, the sounds of the party inside had all but disappeared.

"Run for it, before somebody comes after us," David ordered in an urgent whisper, and they fled like children up the driveway and along the street. Annie started to giggle. It was incongruous to be running away from such an elite gathering.

When they were safe in the car, David laughed with her, and then he leaned back into the seat and whistled a long, low expulsion of relief.

"Lord, I can't stand these things. I don't know why I ever let Calvin talk me into coming tonight."

Annie wriggled her feet out of her high heels and sighed.

"He came over and introduced himself to me, you know, just after that woman with all the teeth dragged you away," she said. "Who was she, anyway?"

"Gillian the barracuda." David groaned at the memory and started the engine, pulling away from the curb with a roar. "On second thought, better forget I called her that. She's the wife of a prominent politician."

He grinned. "You know, I could tell she hated you on sight, Annie." His voice deepened in that intimate way that always thrilled her. "Because you're beautiful and young and soft and sexy and absolutely ravishing in that dress, and she is none of the above."

"Because I was there as your date, more likely." She'd noticed plenty of speculative looks coming her way from women tonight, and it certainly hadn't been her dress that had attracted them.

Not that there was anything wrong with the dress she and Cleo had shopped for most of last week. It was a short, classy white crepe that skimmed down her body and subtly hinted at her generous curves. It felt as sensual as she hoped it looked, but the party had been crawling with outfits that screamed "designer label" and probably cost thousands of dollars.

No, the female attention had been just because of David.

"You must be on Vancouver's most eligible bachelor list, Dr. Roswell. Or did you pose for some calendar you haven't told me about?" The acerbic words were out before she could consider how they might sound.

He laughed. "Not that I'm aware of, on either count."

She knew he was looking over at her, and she kept her attention on the traffic and buildings flashing past outside the car window. Her face felt hot because she realized her statement made her sound jealous and petty.

Well, damn it, she was jealous. Insecure as well, because until tonight she hadn't given any thought to the type of people David knew and felt comfortable around. She'd been too overwhelmed with the feelings he stirred in her to consider the other people in his life.

People like Calvin Graves, for instance. And that elite group of socialites back there.

Writers like her who earned a living but never set the literary world on fire didn't ordinarily rub shoulders with retired doctors, directors of hospital boards, or politicians and their wives.

If tonight was any indication of what that was like, Annie hoped she'd never have to again, either. They seemed to her to be an insular, self-centered lot.

"I'm glad you had a chance to talk to Calvin," David was saying. "I've mentioned you a lot over the past couple of weeks, and he's been eager to meet you."

It sounded natural and friendly when David said it. Why had the actual meeting set her teeth on edge? She struggled with a suitable, polite response.

"It was, umm, interesting, meeting him. He certainly speaks highly of you. He mentioned the transplant unit and how important it was to your career. I got the impression he expects great things from you," she ventured, looking over at his profile in the dim illumination from the streetlights outside and wondering all of a sudden just how much influence Calvin might have on David.

Annie knew for certain that she'd never find much common ground with that cold little man. Any common ground at all, she corrected, and shivered.

David frowned. "I'm afraid Calvin is inclined to be ambitious, not for himself but for me. He's been great at advising me to make certain career moves over the years, and his advice has always been good. Calvin's hobby is taking up causes, and he's making this transplant unit his priority issue at the moment. In fact, he's got some wild scheme for getting me on as an advisor to the Board of Directors at the hospital."

The ambiguous conversation with Calvin slowly began to make more sense to Annie. She'd been right in suspecting that Calvin was warning her off. He obviously had plans for David's career that didn't include a single mother who wrote little books for kids. He probably had the premier's daughter all picked out, she thought with malice.

Another thought struck her. Was Graves the sort of man who automatically considered Jason a bastard because she'd never married? His enigmatic attitude when she'd mentioned Jason seemed to suggest it.

She swallowed the deep anger that attitude always aroused in her and did her best to keep her voice even and casual.

"Is that what you want, David? To be on the Board of Directors, to get involved with the political structure of the hospital?"

His slight shrug was noncommittal. "Actually I hate meetings and hospital politics, but I guess I'd be willing to do whatever it takes to get the unit I want in place and operating, and as Calvin says, the Board is the logical first route."

It was becoming clear to Annie that Calvin Graves had been warning her tonight that there wasn't much room for her in David's future.

They were heading toward the downtown area, crossing Granville Street Bridge.

"Where are we going?" Annie felt the safest thing to do was change the subject, because she couldn't trust herself when it came to saying nice things about someone she didn't like.

"To the restaurant I went to that night I was out with Calvin. The food is great, and it's quiet, and I've been wanting to take you there."

Annie wished they were going to McDonald's instead, because she was pretty certain Calvin Graves didn't eat there.

"SO WHAT HAPPENED NEXT? Where did you go after this wonderful meal at the restaurant?" Cleo demanded.

She and Annie were sitting on the floor in Cleo's living room the next morning just after 10:00 a.m., surrounded by children of varying ages and a mad assortment of toys and kitchen utensils and old junk the kids seemed to love.

Cleo was comforting an eight-month-old baby girl named Lisa, and Annie was adjusting three-year-old Aaron's pants after a recent trip to the bathroom.

"Oh, we drove over to David's apartment," Annie replied, helping Aaron fit an assortment of shapes into a holder, cradling the tiny boy between her outstretched legs and saying, "Look, love, this one's a star. Where does it go? Good boy, that's exactly right." Annie planted a smacking kiss on Aaron's cheek.

"David has a place in one of those anonymous apartment buildings off of Oak Street. Expensive, well cared for, all the same, all decorated by the guys who do dentists' waiting rooms. He's got beige and brown and some glass blocks. And a nice fireplace that doesn't look as if he's ever lit it."

Without looking at Cleo, she added, "And please don't assume anything intimate happened after we got there, because it didn't."

Cleo threw her hands up in dramatic disgust. "I wasn't assuming, I was hoping, for gosh sakes. Talk about wasting precious time! How much longer do you plan to keep this relationship platonic, anyway? How will you ever know you're suited if you don't go to bed together? And what the hell did you do at his apartment if you didn't do . . . *that?*"

Annie ignored the first set of questions. "You've heard of conversation, haven't you? We talked. He showed me his library of books about magic, and helped me choose some that would help with this book of mine. I looked them over this morning, and they're exactly what I needed. There's even an obscure illusion he found for the kid in my book to do."

Cleo shook her head at such a colossal waste of time. "Then we had coffee and talked some more, and then he brought me home. End of evening."

Cleo gave her a look. "Don't snow me, pal. There has to be a part of this you're censoring. I know it."

It hadn't actually been that uneventful. There'd been an intense interlude in David's arms, on his comfortable brown couch, when their "platonic" relationship had come close to changing into a passionate affair.

David had been the one who held back.

"I won't be put in the position of seducing you, Annie, of feeling as though I've brought you here with some sort of goal in mind. I'm falling in love with you. You must know that," he'd said, in a calm way that was much more effective than a passionate outburst might have been. And she'd known by the look in his eyes that his body and his senses were just as inflamed as her own.

"When the time comes, when it's right for you, we'll make love."

All the same, there'd been subdued anger and impatience in his voice. I'm falling in love with you, he'd said.

Those words kept her awake most of the night, and they'd managed to keep her from working that morning, which was why she'd finally abandoned her computer and sought out Cleo and the children.

She'd found in the past that holding Cleo's babies always made her feel better, no matter how serious the problem.

Was having David love her a problem?

Not in itself. It was what she longed for, deep in her soul, because she loved him as well.

But there were many complications. There was Jason and his irrational resentment of David, for instance.

Last night had also illustrated graphically that Calvin Graves could be a problem. And, as David sensed, there were her own deep-seated reservations about entering any long-term relationship with any man. For the tenth time that morning, she tried to explain to Cleo how she felt.

"I've been alone all my adult life. People become more set in their ways as they get older. It would be insane to get into something, and then end up alone all over again, with a broken heart as well as a resentful kid."

Cleo listened and for once didn't comment.

Annie bent her head and pressed her lips against Aaron's sweet-smelling baby hair, and a hot, evil stab of pain in her neck made her gasp and flinch. Beads of sweat formed on her forehead.

"Your back's acting up again, isn't it?" Cleo frowned as she handed Annie a mug of coffee and led Aaron over to the low table where the three other toddlers were making things from Play-Doh.

"Yeah. It's bothered me off and on ever since that first day I met David, and it's been getting worse ever since, for no reason at all. And now David's set up a whole battery of appointments and tests for me with every back specialist in town, beginning next week." Annie gave a disgusted sigh. "I'm not thrilled about it, but he seems to think some medical wizard might be able to help."

She sipped her coffee, and then blurted out in a low voice, "It's probably the best idea, though. You know, Cleo, there are times when I'm scared stiff I'll end up a bedridden invalid because of this stupid thing with my back." She felt tears well in her eyes, and she fought them, disgusted with herself for letting her deepest fears erupt.

Cleo was too wise to offer platitudes. "If you feel that's even a remote possibility, then you have to explore every avenue available in order to find treatment," she advised in her no-nonsense way. "And I can't think of anyone I'd trust more than David to help you."

The phone rang, and Cleo went to answer it in the other room, where she could hear over the babble of children's voices and babies' cries.

Annie talked to the group around the table, admiring the shapeless, lumpy objects they displayed with innocent pride, but her thoughts were a confused jumble.

Cleo's faith in David was well-founded. He was a person who invited trust, both as a man and as a doctor. Therefore, she ought to have confidence in their love for each other, right? Enough confidence to make love with him without reservations.

But it wasn't David she doubted, an inner voice reminded her. It was herself.

Cleo came back into the room excited. "Guess what? That was a guy with a three-month-old baby boy," she explained. "Same thing happened to him as happened to me. His wife walked out on him and his kid. She hasn't been heard from since the baby was two weeks old. The guy's name is Don Anderson, and he says he went on till just lately believing she'd come back. I remember doing the exact same thing, even leaving the door open when I went out somewhere in case Johnny wandered back. Anyhow, Don's over that finally, and now he needs day care for his son, starting right away. He's a cop. He says his holidays and sick time have both expired and he's got to get back to work. And he's finally given up believing she'll come back to him and the baby."

Cleo gave a sound intended as a laugh, but it came out more sad than amused. "I read the other day that there's actually just as many deserted fathers as there are deserted mothers these days. Can you believe there's no dating game to match us up?"

"Did you agree to help him, Cleo? Can you manage one more child, especially such a tiny baby?"

Cleo nodded. "Yeah, I'm sure I can. I can always get a couple of high-school girls to work for an hour or two in the afternoons if things get too hectic. But it's a little complicated because he works shifts, so the baby'll be here overnight every third week. He says he'll supply a crib."

"Make sure you charge enough extra for the inconvenience of having the baby here overnight," Annie warned. "I know you. You're liable to take one look at that sweet little baby and offer to take him for fifteen years or so for free."

"Nope," Cleo said. "After Mag's accident in the park, I started thinking about how important it is to have some sort of emergency fund put away. Sure our medical costs are covered in B.C., but what if the whole thing had been more serious than it was? Say she'd, Lord, I don't know——" Cleo shuddered. "Say Maggie'd lost an eye or something. If she'd needed treatment not available here, or even extensive dental repairs maybe? I simply wouldn't have had the money. So I'm starting to put away a little bit off each check, just in case. It helps me sleep better at night."

"I know exactly what you mean," Annie said. "I used to be terrified of having the dentist tell me Jason needed braces or something, back when we were really poor. Now I do just what you're doing. I keep a special fund just in case."

Annie went back to her quiet house shortly after that, and forced herself to sit in her chair in front of the computer and at least try to get a start on her second chapter.

She finally gave up trying to write, however; it was one of those rare days when nothing triggered the free flow of words.

She turned the computer off in disgust and started reading instead, choosing one of the books David had loaned her.

It was a history of magic down through the ages, beginning with ancient Egyptian lore, and she was soon engrossed in it.

For the rest of the day, while she munched a peanut butter sandwich for lunch, while she nibbled crackers and cheese late in the afternoon, she methodically skimmed her way through one after the other of David's books, not only looking for illusions and facts and ideas that might be helpful with her own book, but also reading with the need to learn more about the man who had collected these books and studied them, the man who had practiced the illusions described until he was adept at performing them.

She was beginning to understand just how much determination and practice were necessary before even the simplest illusion could be performed with any degree of competence, and her respect for David's skill as a magician as well as a new insight into just how determined he must be grew with every page she turned.

Sorcery had introduced her to David. Reading his books made her feel that she was getting to know a special part of him.

When Jason came home from school, she showed him some of the books. He paged through them, and Annie became engrossed again in a fascinating account of how modern illusions had almost all evolved from ancient times.

"I'm going down to the kitchen to make a sandwich, Mom," Jason announced. "Maybe I can read some of these before you give them back, okay?"

"Sure. Don't eat a whole loaf of bread. I'll make supper in about an hour."

Jason clattered down the stairs, and Annie was once again drawn into the world of illusion. The phone rang once, and Jason must have answered downstairs, so Annie went on reading.

"Mom?"

She looked up. Jason was standing in the doorway, and there was something about his expression that got Annie's full attention.

"Yes, Jase?"

"There was a man on the phone just now. He...." Jason's hands were curled into tight fists at his sides, and he was flushed and breathing hard, as if he'd been running.

Annie suddenly knew exactly what he was about to say, and she also knew that it was inevitable that this happened sooner or later. She ought to have expected it, prepared for it.

"It was my father on the phone, Mom. Michael McCrae, my biological father. How come you never told me he's been calling here and wants to see me, Mom?"

Annie felt her abdomen grow tense with apprehension, and hot anger and outrage rose in her throat. Michael McCrae had absolutely no right to do this to her.

"I didn't know he wanted to get to know me." Jason's eyes were full of blame. "You shouldn't have kept the whole thing secret from me, y'know," Mom. You never talk about him or anything with me, and I mean, can't you understand?" His voice squeaked out of control. "He's my...my father, for cripes sake. I have a right to know about him." Jason's face was crimson.

The raw emotion contained in the statement struck terror in Annie's soul. Jason didn't sound anything like a child making childish demands. He sounded mature and outraged, like a person demanding what he knew to be his birthright.

He sounded like an angry adult, and the person he was angry at was her. She wished now that she'd discussed with Jason the things David had confided, the confused facts Jason had gathered somehow about Michael.

But she hadn't.

She'd thrust it to the back of her mind instead, hoping that if she ignored it, it might just disappear.

It had been both foolish and dangerous of her. She saw that now as words burst out of her son, words that must have been building inside of him for a long time.

"Even people who get divorced, like Frankie's parents—they got divorced—well, he still gets to see his father. He knows where he lives and what kind of guy he is and everything."

Jason's voice was intense and trembling. "Y'know, I used to think maybe my father was in jail or he'd done something awful?" Jason's dark brown eyes looked wounded, and Annie felt like weeping.

"I figured he must have, because you never would talk about him at all."

Annie gathered her wits and tried to explain. "Jason, your father was in India until just recently. You always knew that. I didn't realize . . . I guess I thought there's absolutely nothing about your father to be ashamed of. You have to understand, I . . . I just didn't know until, until just recently, that you even thought about him that much." Annie felt as if her heart were being torn in two.

Jason stood there, fists clenched at his sides. "So then why don't you want me to see him? He said on the phone just now that he'd like to get to know me. Why don't you want me to get to know him?"

Annie didn't know what to say. The deep-seated feelings she had about Michael McCrae were far too complex and even irrational to put into any words her son might understand.

Once again, as she had more and more often in the past few weeks, Annie felt her life slipping out of control, felt herself pressured into things she wasn't certain about, forced into facing a situation she didn't want to experience.

But looking at her son's contorted face, hearing the raw pain and troubled confusion in his voice, she had no choice but to face this.

"It's complicated, Jason," she heard herself saying. She felt defeated and old. "You and I have a pretty stable, happy life. It...it could make life a lot more difficult if your, your... father...got involved."

"I don't get it." He was looking at her with such cold accusation in his eyes. "How could knowing my dad make things different around here? You and I live here, I'm not even saying I want to go live with my father, Mom."

Jason, live with Michael? The thought had never crossed her mind, but now that he'd tossed it out, Annie began to wonder if her son didn't toy with the idea now and then.

A new and different apprehension came alive in her, and it made her much more impatient with Jason than she'd intended because it stirred overwhelming fear inside of her.

"I don't want to discuss this right now, Jason."

He didn't revert to the child who accepted her decisions, complaining sometimes, but recognizing her authority as his parent. Instead he stood planted, firm, frowning at her, and the new determination in his gaze, the patent lack of trust in his expression, frightened her more than she'd thought possible.

What had become of the little boy she knew and loved, the little boy who trusted and loved her more than anyone else in the world? He'd disappeared in the space of a phone call.

All Jason said now was "I want to see my father, Mom."

And then he stood there, stubborn, unmoving, waiting for her to give in to him.

CHAPTER EIGHT

"YOU CAN GET DRESSED NOW, Ms Pendleton, and then I'd like to see you in my office, please."

Annie waited for Dr. Kendrick to close the door before she climbed stiffly down from the examining table. During the past three days she seemed to have done little else but climb on and off examining tables.

Assorted doctors had performed endless tests and examinations, poked and prodded and questioned. Many of the procedures they put her through resembled medieval torture more than modern diagnostic medicine, and she was convinced the ever-increasing pain in her neck was being amplified by the medicine men who were supposed to be interested in curing it.

But this morning, the endless tests were finally over. Dr. Kendrick was the doctor she'd seen first, the coordinator of the series of tests David had arranged for her to have, and Kendrick was also the one who would give her the results of the whole, pointless—in Annie's estimation—series of tests.

Moments later, sitting in the comfortable and rather worn chair in the older doctor's office, Annie was disappointed but not surprised at his diagnosis.

"I hate to admit this, Ms Pendleton, but after all these disagreeable things we've put you through, we can find absolutely no physical cause for this pain in your neck."

The balding, pleasant-faced man frowned and toyed with a paperweight beside the fat file folder with Annie's name on it.

"Now just because the pain you feel isn't life threatening and doesn't seem to have a physical origin related to injury, don't think I'm suggesting for a moment that it doesn't exist."

He tipped his chair back and folded his hands over his generous middle. "It causes you discomfort, and that's all that matters. However, we doctors tend to prefer a concrete reason for everything, simply because if we understand the origin of the problem, solving it becomes less difficult. With your particular problem, we are unable to pinpoint any cause, so therefore we'll deal with the pain itself.''

He paused again and seemed to study her before he continued.

"Pain of this sort, pain which we consider psychosomatic in origin, for lack of any better label, can sometimes be controlled in much the same way we control physically-based pain.''

"With prescription drugs,'' Annie supplied with a dejected sigh and a grimace, as bolts of white hot misery shot through her neck.

It seemed as if her body were taunting her, underlining the doctor's words in ironic counterpoint.

Psychosomatic pain. Was he hinting that she needed a shrink?

All of a sudden she felt rotten, drained and frustrated and angry, because after hours of submitting to every stupid test under the sun, still no one could say what was really wrong.

Some part of Annie had gone on hoping that David would be right, that new diagnostic techniques would reveal a physical reason for the persistent agony that plagued her. She'd been hoping that somewhere in the annals of medicine there would be a cure.

Now she felt utterly defeated. Dr. Kendrick was telling her, gentle as could be, that the real cause of this infernal thing was mental, that she was doing this to herself for some unknown reason.

"Sometimes we recommend drugs, but not exclusively,'' Dr. Kendrick was still explaining. "There are other methods that don't have the side effects drug therapy often does. There's biofeedback technique, for instance, and auto suggestion, often effective in controlling the discomfort. Another method is hypnotherapy. Many of my colleagues don't agree with me on this issue, but I've had remarkable results from patients who've tried hypnosis.''

He gathered together pamphlets that described each system and scribbled several numbers on a paper and handed it to her.

"Read all the information. These are the places you can go to learn biofeedback. There's a center on Broadway, if you want more information, stop in there and pick up some pamphlets. If you decide to try hypnosis, then Dr. Steve Munro is the hypnotherapist I most often recommend. Think it over and then let me know. Whatever you decide, I'll arrange an appointment for you promptly.''

Annie took the papers and stuffed them into her handbag, feeling as if the time she'd spent on the tests had been wasted.

It would be, if she walked out of here and let it go at that. She might as well waste a bit more and at least try this hypnosis thing, she decided on sudden impulse. She might as well explore every avenue available, because her neck wasn't getting a hell of a lot easier to bear.

"Make an appointment with this Dr. Munro for me, please,'' she instructed, and Kendrick immediately used the intercom and told his nurse to arrange it.

"He has a cancellation tomorrow at ten. Will that be convenient?''

Annie hadn't expected it to be so soon, but she agreed. The appointment was made, and she got to her feet.

Dr. Kendrick did, as well. He reached across the desk and shook her hand, his lined face a mixture of regret and resignation.

"Thank you for all the trouble you've gone to on my be half,'' Annie said, giving him a strained smile. After all, it wasn't Kendrick's fault that nothing had been solved by all this. He'd done his best for her.

"My dear, I wish we could have helped you more than we have,'' he said with a rueful sigh. "We tend to believe that modern medicine is far advanced, but personally, I believe we're still in the sandbox stage, not even in kindergarten yet. There's so much we don't know. Will you let me know if the hypnotherapy helps at all?''

Annie was skeptical about even trying it. She knew precious little about hypnosis, but she nodded anyway and walked out into the brilliance of a sunny Vancouver day, struggling to throw off the depression and frustration she felt.

She was meeting David at a small café nearby for lunch, and she wanted to be cheerful and upbeat for him, despite the negative results of the assessment he'd arranged. She didn't want to spend the brief time they had together complaining.

David spent enough time with those who were depressed and ill during his working hours, she lectured herself. He didn't need more of the same from the person who loved him—who hadn't told him yet that she loved him. She'd only admitted it

to herself that very week, while she was waiting for some procedure and had plenty of time to think.

Well, damn it all to purgatory, when had she had time alone
with him to tell him anything lately?

She lifted her free hand and irritably massaged the base of
her neck, the place where the pain seemed the worst.

Psychosomatic. If that was true, then she had to be a real nut
case, creating this kind of problem for herself.

And if this was all some warped product of her imagination, she ought to be bloody well writing Stephen King–type
horror stories instead of children's literature.

If she was disturbed mentally and didn't even know it, she
was no fit partner for David, either, was she?

She strung together a pithy group of the worst words she
knew, and repeated them under her breath until she felt better.

DAVID FELT as if he'd never manage to escape from his office
in time to meet Annie for lunch as he'd planned. Two telephone calls came just at the last moment. Both were from parents anxious about children who were slated for surgery, so
David spent precious moments explaining exactly what was
going on with their kids.

When he finally hung up after the second call, he instructed, "Phyllis, absolutely no more calls. I'm not here to
visitors. In fact pretend I'm not here at all. I'm leaving as soon
as I grab my jacket."

He washed his hands and doffed the white lab coat for his
light tweed sport jacket, squinting at himself in the mirror over
the sink. He still hadn't found time for a haircut, and his hair
was now curling far below his shirt collar.

Well, what the hell. At least it wasn't falling out the way it
was for some guys his age. He shoved his damp fingers through
the sides of his hair, smoothing them back, and promptly forgot all about haircuts as his mind went to his luncheon with
Annie.

She'd have the results of the assessment by now. He was eager to find out what George Kendrick had recommended.
Bull. He was just eager to be with the woman he loved.

He was thrusting his arms in the sleeves of his coat when
Calvin walked through the doorway into the office.

"Well, seems I caught you just in time. How are you, David?"

"Great, Calvin. And you?" David forced a grin and shook the hand the other man proffered, but inside he felt a little irritated. Why did it seem as if everything conspired against his time with Annie?

"I've been trying to get in touch with you so that we could talk. I came by hoping you might be free for lunch today. There're several matters I need to discuss with you before that dinner meeting on Friday. You do remember agreeing to attend that meeting, David?"

David had forgotten all about agreeing to attend the damn thing.

"I'll be there," he promised. "But as far as today goes . . . well, the fact is, Calvin, I'm meeting Annie in a few minutes."

"I'm sorry to be insistent, my boy, but there are matters that I absolutely must talk over with you. Today."

David couldn't help but suggest, "Well, then, would you care to join us for lunch, Calvin?"

He found himself hoping that Calvin would refuse, but the other man considered it for a long moment with his head tipped slightly to the side, and then nodded, rather as if he were doing David a favor.

"Actually I suppose that will be fine, David. I have a meeting at two this afternoon, but until then I'm free."

David couldn't stop the rush of disappointment and irritation he felt at Calvin's acceptance.

"Fine, let's get out of here then. The café is just three blocks from here, so we might as well walk."

It was a small and petty rebellion against the older man. David knew perfectly well that Calvin was less than enthusiastic about walking anywhere except out of his car and onto a golf green, where he immediately rented a motorized cart.

Calvin drew his mouth down in disapproval, but he didn't say anything. David was forced to shorten his long, impatient strides to match his friend's more sedate pace once they reached the sidewalk, and it simply added to David's impatience to have to creep along amidst the bustling crowds as Calvin went on and on about this committee, that association, the need for courting some official.

David saw Annie when they were still half a block away, and his heart opened and his soul lifted at the sight of her.

She was wearing a vibrant yellow dress, sitting at one of the outside tables with her chin propped on her hand, her body not relaxed but tense, waiting for him.

It pleased him that her waiting was visible to him. Her gleaming hair was caught up in a rich, high knot at the back of her head. She was wearing sunglasses, but David knew she was watching the crowd, watching for him.

He also knew that she stiffened a trifle when she saw Calvin beside him. She hid her reaction well, however, and smiled a welcome when they drew closer to the table.

"Hi, Annie. You remember Calvin." David did his best to convey subtle apology in the simple greeting, and she slid her glasses to the top of her head and took the limp hand Calvin extended.

"How nice to see you again," Calvin said with a jovial smile. "I hope you don't mind my joining you. I'm afraid I appeared in David's office at the last moment and he had no choice except to invite me."

David drew up two chairs and sat down close beside her.

"Of course I don't mind," Annie lied, and when Calvin turned his attention to the exuberant young waiter who'd appeared at his side, David gave her a quick, reassuring wink and then leaned over and planted a slow, luxurious kiss on her full, red mouth.

He regretted the impetuous action when fullness and heat surged in his groin, making him shift in his chair.

But he loved the way her eyes softened and slow color rose in her cheeks. She glanced over at Calvin, who was now drilling the waiter over precisely what kind of mustard they used in the sandwiches. If it wasn't Dijon, Calvin insisted they leave it out. He ignored the kiss as if it had never happened.

"I'll have deviled egg on whole wheat, and iced tea," Annie ordered when the waiter turned her way, and David, disinterested in food, simply said he'd have whatever Calvin had ordered.

It turned out to be a good choice; German beer with a fat ham on rye, but while they ate, David grew more and more uncomfortable.

Calvin was acting as if Annie wasn't present at all, and she was sitting silent, not eating, not talking.

Even though David understood his friend's single-minded fixation on getting things in order and settled, still he resented the way Calvin narrowed the conversation to include only himself and David.

"I think it's time we moved ahead as planned on your campaign, my boy. Summer's over, which means everyone's back in harness. The first general meeting of the hospital board is less than three weeks away, and it's time to concentrate on strategy. There are several social functions coming up that I feel you absolutely must attend. The first is a black-tie dinner, I've already arranged for invitations...."

"You remember I mentioned that Calvin wants me to campaign for the position of advisor to the Board of Directors at the hospital," David explained to Annie, using one hand to eat his sandwich. "I've more or less agreed." He reached across the checked tablecloth and grasped Annie's cold fingers in his, giving them a reassuring squeeze and holding on when she tried to pull away.

He wanted contact with her, but he also wanted Calvin fully aware of his feelings about Annie. He wanted to force his friend to acknowledge her.

"Now the other area we have to address if this is to work is that of public support. Television interviews, newspaper coverage, that sort of thing."

David wished Calvin would shut up. He wanted to know how the morning's assessment had gone for Annie. He wanted to sit in the sunshine and the open air and simply enjoy being with her, tell her how pretty she looked in that daffodil-yellow dress.

He didn't want to be bothered today with publicity, or blacktie dinners that he knew would bore him cross-eyed, or anything else Calvin considered earth-shattering enough to discuss here in the sunshine on a hot hial afternoon.

But it was also unfair to agree to play the game and then leave Calvin out there doing it alone, wasn't it?

When he'd made up his mind to go ahead and let Calvin put the machinery into operation, David had thought of the meetings he'd have to attend, the hours of precious time that would be taken up with senseless politicking, and at first he'd told himself he couldn't go through with it.

But then he thought again about perhaps being in a position to influence the power makers into allotting funds for the unit.

Most of all, he thought about Charlie and his baby sister, and he'd given Calvin the go-ahead.

David had always been a man who made decisions quickly and surely and stuck by them, but he already regretted this one.

Calvin subsided finally, looking more than a little grumpy at David's obvious lack of interest.

David noticed Annie had been unable to eat even half of her sandwich. He still had her hand trapped in his, and now she glanced at her watch, extricated her hand and stood, looping her purse over her shoulder and wincing, then taking the bag in her hand instead.

David guessed that she was in pain again. There was something else as well, some tension in her that he couldn't identify.

"I've got to go, David. I . . . have a lot to do this afternoon. My editor will be phoning around two."

He'd been foolishly hoping that they could linger until Calvin was forced to leave, and then salvage something out of the day for themselves. Feeling as if their time together had been ruined, David stood as well.

"I'll walk you to your car," he said, and when she began to protest, he ignored her and turned to a disgruntled Calvin.

"I won't be long. Order me a coffee, would you?"

When they were out of earshot, he swore. "Damn Calvin and his persistence. I wanted to be alone with you, Annie. How did the tests go?"

He'd be phoning Kendrick, but he wanted to hear her reaction.

"About what I expected." She told him the details, careful to hide her own disappointment at the inconclusive diagnosis. She skipped the psychosomatic bit and the suggestions about hypnosis. They could discuss that later.

He was holding her hand in his; the sun was bright, and they were together. Everything else was unimportant now.

The parking garage where she'd left her car was nearby, and she paused outside the entrance. "My car's just inside on the first level. Don't bother coming in." She couldn't help adding with a touch of malice, "Calvin will be getting impatient."

"To hell with Calvin. I'll see you tonight. It might be after nine because I've got a late meeting," he explained, leaning forward to kiss her, not trusting his body's reactions should he take her in his arms on the busy street and hold her tight against him the way he wanted to.

He waited while she retrieved her car, and he paid the attendant when she presented her ticket.

She smiled and blew him a kiss as she drove out into traffic.

He watched her drive away, and then, with a reluctance he'd seldom felt before, he made his way back to Calvin.

ANNIE HAD STRETCHED the truth a little in order to escape. Her editor had said she'd call, but no time had been set.

Gritting her teeth as she inched her way through heavy traffic and along the busy streets toward home, Annie couldn't shake the anger and outrage Calvin Graves had once again managed to stir in her.

How dare he horn in on one of the few times she and David had managed to arrange to have lunch? How dare he act as if she were the intruder, and not him? How dare he usurp their precious hour together with his blathering about meetings and dinners and appointments?

Lord, she didn't like that man. She'd have to tell David sooner or later, explain that she didn't ever want to be in Calvin's company again. How could David . . .

Her train of thought came to an abrupt end as she pulled up in front of her house, turned off the key and sat motionless as she reasoned through what she'd been thinking.

What right did she have to be critical of David's choice of friends? What if David had acted this way about Cleo?

She pushed the idea away, telling herself how warm, how vibrant and friendly and nice Cleo was compared to Calvin.

Honesty made her stop short again. The simple fact remained: Cleo was her friend, and David had done his best, gone far out of his way, to accept her friend.

Calvin, for whatever complex reasons, was David's friend. Surely she owed him the same courtesy he'd given her—an honest attempt to accept the other people in his life.

Damn it. She banged an angry fist against the steering wheel. Damn it all to Hades and back again.

Was this what being half of a couple meant? Wasn't this the thing she'd been avoiding by staying single and apart all these years, this compromising of her instinctive feelings? Was it worth any amount of compromise to be in love with David, to have his love in return?

Her mind, her heart and her soul answered without a single hesitation, immediate, deep and irrefutable.

Yes and yes and yes.

She loved David, and that was that.

So she'd simply have to try harder with old Calvin Graves, wouldn't she?

Feeling weary to the very bone, she got out of the car and went into the house, then put the kettle on and made a pot of tea to take up to her workroom, where she turned on the computer.

She stared at the words on the screen, trying to get out of her own way so the story could continue. If only there was secret knowledge buried inside of her, the way there was inside of her young hero.

Annie's proposed book was about a boy named Seth, born with a deformed arm and hand, who would become fascinated with magic.

Although he could only perform the simplest of tricks because of his limited dexterity, in his dreams Seth saw himself performing one specific, complex illusion, a trick he couldn't remember ever having witnessed.

He would visit the Magic Store, a strange, musty hole-in-the-wall establishment that proved to have every magic book ever written, but when he tried to find a description of the dream trick in books, or locate a magician who performed it, Seth would realize that no one had ever heard of it.

The illusion would become an obsession to the boy. Although he remembered the essentials, there would be portions of the trick missing from his dream, parts Seth knew he could figure out if only he could truly practice magic.

If only he weren't handicapped.

The eccentric old magician who ran the Magic Store would insist that Seth stop talking about why he couldn't do magic, and just see himself doing it the way he did in his dreams.

Seth slowly would begin to try. By the end of Annie's book, real magic would happen.

By believing absolutely that he could perform the illusion, and reaching a point in his mind where he no longer doubted in any way, Seth would do the impossible.

Annie skimmed the outline, locating the scene she was developing.

She'd been working for over an hour, using pure force of will to shove everything but the story out of her mind, and after a while she'd even managed to block out the insistent ache in her neck. She was typing in a furious rush when the doorbell sounded, and she swore with disgust.

She ran down the stairs and threw the door wide, wanting to get whatever it was over with fast. Two uniformed policemen stood there, and between them was her son.

"Mrs. Pendleton?"

Jason's face was a tight mask, rebellious and closed.

"I'm Constable Marsh, and this is Constable Stevens. Could we talk to you for a few minutes?"

"Come in," Annie managed. When they were in the hall she shut the door and turned, terror making her whole body stiff. "What...what's happened?" She looked at the policemen, and then at Jason, but he let his glance slide away from hers.

"We caught your son and one of his friends an hour ago sneaking into a movie theater downtown, without paying. We'd already been notified that they'd done the same thing at a different theater, earlier today."

"But today's a school day," Annie said. "He's supposed to be in school." She realized how stupid that sounded, but she couldn't seem to grasp what was going on.

"I thought he was in school," she heard herself repeating like an idiot.

"Exactly," Constable Marsh confirmed.

Constable Stevens took over. "Jason assures us that he's never been in trouble before. Is that right, Mrs. Pendleton?"

"Yes. I mean no, he never has. And it's Ms Pendleton." Her brain was beginning to function again, but she was out of her depth here. "Is Jason...what will happen..."

"We found him committing an act of juvenile delinquency. And of course you're aware that the downtown theater district isn't a healthy place for a kid as young as Jason to be hanging out."

Annie actually felt as if she might faint.

"Because he hasn't been in trouble before, however, the police aren't going to press a charge in this instance. But should he come to our attention again, we would take him before a juvenile court."

Annie realized she and the officers were talking as if Jason wasn't right there, listening to all this.

"Jason?" she questioned.

She looked at her son. His freckles were standing out against the whiteness of his skin, but he wouldn't meet her eyes or deny what was said.

Juvenile court. Delinquent. It was a nightmare.

"Our suggestion to Jason is that he make some effort to repay the theater, perhaps by volunteering to do several hours of work for them, cleaning up or something."

"Yes, yes of course," Annie agreed. Jason still wouldn't look at her, still stood immobile between the officers. Annie felt as if they'd all been standing there for hours like that, and she wanted these men to go, to walk back out the door and leave— leave her alone with her son, so they could work this out somehow between them, so Jason could tell her what had really happened.

At last, they did. They left a card with their names on it, and said to call if she had any questions. The door closed behind them, and still Jason stood unmoving.

"Jason?" Annie's voice was trembling, but she couldn't seem to control it. "Jason, why? Why did you do a thing like that? You have your own money, you're allowed to go to movies on weekends. But to play hooky, to sneak in . . . I never thought you'd . . ."

Do something like this, Annie's mother used to say, voice trembling with deliberate pathos. I never thought my own daughter would do something like this. To me.

The whole time Annie was growing up, over every smallest transgression, that had been her mother's cry. Every large one as well, including that one last time when she'd refused to marry Michael, when she was pregnant and already in disgrace.

Her mother had said then exactly what Annie had been about to say to Jason.

"Come in the kitchen and we'll have a glass of milk and talk about this," Annie substituted, her tone as reasonable as she could manage.

But Jason shook his head. His face was shuttered. He brushed roughly past Annie and a moment later, the door to the basement opened and slammed.

Fury exploded inside of her. She raced over to the door, tore it open, and shrieked like a madwoman at his disappearing back, "You get back up here, young man, if you know what's good for you. Don't you dare walk out on me, do you hear? I want to know what you think you were doing today."

He stopped and turned, and came inch by inch back up the steps. When he reached the top, he looked her in the eye for the first time, and she could tell behind his mute show of bravado that he was afraid and alone. Behind the thrust out lip and the rebellious eyes, a frightened child was hiding.

Annie melted.

"Oh, Jase . . ."

She reached out, took his shoulders in her hands and drew him toward her to hug him, but he pulled violently away, moving behind the table as if it were a shield and she were the enemy.

"Jason, what's going on? I don't understand any of this. What's happening to you? You're changing. I don't feel I know you anymore."

He seemed to be holding his breath, but then it let go in a torrent of words that started low and intense, and increased in volume as his boy-man's voice traveled from bass to squeaky soprano and back down again.

"It's not me, Mom. You can't just blame me for everything around here. You do things, too, you know. You promise things and then you never do them. All you think about is your stupid boyfriend these days. You never think about me anymore, or do what you promise."

It took willpower, but Annie controlled her own voice. "What have I promised and not done, Jason?"

He sounded so angry, and his words tore at her. His control evaporated, and tears began rolling down his cheeks. His voice rose to a shriek.

"You promised me you'd see about letting me meet my father. You promised and then you never did it, and I hate you, you know that? I hate you, hate you, hate you."

He knocked over a chair on his flight to the back door, and by the time Annie could make herself move, he was out the back gate and running down the alley.

There was no way of ordering him back this time, and she couldn't have anyway, because her sobs were choking her.

CHAPTER NINE

THE TROUBLE WITH RAISING a kid on your own, Annie told herself as she struggled for control, was that you had only yourself to blame for the mistakes you made.

And you had to wait alone for him to come back when he ran away like this.

Half an hour had gone by since Jason slammed out the door, and she'd just managed to stop crying. She blew her nose hard and filled the coffee maker.

There was a sharp, familiar tap on the back door and Cleo came in, giving Annie's arm a sympathetic squeeze and acknowledging in silence her tearstained face and reddened eyes.

"The kids heard Jason having a fit a while ago, and they said he ran off down the alley. Maggie followed him. So I called Jeff's place. So I called Jeff's mother and acted real casual. I said that Maggie was looking for him, and she assured me the boys were downstairs watching *Star Trek*, just so you know where he is."

Annie breathed a sigh of relief. She'd been trying to decide what she ought to do to find him.

"Thanks." The tears she'd managed to stifle now rolled down her cheeks all over again. She used her hands to wipe them away and sniffed.

Cleo handed her the box of tissues. "I figured I'd come and have coffee with you before we head for the bridge."

It was an old joke between them. Early in their friendship, Cleo had gone through a particularly bad time, with one calamity right after another. One morning, she'd burst into Annie's kitchen and collapsed in tears, announcing hysterically that she was fed up with it all, that she couldn't take anymore, she was about to jump off the nearest bridge and be done with the whole mess.

Annie had suggested they have a cup of coffee first, and then she'd drive Cleo to the bridge. After all, somebody had to bring the car home and feed the kids lunch.

They'd ended up laughing like a pair of maniacs, and then they'd talked over Cleo's problems and come up with a temporary solution.

Now Annie managed a shaky smile.

"Jason's getting harder to manage every single day," she said in a small voice. "The police were here. He skipped out of school and sneaked into a movie without paying. Two movies, in fact."

Cleo took mugs from the cupboard and filled them from the coffeepot.

"Two, huh? Jason never does anything by halves. Well, I did that a couple of times when I was a teenager, not sneak into movies, but skip out of school. I was mad at my mother."

"He's mad at me because I haven't let him meet Michael."

"I figured it was probably something like that."

"I told Jason I would, and I've been putting it off. I guess I have to call McCrae and get it over with."

Cleo sipped her coffee. "I guess you do."

Annie shuddered. After a moment, she said, "You know those doctors I saw this week? Well, their diagnosis was that there's nothing wrong with my neck. According to them, the pain is psychosomatic. And after this fiasco with that kid, I'm ready to accept that my head is on crooked."

Cleo snorted. "So what do they know? I actually had a doctor tell me the same thing about childbirth. What I thought was pain was purely psychological, he said. I was having contractions, no pain allowed, thank you very much."

Annie met her friend's eyes. "The thing is, maybe they're right about me, Cleo, because I do feel like a psycho about this Michael McCrae thing. I get physically sick when I have to talk to him on the phone. I can't bear the thought of actually meeting him face-to-face. I actually have nightmares of him chasing me with intent to murder. Why should a middle-aged man I haven't seen in years affect me this way? Maybe I am a bit mental. After all, why should I still feel so emotional about him?"

Cleo shrugged. "Who knows? Maybe after you do meet him again, you'll find out it isn't as bad as you thought. Sometimes we build things up, in our heads, and they're really not as bad when they happen."

Annie gave her a baleful look. "Don't feed me that, Cleo. Usually they're worse."

The back door opened, and Maggie stuck her head in, the bandage on her temple now reduced to a giant-size Band-Aid. She was wearing her prissy, managing expression.

"That man's at our house with his baby, Mommy," she announced. "I'll tell him you're coming right now, okay?"

"Never a dull moment," Cleo sighed. "That's my deserted father with his kid. I better go convince him I'm a stable, responsible human being, which isn't going to be easy." She got up and followed her daughter out the door. "Let me know if there's anything I can do."

The telephone began to ring, and Annie called a hasty thank-you after Cleo and lifted the receiver.

It was Jason. "Ma, I'm over at Jeff's house. I figured you might be worried." He was doing his best to sound offhand and tough, but the tension was there.

Annie kept her tone as even as she could.

"Under the circumstances, Jason Pendleton, I think you'd better come home right away."

"Whatever," he said in a bored, gloomy voice.

"No whatever about it. Home, now."

She'd sit him down and they'd have a long, honest talk.

BUT SOMEHOW IT DIDN'T WORK. They sat, Annie talked and Jason did little more than nod and grunt a few times.

There was no way she knew of to make a thirteen-year-old talk when he chose not to. He nodded when she said he was to apologize to the manager of both theaters and offer to work off his debt. He nodded when she said she would not have him bully her, his mother, through misbehaving, into doing what he, Jason, wanted her to do.

And, she concluded—and this was much more difficult—despite what Jason thought, she'd meant to keep her word about getting in touch with his father. She would phone, tonight, and set up a meeting, for tomorrow if that was possible.

But the final decision about that was still hers to make, not Jason's. "If, for any reason, I feel it's not a good idea to involve Michael McCrae in our lives, I expect you to accept that without giving me a lot of grief over it,'' she said.

He met her eyes for the first time. "That's not fair," he stated flatly.

Annie came near to losing her temper all over again.

"Fair or not, that's the way it's going to be. I happen to be the adult in this family, and I still make the rules.''

He rolled his eyes and went off to his room without another word.

DAVID PHONED LATER that evening, and talked fast because he was stealing the time from a meeting he was supposed to be in.

"Annie, this infernal thing is running late. In fact, it looks for all the world as if it's going on into infinity. I want to see you, but I had the feeling today you were really tired. Instead of coming over tonight, how about having a real, honest-to-goodness date with me on Saturday night?"

Before she could do more than smile at the idea, he hurried on, "I'll spring for chocolates, flowers, wine and a fancy dinner, with dancing thrown in as icing on the cake. I'll even get a haircut,'' he promised with rash abandon, and she laughed, the first time she'd really laughed that whole long, miserable day.

David touched her heart without even trying.

"Get a haircut and the deal's off, buster. Don't you know it's that romantic, untamed hair that I fancy?''

Disappointment mingled with relief when she hung up. Much as she would have liked to see David that night, she'd about had it.

She put the next phone call off as long as possible, but finally she forced herself to dial the number her son had scribbled all over the pad beside the phone. Michael McCrae answered, and she made arrangements to meet him and his wife on Thursday afternoon, being as brisk as she could.

Thursday was tomorrow.

Annie hung up the phone, wondering what was wrong with her head. She had to go to the hypnotherapist in the morning, and now she was committed to meeting this man she detested in the afternoon. It wasn't going to be one of her better days, for sure. But then, neither had today been anything but disastrous.

As if she could scrub off the residue of the day's calamities, she ran a tub of hot water and rubbed soap on a cloth and then all over herself, over and over again. She was in bed and asleep by ten-thirty.

SHE REALIZED it was a dream, because part of her knew she was lying in bed asleep while it happened. Her right hand was outside the covers and cold. But another part, just as much her, just as real, was in another place. Another time.

The whitewashed room was small, the walls were thick stone. There were two windows. There was a fireplace on the inside wall, and the stone chimney formed the division between the kitchen and the room where she now sat in a comfortable rocking chair, holding a sweet-smelling, dark-haired child and singing her to sleep.

It was evening, a late summer evening. The soft rosy light coming in the windows would soon give way to darkness. The cow was milked, the chickens locked in their shed for the night.

She was alone. She was lonely, but there were worse things than loneliness.

The child's father was gone, had been gone for a long time now, almost since the war began, and it was a tremendous relief to her. She didn't miss him, even though she had to work hard to keep the small farm in order, even though she was often frightened when she felt rather than heard the far-off booming of the guns and thought about what would happen if the fighting came closer.

So far, they'd been lucky in this tiny hamlet.

The child stirred against her breast, and she bent and put her lips to the velvet cheek. This child was the best thing that had come out of her marriage. She ought to put her in the bed, but there was such comfort in the feel of the small, warm body.

Suddenly there was a knocking at the seldom-used door at the far end of the room.

Alarmed, she got up with the child cradled in her arms, moved into the small adjoining bedroom and laid her carefully in her bed.

Then, heart hammering, she hurried to the door and opened it, just a crack. These were troubled times.

The man, the tall foreign man, smiled at her in apology, and it seemed as if her heart would pound its way out of her chest as she looked up at his face. His eyes were a deep and smoky blue, like the sky over the Seine just before the darkness fell, and there was a sadness in the lines of his face.

Her fear had evaporated as soon as she looked into his eyes. She wanted to stretch out a hand and smooth the lines away.

Annie moved in her sleep, her cold hands grazing her cheek, and the part of her that was dreaming thought the face was his and it confused her, just for an instant, in the time it took to cross the boundaries of the dream and come half awake. It was familiar. She remembered the path below the house, beside the river . . . She'd been in that dream before.

Moments later, she slept again, and the dream was forgotten when morning came.

AT NINE, waiting in Dr. Steven Munro's unpretentious office, Annie felt nervous and out of place. She wished with all her being that she'd never agreed to this appointment.

The waiting-room receptionist was a plump, motherly woman and the whole place had an air of casual messiness. Magazines were scattered in haphazard disarray across a battered table, and there was a blue-and white budgie in a cage in the corner, hopping from perch to perch and shrilling out indecipherable noises.

The atmosphere reinforced Annie's feelings about hypnosis in general; that there was nothing professional about the process, and that it could hardly result in anything that would benefit her miserable neck pain.

She came close to walking out after she'd waited ten minutes past the hour set for her appointment, but just as she was making up her mind, the woman at the desk smiled and said, "Steve will see you now."

Steve? Annie's expectations were well below zero when she walked into the inner room that, just as the rest of the place, looked more like a cozy, messy, artist's study than a doctor's office.

"Hi, Annie. I may call you Annie? I'm Steve. We're pretty easygoing around here. That's my wife, Edith, at the front desk."

He wore an ash-stained electric-blue tie, wide and garish, and a green shirt that clashed with everything else. His sleeves were rolled up past his elbows. His jacket was slung across a chair and his pants bagged at the knees and backside. He was short and stocky, and it was hard to say how old he was. He wore small reading glasses on a blue string around his neck. His bushy black hair was receding, his nose was large and his soft, dark eyes could have belonged to a young child. They were gentle, questioning, and they seemed to take her in and accept her without criticism.

It was impossible to be nervous around Steve Munro, and Annie felt the tension begin to flow out of her as he motioned her to a seat on a battered gray couch along one wall.

To Annie's surprise, he knew without referring to any chart exactly why she was there, the nature of her neck problem and the tests that had been done during the past days.

Steve Munro did his homework, and it restored Annie's confidence somewhat.

He chatted about the weather, asked her what she worked at, and seemed fascinated by the idea of her being a children's writer. Finally he said, "How much do you know about hypnotherapy, Annie?"

"Not much at all," Annie confessed. "Practically nothing, in fact. I know hypnosis is used as a magician's trick at times, but beyond that...."

"It sounds like a lot of mumbo jumbo to you?" he inquired with a crooked grin that revealed a chipped front tooth. She felt herself flush.

"Yeah, pretty much." No point in lying. He might as well know from the beginning that she was dubious as hell about this whole thing.

"Well, I thought the same until a few years ago. I was trained as a clinical psychologist, you see, conventional, formal, emphasis on scientific method, reverence for Freud and the rest of the big boys." He smiled at her, an endearing, humble smile. "Unearthing subconscious material and bringing it to the surface where it can be dealt with works. We all know and accept that." He strolled around the room as he talked, and Annie decided she liked his voice. It was deep and musical, at odds with the unassuming figure it came from.

"Trouble is, analysis is a long, expensive process. I found myself wanting a shortcut to the inner mind, and along with a lot of other people in my field, I started studying hypnosis as a tool that would speed up the process."

"It's a fairly new idea, isn't it?"

"Nope," he declared. "Hypnosis is as old as Methusela. It's been employed as a tool since the beginning of history. There were famous sleep temples in ancient Greece and Rome, and the priests used hypnotic procedures. Many passages of the Bible refer to it. The British Medical Association in 1955 and the American Medical Association in 1958 gave hypnosis official sanction. Even old Freud, at the end of his long career, stated that hypnosis, because of its efficiency, was the key to helping people. My attitude has always been, if a thing works, use it. So I learned hypnotherapy."

"And do you find it effective?"

"Yup." There was total conviction in his answer. "I've used it for years now, and I'm convinced it's helped countless patients." He collapsed like a boneless puppet into an armchair every bit as battered as the couch, facing Annie.

"What we'll attempt to do for you, Annie, is instruct the subconscious mind to relieve that pain in your neck, and maybe also we'll be able to uncover some reason for it that you've decided to bury deep in your memory, some trauma that you don't remember at all."

"Is that what you think I've done, suffered some awful experience and then shoved it out of my awareness?"

He shrugged. "It's certainly possible."

"I doubt it. My childhood and adolescence were pretty ordinary and easy." Annie was still dubious. "But I'm willing to give this a try, so do me and let's get it over with," she said in a tone of resignation, settling back stiffly on the couch and closing her eyes.

Munro's laugh was big and musical.

"Not so fast. You're too quick for me. This isn't a shot in the arm. Let's talk a bit more first. I have to lead up to this a bit slower. I'm a slow sort of guy. Tell me why the thought of being hypnotized scares you witless."

Annie opened her eyes and stared at him. "But I didn't say that it did."

He grinned. His teeth were stained from smoking. "If it doesn't, so much the better. Most people have a deep fear of hypnosis, of giving up control to someone else. They worry about losing consciousness, not knowing what's happening, having the hypnotist plant macabre suggestions in their poor minds."

It was uncanny, but he was describing exactly the half-formed concerns Annie had been trying to ignore.

For the next half hour, Annie listened again and asked questions as Steve dispelled every one of the fears she hadn't wanted to put into words.

"First of all, you don't lose consciousness the way you do when you're sleeping. You enter a deeply relaxed state, and you begin to focus more and more inwardly. You'll always be aware of me guiding you to some degree. But your conscious and subconscious mind are in control, not me."

At last, when every one of her questions were answered, he casually suggested she stretch out on the couch and relax.

Annie found she was tense and shaky again when they reached this part of the procedure, but Steve's deep, resonant voice instructed her to concentrate only on her breathing and its rhythmic pattern: in, out, in, out.

"Relax your scalp," he went on, and continued with all the muscles of her face, neck, shoulders, and on down her body, until Annie was only aware of a deep, tranquil sense of total peace.

"This process will become easier and easier to accomplish as our sessions go on," he reassured, and she could feel herself silently agreeing. It was such a pleasant, floating sensation, such an untroubled place to be.

He took her to an imaginary garden, a place of placid beauty, and used the various senses, one by one, to experience the scene. She smelled a rose, saw the rainbow of colors before her, heard the gentle song of birds and the trickle of water from a nearby stream.

By now Annie felt more than half asleep, comfortable, warm, lost in a wonderful daydream as he had her imagine pure, clear white light flooding through her, cleansing her, before he led her to examine her body from outside herself.

"The pain you experience in your neck is visible as a hard, red knot. Concentrate on untying that knot, Annie. Smooth it out, see it uncurl, and watch the red give way to healthy pink. The pain is going, and each time you concentrate on this image, it will diminish more and more."

Annie followed the suggestion. It actually seemed as if the nagging discomfort diminished.

"We're going to travel backward now, Annie. As I count backward you will envision the years of your life and travel down them, back to childhood times.

"Thirty, twenty-five, twenty..."

"WHAT WENT WRONG? Why did I just come out like that?"

Annie was sitting up again, having a cup of tea Edith had just brought in.

She was beginning to anticipate the wordless shrug Steve used so graphically. "Haven't got a clue. It happens. Next time will be easier, and the next easier still. That is, if you decide to continue."

The hypnotic session had ended abruptly when Steve was guiding her somewhere through her early twenties. She'd suddenly felt a strong urge to escape the images he was encouraging, and she'd promptly opened her eyes and sat up.

"I don't want to do this anymore," she'd announced with childish determination.

"No problem," Steve had said agreeably. "We made good progress anyway for a first session. How's your neck?"

Annie rolled her head from side to side, waiting for the shaft of pain that always accompanied the movement. There was a faint discomfort, but the sharp knifing sensation that had been there when she arrived this morning was gone.

"Why, it's lots better." She gave him a grateful smile. "I definitely want to try again, Steve."

"Great. I want you to take these tapes home with you and use them. They're deep relaxation tapes. Try them a couple of times a day and always end with the auto suggestion I gave you for your neck. Next time, they'll make the hypnosis easier because you'll be able to relax much more quickly. Make a date with Edith, and we'll have another go."

When she walked out of the building and retrieved her car, she was astonished to find that she'd been gone two and a half hours. There was time for a quick lunch at a muffin spot, and then she made her way across town to the area where Michael McCrae had an apartment.

Annie checked the address she'd written down the night before, and tried to subdue the anxiety this forthcoming meeting aroused in her.

She still wasn't at all sure what it was she needed to know about Michael McCrae or his wife, and the peaceful calm she'd felt after the hypnotic session disappeared when she found the street she was searching for.

It was an old neighborhood, prestigious at one time, but now all the stately old mansions had been converted to apartments. Tall oak and cedar trees still lined the boulevard like sentinels determined to keep out intruders.

She felt like an intruder. She should have insisted they come to her. But wouldn't that be worse, having them in her home?

And how was this wife of Michael's, this Lili, feeling about meeting a woman who'd borne Michael's son? Wouldn't she be resentful? Annie thought of someday meeting David's ex-wife, and shuddered. Lord, this was awful. It couldn't be anything but awkward and embarrassing for all of them.

Annie pulled in under the trees and parked her car, staring up at the three-story monolith behind the stone fence.

We're on the main floor, Michael had said.

Annie walked up the wide steps and a surge of nausea rolled over her as she pushed the doorbell.

The door opened almost immediately.

"Please, won't you come in? I am Lili." The woman smiled and put out a narrow hand, taking Annie's in a welcoming grasp and drawing her into the hallway.

Lili was perhaps forty, dark and exotic. Her long hair was drawn back in a high knot, and she wore black pants and a silky patterned blouse.

Annie noticed that her narrow feet were bare, the toenails painted a soft rose. There was something vulnerable about those bare feet, and Annie felt a little less nervous for a moment.

Although she wasn't beautiful, Lili gave the illusion of both grace and a kind of humorous vivacity. If she felt any animosity toward Annie, she hid it well.

"It's most kind of you to come here. What do you prefer I call you?" Lili's voice was well modulated and pleasant.

"Oh, just...call me Annie." She swallowed and did her best to smile, but her palms felt wet and her heart was racing in a crazy rhythm as a tall male figure came around the corner from another part of the house.

"Hello, Annie. Thank you for coming." The deep male voice was Michael's.

It was the moment Annie had dreaded most, the first time she'd seen him since the scene in front of the courthouse all those years ago.

I'll kill you for this, you bitch....

Annie almost panicked as he put out a hand toward her. She curled her fingers into fists and pressed them into her sides. She couldn't bring herself to touch him.

It was an awkward moment. He dropped his hand, but went on smiling at her.

Annie forced herself to look full at him, and it shook her to see traces of her son's face reflected there, in cheekbones, the way the ears were shaped, the set of the jaw. It shocked her, that physical resemblance. And it galled her to have to admit that Jason was indeed his father's son.

But Michael was different from her memory of him. He was older, certainly; he'd been twelve years older than Annie, which made him...she added rapidly as they moved through the hallway, the two of them drawing her with them into their home.

Michael was now forty-six. He looked his age. His rather long, straight hair was peppered with gray and there were deep lines running across his forehead. But it was a nebulous air of tranquillity about him that Annie found foreign.

Michael had been a quiet man, but certainly not tranquil. "Please, sit down," Lili seemed to glide instead of walk, and she gestured to a deep armchair. Annie slid down into it, facing the sofa where Michael and Lili took seats side by side, close together.

There was a tray on the low table separating the seats, and Lili leaned forward, indicating a coffee carafe and a teapot.

"Would you care for something to drink?"

Annie began to refuse, but changed her mind. It would give her something to do with her hands.

The pain in her neck was there again.

"Coffee, please," she said, and Lili poured some into a delicate china cup and set it in front of Annie.

After the cream-and-sugar ritual, there was a long moment of silence. Now Annie was afraid to lift the cup in case her trembling hands spilled the hot liquid.

"This is really difficult for you, and we appreciate your coming here, Annie," Michael said at last, as if it were a formal speech he'd rehearsed.

Annie's nervousness turned to sudden anger, and her voice was hard-edged and spiteful. "It wasn't planned, it just happened. You deliberately forced the issue by talking with Jason on the phone that day."

He stayed calm. "It wasn't planned, it just happened. He answered, and I couldn't hang up. I want to get to know him. He said the same thing about me."

Annie's emotions choked her. She reached for her cup and took a gulp of the coffee, but she had to force it down her throat. She set the cup back on the table with a clatter.

Lili was sitting motionless, her dark eyes going from her husband to Annie. How much had Michael told her about the things that had happened between them? Annie wondered. How honest was he capable of being?

"Why now, Michael?" she burst out. "Why now, after all these years, why come back and bother me now? I've raised Jason. What makes you think there's a place for you in his life?"

She understood that she was deliberately trying to hurt him, to cause him pain, but she didn't care. "You and your wife have no children. What makes you think you even know how to relate to a young boy like Jason? I thought I made it plain years ago that I preferred to raise him alone."

The Michael she'd known long ago had no gift for introspection. He'd had a volatile temper, and he would have quickly met anger with anger. He'd been stubborn, determined, and certainly not given to expressing feelings in words.

She remembered his animal strength, the way his fingers had dug into her shoulders, and she shuddered, glancing involuntarily at his large hands. Lili was holding one of them, and it reminded Annie of the way David had held her hand not long before, aligning himself with her instead of with Calvin. That gesture of affection angered her even more. Michael didn't deserve love, certainly not from Jason.

"Years ago, you hurt me and I guess all I wanted to do was hurt you back," he said after a long pause. "I'd like to think I've grown up since then." There was strain in his voice.

Annie guessed that Michael still wasn't good at expressing emotion in words. The amazing thing was that he was trying.

"Back then I wasn't thinking of Jason as much as I was wanting to just pay you back."

Annie nodded, an angry pulse hammering in her ears. She'd always known his lawsuit was vindictive.

"I'm older now, Annie. Maybe a little wiser?" He raised an eyebrow, and attempted a smile. "I'd like to think so, and it's thanks to my wife. She's helped me understand a lot of things. Oh, I don't pretend to know much about a thirteen-year-old boy, but I'm anxious to learn. Lili and I simply want to be part of Jason's life, be his friends, if that's possible. We're not trying to take over as parents, or anything like that. We're just ordinary people, leading ordinary lives. We'd never undermine you in any way, if that's what you're concerned about."

Until now, Lili had been quiet. In her soft, slightly accented voice, she said, "Please, if there is anything you wish to ask me, Annie, feel free. I will have close contact with your son if you allow him to know us, and if there are problems with my being from another culture, perhaps we could discuss them now?"

Her openness was disarming. What could Annie say? There wasn't anything about Lili she objected to, except that she'd married Michael.

And that was ridiculous, because there had been a time when Annie herself had almost done the same thing. There'd been a time when she had thought it necessary to marry him.

What had she been hoping to find here? Roaring alcoholism, insanity, drugs, perversion? Her honesty forced her to admit she had been hoping for something like that. Anything to justify forbidding them any association with Jason.

But she'd learned, this past week, that Jason had a mind of his own about this. Besides, there was nothing here to object to. She felt defeated, old and tired.

She got to her feet, holding her body stiff against the accelerating pain in her shoulders. "When do you want to see him?" Her voice was a monotone.

Michael had risen, his arm around his wife. "As soon as possible," he said, giving Lili an exuberant squeeze. "Thank you, Annie."

Lili's face was shining with happiness, her eyes soft and liquid when she looked up into Michael's face. Obviously there was love between them, and that was more reassuring than anything they could say.

"Sunday, then," Annie forced herself to set a date and make the whole thing official. Jason would ask her anyway, first thing—when, when, when?

Best to get it over with quickly, now that it was decided. "Perhaps you would come with Jason and share dinner with us on Sunday?"

Annie was touched by Lili's invitation, but she shook her head. "I think it would be best for him to meet you alone. I'll drop him off here around noon, and you can bring him home."

If was done. Annie drove home, and Jason met her at the door. His face was one large question mark, and when Annie told him, he threw his arms around her and squeezed until she winced.

"Thanks, Mom. Hey, thanks. And, Mom?"

"Yeah, Jason. I'm here."

"I went to see the manager of those theaters. I'm gonna run errands and clean up junk for them, starting next weekend."

"That's a good idea. Did you also talk to your teacher and get the work you missed yesterday?"

He nodded. "Yeah. She gave me a detention for skipping school. And, um, Mom?"

Annie recognized the tone, the determination combined with uncertainty. "Did you, uh, did you tell my, my....dad...about what I did, about the, the. . .cops and all that?"

Shock went through her that he would even think of such a thing. Worse than that was the fact that he would call the man he'd never even met yet "dad."

"Of course not, Jason. I wouldn't do a thing like that."

His shoulders slumped with relief.

"It's just that I'd like him to sort of, kinda, well, develop his own opinion of me, know what I'm sayin', Mom?"

The enormity of the boy's vulnerability overwhelmed her. It ripped her heart to shreds because she'd been so certain all along that the environment she provided for Jason was all he'd wanted or needed.

As it had been doing with increasing regularity, Annie's world and the security she'd always found in it seemed to shift and re-form like the images in a dream.

CHAPTER TEN

THE TELEPHONE RINGING on the nightstand beside the bed finally penetrated deep, thick layers of sleep, and David rolled over and lifted the instrument to his ear.

"Yeah, hello?"

He cleared his throat and pulled himself into a sitting position, squinting with bleary eyes at the darkness outside his bedroom window. The clock read two forty-five.

The middle of the night. Saturday morning?

It was his answering service.

"Sorry to bother you, Doctor, but an urgent call just came through long-distance from a Mrs. Vance in Enderby, B.C."

David swung his legs out of bed and grabbed the pen and pad from the night table. "What's the message? And give me her number."

"Message reads, 'Charlie running a high fever.'"

David scribbled down the number and dialed it the instant the line was clear.

The young mother's voice was strained and thin when she answered the phone. It rang only once before she came on the line, and it was obvious from her voice that she'd been wide-awake, waiting.

"Thanks so much for calling me back, Dr. Roswell. I'm sorry to wake you up but I'm awfully worried. Charlie seemed to have caught a little cold two days ago. I took him straight to the doctor here, and he put Charlie in hospital just to be sure." She gulped in air, and hurried on. "But about six last night, his temperature started going up, and now he's running a fever and I'm not sure what I ought to do. Our doctor will be phoning you later this morning, but I couldn't sleep all night. I had to talk to you and see what you think."

David thought hard for a moment. Charlie was listed as urgent on a North America-wide waiting list of possible liver transplant recipients. When a suitable organ became available, he would be flown by special plane to the Pittsburgh hospital where such procedures were performed.

David would check immediately, but it wasn't likely anything would happen within the next day or two, either, so sending Charlie down to the U.S. medical center was probably useless at this time.

Charlie's situation, although it was urgent, was not yet life threatening; the liver disease he suffered from would slowly cause his death, but David had believed it would be some months, perhaps a year, before that happened.

Time. They needed time to get all the details in order, time to find a suitable organ for Charlie.

The question was, what exactly was wrong with Charlie now, and how equipped was the tiny medical facility in the small town the Vances lived in to cope with Charlie's problem?

"I'll call your doctor immediately, Mrs. Vance, and see what he says. Do you have his home number handy? Thanks. I'll ring you straight back, and we'll decide what's best to do."

When he'd finished the second call, he got up, pulled on a pair of sweatpants and a top and walked across his cluttered bedroom to the window, trying to make the wisest decision.

Streetlights cast a faint glow over the peaceful neighborhood. The streets were deserted, and a feeling of intense loneliness came over David. Since Annie had come into his life, he found himself longing to have her with him at times like this.

The young doctor he'd just awakened and spoken to was bright and anxious to help, but he stated in no uncertain terms that he felt the tiny hospital was out of its depth should Charlie become seriously ill during the next few hours. His temperature was still high, but not dangerously so.

If the child were to be moved to Vancouver, where sophisticated help was available should the situation get worse, now was the time to act.

David weighed the possibilities and made a decision. He dialed the Vances' number again, and gently, trying not to upset the young mother more than she already was, instructed her to make arrangements for bringing Charlie to Vancouver.

David knew the trip would be harrowing for Mrs. Vance, and for Charlie as well. It would involve an hour's car trip just to reach the nearest airport, and then another hour of flying time.

It meant arranging care for her baby daughter, as well as coming up with the money for the trip. It was a major upheaval, and that was why David had hesitated over whether or not it was necessary.

He'd have an ambulance waiting at this end, David assured Mrs. Vance, and he'd instruct the airline that serviced her area that this was a medical emergency, so there would be no problem getting a seat on the first flight out that morning.

He'd see her about noon, he promised, at the hospital.

It took him another hour of phone calls to make every possible arrangement, and when he was finished, it was just past five in the morning. He was wide-awake. There was no point in trying to fall asleep again.

He went into the small galley kitchen and boiled water for instant coffee, still going over the decision he'd made and hoping he wasn't disrupting the Vances' life and causing them financial problems if it wasn't absolutely necessary. But how the hell could he know for certain? Making judgments like this one was by far the hardest part of being a doctor.

Sitting drinking the bilious liquid he'd made, he came to the sudden conclusion that he was fed up to the teeth with living alone. He wanted Annie's warm body next to him in that damned bed, he wanted her to talk to at times like this, to sit with him here in the kitchen in the gray dawn and tell him he'd made the right decision, even if he hadn't.

He wanted Annie in every way a man could want a woman. He wanted to share the rest of his life with her. He'd known that on some level, ever since the afternoon he'd taken her home and watched her while she slept.

The trouble was, more and more obstacles seemed to get in the way of their romance. There were the demands of his job, the new drain on his time that all these damned meetings and social engagements were creating, and on Annie's side there was her reluctance to commit herself to any relationship. Of course part of that reluctance involved her son, Jason.

The boy had made it crystal clear that David was unwelcome in his life. David couldn't help feeling irritated with the kid.

He made toast and ate it, hoping that, despite the way the day had started, it would smooth out enough so that his date with Annie tonight worked the way he wanted it to.

THE MORNING BEGAN GRAY and rainy, but by afternoon it had cleared. Annie spent most of the day in her study, although she was careful to allow herself plenty of time to get ready for her date with David.

The ritual of grooming and dressing was drawn out and delightful when the entire purpose was to be lovely for him. She bathed and shaved her legs, rubbed perfumed lotions into her skin, slipped on satin underwear and the simple lime-green dress she'd decided on. She spent forty minutes making her mass of hair look as if she'd just stepped out of bed.

Her reward was the open admiration on his face when she opened the door at his knock. His eyes roamed over her and his mouth pursed in a silent whistle. He had a bouquet of violets and small yellow roses in one hand, and a huge box of chocolates in the other. He half bowed and handed them to her with a grin.

"You didn't have to bribe me, but I love it," she told him.

Her gaze went to his hair. "You didn't get a haircut," she said with a catch in her voice.

"This lady I know told me not to," he teased and they stood and smiled at each other.

The truth was, David had forgotten all about a haircut. He'd spent most of the afternoon at the hospital running tests on Charlie. The boy was still feverish, the tests had been inconclusive, and David was carrying a beeper in his jacket, just in case there was any change in the child's condition.

Jason was watching television. He waved a hand at them when they left; he was expert at being polite to David while making it clear he'd rather not bother.

The restaurant was one Annie had only read about, new and trendy, welcoming and expensive. It overlooked the ocean, with a view of freighters and the promise of a spectacular sunset over the North Shore mountains. David had managed to secure a table by the window wall.

The background music was soft, the tables far enough apart for private conversation, and Annie felt pampered and full of anticipation for the evening ahead as David carefully seated her, his hand caressing her arm and lingering on the soft skin bared by her lime-colored summer dress.

"How lovely you are," he said, a note of quiet wonder in his voice. The wine was poured and he'd approved it so the waiter would leave them in peace. His eyes seemed to caress her, and a lovely tingle of awareness and pleasure traveled down her body.

The problems and tensions of the past several days faded as she sat across from him, and they chatted and laughed over inconsequential things as their dinner was served, admiring the view, speculating over where the boats outside were heading.

"I followed Dr. Kendrick's advice and went to see the hypnotherapist he recommended," Annie finally confided over dessert. "His name is Steve Munro. You probably know him."

It was sort of a weird experience.

She rattled on for several minutes, relating details of the hypnotic session before she realized that David wasn't saying anything. He was frowning a little, so she stopped the free flow of words.

"What's the matter, David?"

"I should have guessed that Kendrick might suggest something like hypnosis. I remember now we got in quite an argument about it one day. I have to admit it's not a treatment I agree with, Annie. And neither do a great many medical people. There's a lot of controversy surrounding its use, outside of strictly controlled instances."

Annie felt a twinge of irritation. "Well, it's far too soon to tell whether it'll help my neck or not, but certainly the doctors didn't have much else to recommend, except good old painkillers. My attitude is, if hypnosis will help, I'll use it."

"The problem is," David began to explain, "they're starting to use all sorts of questionable hypnotic techniques, like…"

The raucous sound of the beeper in his pocket startled them both. David got to his feet. "Annie, excuse me. I'll have to find a telephone."

She was aware of the sudden tension in his body and voice as he asked directions of the waiter and hurried off.

THE NEXT FIFTEEN MINUTES were frenzied. David strode back to her, and explained that there was an emergency and they'd have to leave, right away.

He paid the bill and they all but ran to the parking garage. Once they were in the car, he sketched in what had happened earlier that day, explaining the problems Charlie was having. "With kids like this, poisons build up in the bloodstream as the liver malfunctions and enlarges. We figured we had a bit of time with Charlie, but now it seems the process has suddenly accelerated, heaven only knows why." He reached across and touched her arm, caressing it lightly with his fingertips.

"Honey, I'm sorry about this, but the resident feels the little guy's in serious difficulty. We've been in touch with the medical center in Pittsburgh. They're frantically trying to locate a donor organ, and we have a plane standing by. Our Canadian centers have nothing suitable. Anyhow, we have to stabilize Charlie before he can even be flown down. I'll make arrangements for a taxi to take you home once we're at the hospital."

An hour later, Annie knew she ought to have done what David had suggested and taken a cab home, but still she lingered in the bright waiting room on the ward, where a young resident had been waiting for them.

He and David had hurried down the hallway and disappeared, and Annie had been about to use the phone for a taxi when she saw an impossibly young woman come out of the intensive-care unit into which David had disappeared.

Annie watched as she stood in the hallway for a few moments, leaning against the wall with her head down. Then she made her way into the waiting room and took a seat on the lounge where Annie was sitting.

Her pale blond hair and thin face and body made her seem fragile. She looked the way Maggie might in a few years, with her round blue eyes and pretty, dainty features.

She wore a faded cotton skirt and a pink shirt, and she was crying silently, her face an impassive mask as the tears dripped down her cheeks and off her chin. She sniffed once or twice, and swiped at her face with her open palm.

Annie dug into her purse and produced a small pack of tissues. She extracted several and handed them over. The girl took them without looking at Annie, wiping her face and blowing her nose like a dutiful child.

A nurse appeared in the doorway. "Mrs. Vance, it's going to be a while before you can go in again. The doctors are busy with Charlie just now. Why don't you go to the cafeteria and get a bite to eat? I'll come down for you if there's any change at all."

Mrs. Vance shook her head. The fear in her eyes was naked and horrifying when she looked up at the nurse. Charlie's mother.

She didn't look old enough to be anyone's mother, but her utter aloneness made Annie want to reach out and put her arms around her. She felt an overwhelming affinity for the young woman, a deep sense of kinship and a helpless need to do something . . . anything . . . to help her, comfort her.

She was a mother, too. What if it were Jason, or Maggie, or Paula, in that room down the hall?

Annie shuddered and swallowed hard. Her own eyes were damp.

"Excuse me," she said at last in a soft voice, after the nurse had gone. "My name is Annie. I came with Dr. Roswell. I'm not . . . not a medical person or anything, but I'm a mother, too. Won't you let me get you a coffee, maybe, or a sandwich?"

The woman looked at her, and tried for a quavery smile. She failed, and reached for the tissues again to mop her face more thoroughly this time.

"Gee, I can't stop crying. I'm so scared. You, you're Dr. Roswell's wife?" Her voice was soft but full of reverence for anyone who knew David.

"He's such a wonderful doctor," she went on, gulping her sobs back. "He's been really good to us. I'm Linda Vance. I don't think I could stand all this, with . . . with Charlie, I mean, if Dr. Roswell weren't here for him. I just have so much faith in him. But it's so hard to know what to do. Like I keep thinking I should have seen that Charlie was sick sooner, y'know?" She bit her lip hard before she could continue. "I should have brought him here to Dr. Roswell right away . . ."

Annie hurried to explain that she wasn't married to David, but was a friend. She added that she, too, thought he was a great doctor, and that he'd told her what a fine boy Charlie was, what a personality he had.

Linda did smile at that, a tender, maternal smile. She drew a dog-eared photo out of the pocket of her skirt and held it out to Annie.

"This is him on his second birthday. I swear he was born smiling that way. He's so spunky, that little kid. He's had to go through so much in just two years."

Her face crumpled, and Annie saw the cost of love and fear and worry in the deep marks beside the wide eyes, the ridges around the tender mouth.

"Charlie can be hurting real bad and yet he's always got a smile for everybody. Dr. Roswell says Charlie has what it takes to come through all this. He says if we can only hold on till there's a liver available...."

For the first time, Annie truly understood the frightful burden of trust placed on David. *Doctor, make him well. I know you can, I have to believe you can, because I have nothing else to cling to. How did David stand it,* the wordless haunting plea in eyes like Linda's?

Shaken, Annie could only encourage Linda to talk about Charlie, and then about her new baby girl, Angela.

It was significant that Linda didn't reveal what David had already told Annie, that Angela was in the same danger Charlie was. Instead the pale young woman talked about Enderby, the small interior town she came from.

Linda had been born there, gone to school and married her high-school sweetheart, Rudy Vance. Rudy was a truck driver, but was taking night school courses to better himself, she said with pride.

A tiny bit of the awful tension in the young woman's body eased as she talked in a steady stream. "Rudy's mother offered to keep Angela, so Rudy's coming down. He's driving. We couldn't afford for both of us to fly. He won't get here till late tonight. It's so much easier if he's here with me," she sighed.

Annie went for coffee and sandwiches, and brought them back on a tray. Linda drank the coffee and barely nibbled at the sandwich. There were huge dark rings under her eyes, and finally she nodded off to sleep while Annie was telling her about the books she wrote.

Annie got up and found a phone in the hallway. She called Cleo, outlined what had happened and asked her friend if she'd mind checking on Jason.

"I'm sure he's fine. Probably he's already gone to bed. But I'm liable to be lots later than I planned."

"I'll bring him over here for the night. He likes sleeping in a sleeping bag down in the TV room. Don't worry about him, Annie."

Annie made her way back to the room where Linda was now slumped in a heap across the arm of the sofa, still asleep.

Picking up a magazine, Annie flipped through the glossy pages, hoping that Linda would rest for a while. But it was only fifteen minutes before the nurse who'd been in before appeared, hesitated and sighed, and then gently touched Linda's arm.

"Mrs. Vance, Dr. Roswell wants you to come back in now."

Linda leaped up and staggered, her eyes wild, and the nurse had to hold her arm until she regained her balance.

"Is . . . is he better?"

Annie noted that the nurse avoided the question, listing instead what was being done for the boy in medical terms that Linda obviously found familiar.

It sounded formidable.

Linda hurried down the corridor, and Annie waited.

Time passed, more than an hour.

Then, activity increased. Nurses and several doctors swept past, disappearing into Charlie's room.

It was much later when a flurry of activity startled Annie out of a half doze. Dread filled her when a nurse half ran down the corridor, and another accompanied her back through the swinging doors. After an interminable period, doctors and other medical personnel began to pass the waiting-room door. They were leaving the intensive-care area where Charlie was.

They were all ominously silent, shoulders slumped, expressions strained, and now there was no urgency to their gait.

Annie felt nauseated and her blood pounded in her ears. She paced the hall as more time passed and it seemed she couldn't get air deeply into her lungs.

It was after three before David appeared. His curly hair was on end, and his face looked haggard. "One of the nurses told me you were still waiting," he said, his voice was rough and strained. "You shouldn't have. Anyway, let's go now."

Annie could hardly make the words come out.

"Charlie Vance? Is— How—"

She stopped and looked at David's face. It was stiff and unyielding, as if the muscles underneath were frozen in place.

"We lost him," David said with awful calm. "Nothing we did helped. It's like that sometimes."

The terse words knifed into Annie.

"Oh, God, David, that's terrible. But Linda, his mother. I was talking to her a while ago. I should go talk to her."

And say what? What words or actions could possibly help that fragile girl now?

"We had to sedate her. One of the nurses is with her. Her husband should be here soon." David's harsh tone softened a little, "There's nothing to be done, Annie. Absolutely nothing, believe me. Let's go now.' "

He walked ahead of her toward the elevators, and stood, hands thrust into trouser pockets, jingling his keys, during the ride down. He didn't say anything, and he didn't look directly at Annie even once. He seemed lost in his thoughts, faraway and impassive.

It had started to rain outside, a dismal, typically Vancouver downpour that obscured the windshield when they pulled out of the underground garage. The lighted parking areas around the hospital looked forlorn and eerie; the gray streets were nearly deserted in the early dawn.

Annie thought about Linda's husband, young and frightened, driving alone through this wet darkness, perhaps getting lost in the strangeness of the huge city, still unaware that his baby son was gone.

She remembered a time when Jason was about three, and she'd just moved from one apartment to another. She didn't know anyone in the new building, and the first night there, Jason had run a fever that had gone higher and higher despite all her frantic sponging with cool water and dosing with baby aspirin. Her telephone wasn't connected yet, and she had had to bang on a neighbor's door and ask if she could use theirs. The neighbor was old and angry at being awakened.

She'd called her doctor, but he was away. The doctor taking his calls was obviously at a party, and considered her a panicky bore.

"If you think it's necessary, take the child to emergency," he'd finally directed impatiently when she tried to explain how frightened she was.

She'd spent the night holding Jason in an apartment where everything was still in boxes, bathing him, agonizing over whether or not to awaken the neighbor again in order to call a cab. It meant taking her baby out in the freezing rain, and probably waiting for hours in the chaotic frenzy of a big city emergency unit. What if she did, and Jason got a chill?

What if she didn't, and he died in a convulsion?

That had been one of the loneliest nights of her entire life, and it came to symbolize for her the magnitude of being solely responsible for a child.

Linda and her young husband must be feeling just that way about their children, Annie knew, except that their problems were much greater than Annie's had been with Jason.

David drove the sleek gray car fast, braking hard at stoplights, squealing the tires around corners, making Annie's heart race as he dodged recklessly around even the few cars that were on the streets at this hour.

She bit her tongue and swallowed the words of caution she longed to say.

He pulled up in front of Annie's house and left the engine running. "Won't you come in, David?" she asked. "I'll make you coffee or something to eat." She needed to talk.

He shook his head, one decisive shake.

"Can't, Annie. Sorry. I'll call tomorrow." He reached across and touched her cheek with his fingers, but that was all. No eye contact, nothing except the controlled quiet voice.

Defeated, let down, Annie got out and made her way up to the door. As soon as it was unlocked and she had stepped inside, David roared away, his taillights disappearing as he careened around the corner.

Annie felt empty. She slumped against the door, tears burning behind her eyes. But then a mixture of total frustration, sorrow and nameless rage began to build inside of her.

How dare David close her out this way? How could he pretend to care for her and then the first time something like this came along, something terrible that affected him deeply, how could he just lock her out of his emotions, drive her home and tear off the way he'd just done? Didn't he think she had any feelings about what had happened that night?

She tore up the stairwell and into her bedroom. In a kind of frenzy, she stripped off her dress, her high sandals and her panty hose. The delicate hose ripped and she threw them violently to the floor.

She was shaking with the force of her anger. She tore off her bra and panties, stormed into the bathroom and started a tub of water running. Her eyes were hot and dry, and her breath came in short, angry gasps.

He'd done this before, hurried off and left her to deal with her emotions alone.

She didn't stop to wonder when.

It took several moments before she was aware that someone was leaning on the front doorbell. She turned the water off and listened.

Then she grabbed the worn blue robe hanging on the hook behind the bathroom door and wrapped it any which way around her.

She didn't remember going down the stairs, or unlocking the door so David could burst in. She only knew that he was kissing her all over her face, wild kisses that tasted of her tears and his agony. The smell and feel and taste of him engulfed her.

He used one arm to shove the door shut behind them.

"Annie, my Annie, I need you." The words were torn from him, raw and full of pain.

"Jason's next door for the night," Annie managed to whisper.

Somehow they climbed the stairs, his arms still locked around her.

CHAPTER ELEVEN

ANNIE LED THE WAY into her bedroom, his hand in hers.

The small lamp she'd turned on earlier revealed her clothing, tossed at random across the bed and on the floor, ivory bikini panties, matching lacy bra, satin slip...she'd forgotten about tearing them off and throwing them everywhere.

It was embarrassing.

She made a move to gather some of it up, but David's arms came around her from behind, holding her with fierce strength against his body, shoving her loose hair aside and bending his mouth to her neck. His lips burned a trail across the tender flesh, and his breath was hot and urgent in her ear.

"Love me, Annie. Just love me, please love me...."

She turned into his embrace, her lips opening to him, longing to heal the damage this night had inflicted on each of them.

There was reassurance in the surging heat that traveled through her body, in the answering passion conveyed by his hands, his mouth, the hard pressure of his erection against her abdomen.

The edge of the bed was pressing against the back of her legs, and Annie allowed herself to collapse onto it, squirming backward until her whole body was stretched out, waiting.

"Come to me," she whispered, and David seemed to strip in one graceful motion. Shirt, pants, shoes, underwear came off and joined her own discarded garments on the rug.

She gazed at him, reveling in his beauty, remembering...

He was finely made, long, sinewy bones knit together with elegant grace, overlaid with smooth muscle and tawny skin. His chest had a curly, dark mat of hair, and his need for her was evident in the swollen, pulsing maleness that thrust from the apex of his thighs.

He knelt over her, cupping her face in his palms, and the tip of his tongue closed each eyelid in turn with a soft, exotic caress that then traveled down the length of her nose, and outlined her lips with careful, erotic attention to the deep indentations that bracketed her mouth. He nuzzled her chin, trailed his mouth, hot and wet, down her throat, and made her wriggle and sigh with impatience before his mouth again captured hers, tongue promising.

Her body filled with hot liquid desire. She could sense the female parts of her swelling, opening, lips parting to welcome him. But he forced her to wait.

He unknotted the belt at the waist of her robe, and when the garment fell free of her heated body, he slid his hands under the lapels, his long, sure fingers exploring her swollen breasts with tender, teasing strokes and easing the robe off at the same time.

She gasped and he lowered his head, again using his tongue and his lips to suckle and tug and tantalize.

"Annie, my dearest Annie, beautiful Annie...."

He knew exactly when her nipples began an agonized throbbing, linked in some invisible fashion to the burning pulse hammering at the core of her body, and he slid his hand down to the soft nest at her thighs, his fingers parting her with gentle intent and finding the bud that at first seemed too sensitive for even his sure touch.

She cried out, and he gentled her with soothing noises that made words unnecessary.

He released her wetness and stroked it up over her, making the movement of his fingers like satin slipping over velvet. He knew the exact pressure she needed at all the right moments, slow, soft, indistinct; then firmer, more direct, faster...and all the time his mouth rehearsed the movement of his fingers, drawing the hardened tips of her nipples one by one deep into his mouth, flicking with his tongue, wetting and drawing, releasing, until she felt the knot of orgasm beginning to come undone deep within her.

She wanted him to go on, more than she could ever remember wanting anything. She needed him to suck the engorged nipples, torture her until release came.

Her body thrust up toward him, helpless with hunger, and she moaned, out of control. It was her turn to beg, "David, please, love me...."

"David?"

She opened her eyes and stared up at his face, unable to form other words that would tell him of her delight, of the burning need that soared in her.

His eyes seemed to have become darker, the pupils huge and almost drowning out the surrounding blue. Deep lines etched his face into stark and bony elegance, lines which might have been agony but were instead the marks of rapture.

In the midst of her craving she felt replete, because he'd forgotten everything but her. In the universe, there was only the two of them.

She moved her legs farther apart, inviting him, and in one surging motion, he lowered himself and thrust high and deep into her body. She drew him still farther with her muscles, enclosing him with her legs. And almost at once, she felt the scalding spurt of his fluid begin. Now his motions were also without control, his body taut and melded with her own, his sobs echoing those rising from her throat. His wild and savage thrusting exactly matched the depths of her hunger, and finding the elusive pinnacle they sought was the easiest of tasks.

He sought her mouth at the last instant, locking her lips to his so the primeval sound they made seemed to issue from one throat.

After an endless time, he rolled them to one side, cradling her.

"Annie. I love you more than I dreamed possible," he murmured, and for a long while they rested in silence, floating in and out of sleep.

She could tell exactly when the tension began to build in him, when the euphoria of their lovemaking faded a bit and the devastating memories of Charlie's death crept back.

"I'm ashamed," he finally said, just as if they'd been involved in a long and complex conversation.

"Ashamed of what?" She waited, feeling the tension build in her as well.

"Oh, of being a doctor, and not being able to do more than I did tonight." He smashed a sudden, violent fist into the mattress, and she jumped.

Rage and grief and impotence mingled in his low, passionate words. "If we just had a damned transplant center here in Vancouver, the way we ought to. We've got an organ bank.... Maybe the boy would still have died, but I'd feel as if I'd done more for him and his parents than just promise and not deliver. I'm ashamed of our limitations, Annie, because they're not necessary. We could do better. We have to do better."

He sat up, shoulders slumped forward, still holding her hand, but alone now with his thoughts, his mouth curved into a bitter, sardonic line. "I failed those people tonight. I failed Charlie."

Annie sat up beside him. "David, you did everything possible for him. No one can work miracles. Those parents are aware of that."

Beneath the reason and the quiet assurance she offered him, a torrent of emotion was building inside her, feelings Annie didn't want to explore, couldn't explore just now.

David was telling her he felt like a failure. He'd been Charlie's doctor, he'd had a long-standing relationship with the boy and his parents, and he had every right to be this disturbed over the boy's death. Annie felt that her role ought to be simply that of comforting and loving David.

But the truth was, she felt like a failure, too. Charlie's death had affected her, bringing to the surface feelings that had been building in her for days, and striking at the fragile framework of her love for Jason, her role as a mother, her thoughts about death, her feelings about life.

The truth was, Jason's eager joy at meeting Michael was tearing Annie to bits. She felt betrayed, deserted. She felt the same sense of failure that David was feeling, and she tried to stifle it because it seemed trivial in comparison to his.

The deepest fear a parent had was that a child would die, because death was the final loss, the cruelest of all. But Annie realized there were other losses besides death. There was, for instance, the pain of having a son transfer his love and loyalty to a stranger, a man who'd accidentally fathered him fourteen years before.

"We train ourselves not to become emotionally involved with patients, because of this very thing," David was saying. "But damn it all, it happens anyway. I cared about Charlie, I…" His voice broke, and he cleared his throat gruffly, reaching out with a tortured groan and pulling Annie into his arms.

"I'm sorry, love, going on like this. I never intended our first time together to be anything but joyful. I've dreamed of holding you, making love with you, laughing together. Not this way."

Annie pressed her cheek against his chest, willing away the storm building inside her.

"Tears count every bit as much as laughter," she managed to say, and then the burning ache in her chest erupted, and violent sobs tore from her throat.

"Annie, don't." David clasped her tight against him, cursing aloud as she wept on and on. "Sweetheart, I shouldn't have let you stay there tonight. I should've seen to it you went home. It wasn't fair to expose you to all that. It's my work, I've had more experience at handling it than you." He swore again.

Annie pulled herself away from him, drawing the sheet up and locking her arms around her knees against the torrent of emotion.

"It's not...it's not—just—Char-Charlie," she managed to choke out. "It's...oh, damn, it's Jason, and all...all the things that have been happening."

Unable to stop herself, she blurted out how the past hours had made her feel—her awful, helpless compassion for Linda, and her realization that her own role as a mother was changing, that she was losing Jason.

As if a dam had burst, she spilled out the problems of the past few days, the awful way Jason had been acting and the reasons for it, her own reluctance to let Michael be involved in his son's life.

David listened.

He stopped her several times to ask puzzled questions, and Annie realized how little she'd confided in him. She found herself having to go back to the beginning, describe in detail the battles she'd had with Michael over custody, her very real fear of him, the horror of the court battles fought to keep her son.

"Now Michael's taking Jason anyway, without any effort. Jason's made it plain he wants to be with his father, and it hurts." She knew she sounded hysterical.

"Come here," David said, and she allowed herself to be drawn into his embrace.

"Love isn't a limited quantity, Annie," he said with quiet assurance, holding her and stroking his hand up and down her back in a soothing gesture. "Just because Jason wants to know his father doesn't mean he's going to stop loving you."

She nodded. She knew with her brain it was true. Her heart didn't seem to agree.

"It's just that seeing Michael again reinforced all the bad feelings I have about him. I still don't trust him, and I don't like the thought of him being around me or Jason. The feeling hasn't changed even after all these years. He gives me the creeps."

"Give it time, Annie."

They were quiet for a while, exhausted, empty of emotion. Gradually David's stroking became more purposeful, and once again shivers of longing soared in Annie. This time, their loving was less desperate than before.

As the hours of the night gave way to dawn, they loved again and again, and with the physical joining came peace and a measure of self-forgiveness.

"HOW COME Dr. Roswell's car was out in front of our house all night?"

Annie was making toast, and Jason's question caught her unawares. David had left shortly after five that morning because Annie had wanted to avoid this very thing with her son. David had seemed to understand.

It was now ten-fifteen, and Jason had been home for an hour. Why hadn't he said something before now?

"His car was here because David spent the night here, Jason."

"So I guess he's gonna be around here all the time from now on, then. Are you gonna live with him or just have an affair?" Annie held on to her patience, forcing a reasonable calm in her voice that she didn't feel, and doing her best to ignore the aggressive and insulting tone Jason was using.

"We're just close friends, Jason. For the moment that's about it."

"You wouldn't marry him, would you, Mom?" There was a plaintive appeal in his voice. "I mean, then I'd have a stepfather. Yuck."

Annie's patience slipped a bit. It wasn't easy to vocalize something she hadn't allowed herself to even dream about.

"Adults do get married, Jason. Just because I never have doesn't mean I'm never going to. But at the moment, I haven't any plans."

"Well, I hope if you ever do, it's not Dr. Roswell I get as a stepfather."

Annie's control snapped. "Jason, that's enough."

Knowing he'd gone too far, Jason slid out from the table and headed for back door. "I'm gonna cut the grass until it's time to get ready to go meet my father."

"Right. That's a good idea." Annie smeared apricot jam on her toast and felt like collapsing as she slammed the door behind him. She heard him whistling as he rummaged in the shed for the push mower.

She took one bite out of the toast, and dropped the rest in the garbage, resting her head in her hands and fighting tears.

The events of the past night had left her drained. The lovemaking she and David had shared was overpowering, frightening, because it marked the beginning of a drastic change in their relationship.

Before, Annie could still pretend that her soul wasn't linked with David Roswell's, that the insistent sense of destiny she had about him was just the product of a writer's fertile imagination.

This morning, that rationale was impossible.

She belonged to David, heart, soul and body, and that was that, which raised a whole lot of questions she didn't have answers for.

Questions such as whether or not she could override the convictions she had about staying single, and marry him. What kind of father figure could David be to Jason when Jason made it clear he hated him?

What the hell was she going to do about that kid?

"SO THE POOR little boy died. God, Annie." Cleo's eyes were swimming with tears, and Annie felt herself choke up again at the painful images the conversation was evoking. She'd been telling Cleo what had happened the night before at the hospital, and the telling was painful.

It was afternoon. Annie had dropped Jason off at the McCraes' around noon, and it had been traumatic, not only for her, but also for Jason. He'd showered without being nagged, changed his striped rugby shirt twice before they left the house, and made a touching effort to smooth down his unruly shock of hair. The boy was in a state of near hysteria on the long drive across town.

Michael had been waiting out in front of the apartment, and Annie didn't want to see any more than she had to of the first meeting between him and Jason. She dropped her son off and drove away, tears blurring her vision.

It was stupid, but she felt as if she were delivering her beloved son into the hands of the enemy.

Now several hours later, she was peeling apples in Cleo's kitchen. The mother of one of Cleo's day care youngsters had given her a bushel of late apples, and Annie had offered to help peel and make applesauce.

It was therapeutic, the kind of mindless busywork that Annie welcomed today. She'd tried and failed to write even one page of her book. Images of Michael, of Jason, of Linda Vance, and always, superimposed on everything, of David loving her, intruded between her and the computer screen until she'd turned the machine off and escaped next door.

"The thing is," Cleo said now, "the whole time you were talking, I've been thinking about this organ donor thing. It's really tough to figure out whether or not I'd be able to donate my kids' bodies for organs if something happened to them. My own body, fine. But my kids'? I'm not sure I could carry through with that."

"I know. Reason tells you it's the only ting to do, but I'd find it hard if it were Jason. But then last night, I saw it from the other side, from the point of view of a child needing the transplant if he were to live."

"I'm gonna have to give this lots of thought. It's exactly like the emergency fund I started," Cleo said. "It's something you ought to set up ahead of time. Heaven forbid we'd ever have to make the decision about organ donation, Annie, but it's better made when you're calm."

Annie couldn't help but consider all the decisions she'd had to make the past week; meeting Michael again, dealing with Jason, taking the final step in loving David. She couldn't say she'd been calm about any of them.

And then there was the pain in her neck. It was driving her nuts again this morning.

They worked in silence for a time, slicing and peeling.

"Cleo, what do you know about hypnosis?"

"Hypnosis?" Cleo shrugged and tossed a long strip of apple peel into the garbage bag, then dumped her basin of apples into the huge kettle steaming on the stove. "I've read the odd thing, and once a couple of years ago I went to see that show— you know the guy who hypnotizes people on the stage? It was kind of scary. Embarrassing and silly, too, because the people he called up out of the audience sang and did dumb things they'd never have ordinarily done."

"I'm going to that hypnotist they recommended for my neck pain," Annie admitted. "Actually he's called a hypnotherapist. I've only been once, but I'm going again next Tuesday. He says that stage hypnotists abuse the real power of hypnosis, and exploiting it as a game can be dangerous."

"Ask him if it's possible to hypnotize a person into believing that the cellulite on her butt is actually an aphrodisiac to a lover, and I'll make an appointment."

"You're a hopeless case," Annie said. "Truthfully I'm not at all sure if I want to try this, but there isn't anything else, and I'm sick of this miserable pain."

"So if there's a chance it will help, like I told you before, go for it. But I want to know every last detail of every last visit, starting with the one you already made. Start talking, pal."

Cleo's blatant curiosity made Annie smile, the first time she'd felt like smiling all day.

"This first session, did it help at all?"

Annie shrugged. "It's too soon to tell, but my neck has felt better until this morning. I just started treatments a couple days ago." She explained in detail exactly what Dr. Munro had said and done and Cleo listened with avid attention.

"Is this Munro good-looking?"

"Nope, and he wears a big fat wedding ring as well, and his wife works in the office. But he's the easiest person to be around, really laid-back and accepting of everything. Open. He makes you feel safe and secure."

"Lord, I wish I'd meet an eligible man who's uncomplicated and offered me security and sex. The ones I fall for are so damned unreliable."

"So who have you fallen for lately, Cleo?" Annie's question was flippant, teasing.

Cleo tossed the paring knife down on the pile of apple peelings and slumped back on her chair with a morose expression on her face.

"It's the cop I told you about, Don Anderson. The one whose wife left him to care for their baby? He came by that day and we had coffee. I figured Don would go on and on about this bitch who walked out on him, real bitter, you know, but he never said a word beyond mentioning that he's started divorce proceedings. We got talking about his work instead, the people he meets.... He's got a great sense of humor, and he's kind of shy and gentle. He's maybe six feet tall, and really strong—big muscles. And he's got this thick blond hair and green eyes. And I fell in love with the baby. He's the sweetest little guy! His name is Ben. He smiles at you all the time. And now Don's asked me out for dinner next week."

Annie felt out of breath just listening. "So where's the problem?"

"There are two dandies. One, Don's twenty-four years old and you know I'm thirty-two. Now I know Mary Tyler Moore's made a success of the older woman, younger man relationship, but she's cute and petite and rich. I am none of the above. By the time I'm forty I'll probably look forty-five. I don't have money or time enough for maintenance stuff like collagen creams or, heaven forbid, plastic surgery." Cleo's litany was humorous, but underneath it Annie sensed real turmoil.

"And he'd be what when I'm forty?" Cleo continued. "The age I am now, thirty-two. Sexy, macho, dealing every day with bimbos who trade off sex for a canceled parking ticket."

"Cleo, that's ridiculous."

"Maybe so, but that's not even all. See, Annie, I don't want to get mixed up with a cop, for Pete's sake. Have you any idea how many cops have been shot in the line of duty over the past year or two? Granted, Vancouver isn't Chicago, but there's still a high element of danger. I had one exciting, dangerous, disappearing man in my life and I don't want another one, for any reason. I couldn't stand it." She pursed her lips. "Why I couldn't have married a nice steady, reliable, boring guy the first time is beyond me, but no, I had to have excitement. Next time, I want a marriage that I can count on. I couldn't stand sending a man off to work and spending all day worrying over whether or not he's getting shot at."

"So when did this Don ask you to marry him?"

Cleo stared at Annie as if she'd gone berserk.

"He didn't, you imbecile. I've only known him a week. He hasn't even kissed me, although once there we were breathing pretty hard when I handed Ben over."

Annie held out sticky hands, palms up. "I rest my case. The poor guy asks you out for one innocent, enjoyable evening, and you've got him married off to a forty-year-old hag who lost her bottle of moisturizer as well as her sense of humor."

Cleo threw a handful of peelings at Annie's head, and they both started to laugh.

It felt wonderful.

ANNIE WENT HOME SOON, but that conversation with Cleo lingered in her mind.

It was ironic, but she was guilty of doing exactly the same thing she'd accused Cleo of, crossing bridges before they even appeared.

She was anticipating all sorts of problems with Jason over this meeting with his father. Instead she ought to just go along and deal with problems as they arose, instead of creating them in her imagination, she lectured herself.

And she ought to do exactly the same thing with what was happening between her and David.

HE CALLED just as she was about to drop off to sleep that night. She'd listened to the tapes Dr. Munro had given her, so her body was limp and relaxed, her mind in neutral.

"Hi, gorgeous," David said when she mumbled hello. "I wanted you to know I've thought of you all day. I was over at the hospital with the Vances most of the morning. I called this afternoon but you weren't home."

"I was over at Cleo's. I thought about you too, David."

"Listen, I've got two heavy days at work, Monday and Tuesday. But I wondered if you could take Wednesday afternoon off and spend it with me?"

"I'd love that."

They chatted on. David asked about Jason's visit with his father.

"He was really quiet when he came home tonight," Annie related, a trace of worry edging her voice. "I thought he'd be going on and on about what a wonderful time he had, but he didn't say very much at all, except that his father seemed 'okay,' Lili seemed 'okay,' and the dinner they had was 'okay.'"

Annie hadn't known what to make of Jason's reticent mood.

"It's pretty difficult, meeting someone you've only imagined. Maybe Jason's having a tough time adjusting to the real person."

It made sense, and it relieved Annie's concern somewhat.

They talked then about the night they'd spent together, lovers' words that they both needed to hear and say, affirmations that what had happened between them was new in both their experiences.

Before they hung up, David said, "Annie, I love you very much. I'm so glad I found you."

"I'm glad, too. I love you, David."

She hung up and began the slide down into sleep, warm and full of emotion.

I'm glad I found you, he'd said. She was glad, too, that he'd found her...again.

ANNIE'S APPOINTMENT with Dr. Munro was for 9:00 a.m., Tuesday morning. She was there ten minutes early, and this time it felt easy to walk into the cluttered office. Edith greeted her like an old friend and offered her a cup of coffee, which Annie accepted gratefully.

Steve Munro was just as disheveled as he'd been the first time, and just as easygoing. He was finishing a Danish pastry when he called Annie into his inner office, and his shirt—yellow today—had a small coffee stain down the front. He brushed crumbs off his jacket, missing half of them.

"We'll try age regression again, Annie, and see if we can find the specific time in your life when this bothersome pain first affected you."

Annie took her place in the reclining chair, and was guided through the relaxing techniques, which were becoming familiar from the tapes.

"Let go. Relax. Permit all tensions and anxieties to flow out of the body..."

Steve's voice droned on, and Annie felt herself letting go, slipping into a detached, floating trance.

"Relax more deeply..."

Annie felt herself dropping easily into a deep and utterly peaceful state.

"Imagine yourself getting on a train, Annie. Take a seat facing the rear."

Annie could see herself stepping up the high step, she could smell the faintly musty smell of the coach. She sat down in one of the seats, facing the back of the train.

"Outside the window is a sign with today's date on it."

Annie looked, and the sign was there.

"The train is starting to move. Now there's another sign with yesterday's date . . ."

The signs flashed past. The train built speed. The past dates went by faster and faster.

"Stop at the scene where the problem with your neck origi-nated, Annie."

She could hear the instructions, coming from a great dis-tance. But she couldn't stop.

The signposts were blurring, the train was hurtling her through time and space at a speed she couldn't control.

And then Steve's voice faded, and she was falling head over heels, down and down a long, dark tunnel.

CHAPTER TWELVE

STEVE MUNRO FROWNED as Annie gave a frightened, drawn-out cry and then was silent.

"Annie, you're perfectly safe. Stop at the time the pain in your neck began," he repeated again, watching her with a frown.

She gave no sign that she'd heard him.

She'd dropped spontaneously into what was known as third-stage hypnosis, where the subject has no memory of what is said by the hypnotist. Annie was proving to be a deep-trance subject.

Watching her every moment, Steve leaned over to the nearby desk and pressed a button, turning on the tape recorder he kept there.

Wherever Annie was, she'd likely be interested in hearing about it when she awoke. As he turned back to his patient, he was startled to find that her eyes were open and she was sitting up, although she was obviously not seeing him or the office.

Instead her gaze was inward, staring hard at some scene invisible to him.

"Annie, tell me where you are." He repeated the demand several times with no effect. But what happened next sent a shiver of excitement down Steve's back.

The voice his patient replied in was deeper and more throaty than that which she normally used, and her diction was different as well.

"My name's not Annie, it's Bernadette. Bernadette Desjardins. How is it that you don't know my name?"

There was a trace of irritation in the statement.

Steve studied her, uncertain of what was happening or exactly how he should proceed.

"My mistake. From now on it will be Bernadette," he apologized.

She nodded, and settled herself with precise little movements, more comfortably on the couch. There was a subtle difference now in her body movements. Annie was graceful and moved with deliberation. Bernadette had a quick, impatient way of moving.

"Now, umm, Bernadette..." Steve debated what to ask that would best reveal where the scene she was obviously watching might be taking place.

"Can you tell me what clothes you're wearing?"

She was aware of the voice, coming from a distant place. She felt a need to answer it, although she wasn't certain why. "What I'm wearing? Why, my everyday clothing, of course," she said. "The old brown skirt with the pockets, this pale yellow blouse that I made, oh, two summers ago. It's faded now." She looked down at her feet, and noticed the heavy work boots she hadn't taken off yet.

"Oh, these boots, soiled from the barnyard. I must take them off." She bent and went through the motions of tugging them off, grimacing at the dirt that clung to her fingers. She appeared to peel off some stockings and rubbed her hands down her skirt before pulling something soft over her feet.

"How old are you, Bernadette Desjardins?"

Such strange questions. She thought about it. Strange, not to be certain of her age. But it came to her after a moment.

"Well, I was born in 1892, and this is 1917. So I am twenty-five, yes?"

"Where do you live?"

Really, this was quite ridiculous, and her voice reflected her irritation. "I'm at home, here on my farm in Normandy, where I've lived since I was born."

"You're not married, then?"

The questions were disturbing, and for an instant, she tried to juggle the two realities occupying her mind, the dreamlike knowledge that it was Steve asking her these things, that Bernadette was the vision and Annie the reality. But the effort was too great.

Bernadette triumphed.

"Of course I'm married. I have a child."

"How long have you been married?"

She sighed. "Oh, forever. It seems forever. I was just eighteen. Too young to marry."

There was a deep sadness in the response. She hadn't really wanted to marry Jean Desjardins, but what choice was there? Her parents were old and poor, and there was no chance of going to Paris, to art school, as she'd dreamed of doing. When she finished all the schooling the tiny village could offer, there was little to do except work on her parents' farm and marry. It was what girls were expected to do, in this place.

She explained it as best she could, and Steve encouraged her to tell him more of the story.

"Jean was always around. He was ten years older than I, a neighbor who helped Papa when the old man couldn't manage the heavy farm work on his own anymore. Finally Papa became too sick to manage at all, and then he died. I had no brothers or sisters to help, you see, so Jean took on the full responsibility of the farm for me and my *maman*. She was difficult, *Maman*, as she grew older."

Bernadette's face was somber as she related her history.

"You fell in love with him?"

She became helpless, like a little child. Her mind was gone toward the last. She wandered away, and she had to be watched every moment. And—" she paused and shrugged, an expressive movement Steve was beginning to recognize as distinctive of Bernadette "—and Jean was always there to help me, a strong, quiet man, never saying much."

"You fell in love with him?"

She frowned and shook her head. "He represented security to me. He proposed, and with some reluctance—I'd hoped like any romantic girl that there would be more than this—I accepted."

"Was it a mistake?" Steve asked, caught up in the story.

That shrug again. "Yes, and no. How was an innocent girl to know what the needs would be of the grown woman?" Bernadette portrayed stoic acceptance. "It wasn't always good for me, no."

She brightened a little, and with a half smile added, "But how many marriages are perfect? At least I have my daughter. I was fortunate. Nicole was born after only a year, my beloved little girl. She's a joy to me. I have so many dreams for Nicole. I want her life to be different from what mine has been."

"How old is Nicole now, Bernadette?"

"Seven, last month. Lorelei…she's my friend, the village midwife…she brought me sugar so I could make Nicole a cake. We don't have much money for such things. Times are difficult. France has been at war for a long time." She shook her head. "All of Europe is at war."

1917. Steve remembered sketchy descriptions of the devastation the First World War had wrought on France.

"Is your husband home with you, or did he go off to fight?"

"Oh, he's gone. I thought you knew that. Jean resisted, but finally he had no choice. He had to go. He hated to leave us alone here. He believed the work would be too much for me."

"And is it?"

There was scorn in her voice. "No, of course not. The truth is, it was only a matter of weeks after Jean left that I began to realize I'm not nearly as lonely with him gone as I had been living with him. There's more work, but I don't mind."

She paused and added contritely, "It's probably a blessing I feel this way, because he's almost certainly dead, poor Jean. A telegram came twenty-two months ago. He was reported missing in action and by now he's presumed dead."

"Do you think you'll ever marry again?"

"Never." The denial was swift and absolute. "I've had enough of marriage to last me a lifetime. Oh, I feel bad inside, that I can't grieve properly for Jean or long to have him back again. The child misses him, and for that I'm sorry. But for myself, marriage was a mistake I'll make only once." Her mouth set in a determined expression.

"How do you live? How do you earn enough money for your needs?"

She shrugged again, that delightful Gallic shrug.

"Oh, the farm provides most of our food. There are apple trees out there in the orchard. See, through that window?"

She gestured, and Steve was so caught up in the story he almost looked where she pointed.

"There's the garden, the chickens, and the cow, of course. I sell eggs to the inn at the village, and butter as well. And I go out and do housework, cooking, cleaning, when someone has a baby and needs help for a time. I earn a bit of money that way. Lorelei gets me those jobs."

It was a scanty living at best, and making ends meet was a constant worry to her.

Steve decided to carry her along to something besides the day-to-day running of the farm.

"I want you to go ahead in time, Bernadette, to an event that's important in your life. You're moving ahead in time..."

It was confusing to her. Her thoughts seemed to blur, and when they cleared again, she was sitting in the rocking chair in the early summer evening, in the large front room of the stone cottage, singing to the freshly bathed little girl on her lap.

The child was sleeping, her dark head curled in sweet innocence against Bernadette's breasts, and outside, darkness was beginning to overcome the soft summer twilight.

Bernadette cradled the child, burying her nose in the warm, moist perfume of Nicole's hair.

She jumped, startled, when a sharp knock sounded on the front-room door, and fear made her heart beat fast.

No one she knew ever came to that door. Everyone used the kitchen door at the back. With so many soldiers around, one had to be careful.

She got to her feet, balancing Nicole's slight body, and went into the little ground-floor bedroom where the girl slept. She laid her on the narrow cot and covered her with the sheet. Bernadette smoothed her own dark brown hair back—wild curly tendrils always escaped the thick braid she fashioned each morning and coiled at the back of her neck. Then she took the steel poker from the grate and moved nervously to the door where the knocking sounded again, more insistent this time.

She opened the door only about six inches, holding the poker behind her, concealed in the folds of her skirt.

The tall young man standing there looked at her with a gentle expression, studying her for a long, silent moment before he smiled, and any fear she'd felt was gone in an instant. But her natural wariness lingered, and she peered out at him without widening the opening or dropping the poker.

A woman alone with a child couldn't be too careful.

"Excuse me, *mademoiselle*. I'm sorry to disturb you...."

He was wearing an army uniform, not French, though, with the chevrons of rank on his shoulder.

He had a delightful, crooked grin, and he snatched his hat off and held it in his hand. His face was craggy, with deep lines beside his eyes and mouth, but there was a tired grayness to his complexion.

In fact, Bernadette thought as she went on looking, his skin was pasty underneath. Exhaustion? Illness?

"I'm afraid I've managed to lose myself thoroughly...."

His French was good, but he had a strange accent, and she couldn't help but be amused by several of his expressions as he explained that he'd taken the train to Rouen and then arranged to borrow a car, planning to spend his leave at a remote country inn.

"There were a dozen crossroads, however, and I must have taken several wrong turns somewhere back there," he added, gesturing over his shoulder with his cap.

"My name is Paul Duncan, Dr. Paul Duncan," he added, smiling again. His efforts at being cheerful didn't alter the pale, sickly color that showed through the faint tan of his skin.

"American, Monsieur Duncan?" It was the first thing she'd said, and she knew she sounded wary.

"Yes, although I'm with a British medical unit, number twenty CCS. We're stationed at the Somme. I had a couple weeks leave coming, and I wanted to get completely away. It's a—" He broke off what he'd been about to say, substituting, "Call me Paul, please."

A doctor. Certainly, Bernadette was cautious about soldiers—any respectable woman living alone was—but there was something reliable about Dr. Paul Duncan.

There was also an awareness, from the beginning, that he was male and that he thought her attractive. It was in his shy, hon est glance.

She made an uncharacteristic quick decision, stepping back as she opened the door wide, setting the poker on a stool before she could see she held it.

"The inn you're looking for is quite a long distance away, Monsieur Duncan. If you come in, I'll draw a map that might help." She stood back from the door, and he came into the room.

His hair was golden and curly, mussed from the hat, cut short in the military manner. He pushed his fingers through it, setting it on edge.

It gave him an endearing boyish look.

"Thank you so much." He drew in a deep breath and added, "It smells delicious in here."

She smiled up at him, shy but pleased. She was cooking a stew for her dinner, and the fragrance filled the small stone house.

He was the most handsome man she'd ever met, and it made her more nervous than ever.

"Please, sit down." She gestured toward the broken-down sofa in the corner, and he folded his long body down to the seat, still holding his cap in one hand. He seemed to dwarf the furniture and the small room.

"You have a comfortable home, *mademoiselle*."

"*Madame*. My name is Bernadette Desjardins. My husband's name is Jean."

It was probably wise to tell him that she was married. Was she still married?

He made a polite move to get to his feet, acknowledging the introduction, but she waved him down again. "I will find a paper. Excuse me. . . ."

She hurried into the kitchen, to the drawer where the paper and pencil were kept. The stew she'd been simmering for hours bubbled on the wood stove in the corner, giving off the savory, rich odor he'd commented on, and she gave it an absentminded stir as she passed.

It would be outrageous, unthinkable, to ask him to share her simple meal.

But how wonderful it would be to sit across the table from him and talk. She loved the way he spoke, with that strange accent. Apart from Lorelei, she seldom had company for a meal.

He had the bluest eyes she'd ever seen.

Perhaps he'd tell her about America, describe it for her. . . .

No. What was she thinking?

She took the paper and went back into the other room.

He was standing at the window, his hands folded behind his back, gazing out over the fruit trees that marched in orderly rows down to the banks of the Seine, their branches laden with the promise of a good harvest in another month or so.

There was just enough of the sunset glow left to illuminate the orchard and turn the water of the river the color of brass.

"*Madame* . . . Bernadette, please, may I call you Bernadette? Your farm is the most beautiful thing I've seen in weeks. It's so peaceful here, I can hardly believe it's real. I feel as if I'm dreaming. It's hard to believe this exists, after . . ."

Again, he didn't finish the sentence. His voice died, but she knew what he meant when she looked into his face.

Horrible stories of the war and the battles of the Ypres Salient filtered through every day, even to this backwater area.

She felt her heart contract as she looked fully into his face. His eyes held an almost desperate appeal, a pain that reached past her thoughts of propriety and decorum, reached the loneliness that was her silent companion as well as his.

"It will be a long journey to the inn you want to reach, *monsieur.* Their kitchen will undoubtedly be closed. Would you..." She stumbled over her words, desperate and shy all of a sudden, horrified at her boldness. A blush crept up her neck and suffused her face. She could feel it burning all the way to her hairline.

What would he think of her? Would he think she was suggesting more than just a meal to him, here all alone as she was?

She hadn't yet told him Jean was gone.

"It's only stew, not at all fancy," she stumbled on. "Would you like to...to share supper with me before you drive on?"

His face lit up, and his tone was sincere. "There's absolutely nothing I'd like more. Thank you."

Because his pleasure was evident, she relaxed a trifle.

He took his tunic off and tossed it over the back of the sofa. In his shirtsleeves he came into the kitchen, offering to help set the table, and she handed him the plates and cutlery, careful first to spread her best embroidered cloth on the battered wooden table.

"Your husband isn't here?" He was placing the two plates and cups she'd given him on the cloth.

"No. No, he's...Jean's been gone for two years now, missing in action. I'm not—I haven't heard if he's...alive. Or not. The authorities think not. I think not, either. I would have heard before now."

"I'm sorry." The simple words were sincere. "It must be hard for you, alone here."

She shrugged. "It's not always easy, but I have my little daughter." She told him of Nicole, and made him laugh with a funny anecdote about the child.

"Where are you from in America?" she ventured next.

He described what he labeled a medium-sized town in a place called Ohio, where there were lots of farms. "My father-in-law and I have a small medical practice there."

So he was also married. The strange twinge in her chest couldn't be regret...could it?

She sliced a loaf of her heavy, dark bread, and was thankful that she'd churned earlier that day, so they had fresh, sweet butter to smear on the thick slices. Soon they were laughing and talking together like old friends over the simple meal.

In every way, they were different: language, homeland, education, experience. Yet something between them meshed to perfection. And between them was that ever-increasing awareness of each other, male to female.

The slightest brush of his hand against hers, passing a bowl, caused quivers in all the nerves of her body. And while he spoke of Paris, of the chestnut trees, of how he'd gotten hopelessly lost in the complexities of the Métro system, his wonderful eyes were telling her he found her attractive. Desirable.

It was new to her. She'd never experienced anything like this with Jean. Coupling with him had been a marital duty performed without much feeling on her part, and she'd sometimes longed for the sort of love depicted in the romantic novels Lorelei loaned her.

Every cell in her body reacted to this man. Sensations that had been dream remembrances surged into forceful reality.

She leaped up to clear the table and he helped with clumsy goodwill. "I must go and shut the door on the henhouse. I forgot earlier. There's a fox, and he's already had two of my new pullets," she explained.

"I'll come with you, and then I suppose I should be going," he said.

She checked Nicole. The child was sound asleep, and Bernadette pulled the handmade quilt higher under her little chin, pressing a kiss on her forehead.

He was waiting by the kitchen door, and they walked through the summer darkness to the shed. She secured the door, aware every moment of him, not touching her, but close at her side.

There was a moon, spilling liquid silver over the countryside. Birds called from one tree to the next. A dog barked on a neighboring farm, and the air smelled of growing things.

"Bernadette." His voice was hesitant. "Would you walk with me down by the river, just for a short way? I'd like to remember this idyllic place, when I have to go back to the front lines."

He reached out and found her hand, and the simple touch of palm to palm made her shiver.

Hand clasped in his, she guided him down through the orchard, to the path that traced the loops of the Seine, a trail she sometimes walked along in the evening.

They walked without talking, absorbing the peace and tranquillity of the silver ribbon of river and the dark trees silhouetted by the moon.

"Would you mind if I dropped by to see you on my way back from the inn?" he asked after a time. The words were polite, questioning, but there was a desperate intensity in his tone.

She ought to say no.

"I think I should like that, very much," she answered with prim decorum, while her heart beat a frantic tattoo.

And then he stopped, and put his hands on her shoulders.

"Bernadette, I have no right. We've only just met. But I think I'm falling in love with you. It happened the moment you opened that door tonight, and I saw your face, your huge gray eyes, so frightened of me."

He made a low, lost sound in his throat as his arms came around her, drawing her in to him, and then he kissed her.

It was inevitable. It was what she'd wanted from the first moment she'd laid eyes on him.

His lips opened and encompassed her, tugging at her soul, and she wanted all of him with a sudden, fierce passion she'd never dreamed existed in her traitorous body. If he'd gone on kissing her, and lowered her to the moist earth, she'd have welcomed him.

But he didn't. He drew away, and she understood the effort of will it took. She resented it.

And when he drove away a short time later, Bernadette knew that he'd be back. Soon.

HE APPEARED the very next forenoon, a trifle shamefaced when he confessed that he'd gone no farther than the nearby village, where he'd taken a room for the duration of his leave.

"How many days?" She didn't try to disguise the eagerness in her voice.

"Fourteen."

And one was already gone.

Nicole was playing with a doll when he came, and she ran to hide behind Bernadette, clutching her mother's skirt in both hands, her dark eyes huge with apprehension.

He'd brought a bottle of wine and—unheard of luxury—packets of chocolate and fancy biscuits. He set them down on the table, and then bent down so that he was at the child's level.

"Look what I've found, little one," he said, voice full of excitement, and to Bernadette's amazement, and her daughter's delight, he skillfully made it seem as if a bright red hair ribbon had unfurled from inside Nicole's ear.

"A ribbon for your pretty hair, hiding in your ear."

"How did you do that? You are a magician?," Bernadette clapped her hands with pleasure. She was as thrilled and amazed as her child.

"It's my hobby, magic," he confessed. "And I'm afraid I'm very limited at it, so don't expect much."

But the females made it plain they thought he was wonderful, and for the next fifteen minutes, he performed other tricks, using a pack of cards and ordinary things from Bernadette's kitchen to astonish and delight them.

Bernadette tied the ribbon in her daughter's hair, and from that moment on, Nicole adored him. Watching Paul with Nicole, she saw the love he had for children, the pleasure in his eyes when the shy little girl put her arms around his neck and kissed him.

Grace, his wife, was fragile and often ill, Paul explained, and so terrified of childbirth there had never been any question of their having a family.

PAUL AND BERNADETTE became lovers the second night. After that, he didn't bother going back to the inn. Time was far too precious to waste.

There was always work on the farm that had to be done, and he helped Bernadette, seeming to welcome the earthy tasks, shoveling out the manure or putting out fresh hay. He mended the door to the stable, and nailed new perches up for the chickens. Bernadette helped and Nicole ran errands, bringing a drink or more nails from the shed.

And the three of them, man, woman and child, laughed and teased and played childish games, so the work seemed nothing at all.

In the long, twilight evenings, after Nicole was asleep, they strolled along the Seine, drinking in the sunset, glorying in the growing love between them.

They made love there, under the sheltering branches of a huge old tree, cushioned by the mossy earth. All around them was the smell of growing things, and Bernadette marveled at the aching fulfillment he brought her, holding himself back until she arched and cried out.

Later, Bernadette and Paul would go up to her bedroom under the eaves. She didn't think of it as Jean's bedroom anymore, she'd been so long alone.

It belonged only to her and Paul. There they held each other and made passionate love, and they talked, hour after hour, about secret things from the depths of their beings.

She told him of her convenient marriage to Jean, and how she hadn't known what to wait for. "But then, you might never have come at all, and I wouldn't have had Nicole, so probably it was all for the best," she added with the French practicality that made him laugh.

His marriage was complicated. Grace's father, Martin Oakley, was Paul's dearest friend, an older doctor who helped Paul through medical school and then made him a partner in his practice. And somewhere along the way, it became understood that Paul would marry Grace.

"It was a mistake," Paul said with sadness in his voice. "But when there's no one you truly love, it doesn't seem to matter as much, marrying someone for other reasons. It's only later . . ."

"I know, my dearest. How well I know."

His arms came tight around her, and she pressed herself against him and thought of the innumerable nights spent sleeping in this bed with Jean, hoping that he wouldn't turn toward her.

"I felt as if part of me was dying, withering away in that tidy house, with dinner always at the same time, formally set in the dining room, and conversation that never touched on anything remotely personal. When the war began, I couldn't wait to go. That's why I volunteered with a British medical corps."

"And your father-in-law? He was not happy?"

Paul laughed, but there was a bitter undertone. "Understatement of the century—he was not happy. He was furious. We had our only serious quarrel ever. But there was nothing Martin could actually do, and eventually he agreed to run the practice until I go back."

His words evoked thoughts of his leaving, and they turned to each other yet again, searching in the solace of their passion for forgetfulness. Already, neither could bear the thought of that eventual parting, although both knew it was inevitable.

Even the days of Paul's leave were dwindling; seven, five, then three. Bernadette slept locked in his arms, and it seemed to her she'd stolen more happiness in these few days than she'd had in the rest of her life. She wanted them to go on forever.

But there was a voice in her dream . . .

"ANNIE, ANNIE PENDLETON, I'm going to count backward from fifty to zero, and with the descending numbers, you will slowly return to the present. You will leave behind the person- ality of Bernadette Desjardins. You will remember what has occurred, and remembering will be a positive impression. Fifty, forty-nine . . .''

She was far away and reluctant. She snuggled closer to Paul, trying to ignore the summons, but at last she was compelled to obey the voice.

"Thirty-eight, thirty-seven . . ."

It seemed a long time before she was aware of the office couch, her body, the figure of Steve Munro standing over her.

"Three, two, one . . ."

For an undecided moment, she wanted only to return to the bedroom of that cottage in France, to the arms of her lover. She could still feel the hot length of his body close to her. His unique male scent lingered in her nostrils. And she felt bereft, as if part of her soul had been torn away. . . .

"Zero. Annie, are you here?"

Then, distance intervened. She was fully Annie again, and she was trembling in violent spasms and starting to cry. Tears cascaded down her face, and Steve offered tissues and took her hands in his in an effort to console her.

"It's fine. You're doing so well, I'm proud of you, Annie." There was raw excitement in his voice. "Annie, how excit- ing. You regressed spontaneously into another life. You're a terrific hypnotic subject, for this to happen the way it did to- day, and after only one other session. I don't know what your views are on reincarnation—but the scenes you described were certainly vivid and real to me. Hey, you need some tea. How do you feel?"

Annie controlled the tears with a great effort, mopping her face and blowing her nose before she attempted an answer.

"I feel weird. Shaky. And cold. And I don't . . . I don't even believe in this reincarnation stuff, so how could this happen to me?"

She shivered, and Steve brought a flannel blanket and draped it over her lap, then handed her a steaming cup of sweet tea.

"Believing isn't necessary. Annie, do you understand what happened to you?"

She shook her head. "Only that I was someone else. But not really someone else, because that woman, Bernadette...I felt I was Bernadette. I know I was."

Steve nodded. "I believe you were, too, in another time frame. I do believe in reincarnation, and I've deliberately age-regressed patients before with varying degrees of success. But you surprised me. You did it so fast and all by yourself. You were phenomenal."

Annie took grateful sips of the tea, using it to wash away the tears that clogged her throat.

Steve took the tape out of the small recorder.

"When you feel up to it, listen to this. I know you remember what was happening, but it's interesting to hear yourself as you sounded to me."

She accepted the tape and tucked it into her purse. The emotions Annie had experienced as Bernadette were still vivid in her mind, and in fact seemed more important and urgent than the events occurring now.

"Why, Steve? Why do you think this happened to me?"

He was his relaxed self again, sitting at his cluttered desk drinking his own tea.

"Because I told your subconscious to go to the scene where the neck problem originated." He shrugged and grinned at her. "Obviously it didn't originate in this lifetime, so you just did as you were told and went to the one that mattered."

Annie sat up straighter, setting her cup on the couch beside her. She was angry and confused, and she opened her mouth to deny what he was saying, to tell him that the whole thing was ridiculous.

Preposterous. Unbelievable.

But being ridiculous, or preposterous, or any one of a dozen different adjectives she could apply to this experience didn't change what had happened.

The fact remained that it had happened.

And deep inside, she had to face the fact that it was real. She knew every detail of Bernadette Desjardins's life to the point when she'd obeyed Steve and come back here. She knew how the French woman felt and thought, she knew how she made love, and how it felt to have Paul inside her.

Annie flushed at the memory. She swung her legs over the edge of the sofa and got unsteadily to her feet.

"Here's an assortment of books on reincarnation, and on how regressive therapy unlocks the memory of other lives. Remembering allows us to heal old wounds, Annie. Read these. I brought you out today before you had a chance to explore what happened to your neck in that lifetime. But I feel sure that if we pursue this, if we keep going with it, we'll discover the root cause of your problem. And once that happens, I can almost guarantee that you won't be bothered with neck pain ever again." Steve handed her a bag stuffed with books.

"And Annie, more memories will probably come to you spontaneously over the next few days. Don't let them upset you. Remember that whatever happened back then is part of history. It can't be changed, but neither can it hurt you any longer. Accept the memories as a valuable learning tool about your own psyche."

She left in a daze, astounded when she found the same sunshine outside that had been there at nine, when she'd gone into the office.

Now her watch read twelve-fifteen.

Three hours. She'd wandered through time for three hours. She shuddered and walked off slowly to find her car.

The significant thing was that she'd stopped of her own free will at Edith's desk and made another appointment. After all, she couldn't just leave Bernadette there, without knowing what had happened to her and to Paul. Had they found any sort of future, or was their love as doomed as Bernadette had seemed to think it?

Annie unlocked her car and slid in behind the wheel. Her lips twisted in a grim smile. *Tune in again next week, folks, for the dramatic conclusion.*

Then she put her head down on the steering wheel and started to cry all over again.

CHAPTER THIRTEEN

ANNIE DROVE HOME, took one look at her empty house and headed straight toward Cleo's back door, carrying the shopping bag full of books Steve had loaned her. If ever she'd needed a friend to talk to, she needed one now.

"I stopped off on my way to the bridge," she joked in a shaky voice as she came through the door.

"Good thing. I sure don't feel like raising all these kids plus Jason on my own," Cleo quipped. "C'mon in and sit down."

She was feeding babies, one in a high chair and one cradled on her lap. She stopped long enough to toss a pile of magazines off a kitchen chair for Annie, and both babies instantly began to howl.

"Boy, are you guys single-minded," she accused, making a face at the wailing infants.

"Sit down here and tell me what's up, pal," she ordered Annie over the din, spooning mashed peas into both tiny mouths, stopping the racket in midcry.

"Well, I went back to that hypnotist I told you about, and after what happened this morning, I think I know why I had that feeling about David the first time I saw him, at the magic show. Remember I thought I knew him?" Annie began.

"Sure I remember. I'd never seen you that way about anybody before. So where did you know him from?"

Annie put her elbows on the table and rested her chin on her palms while she tried to figure out how to best explain what had happened to her. Then she just went ahead and blurted it out. There was no best way with something as bizarre as this.

"I think he was someone I met in another lifetime, Cleo. He was a doctor then, too," she began, realizing as she went on with the story what it was about Cleo that made her a wonderful friend.

Cleo had the gift of active listening; instead of the understandable, vocal skepticism Annie might have expected, Cleo just blinked once with surprise and didn't say a negative word. She leaned forward in between spooning, her entire body alert, eyes wide and waiting, expression eager.

"And did you love him then, too?" she prompted.

Annie nodded. "This is how it happened," she began, and through it all, Cleo tended the babies with absent, practiced ease and listened, nodding and asking questions now and then, but allowing Annie to finish the story before she said much.

"Lord, that's amazing. The only other thing I've read about something like this was a book a long time ago called *The Search For Bridey Murphy*," Cleo finally commented when Annie reached the point where Steve had called her back to reality.

Cleo used a washcloth on both dimpled chins and planted a smacking kiss on two tiny faces before she set each roly-poly baby on the floor with a stack of plastic toys to play with.

"I figured it was just a story somebody dreamed up. But come to think of it, there's lots of stuff now about parapsychology and channeling and all that in the bookstores. I just never wanted to know much about it."

Cleo plugged in the electric kettle and made tea. "Same thing as the organ transplant donations we talked about—it only gets to be a personal issue when you do more than just read about it, when you know about someone like little Charlie and his mother. Your ideas change fast when you get involved."

She slapped together two fat egg salad sandwiches, despite Annie's insistent claims that she couldn't eat a thing.

"Eat. Even people heading for the bridge can die prematurely from starvation. Could I borrow a couple of these?" Cleo was shuffling through the bag full of books that Steve had sent with Annie.

"Sure, take as many as you like. I'm not ready to get into reading about this right away. It was enough to have it happen to me."

Cleo shuddered. "I guess. Tell you the truth, I'd rather not know if I lived before or not. There's enough to worry about with one lifetime, never mind two. Eat your sandwich. It'll make you feel better."

Annie did, and Cleo paged here and there through one book after the other. "There're books here about life before life, life after life, using hypnosis to access past lives. Pretty esoteric ideas, but it looks as if this regression thing happens to lots of people."

Cleo closed the books and concentrated for a moment. "When you were, ummm... when you thought you were in that other woman's body, Annie, did it feel as if you were eating real food with this guy Paul? Remember you said you invited him for supper?"

Annie swallowed a mouthful of egg before she answered.

"Cleo, it was so real I can remember the exact taste of that stew. It was seasoned with garlic and thyme, and I added lots of parsley just before I served it, and a handful of what smelled like sage. I liked to cook then just as much as now, but now the ingredients are easier to come by. Digging them out of the garden was a heck of a lot harder than buying them at the super-market. I remember looking down at my hands, and they were all stained from the earth, and my nails were rough."

Cleo stared at Annie. "Garlic and thyme, huh? Well, even now you're a kook about spices." She thought for a moment and added, "I don't suppose you remember having to go to the bathroom while you were this Bernadette woman?"

Annie giggled, the first time all day she'd even come close to laughing. Trust Cleo to get down to absolute basics.

"As a matter of fact, yes, I went out behind the house to a privy. It had two holes and a sort of wooden platform. It wasn't very pleasant. There wasn't any proper paper, just ripped up rough stuff."

Cleo's mobile features lit up with excitement and she snapped her finger and thumb together.

"Annie, as far as I'm concerned, that does it. You were there, all right. That one detail convinces me more than any-thing else could, more than any of the rest of this professional garble in these books. I'll bet you never used one of those kinds of toilets in this life, right?"

"Right," Annie agreed with feeling. "And from what I re-member, I'd just as soon not use one again, then or now."

"When do you go to see Munro again? Because I think you're on to something that's really important to you here."

Annie groaned. "Getting used to outdoor privies and visit-ing the twilight zone have to be high points in anybody's life all right. I made another appointment for next Tuesday."

"Y'know, it might be neat to find out that what's happening in our lives made sense on some grand scale, that it was all linked to the past in a pattern instead of being just a big, ironic accident. If you did know David back then, well, maybe there's a good reason for knowing him again now," Cleo mused.

"What if the people we meet and fall in love with are all people we loved before? If we found out where we screwed up in the past, would we still agonize so much about whether it's right or wrong to fall in love with somebody again?"

Annie studied her friend, recognizing something under the surface of the words, something that was disturbing Cleo.

"Did you go out with Don Anderson yet?" she hazarded, knowing she'd struck a nerve when Cleo's face flushed crimson.

"Yeah, last night. We took all the kids to a drive-in movie. It felt like a family, with the baby in the car bed and the girls asleep in the back seat. We ate popcorn and laughed a lot."

"And?"

Cleo got up and began to scrub the countertop hard. "And what? He's a super guy, he's still as young as he was a week ago and he's still a cop."

There were tears glistening in her eyes when she turned and gave Annie a helpless look. "And I'm afraid I'm falling in love with him, damn it all to hell."

Annie got up and wrapped her arms around her friend.

Before today, she'd have advised Cleo to be careful, to hold herself back in an effort to avoid hurt.

But the memory of Bernadette, the power of the love she'd shared with her Paul were still so fresh in Annie's mind that all she could say was, "Give it a chance, Cleo. Who knows? Maybe this is the guy you've been waiting for."

She went home shortly afterward, but she found she wasn't able to concentrate on her book at all, even though her editor had called with an excited message about going straight ahead with it, that she was mailing a contract immediately.

Normally that news had Annie on a high for days. But now she felt as if a vital part of her belief structure had been turned upside-down. Selling a book was exciting, but finding out she'd maybe lived before was earth-shattering.

SHE WAS STILL OFF BALANCE when Jason breezed in from school that afternoon and announced that his father—Annie still had difficulty with that label—had promised to come and watch his rugby game later that afternoon.

"When did he promise, Jason? You know I explained that arrangements like that have to always be made with me, so that I know ahead of time. Your father hasn't called. I was out this morning, but there's no message on the answering machine from him because I checked."

Jason's face fell, and he gave her the pleading look she had such trouble resisting.

"I called him from school at noon today. My friend's father is coming to the game and we thought it would be excellent if my father could come, too. Jeeze, Mom, it was my idea. Don't blame my father, okay? I wanted the guys on my team to meet him. Their fathers are around all the time."

There was a deliberate plaintive note in his voice when he talked about other boys' fathers. This kid of hers was getting adept at heavy guilt, Annie concluded, glancing at him narrow eyed.

The whole issue of Michael was getting more and more complicated. Now she'd said out-and-out mean if she said no about tonight. And anyway, how could she? A rugby game wasn't exactly limited admittance. If Michael wanted to turn up at the field where Jason played, she couldn't stop him.

"All right, Jason," she said with obvious disapproval. "But from now on, talk to me first, understand?"

He agreed with apologetic enthusiasm, and the telephone rang.

It was Michael. He told her word-for-word what Jason had just related, adding that he was concerned about not letting her know ahead of time. Then he asked if he could possibly take Jason and his friend out for hamburgers after the game.

"I'll make sure he's home at a reasonable hour."

What was there to say? It was a logical thing to want to do, and Jason had stood three inches away during the whole conversation, eavesdropping and making excited faces, nodding with wild enthusiasm each time Annie looked at him.

Annie repeated to Michael what she'd just said to Jason, using the same tone, stressing that she needed to know about things like this ahead of time, that it was inconsiderate and unacceptable at the last minute.

Michael agreed with the same apologetic enthusiasm Jason had used. "Also, Annie, he's going to be asking you if he can start spending some weekends with us, staying over from Friday till Sunday. I was firm about him having to ask you first, but of course we'd like it if it's possible."

Her first reaction was to scream no, no, and no again. But now that she'd allowed the relationship to begin, how was she to say that three hours was acceptable, but two days wasn't?

Her brain told her that the sensible thing to do was to allow Jason time with Michael, as much time as he seemed to require. But every one of her insecurities hurt like a toothache at relinquishing her son to this man.

Annie swallowed hard, said it would be all right and hung up in total defeat as Jason went charging downstairs to gather his rugby equipment.

Her son had just left when David walked in the open kitchen door a half hour later, and Annie's flagging spirits went soaring just at the sight of him.

"I've been thinking of you all afternoon, and I got out of the last meeting earlier than I figured," David explained as he wrapped her in his arms and kissed her. Their love and mutual need for each other blazed out of control as their lips met again and again.

"Jason?" David whispered as the spiral of desire began to soar between them in a pulsing arc.

"Out, until nine-thirty," Annie murmured, and they hurried up the stairs to her bedroom.

But as David undressed her and then himself, using his lips and hands to caress her pulsing body, Annie couldn't stop the images that crowded her mind, images of another man and woman, making love just the way she and David were now.

And when her climax began, it was as if she and Bernadette rode the tumult together, their bodies one, just as the men loving them were one. And at that moment, it didn't matter where or when the eternal bond uniting their souls had begun. To Annie, the only thing that mattered at that moment was that their love be truly eternal.

DOWNSTAIRS AGAIN, Annie made them each a drink, and then she related the details of her hypnotic session to David.

He listened without any of Cleo's responsiveness, and Annie grew more and more ill at ease, beginning to stumble over her words as his face set in stiff, disapproving lines.

Finally she gave up trying to describe the occurrence and instead simply slid the tape Steve had made into her recorder and pushed the play button.

The moment she did she found herself wishing she'd never brought the subject up at all with David. Steve's deep, resonant voice filled the room, instructing her, reassuring her, and Annie, glancing up at David's frozen expression, began to tremble.

She hadn't realized what an effect the tape would have on her, or him. She was frightened, so frightened her insides felt cold and empty. Why was she so afraid to hear this? Was it only David's presence that inhibited her? She fought the sudden, irrational impulse to reach over and switch the machine off.

It took several moments before the sound of a woman's voice registered as having had to come from her own throat, and the profound shock that voice gave Annie rendered her immobile.

The voice was deep and musical, the timbre and quality very different from Annie's, and yet she knew it was her. Or someone who had been her. She stole another glance at David. He was rigid, his mouth a long, hard line, eyes narrowed as the woman who called herself Bernadette described the scenes that even now Annie could see as well in her mind's eye as she could see the pattern of the shawl on the back of the sofa where they sat.

Annie began to shake as the tape continued, and a pulse throbbed in her forehead. She wanted to move over closer to David, press her body against his warmth and know the reassurance of his smile, his arm around her.

She longed to have him give her some logical, medical explanation for what was happening on that tape.

But for the first time since she'd been with him, David was somehow closing himself to her, holding himself away even though they sat just a few feet apart.

What Annie found most disturbing about the tape was the emotion, the depth of honest feeling in Bernadette's voice as she talked about her lover, her child, matter-of-fact yet somehow eloquent in her simplicity, with an undercurrent of hope and desire and longing.

The sentiments expressed were very like those she felt for David, or Jason, and they struck a deep responsive note inside her. Her voice and Bernadette's might differ, but their souls were one.

At last a whirring emptiness filled the room and then, with a sharp click, the tape recorder shut itself off.

Annie was the first to speak. "Well, what do you make of that?" she asked in as normal a tone as she could manage. Her voice shook anyway.

David was still seated on the sofa beside her. He reached for the glass of Scotch Annie had poured him earlier and took a long, hearty swig.

"David, what do you think about all this?" Annie asked again.

He set the empty glass down on the coffee table, still without saying anything to her or even looking at her, and Annie felt as if she were shriveling up inside.

He turned at last and gave her a long, searching glance, one she couldn't interpret. Then he stood and picked up his glass, heading for the kitchen where Annie had left the Scotch bottle on the counter. She heard the liquor splash, the gulp of sound as he added water.

She waited for him to come back, every nerve ending alive. He didn't sit down. He walked over to the window and stood as if he were staring out at the twilight.

When he did speak, his voice was careful and controlled at first. "I wish you hadn't gone along with this nonsense at all, Annie. I have to say I not only believe it's absolute hogwash, but I also think it could be harmful to you." The control disappeared, and he sounded angry and disgusted when he added, "I've never heard such a bunch of garbage in my life."

The condemnation in his voice shocked her.

"But Steve explained to me . . ."

"I don't give a good goddamn what this Munro told you."

He whirled around, his blue gaze icy and hard.

"I'm telling you I don't approve, Annie, from either a medical standpoint or a personal one."

She flinched as if he'd struck her.

Annie shuddered. He'd never looked at her in quite that way before, as if she were a stranger he didn't consider quite bright enough. "Why . . . why are you reacting this way, David? I just wanted you to hear what happened to me, and give me an opinion on what went on today.''

"That's exactly what I'm doing, Annie. I'm a doctor, and I'm telling you I think this nonsense has gone far enough.''

Annie was shocked and angered at the harshness that had once again crept into his tone. Her hands knotted into fists, but she kept silent as he went on talking, striding up and down the room in an agitated way.

"I'm willing to concede that hypnotism has its place as a tool in modern medicine. I've seen it used effectively with children when they have to undergo painful procedures. But what you're fooling with here is preposterous. Surely you understand that after listening to the garbage on this tape. All that's happening is that you're dredging up some buried memories from a movie you've seen, a book you read, a conversation you overheard as a young child. And because you're vulnerable, and innocent, you believe it's happening to some person who lived seventy or eighty years ago, some woman you think was you. You're far too gullible, Annie.''

He thrust one hand and then another through his hair, setting it on end in wild clumps.

"I want you to give this up. If you feel that ordinary hypnosis helps your neck in any way, I'll be glad to find a therapist who doesn't carry the procedure to the extremes this Munro obviously does.'' His voice was hoarse, filled with passion and anger. "The man's a fanatic. I don't want you near him again.''

Annie stared at him, at a loss as to what to say.

He stopped in front of her, reached out and clasped her shoulders with his palms. She felt the warmth that emanated from him, the texture of his skin through the thin blouse she was wearing. She also felt his agitation in the almost painful bite of his fingers on her flesh.

"Annie, love, I want you to promise me that you won't go along with any more of this,'' he begged. "Will you do that, for me?''

She felt as if she'd ended up in a conversation with a stranger. The overwhelming love she felt for David, the desire to please him, the respect she had for his ability as a doctor, were all at war with an automatic, deep-seated conviction that what he was asking her to do wasn't based on logic, and also wasn't some-

David was reacting from some deep emotional level she didn't understand. She suspected he really didn't understand it, either.

She summoned up all the logical words she could think of to try to explain that to him. "But what happened to me was real, David, whatever the reason or the cause. It wasn't fraud, or imagination, or something I read. I can't explain it except to say that just as I know I'm alive now, this minute, so I also know I was alive then. I remember the emotions very strongly. There were things I didn't or couldn't explain on that tape, the way there are emotions inside of me I can't explain now." She frowned up at him.

"I don't understand exactly what you're warning me against, but I don't like it. Dr. Munro is a competent person, or he wouldn't have been recommended. What's more, I like him a lot and trust him. There's no physical danger, he assured me of that. Are you . . . afraid that I might get trapped somehow and not be able to come back?"

That sounded so much like science fiction it embarrassed her.

David let her shoulders go and stood straight, staring down at her. His words were passionate and again, angry. "What you're doing is mentally dangerous in my opinion. Already you seem to be fully accepting some ridiculous explanation for all this, willing yourself to believe it's all valid. Why do you really want to go on with it, anyway? There wasn't one single reference in all that—" he gestured toward the tape recorder "—about the real problem this Munro is supposed to be treating, namely your neck spasms."

She swallowed. Her throat felt parched and fear was clutching at her stomach. In this mood, David was intimidating.

"Steve felt that the reason I ended up back there was that something happened at that time that caused the pain I'm having now. He says I've only begun to explore the reasons."

"Ahh, hogwash," he said in a tone of absolute disgust. She could see he thought her explanation ridiculous, and helpless frustration welled up in her.

Lord, she loved this man. The intensity of that had never changed, never lessened one iota over the time she'd known him.

She didn't want to quarrel like this, didn't want tension or bad feelings between them. For an instant, she considered doing what he wanted, canceling her next appointment, trying to forget the powerful emotions she'd experienced as Bernadette.

But she simply couldn't do it. Somewhere between the time she'd left Steve's office and now, the decision to go on with the hypnotic regression had firmed and stabilized in her thoughts. She had to explore the astonishing possibility that somewhere in the annals of time, she'd lived before, and she would do that research with or without David's approval.

It didn't seem a decision she'd had any choice in making, anyway. The regression to Bernadette had been automatic, as if she were being led toward an experience she needed to remember. Just as she had to know what would happen next.

"David, I'm sorry, but I have another appointment in a week, and I plan to keep it," she said with conviction.

She could see the effort he put into controlling his reaction. She knew that he was forcing himself not to reveal the true depth of his anger, not to lash out at her in rage.

She didn't understand his objections now any better than she had when he first made them.

"Then there's no point in discussing it further, is there?" he said in a clipped, distant tone that she'd never heard him use before. He glanced at his watch, and her heart sank. She'd driven him away.

"I'd better be going. I told Calvin I'd drop by and have a drink with him tonight if there was time. There's some committee planning meeting he wants to discuss."

"Are . . . are we still spending tomorrow afternoon together, David?" Annie hated having to ask, hated the feeling that she was begging him for reassurance.

"Of course. I'll come by and pick you up just after one. We'll have dinner out, if you can arrange something for Jason."

It should have made her feel better, but it didn't. Neither did the perfunctory kiss he planted more or less on her mouth before he hurried out, closing the door firmly behind him.

DAVID DIDN'T GO to Calvin's, however. Instead he drove in the direction of the ocean, braking with a jerk each time a light was red, pulling away with an angry squeal of tires and accelerating with reckless abandon when he reached the long stretch of road that bordered the water.

An irrational need to get away drove him, but what was it he needed to escape?

Annie? He loved Annie.

Whatever it was, it possessed him, kept him from stopping and parking on the all-but-deserted beach. He needed to go on driving, putting distance between himself and the scene he'd been through back there.

Anger and puzzled frustration mingled inside of him, and driving fast released only a tiny portion of the tension that had been building inside of him ever since Annie had played that damnable tape. The moment it started, he began to feel physically ill.

What had caused the deeply rooted fear, the terrible anxiety and sense of failure and frustration he'd experienced when he listened to the damned thing? To her, that woman who called herself Bernadette.

Chills had gripped him when her voice first sounded, and then foreboding and regret had knotted his gut as that haunting familiar voice with its lilting French intonations went on and on. He knew that voice, damn it, knew it in the depths of his pores. It was a voice in a dream he never remembered on waking. He couldn't explain it, and neither could he control the reaction it caused.

He'd channeled his feelings like an idiot into the harsh things he'd said to Annie, but they expressed exactly the way he felt about this whole process she'd bumbled into.

It had to be garbage, didn't it? It had to be a clever fraud perpetrated by her subconscious, or his, or by this jerk Munro. By somebody, damn it, because there wasn't any other explanation.

He'd had to tell her how he felt, he rationalized. *But you didn't have to hurt her doing it, Roswell.* Her soft eyes had widened and then filled with hurt, and it tore his gut apart to see what he'd done with his tirade. What made him act that way, for pity's sake? She was the one person he never wanted to hurt.

All at once a sense of utter desolation rolled over him. He loved Annie, as he'd never loved another woman in his life. But sometimes, sometimes like now, this minute, but also during the entire time it had taken that hellish tape to run its course, he had the feeling he'd lose her somehow. He became convinced he'd eventually end up spending a large portion of his life without her—empty years, lonely years. Long and straight and dusty, leading only to the grave. Who the hell had said that, anyway?

He was past the beaches, back into a suburban area near the university.

All at once he wheeled the car into the parking lot of a small pub he'd never been in and before he could change his mind, he walked through the door into the smoky noise.

He took a stool at the bar and ordered a Scotch.

What he had to do was somehow find more time to be with Annie, put more effort into breaking through the wall Jason had erected to keep him out, and through Annie's own reservations and doubts about their relationship being permanent. He needed time to court her, time to let her get to know him and trust him.

Time. With Calvin pulling strings to get him invited to every bloody business meeting in the western hemisphere, time was the one thing David didn't have.

The bartender put a glass and a pitcher of water in front of him. David ignored the water, lifted the glass to his lips and shuddered as the liquor burned its fiery way down his gullet.

It was sad and ironic that a man with as little spare time as he had should be wasting that precious little sitting alone in a pub trying to drown the haunting memory of a voice he could have sworn didn't belong to Annie, and yet did.

And if it didn't sound like the woman he now loved, then why the hell should it affect him at all? Why should it make him feel as if nails were scratching in slow motion down the blackboard of his nervous system?

"Bartender, another Scotch, please. Make it a double."

He was going to have one bitch of a headache in the morning. With savage intent, he drank the second whiskey and ordered again.

ANNIE WAS READY when David drove up in front of the house the next afternoon. She'd been ready for a nervous half hour, and she didn't wait for him to get out of the car and come to the door.

Instead she hurried out and slid into the seat beside him.

The events of the previous evening and the long, dream-thick night that had passed since their quarrel had given her time to think, time to plan some sort of strategy.

She'd decided the best thing to do was avoid the whole topic of regression and hypnosis with David, and that's what she intended to do this afternoon. They had little enough time together, she reminded herself over and over, and she wasn't about to spend the afternoon quarreling. She only hoped David felt that way, too.

"Isn't it a great day? We're having a real Indian summer this year," she remarked with forced cheerfulness, turning to smile at David as she looped the seat belt across her and fastened it. He was looking out the side window, away from her, staring at two children tossing a ball on the sidewalk.

"Bet this is some sort of record for the Coast. We've had so many days without rain." My gosh, it sounded like the type of conversation she might have with a perfect stranger.

It was hard to read his expression even when he finally turned his head toward her. He was wearing dark glasses that shrouded his eyes, but he attempted a polite smile and agreed before he pulled the car smoothly away from the curb.

"I thought we might take a drive out to Steveston," he said in the same polite, impersonal tone she'd been using.

"There're lots of places to walk beside the river, and the village is fun to explore. Also, someone mentioned a great seafood restaurant where we could have an early dinner later on."

Annie agreed with enthusiasm, doing her best to fill the awkward silences that fell between them as he maneuvered through traffic and over bridges, heading south of the city toward the municipality of Richmond.

There had never been these silences before between them, and it bothered her that there were now. It tore at her, and she wondered if the entire afternoon would be this way.

She'd take a bus home if it didn't improve, she told herself. She couldn't stand being with him, loving him, and having this tension between them.

He was an impossible, pigheaded man, she fumed.

They were driving past fertile vegetable farms whose silt-rich fields were dotted with workers in conical straw hats, crouched along the long straight rows weeding the healthy-looking plants. It might have been a scene from Bangkok.

"...and my editor called and said she loves my proposal, and I finally hit some sort of breakthrough with the character of the boy," Annie heard herself chattering, filling empty air with senseless words. "I was up really early this morning..."

She'd wakened with a violent start at half past four out of a dream she couldn't remember, unable to go to sleep again. So she'd gotten up and gone into the study, turning to her work to stop the parade of confusing images that had marched all night through her dreams.

"...and all of a sudden, I realized what needed to be done..."

She stopped, because David had pulled the powerful car out of the speeding lines of traffic, steering over to the shoulder of the highway and braking with an urgent jolt.

The engine idled and cars sped past as he turned toward her, releasing his seat belt and stripping the dark glasses from his face, revealing bloodshot, weary eyes.

"Darling, I'm sorry." He reached out to draw her into a rough embrace.

His arms encircled her, but the seat belt stopped her. It took her a moment to fumble it open, and then she moved deeper into his arms with a mixture of relief and happiness and overwhelming love for him flooding through her like liquid sunlight.

It was going to be all right, after all.

"Annie, my dearest," a still, small voice inside of her whispered. His mouth was close to her ear, and his gruff words tickled. "Whatever happens between us, remember that I love you. I'll always, always love you," he said, holding her against him with a ferocity that made breathing difficult for her. "Annie, I'll love you till I die."

And afterward, a still, small voice inside of her whispered.

She lifted her head and put her mouth on his, drinking his feverish kisses, running her hands over his face and chest and shoulders, reassuring herself that he was really there for her again.

She wanted to forget the harsh words he'd used the night before, the resentment she'd felt when he walked out the way he had.

"I love you, too, David, more than I can ever tell you."

As they wandered hand in hand through the quaint Japanese fishing village of Steveston and ambled along the shoreline of the Fraser River that day, he wanted to tell her about the dream he'd had the night before.

Nightmare, he corrected himself. He'd never had a nightmare in his life, he'd never understood how unsettling they could be, but if anything was to be labeled nightmare, it would be this infernal demon, which had left him shivering and icy cold with sweat at 3:00 a.m. It must have happened as a result of the whiskey he'd consumed. It had to be the liquor that had caused it.

Maybe if he talked it over with Annie, and they laughed at the ridiculous power dreams seemed to possess in the lonely hours just before dawn, it would lose its importance, fade from his consciousness. But he couldn't bring himself to talk about it, even to Annie, and it settled into his awareness like an invisible albatross.

He'd left the pub just after midnight the night before with enough sense to know he'd had far too much whiskey to make driving possible. So he'd called a cab from the pay phone out front, hoping his car would be safe in the lot till morning.

During the taxi ride home, the alcohol he'd consumed had caught up with him, and by the time he reeled into his apartment, it was a major task just to get out of his clothes and tumble into bed and blissful oblivion.

Drugged sleep enveloped him in an instant.

He wasn't sure when the dream began. He only knew with sudden clarity that he found himself in a large, gracious old house. He wanted to buy it for himself and Annie. They'd be happy there, and he felt excited and eager because now that he'd found them a suitable place to live, there couldn't be any more obstacles between them. More than anything else, he wanted that, needed that permanence.

This house was perfect, he was sure of it. He toured the ground floor, reveling in the gleaming old wood, the size of the rooms, the huge old-fashioned kitchen. Annie would adore this house.

He started up the winding staircase to the upper level, and the first tiny threads of illogical fear began to weave their way into his sleeping mind, but he ignored them, shoving them aside as he moved through the bedrooms and bathrooms, noting the fine polished oak floors, the wide casement windows, the large east bedroom that would serve as a perfect writing studio for Annie.

Then, all of a sudden, he came upon another stairwell, hidden in a shadowed corner, and David knew it led to the attic above. He knew, too, that the time had come to explore that area, and the tiny licks of fear he'd experienced earlier became stronger as he stood at the bottom of the narrow steps looking up at a closed door a dozen steep steps away.

Behind that door lurked horror.

For some unaccountable reason, he was terrified of that door, and of whatever ghastly, unmentionable menace lurked in wait for him behind it. He knew there was something unspeakable up there, and he wanted to escape, leave the house without finding out what it was. But he couldn't go anywhere but up.

The dream twisted, confining him as he forced himself to take one step up those attic stairs, and then another. He was frightened, but he didn't want to acknowledge that fear even to himself. He was a man, and deep shame filled him. Men shouldn't be afraid. Especially of a thing he couldn't even see.

He felt his heartbeat accelerate. *One. Two.* One step after the other, he forced himself to climb. The dream atmosphere was now heavy and ominous; an unimaginable terror held him in its grip, making it hard to breathe. His chest hurt as he inhaled and exhaled. And he could smell his own fear, rank in his nostrils.

The steps narrowed as he neared the top. Now his heart was thundering, and cold sweat broke out on his body.

David had never before believed he was about to die, but he believed it now. With every ounce of willpower he could manage, he reached for the door handle to that attic, forcing himself to turn it....

His scream was still echoing through the apartment when he awoke, and the paralyzing fear took several moments to begin to fade. He was sitting bolt upright in bed, and his body was trembling, drenched with sweat.

He couldn't breathe at first. His heart thundered hard enough to make his chest ache, and the relief he felt at getting out of the dream before that attic door opened made him weak.

Dawn was barely a suggestion in the sky outside his window, but he didn't even try to fall asleep again. He didn't dare chance falling back into the dream, even though the whiskey he'd consumed made him long to throw himself back on the bed and sleep until his eyes and head were better.

Instead he perked coffee, and after the first mouthful, bolted to the bathroom and threw up.

He'd been awake ever since.

ON THE SURFACE, the day Annie and David spent together was a success.

They wandered like carefree lovers, laughing together at nonsense, stopping in secluded places to kiss and hold each other.

David insisted on buying her a teardrop-shaped crystal on a silver chain in a strange little jewelry store hidden down a lane in the village. "It will bring happiness and much luck in love," the Japanese proprietor promised.

Annie figured she needed all the help she could get as David fastened it around her neck, letting his fingers trail across her neck and shoulders.

They ate a delicious seafood dinner in a restaurant overlooking the pier, where dozens of fishing boats rocked at anchor. Annie fed David bits of her lobster and smiled into his eyes, pushing aside the sad knowledge that, despite all their efforts, there was new tension between them now, tension that hadn't been there before the previous evening, tension that must remain unresolved because now there were subjects they simply couldn't discuss without quarreling.

Subjects like hypnotism, regression, reincarnation: offbeat subjects that only a short time ago, Annie wouldn't have thought of discussing anyway. And of course there was the ever-increasing drain on David's time and energy. They couldn't be rational about that, either, because Annie was anything but rational when it came to a situation she felt Calvin Graves had engineered.

Now these matters loomed large and ominous, important, in her life, in her brain, in her subconscious, and she had to be very careful about not mentioning them at all, because they were right there every minute in her thoughts. They put an invisible barrier between her and the man she loved.

DAVID DROPPED HER OFF at dusk. He had to check on a small patient at the hospital, and they both felt a little cheated at not being able to make love that evening.

Jason had had dinner with Cleo and the girls, and he was engrossed in an episode of *Star Trek*.

Annie turned on the answering machine. There was a message from her editor, two hang ups, and then a pleasant voice with a slight accent said, "Annie, this is Lili McCrae. I wondered if you might have lunch with me, perhaps Friday this week? Call me."

Annie frowned down at the machine. Did she really want to put herself through still another awkward situation?

But Lili must have a good reason for wanting to invite her to lunch. Perhaps she and Michael were having some problem with Jason, and Lili wanted to discuss it?

In slow motion, Annie lifted the phone and dialed the number that was becoming all too familiar to her.

It was a small relief when Lili answered instead of Michael, and Annie agreed to meet the other woman Friday at a restaurant on Broadway.

When she hung up, Annie reflected that her life was beginning to resemble the description of plotting she'd once heard a well-known writer deliver at a seminar.

"Plotting a book," he'd said with a beleaguered sigh, "means having one damn thing happen right after another."

It fit the pattern Annie's life was taking, all right. One damn thing happened to her right after another.

CHAPTER FOURTEEN

ANNIE HURRIED in to Lothario's Bistro on Friday at twenty past twelve.

Lili was already waiting at a table near the window.

"Sorry I'm late," Annie apologized as Lili stretched out an elegant, slim hand in greeting.

"But you're not at all," Lili smiled. "I'm compulsive about appointments. It's only by the greatest act of will I avoid getting anywhere two hours too early."

Annie took the chair the waiter was holding, feeling a bit apprehensive about what was to come.

Lili was sipping a glass of white wine, and Annie ordered the same. Once the waiter was gone, she took a moment to study the woman across the table.

Lili was wearing a brightly-patterned narrow skirt and a rose-shaded silk blouse. She had silver hoops in her ears, and her hair was styled as Annie remembered, a dark glossy mass drawn into a high dramatic knot. She wore subtle makeup, but it was her eyes that commanded attention, deep and soft and gentle. Lili was ageless. She'd probably look much the same when she was eighty.

"You must wonder why I asked you here today," Lili said with the forthright manner Annie remembered from their first meeting.

"I know we share a delicate acquaintance, but I thought it wise for us to know each other at least well enough that phone calls and the necessary communication we must make because of Jason might be comfortable instead of strained between us, no?"

The old resentment rose in Annie for a moment, the feeling that these people, Michael and this wife of his, were usurping her place with her son.

But hard on that thought came the realization that the whole situation wasn't exactly easy on Lili, either. It was a wonder she didn't bitterly resent both Jason and Annie because of their ties to her husband. Yet she didn't seem to at all. Her words were positive and totally free of undercurrent as far as Annie could tell.

"I have had little to do with growing boys, you see, and I need to ask you questions about Jason, so that I won't undo through my stupidity things you have set in place. He'll be coming to spend the weekend with us soon, and I need to know what foods he likes, besides hamburgers—" both women grimaced "—and also what rules you feel are important for him."

Before they could talk further, the waiter brought the wine, and they studied the menu, trying to ignore his ongoing litany of what was delicious today.

Annie ordered a croissant stuffed with crab, and Lili decided on linguine with seafood sauce.

Lili leaned across the table when the waiter left and confided in a low voice, "Food is my great weakness. Do you know I have almost seventy cookbooks? I read them like novels. When I was learning English at school I used to study cookbooks, so instead of being able to say—" she frowned, trying to remember "—oh, things like 'my uncle's dog is staying with my cousin'—instead I was spouting 'separate the eggs and whisk in cream.'"

Annie laughed. "I can't resist cookbooks, either. Jason literally drags me past displays of them in the supermarket."

Until their food arrived they talked about cooking and recipes, and Annie found she was enjoying herself.

Lili was intelligent and quick-witted, with a wry sense of humor and, just as she'd admitted, a healthy appetite. She attacked her food with honest hunger.

"I think I must have died of starvation in some other life, to be such a glutton in this one," Lili sighed, spooning up the rich creamy sauce and buttering a thick slice of fresh hot bread.

Annie suddenly lost her appetite, but her attention was fully on the other woman. "Do you believe in reincarnation, then?" she managed to ask.

Lili swallowed a mouthful of food and then raised her wineglass and sipped. "I never give it much thought. It's part of our Eastern belief structure, of course, but—" she said matter-offactly. "—I'm afraid I neither believe nor disbelieve. We weren't a particularly religious family, although I was taught the basics. Reincarnation is linked with karma. You understand the concept of karma?"

Annie shook her head. "Not really." Over the weekend, she'd skimmed through one of the books Steve had loaned her, but her emotions were still too ragged to allow her to concentrate on theory. She was still feeling rather than thinking.

"Doesn't it have to do with—?" Annie searched for a cloudy dictionary definition "—with destiny?"

Lili reached out and refilled their wineglasses.

"In a way. It's simply cause and effect, a belief that our lives have purpose and we come back each time to learn lessons that have escaped us the time before. Karma can bring happiness or sadness, depending on the results you've learned by your choices."

There was something that was concerning Annie more and more. "Do you think, Lili, that when—if—we do reincarnate, that we come back here with the same people?"

Lili shrugged. "It makes sense, of course. The theory is that we're here to learn lessons of love, and if we love the same people again and again, we'd be able to work out problems that defeated us the last time 'round."

Annie wanted to ask if Lili had ever felt that she'd known Michael before, but the complexities of the relationship between her and Lili and Michael and Jason stopped her.

Annie leaned forward, about to ask one of the dozens of other questions Lili's words had evoked, but she was interrupted by the cheerful young waiter.

"Would you ladies like to see the dessert menu? We have the most amazing selection today." He rattled off at least a dozen choices, and Annie met Lili's amused glance and rolled her eyes.

"I can't remember all that. Perhaps I'd better see a menu and study this decision properly," Lili teased him.

When the young man had left again, Annie remarked, "I have a friend who says things always go from the sublime to the ridiculous. Here we're talking about karma, and he's talking about dessert."

Lili's eyes sparkled with humor. "Isn't that true? But perhaps it's a warning that if I keep eating this way, I'll come back with a serious weight problem."

The waiter appeared yet again and placed huge menus in front of each of them. "The chocolate cheesecake is divine, and there's *crème brûlé . . .*"

Somehow, by the time they'd each chosen, the plates had been cleared, the dessert served and coffee brought, the conversation had turned to Jason and the matter of karma wasn't mentioned again.

Annie found that Lili already had a perceptive understanding of her son, and what seemed to be an honest and growing affection for the boy. She asked questions about school, about what special areas Annie was concerned with, about his day-to-day schedule. It was obvious that Lili cared how the relationship progressed, and wanted to conform to any firm rules Annie had.

"The incident with the rugby game concerned me. It's important we have a clear-cut understanding about these matters," Lili said, and Annie agreed.

When the luncheon ended, Annie was the one who offered her hand to Lili. "Thank you for arranging this. You're right, you know. It makes it much easier now that I know you a little."

"For me also. Thank you for coming."

Under different circumstances, Annie thought, she and Lili might have been good friends. But it was impossible, because of Michael, because of the resentment and fear he still sparked in Annie. Neither woman had mentioned him at all today, intuitively aware that he was an invisible presence anyway at the luncheon. Because of him, they'd never be close friends. Instead they shared what Lili had aptly labeled a "delicate acquaintance." Lili loved Michael, and Annie came near to hating him. It left precious little room for a meeting place.

DAVID HAD CALLED while Annie was out, and his rapid-fire message resulted in a lonely weekend.

"Annie, Phyllis just reminded me that I signed up for a seminar in Los Angeles this weekend. There are a couple of doctors attending whom I especially want to talk to about this organ transplant thing. I thought of asking you to come, but these things are a big bore if you're not involved, and you'd spend most of your time alone. I'm booked on a seven-thirty flight out tonight, so I'm hitching a ride to the airport with another guy who's going. Be back Monday. I lo…'' The tape ran out before he could add what Annie considered the most important part of the whole thing.

When she thought about it afterward, Annie wished he'd asked her to go anyway. At least they'd have had the nights together.

Jason spent Saturday playing rugby and Sunday with the McCraes, and Annie tried to devote most of her time to her book.

David didn't phone until late Monday night. He was at his apartment, and he sounded tired and out of sorts. His flight had been delayed for over three hours in Los Angeles, and he'd missed the connecting flight from Seattle, so he'd just gotten home.

"Damned hotel beds. I couldn't get much sleep at all. I missed you, Annie. Tomorrow's frantic. I've got a surgical conference first thing and one of my patients, a kid I operated on for ruptured appendix late last week, has started hemorrhaging so I'm heading straight down to the hospital now.''

GETTING READY for her appointment the next morning with Steve Munro, Annie worked herself into a nervous state. She felt cold and hot by turns, and she was shaking with apprehension as she dressed and drove over.

No one could stay uptight long around Steve, however. He was so relaxed himself, it simply rubbed off on anyone around him.

"How's your neck pain been?'' he asked, taking a seat as he talked and tipping his chair back as far as it would go.

He wore what Annie now recognized as his uniform: baggy, wrinkled navy polyester trousers, a tweed sport jacket much the worse for wear, and a shirt, gray today, with several indecipherable stains down the front.

"It comes and goes. It was good after my last appointment, but yesterday and today it's there again, as bad as ever. I've been using the relaxation tapes.''

"Good. Now about this session. When I hypnotize you, I'll strongly suggest you return to the same time frame you visited before, Annie, but I have to warn you, sometimes it just doesn't work. We'll do our best and see what happens.''

Annie was alarmed. "But I want to go back there, to France," she told him as she settled more comfortably on the couch. "I want to find out what happened to Bernadette."

She added in an urgent tone, "I have to find out, Steve. She's haunting me."

"Have any more memories come back to you, in dreams or just in flashes of awareness?" he asked.

Annie nodded. "That man I loved, Paul. He's someone I know now. Someone I'm in love with now."

Steve nodded, not at all suprised. "That's quite usual, recognizing people from the past as part of your present life. Did you have a chance to read any of those books I gave you?"

"I looked through them. I plan to begin studying them this week."

"I think you'll find in your reading that it would be highly unusual not to recognize at least some of the same people you knew in that other lifetime. If the purpose of rebirth is learning love in all its complexities, then we probably need a lot more than one lifetime to do it in."

He grinned, which made him look like a friendly leprechaun. "Unless everybody's a lot better at learning than I am, that is. I've been regressed numerous times, and I've remembered a whole series of different lifetimes."

Annie thought of the tangled web of relationships that surrounded her, the tangled memories she'd already relived as Bernadette, and she shuddered.

"Reliving just one is quite enough for me," she decided. "Shall we begin, then?"

Her courage deserted her all of a sudden.

"Steve, I'm scared...."

"It's natural. What you're experiencing is a whole new frontier. You're like an explorer without a map, Annie. And I can't promise that the memories won't hurt. All I can promise is that I'll do my best to guide you through them."

Her heartbeat accelerated, but she leaned back and closed her eyes as Steve's voice began the now-familiar relaxation procedure.

SHE WAS AWARE first of all of the river, the constant, soothing rush of water flowing close to where they lay sheltered beneath the overhanging branches and leaves of a huge old willow.

Much time had passed. The awkwardness of first love was gone for her and Paul, but not the intensity. Paul was no longer a stranger; they knew each other well by now.

The number of days they'd managed to spend together was pitifully few, but every chance he'd had, Paul had somehow managed to find a way to come to her.

It was autumn and the leaves were falling. They formed a thick, crackling carpet that both cushioned and prickled Bernadette's nearly naked body through the thin folds of the old blanket she kept hidden behind a fallen log for just such times as these.

She lay curled in Paul's arms, head resting on his shoulder, and she was staring up at the blue sky and white clouds dancing across the heavens through the lattice of branches overhead.

They'd made love only moments before, and her body was still throbbing from the joy of fulfillment. Even after all this time, it still amazed her that she'd performed this act all those years with Jean without ever feeling once the way Paul made her feel every time.

"My love, we have to talk," he was saying, and she wished he wouldn't. She knew what he insisted on discussing, and they never managed to reach a solution. "The war is nearly over," he went on.

His deep voice rumbled through her head, a sensation felt rather than heard, using sounds she didn't want to make sense of.

"I'll be leaving soon, first back to England and then, eventually, on a troop ship to the States."

She lay without moving, and he reached a finger to stroke the line of her jaw.

"Bernadette, I can't bear the thought of leaving you behind. Please let me begin to make arrangements for you and Nicole to emigrate." His tone was persuasive, insistent, the way it was each time this subject arose between them.

It had come up more and more often in the past two months. "There are certain people I know here who could help, who'd speed up the whole process for me. Once I'm back in the States it'll take longer, be more complicated than if we push things from this end, now. After the war ends, there'll be chaos and confusion. Paperwork won't get done as quickly."

Bernadette's heart sank. It was a subject they ended up arguing over each time they were together these days, and she hated hearing him bring it up now while her mind was still floating from his lovemaking. She tried to distract him by nibbling at his chin, but it didn't work.

"I'll start divorce proceedings as soon as I get back, and when I'm free, we'll marry," he persisted. "In the meantime, I'll support you and Nicole, you know that. Lord knows it's not an ideal solution, but it's the best I can do at the moment."

Silence fell, and she could see a lark winging high overhead. After a moment, he grasped her chin gently and turned her head so he could look into her face.

"Bernadette? Do you hear me?"

She pulled away and sat up, pulling her dress on over her head, tugging on the rest of her clothing, avoiding his eyes.

"I cannot," she finally said in a soft, sad voice. "This farm, this land...it's all I have, Paul. It's my home. It's a big decision, what you ask of me. I need more time than this. I would have to try to lease the land, or sell, and in these times it's difficult."

He grew angry, cursing her stubbornness under his breath. "Damn it, Bernadette, be reasonable. Once I'm gone, it'll take months, perhaps years, to arrange visas and do all the bloody bureaucratic nonsense they'll require. I've looked into it. While I'm here I can pull strings for you, but afterward..."

Afterward. She tried never to think about that. On her knees, she moved close to him, wrapping her arms around him, breathing in the musky scent—her scent—that lingered on his skin.

Words didn't work when they talked about this. She couldn't explain that the real reason for refusing what he wanted was fear. With inborn French practicality, she knew that here, he belonged totally to her. Here, love overcame all doubts.

The only people she and Paul had any contact with here were Lorelei, and occasionally, Marc Cerdan, the doctor Lorelei worked with.

Dr. Cerdan had asked Paul to assist him several times with patients from the village, once with a difficult cesarean birth, and twice more with injured farmers.

The villagers gossiped, and knew the handsome young foreigner stayed with Bernadette, but she had little to do with them, so it really didn't much bother her. Nothing bothered her as long as she had Paul's love.

But once he was back in the United States, then more people would become involved. Paul was a married man with deep financial and emotional ties not only to his wife, but also to the shadowy, ominous father-in-law, this Martin Oakley, to whom Paul felt he owed so much. And because of his skill as a doctor, Bernadette realized he would be well-known in his town.

How would these foreign people feel about a French woman and her child?

Going with Paul as he wanted her to do meant trusting him totally. Here, he was simply an army doctor, doing his best to repair the frightful horrors that war produced.

But back there . . . ahh, back there his life was unknown to Bernadette, with responsibilities and pressures she couldn't begin to imagine, people by the score she didn't want to encounter.

Trusting someone completely was a thing she'd never been able to do. And ever since the war had begun and Jean had left, she'd had to be self-reliant and strong. She'd made this small acreage support her and Nicole. The land was her only security; it was literally all she had in the way of worldly goods.

"My marriage to Jean was a mistake, and you say the marriage you made is the same, a mistake," she said now, holding Paul, feeling the strong muscles in his body knot with frustration and anger, anger she knew was directed at her.

It wounded her, and she shuddered. They had only a brief time left. She couldn't bear having him angry, and struggled to make him understand.

"Paul, listen to me, please." He began to protest, but she laid her fingers over his mouth, insisting. "What if I'm the type of woman who shouldn't marry, what if once we're able to be together all the time, we find we've made yet another error? Have you considered this? Marriage is not a thing that should be decided in haste. Both of us know that. We've had only scraps of time together, days and hours here and there, not enough yet to base a lifetime upon."

It wasn't quite the truth. The fact was, she knew in her soul that being with Paul for the rest of her life was all she wanted, all she longed for.

But she'd come to understand him in the months since they'd met. Paul was an honorable man, a man with a deep sense of commitment and a powerful compassion for those weaker than himself.

He'd told her his wife was frail, that he owed a great deal to his father-in-law, and that their business partnership was complex.

If she and Paul were ever to be truly happy together, Bernadette knew that he would have to settle his other life in his own way, without the influence of herself and Nicole hanging like millstones around his neck.

Here, she was independent. There, she would be totally reliant on Paul, and Bernadette sensed that was dangerous.

She tried again. "If there was only myself, perhaps, but I have Nicole to consider. She's in school, and uprooting her is hard. Paul, my darling, I love you with every fiber of my being, but this . . . we cannot do this in haste. Surely you can see that?"

He couldn't, though. He was furious with her. He took her clinging arms in his and peeled them from his body, getting to his feet with the easy grace she admired even now.

His face was etched in harsh lines as he yanked his clothing on — the yank of each garment betraying his anger.

Bernadette watched, her stomach in knots. She tried twice to reason, even to beg, but as soon as he was dressed, he stalked away from her down the river path, each long stride taking him farther away from her.

She knew he had to return to his unit by evening, that he had to leave soon in any event. But to have him leave this way, angry, hurt; she couldn't bear it.

"Paul, please, Paul, come back, just for a moment, my darling, please . . ."

He didn't turn.

Bernadette dropped her face into her hands and allowed the pent-up sobs to explode from her throat in a torrent of anguish.

WATCHING HER CRY, hearing the agony in her harsh exclamations of grief, Steve intervened.

Drops of sweat had formed on his forehead, mute testimony to the tension of the scene she'd been describing. Steve wiped his head absently with a tissue, watching his patient every moment, noting the gamut of emotions on her features as she related to him what was happening to her.

Regression as successful as this was an eerie experience, even for a therapist who'd witnessed it many times before. No one watching and listening to Annie could doubt that the places and the things she spoke of were less than real. And most touching of all was the emotion she evinced.

She was still sobbing as if she'd never stop, deep gut-wrenching sobs that had to hurt her chest.

It was time to move her forward, to explore the consequences of her decision to remain in France despite Paul's desperate efforts at changing her mind.

"Annie, move ahead, away from this sad time. I'm going to count to three. At three, you will move ahead in time, move ahead to another major occurrence in the life you're experiencing as Bernadette. One, two, three. . . ."

The sobbing gradually abated, and Steve said, "Now can you tell me where you are, what year it is?"

Annie sighed, and seemed to take a long time to assimilate whatever she was experiencing. "The war is over, just as Paul predicted. It's spring, it's . . . I guess it's April now."

Her voice was subdued, lacking the vibrancy that had been evident up till now. "The calendar on the wall says 1919. Apple trees outside in the orchard are in bloom again." She sighed, as if the beauty was no comfort, and her whole body slumped.

"He's gone, you know. Paul's gone," she confided. "Since last December. He managed to stay a little longer because he volunteered to stay with the worst of the injured soldiers, the ones who couldn't be moved. But finally, he had to go."

"And how are you managing without him?"

The voice seemed to be inside her head. Bernadette tried to figure out where the questions came from, but she felt muddled, as if her head were full of cotton wool.

She was tired of being weak, of feeling drained and ill. She had little patience for all this talk. Who was this, asking questions? She looked around.

Lorelei Dupré was seated on the chair across the kitchen table from her, and Bernadette thought of asking her if she heard the voice, too, but it seemed too much effort to explain.

Anyway, Lorelei knew that Paul was gone. She knew everything. She was like a sister.

Bernadette was pregnant with Paul's child, and Lorelei came by almost every day, riding her rusty old bicycle along the lane. The two women were closer than they'd ever been, perhaps because Lorelei, too, was in love, and the relationship was complex.

Lorelei was married to a man much older than herself. Years before, she'd come to the village from Paris to live with an old aunt. Her parents had died that year, when Lorelei was twelve, leaving her penniless and terrified of being sent to an orphanage. She'd told Bernadette many times how grateful she'd been to her aunt for bringing her here and caring for her.

Pierre Dupré was a wealthy shopkeeper in the village, and he'd courted the teenage girl despite the fact that he was forty years her senior. Encouraged by her aunt, Lorelei had married him when she was barely fifteen, and she'd been a dutiful wife.

But the war changed everything, just as it had for Bernadette, and Lorelei fell in love.

His name was Tony Briggs, and he was English, a squadron commander who'd crashed his airplane during a thunderstorm one evening in a rocky field five miles out of the village. It happened during the final days of the war.

Dr. Cerdan had been called to treat the injured man, but as usual lately, the doctor was far too drunk to respond. Lorelei had gone to administer whatever help she could, and she talked a local family into taking the unconscious man into their home.

Dr. Cerdan eventually sobered up enough to set his broken arm and leg. Lorelei went on nursing him, and by the time Tony could have been shipped back to an English hospital to recuperate, he and Lorelei were lovers. He stayed on in the village as the war came to an end, and lingered during the confusion that surrounded the military afterward.

Tony was single, and he urged Lorelei to leave her aging husband and come away to England with him. Lorelei was torn, wanting to go, but at the same time feeling responsible for Pierre, who loved her like a child and relied on her more and more as he grew older.

Tony finally was forced to leave, but he'd managed to come across from England twice since in order to see Lorelei.

Bernadette thought it would have been wonderful if Paul could come back, even for a day. She said as much to Lorelei.

"If he were the one pregnant, he'd be back for longer than that," her friend declared with typical cynicism. "Is the nausea any better?'' Lorelei had poured them each more of the herbal tea, which seemed to be the only thing Bernadette's stomach would tolerate these days.

''I think so,'' Bernadette lied, turning aside for a moment to admire a picture Nicole had drawn with one of the colored pencils Paul had brought her on his next-to-last visit.

''Look, Maman.''

''It's a beautiful drawing, chérie. I see the trees, and the river. What is this, here, then?'' She pointed to an uncertain group of shapes in the center of the paper.

''It's Paul, Maman, coming here to see us, in a wagon. See the horses pulling him? When will he come again to see us, Maman? I miss Paul. I miss the magic tricks he used to do. And he made my head better the day I fell down.''

Nicole had been climbing on a fence once when Paul was visiting, and she'd fallen and split her head open. The blood had terrified Bernadette.

Paul, with infinitely gentle skill, had stitched the child's head and then spent all day acting as a willing slave to her, carrying her around and doing all sorts of magic illusions to amuse her, even making one of the farm rabbits appear out of an old hat. He'd rocked her to sleep that night, humming a bawdy American folksong instead of a lullaby.

Pain overcame Bernadette, and her eyes filled with the easy tears that seemed to hover all the time behind her eyes these days.

''I miss him, too, chérie. Go draw another—one for Lorelei, perhaps?''

The little girl trotted off, and the women were silent for a moment.

''I shouldn't be hard on him. He really had no choice, and you were far too stubborn. You should have gone with him when he asked. Have you had another letter?'' Lorelei added in a softer voice.

Bernadette nodded. ''Yesterday. And money, as usual.''

''Thank heaven he's generous. At least you can rest the way you need to, instead of having to do laundry and scrub floors for sour-faced old bats, the way you would have to if he didn't send money.''

''He's generous, as you say. From the very beginning he brought me food, books for Nicole I couldn't have bought. And when he left, there was that account.''

Paul had thrust the bankbook into her hand a moment before that final leave-taking, his face contorted with the effort of holding back his own tears. And the balance in the account had staggered her. It had also given her a measure of security.

In postwar France, there was no room for false pride. Life was difficult, supplies, apart from the barest essentials, almost impossible to obtain, and the money Paul left allowed Bernadette to relax from the constant weary struggle to make ends meet.

It was fortunate, because she couldn't have worked hard, no matter how desperate the need. Paul's child was making her sick in a way she'd never been with Nicole.

"You still haven't told him, in your letters?"

Lorelei disapproved of Bernadette's firm decision to keep the pregnancy a secret from Paul. Lorelei felt Paul should have been told about the baby before he left; Bernadette had known for several weeks by then that she carried his child.

Bernadette shook her head. "It would be wrong to tell him now. He's far away. He couldn't come racing back here. And there's nothing he can really do. As sick as I am, I'll probably never carry this child to term anyway."

Lorelei said nothing, but her soft green eyes met Bernadette's in a telling glance. They both knew that miscarriage would be a blessing in these circumstances.

When Bernadette first knew she was pregnant, Lorelei had offered help if she wanted to abort the child. It was proof, if Bernadette had ever needed it, of the other woman's love for her, because Lorelei adored children. Her job was bringing them safely into the world, and Bernadette knew her friend would never consider doing such a thing for anyone but her.

"This last letter is disturbing, Lorelei. Paul's father-in-law, this Martin Oakley, has had a slight stroke, and Paul's...wife, Grace, has fallen ill with flu. Apparently she's very sick indeed. Paul says this flu is causing many deaths in North America just as it is here in Europe."

Lorelei made a disgusted noise in her throat, and Bernadette didn't have to add that discussion of divorce between Paul and Grace was obviously out of the question at the moment.

"This Grace won't die, worse luck," Lorelei fumed. "From what Paul told you about her, this is a woman who can become ill whenever it suits her. Such women hold their men with yokes of guilt and duty." Her face grew rebellious and a little guilty. "Not only women are capable of that. Pierre, too, keeps me tied to him that way."

"Even now Paul begs me to come to America," Bernadette said in a soft, choked voice. "How I long to do exactly that."

Now she tossed and turned through the lengthening nights, cursing herself for not making the decision to go with him when he had asked. The loneliness she felt was like a cancer eating at her heart. Sometimes it overcame her, and she had to creep into Nicole's tiny bedroom and crouch beside the child's bed during the black night hours, reassuring herself that she wasn't really alone, holding the sleeping child's hand for comfort.

Now, of course, it was too late to go to Paul. She was far too ill to travel even to the village, let alone begin the complex machinations that were necessary if she were to emigrate to the United States.

But after the child came, she promised herself with fierce intent, then she would go.

Nothing would stop her after the child was born.

When the retching was too severe to allow her to even lie down, she would sit propped against pillows with paper and pen, and write long letters to Paul, to the work address he'd instructed her to use.

She wrote cheerful fantasies, little anecdotes about herself and Nicole, regards from Dr. Marc Cerdan, reports on the farm animals, the latest story from the postman, who cursed about everything.

She told him of the late produce from the garden he'd helped her plant, of the kittens the barn cat produced, and always, of how she walked daily along the river path where she and he had walked, thinking of him, pausing under the tree where they'd made love.

Here, she felt closest to him. Here, too, she missed him with a desperation close to madness. She'd left the blanket behind the fallen tree, where they'd folded it the last time they'd made love there.

She never told him that she seemed to have become a bottomless well of tears that flowed in endless rivers down her face as she followed their path and imagined him at her side. Her eyes burned and stung from crying, and she felt sick all the time.

TEARS WERE AGAIN POURING down Annie's cheeks, and Steve, with gentle care, blotted them away using a handful of tissue.

It was once again necessary, he decided, to suggest she move ahead through time.

"You carried the baby to full term?"

She nodded.

"Move ahead to that time, then. What are you aware of now?"

Her tears stopped, and her voice became thin, as if she were tired, very weak, and worried. She didn't talk about the child right away.

"The letters have stopped, you know—Paul's letters. I've had no word from him for over three months. I'm insane with worry. Do you suppose he's forgotten me? I can't bear to think he's forgotten me. It must be something else, don't you think?"

The pathos in her voice touched Steve's soul.

"I was ill after the baby came. I truly thought I would die and I didn't care. I suppose I might have died, without Dr. Cerdan and Lorelei. She moved in here with Nicole and me, and nursed me and the baby. But I did such a stupid thing then, while I was sick. I wrote Paul. I told him everything, about the baby, about how ill I was, everything. I sent the letter to his home address."

Annie's breath caught in a gulp, and she wrung her hands.

"I told him that I couldn't go on without him, that I'd come to him as soon as the baby was old enough, if he would arrange it. I love him. I love him so much, I can't bear to live like this, without him. I would rather die than live my life without Paul."

The vehemence faded and Annie's body became still in the reclining chair. "Lorelei posted the letter, and I waited. I waited week after week, but no answer ever came. I've stopped waiting now. Inside of me, my heart is dying. I should never have told him. Perhaps he thinks I'm trying to trap him. Or he's simply forgotten me."

Steve's own voice was thick with emotion. "What about the baby? Is your baby healthy?"

She didn't smile, but there was tenderness in her tone this time, and she gazed down at her lap as if she were looking down at a baby.

"My son is very tiny. How could one this tiny cause such difficulties? Lorelei says it was the hardest labor she's seen. She was furious with Dr. Cerdan. He was drinking all that day and was no help to her at all.''

Steve's face twisted with compassion, and he swallowed hard as she went on, ''I lost a great deal of blood. It seemed to go on forever, and then, this small one decided to be born, after all.''

She chucked her tongue the way all mothers do at their babies. ''Nicole adores him, she's like a little mother herself with him. His name is Marcel, after my grandfather. I wanted at first to name him Paul, but Lorelei said the child needs his own name, not one that reminds me every second of...'' Her voice broke, and her face crumpled. Then she seemed to muster her strength, becoming almost businesslike, although her tone was still weak and reedy.

''He's five weeks now. I'm feeding him, although sometimes there's hardly enough milk...'' Her voice trailed off, and she tipped her head to one side as if she were listening.

''What is it?'' Steve asked. ''What's happening now?''

''I hear someone, at the door. Someone...''

She sounded puzzled and a little apprehensive. Steve waited, curious about this new development.

The fearsome cry that came from Annie resounded through the room, and Steve bolted from his chair, staring down at her.

''Whatever it is has no power to hurt you any longer, do you understand?''

He forced himself to sound calm and persuasive. She was breathing rapidly, cowering on the couch, an expression of extreme fear on her face.

''Ann...Bernadette, whatever is occurring is already over. Move through it. It can't hurt you because it's over. Do you hear me? Move to the other side of the experience.''

Her hands were trembling, and every faint trace of color had fled from her face.

''What is it? Can you describe it to me now?''

She tried to speak and couldn't. Finally moistening her lips, she managed.

''My God! My God, it's my...it's Jean Desjardins! He came walking through the door just now. He has come home. And I was...was sitting here, nursing this child.'' Her voice dropped to a whisper. ''It's not Jean's baby. He couldn't have known about him. I was...nursing...Paul's baby...and the man...who was my husband came...came...home.''

She spoke in staccato gasps, and Steve was concerned about the violent emotion Annie was reliving. He debated whether or not he should allow her to continue, and decided against it.

"Leave the emotion back there where it belongs, Annie. It has no power to hurt you anymore. You are Annie Pendleton again. You're waking up now. At the count of three, you will awaken, and you will remember these things with understanding, without pain, knowing how they relate to your present life. Coming out now, one—two—three—"

The total silence was marked only by the faraway ringing of the telephone in the outer office and Edith's muffled voice as she answered it.

Steve waited, apprehension knotting his gut.

After what seemed an eternity, Annie opened her eyes, the anguish and fear slow to fade from her features.

"Now I know who he was," she said at last, looking up at Steve with eyes still half in another world. "I know who he is in this life, and I know why there are bad feelings between us. I know now—I understand why I couldn't marry him again."

"What do you understand, Annie?" Steve smiled at her, reassuring her, relieved more than he could say that she was back. The depth of the trance she attained was worrisome at times like this.

"I know," she said again, drawing in a ragged breath, "that my husband back then, Jean Desjardins, is someone I know well in this life. His name—" she swallowed and tried again "—the name I know him by in this life is Michael McCrae, and he's the father of my son, Jason."

CHAPTER FIFTEEN

"STEVE?" Her voice was urgent and her eyes begged for reassurance.

"Yes, Annie, go on. I'm right here, listening."

Her breath caught in a sob. "I'm terrified of him. I always have been. Jean, Michael, whichever name he has. I was afraid back then, at that dreadful moment when he walked in the door, but I've felt that way about him in this lifetime, too."

She drew in another breath, and Steve asked, "Can you tell me exactly what happened to you? You were frightened, and I felt there was a great deal of the story missing."

Steve hoped that the telling would let her release the pain of the memory.

She stared at the opposite wall, but he could tell she wasn't seeing it at all.

She was seeing Jean Desjardins. Her voice was almost a whisper when she began. "He was so angry, he looked quite insane. He stood there clenching and unclenching his fists and staring first at me and then at the poor tiny baby, as if he hated us both."

Annie shook her head, trying to explain to Steve the rest of the traumatic scene she'd just experienced, which still seemed powerful and real.

"I was breast-feeding the baby. I couldn't move when he came toward me. I sat there as if I were paralyzed, and he came across the kitchen, step by slow step."

She shuddered, and cold drops of perspiration dotted her forehead. Even with Steve's suggestion that she move beyond the emotion, all the feelings still lingered, mixtures of fear and sorrow and terror, and worst of all, that deep, maternal protectiveness toward the tiny infant she'd held in her arms.... It seemed only moments ago.

Her breasts still ached with the fullness of the milk. She could smell the clean baby scent, see how the fine hair on the top of the fragile skull whirled into a peak beneath the blue-veined skin. She could feel the overwhelming mother love for the child she held. It almost choked her, even now.

And she could see that threatening man . . . her husband . . . coming toward them.

She began again, trying to keep her voice steady and failing. "Jean, he—Jean looked barely human, skeleton thin, hair shaved off, dirty." She shuddered again. "I learned later that he'd been in a prison camp, close to death for many months, and he had suffered a sort of mental breakdown there. When he saw me with the baby, I believed for a moment he was about to kill us both, Steve. His eyes were bloodred, and his whole body shook as he came toward us." Annie shuddered, clasping the welcome cup of tea Steve handed her.

"Nicole came running in just then, and the expression on her little face stopped him. 'Who is that man,' she kept asking me. 'Is he going to hurt our baby? Don't let him hurt our baby, Maman.' And I couldn't answer. I couldn't tell her it was her father. I couldn't even seem to get it through my own head that this awful creature could still be my husband. It didn't seem possible."

Annie's eyes closed as the horror of the situation rolled over her. "You see, I felt that I belonged, body and soul, to Paul Duncan, regardless of whether we were married or not."

Just as she felt she belonged to David, here and now, whether he was with her or not.

"I know them all again—that's what's so awful," she burst out. "I know both my husband and my lover from that other life, Steve. I'm involved with them all over again in this one. I love David just as passionately as I loved Paul, and years ago I was involved with Michael. He fathered my son, and I gradually began to hate and fear him. I always believed it was illogical, my deep-seated feelings about him, and yet now I see that what happened before had bearing on what I feel for him now."

Steve nodded. "Of course it does, Annie. Remembrance can bring new insights into our lives, and it can also bring the memory of great suffering. Understanding is the true benefit of all this, because with knowledge comes the power each of us has to change the outcome this time around. Perhaps we can prevent further harm," or make up for old wrongs. It all comes down to choice."

Annie listened, not just with her ears, but with her whole being. Because of what she'd experienced, she understood as never before the reservations she'd had about marrying Michael years ago.

She poured it all out to Steve. "I was married to him once already, a hellish marriage, that lifetime ago. It was a monstrous mistake. At least I had sense enough not to do it again this time."

Steve waited. When she didn't go on, he said, "But this time you had his son, didn't you?"

And, her relentless mind prodded, wasn't it a kind of divine justice for the son to be Michael's this time, having to adjust to David much the same way he must have had to adjust to Jean in another lifetime?

And why did Paul desert her back then? The devastating sense of loss and heartbreak she'd experienced as Bernadette lingered in her very pores, and when she thought of it a sore knot formed in her chest, and resentment grew.

Resentment toward David?

Yes, she admitted silently. Knowing what she knew did make her resent him, however illogical that might seem. No matter what, he shouldn't have deserted her the way he had.

There was a pattern forming again, of strong influences in David's life that pulled him away from her. It was his same deep-seated sense of responsibility, of needing to help those who depended on him, that was tearing David away just as it had done with Paul.

Would it happen again, here and now? Would David leave her this time, too? Their love was under severe strain, just as it had been then, and the problems weren't only on her side.

She often felt as if she and David were worlds apart emotionally, as they had been physically in that other life. She listed to herself the other concerns that nagged at her day and night. David was totally dedicated to his work, to the exclusion of all else at times. More and more, she was convinced there wasn't room for her. And what about Jason, who stubbornly went on rejecting David? And then there was Calvin Graves and his ambitions for David that didn't include her.

Somewhere too deep for rationality was the conviction that no matter how much she loved him, David would abandon her again.

The echo of that tragic life in France was haunting her. It was haunting all of them, whether they realized it or not.

Were they fated to relive that other sad time? If only David would listen to the story, she could perhaps somehow convince him that they'd destroyed the love they'd shared once already, and that they mustn't let it happen again.

"How can a person persuade someone else that it's really possible to experience this, Steve, and to learn from it?"

Surely Steve must know of a way that would work. She stared up at him, begging for an answer.

But he shook his head. "Annie, only personal experience works. If I'd told you the first time you came here that this was going to occur, you'd probably have walked out in disgust, and labeled me a fraud. There are books, like the ones I loaned you, but they have to be read with an open mind. If the other person has a strong enough block against such material, there really isn't any way I know of to make him think otherwise. He has to come to it on his own. We all do." He added after a long, silent moment, "There's an old adage that says, 'When the student is ready, the teacher appears.'"

That was no consolation at all. She folded her arms against her chest, trying to hold in the agony inside but failing.

"Steve, I won't be back after today. I can't go through this any longer. I can't stand the pain. I'd rather not know if it's all going to happen again, or how it all ended back then."

She looked at him, her eyes swimming with tears so that he seemed shimmery and insubstantial.

"I just can't do this anymore. I can't stand this feeling that lasts even after I come out, as if the only person I've ever totally loved has—" her voice broke again "—has deserted me forever. See, Steve, it makes me certain that he'll do it all over again, and I can't bear that."

Her face was ravaged, a kind of agony contorting her features.

"Now that we've found each other, I can't stand the thought of living another lifetime without him, and yet deep in my heart I'm afraid that's what's going to happen. But I can't be absolutely certain, you see, because I can't see the future. I'm so glad I can't. At least I can dream. I can hope."

Her eyes met Steve's, and his heart contracted with pity for her.

"Back there, there wasn't even one shred of hope. And that's why I can't go back again. Oh, Steve, I'm such a rotten coward."

Steve reached out and took her hand. "You're a brave woman, Annie. Few of us have the courage to look at ourselves the way you're doing."

She made herself unknot her fists.

"Isn't this ironic? We go through life wishing we knew more about ourselves, and now I'm scared witless because I think I do." She gave a laugh that sounded more like a sob.

Steve came and took her shoulders in his hands. "Annie, I have to say I think it's a mistake to come this far and not see it through. We haven't reached the core of the problem with your neck yet, and I know it's buried back there, in that awful time. Annie, don't make a final decision now. Wait a few weeks until the memories are easier to handle."

She shook her head. "They never will be. They're burned into my brain and they just go on hurting. Nope, I'm finished, Steve. I should have listened. David told me I was fooling with stuff I didn't really understand. Now I'm inclined to believe him."

"Does it help to tell yourself that everything that happened back then is over now—it's part of your personal history?" Steve pleaded. "You can't alter the past, Annie. But you can change the present. If you choose to stop now, that's entirely your decision. You're entitled to do whatever you think best. But if you ever feel you need to come back, remember that I'll help all I can."

Steve watched her gather up her purse and sweater.

"Goodbye, Steve. Thank you."

ALL THE WAY HOME, Annie thought about what had happened.

She had to try again to talk this over with David—she simply had to. She'd tell him of her decision not to go on with it, but she had to confide in him, let him know what she'd learned about their common past, because she was convinced it was his past as well as hers.

Jason would be spending next weekend with Michael and Lili.

If she made a special dinner, and she and David had time together, if she introduced the regression logically, without negative emotion or pressure, maybe it would work?

She called David at his office as soon as she got home, and her heart sank when she got Phyllis on the line.

"He's not available at the moment. He's in an important meeting," Phyllis said with more than her usual brisk impatience. "I'll give him your message, but his schedule is tight today, Ms Pendleton. He has several late appointments after this." She was both snippy and dismissive, and made Annie feel like a teenybopper hounding a movie star.

"Well, this is important, too," Annie forced herself to say. "Just tell David I called and that I'd like to speak to him as soon as possible."

The secretary's manner never failed to put her on the defensive. As she hung up, Annie mentally added Phyllis to the list of obstacles that loomed between her and David.

AS ALWAYS, when he appeared at her door later that day, every problem seemed insignificant in relation to the love between them. She flew into his arms, and he held her for a long, silent time as the invisible bond uniting them strengthened with the contact of their bodies.

"I missed you so much, Annie. Want to come away to a desert island with me?"

How she wished it was possible.

They settled on Sunday evening for a quiet, home-cooked dinner, because, predictably, David was committed to various appointments and dinner meetings for the rest of the week, including both Friday and Saturday.

Of course, they'd spend some evenings together before then, but it was always late by the time David was finished with his workday.

"How's the child you told me about who was hemorrhaging?" Annie asked.

"Took us most of the night, but we got him stabilized. He was a street kid, thirteen years old, and he waited too long to come in, so his appendix had burst. Then he developed stress ulcers in his stomach, and the ulcers bled. We nearly lost him. I was at the hospital at five this morning.''

For a fleeting moment, Annie had considered trying to talk with David that night about the regression session, but she gave it up fast as a bad idea. His eyes were bloodshot and he moved as if he were exhausted.

She made him hot chocolate and a thick ham sandwich, and they talked about pleasant things.

''You will come with me to this luncheon deal on Saturday, love?'' David coaxed. ''It's the only damned thing all weekend that might not bore you to death.''

Annie agreed to go.

Beggars can't be choosers, she reminded herself. If she wanted to share in his life, she'd better learn to look as if she enjoyed chatting to people she hoped to never see again.

THE LUNCHEON ON SATURDAY was held at one of the huge downtown hotels, and during the social hour, David became engrossed in a technical discussion with three other doctors.

Annie listened for a while, but when the terms became indecipherable, she moved through the crowd to the wall of windows, to admire the breathtaking aerial view of the city and the nearby park.

A tall, older man with pepper-and-salt hair and kind eyes stood near her. He, too, was gazing out with a wistful expression.

''It's a pity to be trapped in here when we ought to be down there in the sunshine, don't you think?'' He motioned with a stemmed glass toward the walkway that bordered the ocean.

Annie agreed, and they chatted for a few moments about Vancouver's weather.

''I'm from Seattle, and our climate is much like yours. My name is Abraham Caldwell.'' He glanced around the room at the groups of people intent on being social. ''And medical gatherings are much the same everywhere. Are you a physician, Ms...uh....?''

His eyes scanned her shoulder for the name tag that wasn't there.

''Annie Pendleton, and no, I'm not a medical person. I write books for children.'' She half expected his eyes to glaze over before he moved away, searching for a more kindred soul to chat with. But instead he stayed and asked intelligent questions about the publishing world and being a writer.

"You're a doctor?" she inquired after ten minutes or so. He was a good-looking man, she noticed now, tanned and fit, with an appealing open smile.

"I have a medical degree, yes. I work as a professor, however. I'm here today to give a short luncheon address on holistic health."

"Which is . . . ?" Annie felt enough at ease with him to reveal her ignorance about most things medical.

"Quite simply, the healing of the whole person, mind, body and spirit, using techniques such as acupuncture, visualization, therapeutic touch as well as more mundane methods. Our attitude is, if it works, use it, regardless of how unusual it might seem. Our success rate is our best advertisement."

He smiled again, and there was a touch of irony in his tone. "Medical science values the scientific, provable approach to problems. There's usually a fair amount of dissension and resistance among medical people when it comes to alternate methods." His eyes were full of gentle humor. "In fact, it might be wise not to sit too close to me at lunch, in case some good doctor throws a tomato or two during my address."

Annie felt a shudder of recognition go through her. She'd wanted more than anything to forget the regression last Tuesday. Yet here was Caldwell reminding her once again that all things were possible.

"What are your views on regressive hypnosis as a method of treating psychosomatic problems?" Annie's heartbeat had accelerated, and now her full attention was centered on the tall man at her side.

"I'm very much in favor of it. I feel we've only begun to explore the possibilities it affords. I refer a great many people to trained hypnotherapists, and the results are positive in an astonishing percentage of cases. In fact, I'll be mentioning that particular method in my talk later."

Annie had an eerie feeling that the powers that ran the universe kept leading her, like the proverbial horse, to water and daring her to drink.

DAVID WAS AWARE OF ANNIE every minute. He knew exactly when she became deeply engrossed in conversation with the distinguished professor, and he could feel his blood pressure rise.

Irrational jealousy stabbed him, tore at his guts, making him want to rush over and plant a fist in the professor's face and then drag Annie away, to a place where there were just the two of them.

His mouth twisted at the thought of Calvin's horrified reaction to a spectacle like the one he was contemplating. In fact, David had the uncomfortable feeling these days that Calvin was subtly turning him into a far too civilized version of himself. He also had the distinct impression that Calvin's plans for him didn't always include Annie. David was going to set Calvin very straight on that at the first opportunity.

Why was he haunted lately with this fear of losing her? He wasn't altogether certain, but it seemed to have something to do with that infernal nightmare that had torn him from sleep more times than he cared to count.

IT WAS AFTER MIDNIGHT, and they were wrapped in each other's arms, bodies still joined after loving, sweaty and slick from love's fervor.

"You made a real conquest at that luncheon today," David murmured, nibbling her ear. "Professor Caldwell was obviously longing to take you back to Seattle with him."

"Jealous?" she teased, raining kisses down his cheek and keeping her legs tight around him.

"Damned right," he growled, and she giggled, sobering when he added, "The professor's taste in women is first-rate, but his talk didn't impress me at all. Medicine is medicine, and magic is magic. I'm well qualified in both, and believe me, they don't belong under the same shingle. I get furious when I'm tricked into listening to garbage like he was spouting today."

Annie's heart sank. She'd been hopeful that Professor Caldwell's talk might open the door just a bit for her own discussion with David.

Passionate words sprang to her lips, defense of all the things David was denying. But she remembered that she had a good reason to keep silent, to save all her arguments and convictions to use where they'd do the most good; in an effort to get him to listen, really listen and absorb, the things that were important to both of them. And now was not the right time.

So she curled tighter against him, sliding a wicked hand down between them and cupping the part of him that gave her such pleasure.

He drew his breath in and covered her mouth in a kiss that was a prelude, and soon Annie forgot everything except his body, invading hers, joining with hers in an ancient dance that made them one flesh. The act of love allowed her the balm of forgetfulness for a tiny stretch of time.

SUNDAY MORNING, they got up early and rode bikes down to Granville Island and the huge farmers' market that was centered there. They breakfasted on croissants and fruit from stalls in the covered market, and Annie carefully shopped for the freshest produce and meat she could find for the dinner they'd share later that evening.

They rode home, puffing and laughing their way up hills because of the loaded string bags of groceries Annie had bought. At home, David helped her unload and shortly afterward left for his appointment.

He hadn't been gone fifteen minutes when Cleo gave her distinctive short rap on the back door. She was carrying two of the books she'd borrowed.

"The girls have gone to a birthday party, and I saw David drive away. You busy? If you don't feel like company just say the word."

"I'm about to do a massive cook scene here. C'mon in and help me prepare vegetables."

Annie put fresh coffee on, and together they scrubbed and chopped produce for the stew Annie planned.

"So how's it going?" Cleo raised an eyebrow and waited.

"Which particular 'it' are you talking about? There's David, there's Jason, there's Dr. Munro. My life is a mass of 'its' at the moment."

"Start with Munro. Don't you call him Steve? Have you learned any more with the regression?"

Annie quickly sketched in the latest developments from her last session, able to control her voice and minimize the trauma of what she'd gone through.

It was like a dress rehearsal, she told herself. She'd have to keep it light if she wanted David to listen to the whole thing. She concentrated on telling the story, trying to divorce herself from the emotion as much as possible, concluding by explaining the link between Michael in this lifetime and Jean in that.

Cleo listened. When Annie was done, her friend whistled in amazement.

"So there you were, with a husband back from the war and a kid who wasn't his. And when you think about it, it's obvious that Jean would turn up again as Michael. No wonder you feel the way you do about him."

It was absurd, but finishing the story had made Annie choke up with emotion all over again. She bent her head over the carrots. "I guess it was pretty hard on him, too, come to think of it."

"You know, these books explain a lot of things I've always wondered about," Cleo remarked. "Such as why bad things like that happen to us, and why the same damn situation keeps popping up over and over again in our lives. Apparently all we're here for is to learn lessons we've been too boneheaded to learn before. Which puts paid to my idea that we're here to have a good time. Anyway, what I still don't understand in this regression you've had is how it's related to the pain you get in your neck. Nothing's come up about that, has it?"

"Not yet," Annie admitted. That lack was beginning to seem the weak link in the whole thing. "I asked Steve about it, and he seems to think there has to be an incident of some sort in that particular lifetime that was the root cause of my neck problem, because my subconscious returns over and over again to that experience. Whatever it was, we haven't gotten to it yet. And we're not going to, either." She scooped up the neat carrot strips and dumped them into a bowl.

"What do you mean, 'not going to'? I'm waiting with bated breath for the next episode."

Annie shook her head. "Nope. I've decided not to go back for any more of this stuff, Cleo. I—I just can't handle remembering anymore, I guess."

Cleo studied her a moment and then nodded. "Yeah, I sure can see that. It must be scary. I don't think I'd ever have the guts to go through it. I still figure I'd rather not know who I was or what I didn't do last time around." After a moment she added, "Besides, I'd say having this Jean guy turn up like that is enough to give anybody a pain in the neck, wouldn't you? A pain in your backside as well."

Annie smiled a shaky smile and attacked the onions, holding them as far away as possible as she stripped off the papery skins.

"Ain't it the truth? But seriously, the pain is lots better. I've been using the relaxation tapes and the meditation exercises Steve recommended, so the whole thing was worth it."

They peeled in silence for another few moments while Annie wondered whether or not to reveal something else that had become apparent to her after the last session.

"I know you said you don't want to know, but you were my friend back then, too, Cleo," Annie ventured. "I'm pretty certain you were Lorelei Dupré."

Cleo tossed some celery into the bowl. "I sort of thought so myself," she mumbled, not looking at Annie. "I had a funny feeling each time you mentioned her." There was a long pause, and then Cleo asked in a small voice, "If you find out anything bad about her, don't tell me, okay? I mean, part of me would like to know if she ever got up enough gumption to take off with that young pilot, but another part doesn't have the stomach for it, see?"

"I understand, only too well. Why do you think I can't bear going back and finding out anymore?"

Cleo tossed her knife down and slumped back in her chair.

"I probably didn't do anything but mope around like a sick cow back then. That's typical of me. I'm not any braver this time around, either."

"Do you mean Don?"

Cleo nodded and bowed her head. She hesitated before she answered.

"I really like this guy, y'know, Annie? He's intelligent and sexy and sweet. And he's interested in me. But for all the yapping I've done about finding a guy I could love again, now I'm scared of getting involved. That's what's underneath the noise about his age and being a policeman and all that. That's not the reason at all. I'm simply scared of getting hurt again."

"Well, you got really hurt when your husband walked out," Annie reasoned.

"Yeah, but wouldn't you think I'd be over that by now? I thought for sure I was until Don came along. I really wish I knew how to stop feeling this way."

"Give it time, Cleo," was all Annie could find to say. Who was she to advise anyone on matters of the heart? She felt just as uncertain about David as Cleo did about Don Anderson.

And in an eerie fashion, it was for the same reason as Cleo. She'd had her heart thoroughly broken the last time around, and she was scared spitless it was going to happen again. It didn't matter one bit that the last time had happened to her over seventy years before.

THE DINNER was going to be a triumph, she told herself as she made the final preparations after Cleo had gone home.

She'd put together a thick, exotic stew with beefsteak simmered in red wine, herbs and fresh vegetables. She baked a loaf of crusty bread, and made a crisp salad, with apple pie and thick cream for dessert.

She placed the regression tapes in the machine. They would need only a touch to turn them on.

The problem was trying to figure out just when it would be best to broach the subject with David.

Perhaps before dessert? Or after, when they were having coffee?

She set the table with extra care, opened a bottle of fine French wine to let it breathe and dashed upstairs at the last minute to shower and change into a pair of silky black pants and a blue jersey top that hugged her breasts. She brushed her hair up and twisted it into a knot, then fastened the crystal pendant David had given her around her neck, adding a pair of tiny pearl earrings.

"Annie? Hey, darlin', get down here and kiss me." David's voice was full of exuberance, and she bounced down the stairs to greet him with the long, passionate kiss he'd requested. David held her tight, and words poured from him.

"I stopped off at my apartment to pick up the phone messages, and there was one to call Calvin. Apparently he's managed to get me on the finance committee, which means I also become an advisor to the Board of Directors. Annie, my love, it looks as if I might get a chance to have my say, after all."

He held Annie around the waist, and she looked up into his eyes. They were like blue flames, full of light and animation and love for her, with a touch of self-mockery. He announced his news.

"Calvin was as close to gleeful as I've ever heard him."

Annie thought that would really be something from a near cadaver like Calvin, and then felt ashamed of herself.

"This is the all-important first step toward eventually becoming a full board member, Annie, and being able to really carry some weight when it comes to decisions such as whether or not we need an expanded transplant facility. I feel as if I'm actually doing something at last instead of just making empty noises nobody hears."

"Oh, David, I'm happy for you. I'm thrilled, darling." She hugged him and soon the kisses they shared grew heated and full of desire.

"Maybe ... we ... should ... just ... go ... upstairs ... and ..." With each word, he walked her backward toward the stairs, kissing her face and throat wherever his lips landed, pressing his hips against her with urgent need.

Annie finally tore her mouth from his and resisted his backward path by going limp in his arms.

"Stop, you lunatic." She grabbed his hand and tugged. "Come in the kitchen and behave yourself. Dinner's all but ready, and you can have a drink while I put the finishing touches on the food."

"But man doesn't live by liquor alone," he teased, pretending to ruffle her hair and then managing to make it seem as if he'd pulled a long-stemmed red rose out of her upswept knot.

He looked comically amazed at his own sleight of hand, and then bowed and handed her the flower. She was thrilled and amused; she couldn't figure out where he'd had it hidden, and of course he wouldn't tell her.

"Sorcerers never reveal their secrets, my pretty one," he hissed, pretending to twirl an imaginary moustache. "However, it you should change your mind and come upstairs with me, I could probably be seduced into..."

She tossed a tea towel at him.

He made her laugh all during dinner with gross, exaggerated tales of the women's auxiliary meeting he'd addressed.

When she served the warm apple pie with thick slices of cheddar cheese and a bowl of cream, he reached across the table, took her hand and brought it to his lips.

"Annie, this is a meal fit for a king. Thank you, sweet, for going to all this work for me. I wish we could have evenings like this more often. The schedule of committees and meetings that

Calvin has me roped into isn't my idea of how a person spends his free time, and I promise you it won't always be this way."

"Will the meetings ease off now you're an advisor to the Board?" Annie was pretty certain they wouldn't, but there was no harm in hoping.

He grimaced and shook his head. "It's unfortunate, but no."

For the first time that evening, a look of strain came over his face. "I've said I'll do this, Annie, and I will. But if I'd known what a drain it was going to be on our relationship, on my time, even on my job, I'm not sure I'd have gotten myself into it..." His voice trailed off.

"David, are you dead certain this is what you really want?" The question popped out, probably because it had been hovering under the surface for a while. "Or are you going along with it because it's what Calvin Graves wants for you?"

Whispers of another time, of a man named Martin Oakley, rose in the back of her mind. Although she couldn't be sure, she had the feeling that Oakley had had something to do with deserting Bernadette.

"What do you mean, because it's what Calvin wants?" There was harshness in his answer all of a sudden. "That's a rotten thing to say, Annie. Of course it's my own choice to do this. I thought you knew that without having to ask.

"After all, the committees I'm on now are just learning tools," he rationalized. "I plan to head one in the near future that studies the feasibility of an extended organ transplant unit and devote all my spare time to that one issue. The rest of all this is unimportant."

Unimportant? Then why was he doing it, she wondered? Was never having time with her unimportant? Irritation grew in Annie until she couldn't stifle it.

"But David," she burst out, "it's eating your life just the same, and affecting my life, as well, because I love you. I want to spend time with you, and there isn't room for that. How can I share what's happening to me when I never see you?"

Damn it all, this wasn't what she'd planned to talk about. But now that it had surfaced, maybe it was important that he know how she felt.

He sighed. "I know it seems impossible just now for us to have much time together, and believe me, I want time with you, Annie. I want us to spend the rest of our lives with each other."

Annie felt her heartbeat accelerate, and she knew what he was going to say. David was about to propose to her. And what was she going to answer when he did?

His words were quiet and emphatic. "Annie, I want to marry you." The statement was matter-of-fact, purposeful, and as if he read her mind he added, "You may not be ready for that yet, but I am."

His blue eyes seemed to pin her to her chair, blazing with intent. "See, I want to come home each evening and find you there for me. I want to be around when you need me. It drives me nuts, not having enough time to court you the way I want to. It's a real problem, and I take full responsibility for it."

His tone took on a harder edge. "But there's a hell of a lot more to this than just the demands on my time. The problems aren't all on my side. You know as well as I do that Jason resents me, that there's no way in the world he'd accept our being together without causing us both a great deal of trouble. And believe me, a thirteen-year-old boy can make life pretty miserable if he decides to."

She did know that. She'd been hoping that Jason would improve, but he hadn't.

"I've tried to be reasonable, tried to explain to him that adults need relationships, but he's just not ready to accept...," she began, but David slammed his hand down on the table, silencing her.

"There's a point where a boy Jason's age needs more than sweet reason, damn it. He's manipulating you, doing his best to control the situation. Don't you see that, Annie? He's a bright kid, and he's strong. Right now he needs a stiff dose of tough love, ultimatums about behavior and consequences. Stop shielding him, stop letting him make you feel guilty for loving me. He's had you to himself far too long. It's natural, but it's as dangerous for him as it is for you if you let him win."

His harsh criticism wounded and angered her. She knew there was truth in some of what he said, but his absolute assurance that he knew all the answers enraged her. Jason was her son. David had never had a child, had no idea of the pitfalls involved. Yet here he was, lecturing her on how it ought to be done.

"Is that what this is, David?" Her voice was dripping with sarcasm. "Some sort of competition between you and Jason with me as the prize?"

She was trembling. She folded her hands in her lap so he wouldn't see.

"Don't be ridiculous." He scowled at her. "I'm just telling you it's wrong to let the boy run your life."

"Run my life? He's a huge part of my life. We've been alone together since he was born, and I know him better than I know you."

Annie saw David flinch at that, but she was far too angry to back off now.

"Don't you think that it might be a good idea for you to get to know Jason before you make all these assumptions about him? You're full of suggestions, but you're never around to spend any time with him."

"Damn it, Annie...."

She knew he was about to say that time was one thing he didn't have, but they'd been over that already. Besides, that was his concern, not hers.

He looked exhausted, all of a sudden, and maybe ashamed of his bad temper.

But what she said was right, Annie reassured herself. He had no right to criticize Jason if he didn't also put time and effort into helping the boy.

As if they'd conjured him up, a car door slammed out front and Jason's voice hollered a cheerful goodbye. A moment later, he came in through the back door. Annie and David waited, tension thick between them. Jason appeared in the dining room doorway, sports bag slung over his shoulder, red hair on end.

"Hi, Mom, I'm home. I'm going downstairs to do homework." There was much less enthusiasm as he added, not looking at David, "Hi, Dr. Roswell."

His negative attitude was palpably evident.

"How was your weekend?" Annie's voice sounded strained even to her own ears.

"Ace, just ace. My dad and Lili—I guess I should call her my stepmother, eh Mom?—well, we went hiking up in North Vancouver, by the reservoir, and there's this suspension bridge, and she was scared to go over it. My dad and I had to take her hands and lead her across. And then we made all these weird things for dinner—*chapatis* that you fry, like flat bread. Man, they're good. Maybe you oughta get the recipe, Mom. Well, see ya.''

He clattered down the stairs to the basement, whistling tunelessly. There was silence for a long time after Jason disappeared.

Annie's shoulder and neck were throbbing all of a sudden. She felt as if her face were frozen with the effort it took not to show she was in pain.

David studied her expression. Then he swore and got to his feet, knocking his chair over behind him. He ignored it and drew Annie into his arms, stroking her back.

''I'm a rotten-tempered ass, darling. I haven't been sleeping well lately, probably—,'' he held her away and looked down into her eyes, making a joke of it ''—probably because you're not lying there beside me. Anyhow, I'm sorry if I hurt you with what I said. I sounded like a know-it-all.''

''But you were right about a lot of it,'' she said in a small, dreary voice. ''It's just that I'm defensive when it comes to Jason, I guess.''

''Well, in the next few weeks I'm going to do what you suggested—try to get to know him and let him know me.''

She didn't ask when he'd find the time for it, because she simply didn't believe him. His intentions were without doubt the best, but she knew from experience it wouldn't work. After all, there were only so many hours in a day or a week.

David helped Annie tidy the kitchen and load the dishwasher. They both did their best at being cheerful and they even managed to laugh a little, but David left early.

''I've got surgery first thing in the morning, and I'm beat,'' he explained, kissing her at the door, and Annie felt only relief when his car sped away. The strain was obvious between them, and tonight she didn't feel able to cope with it any longer.

Annie knew it was ridiculous, but she felt wounded and threatened by Jason's account of the weekend with his father and Lili, coming as it had on the heels of David's criticism.

All in all, the evening hadn't been a success. In fact, it had come near to being a total disaster. And she hadn't even mentioned the hypnotic tapes to David the way she'd planned.

That, she decided as she dragged herself up the stairs to her bedroom, was most likely a blessing. They sure didn't need one more thing to argue about, and she didn't have one shred of energy left to do it with anyway.

It wasn't until she was almost asleep that she realized the meal she'd made for David tonight was almost a replica of the one Bernadette had shared with Paul. The more things changed, the more they stayed the same.

HALFWAY THROUGH the following week, David called and asked to speak to Jason.

Annie could tell by the monosyllabic answers her son gave that David was asking him to go somewhere, and she held her breath until Jason finally, grudgingly, agreed.

"What was that all about?" Annie couldn't help asking when the boy hung up.

"He wants me to help him at a magic show he's putting on next Saturday," Jason said with such nonchalance that Annie knew Jason was thrilled despite his animosity toward David. He'd never break down and admit he was pleased, though.

Annie wanted to throttle him.

"Is it okay if I go practice with him tomorrow after school? He said he'll teach me a couple of tricks to do on my own."

"Sure, that's fine." Annie was as careful as her son to sound offhand about the whole thing, but she felt a warm rush of love and gratitude toward David for keeping his promise about getting to know Jason better.

Maybe Sunday evening hadn't been quite the disaster she thought it had.

CHAPTER SIXTEEN

"Now, Jason, this next illusion is called 'Dozens of Eggs from a Hat.'"

They were in David's apartment, and the entire living room area was a carefully congested mass of different magician's equipment that David had been demonstrating for Jason.

"Because the show we'll be doing is for kids of about six to ten, they ought to love this trick," David went on. "If you and I are adept enough to pull it off, that is, without scrambling the eggs ahead of time."

David grinned at the boy, and began to explain the secret.

"What we do is call somebody up from the audience to examine this top hat inside and out, and of course they won't find a single egg anywhere in it. Then you, my trusty assistant, walk casually out from stage back holding a huge piece of oilcloth, which you hold up boldly to convince the audience there's nothing in it, either—it's just to protect the floor from the eggs. As soon as you walk on stage, I'll pass behind you to stand at your side... and remove the silk bag of eggs pinned to your back. Then just as you hold up the oilcloth, I'll slip them neatly into the hat. Let's give it a try."

Jason's face was radiant, and he grinned as David walked him through the procedure.

"Hey, this is bad."

It took David a moment to realize that bad meant great.

"This is real bad," Jason enthused. "We're gonna pull this off like nothin'."

"Right you are. Just don't make any sudden moves with those eggs hanging down your back, partner."

They both laughed.

"Y'know, magic is weird, isn't it?" Jason commented. "I mean, it all seems too easy when you know the secret of the trick, right?"

During the drive over and the first ten minutes there, Jason had been sullen and silent. But David had set the stage for this meeting with extreme care. He'd selected books about magic that would fascinate any boy who had the vaguest curiosity about the art, and had scattered them on the table and the arms of the sofa.

And he'd decided on some not-too-complex illusions that needed an assistant—with a bit of showmanship and sense.

He was beginning to suspect Jason had both traits in abundance, and by now David was enjoying himself just as much as Jason was.

"I want you to perform a trick on your own in the middle of the program," David told the wide-eyed boy. "It'll act as a filler while I'm getting ready for the more elaborate act to follow, but the one I have in mind is punchy and surprising. It's called 'The Glass of Water and the Hat.' This is what you do."

Another two hours sped past without either of them realizing.

"Well, that's about it. I'd better get you home," David said at last. "How about a burger and fries on the way? I'm starved."

"Me, too! I'd really like that, thanks."

The conversation flowed now, centered mostly on magic, and by the time they pulled up in front of Annie's house, David felt there was a new warmth between them.

He soon realized he was mistaken, however.

"You're not comin' in to see my mom tonight, are you?"

There was a less-than-subtle change in the boy as he asked the question.

Open resentment came through in his tone. It was clear that any understanding between them didn't include Annie as far as Jason was concerned.

David sat with his hands on the wheel for a long moment, feeling defeated, and then he decided that win or lose, the time had come to talk to Jason.

He turned and looked at the boy—a long, thoughtful look.

"There's a few things you and I have to get straight between us concerning your mom," he said. "So we might as well sit out here and hash it out right now, Jason. Man-to-man."

David kept his gaze on Jason. "The bare facts are, I love your mother, and I intend to marry her someday soon, if she'll have me. You don't like that idea one bit, and you're putting up a fight."

David stated the facts, keeping his tone as neutral as he could. "I warn you, I'm going to win, regardless of how you feel. But I'd rather have you as a friend than an enemy, Jason. After all, we both love the same lady, don't we?"

Jason's face was stiff and remote, as if he'd removed himself in spirit. It was like giving a speech to an empty room, David decided, trying to talk to this boy. He forged on anyway.

"One of the things we have to learn to do as we grow into men is to begin to think about the consequences of our actions."

Damn. That sounded pious and superior enough to make a kid want to vomit, although Jason didn't look nauseated; he looked more like a marble statue.

David tried again. "What you're doing, see, is agreeing to take on full responsibility for your mom as long as she does what you want, which is dump me and go on with the safe and comfortable life you've shared up till now. You think that's what you want, but there's always a price if we get what we want, Jason."

The boy was staring out the side window, a study in boredom.

"That price is usually our freedom," David said, wondering why the hell he was bothering. "You're growing up. You'll want to be out on your own eventually, living life your own way. If you win this fight with me and get your mother all to yourself again, you'll always be aware that Annie's alone not through choice, but because you manipulated her into it." David made the words emphatic. "And believe me, that's going to bother you a whole bunch."

"That's a big fat lie." Jason had suddenly come to life. Now his face was scarlet, and he was glaring at David with unconcealed anger. "I never manipulated my mother into anything. She can do what she likes. She's an adult. I'm just a kid."

A kid far too smart for his own good, David thought.

"You're her son, and she loves you. What your mom wants is to make certain you're happy, and you know that better than anybody. That's your ammunition in this fight," David said with firm emphasis. "Now if you and I really didn't get along, if we hated each other's personalities, that's one thing. But the fact is we do get along. I think you're a fine guy. The only time there are any bad feelings between us is when your mom's involved. And," David concluded, angry now, "at the same time you're doing your best to restrict her life, you're demanding freedom in your own life. Is that fair?"

"I don't do that. I do not!" Jason objected, sounding close to tears. "I'm just a kid. Kids can't go around demanding things."

"Come off this 'just a kid' nonsense," David said with disgust. "You've got lots of clout and you use it all the time. Of course you demand things," David was remorseless. "You wanted to get to know your father, for instance, and you were pretty adamant about getting what you wanted."

"That's different. That's personal. And lay off my father, you hear?" There was a note of near hysteria in Jason's tone.

David knew there was no point in coming this far and then backing down. "We're not talking about your father, we're talking about you. I'm criticizing you, Jason Pendleton. Think about it. You wanted a relationship, your mom wants a relationship. What's so different about the two situations?"

Their voices were both loud by now, as words flew back and forth. They glared at each other for several moments, both breathing hard.

"You finished this lecture, Dr. Roswell?" Jason's voice dripped venom, and he made a move to get out of the car. "Cause I've gotta go in now."

David gave up. There was no more he could say that would help. He dropped his head back on the padded headrest for a moment, wondering why he'd tried at all.

"Yeah, I guess that's the whole business." He added with no hope at all, "After this, are we still on for next Saturday?"

The answer would determine a great deal on whether he and Jason would ever be friends.

A long, tense moment crept past, and then Jason surprised him. With a visible effort, the boy nodded. "Yeah, I suppose so." As if every word were a tooth being extracted without freezing, he added, "I'm not saying you're right about any of this, Dr. Roswell, but I guess I'll think it over. Maybe."

David could hardly believe his ears. He forced himself to keep his voice noncommittal. "Great. That's all I want you to do. So now let's go in and see your mom. And Jason?"

"Yeah?"

David had to hide a smile at the boy's world-weary tone. It seemed an echo of David's own just a few minutes before.

Obviously Jason was expecting a continuation of the lecture.

"How about calling me David from now on?"

SATURDAY'S MAGIC SHOW was a resounding success. Annie took Cleo and the girls, and they sat up front, close to the stage.

Maggie and Paula were nearly incoherent with the excitement of seeing David as The Sorcerer with Jason as his assistant.

When David called for volunteers to check out his hat in the Dozens of Eggs illusion, Maggie went forward, and Cleo and Annie had to smile as they watched her check out the hat in her own thorough fashion, holding it upside down and reaching her hand inside several times to make certain it was empty.

She was such an earnest child.

"There was nothing in it. I saw with my own eyes it was empty," Maggie told her mother. And then she watched in utter disbelief as David pulled one egg after another out of the tall silk hat.

"He really is magic, isn't he, Mom?" Maggie sighed in ecstasy.

After the show, David invited everyone to McDonald's, where he and Jason refused to reveal any of the secrets of their act, and the laughter and teasing at their table made half the restaurant look their way and smile.

Annie watched her son and the man she loved, noting the warm camaraderie that seemed to have sprung to life between them, and she allowed herself to half hope that the complications of her life were all going to sort themselves out the way this one seemed to have done.

That hope died during the next weeks, however.

David became more embroiled than ever in the endless meetings and dinners that went along with his new appointment.

Annie went along to two of his business dinners, but it was evident that the only person who wanted her there was David. She ended up being seated at the opposite end of the table from him on both occasions, and the time spent on social niceties with strangers seemed to her to be a total waste. Her book was due in another month, and she felt irritated at spending precious hours socializing with people she'd probably never see again.

Calvin Graves was present at that second dinner, and he reinforced all of Annie's misgivings. He was suave, charming and, Annie concluded later, not subtle at all in his dismissive attitude toward her.

"He's a young man on the move, don't you think?" he purred into Annie's ear as David made some clever remark that caused an outburst of laughter from the group around him. "I feel David has the makings of an excellent politician in years to come."

"Yes, I suppose he has," she said with little enthusiasm.

"And how is your little book coming along?" he asked next.

He was both patronizing and as phony as a three-dollar bill. She also had the distinct impression that Calvin felt he could afford to be magnanimous toward her because David would soon be out of her life permanently. Trust Calvin to sense the widening gap between herself and David.

Annie certainly did, no matter how she tried to deny it. Their lives were moving in different directions, and she told David exactly that when he drove her home after the second dinner.

He was silent for a long time, and when he answered it was obvious to Annie that he was impatient with her attitude.

"These affairs aren't exactly fun for me, either, but I thought spending the evening together was worth it."

"David, I hardly had a chance to say two words to you all night. I don't consider that spending the evening together. And half the time I don't even know what those people are discussing. I'm a dead loss when it comes to politics and stock market deals, you know that. I simply don't give a damn about those things."

"I know. But this happens to be the best I can do at the moment socially, if we're going to see each other at all," he said with icy precision, and misery filled her.

"I'd rather you attend these things alone from now on. I'm under pressure to finish my book, and I just don't enjoy this." He didn't answer, and he didn't ask her to go with him again.

AFTER THAT the time they had together, always limited, seemed to dwindle until most of their contact was on the telephone.

Annie worked hard on her writing and tried not to mind the long evenings alone, tried not to recognize what was happening between them.

Or not happening, she corrected with black humor.

They managed to spend four nights together out of fourteen, and on each occasion David arrived near midnight when they both were exhausted, and all either of them wanted to was to lose themselves in the glory of loving and then fall asleep in each other's arms.

But on one of those nights, Annie was startled awake in the dark hours before morning as David flung himself to a sitting position and cried out in such a lost, terrified way that Annie felt paralyzed by nameless dread.

His entire body was soaked with sweat, and she could feel his heart pounding in a frenzy as she touched his chest with her hand. She fumbled with the bedside light and at last its soft glow illuminated the scene.

"David, darling, wake up. What is it?"

Her own heart was pounding with fear. He brushed her arms away with a violent movement, and although his eyes were open, it was obvious he was still unconscious.

"David, wake up! Please wake up,"

When she finally managed to awaken him, he looked at her with crazed, staring eyes, terrifying her for what seemed an eternity before he realized who she was and what was happening.

"David, good grief! What were you dreaming? You scared me half to death."

Annie was close to tears, and her entire body was shaking.

He gathered her close, full of apologies, but refused to say what the nightmare had been about, and Annie felt like a stranger.

It happened the next time they slept together as well, and that time David insisted on getting up and going home at 3:00 a.m. when it happened.

That heralded a new and even more disturbing pattern between them. David still stole hours at night to be with her. He made love passionate, wonderful love to her, and he assured her he loved her. But after their lovemaking he didn't stay the night as he'd done before. Instead he got up and dressed, using the excuse of early surgery or breakfast appointments so that even their stolen half hours over coffee in the early dawn, and the conversations they'd shared in those intimate morning moments became a thing of the past.

Annie was resentful and angry, puzzled and helpless as well as lonely.

What was haunting David? What demon caused the violent nightmares, and why wouldn't he talk about it with her? The strange new problem was one more wedge in the gulf forming between them.

ANNIE AND JASON were having supper one evening, both lost in their own thoughts, when Jason broke the silence.

"Mom, did my dad talk much when you knew him in the old days?"

The question dropped into the pool of quiet, surprising Annie with its intensity as well as its content. She looked at her son, trying to see him as a stranger might.

Jason was changing. Meeting his father might have matured him in some indefinable fashion, but he was changing physically as well. The traces of little boy softness were disappearing from his features. His face was taking on more angular lines, and where his hands and feet had seemed too large for his frame just months before, now it was his nose and ears that were out of proportion. His hair had darkened to an auburn shade, closer to the color of Annie's.

"Well, Mom?" His voice was impatient. "I asked you if my father was very talkative when you used to know him."

"Yes, I heard you, Jase. The answer is no, he never talked a whole lot. Michael was . . . I guess you'd say he was always a quiet man."

Sullen, Annie added to herself. Michael was sullen. The same as Jean had been.

"Yeah, well, I don't know how to take him sometimes, y'know? I'll be talking away, and it's like he doesn't hear me or something. It really bugs me. I mean, you'd think he could answer me at least. I mean, he wanted to get to know me, right?"

Annie couldn't believe her ears. This was the first whisper of criticism she'd heard about "my father."

Jason had been spending every other weekend with the McCraes, and the reports till now had been glowing, so much so that Annie had begun to wonder in her darker moments if the time might come when Jason would decide to live with Michael and just visit her.

"Lili says Dad's paying attention all right. She says that's just how he is, and in families you have to accept differences in people's natures. You figure that's how it really is, Mom?"

"Yes, I think she's right," Annie agreed after a moment's thought.

"Lili's pretty smart, isn't she, Mom?"

Lili was bloody brilliant, mediating between her husband and his son with such tact. Annie nodded reluctant agreement.

Jason gave her a measuring look, and then added, "Lili and my dad are pretty close, y'know, Mom? Kind of like best friends or something. It kinda made me feel left out at first, 'cause I'm used to there being only me and you—y'know how we are with each other? But Lili noticed I felt left out, and we talked about it, and now she always makes me feel part of whatever's going on. It's real strange, though, to be around a place where there's two adults, and they talk and laugh and stuff. And even kiss, sometimes." The disgust in his voice was patently phony.

An ache began in Annie's chest. Jason was describing a union based on love, she suddenly realized. He was describing a family—man, woman, child. Complete.

Not like here, with just the two of them.

What harm had she done to her son, denying him that family feeling?

He was staring at her, and he seemed to somehow know she was hurting. "Don't get me wrong, Mom. I figure we have lots of fun, just you and me," he assured her.

She met his concerned glance and forced herself to give him a jaunty wink. "Let's really have fun and get these dishes cleared away," she teased.

When they were clearing the table, he said, ultracasually, "What do you do all the time I'm gone to my father's anyway, Mom? And tell me the truth."

The truth. Careful, Annie. It would be so easy to sow the seeds of guilt here. And, Lord, it was tempting to admit she was lonely.

"The truth? The truth is I can't wait to boot you out the door, kid. I'm on a deadline with this lousy book. You know that. So I work and don't worry about the human food machine and what it's going to eat for supper, and I actually find there's hot water because some shower maniac hasn't used it all up, and I tidy the house and no teenage earthquake disrupts it.''

He wasn't fooled. ''But you don't see much of David anymore, huh? How come you don't spend much time with David, huh, Mom?''

It was revealing that Dr. Roswell had become David.

Just when she almost needed an introduction to the man because she saw him hardly at all, here was her son, on intimate first-name terms, asking where he was, no less. There sure as hell was no justice.

''Oh, I see him now and then. You know he spends the occasional night here. He's a busy man.''

''You gonna marry him, Mom? He told me you guys were gonna get married.''

Annie stared at her son, all her defenses up.

''He did, did he? Well, maybe he was a bit premature telling you that. We haven't settled it between us, and it's customary for the lady to make her own decision about things like that.''

''Jeeze, Mom. Don't get all huffy, okay?'' Jason frowned at her. ''He told me he'd talked it over with you, and if you wanna know what I think, I figure if he asks you again, maybe you'd better go along with it. It's not a bad idea, y'know. Like, you're not exactly twenty. How many more chances are you gonna get?''

Annie opened her mouth to blast him and realized that his brown eyes were dancing with mischief.

''Rotten brat,'' she said with feeling. ''I work my fingers to the bone for you, and what do I get?''

''Bony fingers,'' he sang, off-key.

He danced out the door ahead of the dishcloth she aimed at him, but for all the fooling, Annie recognized her son's real concern. He was worried about her. He felt guilty about leaving her alone on the weekends.

Because he wasn't around to bring her breakfast in bed on Saturday or Sunday the way he'd always done, he had started getting up early some weekdays and making her a tray.

Their roles were becoming reversed in some subtle way. It pointed out as nothing else could have how fast Jason was growing up.

And that remark about her and David getting married. Annie sank into a chair and closed her eyes. Utter desolation swept over her as she admitted how unlikely that possibility had become. She and David didn't have time enough together to discuss the weather report, much less marriage.

With every passing day, it was becoming more obvious that David was out of her league, part of a different world and, therefore, lost to her. It was only a matter of time before he left her.

DAVID STRIPPED off the mask and gown he'd worn in the operating room and, after a long conversation with the parents who were waiting to hear about their son, forced himself to exchange a few cheerful comments with the staff about the success of the tricky operation he'd just completed.

As he washed and dressed again in street clothes, bone-deep weariness and a bleak sense of depression overcame the exhilaration of the operation's success.

"Good work, David." The surgeon who'd assisted clasped a hand on David's shoulder to congratulate him. "When I saw the size of that mess, I figured you'd never get it out clean."

The patient had been an eighteen-month-old boy with a large tumor in his abdomen, a neuroblastoma that turned out to be malignant. It had taken hours of meticulous work, as well as a good dose of luck, to get the thing out intact.

He ought to feel exuberant, but more and more often these days, David just had the feeling his life had gone out of control when he wasn't looking.

"See you at the Parking and Safety Committee meeting this afternoon?" The question came from a man he passed in the hall, a man David couldn't for the life of him identify.

He nodded, smiled and hurried on.

The ever-increasing demands the new appointment made on his time plus the social tap dancing that Calvin insisted upon were wearing him down. He must have six meetings lined up just in the next couple of days, and heaven only knew what Calvin was planning after that.

Worst of all, he was haunted by the sick feeling that he was losing the woman he loved.

There was now a subtle but disturbing difference in Annie. He felt as if she were watching, waiting for something inevitable and final to befall them. She was withdrawing from their relationship. And although he knew it was happening, there didn't seem to be anything he could do to stop it.

He didn't have any energy to stop it. He felt as if he were moving through his days in a slippery thick fog, barely avoiding disaster in every area.

And he knew why he felt that way: he could no longer get a good night's sleep. As a doctor, he understood better than most the dangers of sleep deprivation over a long period, and the very real prospect of a mental breakdown if it went on too long.

The dream that turned to nightmare, the door he couldn't open, now waited for him each time he relaxed into deep slumber. It didn't take a genius to figure out the symbolism of that dream, the fact that there was something in his subconscious he was terrified of facing.

He'd done his best to delve into areas he wasn't too proud of in his life, in an attempt to uncover whatever it was. But try as he might, he couldn't reveal it to his conscious self.

It was obvious something was buried deep in his subconscious that was haunting him, demanding to be examined, yet hiding behind that infernal door. And whatever it was scared him witless when he encountered it in his sleep, so much so that he was avoiding going to bed.

He was ashamed of such weakness, but also unable to pinpoint whatever it was he was blocking.

He was going to have to do something about it, soon. He was still functioning in top form at his work, but even a system as strong and healthy as his would eventually break down unless he managed to get more rest than he was getting.

Phyllis looked up when he walked in the door of his office and handed him a handful of messages.

"You're late, Doctor," she greeted him. "Dr. Graves has called at least four times. He told me to tell you it's very important you speak with him before noon. He'll be at the Faculty Club at the University most of the morning, and you're to call him there the moment you come in. And—" Phyllis tilted her head a trifle higher and managed to convey disapproval, as she always did whenever Annie was involved "—your Ms Pendleton called, as well."

Emphasis on the "your."

David suppressed an exclamation of annoyance with Phyllis's attitude and went into his inner office, shutting the door with a bang and dialing the phone as soon as he sat down. Phyllis had a divorced daughter she'd been trying to interest

David in for years now, and he knew that was why she resented Annie.

Annie had her answering machine on, and when her recorded voice asked for messages, he said, "This is my answering machine calling your answering machine. In the words of a long-ago song, has it told you lately that I love you?"

He cleared his throat and crooned the rest of the message, well aware that he couldn't carry a tune to save his life. "Well, darlin', I'm tellin' you now."

He added, "If you're still there, I'll be here in the office this afternoon. Give me a call, darling, and I promise I won't sing anymore. I miss you, Annie." He hung up wishing she'd been there to really talk with.

Then, with a lot more reluctance, he dialed the Faculty Club and had Calvin paged. The other man sounded almost jocular when he finally picked up the phone after a long delay.

"Hello! Hello there, David, my boy. I'm in the midst of a rather important brunch meeting, so I won't keep you."

I'm busy, so I won't keep you. Calvin's reasoning brought a rather grim smile, but it faded when the monologue continued. "I simply need you to stand in for me later today at the Lions' Club annual luncheon, my boy. It won't cut all more than just showing up for an hour and saying a few brief words about their support for one of my projects. If you have a pen handy, I'll give you the details."

It was probably a result of already feeling pressured and exhausted at barely ten in the morning, but David suddenly found Calvin's manner irritating, as well as his bland assumption that David would drop whatever plans he might have and race off to do Calvin's bidding. Was it his imagination, or had Calvin Graves become much more demanding, telling David what he ought to do instead of asking the way he always used to?

Steady, Roswell. Remember you're not hitting on all cylinders here. David scribbled down the things Calvin was dictating and held back the sharp rebuke on the tip on his tongue. *Calvin Graves is working hard to get you what you most want for this hospital,* he reminded himself, but it was difficult. *Don't be a bastard just because you're turning into a psychotic idiot.*

But when he hung up, he was aware that Calvin never had said just why he couldn't go to the damned Lions' Club meeting himself that afternoon. And he hadn't once asked David to

ANNIE LISTENED to her answering machine later that day and smiled at David's nonsense. She dialed his office number again, and was told in a haughty tone that the doctor wasn't in, and wasn't expected back that afternoon, and no, Phyllis had no idea where he could be reached.

Annie bit her tongue to stop the pithy swearword that best described Phyllis, and then dialed David's apartment, knowing as she did that he wouldn't be there, either.

Damn it all, she wanted to talk with him. A feeling of urgency had been growing in her all week, a need to settle their relationship one way or the other.

She still wanted to talk over the regressions with him. Instead of fading as each new day passed, the memory of that other life they'd shared became more real, more vivid. Details that had escaped her before came to her now with spontaneous impact, in dreams at night but also like misplaced wisps of memory when she was wide-awake.

If they discussed it, David would see the connections, the parallels between then and now that were recurring. Maybe together they could figure out how to avert the parting that Annie sensed was becoming inevitable.

But the phone rang and rang, and finally she hung up.

David might turn up late that evening, for an hour, maybe two or even three. But stolen hours late at night when they were both tired didn't leave time to properly satisfy the body hunger between them, much less allow room for discussion of anything serious. And he was so tired all the time.

DAVID CHECKED with his answering service when he finally managed to escape the Lions' Club meeting late that afternoon. He was frustrated, embarrassed and more than a little furious with Calvin Graves.

Far from being the lightweight social event Calvin had led him to expect, the members of the service club had asked difficult and penetrating questions, and David, naturally, hadn't been prepared. Besides, he'd overheard two members speculating as to why Calvin himself hadn't appeared. One of them seemed quite certain it was due to a golf tournament being held that afternoon at the University links.

The two hours David had counted on for the meeting had stretched to four, and there were urgent matters at his office he'd still have to contend with before he could think of going home.

"You've had calls repeatedly from a boy named Jason Pendleton, at this number," his service reported.

David frowned, and his fingers knotted around the receiver. The number Jason had left wasn't Annie's.

Anxiety knotted in his gut as he dialed. If something had happened to Annie, and he wasn't even there to help...but the jaunty excitement in Jason's voice when he finally came on the line was reassuring.

"Hi! Hey, David, I've been trying to get you all afternoon. I'm at my friend Jeff's. There's something I need to ask you, David, and it has to be kind of a secret, so I didn't want to call from home."

David felt his muscles unclench, and the adrenaline that had spilled through him drained away, leaving bone-deep weariness behind. He slumped against the rough cement wall beside the phone, trying to keep his voice from revealing how he really felt.

"Fire away, Jason. I'm good at secrets."

"Well, there's this fund-raising fair at my school the end of November to get money for our rugby team to go on tour, see. And I sort of told Mr. Albright, he's the coordinator, that you and I had done that magic show and it turned out ace, and maybe if I asked you we could put on one for the fair?"

Jason's voice went up the scale and back down, his eagerness and uncertainty painfully obvious to David.

"We'd be the main attraction. Well, you'd be, of course. I'd just be helping like last time, but Mr. Albright said it would be terrific if we could do it. And the reason it's a secret is, I thought maybe I could invite everybody at the last minute—Mom and Cleo and the kids and...and maybe my dad and Lili, too—and not tell them we were the main attraction till they got there, right?"

Wrong. David screwed his eyes shut and shook his head from side to side. Wrong, wrong, wrong.

The idea was impossible. A magic show performed with any degree of professionalism would require untold hours of practice, especially if Jason were involved to the degree that was necessary here. David didn't have time to go to the bathroom properly these days, much less spend hours on magic. It was out of the question and that was that.

When David still said nothing, Jason recklessly added, "See, right? And now you don't see much of each other anymore and I figured you and my mom sort of got together at a magic show, I feel bad about that, so maybe. . ." Jason's voice trailed off, and David could hear him breathing into the receiver as if he'd been running.

It took a long moment to register, and then the words hit David like a blow in the chest. Unless he was mistaken, this crazy, wonderful kid was actually trying to put him and Annie back to the beginning, when they'd first fallen in love, when things were near perfect between them and a future seemed possible.

After months of stonewalling, Jason was playing matchmaker.

David thought of the gut-wrenching meeting he'd just bungled through, of the appointment calendar so full it depressed him just to think about it. And he thought of Calvin and the cavalier way he'd sent David off to fill in for him today, just so that Calvin could play golf.

"What do ya think, David?"

He thought he had to say no. He had to let Jason down because there was no way humanly possible to fit this into his life.

Was there? And then he heard himself saying, "Tell Mr. Albright he's got himself a magic show, Jason. The Sorcerer and his Apprentice. But we'll have to set aside several hours at least twice a week to practice, you understand that? We don't want to look like a couple of bumbling fools up there, do we?"

The victory yell that came over the line almost deafened David, but for the first time since surgery that morning he actually felt good about something as he hung up the phone.

If he could only sleep one whole night through, he might start feeling better about the rest of his life as well.

ANNIE'S BATTERED green Volvo was parked across from his apartment building when he arrived home just after ten that night, and for a moment he was elated at the thought of having her there waiting for him.

He was surprised, as well, because in all the time she'd had keys to his apartment, she'd seldom used them.

When he'd called her from the hospital an hour before and gotten her answering machine, he'd smashed his phone down in a rage when her recorded message began, and then reflected how the slightest frustration seemed to make his temper flare these days.

As he fitted his key into the lock, he tried to overcome the overwhelming weariness that plagued him like a virus.

She'd made tea, and when she heard him she rose in one graceful motion from the armchair where she was sitting, and put her mug on the side table so that she could fold herself into his arms for a kiss.

"I needed to see you. I hope you don't mind my coming here," she blurted before he could say anything, and the hint of apology in her voice brought home to him as nothing else had how far they'd drifted away from each other. Only a short time ago, no explanation would have been needed for wanting to be with him.

"I decided to wait here all night if I had to, because we have to talk, David." She tipped her head back so she could look up into his face, and the deep lines and dark shadows there made her lose the resolve that had brought her there in the first place.

"You look exhausted," she murmured, putting her hand along his jaw. "Maybe I'd better go after all...."

His arms tightened around her. "You're staying, love. I'd planned to grab a quick shower and then come over to see you anyway, so this just gives us an extra hour." He held her against him for a long moment, wishing he could absorb some of the fine vitality that always seemed to surround her.

"How about pouring me a drink while I get out of these clothes and put on—" he made an attempt at a leer "—something more comfortable?"

She smiled, but he sensed that she was preoccupied.

"Want to come and talk while I change?" he suggested, but Annie shook her head.

"I'll wait here," she said, and apprehension flared in him.

It was obvious she was there for a specific reason, and he cursed under his breath as he stripped his suit off in the bedroom and stepped into a cool shower.

He wasn't up to a heavy scene, damn it. He was off balance, wiped out from nights with little sleep and days like today when one frustration piled upon another until he felt he balanced the weight of the world on his shoulders.

He toweled off and pulled on worn jeans and a T-shirt. The shower had refreshed him, and a drink might help as well. He began to feel more cheerful about everything.

Annie was once again curled in the armchair, and she smiled as he came in. She'd mixed him a Scotch with just the right amount of water, and he flopped down on the battered sofa and took a long sip, feeling the liquor flow through his veins in a comforting stream and admiring the long, tantalizing length of her legs, bared by the skirt she wore.

"Lord, Annie, I love you." The words were spontaneous, and a sense of well-being he hadn't experienced in days welled up in him, just from the primal joy of being with her.

"I love you, too, David. It's because I love you this way that I have to talk over what's been happening to me. I want you to listen, please, David, with an open mind, because I'm convinced we're making the same mistakes together now that we made once before, and I'm frightened."

Annie's eyes seemed to overshadow the rest of her features, and David could feel the intensity of her emotion like an electrical force field vibrating between them, compelling him with its power.

Instinctively he knew what she was about to bring up, and with every fiber of his being, he rejected another discussion about hypnotic regression and past lives.

He wanted to jump to his feet and roar like a wounded animal would, as the last fragments of his newfound optimism shattered like shards of crystal. He tossed the last of his drink down his throat and grimaced at the raw fire in his chest.

There was a small tape recorder on the side table, and he watched, keeping his features impassive, as she reached out and pushed the button. She'd set it all up ahead of time, and David felt anger and resistance of this whole charade overwhelm him.

Almost at once, that haunting, familiar woman's voice wormed its way into his ears, into his soul, while every fiber of his being rejected the unfolding tragedy that voice revealed.

CHAPTER SEVENTEEN

"DAVID, THAT MAN I LOVED back then was you."

The tape had ended, and Annie's urgent voice filled the silence with still more words David didn't want to hear.

"You were Paul, and I loved you and had your child. Then, for some reason you deserted me. And the man I was married to, Jean Desjardins, came back. David, Jean was Michael McCrae. He was the man who walked in and found me nursing your son."

David's head was throbbing, and the headache seemed to penetrate every muscle in his body as he got to his feet and walked over to stare out the window. It took every ounce of control he possessed not to bellow at her, not to pick up the infernal tape machine and smash it against the wall.

"What you've done here is create an elaborate fantasy, Annie. You're a writer, and you're unusually creative," he began, and every word drove the pain in his head deeper.

"But to blame our current situation on this . . . this day-dream of yours is preposterous. I know things between us haven't been ideal lately, but I promise you they'll get better. I'm trying my best to . . ."

She was on her feet when he turned toward her, and she was tucking the tape in her handbag. He moved toward her, but she avoided his arms and walked to the door.

"Damn it, Annie, sit down." His voice was almost out of control.

"I won't argue with you about this, David," she said softly.

"You don't believe it, and I do. I guess I was hoping you'd be more honest than this with yourself and with me."

"Sit down and try being reasonable about this garbage," he roared, flinching at the ugly flaming bolt that shot through his brain when he raised his voice.

The door closed behind her, and he took two long strides toward it, more angry than he'd ever been with Annie. He'd bloody well drag her back in here, force her to listen to reason. . . .

He slumped against the door, aware that he was thinking like a maniac. Sleep. Damn it, he needed sleep.

He staggered into the bedroom and dug through his medical bag in a frenzy. The sealed packages contained samples of a new pill, one that the pharmaceutical companies assured in their brochure would bring deep, restful sleep with no ill effects to even the most dedicated of insomniacs. He ran a glass of water and swallowed two capsules.

HE DROVE OVER TO ANNIE'S early the next morning and apologized.

"I'm too tired to think straight," he told her, and then he lied. "I'll give this whole regression thing a lot of thought and we'll discuss it another time."

Thus, they made a sort of strained peace between them, but both of them knew they were avoiding any real issues.

The next two weeks stretched David's endurance to the limit. Long, haunted nights when he tried to sleep without the aid of the pills were shattered as he climbed those stairs in his dream and shocked himself awake by screaming. He used the capsules with care at first, aware of how soon dependence could occur, but he was soon swallowing three, and then four.

The nights ran into long grueling days of surgery, office hours and endless, eternal meetings. He stole time from an overloaded schedule to practice magic with Jason several nights a week.

David missed three meetings during those two weeks in order to keep his evenings free for Jason. It was ironic that spending time with Jason meant even less time to spend with Annie. Jason had told her they were planning a surprise, and she accepted that. She was working long hours, as well, finishing the first draft of her book.

The evening David skipped the meeting of the Finance Committee, Calvin called.

Jason and David were perfecting an illusion called Doves in a Box, which involved making two live doves vanish using a folding box. Jason's job involved carrying offstage the flattened box, behind which was suspended a zippered bag in which David had secreted the doves. Like all stage illusions, the success of this one relied on Jason's smooth and innocent removal of the evidence, and the rehearsal wasn't going well.

David knew why. The fault wasn't Jason's; it was his. Magic required perfect timing and quick reflexes, and he was just too tired to be adept. When the phone rang, he was feeling frustrated with his own clumsiness.

"Have a Coke while I answer this, Jason. There's a pack in the fridge," David called as he lifted the receiver and said an impatient hello. His mind was still on the illusion.

"My boy, you are aware that today is Thursday?"

Calvin's smooth voice was sarcastic, and being called "my boy" grated on David's already raw nerve endings.

"Yes, Calvin, as far as I know it's been Thursday since early this morning." He was even more sarcastic than Calvin had been, and it gave him great satisfaction.

There was a discernible pause.

"This is also the third Thursday of the month, David, which heralds the regular meeting of the Hospital Finance Committee. I take it you aren't planning to appear?"

"No, Calvin, I'm not. I had Phyllis call the committee chairman and tell him I wouldn't be there. Is there a problem?"

"The problem, my friend, is the simple matter of your absence from a group that is most influential, and in which you should at this moment be highly visible. Now I had to call in a fair few debts to get you installed on that committee, David, and I'm afraid I don't understand what's going on. You're not ill, are you?"

It was like being caught playing hooky from school, and David resented the implication. His answer was abrupt and his voice revealed his irritation.

"No, I'm not sick, Calvin, although I am fed up to the teeth with meetings. However, we can discuss that another time. I'm busy at the moment, so if you'll excuse me, I'll get back to you tomorrow."

Calvin hung up in his ear with a decisive bang, and David stared at the receiver for a long moment before he set it in its cradle.

Hell. Maybe Calvin had every right to be angry. He had no right at all to be condescending.

It was beginning to sound at times as if David was a property Calvin Graves had invested in rather than a friend he valued.

DESPITE THE PILLS, every time David fell asleep that night the dream recurred, and he jerked himself awake only to fall back into a drugged stupor and have the whole scenario repeat itself.

At last he swallowed two more pills . . . did that make four? Six? His befuddled brain tried to add and failed. Finally oblivion descended, a black unhealthy nothingness that was a parody of restful sleep.

He dragged himself out of it knowing the alarm had been buzzing long ago. In fact, he was almost an hour behind schedule, and the residue from the powerful sleeping drug made him feel as if he were swimming underwater. His eyes were almost glued shut and his tongue had a furry, foul coating. When he raised his head from the pillow a zigzag jolt of pain shot through his skull, a hangover from the narcotic effect of the drug. He must have taken plenty.

He made black coffee and while he choked it down and shuddered at the bitter taste, he admitted to himself that had he been scheduled to perform surgery that morning, he wouldn't have been fit for it.

Hell, he wasn't fit for office routine, either. He dialed Phyllis and canceled his morning appointments.

You're a sorry mess, Roswell, and now you're swallowing pills like some kind of junkie.

If only . . . if only he could sleep.

If you were one of your own patients, you'd prescribe psychological help about now, wouldn't you?

Physician, heal thyself? Something had to be done, and fast.

An idea began to form, murky and flawed, but just maybe possible. Maybe he could kill two birds with one stone here, lay two demons to rest with one blow.

David forced himself to locate his address book, find a number and dial a colleague he liked and respected. David and Mike Dresko had interned together, and although they hadn't been close friends, they shared a mutual respect for each other's ability. Mike was a clinical psychologist.

"SO THAT'S THE PROBLEM, Mike, plain and simple. I can't sleep because I can't make myself open that damned door in my dream. I know the door symbolizes a problem I'm blocking, and I know if I ever manage to face whatever the hell is there, I'll feel better. Just don't feed me your Freudian mumbo jumbo and suggest years of analysis, because I don't have any time for it."

Mike was a tall, gaunt scarecrow of a man, prematurely balding. He'd poured them each a cup of coffee that tasted rather like ammonia, and he gulped his with relish, giving David an amused glance as he took one sip of the vile concoction and nearly gagged.

"You don't recognize good coffee, and you don't listen to what your doctor has to say, either. I guess we'll treat your symptoms by giving you stronger and stronger sleep medication, and just go on hoping the problem disappears before you OD, since obviously you've already decided nothing I can do will work anyway."

Mike's voice was level, but his irritation was obvious. "Why bother coming here if you aren't going to agree to treatment? You can prescribe your own damn sleeping pills, Roswell. You don't need me for that." He shook his head and took another long pull at his coffee.

"I swear doctors are the very worst when it comes to problems of their own. I ought to know by now never to let another doctor in that door in the guise of patient," Mike grumbled. "Every last one of them starts off just like this, telling me what not to do."

He gave David an astute look. "Actually you look like hell, Roswell. If you haven't done any better than this treating yourself, maybe you'd better decide to trust me a little, fill me in on what's going on in your life, and stop telling me how smart you are about psychology. I'd never tell you how to take out my gallbladder."

He was right, and David gave him what passed for a grin and relaxed as much as he could. "Your gallbladder's in danger if this is what you call coffee."

For the next hour, Mike painstakingly found out most of what was happening both on the surface of David's life and below, without seeming to pry too much.

David tried to be as honest and open as he could, within limits. He told Mike about Calvin, about the hopes for the transplant center, and all about Annie, including the fact that they were having various problems, outlining most of them and putting much of the blame on himself. But he left out any mention of Annie's experience with regressional hypnosis.

"Mike, I know the most direct means of breaking down a barrier like this one of mine is by trying hypnosis, right?"

Mike sighed and nodded. "Here we go again."

"Well, I want you to try hypnosis on me, but I want you to go one step farther. If there doesn't seem to be any basis for this nightmare in my past, then I want you to regress me, take me back to birth and before if you can."

Mike frowned and shook his head. "Look, David, it's one thing to come in here and tell me what treatment you expect. But to get into this regression stuff . . . Hell, as far as I'm concerned, the jury's still out on all this reincarnation material, memories of past lives and all that. I've read some of the books, and I know a lot of people are jumping on the bandwagon, but I've never put much faith in it."

"I figured not. Which is exactly why I came to you, why I'm asking you to do this for me. I don't believe either for one second it's possible. But the only way I can be certain is by trying it myself. The fact that you don't believe it, either, is the very reason I'm even suggesting it."

Mike gave him a long, measuring look. "I take it you have a good reason to want to do this, something you're not telling me, and it's connected in some way to this sleep problem you're having?"

"Yeah, Mike, I can't explain how or why, but I know in my gut this dream of mine is connected to the feeling I've always had about hypnosis. It goes way beyond skepticism. I've got a total block about the whole subject."

"Which doesn't exactly qualify you for the procedure," Mike groaned. "You're lucky I enjoy a challenge once in a while. As you know, even under hypnosis, your own subconscious mind is in complete control anyway, so I can't see any harm in trying."

"I probably can't be hypnotized anyhow," David snapped. "I really don't believe in this garbage. And don't ask me to lie down, either. I'm staying right here in this chair."

"For crying out loud, David, this was your idea, not mine. Sit wherever the hell you please—I don't care. I can only try."

Mike sighed, adding under his breath, "Sometimes I wish to heaven I were a dentist."

MIKE'S VOICE DRONED ON in a relentless monotone, and at some point David stopped fighting.

He was tired, so tired. He'd tune Mike out, let him say whatever the hell he wanted, and maybe just take a short nap. This had been a total washout from the beginning anyway. He ought to have known better than to get himself into it.

He allowed himself to relax, and the sensation was delicious. He let himself sink into oblivion....

He was in an office. Not the office he had now, but one that he recognized from somewhere. It belonged to some practice he'd had in the past. He was standing in front of a file cabinet. He pulled out a drawer and selected a yellowed folder.

He opened it, following Mike's instructions.

David's heart thundered in his ears, and he wondered with clinical detachment if he was about to have a heart attack as he stared down at the contents of the docket. Inside was a bundle of letters with foreign postmarks. French postmarks.

David knew he wasn't having a heart attack. His heart was breaking instead, crumbling into dust inside his chest, and he didn't care. He knew only that he truly wanted to die....

MIKE WAS FEELING SMUG and satisfied as he watched David's wall of resistance fade and disappear. This was going far better than he'd anticipated, considering David's attitude. Far from being a poor subject, Mike was beginning to suspect that David was one of those rare people who entered the deepest levels of mind quickly and easily once their initial reluctance was overcome.

"Go to the door in your dreams," and then "Open the door without fear," he'd instructed after careful preliminary cautions were in place. He wanted to explore the cause of David's sleep phobia before attempting anything else. David's suggestions about regression could wait until the major issue was resolved. Then, if he still wanted to pursue it, Mike would help.

They'd agreed on taping the session, and Mike couldn't wait for David's reaction when he brought him out and proved to him how simple the hypnotic procedure had been.

"Are you reading the file now, David?" he queried. What happened next was unexpected. The hopeless, desperate sound that erupted from David rose in volume and became a tortured scream, and what was left of Mike's hair felt as if it were standing on end with horror. A cold shudder ran down Mike's body, and he leaped to his feet and came close to the slumped figure in the leather chair.

"David, move away from this scene. Move back in time. The scene is receding now," Mike instructed urgently.

David's face was contorted, agonized, and the sounds coming from him were desolate, animal-like in their terror.

Mike swallowed hard. "Leave the scene, David. Move back in time. Leave the folder in the drawer and go back, far, far back . . . to the cause of the pain you're experiencing. Go back, David, and find the cause. The pain is gone now, it's receding, and you're going back and back . . ."

The dreadful cry faded and as David relaxed, Mike dragged a chair over close to his patient and sank into it. He hadn't had a scare like this in a long time.

"Tell me where you are, and what's happening to you," he instructed. "Where are you now, David?"

This time, David's voice was controlled, but it held such anger, such sadness and depths of futility that Mike was chilled, listening.

"In a . . . in a tent. Hospital tent. At the front. It's a casually clearing station. We work in these tents," David said in a weary monotone.

"Dismal, dirty tents set in a sea of mud. Men are screaming. I hear them even in my sleep. They found this man I'm working on this morning. He'd been lying out there in the barbed wire."

Mike frowned and shook his head. Whatever was going on here was outside any knowledge he had of David's life. As far as he knew, David hadn't been involved in Vietnam.

"Are you a doctor, then?"

"I'm a surgeon." The weary voice was full of irony. "A surgeon—that's a joke. This place is more like a butcher shop than anything else. A lot of the time there's damned little anyone can do." There was anguish in his voice for a moment, but then David's tone became authoritative, as if his attention were elsewhere and he was instructing a medical team.

"Gangrene's set in here. We'll have to amputate. Make sure there's plenty of chloroform handy." He raised his voice and called, "Nurse, inject these men with five hundred units of ATS. And we need morphine." His voice dropped and he murmured in helpless fury, "He's not a man, you know, he's just a boy. Doesn't even shave yet. Must have lied about his age, because he's only a kid. And he's going to lose both legs. If he even lives. So many of them don't."

Compassion washed over Mike, pity for David, and for the terrifying, vivid scene he was describing.

"David, what year is it?" Mike was perplexed with the sudden change of scene, the depth of emotional intensity his patient was experiencing.

"Year? How the hell can anyone forget the year? It's 1918. I'm thirty-six years old. Thirty-six, going on ninety." He gave a caricature of a laugh.

"The war's supposed to be over, according to the politicians here in France and everywhere else. They mouth that, but they're still sending these boys out there to die. It's all numbers to them. They figure on so many casualties for so many feet of useless mud."

Mike stared at the man before him, unable to speak for a second.

The First World War. David was reliving a scene from the First World War. David had regressed to not only another time, but what had to be another life...a situation which he'd already firmly rejected as a possibility.

Mike had strong doubts about it as well. But no one listening to David right now could possibly doubt that what he was recounting was a segment of his past, a past in a body long dead and buried.

Mike struggled with his scientific beliefs, searching for an explanation he could accept. He knew of Jung's theories about a universal unconscious, of the concept of extra cerebral memory.

But when he thought it over, he realized he shouldn't be as concerned over where these memories were coming from as he was about where they were leading his patient at this moment.

After all, he reminded himself, he wanted David to find the key to whatever was causing the disturbing and dangerous sleep disorder that had brought him to Mike's office.

He'd best use his energies to try to uncover the source of David's problem right here and now, because he was pretty certain when his stubborn, opinionated friend came out of this, he'd never turn up next Tuesday at three for another session. One way or another, this was it.

Mike moved to his desk and punched a button on the intercom.

"Margie, better cancel my next two appointments this morning," he instructed in a soft tone that grew impatient when Margie objected. "No calls or interruptions until I give you the word."

This was going to take time, but it was fascinating. His practice was lucrative, but he did get bored with upwardly mobile women and their sex problems.

He moved back to the large man slumped in the leather office chair.

"David. Can you hear me, David?"

There was silence, broken only by the sound of traffic on the street outside the office window. Brakes squealed and a horn honked.

Mike asked again, and David frowned and moved his head from side to side.

"I hear you, David," he murmured, a puzzled frown creasing his brow. "Can't remember my name. Now why is that?"

Mike cursed his own stupidity and said, "At the count of three, you'll know your name. Someone will call you. You'll hear them call your name. One, two, three . . .,"

"Lord, this hellhole must be getting to me. Of course I know. I'm Paul, Paul Duncan. Colonel Duncan." His mouth curved again in the ironic smile Mike was beginning to recognize. "They've just made me a colonel. The army's obsessed with having the proper rank doing the proper job. Major, Colonel, as if I give a damn about it. As if these soldiers I'm treating care, either."

David's forehead creased again and his fingers curled into fists. "I only wish I could really make a difference here, really do something for these poor suckers."

The more things change, the more they stay the same, Mike thought, remembering David's crusade for a transplant unit. David's need to make a difference for his patients was just as urgent then as it was now.

"If the war's technically over, will you be going home soon? Where's your home, Paul?"

"I'm a Yank, an American, from Columbus, Ohio."

Mike asked questions, and David answered.

"I'm married back there. My wife's name is Grace. Her father, Martin Oakley, and I have a medical practice together. There's talk of shipping us home you know, before Christmas."

Mike watched as his patient frowned, a worried expression creasing the handsome features. "I don't want to go back to the States, but I have to. I have to get things settled once and for all."

"You don't want to go home? Why's that, Paul?"

There was silence for a moment, and then the response came in a rush of words and feelings.

"Because I've fallen in love with a woman here. I never dreamed I'd love anyone the way I love Bernadette. Going back home means leaving her over here until I can arrange a divorce, and I hate the thought of leaving her behind. It tears my guts apart. Oh, I tried writing Grace and telling her, but I couldn't do it properly on paper. I didn't mail the letter,"

There was a pause, and then he said with a sigh, "It's complicated because of my relationship with my father-in-law, Martin. I owe him a great deal. He paid for most of my medical training, and I dread telling him what my plans are. I hate hurting him, but it has to be done. And there's my wife. Grace has never been strong. Martin's always protected her." His head moved from side to side in a despondent motion, and his tone became vehement.

"We should never have married—I know that now. She wants a husband who plays bridge, makes a lot of money, knows the right people. She doesn't want kids. I'm wrong for her. I don't care about any of those things, especially not now, after what I've seen here. It all seems frivolous, unimportant to me now."

He was breathing fast, overwhelmed with feeling. "I'd like a kid of my own. Bernadette has a daughter, Nicole." He seemed to be seeing the child in his mind's eye, because he smiled a little. "I love that little girl."

A sad smile creased his mouth and then was gone again. "Children. They're our hope for the future, when this hell is over. Maybe I'll specialize after this, work only with kids. I'd like that."

"And this French woman, Bernadette. How does she feel about your leaving?"

He became agitated again. "I love her more than life itself. I don't want to leave her even for a day. She's so strong, full of life and laughter, yet there's something wistful about her as well. Meeting her, being able to spend a few days or, if we're lucky, a week together, has made this bearable, you see, this....carnage, this squandering of human lives. She helps me, she makes me feel there's still beauty and peace in the world."

"Where is she now?" Mike was trying to place the characters in this drama.

"On her farm, in Normandy. By some miracle, the place has escaped pretty much untouched. It's a small farm. Her husband was a soldier, but he's dead. He disappeared early in the war. Her life is hard. I spend as much time as I can with them. It's like a different world. I want to marry her, take her back to the States."

Mike listened, and a strong presentiment of tragedy overwhelmed him as he instructed David to move ahead, to a time after the war. He knew it was ridiculous, but Mike almost hated to ask the next questions.

How the hell could he become emotionally involved in a romantic tale seventy years old? And yet he was involved, in a way he seldom experienced with his patients. This was real, and vivid.

"Months have passed, the war is over now. Tell me what's happening to you."

Moments passed again as David oriented himself in his invisible reality.

"I'm back in Columbus. I've been sick." He coughed, a harsh, empty rattle in his chest. "This rotten flu. Everyone has it. People are dying as if it were the plague."

Mike was flabbergasted at how David seemed to change. Even the voice, which had been vibrant and strong was now thin and reedy, almost a whisper at times.

"Grace caught it first, the very week I arrived home. She was dangerously ill, and Martin....good Lord, it shocked me, how old Martin's become while I was away." Silence, and then he burst out, "It's a trap, you know—Grace's illness, Martin's aging. It's an insidious trap, and I'm caught in it." David's fist knotted all of a sudden, and he pounded on the chair arm in frustration. "This place, this place is like a prison to me."

His voice dropped to a near whisper of despair. "Every day, every hour, I feel like walking out of here, taking the first ship back to France, back to Bernadette. But how can I, the way things are? How can I leave now?"

He shook his head in absolute despair. "You'd have to be heartless to walk out on them the way they are. And then, I caught this damned flu, and pneumonia afterward. It was weeks before I was even strong enough to hold a pen and write to Bernadette."

His features contorted with pain. "What did she think, my beloved, all those weeks without a letter from me? Martin took care of me when I was at home. The hospital is overflowing with flu cases. I was delirious. I remember calling out for Bernadette again and again. Heaven knows what Martin thought. He's never said a word about it, and I know I babbled. I worry about the letters that come from her. They're addressed to the office, and Martin must see them—he's taking care of the mail."

David was silent for a time, his face a mask of despair. When he spoke again, there was a dry and hopeless desperation to his words.

"It's hard to accept this, you know. I was always physically strong, but I'm not strong any longer. I can't even walk to the office, just a few short blocks. It's humiliating to me. I took my health for granted. I'm not yet forty years old, but the muscles around my heart were damaged by this flu. Martin called in a specialist yesterday, and he says it's irreparable. I'll be a semi-invalid the rest of my life."

He struggled for a long moment, the struggle of a proud, strong man who wouldn't give in to tears.

Again, Mike moved the scene ahead, half expecting to be told that Paul had died.

"Move ahead in time. Tell me how old you are now, Paul."

"I'm sixty-three."

"And where are you now?"

There was more strength in the voice than there had been, as well as world-weariness and perhaps just a touch of pompos-ity.

"Still here in Columbus, still running the practice. I've been successful in my career. I'm director of the hospital, you know.

Martin got the town to build a new and better hospital. I'm also a member of the town council. The place is growing."

"What about your wife? Do you have a family?" Mike posed the questions with intense curiosity.

"No family, no," the dry voice related. "I live alone." He gave a dry and bitter chuckle. "Grace divorced me several years ago. She got involved in social work and women's rights. Martin was horrified. He came close to disowning her." A stiff little smile came and went.

The irony of it all, that the woman both men had protected had turned against them, brought a wry grin to Mike's face, but he sobered when he asked the question bothering him.

"And what of Bernadette? Did you ever see her again?"

Paul shook his head from side to side and seemed to struggle with his feelings.

"I wrote, but she never answered again. Finally I contacted a friend I'd known in her village, a doctor. He was a chronic alcoholic, but a nice guy. His name was Marc, Dr. Marc Cerdan. I begged him to write and tell me what had happened to her."

"How did you feel about that?"

Anger sparked, the first real sign of emotion Paul had shown for some time.

"How the hell do you think I felt? I was half insane with jealousy and grief. I was hurt, betrayed. She'd assured me her husband was dead. Had she lied, or was this some new man she met and married after me? Was he the reason she refused to come to the U.S. when I begged her? I couldn't stand not knowing, so I decided to go to France and confront her."

"And did you go?" Mike felt deep compassion.

A huge sigh. David seemed to slump. "No. No, I never did. There was always something, work, meetings, illness, never a time when I could get away easily. Martin expanded our practice about then. He had high ambitions for me, and I got caught up in local politics. As time passed, I began to feel that

An enigmatic smile played over David's features. "He wired me back, a short and cryptic message saying that the lady was well, she was now living with her husband, an injured war veteran, still in that same tiny hamlet in Normandy. She had another baby, Cerdan said. He suggested that I chalk up the experience to wartime romance and forget about it. Leave her alone, he all but ordered."

I really had no right to interfere in her life, just as Cerdan said. She had a husband now, and another child. I could only cause trouble for her."

He sighed again. His voice was heavy and sad when he added quietly, "But I never forgot her, either. I never could stop loving her. I love her today, this minute, as much as I ever did. Not a day passes that I don't think of her. For some people, there's only one love in a lifetime, and she was mine. I think of her, and I remember everything, every detail of our time together. I dream of her at night. Ahh, I remember."

He seemed to be lost in memories for a long moment, and Mike didn't interrupt. At last, with a visible effort, David resumed the narrative.

"Martin Oakley died two days ago, you know. I'm in his office. There's an old file cabinet that needs cleaning out."

A warning bell went off in Mike's mind. They'd come full circle, back to the office, the file. He sat forward on his chair.

Sweat suddenly appeared on David's forehead, and lines of tension deepened on his face.

"I don't want to open it," he said abruptly, fear evident in his tone, each word an effort. "I have to do it, but I don't want to."

His clenched fists strained against the chair arms and every muscle in his body seemed to stiffen. Cords stood out in his throat and blood vessels bulged in his forehead.

David was again at the hidden door in his nightmare, and terror was building. Mike prayed silently for the skill he needed to guide his patient through the next few crucial moments in safety.

"David, I want you to remove yourself from the scene and just observe what's happening. Watch without feeling. Allow yourself to move away from the fear, move back from it and observe. Can you do that?"

Sweat streamed down David's face, and his eyes opened, unfocused and wild. It took several seconds for Mike's suggestion to take effect, and then gradually, David relaxed a little.

"Are you feeling safer now? Can you tell me what's happening?"

"Opening . . . the . . . drawer, taking out . . . the . . . folder."

Even with the strong hypnotic suggestion, David still showed signs of extreme stress as he related what was occurring.

"Inside ... oh God, oh God ... letters." David's hands were trembling visibly, his face contorted in agony.

"Bernadette. Letters from her, my letters to her. Martin must have stopped them. I gave them to him when I was ill, but he never mailed them ... How could he do this? How could he?"

A charged silence followed, as if David were examining the contents.

"They're open. He must have read them all. And hers to me. There's one addressed to me at home! She'd never have done that unless she was desperate.... Here, she says ... she writes...."

David's moan of anguish and heartbreak echoed through the room, but now the terror was gone, leaving only a depth of pain that made Mike feel helpless and inept.

"God, I have a son. Our son—the child was mine, Martin knew how much I wanted a child, and yet he never let me know ... and in every letter, every single one, she tells me she loves me. She ... she needs me. See here, this final letter, she's begging me to come to her ... oh God, she needed me. She needed me, and I never went back."

Tears poured from David's eyes, and anguish contorted his features.

"I've wasted all these years. I've wasted my life. I always knew I shouldn't have given up. I let Martin pull the strings that kept me here. Our son, I'll never know my son ... and oh, my Bernadette ... "

Mike's own eyes were damp as he watched and listened to the powerful play of emotions rocking David.

Then to Mike's alarm, David flinched violently and groaned. Mike snatched up his patient's wrist, monitoring his pulse, and was astonished to find it thready and weak.

"What is it, David, what's happening?" he demanded, but there was no reply. David slumped over in the chair as if he were dropping farther and farther into oblivion.

CHAPTER EIGHTEEN

HE'S ONLY REACTING to a powerful memory, Mike reassured himself. A patient in hypnosis is safe from actual physical harm. Still, in another minute he'd have to bring David out, and to hell with theory. A person couldn't actually relive a heart attack or anything like it, could he?

Of course not.

Mike felt beads of anxious sweat form on his own head and drip down the sides of his face as David gasped, "Heart...always weak, white-hot pain, in my chest, down my arm..."

"David, your inner mind will let go of these memories now. This is happening in another time. Let them go, become calm and relaxed, very relaxed. The nightmare is gone. It will never recur because you know now what's behind that door. You will be able to sleep long and restfully from now on, with no disturbing dreams. You will come back to the present. You will wake up now with full recognition of what's happened here, and you will understand and examine these memories and the messages they hold for you in your present life."

Thank the Lord something was inspiring him, Mike thought with relief. The words, the reassurances, were there when he needed them.

David was slow in coming out of hypnosis. He was wet with sweat, and his shirt clung to his chest. He looked gray and weary, and at first he avoided Mike's eyes. He sat immobile and silent, staring with blind concentration at the window, his face a controlled mask.

Mike knew David was struggling with what had occurred, because Mike himself was. He felt as if he'd just witnessed an event that radically affected his professional life and every last one of his personal beliefs. Of all the dramas that had ever been played out in his office, this was the most memorable by a country mile.

At last, Mike couldn't help but ask with gentle curiosity, "David? You remember all that?"

David gave one emphatic nod. "That, and more." He sounded as if his throat hurt.

"Did you die from that attack, David? Your pulse actually had me worried for a while there. There's nothing really wrong with your heart, is there?"

"Nothing. And no, I didn't die the right then. Not from that one," David answered. He seemed to be drained of emotion, his voice was matter-of-fact and without inflection.

"It was the first of several. I didn't really give a damn about living any longer, see. I remember thinking I only wanted time enough to write one last letter to . . . to her. To, ummm, to Bernadette."

He raised haunted eyes to meet Mike's gaze, and in a low, strangled voice he said, "Lord, I loved her, Mike. I love her now. Isn't that a hell of a thing, to love a woman who's been dead a long time?"

The ghost of a smile came and went again. "Except I know her again. I told you about Annie. I know deep inside of me that Annie and Bernadette are the same person. I think I've known a long time, but I kept denying it. It meant facing a version of myself I didn't like much. Mike, I love Annie the same way I loved Bernadette."

A strange, sad envy was born in Mike at that moment. He thought of his pragmatic schoolteacher wife, Sarah, of their three children, their lavish house in Kerrisdale and their secure and predictable life.

He thought of the shoddy affair he was having with Margie, a romance he'd convinced himself was torrid and exciting.

And for the first time in years, he remembered being young and having dreams of a great and memorable love, the way an idealistic young men do. But he'd never found it.

He was an impatient man, greedy for instant reward, and he admitted to himself that he'd never come close to knowing the kind of love David was describing. Was it really out there, for everyone, if they searched hard and waited long enough?

With an immense effort, he brought his thoughts back to David, to what had occurred.

"You had me on pretty strange ground there for a while, partner. Lucky thing I keep up with the journals. At least I had some idea what was going on."

He hesitated, and then asked, "Do you think it was fantasy or actual memory, David? It sure as hell sounded authentic to me. But if it was a legitimate regression, you and I have a lot of revising to do in our belief systems."

"It happened all right." There wasn't a shred of doubt in David's voice. Disgust filled his voice. "Jeeze, Mike, I was a sorry excuse for a man back then. I let my father-in-law coerce and bribe me into becoming what he thought was a success. Why the hell didn't I take charge of my own life?"

David got up from the chair, feeling drained of energy. He walked to the window and pulled back the blind. The traffic outside had accelerated, and the sun's angle indicated that somehow the morning had become afternoon. But inside the office, time had somehow stopped being a factor. In the midst of their clock-regulated lives, Mike and David had created a warp, and neither man felt urgency or pressure or even curiosity about the changing numbers on their expensive watches.

Instead Mike thought about all the things David had experienced, and his wide mouth twisted in a sad, sardonic grin.

"Then or now, how many of us ever take charge of our lives? Life seems to happen, and we're along for the ride. Which makes this reincarnation idea pretty scary, because it throws responsibility back on us. Who the hell else can we blame if we create our own destinies?"

David considered the life he was leading now. He shuddered as he remembered Paul, the tragic man he'd been, and perhaps still was, somewhere deep inside David.

"I chose my life back then, regardless of how much I'd like to blame the whole thing on Martin or war or fate. I could have made a different decision at any time, gone back to France, turned my back on my career. What happened was my choice, mine alone." He was talking more to himself than to Mike. He felt dizzy and light-headed for a moment, and he grasped the back of a chair and bent his head until the giddiness faded.

"I've got the same options now as I had then."

"The thing is, do you figure you'll be able to sleep now without nightmares?" Mike queried.

A weary grin twisted David's mouth. "Nightmares won't be a problem anymore, I know that. I've got some waking horrors to get through, though."

Mike watched as David straightened, reached for the jacket he'd hung on the back of a chair and shrugged into it. He held a hand out and Mike clasped it hard.

"I'm grateful, Mike. You'd better bill me in installments, or sure as hell I'll really go into cardiac arrest when I get your statement for this one." David tried for a light tone and a grin, but he was sweating and shaking again. The session had taken its toll physically. It was all he could do to hold himself upright. Some shred of macho pride in him didn't want Mike watching while he fell flat on his face.

Mike went to his desk drawer, extracted a set of keys and held them out to David.

"Listen, the only thing you're fit to do is rest, and nobody knows better than me how impossible that is at home, with the office or your service calling every fifteen minutes. Besides, you probably shouldn't be driving either. If you go out the front door of this building, you'll see a small apartment complex halfway down the next block. I, ahh, rent a unit there nobody's gonna be using today. Why don't you go over there and sleep for a few hours?"

David gave a good imitation of a grin and shook his head. "There's somebody I need to see right away, while I'm still raw enough to swallow my pride and admit I was wrong about a lot of things. I'll sleep at her place. Thanks, buddy. I owe you one."

As the door closed behind David, Mike mumbled, "Maybe you do. And maybe you don't."

DAVID DROVE with extreme caution along the busy streets, forcing himself to think only of the traffic until he arrived at Annie's house and parked at the curb. He'd never felt more relieved at getting anywhere as he dragged himself out of the car and made his slow way up to the front door.

It was locked. Annie was out somewhere.

For a moment, David contemplated lying down on her front lawn and just staying there until she came back. Then he remembered that she seldom locked the kitchen door, and with slow, dragging steps, he made his way through the side gate and around the back.

That door was unlocked. He went in, and with a slow, single-minded shuffle, he headed across the kitchen to the hall that led to the stairs.

The small watercolor, the pastoral scene of the stone cottage with the river in the distance, hung on the wall by the doorway. David stopped and looked at it for a long time. Waves of recognition rolled through him, along with a sense of grief so overwhelming it was all he could do not to cry.

No wonder Annie had bought the picture. It could have been a sketch of Bernadette's farm in Normandy. He could almost smell the scented air, hear the larks singing in the trees beside the river.

He moved down the short hall to the stairs, taking them the way an old man would, one laborious step after another.

At last, he was in Annie's bedroom. He took off his coat and his shoes and gave up the struggle, collapsing on the unmade bed and rolling on his stomach so he could bury his nose in the scent of Annie that pervaded the pillow. Or was it the clean-washed lemon scent of Bernadette's hair?

Oblivion was immediate.

ANNIE HAD WRESTLED with the increasing pain in her neck for three days, and she'd reached some kind of crossroad during the night while she tossed and turned, trying to find a position that eased the burning sensation.

One of her decisions had to do with David. She couldn't stand one more day of indecision, of sitting waiting for him to make room in his life for her. She was determined to search him out, and force him to spend at least enough time to say goodbye with dignity, if that's all that was left for them.

The other decision was out of her control. She would go back to Steve and undergo regression one last time. Her neck hurt enough to overcome her fear of the past.

She tried to settle the issue with David first, but the problem was the usual one; she couldn't locate him to tell him anything.

Phyllis snapped at her even worse than usual when Annie called the office just after nine.

"The doctor hasn't been in this morning, and I don't expect him."

"Well, do you know where he might be?" It galled Annie to have to ask, but she did anyway. The answer was abrupt and final. "No, I don't."

"You know, Phyllis, it doesn't cost anything to be polite," Annie said.

Click.

At least this time she'd said it, and it made her feel good.

Annie hung up, dialed again, left a second message on the machine at David's apartment and then wondered if perhaps he was with Calvin Graves.

To hell with it. She didn't feel intimidated by anyone any longer. She located and dialed Calvin's home number and actually got Calvin on the phone after the first ring.

If anything, he was in a worse temper than Phyllis had been.

"Unfortunately I have no idea where our good doctor is, or where he can be reached, or even when he might again be available, my dear." His voice was frosty and heavy with sarcasm as he added, "Ironic we should both be ignorant of David's whereabouts, don't you think? Perhaps there's some little thing he isn't telling either of us."

Annie's bravado deserted her. She swallowed the furious retort that Calvin deserved and hung up again, but his vicious innuendo stung.

Did she really know whether or not David was involved with someone else? He certainly wasn't seeing much of her.

Is this what had happened in that life long ago as well? Did the sudden ending to Paul's letters mean that he'd found someone else to love? Maybe, her confused brain suggested, Calvin had given her the real reason for David's absences.

That's absurd, Annie, she reasoned. *You know that's ab-surd.*

But she could no longer tell what was logical and what wasn't. The shafts of pain in her neck accelerated until they were agonizing. She switched on the relaxation tape and tried to concentrate, but the pain was now uncontrollable. In desperation, she picked up the phone while she could still function, and dialed Steve's office.

She'd spent a great deal of time in the past weeks reading the books he'd given her, learning more and more about the strange phenomena of past life regression, and more as well about the lessons to be learned from understanding reincarnation.

The message that came through loud and clear was that there were no accidents in the universe, that each person chose every detail of the life they lived: past, present, future. Hiding from the truth was impossible. Sooner or later, every challenge had to be dealt with, every pain expiated, no matter how many lifetimes it took.

During those weeks of reading, she'd resisted what she knew was necessary, but now the time had come for her to learn the ending of that other life, regardless of how painful it might be.

She might as well get it over with this time around. She might as well find out once and for all why Paul had deserted her.

"Come right over, Annie. I know Steve will see you right away," Edith said immediately.

Within an hour, Annie was lying back on the now-familiar battered couch, and she knew it would be a simple matter to find the familiar tunnel that led into that other life. Whatever scenes awaited there would be anything but simple, however.

"I'm petrified, but I want to know what became of me, of all of us back then," she told Steve, and he agreed.

"I'll take you over the years that intervened, but I'll try to have you view them as an observer, so the experiences aren't as painful. Then I'll guide you to the last day of your life as Bernadette," he promised. "Relax, Annie. It'll all be over soon."

WITHIN MOMENTS, Annie once again saw herself as Bernadette. Years had passed since Paul left, and she never heard from him again. She never forgot him, either. As long as she lived, her heart would belong to Paul.

She lived in two worlds all those years, and in halting, pain-filled phrases, she explained it all to Steve.

"In one way, I was Jean's wife. I worked hard, cared for my family. But in some other reality, in my dreams, Paul and I walked hand in hand forever along that tree-lined path by the Seine, the way we had so many times when we were together. Every day, after my work was done, I'd go there."

"Wasn't your husband jealous? He must have known you thought of your lover."

She shrugged. There was a touch of disdain in the movement and in the tone of her voice when she said, "What could he do? He thought he owned my body, but he couldn't control my mind, could he?''

Jean Desjardins had grown physically strong again. Lorelei had used all her considerable nursing skills to help him recover in the weeks after he came home, and she was a positive influence on his mental state as well.

After that first terrible encounter the day Jean arrived home, Bernadette fled with her children and went to stay with Lorelei and Pierre Dupré, desperate to escape Jean's presence and his rage. Lorelei had reasoned with Bernadette, convincing her that she should go back and make the best of it. Inside herself, Bernadette knew she really had no choice in the matter, with a new baby and little money left from the amount Paul had given her.

And she couldn't go on staying with Lorelei and Pierre. Lorelei, too, lived a married life far from ideal. Pierre Dupré was a sad, dependent old man, clinging to Lorelei like a child, and just like a child he was jealous of his wife's attention.

There was really nowhere else for Bernadette to go but back home.

"To give him credit, Jean did his best to accept what had happened. Basically," she admitted with some reluctance, "I suppose he was a good man in some ways."

But living with Jean and loving Paul was slow agony for her. Gradually Bernadette compensated by lavishing her affection on her children, particularly on her son . . . Paul's son, Marcel.

Jean's daughter, Nicole, was a serious, responsible child. She looked like Jean, and the physical resemblance reassured and pleased him. He set out to win the little girl's trust and affection in the weeks after his homecoming.

A frown came and went as she tried to explain the complex relationship among the four of them. "It wasn't that I didn't love Nicole," she said at one point, as if defending herself against an accusation. "But Marcel was conceived of the love Paul and I shared, and there was a special feeling for him. Jean knew this. I kept the boy away from him as much as possible."

Jean at first ignored Marcel completely, the hurt of having another man's child around almost more than he could bear. But as the years passed, he did try his clumsy best to form a relationship with the boy. He never succeeded, and Bernadette had to accept much of the responsibility for that failure.

Marcel was very much like his father, Paul, in appearance and in disposition. Thus, he seemed totally foreign to Jean. The boy, bright and charming, handsome and quick-witted, soon was aware that he always had his mother's support in any dispute with Jean. As a result, Marcel became headstrong and willful.

As Marcel grew, Bernadette was aware that her son was a constant, visible reminder to Jean of her love for another man. Marcel caused a great deal of trouble in the family by his very presence, but also because of his actions. He was rebellious from an early age, and at times his mischief sparked an insane, blinding rage in his stepfather, Jean, and then Bernadette would come rushing to her son's defense.

"Several times, Jean goaded me, telling me that my American lover had deserted me and my bastard son, and now he was stuck supporting us. I hated him when he was like that."

Annie recounted these situations for Steve in a matter-of-fact way, but there were undertones of both growing fear and increasing sadness in her voice as she again took up the story. Steve noted that the role of impartial observer had disappeared, and once again, Annie was Bernadette.

"Marcel is now twenty and two weeks ago, against my wishes, he ran off to join the army," she said in a quavering voice. "We are once again in another war, you know."

"And your daughter? Where is Nicole now?" Steve prodded.

"Gone away as well, to train as a nurse." Weary desolation filled her voice. "I'm more lonely than I've ever been before. It's like a cancer in me."

"What about your friend, Lorelei? Don't you have her to talk to?"

She shook her head. "Lorelei's dead. She left here years ago, two years after Jean returned. Her young lover, Tony Briggs, gave her an ultimatum, and she went off to be with him. But it didn't work out. He fell in love with another woman and left her, and it broke Lorelei's heart. She stopped writing after that. The last letter I had of her, she was working in an orphanage in Paris. Dr. Cerdan went to find her, and he brought me the news that she had died. Consumption, he said. I miss her so."

Steve decided the time had come to move forward.

"You will go now to the last day of your life as Bernadette. You will remember without pain what occurred that day. You will exorcise the soul memory once and forever...."

The words penetrated her deepest consciousness, but even powerful hypnotic suggestion couldn't defeat the horrors of that awful day as she allowed herself to remember.

At first, excitement and apprehension seemed to overcome her.

"What's happening now?" Steve asked, curious at the sudden change in her body language.

"A letter." Her voice was breathless. "A letter from the United States. From—" tension filled her "—from a lawyer?" There was a pause, and then her hands clasped and she slumped as if in pain.

"Paul. Somehow I knew it," she whispered at last. "It says here that Paul is dead. My love is dead, forever gone from me." Her arms folded around herself in a lonely, pathetic gesture that wrung Steve's heart. "The lawyer encloses a letter Paul gave him for me, and a bundle of faded envelopes...."

"Open the letter," Steve instructed with gentle insistence. She shook her head, her breath coming in short, agitated sobs.

"You must open the letter Paul wrote, Bernadette," Steve said again, "and read it to me."

"My... my dearest love...," she began at last, so low Steve had to lean forward to hear.

In a few terse phrases, the words described Paul's life, how circumstances had prevented him from coming back, the maze of complications and errors of judgment that finally prevented him from returning at all.

"His father-in-law hid these letters, all of them," she said dully. "At least now I know—I know he didn't stop loving me." And then, with heartbreaking tenderness, she began to read aloud. "The memory of the love we shared is etched indelibly into my soul, beloved. How I long to see you just once again before my life ends. How bitterly I resent the accidents of chance that have kept us apart." Her voice broke, and she reached a finger up and rubbed away a single tear that trickled slowly down her cheek.

"I realize now I should have put everything aside and come to you, Bernadette. I know that now, when it's too late."

A deep, silent sob shook her, and she bit her lip before she could go on. Steve was shaken and deeply moved by the scene.

"Bernadette," she read on, "I have the strangest conviction that we've loved many times before now. Remember how we used to talk about the feeling that we'd known each other before? And so I can only hope that we'll meet again, in another time, another place. Until then, my darling, hold me in your memory the way I've held you all these long empty years."

Her voice broke again, and she choked out the final words. "Dearest Bernadette, remember me. Remember me as I do you. Yours eternally, Paul."

Tears were flowing down her cheeks, and once again she raised her hand, brushing the wetness away with her knuckles. "You see, Jean?" she cried out all of a sudden, with a passion and a depth of anger that startled Steve. "You see? He loved me after all, during all these years he loved me, and that's all that matters to me now."

Listening, Steve was appalled, and a foreshadowing of awful tragedy overcame him.

"Bernadette, is Jean there with you? Did he hear what was in that letter??"

When she nodded with proud defiance, Steve felt his stomach clench with fear. Despite it, he instructed, "Move ahead now. Tell me what happened next."

"I can't stand the pain of knowing what might have been for Paul and me. It's tearing my soul apart, and Jean is watching with that awful burning look on his face."

Her words came faster now. "I run from the house. I run to the path by the river...where Paul and I...made love under the trees." She was panting, and her breath was coming in short, sobbing gasps.

Then, for an instant, the anguish contorting her features seemed to be smoothed away, and she said in a lilting, girlish voice, "Paul? Is that you, Paul...?"

Her tone was full of wonder, her expression one of surprise and joy that changed in an instant to a look of horror as Steve watched and waited.

"Jean," she gasped, her eyes wide open and filled with horror. "Jean, don't, I..."

"Tell me what you're experiencing," Steve ordered firmly. "Try to stay relaxed and calm and tell me what's going on."

"He...I...I thought it was Paul, but it was Jean," she gasped. "Only a step behind me, and I turned and....oh, his face! Jean's face is full of rage...and I'm frightened. Oh, Lord, he's got my arms now and he's shaking me...shaking me back and forth, and...I'm struggling...he's strong...my body, my head, jerking...back...forth...can't...."

Steve crouched down beside her and took her hand, but there was little more that he could do but listen and try to comfort.

This was it at last. This was the buried moment from long ago, the traumatic moment that Annie had carried with her through death, through birth, through her entire present life. This was where the pain had originated.

"Stay very calm and very relaxed, and describe what happens next," Steve said.

"Pain," she gasped. "Terrible, burning pain in my neck, my neck.... Stop him, oh, stop....God, help me...shaking and shaking me...I can't stand it...ohhh, this cracking noise... filling my head..."

The last wailing cry she then made rose to a peak, filled the room and then faded, and Steve knew with sick horror that somewhere in the past, and eerily again here in his office, Bernadette Desjardins was dying of a broken neck.

SHE FELT HERSELF TUMBLE to the earth.

The red-hot agony in her neck and upper back engulfed her, but soon it passed into darkness, and she moved up, into a brilliant tunnel of light. A tiny part of her was aware of the tormented figure of Jean, far below, shaking the body she'd left behind, roaring out his fear and pain and grief like a wounded animal, then running toward the riverbank and plunging into the swollen spring waters of the Seine.

Steve took charge again as her whispered words ended. He had to swallow several times to make his voice behave.

"You're going to receive more and more insights into this other life during the next few weeks, but now I want you to come back to being Annie. I'm going to count from ten to zero and I want you to come back, remembering what you've learned today."

"My neck hurts," she moaned, still deeply hypnotized.

No damn wonder, Steve thought, awed by the power of the scene she'd recreated. You've just had your neck broken. No damn wonder it hurts....

"This is the last time it will ever hurt this way, Annie," he assured her. "You now know the reasons for the pain, and you can leave it behind forever." With care, he brought her out of the trance.

The pain in her neck began to ebb, pain from a long-ago tragic death. The last burning traces faded along with her tears, and Annie knew with deep conviction that the problem she'd had all her life would never trouble her again.

She knew as well that the neck pain had become a secondary issue in this search for truth. She'd begun the journey with single-minded purpose, to help with a physical problem. Now she'd ended it, and the physical relief seemed minor in comparison to the emotional knowledge.

"I understand now the feelings I've always had about Michael, the fear and distrust, and even why I was both attracted and repelled by him when we met again in this lifetime."

Annie shuddered as she thought over the mistakes she'd made as Bernadette, the countless small ways she must have wounded Jean over the years. And the selfish way she'd clung to Marcel and spoiled him, excluding any relationship the boy might have formed with Jean.

Steve listened as she verbalized her experience.

"As Bernadette, I was unfair to my husband, you know. He was basically a good man, and I knew deep inside myself that he loved me, even though his nature wasn't expressive. I shouldn't have stayed when I couldn't love him back. It was almost as if I taunted him at times with Paul's son, with the enduring love I felt for Paul and not for him."

It was ironic, this feeling of regret, and even shame, for the way another version of herself had acted so long ago.

"Maybe through Jason, we can learn to forgive each other this time around," she mused. "I feel easier about Michael now. You'd think knowing what he did to me would make me hate him, but instead it's myself I blame. With Jason," she went on, "I've come close to making the same selfish mistake again, keeping Jason from Michael. This time Michael is his natural father, and yet I've resisted the idea of letting the two form a bond."

She thought for several moments. "How strange, and yet how just that David . . ." She'd been about to say that David would be the boy's stepfather this time, but she stopped before the words were out.

Familiar anxiety filled her as she admitted that it was far more probable that David would disappear from their lives forever, just the way he had the last time.

She could alter only her own reality, but not David's. He had free will, and she couldn't influence the choices he'd make. Judging by the way things were going between them, it seemed unlikely he and Annie would ever make a life together.

How that hurt. Her mouth twisted with pain as she thought of living the rest of this life, too, without the man who seemed to be the missing half of her soul. *David*, she thought in agony. *If only I could make you understand these things, see them as I've been allowed to do.*

"Do you know what became of Marcel and your daughter, Nicole?" Steve's question was a welcome distraction.

Annie closed her eyes and nodded. "It seems they died in that second war. Those were terrible times, for us, for France, for all of Europe. When I left that body, it seemed to me that I could see both the past and the future, and my children didn't survive the war."

Tears filled her eyes again, and regret filled her heart. She hadn't been the best of mothers to Nicole or to Marcel. She'd spoiled Marcel, allowing Nicole to take a secondary role. The girl had been sweet and undemanding. Annie felt stricken with guilt while realizing how fruitless the feeling was.

"Do you have any idea if Nicole is part of your life again this time?"

Annie shook her head. "I've thought about all of them, trying to place them in this incarnation. I can't figure it out for sure, except for Paul and Marcel. And Lorelei, of course, dear Lorelei. She's Cleo, my best friend all over again. But the others . . ." She frowned, puzzled.

"Give it time—it'll all come clear. The important thing is not to agonize over what happened, but to learn from it and apply the lessons here and now. I believe that's why this gift of memory is sometimes granted to us, to help us along the path to knowledge a little faster than we'd progress otherwise."

They talked a long while over the usual cups of hot, sweet tea. The cycle was at last complete.

He took both her hands in his when she said goodbye, and his ageless eyes met hers with compassion and deep caring.

"May this life be filled with love and happiness, Annie."

"Thank you, more than I can say. Goodbye, Steve."

This time, they both knew she wouldn't be back.

"MAY THIS LIFE BE filled with love and happiness." Steve's words lingered like a benediction in Annie's mind as she shopped for groceries, returned library books and went through all the mundane activities she had to get through during the remainder of that afternoon.

Jason was going to a friend's house for supper, and then to an exhibition basketball game, so there was no real reason to hurry home.

Annie drove to a stretch of beach deserted on this cold October afternoon, parked and locked her car and went for a long walk along the shore of the inlet. The brisk cold air and the rhythmic sound of the waves gradually overcame the turmoil of her thoughts, and a strange sense of peace filled her.

Nothing in her complex life had really changed, and yet everything seemed clear to her now. Not happy. Just . . . clear.

She drove home just before darkness fell. Astonishment filled her when she recognized David's car parked at a crooked angle in front of her house. She couldn't remember the last time he'd come by this early to see her. And she hadn't been home.

She raced up the stairs and fumbled with the lock.

"David? David, I'm back."

There was no answer, and no lights on anywhere inside. A deep stillness surrounded her as she hurried from one room to the next, searching for him.

She found him fully clothed except for his jacket and shoes, and for an awful moment she was frightened. He was limp and still. He hadn't even heard her come in. He didn't hear her now.

But then she saw the almost imperceptible rise and fall of his chest. He was asleep. It had been a long time since he'd slept in her bed, and an aching tenderness came over her, as well as the strangest feeling that everything was going to be all right now.

She had no idea why he was there, but as always, just having him with her was enough.

She tiptoed back downstairs and scribbled a note to Jason, asking him to be quiet when he came home, since David was resting. Then she went back upstairs, stripped off her clothing and slid her naked, chilly body carefully into bed beside him.

He still didn't awaken, but he turned in his sleep and mumbled, hooking an arm around her and drawing her into the curve of his body, warming her, holding her as if he would never let her go again.

"Bernadette," he murmured, burying his face in the spill of her hair. "I love you, Bernadette."

Annie let the words sink deep into the raw wounds in her soul, and she felt them beginning to heal. "I love you, too," she whispered, folding her hand inside his.

Then she let the balm of sleep wash over her, secure in the arms of the man she'd loved through many lifetimes.

CHAPTER NINETEEN

THE SCHOOL AUDITORIUM was packed that late November evening, and the variety show was drawing to a close.

Jason and the other members of the rugby team had done a fine job recruiting an audience for the benefit, Annie decided as she glanced around the crowded, stuffy room.

Still, if all the other boys had as many people to bully into buying tickets as her son did, the size of the crowd was understandable.

Jason had high-handedly reserved the best seats in the house for his "family." They occupied an entire front row of folding chairs. Annie was flanked by Cleo on one side and Maggie on the other, Don Anderson was at Cleo's other side, holding a sleepy Paula on his knee, and somehow managing to hold Cleo's hand at the same time. They'd left the baby with a sitter tonight. And beside them, Michael and Lili were also hand in hand.

The young master of ceremonies, resplendent in top hat and tails, bounded out on the stage and the room grew quiet. "It gives me great pleasure," he boomed into the microphone, "to introduce the grand finale of the evening. Ladies and gentlemen, our feature attraction, an act that has amazed and delighted royal audiences all over the world, and which we are proud to have here tonight at Kitsilano High. May I present..."

The school band, heavy on brass, gave a drumroll that Annie felt reverberate up through the soles of her feet.

"Jason and The Sorcerer."

A tall figure and a shorter one strolled out of the wings, one from each corner of the stage. Both were dressed in casual jeans and matching rugby shirts, but each wore a magician's signature top hat on his head.

In unison, they met at center stage and turned toward their audience, swept their hats off, and bowed low.

David looked astonished when out of his hat jumped a live rabbit and then another. Jason peered at the crowd, and nonchalantly produced a bundle of huge carrots from his own hat.

The audience roared with laughter, and the two performers began a quick routine that combined humor with clever variations of the usual stage illusions magicians performed.

They were good. Annie's nervousness faded and her heart swelled with pride.

"Annie, look what they're doing now. Jason's taking a balloon out of David's ear." Maggie's freckled face was alight with wonder, and she clapped her hands and giggled, making her blond braids bounce. "It's blown up, too. How could it come out of his ear, Annie?"

A small, timid girl cowered behind her mother's skirt in the warm farm kitchen. The tall, uniformed man with the deep blue eyes bent down and seemed to draw a bright red ribbon out of the little girl's ear. Then tied it in a clumsy bow in her dark curls....

Annie's heart seemed to turn over, and she reached out and squeezed Maggie's hand.

The memories came when she least expected them, these moments of recognition she was learning to trust. David had them, too, wisps of memory that came and went like dreams. They'd been able between them to piece together the jigsaw of that lifetime in France. There were only a few pieces still missing, and this was one.

So the earnest little girl who'd been Nicole was now Cleo's daughter, Maggie. And Annie was being given a second chance with her, not as her mother this time, but as a beloved friend.

Maggie leaned her head against Annie's shoulder for a second and whispered, "I'm glad you're gonna marry David, Annie. I like him a lot. He's the best magician, isn't he?"

"Yes, Mags, he is," Annie said through the lump in her throat. And the best doctor, and the best lover . . . and she had not a single doubt that he'd also be the best of husbands.

It would be a Christmas wedding, small and informal, in the living room of Cleo's house with all the children present. Jason had asked for and been given permission to invite Michael and Lili, which, along with the prospect of Jason givin his mother away in the traditional ceremony Annie planned, appealed to Cleo's sense of the unorthodox.

"Jason can give me away, too, when the time comes," Cleo insisted. "It's only fair, having had to go through adolescence with me. But just don't try to locate that rotten ex of mine to invite to the wedding. I'd rather not have him there when Don and I get married."

Cleo laughed at the scenario, but Annie's smile was always strained. Annie wondered a lot about Pierre Dupré and Tony Briggs. What roles were they now playing in Cleo's life? Which one had returned as the young and handsome Don? And as Lorelei, which man had Cleo deserted?

THE MAGIC SHOW was almost over. The audience watched with delight as Jason carried a small wooden table out from the wings and put it center stage. On the table was a bird cage, and Annie raised her head and met David's eyes.

"They're gonna make the bird cage disappear. 'Member how David did this at that magic show before, Annie?"

She hadn't known until this moment that David had taught Jason his special illusion. She remembered David's refusal when she'd asked him long ago to explain the secret of the trick so she could use it in her book.

"The bird cage is unique, Annie. Sorry, but it's a trade secret, sort of a magical legacy, the sort of valuable secret I'd hand down to a son if I had one. I can't let you use it in a book. It's the only trick I never explain to anyone. I'll find another illusion for you, though...."

Here was tangible evidence of the bond that united David and her son.

David was asking for young volunteers to come up and help with the illusion, to hold the bird cage down.

"I wanna go up. It's okay if I go, isn't it, Annie?"

Maggie raced to the stage, and soon a ring of children had their hands on the cage containing the canaries. In unison, Jason and David raised their hands high over their heads, and with perfect timing, brought them down. The bird cage and its contents disappeared.

A magic incantation was recited in tandem, and the cage and its contents were back again.

The audience roared its appreciation. Jason and The Sorcerer had them under their "fluence."

"WASN'T I JUST EXCELLENT, Mom? Did you hear how we made people laugh? It was awesome, just awesome. We were ace, right? And how about that one we did...."

Jason and David had done a quick job of packing their equipment after the show, and now they joined the group waiting for them in the hallway outside the stage door.

"You were totally awesome, all right, kid," Annie agreed.

"And not only are you an ace performer, you're so modest as well," Annie teased, rumpling his thick hair.

"Ahhh, Mom."

Michael and Lili moved up just then to give him hugs and extravagant compliments, and Annie could return Michael's proud glance without a trace of resentment for either the man or his affection for the son they shared.

Annie's inner reaction to Michael was not exactly one of friendship. It was rather a deep and compassionate recognition of the law of cause and effect. It was one of tolerance, forgiveness and peace. As far as she was concerned, they'd settled the debts and credits between them.

David slid an arm around Annie, and she felt the warm rush of joy that filled her whenever they were together, the sense of unity that bonded them.

"How about a hamburger, everybody?" David suggested. When they all agreed, Annie noticed David slip folded money into Jason's hand, and the two exchanged a conspiratorial glance as arrangements were made about where to meet.

"WHAT WAS THAT all about?"

Somehow, Annie and David had ended up alone in David's car. Jason had decided to ride with his father.

"Just a gentleman's agreement Jason and I made," was all David would say. But Annie noticed they weren't going in the direction the others were. They were heading for David's apartment.

"I CAN'T BELIEVE you did all this by yourself."

Annie was relaxed on the couch with a glass of wine in her hand. A fire blazed and crackled in the fireplace, and on the low table in front of her sat an assortment of fresh fruit, pâté and cheese. The food shared space with a mass of daffodils and tulips jammed any which way into a plastic pitcher.

David was in the galley kitchen, adjusting the oven with the same intensity he must apply to major surgery. He had a list tacked to the fridge, and he consulted it several times as he slid a pan of rolls in and took a covered casserole out, swearing under his breath each time he burned himself.

"Ahh, you underestimate me. I'm a magician, remember?"

He swore again, out loud this time, and almost dropped the casserole before he got it safely to the table. "Dinner's almost ready," he announced with enormous relief.

Annie glanced at the assortment of containers jumbled on the counter, all bearing the logo of Vancouver's most elegant catering service.

"Bet you're a rich magician at that," she teased, watching the performance he was going through just to serve her dinner.

"You've gotta be rich to afford Lazy Gourmet."

"I once promised you dinner, dancing, wine, flowers, and chocolates," he'd explained when they arrived. "But unfortunately, the evening didn't turn out as I planned. So I'm going to keep my promise tonight."

She was thrilled to the core, and touched that he would somehow find time to make these arrangements in the midst of what was still a brutally busy agenda.

Not quite as busy as it had been, however. David had resigned from most of the committees during the past weeks, and there'd been a dramatic showdown with Calvin. Annie didn't know all the details—David had just told her he was no longer a candidate for any sort of office, and Calvin was raving mad at him as a result.

"Can you salvage your friendship with him, David? After all, he's been part of your life for years."

"A lot more years than he realizes. It's up to him now. Annie. I'm not certain Calvin understands friendship as well as he understands manipulation and power. It's a lesson he'll have to learn on his own."

Knowing Calvin, Annie wondered how many more lifetimes that was going to take.

"How's your wine, pretty lady? Time for one more small glass, and then we'll eat before this mess gets cold."

She held out her glass for him to refill. He reached over and plucked a card from a pile of mail on the stereo stand and handed it to her.

"This came yesterday. It's from Mrs. Vance, Charlie's mother."

The message on the outside of the card just read, Thank You. Inside was a note and a snapshot of a little boy with laughing eyes and a smile that reached out from the picture and wrapped itself around Annie's heart. It was the photo Linda Vance had shown Annie with such pride that long-ago night at the hospital.

"Dear Dr. Roswell," the note read. "We want to thank you for all you did for us. Like you said, you can't promise things will be different for our baby girl, but we have complete trust in you. We know you will do everything possible for her, just like you did for Charlie. Wherever he is, I know he thanks you, too. I thought you'd like to have his picture."

Annie slid the card back in the envelope and handed it to David. "They'll have to take her to Pittsburgh, won't they?"

David nodded. "I've accepted the fact that a full transplant unit is still very much in the future. But we're making progress here all the same. There's the Organ Retrieval for Transplant facility, and the public's becoming more aware of the need for donor organs."

He poured himself a glass of wine and perched for a moment on the arm of the couch as he drank it.

"I feel differently about it now than I did before. The sense of desperation is gone," he admitted. "Part of it is understanding that a lot of the frustration I feel is linked to that poor bastard doing surgery in a tent back in France, trying to patch up young soldiers as best he could and failing more often than not."

It still amazed Annie, having David accept and talk about this concept of other lives.

"But the biggest change is knowing for certain that life is eternal, that little old Charlie is out there somewhere right now, and that maybe the next body he gets will work better than the last." He smiled down at her, that wide, crooked smile that always reminded her of Paul.

"It's knowing, too, that kids like Charlie choose their bodies for a reason—that there's a rational purpose to it all. It makes my job a little easier, understanding that."

Her heart full, she reached up and wrapped her arms around his neck, pulling him down on top of her, spilling what was left of his wine all over her dress and not caring at all.

He let the glass fall to the carpet and settled her more comfortably beneath him.

"David, you're such a fine man, such a good doctor."

"Not yet, my love. But I will be, even if it takes another dozen lifetimes. With you."

He kissed her, and profound peace and soaring joy filled Annie's heart. She and David had been born again, to find a way to be together, and now at last the sad and lonely images of Bernadette and her Paul could be laid to rest. Yesterday's debts were paid. There was only love on time's ledger now, to look forward to. To remember and enjoy again, after this lifetime was ended. Love was eternal; yesterday, tomorrow, forever.

She wriggled underneath him.

"Enough, woman. My dinner is gonna be ruined if you distract me this way."

"Woman does not live by food alone," she breathed in his ear.

"I heated it up, and you're going to eat it," he insisted, and kissed her again.

"Food now, love and dancing later," he promised.

There was plenty of time.

HARLEQUIN CELEBRATES
THE SEASON OF SHARING
AND FAMILY WITH

Friends, Families, Lovers

Harlequin introduces the latest member in its family of
seasonal collections. Following in the footsteps of the popular
My Valentine, Just Married and *Harlequin Historical Christmas
Stories,* we are proud to present FRIENDS, FAMILIES,
LOVERS. A collection of three new contemporary romance
stories about America at its best, about welcoming others into
the circle of love…. Stories to warm your heart…

By three leading romance authors:

**KATHLEEN EAGLE
SANDRA KITT
RUTH JEAN DALE**

Available in October, wherever
Harlequin books are sold.

Take 4 bestselling love stories FREE

Plus get a FREE surprise gift!

Special Limited-time Offer

Mail to Harlequin Reader Service®

3010 Walden Avenue
P.O. Box 1867
Buffalo, N.Y. 14269-1867

YES! Please send me 4 free Harlequin Superromance® novels and my free surprise gift. Then send me 4 brand-new novels every month, which I will receive before they appear in bookstores. Bill me at the low price of $2.71 each plus 25¢ delivery and applicable sales tax, if any.* That's the complete price and—compared to the cover prices of $3.50 each—quite a bargain! I understand that accepting the books and gift places me under no obligation ever to buy any books. I can always return a shipment and cancel at any time. Even if I never buy another book from Harlequin, the 4 free books and the surprise gift are mine to keep forever.

134 BPA AJJC

Name	(PLEASE PRINT)	
Address		Apt. No.
City	State	Zip

USIP-83R

©1990 Harlequin Enterprises Limited

1993 Keepsake

CHRISTMAS

Stories

Capture the spirit and romance of Christmas with KEEPSAKE
CHRISTMAS STORIES, a collection of three stories by favorite
historical authors. The perfect Christmas gift!

Don't miss these heartwarming stories, available in November
wherever Harlequin books are sold:

ONCE UPON A CHRISTMAS by Curtiss Ann Matlock
A FAIRYTALE SEASON by Marianne Willman
TIDINGS OF JOY by Victoria Pade

ADD A TOUCH OF ROMANCE TO YOUR
HOLIDAY SEASON WITH KEEPSAKE
CHRISTMAS STORIES!

HX93

Once upon a time...

There was the best romance series in all the land—Temptation.

You loved the heroes of REBELS & ROGUES. Now discover the magic and fantasy of romance. *Pygmalion, Cinderella* and *Beauty and the Beast* have an enduring appeal—and are the inspiration for Temptation's exciting new yearlong miniseries, LOVERS & LEGENDS. Bestselling authors including Gina Wilkins, Glenda Sanders, JoAnn Ross and Tiffany White reweave these classic tales—with lots of sizzle! One book a month, LOVERS & LEGENDS continues in November 1993 with:

#465 NAUGHTY TALK
Tiffany White
(Sir Gawain)

Live the fantasy....

HARLEQUIN

Temptation

LL11

◈ HARLEQUIN®

Are you looking for more titles by

ANNE STUART

Don't miss these additional stories by one of
Harlequin's most distinguished authors:

Harlequin American Romance®

#16361	ANGELS WINGS	$2.95	☐
#16374	LAZARUS RISING	$2.95	☐
#16398	NIGHT OF THE PHANTOM	$2.95	☐
#16413	CHASING TROUBLE	$3.29	☐
#16434	HEAT LIGHTNING	$3.39	☐
#16453	RAFE'S REVENGE	$3.39	☐
#16473	ONE MORE VALENTINE	$3.39	☐

Harlequin Promotional Titles

#83257	MY VALENTINE 1990	$4.99	☐

(short-story collection also featuring Judith Arnold,
Anne McAllister and Linda Randall Wisdom)

(limited quantities available on certain titles)

TOTAL AMOUNT	$
POSTAGE & HANDLING	$
($1.00 for one book, 50¢ for each additional)	
APPLICABLE TAXES*	$
TOTAL PAYABLE	$
(check or money order—please do not send cash)	

To order, complete this form and send it, along with a check or money order for the
total above, payable to Harlequin Books, to: *In the U.S.*: 3010 Walden Avenue,
P.O. Box 9047, Buffalo, NY 14269-9047; *In Canada*: P.O. Box 613, Fort Erie, Ontario,
L2A 5X3.

Name: _____

Address: _____ City: _____

State/Prov.: _____ Zip/Postal Code: _____

*New York residents remit applicable sales taxes.
Canadian residents remit applicable GST and provincial taxes.

HASBACK1

Are you looking for more titles by
JAYNE ANN KRENTZ

Don't miss this chance to order additional stories by one of
Harlequin's most favorite authors:

Harlequin Temptation®

#25441	TOO WILD TO WED?	$2.95	☐
#25477	THE PRIVATE EYE	$2.99	☐

Harlequin® Promotional Titles

#15158	THE FAMILY WAY	$2.99	☐
#83239	JAYNE ANN KRENTZ 2-IN-1	$4.59	☐
#83244	DREAMS PARTS ONE & TWO	$4.59	☐

Best of the Best

#83268	TWIST OF FATE	$4.50	☐
#83269	THE TIES THAT BIND	$4.50	☐
#83270	BETWEEN THE LINES	$4.50	☐

(limited quantities available on certain titles)

TOTAL AMOUNT	$____
POSTAGE & HANDLING	$____
($1.00 for one book, 50¢ for each additional)	
APPLICABLE TAXES*	$____
TOTAL PAYABLE	$____
(check or money order—please do not send cash)	

To order, complete this form and send it, along with a check or money order for the
total above, payable to Harlequin Books, to: *In the U.S.:* 3010 Walden Avenue,
P.O. Box 9047, Buffalo, NY 14269-9047; *In Canada:* P.O. Box 613, Fort Erie, Ontario,
L2A 5X3.

Name: _____

Address: _____ City: _____

State/Prov.: _____ Zip/Postal Code: _____

*New York residents remit applicable sales taxes.
Canadian residents remit applicable GST and provincial taxes.

HARLEQUIN®

HJAKBACK1